REGENCY

Marriages

Elizabeth Rolls

MILLS &
BOON

Mills & Boon, an imprint of Harlequin (UK) Limited,
Eton House, 18-24 Paradise Road, Richmond, Surrey TW9 1SR

REGENCY MARRIAGES © Harlequin Books S.A. 2011

The publisher acknowledges the copyright holder of the individual works
as follows:

A Compromised Lady © Elizabeth Rolls 2007
Lord Braybrook's Penniless Bride © Elizabeth Rolls 2009

ISBN: 978 0 263 88740 2

052-1111

Harlequin (UK) policy is to use papers that are natural, renewable
and recyclable products and made from wood grown in sustainable
forests. The logging and manufacturing processes conform to the legal
environmental regulations of the country of origin.

Printed and bound by
CPI Group (UK) Ltd, Croydon, CR0 4YY

A Compromised Lady

For Linda.
Who waited. And waited.
And then waited some more.
She even gave me another contract!
And for all the readers
who kept asking about Richard.
Thank you.

Chapter One

'David—he can't be serious! Why does he suddenly wish me to return after all this time? Nothing has changed! Nothing!' Thea dragged in a breath. 'I am still—' At the sight of her brother's taut mouth, the sudden tension in his clenched fists, she changed what she had been about to say. 'I am still of the same mind—I have no desire to return. What has changed Papa's stance?'

David's mouth opened and then closed, as though he too had thought the better of something. Then, 'I don't know, Thea. Not definitely. I have a suspicion, but since he didn't tell me anything beyond that I was to bring you back to town with me, I'd prefer not to say.'

Exasperated, Miss Dorothea Winslow stared at her brother across the confined gloom of their aunt Maria's parlour. If David's unannounced arrival in North Yorkshire from London had been unexpected, the news he bore was doubly so. She clutched the warm shawl closer, shivering despite the warmth of the fire crackling in the grate. Twenty minutes ago she had been knitting socks, a pot of tea beside her, quietly content and perfectly warm. Now the chill of the bitter rain gusting against the windows had seeped into her bones and the old panic stirred restlessly.

'Papa was more than happy for me to stay out of the way for the past eight years.' She added, 'He wouldn't even let me journey south to attend Mama's funeral. Why now, David? Don't tell me he wants me to be a comfort to him in his old age!'

David snorted. 'Hardly.' He stared into the fire for a moment. 'He is talking of a match for you, Thea.'

Her blood congealed, along with her forgotten cup of tea. *'What?'* Her breath came raggedly. 'But—'

David said, 'At Mama's funeral eighteen months ago, several people asked where you were. Remarked upon your long seclusion. Thea—burying your heart in the grave with your betrothed does not constitute a sufficient reason for not marrying. If people ask enough questions—' He broke off.

She steadied her breathing. 'I see.' *If people asked enough questions, someone might hit on the truth...*

He stood up abruptly and said, 'Our father fears the gossip. Which is at least part of the reason that he is essentially compelling you to come to London for the Season.'

'Compelling me?'

David nodded. 'He has instructed me to inform you that if you do not, you will receive no allowance at all.' His expression was grim.

Thea bit her lip. And then she gritted her teeth. 'I can still remain here with Aunt Maria.'

'He has already written to her—telling her that you are to come to London. Do you imagine she will defy him? She depends on his support.'

'But why? If I remain here—'

His grey eyes were flinty. 'As far as our father is concerned you have had ample time to recover from your...' He hesitated and then said, with an edge of violence, 'Your disappointment.'

Thea made a sharp movement and the now gelid cup of tea beside her crashed to ruin on the floor.

She ignored it.

'I see. Of course, eight years is ample time to recover from a *disappointment.*' She laid her hands carefully in her lap to prevent them clenching into fists. 'Especially a *disappointment* that never happened, according to one's point of view.'

He returned no answer to that.

'David, can't you—?'

'Damn it, Thea! Do you think I didn't try to talk him out of it?' David surged to his feet and prowled about the parlour, his movements jerky. 'I know this is not what you want, and if what I suspect is true, then in part it is my fault, but nothing would sway him.'

'And you aren't going to tell me?'

He shook his head. 'Better not.'

She shivered. There would be compensations. To hear good music again, visit Hatchards…and apparently she had no choice. But living in her father's house again…

'I suppose a chaperon has been arranged?' she said with forced calm.

David's mouth twisted. 'It is arranged that you should stay with Lady Arnsworth for the Season, and that she will chaperon you.'

Thea let out a sigh of relief, but said nothing; she merely knelt down and began carefully picking up the shattered porcelain. Aunt Maria was going to be most annoyed at the desecration of her best tea service.

Aunt Maria sat in a chair by the rarely lit fire as Thea packed later that evening. 'Certainly not, Dorothea!' she snapped, diligently folding handkerchiefs. 'Aberfield,' she continued, 'is obviously lost to all sense of decency and propriety!' She shot a hard glance at her great-niece. 'However, it is not for me to gainsay him; so, no, Dorothea, I will not attempt to change his mind.'

Along with her back, her lips were ramrod straight. 'Let us hope that your sense of duty to your family has increased in the past eight years. I say no more than that *I* have done my best to ensure that it should be so.' Her tone suggested that she doubted her best had been anywhere near good enough.

'But, Aunt—'

Miss Maria Winslow flung up her hand. 'No, Dorothea. Aber-field,' she proclaimed in the tones of one invoking a deity, 'is your father, and Head of the Family. It is not for me to argue with him. You will do as you are bid.'

No choice at all. With no money and no refuge, she was going to London. Thea laid her best gown, the dove-grey silk reserved for expected visitors, carefully layered in tissue paper, in the open trunk on her bed. She doubted very much that she would wear it again more than once or twice. What was adequate for the depths of rural Yorkshire would be despised in London. Thea stared at the gown. Three years she had been wearing it. Only yesterday when she had changed to greet the rector's wife, she had put it on with loathing, longing for something pretty, some-thing *pink,* instead of the never-ending grey. Now it looked safe, secure. Anonymous. All of which were about to be torn from her.

In the corner of the post-chaise rocking its way down the Great North Road towards London, Thea sat straight and stiff, a book open and forgotten on her lap. David lounged in the opposite corner reading a newspaper. Outside, northern England fell away behind them, every mile, every hoofbeat taking her closer to London...

'I have been thinking, David.'

He looked up from the newspaper. 'I assumed there was a reason you hadn't spoken or turned a page in half an hour.'

She gave him a rueful smile. 'Was I being rude?'

He grinned comfortably and laid the paper aside. 'No. I'm your brother. It's not technically possible for you to be rude to me.'

Despite the roiling tension, she chuckled. 'Oh? You were used to be rude enough to me!'

'That,' he informed her, 'is different. Brothers exist only to be rude to and, on occasion about, their sisters. What were you thinking?'

Slowly, she said, 'Papa cannot want me quartered on him in London for ever—even at Arnsworth House.'

'No,' said David. 'He doesn't. He's counting on your marriage.'

She twisted her battered old gloves between her hands. 'It won't happen,' she said shortly. 'He may force me to London, but he still can't force me into marriage. If I do not marry by the end of the Season—surely once he realises—'

'Do you think,' asked David, his voice diffident, 'that you might, our father's machinations aside, find some fellow to care for? One who will care for you?'

Leaning forward, he reached out and covered her hand with his.

She couldn't help it—instinctively, she jerked back, every nerve jangling at the unexpected touch.

Very slowly David sat back, his eyes shuttered.

Silence grew and stretched. When Thea spoke it was as though the words dropped into an abyss. 'I hope to God that I don't.'

'Really, Richard! What were you thinking? Seventy thousand pounds! Of course it was snapped up! And after all my efforts to cultivate the connection, where were you? In Kent!'

With forced patience, Richard Blakehurst listened to the continuation of his aunt Almeria Arnsworth's tirade. He had heard most of the countess's diatribe before and this particular version had been running—with minor variations upon the original theme—for the past several months.

'I *wrote* to you, explaining the urgency! And now the wretched girl is betrothed! To someone else.'

With a silent prayer of thanks to a benevolent deity for this circumstance, Richard settled himself as comfortably as possible in an Egyptian-style gilt chair built for a female form rather than a six-foot male and cast a considering glance at the decanters gracing a console table supported by a pair of sphinxes. His cup of tea wasn't quite hitting the mark under these circumstances. It was weak to start with and Almeria had put sugar and what tasted like half a cup of cream in it.

No. It would be extremely bad form to dump the tea and stalk across the Dowager Countess of Arnsworth's drawing room for the brandy. Even if she was his aunt and godmother.

Sweet, weak tea and good manners were not much to fortify a fellow against a determined assault on his bachelor status. It had been bad enough before, but the betrothal last week of a major heiress to someone other than himself, appeared to have escalated the crisis in Almeria's view.

'After all, Richard,' she went on, 'if you are not to inherit the earldom, due to Max's *selfish* marriage, then you must be established in some other way and how better than—'

'*No.*' Before she could get into her stride again, he said, 'Almeria—I do not lack for money, so I have no need to marry a fortune.' The jibe about his twin's marriage stung. He added, 'And no one could be more delighted about Max's marriage than I am. He's happy. You must see that.'

His godmother's glare consigned that hope to Hades and beyond.

'He hasn't even come up to town this year!' she snapped.

Richard gritted his teeth. 'No,' he said patiently, 'because Verity is increasing. He wanted to stay with her. Braybrook promised to keep him abreast of all that takes place in the House. He will come up if he is needed.'

Apparently knowing that her other nephew, Earl Blakehurst, was not completely neglecting his parliamentary duties didn't help at all. Almeria's nostrils flared.

'Richard—you must marry. It is your *duty!*'

His *duty?* To whom? To *what?* Duty was reserved for heirs. He'd only just purchased his own small estate. Surely it wasn't quite that desperate!

He voiced the question. 'Er, Almeria—to whom do I owe this—?'

'The earldom!' she said, replacing her teacup in its saucer with a decided click.

Richard felt his jaw sag. The *earldom?* That was a bit much to swallow. With two brothers originally between himself and the blasted earldom, he'd never *expected* to inherit. Or wanted to. Especially not since it would mean the deaths of his brothers. Abandoning the tepid cup of syrupy tea, he limped over to the decanters and poured himself a glass of brandy. He ignored Almeria's obvious disapproval. A little early, but with Almeria in this frame of mind he needed more fortification than a cup of tea would provide, if he were not to deal her a resounding set-down.

Reseating himself, he sipped the brandy, and said mildly, 'Almeria, Frederick's death was a stroke of misfortune.' He resisted the temptation to emphasise *mis*. 'You can hardly fear the same sort of accident happening to Max! Besides, he is married. And Verity is on the point of giving birth to their first child. How the devil can it be *my* duty to marry?'

'It might be a girl,' said Almeria hopefully. 'In fact, I wouldn't put it past that…that *hussy* to present him with a score of daughters!'

'Verity,' said Richard between clenched teeth, 'is *not* a hussy.'

Almeria had the grace to look slightly abashed. 'Oh, very well, but even so, Richard—there is no guarantee there will be an heir!'

No, there was no guarantee. Indeed, given his twin's current state of terror over his adored countess's perfectly normal pregnancy, it was entirely possible that he'd already sworn an oath of eternal celibacy. Not that one should dismiss the risks. Childbirth was childbirth. Risky. But still…

As if reading his thoughts, Almeria continued. 'And childbirth—why, you never know what might happen!' she said hopefully. 'Really, Richard! You are being most unreasonable about this.'

Forbearance crashed into smoking ruin. He nearly spat out the brandy. 'Max is my twin, ma'am,' he grated. 'I have a considerable affection for both him *and* Verity. You can hardly expect me to be reasonable about a suggestion that I ought to be counting on her death in childbed!'

He noted Almeria's flush with grim satisfaction.

She recovered and rattled in again. 'But, Richard—'

He flung up a hand. 'Enough, ma'am! I've every intention of marrying.'

She blinked. 'But *who?* There were several eligible girls out this year, and they are, each and every one, snapped up, while you sat in Kent!' She counted the eligibles off on her dainty fingertips. 'Lady Sarah Wilding, Miss Creighton, the Scantlebury chit—' Her lip curled slightly. 'Trade, to be sure, but one hundred thousand! I suppose one can make allowances.' She glared at Richard. 'All betrothed! So whom do you have in mind?'

'How in Hades should I know?' he answered with forced calm. Trust Almeria to take him literally! 'All I can tell you is that I am not on the catch for an heiress!' Then, with fell intent to end the conversation once and for all, 'Besides, you know Max. He'll probably give Verity a dozen strapping sons in his image.' He watched, fascinated, as Almeria's colour rose. Judging by the peculiar sounds emanating from her, it was entirely possible that she was actually choking. His baser self stirred. 'I mean, it didn't take him long this time. They'll barely have been married nine months.'

She favoured him with a look that would have felled a dragon and said, 'I do *not* consider this a suitable topic of conversation. And if you had the slightest regard for one who has only your well-being in mind—' She halted mid-flight and drew a deep breath. 'Well, that is neither here nor there. Now tell me, you arrived yesterday; where are you staying?'

At the sudden change of tack, the back of his neck developed a most unpleasant prickling sensation.

'With Braybrook, just for the moment,' he said. 'I mean to be up for a few weeks though, so I'll probably take lodgings.' No need to tell Almeria that in addition to the small estate he had bought the previous year, he was in the process of purchasing a small town house—she was likely to go into convulsions when she did find out. Bloomsbury was not on her list of eligible addresses for a gentleman.

'And you mean to take part in the Season?' She sounded as though she held out little hope in this direction.

'Actually, yes,' he confessed.

She blinked. 'Really? Well, then—you must stay here.'

Richard stiffened. 'Here?'

'But of course!' she said. 'Lodgings!' She shuddered in distaste. 'Quite ineligible. Of course you must stay here!'

He thought about it. He preferred lodgings. Much safer. He knew the signs. Almeria was up to something. Something that involved him.

Oh, for God's sake! As if he couldn't dodge yet another of Almeria's matchmaking attempts! Even if it was compounded by his own intent to seek a bride this year. Besides which, staying with Almeria, he might be able to give her thoughts about Max and Verity a happier turn. If she could see that he really didn't mind, had never considered the earldom his, then perhaps she would become reconciled to the match. Spending a few weeks at Arnsworth House would be a small price to pay for healing the breach in the family.

Taking a deep breath, he said with a tolerable assumption of pleasure, 'That is really very kind of you, Almeria, if I won't be in your way.'

She waved that aside. 'Of course not, Richard. Shall you be in for dinner this evening?'

Richard shook his head. 'No. I'm promised to Braybrook for the evening. I'll stroll back to Brook Street shortly and have my man bring my things over, if that's convenient.'

Lady Arnsworth looked like a cat drowning in cream. 'Perfectly. Myles will give you a latch key.'

Suspicions redoubled, Richard simply nodded. 'Thank you.'

She waved his thanks aside. 'Oh, nonsense, Richard. And you must not be thinking that I will for ever be expecting you to dance attendance. You may not have realised, but I will be chaperoning Dorothea Winslow this season.'

Richard stared. 'Chaperoning Thea? But…didn't she—surely she must have married years ago?'

Almeria's eyes opened wide. 'Dorothea marry? Dear me, no. Such a sad story… I dare say you will recall she was betrothed to one of Chasewater's younger sons?'

Richard remembered that only too well. At not quite seventeen, Thea Winslow had been betrothed to the Honourable Nigel Lallerton, third son of the late Earl of Chasewater. As a gentleman set for a career in Parliament, naturally he required a well-dowered bride. Thea had been it.

But Lallerton had died in a shooting accident.

'I assumed she'd recovered from her disappointment and married,' he said. He had been abroad himself for some years after that and had heard nothing more.

Almeria's metaphorical whiskers positively dripped cream. 'Sadly, no, Richard. Such affecting loyalty! Naturally one sympathises with her, but, goodness! It must be several years since poor Nigel Lallerton died.'

Richard stared. He remembered that Thea had retired from society after Lallerton's death. Understandable if her affections had been engaged. But never to marry? Had she then cared for Nigel Lallerton so deeply that she had retired completely from society after he had died? He'd not had much time for Lallerton, himself...a bully, as he remembered. He stepped back from the thought. The man was dead after all. And perhaps Thea had seen a different side of him... Still, never to marry...

Almeria spoke again. 'She cannot mourn for ever and I dare say Aberfield considers the time right...'

The sentence remained unfinished, but Richard had no difficulty filling the blanks: Thea Winslow could not be permitted to inter her heart or, more accurately, her hand in marriage, permanently in the grave. She must take a husband. Her father's political ambition required it.

'Of course she must marry,' said Almeria, echoing his cynical thoughts. 'Probably Aberfield would have brought her to town last year, had they not been in mourning for poor dear Lady Aberfield. 'Tis positively unnatural for Dorothea to waste her life because her first choice met an untimely end!'

Something about Almeria's airy tone of voice sent awareness prickling through him, like a hare scenting the hounds.

'Oh?'

She sighed. The sort of sigh that would have reached to the back seats in Drury Lane. 'Naturally Aberfield wishes her to make an advantageous match. Of course, Dorothea is not a beauty. She was used to be well enough, but at twenty-four she really is past marriageable age, and one must expect that the bloom has faded. Still, I dare say she will attract *some* offers.'

The prickle intensified. 'You are not envisaging me as an eligible suitor here, are you, Almeria?' he asked bluntly.

Almeria's eyes widened. 'Good heavens, no, Richard!' she exclaimed. 'Partial though I am, I cannot persuade myself that Aberfield would look on your suit at all favourably.'

'My suit?' Richard wondered if he had misheard. 'My *suit*, did you say, Almeria? I wasn't aware that I had one.' Under the circumstances he considered the even tone he achieved did him great credit.

'Of course not,' said Almeria crossly. 'How you do take one up! Naturally when Aberfield wrote to ask if I would chaperon Thea, I thought of you. After all, you were used to be fond enough of her.'

'She was a child, Almeria,' said Richard, striving to maintain his calm. 'I wasn't thinking of her in terms of a bride!' In fact, he'd been disgusted at the announcement of the betrothal.

Almeria waved dismissively. 'Oh, well. No matter. I understand Aberfield has already put out feelers. He is looking for a political alliance to a man of far greater substance, you may be sure.'

'How very sensible of him,' he murmured, tamping down a sudden flicker of anger at the thought of Thea being used as the glue in a political union. Again.

Apparently oblivious to the edge in his voice, Almeria went on to enumerate all the eligible men of rank and fortune who might reasonably be expected to have a chance of securing the daughter of an influential viscount. 'For you know, she will arrive in town this afternoon, and I must be prepared,' she said.

Again an odd flicker. This time of interest. Aberfield House was just across Grosvenor Square. Perhaps Thea would call. It would be good to see her again…

Aberfield House had not changed in the slightest in the eight years since Thea had seen it. Carnely the butler had a few more wrinkles, but otherwise she might have been stepping back in time. Thea checked her appearance in a pier glass in the hall as David knocked on the door of the library, reflecting on the futility of this even as she straightened her bonnet and tried to tuck a curl back into it. She was tired and travel stained, dusty from the journey. She wished that she could have gone to Arnsworth House first to change and wash, but apparently her father insisted on seeing her first. Perhaps it was better to get it over and done with. Besides, Lord Aberfield would find fault with her appearance, or, failing that, with her very existence no matter what she did. Grimly she reminded herself that even if Aberfield House had not altered, she had. The despairing young girl who had left here eight years earlier was gone.

David's light knock on the door was answered by a loud injunction to enter. She did so, reminding herself to keep her face blank, her eyes downcast.

A swift glance located Lord Aberfield seated before the fire, one foot heavily bandaged, resting on a footstool. Thea uttered a mental curse: gout. He'd be in a foul mood.

David escorted her over to a chair. He smiled at her and cast a warning sort of glance at their father.

'Good afternoon, sir.'

Aberfield shot a glare at David. 'Took your damn time, didn't you?'

David looked amused. 'Next time I'll arrange winged horses, sir.'

Aberfield scowled and turned his gaze to Thea. 'Sit down. Hurry up. I've not got all day to waste on this. As for you, sirrah—' he turned to his son '—you may wait outside to take her over to Almeria Arnsworth. You've no more to do here.'

'I think not, sir,' said David calmly. 'I'll stay.' Grey eyes snapped fire.

'The devil you will,' said Aberfield. 'You've interfered quite enough. Writing your lying letters.'

A satisfied look of understanding came into David's face. 'So *that's* it. He *did* receive my letters before he died!'

'*Out.*' The softness of Aberfield's voice did not disguise his fury.

'Go to hell, sir.'

Thea blinked as she sat down. David's tones were as polite as they had been when he bid their father good day, and she didn't understand in the least what they were talking about. To whom had David written and what did it have to do with her coming to London?

Unable to quell his only son and heir's outright defiance, Aberfield snapped his attention back to Thea. 'Get that mealy mouthed look off your face,' he shot at her. 'You don't fool me, girl. I know what you—'

'Enough!' said David sharply.

Aberfield's eyes bulged, but he said only, 'Suppose he's told you already why I sent for you? Eh? Interfering cub!'

'No,' said Thea.

'No?' His colour rose. 'If I say he's an interfering—'

'I've no idea why you sent for me,' she interrupted him.

'Don't speak over me!' he snarled. 'Surrounded by worthless fools!' He caught David's eye and took a deep breath, evidently attempting to control himself. He continued in bitter tones, 'Well, he'll have told you that you are to go to Almeria Arnsworth for the Season?'

She nodded. 'Yes, sir, but I don't understand why.'

He snorted. 'Aye. And well you might not! God knows what I did to be saddled with you!' He caught David's eye again and said, 'Everything's different now.' He swept up a sheaf of papers from a wine table beside him and thrust them at her. 'Read those—if you can! What a damned mess! Thought I'd made things plain to the fool; but a few fairy tales, spun by—'

'I did what I thought right, sir,' said David.

An extraordinary noise burst from Aberfield, but he controlled himself and said to Thea, 'David must needs meddle, blast his eyes! I've no choice; but by God, if you're to marry, you'll marry as I say!'

Again she met David's eyes. This time he shook his head, his expression faintly apologetic.

'Read them, Thea,' he said gently.

What had he done?

Leaning forward, Thea took the papers from her father, forcing her expression to utter stillness, her hands to steadiness, despite the shaking of her insides.

The first paper was straightforward enough—a letter from a firm of London solicitors, assuring Lord Aberfield of their humble duty and informing him that it was their sad task to apprise him of the death in Bombay, some months earlier, of his brother-in-law, Theodore James Kirkcudbright. Thea bit her lip. Uncle Theo had been her godfather. She had been his heiress. Once.

She continued reading. The lawyers drew Lord Aberfield's attention to the enclosed copy of Mr Kirkcudbright's Last Will and Testament, which they believed to be rather different from the previous one. There were also two letters from the late Mr Kirkcudbright: one to his esteemed brother-in-law, the fifth Viscount Aberfield, and one to his goddaughter, Dorothea Sophie Winslow, only daughter of the said Viscount Aberfield. They believed the letters would sufficiently explicate Mr Kirkcudbright's intentions and remained his humble servants, et cetera, et cetera.

Puzzled, Thea turned to the letter addressed to herself. Her godfather had not written to her in several years…not since he had written to express his shame and disappointment in her.

My dear Dorothea,

I shall be dead and buried before you read this, and can only pray that your brother has not been misled by his Partiality into overstating your comparative Innocence in the Affair your father related to me several years ago. You will understand that in reinstating you in my Will I have placed the strictest controls upon your inheritance, so that you are not placed in the road of Temptation again. It is not my intention to reward any Transgression, but to show my Good Faith, and give you the opportunity to redress the situation by making a good marriage.

I remain your affectionate godfather and uncle,
Theodore Kirkcudbright

David had persuaded him to reinstate her.

Her stomach churning, she turned to the letter addressed to her father—then hesitated. 'This one is addressed to you, sir—'

'Read the lot!' he said savagely. 'Damn fool! I told him! *Warned* him what you were—and he does this!'

Sick and shaking, Thea looked at the letter to her father. And frowned. She was to have two hundred a year? From her twenty-fifth to thirtieth birthday, unless she married with her father's approval in the meantime, after which she would have the rest of the income...that Mr Kirkcudbright understood from his nephew that not all the blame could attach to Thea...that Aberfield's foolish attitude... She risked a glance at her father over the letter. No wonder he looked apoplectic.

Her world spun and reshaped itself. Two hundred a year—her twenty-fifth birthday was less than three months away...she would be free. Independent. What happened after her thirtieth birthday?

She turned to the will. Apart from various minor bequests, the major one was to herself. And after her thirtieth birthday she received the entire income from the bequest.

Dazed, she looked up and met her father's bitter gaze.

'Well?' he said. 'God, what a coil! I *told* him what had happened! And he does this! Now there's no help for it—you'll have to marry! Almeria Arnsworth will find you a husband.'

'Only if that's what Thea wants,' interrupted David.

Aberfield ignored that. 'It shouldn't be too hard with fifty thousand to sweeten the deal.'

Thea dropped the papers. *'Fifty thousand?'*

Lord Aberfield snorted. 'That's about the figure. In trust, of course. Thank God Theodore retained that much sense, despite David's meddling. And believe me, I'll see that you never get more than the two hundred a year if you don't marry with my permission!'

Two hundred a year until her thirtieth birthday. Thea said nothing, retrieving the papers from the floor. It was wealth. An independence. And it would be hers in less than three months. All she had to do was to avoid her father's matrimonial plans until then. An odd crunching noise distracted her. She looked up. Aberfield was grinding his teeth.

'Don't get any ideas about setting up your own establishment after your birthday,' he warned her. 'You'll be married long before then. In fact,' he said, 'you'll be married by the end of the Season!' He looked triumphant. 'Dunhaven—he'll have you.'

'What!'

This exploded from David. 'Dunhaven? For God's sake, sir! Are you insane?'

Aberfield banged the arm of his chair. 'Who else would have her?' He cast a contemptuous glance at his daughter. 'No point being fussy at this stage. Thing is to get her married off.'

'Thea,' began David, 'you don't have to—'

She waved him to silence and lifted her chin a notch and considered Aberfield from an entirely new perspective—that of having a choice.

Playing for time, she said, 'I assume, then, that Lord Dunhaven is now a widower?'

'Just out of mourning,' confirmed Aberfield. 'And looking for a bride.'

Her mind worked furiously. Appearing to fall in with his plans would be far safer. Safer than outright defiance anyway. He had shown once before that there was little he would not do to force her compliance... If she allowed him to think that she would toe the line...

Calmly she rose to her feet. 'I shall look forward to renewing my acquaintance with Lord Dunhaven then. I won't keep you any longer, sir. I have no doubt that I shall be perfectly safe under Lady Arnsworth's roof.'

David's sharply indrawn breath told her that he had understood her meaning perfectly.

Aberfield's face was mottled. 'Just remember: this time,

you'll do as you're bid. Don't expect me to protect you if you play fast and loose with another suitor!'

Her temper slipped its leash very slightly. 'Nothing, sir,' she said, 'could possibly lead me to expect anything of the sort.'

'Miss Winslow and Mr Winslow, my lady,' Myles announced. His eyes flickered briefly to Richard, with what Richard would have sworn was a look of amused sympathy.

So he'd been right. A trap. And Myles knew all about it. He wouldn't have been surprised had the dainty gilt chair he sat in suddenly sprouted shackles as Almeria rose and swept forward to greet her visitors.

Richard rose automatically as Thea Winslow and her brother came forward. Then he blinked in frowning disbelief. Could this be Thea? Dressed all in grey, not a scrap of colour, not a frill nor flounce relieved the drab, functional appearance of her pelisse and bonnet. She looked more like a governess or companion than an heiress.

Almeria said, 'Welcome, my dears.' She took Thea by the hand and leaned forward to kiss her cheek. 'Dear Dorothea, do come and sit down.' She led her to a chair, still patting her hand affectionately. 'I am sure you are exhausted after your journey. Shall I ring for some tea?'

Even her cheeks looked grey. A pang went through him. Did she still mourn Lallerton?

For an instant their eyes met, and shock hit him as her gaze blanked. She hadn't recognised him.

But would he have recognised her? The soft tawny curls were doubtless still there, hidden beneath the bonnet and cap. And her eyes—perhaps it was the grey of her gown, but he remembered them as more blue than grey. He remembered her face as vivid, expressive—not this blank mask with shuttered eyes. And she was thinner than he remembered.

He could have passed her in the street, even spoken to her, and not realised who she was. Yet now that he looked closely, in some strange way he did recognise her—as one sees the likeness between a waxwork doll and a friend.

The ache inside deepened. Had grief done this to her?

Thea's breath jerked in as she realised that Lady Arnsworth had a gentleman with her.

The gentleman had risen and regarded her with a friendly smile on his face. She lifted her chin a little. Surely he was familiar...tall, a spare frame, dark brown hair, his face lined a little...no, it couldn't be—

'I am sure you both remember my nephew, Mr Richard Blakehurst.'

It was. Richard Blakehurst. Lady Arnsworth's nephew and other godchild. Richard with his broken leg. As a boy he'd spent months here at Arnsworth House recovering after a riding accident that left it doubtful if he would ever walk again without the aid of crutches.

David was the first to speak, his voice coldly biting. 'Blakehurst. I didn't expect to see you here.'

Richard's eyes narrowed at this chilly acknowledgement. 'A mutual feeling, Winslow. How do you do?'

Eyes glittering, David strode forward and took the proffered hand.

'Servant, Blakehurst.' His tone suggested anything but cordiality.

Thea felt her cheeks burn. For heaven's sake! Surely David did not imagine that Richard could possibly have joined the ranks of fortune hunters? Or that he could pose the least danger to her?

Seemingly unconcerned, Richard turned to her.

Swallowing hard, she nodded. 'I...yes. I remember Mr Blakehurst. You are well, sir?'

The dark brows shot up. His eyes. She had forgotten how expressive they were. And she did not remember him as being quite so tall. Or the planes of his face to be so...so hard.

He inclined his head. 'Very well, I thank you, Miss Winslow. Delighted to meet you again.'

Panic flooded her as he came towards her, hand outstretched.

He was going to take her hand. He would touch her. And she had stripped off her gloves in the hall…

Richard. This is Richard…you knew him as a boy… She forced herself to stillness. But Richard Blakehurst was no longer a boy. Tall, broad-shouldered—despite the remaining halt in his stride, Richard was a man…

Deliberately she lifted her chin. She knew Richard; he had been her friend—it wouldn't be too bad… Braced to withstand her usual panic, she held out her hand. A gentle vice gripped it. Her breath jerked in and caught as tingling warmth laced every nerve.

Their eyes met, his suddenly intent, even startled. She was wildly conscious of the strength of his long fingers. They tightened very slightly, as though staking a claim, and an instant later released her.

The sudden silence seemed to hum with awareness as she struggled to understand what had happened.

Lady Arnsworth bustled up. 'Do sit down, dear Dorothea,' she said. 'How nice that Richard was here to meet you. It must be several years since you met.'

'Eight, or…or thereabouts,' Thea temporised, as she sat down. He had attended her come-out ball. Eight years ago, though his touch hadn't seared her.

'Of course,' said Lady Arnsworth. She turned to her nephew. 'Although I dare say, Richard, that you see Mr Winslow from time to time?'

'Not often of late years,' said Richard, resuming his seat.

Thea tried to listen, nodding occasionally, as Lady Arnsworth outlined all her plans for the Season, which were comprehensive to say the least.

Richard must be…two and thirty now, surely. He was about eight years older than she. He couldn't really be any taller than she remembered. It just seemed that way for some reason. She flickered sideways glances at him, trying to understand what it was about him that was so different to her.

Lady Arnsworth continued to expound her campaign. Almack's, of course. There could be not the least trouble in the world gaining vouchers…

Perhaps it was just that he was broader. Yes. That was it. He was a long way removed from the rather slight young man she remembered. She wondered if he still enjoyed chess... He had been a formidable opponent and she did not doubt that he was even more formidable now. Something about the calm self-contained gaze told her that. Still waters...

Only none of that explained why her whole body had seemed to shimmer and leap to life when he took her hand...

Lady Arnsworth preened a little as she listed the invitations they were likely to receive. Once people knew that dear Dorothea was at Arnsworth House, there would be invitations aplenty. And Lord Dunhaven had already left his card.

An odd choking noise came from Richard, and, glancing at him, Thea had the distinct impression that something had struck a jarring note with Mr Richard Blakehurst. His jaw bore a startling resemblance to solid stone.

A glance at David revealed his jaw in much the same condition, which was no surprise at all after what he had said about Lord Dunhaven as they crossed the Square.

Lady Arnsworth sailed on, listing all the more influential hostesses who would be *aux anges* to receive the Honourable Miss Winslow.

The Honourable, *wealthy* Miss Winslow. Lady Arnsworth didn't bother to spell that out.

Mr Blakehurst's fathomless gaze met hers over the rim of his glass. Thea forced herself not to look away, to keep her own expression blank... Richard had...had grown up. That was all. It had been surprise, nothing more. Nothing deeper.

Lady Arnsworth finished, 'I don't doubt we will be invited everywhere. Everyone will wish to make Dorothea's acquaintance, you may be sure.'

'Oh, without a doubt,' said Mr Blakehurst. 'How could it possibly be otherwise?'

Thea's gaze narrowed at the faintly ironic tone, as a spurt of annoyance flared, swiftly suppressed. Control. She could not afford to betray anything.

Lady Arnsworth shot Richard a quelling glare and turned back to Thea.

'Now, my dear,' she said, 'should you like to go up to your bedchamber and rest? Dinner will not be for some time, but perhaps some tea on a tray?'

Another strangled noise came from Richard, but, ignoring this, Lady Arnsworth smiled graciously at David. 'And I am sure, Mr Winslow, that you will wish to inform Lord Aberfield that Dorothea is safely with me. My nephew will see you out. I shall bid you farewell now.'

Chapter Two

There was something distinctly strained about Richard's voice as he assured Lady Arnsworth that he would not be in the least put out, but Thea had no time to ponder on it as she bid David farewell, and Lady Arnsworth led her from the room.

All along the upper hallway, Lady Arnsworth waxed lyrical about the joys of London. Especially for '…a young lady as well-dowered as you, dear Dorothea!'

Thea could not repress a chill, remembering how people clustered around heiresses. Gentlemen, smiling, pretending affection, while all the time… She pushed the thought away. She would manage perfectly well once she was accustomed.

Except— 'I…ma'am, I would really rather not have dozens of suitors tripping over themselves. After all—'

After all, what? What can you possibly tell her that would convince her you don't want a husband?

Lady Arnsworth opened the door to the bedchamber, an arrested expression on her face. '*Dozens* of suitors?'

It was as though the idea had never occurred to her.

Thea flushed. Was she that much of an antidote these days? 'Well, fortune hunters,' she said, following her godmother across the threshold.

A maidservant was already putting her belongings away.

'Fortune hunters? Oh, dear me, no! There will be nothing like that.'

And the sun might rise in the west. 'There won't?'

'Oh, no…now I am sure you will be perfectly comfortable in this chamber. And don't worry about fortune hunters. You may trust me to see to *that*. Why, the very idea! The maid will have your things unpacked in no time,' she said. 'And if there is anything you require, of course you must tell me.'

'Thank you, ma'am,' said Thea politely. 'Er, you seem very certain about the fortune hunters.'

'Ah, the girl has finished.' Lady Arnsworth flipped her hand at the maid. 'That will be all.'

The maid dropped a curtsy and left. Lady Arnsworth turned back to Thea.

'My dear, what a sensible girl you are!' Her ladyship was all smiles as she took Thea's hand. 'While naturally your circumstances will attract a certain amount of attention, you may rest assured that as your sponsor and chaperon, I shall be most careful to ensure that only the most eligible suitors are brought to your notice. Two, perhaps three at the most should be quite sufficient.'

Thea blinked as Lady Arnsworth patted her hand and repressed a shiver at even that simple touch. Two or three? What would her ladyship think if she knew that Thea didn't want *any* suitors?

She tried. 'As to that, ma'am, I have no thought of marriage. I…I find the whole idea…that is—' Her throat tightened.

Lady Arnsworth looked away and fiddled with her rings, turning them to better display the stones. 'Ah, yes. Your father did mention that—

'Of course, such things are not quite unknown.' There was something very odd in her voice, not quite distaste… She met Thea's puzzled gaze. 'Generally one does not approve, but under the circumstances—and your fortune is considerable. I am sure you need not worry.' She fussed with her cuffs, still avoiding Thea's shocked gaze.

Thea said nothing to this, but gripped her underlip hard between her teeth.

'Naturally your years of, er, mourning have given you ample time for reflection.'

'They certainly have,' said Thea, finding her voice.

Looking far more at ease, Lady Arnsworth said carefully, 'Indeed your feelings are quite understandable. I found the marriage act most unpleasant myself. But it is our duty. And once you have done your duty and provided the heir—and a spare, of course—if you wish it, most gentlemen will respect a lady's natural modesty and seek their pleasures elsewhere for the most part. Men, of course, are different. Very different. Now, I must change. I will be out this evening, but tomorrow we will have to do some shopping.' She cast a pained glance at Thea's travelling dress. 'Yes. A new wardrobe is of the first importance! I venture to suggest that you will feel very different when properly gowned!'

And with that, Lady Arnsworth whisked herself out of the room.

Staring at the closed door, Thea faced the fact that her father had told Lady Arnsworth the truth. Or at least the truth as he saw it. And she had the oddest notion that it had not been the fifty thousand pounds that had tipped the balance for Almeria Arnsworth…although that would certainly be the case with most of society. She felt sick to her stomach, thinking of the next couple of months to be spent in the full glare of society and its crowding, jostling throng…all of whom would turn on her if they knew the truth… From nowhere panic ambushed her, sinking familiar claws deep. Her stomach clenched, warding off the striking terror. She forced her body to relax, her lungs to draw breath steadily, blanking her mind. And as suddenly it was gone, a chill warning, leaving her cold and shaking, but free and rational. Free to wonder if she had been completely insane to imagine that she could do this.

As the drawing room door clicked behind Almeria and her houseguest, Richard throttled the urge to swear resoundingly. He could only marvel at the neatness of the trap, as he sat down. A trap compounded of his own good manners. The same good manners that would keep him from strangling his godmother when she returned. Very well, he was fond of Almeria too, and she was family.

'Quite a coincidence that you are here to greet my sister, Blakehurst,' remarked David in biting accents.

Richard's normally even temper flickered. 'Just so,' he said. 'Do take a seat again, Winslow.'

Perhaps he would strangle Almeria. Affectionately, of course. If he lived long enough. Judging by Winslow's narrowed gaze, there was every chance he might not.

'You are staying in town?' David asked, in deceptively casual tones. He remained standing.

Not deceived in the slightest, Richard said, 'I am. Here, as a matter of fact.'

The silence that followed this admission seethed.

Richard sat back and waited. Winslow's grey eyes resembled nothing more than twin blades.

'How very…convenient.'

Richard's temper did a great deal more than flicker. It smoked and curled at the edges. Winslow's attitude reeked of protective elder brother, although why he would imagine that Thea required protection from himself was beyond Richard's comprehension. And there was something else in Winslow's level gaze: scorn.

'Can I pour you a brandy?' he offered politely, damping down his temper.

Winslow declined. 'Thank you. No. I will take my leave of you.'

Richard smiled. 'Then no doubt I shall see you again. You will be calling on Miss Winslow, I dare say.'

'Most definitely,' her brother replied in clipped tones. 'If only to keep an eye on all the scaff and raff who cluster around heiresses.'

Richard blinked. Then anger welled up—it was a very long time since anyone had accused him of being a fortune hunter. And even then, at least he had been well aware of the chit's fortune! This time…

'No need to summon the butler. I'll find my own way out.' David executed a perfunctory bow and left.

Left alone, Richard said several things he had suppressed when Almeria left the room—and a few more for good measure. While he'd known that Thea must at least be respectably dowered, the term *heiress* suggested a great deal more. And while Almeria's penchant for dropping stray heiresses in his path had caused him considerable embarrassment on occasion, he couldn't recall that it had ever put him in danger of his life before. There had been a definite glint of gun metal in Winslow's eyes.

He took a deep breath. And then there was Thea herself. Something had wrought a change in her that went far beyond years. Far beyond the change from a young girl on the eve of her come-out to a young woman. Thea-the-girl had been exuberant, bubbling over with mischief. Thea-the-woman seemed half-lost in shadow…only there had been that flash of light when their hands met—as though something had awakened inside her.

And as for her blasted, hitherto unsuspected fortune— Winslow was right; it would have the fortune hunters out in force.

By the time Almeria returned to the drawing room, he had managed to reduce the situation to its proper proportion. Almeria was matchmaking. No more. No less. He rose as she sailed into the room, saying airily, 'I must have forgot to make clear to you that Dorothea will be my guest for the Season! 'Tis positively shocking how forgetful one becomes as the years advance!'

Despite himself, Richard nearly grinned. 'Quite shocking,' he said gravely. Not that he, nor anyone else, would dare suggest to Almeria that she was advanced in years. Although she must be slipping if she expected him to believe that all this had not been carefully prearranged.

Occasionally a little unsubtlety was called for.

He settled for being extremely unsubtle.

'Almeria—what the deuce are you up to?'

'Up to?' she said with a lift of her brows. 'Why should you imagine I am up to anything? Really, Richard!'

'Fudge,' he said bluntly. 'Don't waste your breath, Almeria. Instead, tell me precisely what is the extent of Thea's fortune. I was not aware she had one.'

Almeria looked a little conscious. 'Her godfather's fortune. *Not* the sort of thing one counts on, although he always intended to leave it to her, but after all, he might have married. And it is not a terribly big fortune as these things go, of course.'

The prickle at the back of his neck escalated into outright alarm bells.

'Just *how* not-terribly-big are we talking about here?' he pressed.

'Only fifty thousand,' said Almeria with an airy wave. 'And derived from *trade,* of course!' This last with a faint grimace.

Fifty thousand? *Only* fifty thousand? Hell and damnation! With that much at stake, it wouldn't surprise him to hear that Almeria already had the special licence in her reticule and a tame bishop in the back parlour.

The suspicion that he had stepped into a well-laid and very sticky trap was unavoidable.

But he could make one or two things plain.

'Almeria—let us be quite clear. Although I intend to marry, I am *not* in the market for an heiress, and—'

'Oh, for goodness' sake!' Almeria settled her skirts with a swish as she sat down. 'Naturally when Aberfield asked that I chaperon Dorothea, I thought of you—since you were going to visit me anyway...' She looked more than a trifle evasive.

'Was I?'

Richard couldn't recall his plans including anything of the sort. Almeria's summons to visit her as soon as he reached town had arrived several days ago quite unheralded. However, that wasn't to say that *Almeria's* plans...

She glared at him. 'Since I was *intending* to invite you—'

The moment she had an heiress staying with her—that went without saying.

'Richard, you must marry sensibly!' she said crossly. 'You need a wife, the right wife. Especially now that you have bought that property in Kent. One assumes you intend to get an heir!'

Wisely, Richard held his counsel. There was nothing to gain from encouraging Almeria. No matter how right she happened to be.

'And as for leaving these things to take care of themselves,' she said, returning to an earlier theme, 'I would have thought the danger of that was made plain by the appalling mess Max has—'

'Enough!' He controlled himself with an effort and said in a gentler tone, 'Almeria, I cannot possibly remain here if you are to criticise Max and Verity. He is happy. Does that count for nothing?'

Goaded, Almeria snapped, 'And how long can it last before she does something disgraceful?'

Enough was enough. 'Like what? Cuckold him? Is that what you mean?'

Her colour rose. 'Exactly!'

He shrugged. 'Then he would have to cope with it. In his own way.' Seeing Almeria's mouth open, he added, 'Just as our father did, in fact.'

Her mouth closed.

'Did you think I never realised? That summer I broke my leg and stayed with you here, I knew then.'

Almeria was scarlet. 'At least my sister was discreet!' she said furiously. 'I do not say that I approved of her behaviour, but she did not bring any disgrace upon the family!' With which she rose, swept past him and left the drawing room again. The door shut with the sort of controlled click that was a well-bred woman's alternative to slamming it. Settling back in his chair, he took a measured sip of brandy and muttered a few things that it was as well Almeria couldn't hear. What the devil was he to do now?

He had to wonder if every god in the pantheon had conspired against him. His laudable plan of reconciling Almeria to Max's marriage was clearly misfiring. Instead of accepting his own delight in the match, the mere sight of him was enough to stir up all her outrage at the ruin of his supposed expectations. Worse, she was now about to fling fifty thousand pounds' worth of heiress at his head. Although probably not with Aberfield's blessing.

In fact, Aberfield would probably succumb to apoplexy if he knew what Almeria was up to. A viscount, and a wealthy one at that, Aberfield didn't have a seat in the cabinet any more, but he wielded a fair amount of influence with those who did.

Almeria was howling at the moon. Aberfield would never accept a match to a younger son, remarkable only for living within his means, his fortune respectable but no more, and about as much interested in a political career as he was interested in succeeding to his twin's title—to wit, not at all. All Richard wanted was a quiet, private life improving his recently purchased acres and reading his books.

Nigel Lallerton was a younger son. He dismissed that as irrelevant. Lallerton had been set for a safe seat in parliament, supporting his father's interest. Not to mention Aberfield's interest. Lallerton's father, Lord Chasewater, had been an old political crony. No doubt the match was stitched up between them as mutually beneficial. It had probably been sheer luck that Thea had cared so deeply for Lallerton.

Stretching out his stiff leg, he considered his options.

If he returned to the country, Almeria would think it was because of what she'd said about Verity. Richard frowned. Max could look after Verity, but even so, he hesitated to expose his sister-in-law to any more of Almeria's rancour. Nor did he wish the rift between Max and Almeria to widen.

Besides, Almeria would be hurt if he left. She was actually fond of him, he reminded himself firmly. When he'd broken his leg, she had come up to town and had him to stay as soon as the doctors said his leg had healed enough for him to travel. Not that a twelve-year-old with a broken leg, wondering if he would ever walk again, had been precisely grateful for that, but nevertheless she had been kind to him. Buying him as many books as he could read, insisting that the kitchen made his favourite cake at least once a day. She had even put up with his dog, although she hated dogs in the house.

He grimaced. His own mother, while professing to be utterly devoted to her sons, had attended a succession of house parties that summer. He hadn't understood why at first…Almeria had taken over. Brisk, no-nonsense and frequently acerbic on the subject of his idiocy in trying to ride that damned hunter in the first place, but she had been there, while his own mother wafted through London several times between gatherings and recommended laudanum when she thought he looked *out of sorts*. She had invariably been accompanied by Lord Ketterley—he grimaced. Ketterley had seemed such a decent fellow…it had been Max, cynical, rebellious Max, who had worked it all out…

Almeria hadn't even complained when she discovered that he had inveigled Myles into playing chess with him. Her face when she caught them, though! Three days later she had appeared triumphantly with her other godchild, five-year-old Thea Winslow, announcing that *Dear Dorothea is come to stay as well, and she is most interested in learning to play chess…* The twelve-year-old Richard had barely choked back his disgust at having dear, *little* Dorothea foisted upon him. He'd taught her to play chess in sheer self-defence.

He found himself smiling as he remembered the little girl who had pored over the chess board, chewing her bottom lip with her untidy curls for ever falling into her eyes. Even at sixteen when she had made her come-out, her unruly curls had tended to escape their bonds. He'd teased her for it… He frowned as something occurred to him; there hadn't been a wisp in sight today. For all he knew, she might be bald under that ghastly bonnet. Not that he understood anything about fashion, but he could recognise an ugly bonnet when he saw one.

An odd thought came to him—could he help Thea?

Help Thea? An heiress?

Even an heiress needs a friend.

He grimaced. Almeria would be looking for every opportunity to throw them together. Was he really going to be so foolish as to assist her? A memory of grey eyes that should have been blue suggested that he was.

He sighed. It would probably be polite to inform Braybrook in person that he no longer had a houseguest.

Julian, Lord Braybrook, received the news that his guest of twenty-four hours would be departing, with a suspicious degree of *sangfroid*.

He laid down his pen, leaned back in his desk chair and said merely, 'Ah.' Not at all as though the news came as a surprise.

Richard eyed him warily.

'Food not up to standard, old chap?' enquired Braybrook in tones of polite interest. 'Bed unaired?'

Richard grinned. 'Indigestible. And damned chilly. How the devil did you find out so fast?'

'Thanks,' said Braybrook drily. 'For God's sake, Ricky! Are you mad? As for how I found out—I have just sustained a visit from the outraged brother!'

'Winslow?'

'She's only got the one,' said Braybrook.

Richard nodded slowly. 'I'd forgotten you were friendly. He's not been in town much the last few years.'

'No,' said Braybrook. 'But he recalled that I was also acquainted with you. You may imagine my surprise when he informed me that you were staying with Lady Arnsworth.' He shot Richard an odd glance. 'I was under the impression you planned to seek out lodgings.'

'It's not what it looks like,' said Richard, rather shocked to realise that his teeth were gritted.

'Of course not. And I do hope you will appreciate my discretion in not informing Winslow that your sojourn with Lady Arnsworth is of such recent date.'

'Dammit, Julian! I didn't even know Miss Winslow was expected when Almeria persuaded me to stay!'

'Then what did persuade you?' He flung up a hand as Richard glared at him. 'Oh, don't be a gudgeon! *I* know you aren't the sort to dangle after heiresses! I even did my best to reassure Winslow on that head; but I will admit to a very human curiosity about what possible cause you could have for staying with Lady Arnsworth!' He grinned. 'Apart from my unaired beds and the indigestible food.'

Despite his annoyance, Richard laughed. Damn. Telling Julian that in some odd way he was worried about Thea would have the fellow leaping to all sorts of unwarranted conclusions. Instead he fell back on his original reason for accepting. 'Almeria is still very bitter about Max's marriage, you know,' he said.

Braybrook looked rather self-conscious. 'So I hear.'

Something about his voice alerted Richard. 'Yes?'

'I had a letter from Serena,' said Braybrook.

Richard nodded. Serena, Lady Braybrook, was the previous Lord Braybrook's widow. Julian's stepmother. Almeria had long considered it her duty to keep the invalid Lady Braybrook fully apprised of her stepson's indiscretions.

'Yes?'

'Lady Arnsworth had written to her.'

Richard suppressed a grin at the irritation in his voice. 'Ah. Giving her advice on how to marry you off?'

Braybrook snorted. 'Precisely. Citing Max as a fearful example of what happens when a man is left to his own devices in the matter.'

'Annoying,' replied Richard, 'but there's nothing new in that. She said as much to me this afternoon. She's doubly furious because of the expected baby.'

The blue eyes narrowed. 'Maybe. Did she also express doubts about the child's paternity?'

'*What?*'

'No. I didn't think she'd have said that to you. Obviously you don't have to worry about it going any further, but she hinted at it in her letter to Serena.'

Richard swore. 'Is she still harping on that? She said something to that effect last year.'

'To you?'

'And Max,' said Richard grimly.

Braybrook's jaw dropped. 'That would explain why Max is at outs with her.'

'Exactly,' said Richard. 'Which is why I agreed to stay with her,' he went on. 'To try to convince her that Max's marriage has not consigned me to poverty, before she says something to create a permanent breach between herself and Max!'

A sceptical brow lifted. 'And questioning the child's paternity to his face hasn't done that already?'

Richard grimaced. 'Not quite. Max doesn't want a breach any more than I do, but if it comes to a choice between Almeria or protecting Verity—' He broke off. 'You know what he will do.'

Braybrook made a rude noise. 'Slight understatement there, Ricky. If it came to a choice between the entire world and protecting Lady Blakehurst, Max would consign the lot of us to perdition!'

Richard smiled. 'True.'

Braybrook looked curious. 'You know, Ricky—I've never quite understood just why Lady Arnsworth was so fixated on Max remaining single?'

Richard frowned. 'Max never told you?'

'I never asked.'

He nodded. 'It was my accident that started it. Mama and Almeria blamed Max for daring me to ride the cursed horse. Never mind that I was perfectly capable of saying no to him, he'd suggested it and therefore it was all his fault. Later, I was supposed to go into the army—Mama insisted that my leg made that unsuitable, and that Max should be bought a commission instead.'

'What else did they have in mind for him?' asked Julian.

'The church, if you can believe it.'

A most peculiar choking sound came from Lord Braybrook.

'Quite,' said Richard. 'I think he preferred the army on the whole. He was a damn sight better suited to it than I was.' He sighed. 'And then Freddy died not long after our father. And suddenly Max was the earl. But instead of demanding that he settle down and secure the succession, both Mama and Almeria decided between them that he owed it to me to remain single!'

'How very melodramatic of them,' observed Julian.

Richard snorted. 'I didn't take it seriously, but Max did. He always blamed himself for my accident anyway and Mama and Almeria had rubbed it in with a vengeance over the years.'

Braybrook's mouth twitched. 'And, of course, it's plain to the meanest intelligence that you yourself are bitterly disappointed in being cut out of an earldom,' he said drily.

'Bitterly,' said Richard, yawning. 'I've enough money for my wants.'

'And if you don't,' said Braybrook, 'you could always marry Miss Winslow.' He grinned wickedly. 'No point cutting off your nose to spite your face, you know. After all, she might be your perfect bride!'

'As long as her brother doesn't shoot me first,' said Richard sarcastically.

Unholy amusement gleamed in bright blue eyes. 'A risk, of course. Mind you, it would certainly calm Lady Arnsworth down to see you safely legshackled to an heiress!' He grinned. 'Proof positive that your game leg and Max's marriage have not combined to blight your life.'

'Oh, go to the devil, Julian,' recommended Richard.

All the same, the flippant advice niggled at him as he blew out his bedside lamp later that night, after walking back to Arnsworth House, as it had done all through dinner and numerous hands of piquet afterwards. A circumstance that had led to Julian relieving him of a vast, if imaginary, fortune.

In the best spare bedchamber, Thea Winslow was probably sound asleep…a thought that had made him very, very edgy as he'd tiptoed past to his own room… It had been a distinct shock to find a sleepy footman waiting up for him. He'd forgotten to keep his voice down as he told the man never to do such a thing again. He hoped it hadn't disturbed Thea… He pushed the recurring thought of Thea away. Thea Winslow, sleeping peacefully just down the hallway, was no concern of his. Or she ought not to be.

No point cutting off your nose to spite your face...she might be your perfect bride...

Leaving perfect out of it, he had always intended to marry. Marriage had always made complete sense—at some dim, unspecified future time. Apparently the future had arrived. With the purchase of an estate and a London house, marriage was becoming, if not imperative, then at least desirable. All he needed to do was choose the right woman—and of course persuade her that he was the right man. Yes, a sensible, intelligent woman with a sense of humour. She didn't need to be wealthy, just someone he liked and respected... His stomach clenched—someone who wouldn't view a child's broken leg as an interruption to her own life. Someone who wouldn't mind that her husband had absolutely no ambition to figure in society, but preferred a quiet life in the country with his books and acres, and was happy to remain there with him for the most part. Happy to remain, not self-sacrificing...not complaining that she had nothing to amuse her, and flitting off to yet another house party with her lover—he slammed a lid down on that; there was no point being bitter about the past, but you could learn from it. He added another criterion: honour. He wanted a woman to whom honour was more important than discretion.

Common sense firmly in place, he permitted his thoughts to turn to Thea. He liked her. He always had. She had always been blazingly honest as a child, and young girl, sometimes when it might have been wiser to dissemble a little. And she was loyal— if she had mourned Nigel Lallerton so deeply, he needed no further proof of that. What if she *were* the right choice for him? The sensible, logical choice...folly to discount her simply because of Almeria's entirely predictable matchmaking.

She was here in the house. It was the perfect opportunity to find out if she really would suit him. He caught himself—if *they* would suit. For all he knew, his bookish habits might drive her to distraction. Or his tendency to leave curls of shaved wood everywhere from his whittling. If their old childhood friendship could become an adult friendship and the basis for a successful marriage…an irritatingly rational voice suggested that perhaps he was being a little bit *too* rational about this, that perhaps he might look for a woman to love…after all, love wasn't ruining Max's life. Quite the opposite.

He rolled over and punched the pillow. That was all very well, but if he hadn't fallen in love in thirty-two years, what were the odds of it happening now? A sensible marriage would be far more…sensible. Logical.

Safe.

His father had loved—and look what that had led to…a totally unsuitable choice. Max had been lucky. Damned lucky.

There could be no harm in spending time with Thea, and renewing their friendship. He liked that idea. What he didn't like was the memory of Thea as he had seen her that afternoon, all the old laughter and liveliness quenched. A feeling that was not in the least sensible stole over him…whatever had been responsible for the grey shadow in eyes that ought to have been blue— he wanted to remove it.

Hours after going to bed Thea lay waiting for sleep. Perhaps she should light a lamp and read for a while. The strange bed unnerved her…but it was so late. Surely she would sleep if she closed her eyes and emptied her mind. She had become very good at that over the years—keeping her mind utterly blank, refusing to allow emotion to creep in.

But now, back in London, among people who had known her as a child, a young girl—even though her body ached with tiredness, the thoughts and feelings held sleep at bay.

A little spark of anger flared in a dark corner of her heart, a corner she never looked into. From her father's point of view, her marriage now was an unquestioned necessity. She rolled over and thumped the pillow. She would *not,* under any circumstances, acquiesce to any match proposed by her father.

The little spark had caught, lighting up the corner. Thea shut her eyes to it, dousing it. She *wouldn't* look there. She mustn't. Better that it remained shadowed. Hidden from the light. If she permitted herself to feel anything again...anger, hurt...even love, she pushed them all away. Safer to remain calm. Unmoved. As untouched as she could ever be.

The news would be all over London that Miss Winslow, only daughter of Viscount Aberfield and heiress to fifty thousand pounds, was residing in Grosvenor Square with Lady Arnsworth. She would be sought out. Courted, flattered, every social distinction pressed upon her.

The thought sickened her.

Money bought acceptance; with fifty thousand pounds, as long as the truth remained a whisper, the past would be ignored by many. Not by all, but many including her own father.

She gritted her teeth. She didn't want that sort of acceptance anyway. Especially not from Aberfield. Uncle James had shown more understanding and affection for her than her own father. He had been prepared to believe her innocence and reverse his decision to disinherit her. Aberfield had reinstated her only because of the money. It was easier somehow to think of him as Aberfield, not Papa. It wasn't as though he wanted her as his daughter. All he wanted was for her money to secure a husband of benefit to himself.

A queer thought came to her—she doubted that her money would buy Richard's good opinion if ever he knew the truth. She could count on his honesty. She shivered, and drew the blankets closer. Why was she thinking of Richard anyway? How could she know what he had become? She hadn't seen him since her come-out ball.

The memory slipped past her defences. He had danced with her that night, laughing because her wretched hair was escaping, enjoying the ball as much as she, although he rarely danced because of his leg. He had danced with her twice, and then she hadn't seen him again until today.

She pushed the memory away. Richard would be revolted if he knew the truth; at best he would feel sorry for her.

She didn't want pity. She wanted nothing of anyone. She didn't need anyone—she could stand by herself. And in less than three months she would be free. Only…what on earth would she do with her freedom once she had it? She would enjoy it, that was what. And in the meantime she would enjoy herself now. Here. In London. She was not going to permit her fears to rule her life—she would not wait for her twenty-fifth birthday to release her, she would begin now. Tomorrow—no, it was tomorrow already. Today. She would begin today. She had put off enough tomorrows.

Thea arose early the following morning and dressed without summoning a maid—she could manage her short wraparound stays herself. Unsurprisingly when she went downstairs, she found the breakfast parlour empty. Having been out the previous evening, Lady Arnsworth would probably not arise until noon. Fully expecting to have to ring for tea and toast, she was startled to find a varied selection of food set out in chafing dishes on the sideboard, including, to her great surprise, sirloin.

Puzzled at this very masculine inclusion, Thea helped herself to toast, poached eggs and ham, and made a pot of tea from the urn steaming in the corner.

She enjoyed a leisurely breakfast, and afterwards sipped her tea with lingering enjoyment, wondering what she might do with her day. A day in which she might do precisely as she pleased.

Contemplating this rare treasure, Thea poured another cup of tea. She might take one of the maids and go for a walk. She could visit Hatchards. She might—

Stare at Mr Richard Blakehurst strolling into the breakfast parlour as though he owned it! At this hour! Swallowing her tea with difficulty, she realised that his limp was far less noticeable these days, more a slight halt in the stride than a limp. The harsh lines pain had etched in his face made him look rather forbidding.

Until he smiled his familiar crooked smile.

Which he was doing now, the corners of his eyes creasing in the way she remembered. His whole face lightened. She remembered that too, Richard smiling at her as he clumsily partnered her in a country dance. But he'd always been just Richard. An extra brother. Someone dependable. A dear friend. She didn't remember that she had ever thought of him as attractive...

'Good morning, Thea,' he said pleasantly.

She found herself smiling back.

Attractive? Surely not.

Oh, yes, he was. Even more so as his smile deepened in response to her own.

'Good morning,' she returned, confused. 'Er, Lady Arnsworth is not yet down, sir.'

His brows rose. 'Just as well,' he said, strolling to the sideboard. 'Or you would have to revive me with burnt feathers.'

A giggle escaped her at the image, and with a perfectly straight face Richard added, 'No proper lady leaves her bedchamber before noon, you know.'

Laughter bubbled up. 'Are you implying, sir—?'

'That proper ladies bore me,' he said, grinning. 'That's better. You should laugh more often. And stop calling me *sir,* Thea. It makes my teeth ache. Now, what have we here?' He lifted the lid of one of the chafing dishes.

She glared at him. 'A trifle early for morning calls, is it not?' she enquired. 'Especially when your aunt is still abed.' Better to ignore the implication that she didn't laugh enough.

He looked around, with a sudden frown. 'She didn't tell you?'

'Tell me what?'

The frown deepened. 'This isn't a morning call. I'm staying here too.'

'*What!*' Her teacup clattered into its saucer. 'Why?'

'Heiress hunting,' he said blandly, carving some sirloin.

'I *beg* your pardon?' she said icily.

'Absolved,' he said promptly. 'I'm sure you didn't mean to be rude.'

Her mouth twitched. She had forgotten his ability to turn the tables so neatly in any verbal sparring.

He helped himself to mustard, sat down and smiled at her

again. 'Don't blame me. Curse our mutual godmother.' He took
a mouthful.

'But why are you staying here?' she asked, refusing to return
that annoyingly infectious smile. Smiles like that ought to be
outlawed anyway!

He finished his mouthful and said, 'Because I have business
in London and Almeria invited me.'

'Oh.' His business was none of her concern. 'Then—'

'I am *not* pursuing you,' he growled. 'And so you may tell
your fire-eating brother! You could have twice the fortune and I
wouldn't be interested in it! I have a little more pride than that!'

For a moment shocked silence hung between them.

Shame burnt her cheeks, and deep inside, coldness spread,
leaching through her, a slow poison welling up. She fought it
down, forcing herself to seem untouched, unmoved.

'I suppose I must thank you for making your sentiments so
plain,' she said stiffly. It didn't matter. It didn't! After all, she
didn't want him, or any man, to pursue her. The chill spread
further. *How* had he known? Lady Arnsworth?

Then— 'Oh, damn!' said Richard. 'I mean, I beg your pardon,
Thea. That was not at all how I meant to put it. What I *meant* is
that I am not on the catch for an heiress. Any heiress. Unfortunately for us, Almeria has other ideas.'

Thea took a shaky breath. She had thought—for one dreadful
eternal instant—that he knew. 'I…very well…' Then his remark
about Lady Arnsworth's plans crashed into her. 'What do you
mean, Lady Arnsworth has other ideas?'

He looked at her in disbelief. 'Thea—stop wool-gathering.
Think—her goddaughter with a fortune of fifty thousand pounds;
her godson and favourite nephew, a younger son with no expectations whatsoever—clearly a match made in heaven.'

Her eyes widened as that stabbed home. Oh, God! Why hadn't
she seen it? No wonder Lady Arnsworth had assured her that
there would be no swarms of fortune hunters! She took a couple
of careful, deep breaths and met Richard's gaze.

He was looking at her oddly. 'Are you feeling quite the thing?'

She took a sip of tea. If she looked as shocked as she felt, then he had some cause for asking. 'Perfectly well, thank you, sir,' she lied. 'Er, thank you for your honesty.' At least he *had* been honest.

He frowned. 'Thea, if you think I am going to call you Miss Winslow and stand upon ceremony with you, then think again,' he said in rising irritation. 'And stop calling me *sir!*'

At this inauspicious moment the door opened and the butler came in with a coffee pot.

'Your coffee, sir.' His tones oozed reproof.

'Ah, thank you, Myles. That will be all.'

'Yes, sir. Very good, sir.' Myles placed the coffee pot before Richard and removed himself with all the air of a man removing himself from potential crossfire.

Thea met Richard's glare head on. 'Mr Blakehurst, you have been so kind as to make clear your position—mine is similar. I have no interest in marriage to you whatsoever. If you are concerned that your aunt wishes to promote a match between us, you may rest assured she will receive no encouragement or assistance from me. Good day. Sir. If you will take my advice, any familiarity between us will merely encourage any mistaken assumptions! In future I shall request breakfast in my bedchamber. It will be far safer for both of us if we are not alone together!'

She stalked out, leaving Richard contemplating his breakfast, furiously aware that he had displayed all the finesse of a cavalry charge. Nor had he made his position clear. Now that he thought about it, she had always been able to get under his skin with the greatest of ease, deflecting him from what he wished to say. And that knack she had of getting the last word was like to drive him insane.

But at least their argument had banished the shadows in her eyes. They'd been positively snapping sparks before she walked out. As though the waxwork doll had come to life or split to let out the old, passionate Thea… She was still too pale—or perhaps it was just the effect of the slightly too big, dull grey gown.

Muttering to himself, he poured a cup of coffee and stirred

in several lumps of sugar. What really annoyed him was that in one sense she was right about them avoiding each other. The last thing Almeria needed was encouragement. She would be having a field day, dropping not-so-chance remarks about duty and commenting on all the advantages of the union—he paused, quite unable to think of any arguments Almeria would be able to advance in his cause beyond the purely mercenary ones. He didn't, however, let that fool him into believing Almeria wouldn't think of some.

He didn't want to avoid Thea. Why the hell should he? They were friends, and how the devil could he discover if they would suit if they were avoiding each other?

Chapter Three

Thea stared at the rose-pink gauze evening gown in the arms of the modiste's assistant. She loved pink and this was, without a doubt, at the very forefront of fashion, but… She gulped—it appeared to be missing its bodice…and the sleeves consisted of the tiniest scraps of gauze…but the way the light shifted on it…as though it were alive. Delicate embroidered flowers decorated the *rouleau* at the hem. Temptation flickered; involuntarily her fingertips brushed over it. So soft, so fine—there was nothing of it at all… She drew back.

'N…no. No, I couldn't possibly wear that,' she said cravenly.

'*Mais, mademoiselle,*' wailed the modiste, 'it is of the finest, ze mos' beautiful—*madame!*' She appealed to Lady Arnsworth who had stepped away to examine a dress length in softest blue merino draped over a chair.

Lady Arnsworth looked up. 'Excellent, Monique. Precisely what she should wear! With proper stays, of course.'

'But, Lady Arnsworth!' protested Thea, ignoring the reference to stays. She hadn't worn long stays in years. They were impossible without a maid. 'The bodice!'

'Bodice? What about the bodice?'

'It doesn't have one!' said Thea. The thought of appearing in such a gown, exposed to the gaze of all—her skin crawled at the thought of people, men, staring at her, leering. Touching her. No. It would be unbearable. But the gown really was very pretty…

Lady Arnsworth examined the gown. 'Dreadful the way some females flaunt their *charms,*' she said, subjecting the non-existent bodice to keen scrutiny. 'If charms one can call them when they are exposed to every vulgar gaze!'

Thea nodded.

'It is of the first importance that you should not draw attention to yourself,' continued Lady Arnsworth. 'But…' She hesitated. 'As an heiress, there will of course be those only too swift to be spiteful, whatever you do! It is a very lovely gown, Dorothea, but if you do not like it…'

Thea remained silent. That was the problem; she did like it. Very much.

The modiste, her mouth primmed in distaste, cast an affronted glance at Thea's grey dress, muttered something that sounded suspiciously like *sackcloth!* and issued a stream of voluble instructions to her assistant, along with the pink gown, which was borne away.

Sackcloth? Thea considered her current wardrobe. Her gowns were all grey…or brown. Discreet, modest, and…dull. No doubt any gowns provided by Madame Monique would be beautifully cut, and the material exquisite…but, did she really want them to be *grey?*

Sackcloth? She swallowed. That *was* the word that came to mind when she thought of her wardrobe. And there were probably some ashes about somewhere as well.

The old, rebellious spark, dimmed for years, flared. After all, she had never meant to dress in grey for the rest of her life. It was just the way it had turned out after…after Lallerton's death. There had been no money with which to purchase other clothes after her period of official mourning…decreed by her father, and enforced by Aunt Maria…even a pink riband for her hair had been burnt.

The spark ignited. How was shrouding herself in more grey helping her to enjoy herself? She took a very deep breath.

'If you please, *madame*—' she directed what she hoped was

a friendly smile at the modiste '—that pretty pink gown—I should like to try it on after all.'

Madame's eyes brightened. '*Mais oui!* But of course.' Now beaming, the modiste continued, 'The colour will be *ravissement,* of course. It will bring out the pretty colour in *mademoiselle*'s cheeks. We will put away *ces robes tristes*. One does not wish to cover oneself in sadness. The pink. *Oui*—the pink. And there are others, *mademoiselle!*' She rushed away.

Others? Thea gulped. What had she let loose?

No. She pushed the doubts away. She might feel alive again in the pink gown. A dangerous thing being alive, but the pink gown beckoned. She would enjoy the pink gown. As for the non-existent sleeves—well, she would be wearing long gloves. It would be concealing enough.

Madame came back, bearing the pink evening gown as tenderly as a babe. An assistant trailed behind, a rainbow of silks and satins cascading from her arms. Thea viewed it all with intense satisfaction.

Her gowns. Her choices.

Her life. To enjoy.

Lady Arnsworth gave an approving little nod. 'Excellent. Very sensible, my dear.'

By the time Thea left the modiste she had ordered an entire new wardrobe from the skin out, and was garbed in a new walking dress and a pelisse of turkey red. She still couldn't quite believe that she had spent so much money. And she felt completely different—just as Lady Arnsworth had predicted.

'That bonnet,' announced the other woman as she settled herself in the barouche, 'is an abomination. It always was, I dare say, but it is far more noticeable with your new clothes. We shall have to buy you a new one. Several new ones. Now.' She leaned forward to give directions to the coachman. 'And afterwards,' she said, 'we shall drive in the park.'

Her old bonnet consigned to a dust heap, Thea found herself being driven at a snail's pace through the leafy green of the park.

Fashionable London had returned to life after the festivities of the previous evening and their progress was impeded by the number of times the coachman was obliged to stop so that Lady Arnsworth might exchange greetings with her acquaintances.

Just as Thea had expected, no one seemed terribly surprised to learn the identity of Lady Arnsworth's companion; most remembered her from her first Season.

The carriageway was crowded, horses ridden by nattily turned-out gentleman and elegant women, weaving between the carriages, chatter and laughter filling the air as society preened itself. A show, she reminded herself. Like a peacock's tail. Nothing more. And she wasn't frightened of peacocks after all.

'Oh!' Lady Arnsworth's exclamation pulled her back. 'Goodness me—'tis Laetitia Chasewater. I dare say given your connection, Dorothea, that she will call. Nothing could be more fortunate.'

Thea's breath jerked in. The lady in question was seated in her own barouche on the opposite side of the carriageway a little further along. Elegantly gowned in soft grey, tastefully trimmed with black, the lady smiled and inclined her head.

'There…there is no connection, ma'am,' said Thea, her stomach churning. 'I should not like her ladyship to feel obliged—'

'Nonsense,' said Lady Arnsworth. 'Why, 'tis common knowledge that poor Nigel was by far her favourite child, and that she was very happy about the match between you. There! She is beckoning to you! Of course you must step over to greet her. Edmund…' she indicated the footman perched up behind them '…will attend you.'

Immediately the footman leapt down from his perch and opened the door. Thea dragged in a breath as she stepped out, bracing herself to greet the woman who would have been her mother-in-law. It would have been quite distressing enough without the awareness that a large portion of fashionable London had stopped in its tracks to view the exchange of greetings. Peafowl, she reminded herself, were harmless.

* * *

'My dear Miss Winslow,' said Lady Chasewater, with a sad smile, holding out her hand. Hesitantly Thea laid hers in it, and thin gloved fingers tightened like claws. 'How delightful to see you again,' said her ladyship. 'I think I have not seen you since, well…' The grey eyes became distant for a moment, before she went on. ''Tis all a very long time ago. I am glad you have come up to town again.' She patted Thea's hand. 'One cannot mourn for ever, my dear.'

No. One couldn't. Nor could one jerk one's hand away from an elderly lady.

Cold and clammy, Thea managed a polite response, her stomach tying itself in knots.

'And how does Aberfield go on? I understand him to be suffering dreadfully from the gout at the moment.' She did not pause for a response, but continued, 'I found some letters from him to Chasewater some time ago.' Her smile became reminiscent. 'After Chasewater died. Such memories as they brought back! All our hopes!'

Nothing in Lady Chasewater's languid voice betokened more than polite interest, but Thea's heart raced.

'Did you, ma'am?' she said with forced calm. 'I am sorry if it was distressing for you.' Of course Aberfield had corresponded with Lord Chasewater…it would have been unavoidable.

Lady Chasewater patted her hand again. 'Oh, no. Why should you regret what is past? I shall do myself the pleasure of calling on Almeria very soon. Now, I must not keep you.' And she gave Thea's hand another gentle pat as she released it.

'Good day, ma'am,' said Thea, relaxing slightly as she stepped back from the carriageway.

The barouche moved on and Thea breathed a sigh of relief, trying to quell the shivering that persisted despite the warmth of the sun and her new pelisse.

Upon reaching Arnsworth House again, Thea retired to her chamber to remove her gloves, bonnet and pelisse. Several dress boxes were already piled on her bed, having been delivered from the modiste's in her absence.

Not bothering to summon a maid, Thea set about unpacking them. These were only a fraction of what she had bought. The rest had required alteration, including the dusky pink evening gown which *madame* had promised would be delivered that same day, assuring Thea that her minions would not rest until it was done.

Thea could only gulp at her expenditure. In one afternoon she had spent ten times more than she had in the preceding eight years. And that was just at the modiste. She had—she was forced to admit—enjoyed it, once she had let herself go. Not that she wanted to fling her money about all the time. After this spree there would be no need. But, oh, it was lovely to know that when she dressed tomorrow morning there would be something pretty to put on. That—

'Ah. There you are, Dorothea.' The door had opened and Lady Arnsworth looked in. 'Do come down when you are ready. I have asked for tea to be brought to the drawing room.'

She looked critically at the new dresses on the bed and hanging over the back of the chair. 'Hmm. That will do for a start. Once a few more invitations have arrived, we shall think again. Do be quick, dear.'

Thea gulped as the door closed behind her godmother. *A few more invitations* sounded as though some had already arrived.

She hurried with the dresses. No doubt Lady Arnsworth had further plans to unveil for the Season. Balls, routs, dinners, soirées, making calls. All the activities of the social whirl. At least she had a day or two before she must plunge into it. Hardly anyone yet knew that she was in town, which meant she was safe for a couple of nights at least…

'Good God! That's…it can't be! Not the Winslow chit!'

Richard, whatever he'd been saying to Braybrook forgotten, stiffened as he heard the middle-aged matron's amazed tones ring out in the middle of the Fothergills' very crowded drawing room that evening. Forcibly he resisted the temptation to turn and stare her down. Whoever she was.

Instead he looked around for Thea. He found Almeria almost immediately, regal in purple, and…

The unknown female behind him continued. 'I had the most *interesting* letter, my dear! Why, she was barely out when…' Her voice dropped, and turning his head slightly, Richard could see several be-turbaned matrons, feathers a-quiver, nodding and casting startled looks at Thea as the knowledgeable one disgorged her burden of gossip.

'And you say there was something more to it? Some indiscretion? I understood that story about her grief to be…' began one. Damn it all! Could a girl not be absent from society for a few years without the tabbies deciding that there must be 'something more to it'? Were their own hearts so withered that they could not understand grief?

Another lady leaned forward, murmuring behind her fan. All he heard was, '*—hurst!*'

'No!' Eyes popping, the first lady cast another, disbelieving look at Thea. '*How* much? And Almeria actually has him staying with her? In the very house?'

There were times when the mercenary tendencies of society amused Richard. This was not one of them.

Braybrook caught his eye. 'People are so predictable, are they not, Ricky? And, no, you cannot tell her off for it. Much less demand satisfaction.'

Richard had to unclench his jaw before he could respond. And Julian did it for him anyway.

'It should be entertaining to watch them all trying to work out precisely how great an indiscretion can be glossed over with fifty thousand pounds.' There was an odd snap in his voice.

'What indiscretion?' growled Richard.

Julian's brows drew together, and he nodded to another acquaintance. Then he said lightly, 'The imaginary one they are talking about, of course, Ricky. And do, please, unclench your fists.'

Looking down, Richard was startled to discover that his fists were indeed clenched. Since Julian hadn't even glanced at his hands... He glared at his friend.

Braybrook raised a dark brow. 'Your voice, old chap. It always gives you away.'

Behind them the matron continued, 'Well, I can't say I should like the connection for Marianne, but—' a tinge of scornful condescension crept into her voice '—I dare say Aberfield can't afford to be fussy getting *this* one off his hands; after all, Dunhaven does need an heir.'

Her companion tittered in agreement.

All consideration of discretion crashed to splinters as Richard spun and skewered the startled women with a glare that could have felled a gorgon. He didn't waste time on words, merely stared at them coldly as they flounced and muttered, before hurrying off through the crowd. Dragging in a deep breath, he turned and looked again...this time he found her.

Every nerve taut in shock, tension rippled through him. What the hell did she think she was doing? No longer the grey mouse who had snapped his head off at breakfast, but a vision in shimmering rose-pink gauze. A soft, dusky shade—exactly like...like something waiting to be plucked. He backed right away from that analogy. The light brown curls were piled high, a pink bandeau holding them in place, gold lights glinting in the blaze of candlelight...but it wasn't the change in her appearance that had fury simmering through every vein.

Aberfield had lost no time at all in offering his daughter up on the altar of political expedience—Lord Dunhaven hovered beside her like a dog guarding a juicy bone.

'Ah.' Braybrook nudged him. 'That is Miss Winslow over there, is it not? In rose pink?' A brief pause and then Braybrook added, 'With Dunhaven.'

'Yes,' Richard grated. Inside him something growled, and Braybrook's less-than-parliamentary remark about old goats went unanswered—Richard was already forging a path through the crowd.

Braybrook blinked. Then his gaze narrowed. How very unlike Ricky not to think a strategy through first. And while a full-frontal assault might be sufficient, a little flanking manoeuvre would not go astray.

Thea had completely underestimated the speed with which news could travel through fashionable society. Any number of people had seen her in the park and realised her identity. And of course all the people to whom Lady Arnsworth had presented her had been only too happy to mention their acquaintance with the latest heiress. Mrs Dallimore had been swift to bear the tidings to her sister, Lady Fothergill, who had dashed off a charming note assuring Lady Arnsworth that *of course* she would be delighted to welcome dear Lady Arnsworth's protégée to her little party that very evening.

In Thea's book, Lady Fothergill's assembly did not qualify as a little party.

She had forgotten what it felt like to be one of three hundred people squashed into one house. The roar of conversation, mingled with the half-heard strains of the small orchestra made it almost impossible to hear what was said to one. And the heat of all those bodies, the mingled aromas of perfume, cologne and overheated humanity, rose in an almost overpowering wave. Chandeliers and wall sconces blazed with wax candles, adding to the heat. At least this was only an assembly. There would be no dancing tonight.

Once that would not have pleased her at all. She had loved dancing. Loved the music, melody and rhythm sweeping her along in delight. Now she fought to keep a polite smile plastered on her face. And the knowledge that the following evening she was expected to attend a ball feathered chills down her spine.

People kept *touching* her, brushing by her. They couldn't help it, of course, in the press, but nevertheless her skin crawled and her stomach clenched, a solid lump of panic churning within. Each time she kicked her chin a notch higher and breathed with fierce determination. It was foolish, irrational—she *wouldn't* give in to it!

As various people greeted them, Thea's nerves began to

steady, and she realised with an odd shock that, although she disliked the crowd, the fear of exposing herself was ebbing. She might be uncomfortable, but she wasn't going to faint or panic, even when one dowager went so far as to prod her with a fan, commenting that it was time and more that she did her duty. She shot a gimlet-eyed stare at Lady Arnsworth. 'And I hear you have that nephew of yours with you. Well, it might be worse!' and stumped off, leaning on a cane.

'Such a *dreadful* crush!' pronounced Lady Arnsworth in scathing tones, as the dowager retreated. 'Really, I wonder that Louisa cares to invite so many. I have not seen a single person I wished to see.' She smiled graciously, inclining her head at another lady. 'Lady Broome! How nice…yes. A frightful crush. I shall look forward to a comfortable cose later!'

Lady Broome sailed away into the seething silks and satins.

Lady Arnsworth shuddered. 'Vulgar creature! Her father was a merchant. I vow she smells of the shop!'

Thea remembered Lady Broome as a very good-natured, un-affected woman—not at all vulgar. And her own fortune, now respectably invested in the Funds, derived from her uncle's involvement with the East India Company. Perhaps Lady Arnsworth's sense of smell was selective…like her tolerance for other failings.

The gentlemen were no less assiduous in their attentions, several claiming to remember her from her brief Season.

She smiled and replied politely to their compliments, vaguely remembering names and faces from eight years ago. The smile was the important thing: vague, gracious, never direct. Let them think her cold, uninviting…

'Oh, goodness me!' muttered Lady Arnsworth, nipping at Thea's arm in warning with gloved fingers.

Thea recognised Lord Dunhaven at once. Slightly above average height, his powerful frame drew attention as he strolled towards them, his expression intent.

'Really! I did not think he could possibly be serious!'

muttered Lady Arnsworth to Thea. Then, in far more gracious tones, 'Lord Dunhaven! How do you do?'

Instantly Thea was aware that although his lordship exchanged polite greetings with Lady Arnsworth, all his attention was on her. Intent, knowing eyes looked her up and down. She stiffened her spine against the tremor that went through her as Lady Arnsworth presented her. 'You recall Lord Aberfield's daughter? Miss Winslow, this is Lord Dunhaven.'

Thin lips curved in acknowledgement. 'Certainly, ma'am. I called on Aberfield earlier and he mentioned that she had arrived.' His gaze returned to Thea. 'Good evening, Miss Winslow.' He extended his hand with all the air of one conferring a signal honour upon the recipient.

Thea repressed a shudder, violently aware of her scanty bodice, as she placed her hand in his. She remembered Lord Dunhaven well; she had never liked him. Lady Dunhaven had always been casting nervous glances at him, agreeing with everything he said.

'How do you do, my lord?' She curtsied slightly as he bowed over her hand, and the odour of his pomaded hair sank into her. Her stomach roiled, but she lifted her chin. His lordship seemed inclined to retain possession of her hand and place it on his arm, but she withdrew it firmly. Something about Lord Dunhaven made her skin crawl, even through her white kid gloves. She quelled the urge to rub her glove as though it might be soiled. There was something about the way he looked at her—assessing, judging, as though she were a filly he contemplated buying.

'It is some years since you were in town, Miss Winslow,' he said. 'I will be happy to act as your guide in some measure. Aberfield was most anxious that your time in London should be spent profitably.'

Thea barely suppressed a snort. 'Really, sir? I am sure we can depend on Lady Arnsworth to ensure that my time is not wasted.'

'Yes, indeed,' said her ladyship. 'I have no doubt that—'

'Almeria! How lovely to see you! And Miss Winslow! How delightful!'

Whatever Lady Arnsworth had meant to say was lost as Lady Chasewater came up to greet them.

'My dear—I cannot tell you how pleased I am to see you again so soon—how much it gladdens my mother's heart.'

Dragging in a breath, Thea pinned a smile in place. 'Lady Chasewater,' she said with a smile. 'How kind of you.'

Something lit in Lady Chasewater's eyes, a spark deep within. 'My dear, you must not feel obliged to me. My poor Nigel— there! his name is spoken between us—let me assure you, he would not have expected you to mourn—now, would he?'

Thea shook her head. God help her, it was the truth.

'Of course not,' said Lady Chasewater. 'And I am so glad you have returned,' she continued, patting Thea's hand. 'People do say such foolish things, you know. But you may count on me to do everything I can. Perhaps if you were to drive with me in the park one day…'

Somehow Thea's heart kept pumping gelid blood around her body. Somehow she held herself still, mastered the frantic need to pull her hands away, and kept a smile frozen to her face as her voice fought its way past the choking blockage in her throat.

'Thank you, ma'am.'

Lady Arnsworth chimed in, 'Yes, indeed, Dorothea will be honoured. An excellent notion and so kind of you, Laetitia. It will do her a great deal of good to be seen with you.'

'Oh, tush, Almeria!' said Lady Chasewater. 'Why, she was to be my daughter-in-law!' Her gaze flashed to Thea. 'I would have been a grandmama by now. And poor Nigel has been dead these eight years, and no one ever speaks of him to me.' A sad smile accompanied these words. 'I know Dorothea will understand! I may call you Dorothea?' As she spoke, she released Thea's hands with a little pressure.

'Of course, ma'am.'

'And you will drive with me?'

A drive in the park. That was all. So why did she feel as though she were being manoeuvred to the gallows?

She lifted her chin. 'Thank you, ma'am. That will be delightful.'

Lady Chasewater inclined her head. 'Excellent, my dear. I shall send a little note round. Now, if I am not much mistaken, Lord Dunhaven wishes to stroll with you, Dorothea, and is wishing me elsewhere.' She cast an arch smile at his lordship, who smirked and disclaimed.

'Aberfield must be pleased to know that Dorothea is drawing such distinguished attention.' She rapped his lordship on the arm with her fan. 'And so pleasant to see you again now that your period of mourning is over. I am sure we *all* hope to see you happy again very soon.'

Lacing her farewells with another gracious smile, she glided away through the crowd.

'If you would honour me, Miss Winslow?' Dunhaven extended his arm, and Lady Arnsworth cleared her throat. He accorded her the briefest of smiles. 'Your ladyship has no objection?'

'Of course not,' said Lady Arnsworth, although Thea had the distinct impression that she would have liked to rattle off several objections.

As they strolled, Lord Dunhaven presenting her to this person and that, Thea could almost feel the whispers eddying in their wake. Faint smiles, half-hidden behind fans, betrayed a cynical acceptance. And as they proceeded she felt colder and colder from the inside out, as though the chill leached from somewhere deep within. She kicked her chin a notch higher, and told herself that a few people sliding away through the crowd at their approach meant nothing, that the speculative sideways glances were mere curiosity, nothing more.

Lord Dunhaven appeared not to notice, as though such things were beneath him. Instead he regaled Thea with an exact account of all the various improvements he had undertaken at his principal country seat, the refurbished stables, the rearrangement of the principal apartments.

'I should like very much to show it all to you, Miss

Winslow,' he said, after telling her how his new billiard room was laid out.

Before Thea could do more than skim over all the possible ramifications of this, she prickled with sudden awareness as a tall figure came up beside her. She turned sharply and warmth flooded her, dispelling the growing chill.

Richard, immaculately turned out in utterly correct evening garb.

'Good evening, Miss Winslow. Servant, Dunhaven.'

Thea blinked. Anything less servant-like than Richard's clipped tones would have been hard to imagine. He sounded as though he'd swallowed a razor blade made of ice. Even his bow held an arrogance that reminded her all at once that he was after all the son of an earl, one of the damn-your-eyes Blakehursts: assured, at home in the *ton* for all his scholarly nature.

The contrast between the two men was startling. Very few would have described Richard's evening clothes as stylish, but somehow the comfortably fitted coat over broad, lean shoulders had a greater elegance than Dunhaven's tightly fitted and, she suspected, padded coat. Dunhaven dripped with expensive fobs, rings and a very large diamond blazed in his cravat. Richard's jewellery consisted of a pearl nestled quietly in his cravat and a plain gold ring.

Dunhaven looked his disdain. 'Ah, *Mr* Blakehurst, is it not? How surprising to see you here.'

A spurt of anger shot through Thea at the sneering tone, but Richard merely looked amused.

'Is it, Dunhaven? I assure you that I overcome my boredom with this sort of thing quite regularly enough for the hostesses not to completely despair of my attendance.' He smiled at Thea. 'Good evening, Miss Winslow. May I take you to find some champagne?'

Thea blinked. As simple as that.

'Certainly, sir. That would be lovely. I'm sure his lordship will excuse me.'

Dunhaven's hand came across and settled in hard possession

on Thea's fingers, clamping them to his arm. 'There is no need, Miss Winslow. I shall be happy to escort you and find you something suitable for a lady to drink. Some ratafia, I think you would prefer.'

Not the usual paralysing fear, but anger surged through her. With a sharp movement, she slid her fingers from under Dunhaven's grip. Telling her what to do was bad enough, but presuming to tell her what she would like was going entirely too far. Besides, she didn't like ratafia.

'Dunhaven! Just the man I was looking for.'

The newcomer was familiar to Thea. Tall, with jet-black hair and brilliant, deep blue eyes—surely… Shock lurched through her—yes, it was David's friend, Julian Trentham…only he had succeeded now to his father's title—Viscount Braybrook.

He smiled at her and bowed. 'Miss Winslow. Braybrook at your service. Friend of your brother's, if you recall? You won't mind if I steal Dunhaven, will you? Blakehurst here will look after you.' He glanced at Richard, 'Won't you, old chap?'

Richard's mouth twitched. 'I think that could be managed.'

Thea's gaze narrowed, despite her suddenly pounding heart. There was something wicked in Lord Braybrook's limpid blue eyes. However, she wasn't fool enough to reject a lifeline, no matter how it presented itself. 'Of…of course.' She seized the opportunity to step away from Dunhaven. Richard caught her hand and set it on his arm, anchoring it there and again that shock of awareness jolted through her at his touch. Dazed, she met Braybrook's gaze, but the bright eyes told her nothing—what would David have told him? Could he possibly know any of the truth?

'You'll excuse us, gentlemen.' Richard's clipped voice shook her back to herself, and he drew her away through the crowd.

'What the devil are you playing at?' he muttered, and nodded curtly at an acquaintance smiling at him. 'Dunhaven, of all men! He's desperate to marry again and sire an heir. He's looking for a bride! A nice, young, *fertile* bride to bear his sons!'

'He's also a friend of my father's!' said Thea, blushing

scarlet at Richard's blunt assessment. 'I can't just cut him, or snub him, when—'

'Then let Almeria do it for you!' came the riposte. 'Trust me, she'll be only too happy to see him off with a flea in his ear!'

She didn't doubt that for a moment, but—

'Even Lady Arnsworth can't do that when my father has practically given his blessing to the match!' she snapped.

'What?' They were near an open door, and Richard whirled her through it and along a corridor. He opened another door and she found herself whisked into the library. It was empty, lit by a single lamp. Even in her annoyance she could not repress a spurt of amusement. Trust Richard to know the location of the library.

He faced her in the dim light. 'What the hell are you talking about? Dunhaven is old enough to *be* your father! You can't be serious!'

Furious that he could even think she might accept such a match, Thea glared at him. 'Perhaps you might care to mention that to Aberfield?'

'I would if I thought it would have the least effect! For God's sake, Thea! Dunhaven's a complete wart. He's so desperate to cut his brother out of the succession, it's a wonder he hasn't found a young enough widow with a couple of brats to her credit!'

The moment the words were out of his mouth he knew he'd said the wrong thing. She flinched, as though he had struck her, and the colour drained from her face.

Something white hot jolted through Richard. He caught her arm, steadying her, feeling her tremble. 'Thea! Are you all right?'

'He *couldn't!*' she whispered. 'Even Aberfield wouldn't do that to me!'

Richard slipped his arm around her waist to support her, and she shook her head very slightly as if to clear it, tensing. Ignoring her attempt to pull away, he guided her to a sofa and eased her down onto it, seating himself beside her.

'Just sit,' he told her.

Her chin came up. 'I am perfectly well, thank you.'

'Dammit, Thea—you are not all right!' he said furiously. 'You nearly fainted!'

'I did not!' she snapped. 'I was merely a little dizzy. It's…it's stuffy in here! Look, I must go back—if we're caught here together!'

There would be the very devil to pay. He'd be offering for her immediately. Surprisingly the idea didn't send the usual battle alert along his nerves.

'I can think of worse fates,' he told her. 'For both of us.'

The mere thought of Dunhaven touching her in any way at all had something growling inside him—a clawed beast with a distinctly greenish cast to its eyes.

Blue eyes snapped fire at him in the dim light. 'But you said *you* don't want to marry me, so—'

'The devil I did!' he growled. And right now, with that pink gown hinting at feminine mysteries, the delicate lace edge at her breasts that tempted a man to slide his finger beneath to tease velvet-soft flesh—he tore his mind free of its imaginings and concentrated on reality.

Reality was glaring at him. 'Yes, you did. At breakfast!'

'I never said that,' he told her bluntly. 'I told you I wouldn't marry you for your fortune. First rule of scholarship: don't tamper with the text!' Or with those silken glossy curls feathering about her brow—or the one lying against the slender, creamy column of her neck…especially not that one. His own collar itched.

A merry voice interrupted. 'Thea! I thought it was you! How naughty of you to hide away here with Mr Blakehurst. And how delightful to see you after all these years! Do you know, I quite thought you must have retired to a convent.' A slender woman stood in the doorway, several feathers nodding in her dark, elaborately coiffed hair. 'I couldn't believe it when they said you were here,' she continued, 'and then I saw you vanishing out of the door! Am I interrupting?' She stepped into the room, leaving the door open. 'Are you about to box his ears?'

Richard recognised the fashionably dressed young matron.

Lady Fox-Heaton's famous smile beamed as she came across the room, holding out her hands to Thea in unaffected pleasure.

Hesitantly Thea placed her own in them and stood up. 'Diana—how well you look.' She smiled. 'You are married, of course?'

Diana Fox-Heaton flushed slightly. 'Yes. Had you not heard?'

At Thea's denial, Lady Fox-Heaton looked troubled. 'Oh, well, I…I married Francis—Francis Fox-Heaton.' She sighed. 'You will remember him, of course—he was friendly with poor Mr Lallerton.'

To Richard it seemed that Thea's expression froze.

'You married Sir Francis Fox-Heaton?' she said carefully.

Lady Fox-Heaton's smile glimmered. 'Oh, yes. And I know what you are thinking! How did I come to marry a mere baronet? We were all going to marry earls at the very least, were we not? But Sir Francis is an MP now! Such consequence!'

Richard repressed a snort. It was rumoured that Diana had outraged her family by dismissing a marquis to marry Fox-Heaton. A love match if ever there was one.

'How lovely for you,' said Thea. But Richard could not rid himself of the impression that she thought it anything but lovely.

'Yes,' said Diana cheerfully. 'It is. But for now, we had better get you back to the party. If I saw you leave, you may be sure others did, and I must say—there are some *very* odd stories circulating anyway.' She gave Richard a severe look. 'I should have thought, Mr Blakehurst, that you had more sense than this.'

Richard choked.

'Odd stories?' Thea's query sounded casual. Too casual, thought Richard. Were she not wearing gloves, he'd swear her knuckles would be showing white.

'Very odd,' said Diana. 'I'll explain later.'

Returning to the party, Richard was hailed by a small group headed by the Marquis of Callington, wanting his opinion on the value of the late King's library, recently presented to the nation by his Majesty. More than happy to promote his belief that the value of the library was immense, he joined them, but discovered to his disgust that part of his mind remained focused on Thea. His gaze kept straying to where she stood with Diana Fox-Heaton and a number of other young matrons, and several men whom usually he considered good enough fellows, but whom right now he would have cheerfully flung through a window. Men who were far too wary to hang around most matrimonially inclined young girls and their mamas—but who might nevertheless be interested in a woman with an independent fortune...

'Well, the last thing we want is a repeat of the tragedy that you say befell the Cotton manuscripts, Ricky,' said Callington.

Richard dragged his mind back to agree with Callington's conclusion that it was of the first importance to ensure that the late King's library was well protected from fire or any other calamity. He breathed a sigh of relief to see that David Winslow had joined the little group about Thea. If Winslow was ready to carve slices out of *his* hide, then he was well able to re-educate the thinking of any other overly libidinous suitors.

Chapter Four

By the end of the evening, Thea felt as though she had been boiled up in a copper with the sheets. She was exhausted, limp, by the time Almeria summoned the carriage to return to Grosvenor Square. But she had survived. She had renewed her acquaintance with a number of women who had been brought out in the same season as herself and had been accepted back into their number.

Her public acceptance by Diana Fox-Heaton ensured that. Diana had accompanied her back to the drawing room. Several women she had known as a girl had come up to her, inviting her to various parties. She thought about Diana as the maid readied her for bed. They had not been close friends years ago, but they had liked each other. And Diana had gone out of her way to help tonight. She had warned her that rumours were circulating. Rumours that suggested Miss Winslow's long absence from society might have very little to do with mourning a lost love…

She shivered. Diana was married to Sir Francis—one of the very few people who could have any inkling of the truth. He had been a close friend of Nigel Lallerton's, that was how she had come to know Diana. They had been part of the same circle. What would he say to his wife's renewed friendship with her?

She slipped into bed and blew out the lamp. Despite her exhaustion, sleep mocked her. Diana had been quite as outspoken as Richard on the subject of Lord Dunhaven… *Francis says he simply wants a brood mare—and that no father of sense will give his consent to such a marriage. You know, there was all sorts of gossip when his wife died—but nothing could be done. No servant would ever speak out in a matter like that!*

Thea shivered. Aberfield, however, *was* willing to promote the match.

A hard-edged face slid into focus. Dark eyes that usually spoke of cool control, self-discipline—eyes that had positively blazed with some violent emotion this evening. Heat flickered, tingling inside her—Richard must really loathe Dunhaven for some reason, she told herself. She didn't think she had ever seen him so angry—except once when he was a boy, and his mother had just visited… She sighed. She hadn't much liked Richard's mother herself and she wondered what the new Lady Blakehurst was like… Richard seemed to like her, even if Lady Arnsworth didn't.

Richard walked back to Grosvenor Square in company with Braybrook. They had ended the evening in the card room, playing piquet for penny points with an added shilling for a game, and a pound a rubber. Richard had emerged ahead by a couple of pounds and half a bottle of brandy.

'The sad thing is,' said Richard, jingling the coins in his pocket, 'that if I played for larger stakes, I'd lose resoundingly!'

'Naturally,' said Braybrook. 'My father always said much the same; you only win when you can afford to lose. Pity he didn't take his own advice speculating. Here we are—Arnsworth House.'

'So it is,' said Richard, inspecting the familiar portico.

A faint scraping sound brought both of them swinging around sharply. A small dark shape detached itself from the steps leading down to the area and resolved itself into a boy.

'What the devil are you doing there?' demanded Richard.

The lad hung back. 'Would one of you be Mr Richard Blakehurst?'

'What's that to you, lad?' asked Braybrook suspiciously.

Richard shook his head. 'It's all right, Julian,' he said. 'Yes, I'm Mr Blakehurst.'

'Note for you then, guv,' said the boy, approaching. 'From a lidy,' and pushed the note into Richard's hand. He was gone in a flash, racing off along the pavement and disappearing around the corner into Upper Grosvenor Street, before either of them could stop him.

Richard stared after him with raised brows. 'Idiot boy,' he said. 'I'd have given him sixpence. Wonder who's writing me love notes?'

Braybrook raised his brows. 'Love notes, Ricky? You?'

Richard grinned, breaking the seal and opening the note. 'Do you think you and Max are the only men in London ever to—*good God!*'

He stared in disgust. Who the hell had penned this filth?

Braybrook twitched the note out of his hand and read aloud, *'How many times will you tup the gilded whore tonight?'* In an expressionless voice, he said, 'Charming, Ricky. Absolutely charming.' He handed it back.

Crumpling the note in his fist, Richard shoved it deep in the pocket of his coat. 'Quite.'

The burning question, of course, was just who was the gilded whore? He hoped, he very much hoped, that he didn't know the answer.

'Sure you won't seek lodgings, old man?' asked Braybrook.

Richard shook his head curtly and limped up the steps, refusing to acknowledge the wisdom of the suggestion.

Thea frowned at the note from Lady Chasewater, inviting her to drive her in the park the following day. Relieved that it wasn't for that afternoon, Thea managed to persuade Lady Arnsworth that a quiet hour in the back parlour would be more beneficial than more shopping.

Reluctantly, her ladyship consented. 'Very well, dear. If you are quite sure it is necessary. You do look pale. And of course you must send a note accepting Laetitia's invitation. She is very influential. And there must be no question of you not being able to attend the Montacute ball this evening, so I suppose…'

Thea assured her that with a little quiet she would be perfectly ready to attend the ball and Lady Arnsworth departed.

Telling Myles that she was not at home to anyone, Thea asked for a pot of tea to be brought to her in the parlour.

Ten minutes later she was ensconced on a sofa with her writing box and sipping her tea. Peace descended in the familiar room. Faint sounds from the street and the mews reached her, but they seemed oddly detached, as though the house hung suspended beyond the noise.

Hastily she wrote a note to Lady Chasewater, assuring her that she would be delighted to drive with her the following day. Then she summoned a footman to take the note. That done, she took out another sheet of paper to write to Aunt Maria.

For a few moments her pen scratched away. Then it stilled as her concentration wavered and she gazed about the familiar room. Little had changed since last she had been there. It was not a public room, and the furniture was rather old-fashioned and crowded. Not a crocodile leg or sphinx in sight, as though the room had been forgotten when Lady Arnsworth redecorated.

Of all the rooms in Arnsworth House, this was the one she had always known best when she visited as a child. Here Richard had spent his days after the riding accident that broke his left leg. Here, she had been introduced to him at the age of five, as a suitable chess opponent. She smiled, remembering. The twelve-year-old Richard had barely choked off the exclamation of disgust. He had, however, taught her to play chess.

She laid the pen down.

What was he really like now? She had known him as a boy, but did she know the man? Perhaps she did. No doubt he still loved dogs. And horses. The fuss there had been when he insisted on riding again after his accident! His mother and Lady Arnsworth would have kept him wrapped in cotton wool on the sofa if he hadn't been so stubborn about it. She couldn't believe *that* would have changed. Richard could make a mule look cooperative.

Which probably meant he was in no danger of being lured into a matrimonial trap with her.

And he was still kind. Protective. The thought stole through her, insensibly warming. He had been protective last night. No, that had not changed. So perhaps she did still know him. A little. Far better than he could know her.

The child who had known Richard was gone beyond recall, as if a knife had slashed the thread of her life leaving it in two utterly separate pieces. Short useless pieces that could never be woven back into the pattern.

No one knew her now. Sometimes she wished she didn't know herself. There was no point wondering about Richard Blakehurst. He was no concern of hers. She thrust the thoughts away and went back to her letter. That was how she had learnt to manage. One thing at a time; concentrate on the task at hand.

The only sound within the parlour was the scratching of Thea's pen as she concentrated on manufacturing neat, ladylike sentences for Aunt Mary.

A light tap at the door disturbed her.

'Yes?'

The door opened and Myles came in. 'A note for you, miss.'

'Oh. Thank you, Myles.'

She took the note with a smile.

'Will that be all, miss?'

'Yes, thank you. I'll ring if I need to send a reply.'

As the door closed behind the butler, Thea looked at the note. A single sheet folded once and sealed with a plain seal. It was directed to Miss Winslow, Arnsworth House, in clumsy, ill-formed capitals. Thea frowned, broke the seal and opened the note.

Time stood still and her veins congealed as the single word slashed her hard-won peace to shreds: *SLUT.*

Who? *Who?*

How long she sat staring at the note, she had no idea, but a deep voice wrenched her out of the nightmare with a shock like icy water.

'What the deuce have you got here?'

The writing box hit the floor, accompanied by the crash of splintering glass and china as the inkpot and teacup broke. Thea found herself on her feet, every sense at full stretch, one fist clenched. Ready to fight.

Richard's shocked face steadied her. 'It's only me, Thea.' Then, 'Damn! Stay still!'

He strode towards her, his expression fiercely intent.

Despite herself, she flinched, stepping back.

'Damn it, woman! *I said to stay still!*' he roared.

She froze in sheer outrage, and he was beside her, his booted feet crunching on the ruins of the inkpot and teacup.

And gasped as she was lifted bodily with ease and dumped back on the sofa with a marked lack of ceremony.

'And *stay* there,' he growled, 'while I send for someone to clear this up. Those slippers won't protect you from a shard of glass!'

She looked down. Broken glass and china sat in the lake of spilled ink and tea soaking into the Turkey carpet. And with them the anonymous note.

Sanity flooded back in some measure, but the violence of her reaction still shook her. 'I...I didn't hear you come in.' She leaned forward and reached for the paper.

His mouth quirked. 'Obviously.' And before she could stop him, he had bent down for the note. 'Here you—' it was open, face up— 'Good God!' he exclaimed, staring at the note.

Then he looked up and Thea's stomach turned over as she met his eyes. Fury, sheer protective fury blazed there.

Oh, God! If Richard tried to find out...

For a moment the shocked silence held, then Richard spoke, scarcely recognising his own voice, soft, deadly. 'Who the devil sent you this?' He forced himself to consider the matter logically, controlling the choking rage. Last night's note had disgusted him, but this! His fingers shook in the effort not to shred the note.

He turned it over. Like his, the seal had been plain, the writing consisted of clumsy and ill-formed capitals...and directed very clearly to Thea. This piece of...of filth had been intended for her. As last night's note had been directed straight to him. His fist clenched, crushing the note. His own note he might have ignored, but if he ever found out who had sent this—he'd serve them the same way. Slowly.

'Who sent it?' he repeated.

'I don't know.' There was not the least tremor in her voice now and her eyes were steady and clear. 'Myles brought it in. It's nothing to fuss about, Richard. Just foolish spite.' She essayed a faint laugh. 'No doubt the rumours of my fortune inspired it. I'd burn it, but the fire isn't lit.'

Undoubtedly the fire was where it belonged. If he had not been watching her for a moment before he spoke and startled her, he might have believed her not to be upset. But he had seen the pallor of her face as she stared at the note, seen her hands trembling. She had been so lost in whatever emotion had gripped her that she had not even heard him enter the room. And now she was trying to hide it from him.

Surely a piece of casual spite would not strike to the heart like that? She had looked devastated. Had she heard the whispers the previous night? Should he mention his own note? Common sense said he should. But...

'Do you receive many letters like that?'

'No! Give it back, Richard. I'll burn it later.'

'I'll deal with it,' he said. 'I don't want you touching it again.' The thought of a piece of vileness like this coming anywhere near her offended him. He put the crumpled note in his pocket.

Flushing, she met his gaze. 'I thought you were out.'

As an attempt to change the subject it was pitiful. 'I came home,' he said. 'Thea, that note—'

'Please—no,' she interrupted. 'I know what you would say—that I ought to find out who sent it, but really, Richard, it doesn't matter. Just burn it for me. It's just someone...someone who doesn't like me, I suppose. Someone...very unhappy.'

'How do you work that out?' he growled.

Her eyes dropped. 'Oh, well...can you imagine a happy person sending a note like that?'

He couldn't, of course. There were times when feminine intuition was absolutely irrefutable. Only he could have sworn she meant something far more specific. Something personal. That she knew who had sent it, or at least suspected.

'Leave it, Richard,' she urged. 'There's no point making a fuss. It was horrid and I admit gave me quite a shock, but that's all.' She smiled at him, eyes steady. 'What brought you in here?'

Another attempt to change the subject.

He didn't like it. Not one little bit. Every instinct told him that Thea was deeply shaken, that her increasing calm was a façade, that if she knew of the note he had received she would be even more upset. For now he would accept her reticence. It seemed more important to distract her from the vile note. And definitely more important to distract her from wondering what he might do about it.

'What brought me in here?' He smiled. 'Myles told me you were here and he swears that Almeria is out.' The mess of ink and tea caught his eye and he reached out to ring the bell. 'So I thought it would be safe to have a game of chess without giving her any encouragement.'

'Chess? In here? Do you...do you think that's wise?' Suddenly self-conscious, she said, 'If Lady Arnsworth has some idea...that is, that we...that we—'

She broke off and Richard had to suppress a grin.

'That we might make a match of it?' he suggested helpfully. 'So she's spoken to you about it, has she?'

She flushed. 'She didn't precisely *say* anything to me. Only...'

Richard laughed. 'Didn't she? You escaped lightly. She said a great deal to me. Very precisely and in detail. You must know that Almeria has been trying to marry me off to the nearest available fortune for the past ten years!'

Something flickered in her face. Pain? This was not the moment to suggest to her that maybe they should give some thought to Almeria's matchmaking. Not when she had just stopped calling him *sir* with every second breath. Instead, he said gently, 'Thea, we need not consider it. You must know that I would never court any woman for her fortune, let alone you. We can still be friends, can we not? Despite Almeria's meddling?'

For a moment Thea hesitated. Friends…it would be safer not… Yet, unbidden, some long-buried, unrecognisable sensation unfurled within her. She nodded. 'Friends. Yes.'

He smiled. 'Good. Then leave Miss Winslow in the drawing room where she belongs.' He rose, stepped carefully over the mess of ink and broken glass and china and went over to a large, old-fashioned chest under the window. 'Now, let's see…'

Leave Miss Winslow in the drawing room…

'What do you mean?'

He shot her a glance. 'Miss Winslow is all very well for the rest of the world. But I've always been quite fond of Thea.'

He knelt down with a muttered curse and pulled out the bottom drawer. 'Ah hah! Here we are.'

Despite her confusion, Thea felt the unaccustomed smile curving her lips, warming her heart. He had found the old chess set he had taught her to play with. And there in the corner, half-hidden behind a fire screen, was the little chess table.

That sensation inside her stirred again, and this time she recognised it with shock. It was happiness. She had been so utterly determined to enjoy herself, even if she had to pretend, and here happiness had been quietly waiting within to be let out. Along with the Thea he said he was fond of? Was she waiting to escape too?

Automatically the old words of challenge rose to her lips. 'No quarter? No chivalry?'

His answering smile flashed, lighting the dark brown eyes. 'To the death!'

Together they set out the pieces, the memories of all the times they had done this stretching back and forth between them.

'You were about five when I taught you how to do this,' said Richard.

She looked up, an answering smile in her eyes. 'You must have thought I was the most frightful little pest.'

'I did. And I was furious with Almeria. I'd been enjoying my games with Myles. He kept having to rush off to do his job, so

I had plenty of time to contemplate my moves. Try to work out what he would do next. And, of course, he could actually play. A distinct advantage.'

'Rather than having to teach me?'

He thought back, pushing out a pawn. 'You learnt fast enough. Once you found your voice and started asking questions.'

'I was terrified your leg would fall off,' confessed Thea.

'What!' A pawn went flying as he spluttered with laughter.

She went scarlet. 'Well, from what Lady Arnsworth told Mama, I thought your leg had been broken off and stuck back on. And my nurse was always saying I could talk the hind leg off a donkey, so I thought if it fell off again while I was there everyone would blame me!' She glared at him, as though daring him to laugh.

Laughter shook him anyway, as he righted the fallen pawn. Amazing how one could laugh at a terror almost twenty years old. At the time he'd still been having nightmares that he would lose the leg after all.

'No wonder you didn't say anything,' he said with a grin.

Bit by bit, the constraint between them loosened and he found himself telling her what he had been doing since last he'd seen her. Learning about the land to be, in essence, Max's steward. 'Since I have now bought my own place, at least I know what I'm doing,' he said.

'Your own place?'

And he told her about the small property just ten miles from Blakeney over the North Downs; the sheep grazing on the uplands and the old house and gardens nestled in their small, hidden valley, sheltered from the worst of the storms that could sweep up the Channel.

'Not grand,' he said, 'but it will be a home. Enough for me.'

'Sheep?' she said. 'You? I thought you would remain at Oxford.'

If Max had not inherited, he probably would have. 'Sheep,' he informed her, 'have a long and noble history in this country. I've been going through the Blakeney papers. Centuries they go back, and sheep are mentioned frequently.' Odd, but he was finding the task just as stimulating as more conventional study at Oxford. He tried to explain that to Thea in answer to her questions, and realised that somehow he had done nothing but talk about his own concerns for over an hour.

He looked at the mantel clock. Well over an hour. 'I must be boring you rigid!' he said. 'Why on earth didn't you tell me to shut up?'

'Because you weren't boring me,' she said. 'Because I was imagining it all, and seeing how right it all is for you. It sounds wonderful, Richard. Peaceful, yet busy. Fulfilling. Something practical to fill your days, and something to occupy your mind. That was always what you needed.'

With a shock he realised that she was exactly right, that Oxford had never quite been right for him because of that. That he had given it up and come home so readily when Max asked, because deep down he had known that.

'And you?' he asked. 'What have your days held?' Too late he remembered that the question might be unwelcome, but it was gone now, and could no more be recalled than a loosed arrow.

Only in the tightening of her mouth did he see the question strike home. She didn't look up from the board, but said at last, 'Very little. After...after I was considered out of mourning I remained with Aunt Maria. She...she required a companion, and since I had—*have*—no wish to marry, it seemed the logical thing.' She moved her knight.

He didn't know what to say. She had said that yesterday— that she did not wish to marry. But surely...

'My brother thought that he would never marry,' he said. 'And I doubt that he has ever been happier than he is now.'

She did look up at that. 'I'm glad,' she said. 'Tell me about your sister-in-law. She is...expecting a baby, is she not?'

He heard the faint hesitation and ached. Was that something she had wanted, and thought now was for ever lost to her? Nevertheless, she had changed the subject, and he could only respect that. So he made his countermove, and told her a little about Max and Verity, that the baby was nearly due, and that Max was terrified. Far more so than Verity herself.

Thea did not look up again, but surveyed the board, apparently concentrating, soft pink lips very slightly pursed. But her hands, resting in her lap, shifted continually, fiddling with her cuffs, turning a small turquoise ring on her little finger.

He should be concentrating himself, predicting her likely move and its consequences. He knew what he wanted her to do, what nine people out of ten would do at this point. Only it seemed unimportant, compared to the stray curl escaping to tickle her face and make her frown. She pushed it back and his own fingers itched to capture the wisp and tuck it in safely. Or to release a few more of her softly curling tresses to twine about his fingers. He leaned forwards…

She glanced up, pushing the errant wisp out of her eyes yet again. Their eyes met, his suddenly narrowed, intent; hers wide and startled. Reality reined in his half-formed desire. What in Hades had come over him? He needed to conduct this courtship logically…and playing chess was a very rational and logical thing to do.

Dazed, he realised that in the space of two hours he'd gone from considering the possibility of a match to courtship. Thea had loved once, and was disinclined to give her heart again. Would she perhaps consider a marriage based on friendship? Mutual interests and understanding? Would that be enough for her?

She reached out and he watched, fascinated, as the slender, graceful fingers hovered over her knight. He rather thought she had seen his little trap. And the next question occurred to him: would such a marriage be enough for him?

The door opened.

'Mr Winslow,' announced Myles.

'David!' cried Thea as her brother stalked in.

Richard looked up. Winslow's eyes glinted gun metal as he took in the scene.

'Good afternoon, Winslow.' For a moment the quiet greeting hung there and then David Winslow seemed to relax infinitesimally.

'Blakehurst.' A rather reluctant smile curved his mouth. 'I remember that you were fond of chess. Am I interrupting?'

Thea glanced back at him questioningly.

'Yes. You are,' said Richard blandly. 'You will have to wait about three seconds for your sister.' He shot Thea a grin. 'It will take her about that long to mop up my king.'

Thea chuckled, an unshadowed ripple of delight that sent streamers of pleasure curling through him. A sudden movement caught his attention. About to seat himself on the sofa, David Winslow's head had jerked up, his gaze fixed on his sister, as though he had only just seen her. Startled grey eyes flickered to Richard, and then back to Thea in wonder and speculation.

'Don't let me disturb you,' he said with an odd smile.

As Richard had predicted, his king fell in short order.

'Ah, well,' he said. 'That will teach me not to underestimate you again. I'll take my revenge on another occasion, Thea.' He rose and turned to Winslow. 'I'll bid you good day and leave you with your sister.'

Winslow stood. 'As to that, Blakehurst…' He hesitated, seeming to consider something and coming to a swift decision. 'I was hoping for a word with you later.'

Richard held his gaze. 'Were you, indeed?' A challenge? A warning?

Winslow looked very slightly embarrassed. Probably not a challenge, then. 'Er, yes. Perhaps you might care to dine with me this evening at my lodgings? I'm in Jermyn Street.' He took his case out of his pocket and handed a card to Richard.

Definitely not a challenge.

Richard took the card. 'Very well, Winslow. What time?'

'Will eight suit you?'

'Of course. I shall look forward to it.' He smiled at Thea. 'Save me a dance this evening, won't you? Or even two.'

'A dance?'

'Yes, a dance.' He grinned at her look of confusion. 'You know what a dance is—something you do with your legs.'

The door closed behind him and Thea strangled the urge to

scream in frustration. Curse him! She knew what a dance was—what she really wanted to know was if he envisioned dancing with her or still preferred to sit out because of his leg. Although…*something you do with your legs*…that did rather suggest that he intended to dance…

Banishing speculation, she turned to David. 'Why do you wish to speak to Richard?'

He didn't answer immediately. Just stared thoughtfully at the chess set.

'I'd forgotten how fond of you he was, Thea,' he said at last. 'I understand he stepped in for you with Dunhaven last night—' he frowned '—even if he did take you off somewhere alone.'

She saw where that was going immediately.

'No!' she said furiously, banishing the memory of the earlier look in Richard's eyes that had for a moment spoken of more than friendship. 'I mean, yes, he did—but don't read anything into it beyond his good nature! He wished to warn me about Dunhaven. Just as you did!'

Not kiss her. And even if he had, any curiosity she might have felt on what it might have been like had been well and truly extinguished years ago. She knew what a man's kisses were like.

'Thea—'

'No!' She ignored the odd little voice that whispered that she wished it could have been different, that she could share the peaceful life Richard was creating for himself. And that she was being illogical in lumping all men and their kisses in the one pile. Richard's kisses might be as different as the man himself.

There was no rule forcing fear to be logical.

Forcing that out of her mind as well, she said, 'You are perfectly right; Richard is *fond* of me. He considers me a friend. Leave it, David. I don't have so many friends that I can afford to lose one.'

'Are you so sure that you would lose a friend?'

She laughed at that. A sound without a vestige of humour. 'Ask yourself how you might react in a similar situation.'

David sighed. 'Very well. Why don't you put on a bonnet and pelisse? I'll take you to Gunther's for an ice.'

She stared. 'An ice?'

He smiled. 'Why not? You like them. Or you certainly used to. And I'm prepared to wager you haven't had one in eight years!'

Richard found Myles in the butler's pantry. This was one of those moments when action was vital. Apart from the need to do something about the letters, he needed something to occupy his mind. Something other than the queer longing that stirred in him at the memory of Thea saying he had found exactly what he needed in life. In one sense she was perfectly correct, but he had a niggling idea that something was still missing. Or if not missing, perhaps unrecognised. Some final colour or shape to complete the picture. One thread to knit the whole.

'Who sent the note, Mr Richard?' Myles looked puzzled. 'Why, I'm sure I couldn't say. Edmund must have answered the door, I believe, since he was on duty in the entrance hall. He came to me with the note, asking where Miss Winslow might be. I took it up to her.'

Richard nodded. 'Very well. Send Edmund to me in my room, please.'

Ten minutes later, Richard swore as his bedchamber door closed behind Edmund. The footman had not seen whoever had delivered the note. It had been pushed under the front door and the bell rung. He'd had a brief glimpse of a boy running off. A dead end. But perhaps he could learn something from the notes themselves.

Frowning, he found the note from last night, pulled Thea's note out of his pocket and spread the pair of them out flat on the dressing table. He'd looked at enough old documents in his life. Surely he could tell something from these?

Not much. Each had been written on the same ordinary, good-quality paper. The watermark wouldn't help. It was common enough. What about the handwriting? A contrived-looking scrawl of capitals, which he suspected was nothing like the writer's ordinary hand. A faint fragrance teased him…feminine, flowery. Frowning, he sniffed at the note. The odour seemed to cling to it…as though the writer had perhaps been wearing perfume—on her wrists, at the pulse points. It wasn't much, but it was something. He was looking for a woman.

He also had the answer he hadn't wanted the night before; the *gilded whore* referred to in his note was Thea herself. Something else from the previous evening came back to him; a woman's voice, dripping with malicious gossip about Thea—*I had the most interesting letter, my dear…* Such a simple way to start gossip if you didn't wish to be identified.

Deep inside he was conscious of fury burning with a cold intensity. When he found the culprit…

Common sense spoke up; unless the sender was foolish enough to send any more notes here to Arnsworth House, it was going to be devilishly hard to find out who she was. His jaw hardened. Difficult, perhaps, but not impossible. And there was something else; with a grim sense of resignation, Richard acknowledged that whatever the wisdom of seeking lodgings all thought of it had been abandoned—he was remaining at Arnsworth House.

Chapter Five

Richard limped up the steps of Winslow's Jermyn Street lodgings, still wondering what might have inspired the invitation. A servant led him to a snug, if rather untidy, parlour, and his host stood up with a friendly smile, which didn't quite disguise the frown in his eyes.

'Blakehurst.' Winslow held out his hand and Richard shook it.

Winslow went straight to the point as the door closed behind the servant. 'I owe you an apology. Brandy?'

Richard raised his brows. 'Oh? Yes, please.'

Winslow looked rueful, as he poured a glass of brandy and handed it to him. 'Yes. I rather leapt to conclusions the other day. Braybrook put me right.'

Richard couldn't quite suppress a snort. 'Don't refine upon it too much, Winslow,' he said. 'By now most of society has leapt to the same obvious conclusion.' Including the harpy who had penned those poisonous notes.

'So I hear.' Winslow gestured to a comfortable-looking leather chair on one side of the crackling fire.

Richard sat down and they sipped quietly for a few moments before Winslow broke the silence. 'Braybrook gave me some advice.'

Richard looked at him carefully. That sounded dangerous.

Julian's advice was frequently sound and always outrageous. 'Did he?' He managed to sound mildly interested rather than suspicious.

'Yes.' Winslow swirled the brandy in his glass, and met Richard's gaze over the rim. 'Apart from convincing me that if you were hanging out for a rich wife Lady Arnsworth would have married you off years ago—'

Despite the simmering remnants of his annoyance with Winslow, Richard laughed.

'He also said that you were in the perfect position to help Thea.'

Richard choked on his brandy.

A moment later, after a helpful bang on the back from Winslow, Richard cleared his throat.

'And just how did he come to that conclusion?' he asked.

Winslow grimaced. 'One, you aren't hanging out for a wife. Two, you're on the spot. Three…' He hesitated and then said, 'Well, I saw that for myself this afternoon. You were always kind to Thea when she was a child. She sees you as a friend. And when Braybrook told me about your run in with Dunhaven last night, he said you wouldn't ask a lot of questions I couldn't answer.'

Richard was silent for a moment, wondering just what Winslow thought he had seen that afternoon. 'Bearing in mind all those questions I am apparently too discreet to ask,' he said, with only the merest hint of irony, 'would you care to explain exactly why Thea might be supposed to require my assistance? And perhaps even what you think I can do?'

'Thea is…disinclined to marry,' began Winslow. 'After her— that is, after what happened eight years ago, she does not wish it. Unfortunately, our father sees matters quite differently. He wants her married.' Narrowed grey eyes glittered. 'I understand you share my opinion of Dunhaven as a *parti* for my sister?'

'I should think it extremely likely,' said Richard evenly. 'He's a wart.' He tried to ignore the response boiling up inside him at the idea of Thea and Dunhaven. *Over my dead body.*

'Quite.'

It took Richard a moment to realise he hadn't actually spoken that last phrase aloud; that Winslow had merely agreed with his summation of Dunhaven's charms. 'There was talk,' he said slowly, 'about the death of Dunhaven's wife.' He loathed gossip and avoided spreading it, but in this instance he'd make an exception.

Winslow said nothing. Just waited. He didn't even look surprised, so there was no point suggesting that he mention this to Aberfield. Aberfield knew and didn't care.

Hell and damnation. 'You know, Winslow, you really didn't need to ask. Did you think I'd let an excrescence like Dunhaven anywhere near her?'

'There'll be others too,' said Winslow quietly. 'He's the worst, I agree. But if she really does not wish to marry, I don't want to see our father force her into it.'

'I beg your pardon?' Richard could not quite believe what he was hearing. 'Why would—?'

'Gossip,' said Winslow savagely.

'What?' That made no sense at all.

Winslow hesitated, as though choosing his words carefully.

At last he said, 'Someone let it out how much Thea's inheritance is. Our father decided to marry her off to his satisfaction before she became a target for fortune hunters.'

Richard frowned. Winslow wasn't telling him everything. But then, he hadn't told Winslow everything...

'Forgive me, Winslow, but I overheard some speculation last night—' Seeing his companion's suddenly narrowed gaze, he said irritably, 'Oh, for God's sake! Take a damper! You've asked my assistance and I'm more than willing to help, but I need to know what's going on.'

Winslow subsided and Richard continued, 'Some of the tabbies were speculating that there might have been a reason other than grief at Lallerton's death, some indiscretion, that has kept Thea in retirement.'

'Were they, indeed?' grated Winslow.

'Yes. And, no, as Julian informed me at the time, we can't call them out over it.'

Winslow gave an unwilling crack of laughter. 'We? Blakehurst, calling someone out on a woman's behalf is usually reserved for her brother or her husband! Or her betrothed.'

Richard ignored that. To his shock, the idea of calling someone out on Thea's behalf didn't feel in the least out of place. Especially if it turned out to be Dunhaven. Banishing the thought, he stuck to the point. 'It strikes me that, given it was Thea's first appearance in years, the gossip was surprisingly fast. Even for London. Which suggests that people were talking even before Thea came to town. Is that part of the reason for your father's determination to marry her off?'

Winslow's fingers drummed on the table, and again Richard had the impression that he was considering his answer.

Finally, 'Yes. He doesn't want any hint of scandal. He's being considered again for a Cabinet position.'

All perfectly reasonable. But why had the gossip started in the first place? *Who* had started it? Gossip was part of life in society, but usually it was about current events. Not a non-existent scandal that was eight years old to boot. Not unless someone had an axe to grind...

'So someone wants to block your father's Cabinet appointment.' It was the obvious solution.

Winslow looked arrested. 'What?' He caught himself hurriedly. 'Well, yes. That...that would fit.'

Except that it was so bloody obvious, Winslow shouldn't look surprised. And where did the notes fit in? And was he going to mention the notes to Winslow? Thea obviously hadn't mentioned hers. If she had, Winslow would know that he knew. Which answered his question.

'Blakehurst?'

He looked up. 'Sorry. Thinking.'

Winslow looked rueful. 'Braybrook warned me about that too. Said you wouldn't ask questions, but that wouldn't stop you thinking them. Shall I ring to have our dinner brought in?'

'By all means,' said Richard. He wouldn't mention the notes yet. The least he could do was tell Thea about his own note before telling her brother. Nor did he consider it necessary to inform Winslow that he had already decided to keep an eye on Thea. Winslow would want to know why, and he wasn't entirely sure he was ready to give that answer. But he was still curious...

Winslow tossed off the remains of his brandy and tugged on the bell pull.

Watching him narrowly, Richard asked his last question. 'Why not you? You are her brother. No one could censure you for protecting your sister from a match with Dunhaven, even if your father is mad enough to think it acceptable.'

'I am afraid, Blakehurst,' said Winslow apologetically, 'that that is one of those questions I cannot answer.'

He'd rather thought it might be. Which meant he'd have to find out by himself. And how those damned letters were connected—if they were. And there was another question he hadn't even bothered to ask—why did Aberfield think Dunhaven an acceptable match for his daughter?

Thea gazed about the rooms Lady Montacute had hired for the evening with a growing sense of confidence. The heavy perfume of hothouse flowers mingled with melting wax, noise and heat. It should have panicked her, and yet it did not.

Madame Monique had sent an exquisite ball gown in a brilliant shade of poppy muslin, trimmed with tiny sprigs of gold and gold lace. 'A bold colour per'aps,' *madame* had said. 'But you are a leetle older. There is not the need to dress *à la jeune fille...*'

She had not been convinced at the time, but now she began to understand what Lady Arnsworth had meant about feeling different with a new wardrobe. Somehow the bright gown was like armour. The young girl might be gone, but gone also was the acquiescent creature who had slowly taken her place. In her poppy-bright gown and matching headdress, she felt secure in a fortress. Of course, she thought with a spurt of amusement, the new, perfectly fitted stays might have something to do with that!

And the dainty fan of peacock feathers was the ultimate weapon in a lady's arsenal...with it one could hold the world safely at bay. And, buoying her courage was the fact that Richard had asked her to save him two dances. Not that he danced very much, Almeria told her. He preferred to sit out and chat to his partners, which suited her perfectly. It meant that she wouldn't have to waltz. She thought she could manage all the other dances, but the waltz terrified her, the thought of being held in a close embrace brushing ice down her spine.

Waving her fan negligently, she smiled at Mr Fielding. She could do this. She just hoped Richard would appear in time for the first waltz.

'No, sir, I fear that I am already engaged for both waltzes.'

Richard, entering the ballroom with Winslow, saw Thea at once and his breath jerked in. Standing beside a potted palm, with Almeria seated on a *chaise* beside her, Thea was the centre of a small group of men, all jostling and vying for position.

'Damn!' muttered Winslow. He started forward.

'Winslow! Might I have word, if you please?'

Sir Francis Fox-Heaton, tall, elegant and frowning slightly, stood just ahead of them. 'I intended to call tomorrow, but since you are here…' He cast a faint smile at Richard. 'Mr Blakehurst. You will excuse us?'

Winslow turned to Richard, his mouth a hard line. 'I'll find you later. Would you mind…?'

'You asked already, if you recall,' said Richard.

A slight relaxation of the jaw that might have been a smile. 'So I did. Thank you.' He turned. 'At your service, Fox-Heaton.'

Richard made his bow to Almeria and to Thea, exchanging friendly greetings with the various gentlemen attempting to capture Thea's attention. Most of them harmless, he forcibly reminded himself, and it occurred to him that she was not paying them a great deal of attention. He had the oddest notion that she was, in some way, not really there. That for all her smiles, and polite responses to her admirers, she was otherwhere, and that gently waving peacock fan had something to do with it.

He saw Dunhaven approach and the growling creature within stirred restlessly. Dunhaven was not harmless, in any way, shape or form.

'Oh, I say, Miss Winslow,' Tom Fielding was protesting. 'It's a great deal too bad! Both the waltzes, and you won't say who has been granted them, so we can—'

'Miss Winslow,' cut in Lord Dunhaven, 'will be dancing the waltz with myself, Fielding. A prior arrangement, you understand.'

The air of assured ownership had the beast sitting up snarling.

'Oh?' Thea's eyes narrowed and the fan stilled. 'A prior arrangement with whom, my lord? I fear it was not with me.'

The beast subsided very slightly. Polite, gentle Thea had just delivered a snub one of the Patronesses of Almack's might have envied.

A smile, and the resumed gentle movement of the fan, served only to hone the edge in her dulcet tones.

Almeria, chatting to Lady Hornfleet, turned her head slightly, clearly listening.

Lord Dunhaven cleared his throat and frowned at her. 'I felt that under the circumstances—I was speaking to your father this afternoon—'

'Were you, my lord?' The cutting edge glittered with frost. 'And how was he?'

'Very well, Miss Winslow.' Dunhaven bestowed an indulgent and proprietorial smile on Thea that had Richard grinding his teeth. Almeria's head snapped around and she stared at him.

Richard clenched his jaw into silence as Dunhaven continued. 'He assured me that you would be most happy—'

'How times change, my lord,' said Richard, his jaw escaping his control. 'Nowadays, whatever customs may have pertained in Lord Aberfield's youth, one solicits the lady, not her father, for a dance.' With a slight bow, he added, 'As I did earlier.' Earlier could mean a great many things, not necessarily that he had been alone with Thea in Arnsworth House that afternoon.

And not for anything would he employ Dunhaven's strategy of forcing Thea into a position where she must either dance or deal him a set-down. They had not agreed on which dances, but if she wished it…

Over the top of that lethal fan, blue eyes questioned him.

He smiled.

'Perhaps another time, my lord,' she said, stepping away from Dunhaven. 'I have indeed promised this dance to Mr Blakehurst.'

Dunhaven's eyes narrowed in dislike as he swung to look at Richard. 'Oh? I didn't realise you *danced*, Blakehurst. How very singular!'

The indrawn hiss of Thea's breath was balm to his cold fury.

'Of course my nephew dances, sir!' snapped Almeria.

'No, my lord?' Richard looked his lordship up and down with mild curiosity, and the earl reddened with annoyance. 'Ah, well, there's plenty of time yet for you to acquaint yourself with all manner of things you don't know. I do dance. Upon occasion. When I consider the effort worthwhile.' He flicked a glance at Thea. 'It's a little like culping wafers at Manton's, you know. I only bother to engage in matches with those I know can give me a halfway decent match.'

Over the peacock feather fan Thea's blue eyes glimmered with silent laughter.

She turned, saying coolly to Dunhaven, 'Perhaps a country dance, my lord. I have promised both waltzes to Mr Blakehurst.'

Richard uttered a mental malediction. He doubted that his leg would survive two waltzes in one evening.

Dunhaven nodded curtly. 'Servant, Miss Winslow.' He nodded even more curtly to Richard, turned on his heel and stalked away. Thea knew a moment's fear. Richard might be the son, and brother, of earls, but Dunhaven was a powerful man—what if he—?

'Shall we, my dear?' said Richard, offering his arm. As she permitted him to steer her through the crowd, he gave a deep laugh. 'Pompous ass,' he said.

'Richard! It's not funny!' she whispered fiercely. 'What if he—?'

'If he tries anything with you,' said Richard, in deadly quiet tones, 'I will take great pleasure in dealing with him.' All vestiges of amusement had vanished.

'I'm not worried about *me!*' she snapped. 'I'm worried about *you!*'

He blinked, patently surprised. And then a quite different sort of smile crept across his face. A tender smile, a smile that spoke of things she had long considered lost to her. Despite the warning bell clanging deep within her, a glowing sensation spread through her, and for a moment there hung between them something almost tangible. She caught her breath...if only—oh, if only!

'Where shall we sit out?' she asked.

'Sit out?' He stared at her. 'We're going to dance.'

'Dance?'

'Well, of course! Unless—' An odd look came into his eyes. 'Unless *you* would prefer to sit out?'

Shock slammed into her. He wanted to dance? Actually dance? She hadn't really believed that he could mean it.

It would be safer not to dance. This shattering awareness of him unsettled her as it was. Dancing, being held in his arms, with music a shimmering web around them, would be twice as dizzying. Like the sudden blaze in the dark eyes as he stared at her.

She had never intended to dance—she had not thought he would want it.

And yet, why should she not? What harm could there be in dancing with Richard? Of all men, he was the one she would feel most comfortable with. She summoned a smile, swallowed the last of her champagne and said, 'I would be honoured to dance with you, Richard.'

He took her empty champagne glass and handed it, along with his own, to a footman. Then, with another devastating smile, he offered her his arm. 'Our dance, I believe,' he said. He steered her on to the dance floor and swept her into the waltz.

She didn't know what she had expected. Not fear. Certainly not that. And not revulsion. Not with Richard. Never with him.

But…the chill…the sense of distance she had learnt to place mentally between herself and anyone who came too close…she had felt it all evening as people jostled around her and she had held them at bay with her fan. Especially with Lord Dunhaven. And now…

Now, in Richard's arms, adjusting her steps to his uneven strides, the fan dangled unneeded from her wrist, and she felt only warmth, and an enveloping closeness. Whatever she had expected, it had not been this.

Held safely by his arms in the surging rhythm of the dance, she was wildly conscious of his strength, his sheer maleness. It brought only pleasure, a purring, purely feminine delight that he had thought her worth the effort. She felt alive, as she had not in years.

She lifted her gaze to his face. It was as if she had never truly seen him before. Strongly chiselled planes, the deep brown eyes set under dark brows. So familiar. And yet new. New lines, graven she thought, by pain. And he was simply older. More mature. To some his face might look forbidding, yet his smile denied that. And he was smiling now. At her. As though having her in his arms was a pleasure. Her breath hitched and she found herself smiling back.

It wasn't supposed to feel like this. Not as far as he could recall, anyway. And it was quite some time since he had danced at all, let alone waltzed. In fact, Thea was one of the very few women he had ever waltzed with.

His stride was as awkward and uneven as ever. That wasn't different. What shocked him was the sheer delight in having Thea's slender, supple body in his arms completely overrode the increasing ache in his leg. Worse, the delight of looking down into her soft blue eyes, seeing the delicate colour fanned on the pale cheeks, and her slightly parted lips nearly made him forget which leg ached.

And then she smiled up at him. A tentative smile, uncertain, as though unsure of its welcome. His breath caught. Never before in his life had he been conscious of an urge to sweep a dance partner out of sight and kiss her, and himself, senseless. With a shock he realised that if he gave in to the urge, he might forget all about sweeping them out of sight.

The music was like a drug, its rhythm one with their shifting bodies. Never had he been so wildly aware of a woman—as a woman. Never had every sense clamoured for more. To be closer, to breathe her soft flowery scent, to hear the soft hush of her breathing. Never had he known the urge to pull a woman closer in the dance so that her thighs shifted against his, so that her breasts touched his coat. Every muscle hardened savagely in the effort not to just do it.

He knew at once when she felt the change in him. The sudden tension in his arms as he fought not to haul her closer, the added clumsiness in his stride, which owed nothing to the ache in his leg.

'Richard?'

Somehow he met her concerned gaze.

'I knew this would hurt your leg! Do you wish to stop?'

'Not in the least,' he informed her. It wasn't his leg that was causing the problem.

'You are sure it doesn't hurt?'

'Quite sure,' he lied. 'It's, er, just a kink. Moving will ease it.' Only not the sort of moving he was doing at the moment. Or at any other moment in the foreseeable future for that matter.

By the end of the dance they were at the far end of the dance floor from the chaperons. Richard was violently aware that Thea was flushed, glowing and radiant. And that he was heated in an odd tingling way that had nothing to do with the heat of the ballroom and everything to do with the slow heat consuming him. Aware that although the dance had finished, music still sang and ached to every heavy beat of the blood in his veins.

He fought for control, reminding himself that it had been a while since he had been with a woman. Casual liaisons with discreet widows had lost their savour some time ago. Apparently with the inevitable result that desire had conducted an ambush in the most impossible, and unexpected, place imaginable. All perfectly logical, if potentially embarrassing.

She looked up at him and his breath caught as their eyes met.

Good lord! What a place to realise that he desired a woman! Especially a woman as untouchable as his aunt's protégée and goddaughter. Unthinkable.

Well, no, not unthinkable precisely, since he was thinking about it. But definitely inappropriate.

Carefully he stepped back, his mind reeling at the wave of tenderness that poured over him. At the sight of her smiling up at him, all shadows fled, just as he had wanted. This was different, somehow—more than desire. Oh, he'd always liked his partners—what was the point in going to bed and being intimate with someone you didn't like? But this shattering ache?

'More champagne, Thea?' he suggested, in as light a tone as he could muster. He'd known Thea for so long—not surprising if he felt protective towards her. She was lovely—desire was not surprising either. But this tenderness, this welling up of delight merely to see her smile…to see her smile in his arms—this was different.

'Good evening, Mr Blakehurst.'

Chill disapproval splintered in the voice.

Richard turned slowly to find Lord Aberfield watching them, his face expressionless. 'Lord Aberfield.' He acknowledged the older man with a bow. Beside him, Thea stood motionless. Silent.

The moment stretched as Richard felt the tension sing between the pair of them. He flicked a glance at Thea. No shadows, but the woman he had been dancing with was gone. In her place stood a marble statue, blue eyes frozen to arctic winter.

Then, in a voice that cut like a polar wind, she spoke. 'Good evening, my lord.'

A perfectly correct form of address…for a perfect stranger. As a young woman's greeting to her father, it was the ultimate snub. And in that icily correct voice, it was a snub with a sting in the tail.

Not surprisingly Aberfield's face turned slightly purple.

Thea continued, 'You are well again, my lord?'

'Very well,' he grated. 'A word with you, Dorothea! In private.'

Her brows lifted. 'Oh? Yes, I think that is possible.'

Aberfield's teeth grated audibly at the implication that Thea might have, if she had chosen, refused his request. 'Perhaps, *daughter*,' he said with silky emphasis, 'you would come with me, then. There is much that I wish to discuss with you. Privately.'

'Now?' Her fan flickered open with a swish, and she disappeared behind it. 'I assumed you meant to call tomorrow at Arnsworth House. Yes, that would be better. Far more scope for privacy there. What time will suit you?'

'Now would suit me!' snapped Aberfield.

Thea's smile was a naked blade. 'I am afraid, dear sir, that Lady Arnsworth would be sadly inconvenienced were I to steal her carriage and return home now. But I am perfectly happy to hold myself at your disposal tomorrow. Call at whatever time suits you. I promise you shall find me home.'

For a moment it looked as though Aberfield might explode, but he nodded and stalked away.

To say that Lady Arnsworth was unimpressed the following morning to hear that her protégée had undertaken to remain at home all day awaiting her father's convenience, would have been an understatement.

'You were to drive with Lady Chasewater, you remember?' said Lady Arnsworth.

'I sent her a note explaining,' said Thea. A very convenient added benefit she had not thought of at the time. 'I felt my father's request must take precedence.'

There was no answer to that, and Lady Arnsworth didn't attempt one, only saying, 'But he gave *no* indication of when he might call?'

Thea contrived to look repentant. 'No, ma'am. He wished to speak to me privately, and at a ball—' She spread her hands. No need to tell Lady Arnsworth that it had been her strategy to avoid leaving the safety of a crowd with Aberfield. She didn't trust him an inch.

Lady Arnsworth pursed her lips. 'Very well, my dear. There

is nothing to be done. I *must* pay some calls this afternoon, and I shall drive in the park afterwards. Naturally I shall give instructions to Myles that he must admit only your father, and any female visitors you might have. No gentlemen, of course, unless your brother were to call.' A very faint smile played about her lips.

'Oh, of course,' agreed Thea.

Lady Arnsworth nodded. 'Yes. And, dear, if you play chess with Richard again, it might be for the best if you were to leave the door open.'

Thea's jaw dropped, as her ladyship continued, 'You may trust Richard, of course, as you would your own brother, but it doesn't do to give the gossips the least bit of encouragement, you know. If anyone were to call and find you together—well!' She patted Thea's hand. 'Your father wouldn't like it at all.'

Chapter Six

'Lord Aberfield is here to see you, miss,' said Myles. 'Shall I show him in here?'

Thea laid down her pen and considered the alternatives. She was in the back parlour, writing a note to accept an invitation to attend a picnic with Diana Fox-Heaton the following week. While being received in there would sting his pride, she hesitated. Somehow the back parlour of Arnsworth House was associated with happy times, with her childhood visiting the house, with Richard teaching her to play chess, with his slightly crooked smile. She did not want Aberfield anywhere within spitting distance of those memories.

'No. Show his lordship into the drawing room, please, Myles. And, Myles—?' An inner demon suggested another way she might infuriate Aberfield. 'Tell his lordship that I will be with him very shortly.'

She heard Aberfield being ushered into the next room, heard Myles offer refreshment, and heard it refused. Deliberately she completed her letter to Diana. And read it over. Then she sealed it, addressed it, rang the bell and waited for Myles.

When he came, she smiled and handed him the note with instructions to have it delivered at once. 'And bring tea to the drawing room in fifteen minutes, please, Myles.'

Then, feeling that she had made her point, Thea settled her elegant morning gown, tucked a stray curl back into place under her lace cap, assumed an indifferent expression, and strolled through the door connecting the back parlour and drawing room.

'Good afternoon, my lord. I've kept you waiting.' It could be construed as an apology. Just.

Aberfield turned and glared at her. 'Where the devil have you been, miss?' His colour was high, and the faded blue eyes glittered at her.

She granted him her most gracious smile. 'Finishing a letter, my lord. Do be seated and tell me what I may do for you.' She sat in a small chair set slightly apart, and waited.

Aberfield didn't waste time on niceties. 'You can tell me what the devil you're playing at with Blakehurst,' he snarled. 'Waltzing with *him* when Dunhaven had honoured you with an invitation to dance!'

So that had got back to him. Lord, he was a fool! Had he learned nothing from the past?

'Playing at, my lord?' she queried. 'Unlike some, I play no games. Mr Blakehurst asked me to dance with him—'

'Asked you after Dunhaven asked you!' snapped Aberfield.

'Not at all,' she said sweetly. 'He had asked me earlier.'

Aberfield looked her over. 'Think you can get him up to scratch, do you?' He snorted. 'I doubt it! Too high in the instep the Blakehursts, even if his brother *has* made a fool of himself.'

Thea froze and Aberfield continued, his voice contemptuous. 'Knew Almeria Arnsworth would try her damnedest to marry you to him, but he's dodged every other heiress she's found. Some of 'em a damn sight wealthier than you!' His lip curled. 'And they weren't some other man's leavings.'

Words, meaningless words. They can't hurt unless I permit it …

Something Richard had said about Dunhaven slid through her mind, displacing her father's barb: *He's so desperate…it's a wonder he hasn't found a young enough widow with a couple of brats to her credit…* What had Aberfield told Dunhaven? She didn't really believe it, not quite. But if she trailed the lure …

'One wonders,' she mused, 'what can possibly have induced Lord Dunhaven to relax his standards.'

The fish rose. 'Dunhaven needs an heir,' he told her. 'For a wealthy bride he knows can breed a brat, he's willing to overlook things.'

'I have no "brat", as you put it.'

Just aching grief and guilt over the death of a nameless child she had neither seen nor held, and the opium-hazed memory of a newborn wail.

Aberfield opened his mouth and shut it again. His gaze shifted and then he shrugged. 'Even if the whelp died, you still went full term,' he said.

Bile rose, choking and sour.

'More than his first wife ever did,' he continued. 'For that assurance and your fortune, it's worth it to him.'

She swallowed the bile, reaching for control. 'I'm sure it is,' she said. 'But tell me, my lord—was it not rather a risk for you, confiding so much in Dunhaven?'

'Why should he talk about his bride?' Cold triumph gleamed. 'No reason for him to talk if you're married. And he's willing to marry you.'

'But if I don't marry him—?'

Aberfield's fists clenched. 'You'll marry him, or I'll…I'll—!'

'You'll what, my lord?' The time for dissembling was past. She stood up, casting aside caution. 'You really have no power left, sir. Do you?' She smiled. 'You may cast me off, but in two and a half months I turn twenty-five and will have two hundred pounds a year. A pittance to you, I am sure, but I will manage very well. And just think of the gossip if you cut off my allowance now.'

Aberfield had risen as well, his face mottled. 'And this is the gratitude I receive for protecting you from your folly eight years ago!'

Thea rang the bell. 'I think there is nothing more to be said, my lord.'

'I'll see you don't get a penny of the money!' he blustered.

She laughed. 'You can't. Under the terms of the will, once I turn twenty-five there is nothing you can do to block the two hundred a year. With that I will be independent and can do as I please.'

Aberfield's colour deepened to an alarming purple. 'You mean to have Blakehurst, then?'

'That, my lord, is not your concern.'

His teeth clenched, he said, 'Make sure he understands you'll not see a penny more than the two hundred before your thirtieth birthday.'

The door opened to admit the butler.

'Ah, Myles. His lordship was just leaving.'

His face stiff with fury, Aberfield stalked out of the room without another word.

As the door closed, Thea sank on to the sofa, all the cold fury ebbing to leave her drained and shaking. But she had done it! Stood up to Aberfield and forced him to realise that he had no power over her any longer. That there was nothing he could do to force her marriage or control her actions. That knowledge had fuelled his anger. His parting shot about only receiving the two hundred per annum until she turned thirty suggested that he accepted that she would not marry Dunhaven. Which left her free to contemplate the sort of life she wanted for herself.

The future stretched out before her, not golden, but peaceful. Or it would be if she could only rid herself of the guilt and pain—the child had been an innocent, blameless of any wrongdoing. Had her actions been responsible for its death? At the very least she had been partly responsible for its unmourned, unmarked grave. *It*. That sounded so cold. So uncaring. Like Aberfield's reference to the child as a brat or whelp. As though its very life hadn't mattered. *It* again. She had no other way to think of her lost baby. A shudder racked her as she stared blindly into the empty fireplace. She was vaguely aware that the doorbell had rung. An annoyed voice echoed in the front hall, followed by the slam of the front door. It wasn't important. Her vision blurred. She didn't even know if her baby had been a boy or a girl…they had refused to tell her.

For the first time in seven years someone had spoken of her

dead baby—as proof of her fertility. Her hands clenched into fists until the nails dug into her palms as she looked back at the mess her younger self had made of everything. If only she had known…had realised in time… She swallowed hard. She could see now what she should have done…and it was far, far too late. She felt cold, cold all over, as though a void inside her had been filled with ice.

The door opened and she looked round. 'Yes, Myles?'

'Your tea, miss.' The old man looked at her kindly. 'If I may say so, Miss Thea, you look as though a nap wouldn't go astray. Why don't you go on up and I'll send one of the maids to help you?'

Heat pricked at her eyes at the kindness in his voice. What a fool she was to feel like crying because of a simple expression of kindness when her father's callous actions merely left her cold with fury.

'Thank you, Myles,' she said, forcing words past the choking lump in her throat. 'I'll do that.' She went over to the door. 'I'll leave the tea for now. I'm sorry to waste your time.'

He shook his head. 'Not to worry, Miss Thea.' He hesitated. 'Lord Dunhaven called. Just after Lord Aberfield left.'

So that was who had owned the loud, blustering voice.

'You denied me?'

Myles's mouth flickered into what in a less well-trained butler might have been a smile. 'No, Miss Thea, although her ladyship had instructed me to do so.' The smile escaped its bonds. 'Mr Blakehurst beat me to it.'

Warmth eased the aching chill within her.

'I am never at home to Lord Dunhaven,' she told him. 'Nor…' she drew a deep breath '…to Lord Aberfield, unless I have informed you of a prior appointment.'

'Very good, Miss Thea.'

She nodded and left the room.

The maid answered her summons and helped her out of her gown and stays. Clad only in her shift, Thea snuggled down under the bedclothes and closed her eyes.

When she opened them again the shadows in the room had moved. She yawned and stretched. She felt better, although she didn't think she had slept for terribly long. A glance at the clock on the mantel confirmed this. She hadn't slept for more than an hour and a half. But she felt refreshed, in spirit as much as body.

It was as though facing her father had drained a poison from her, its passage leaving her cleansed. She was a long way from happy, but there was no longer the sapping despair. Her gaze fell on a carved wooden box beside the armoire. Now there was a task she had been putting off—sorting out her collection of…of what? Rubbish? Tangible memories? Ever since she was a little girl she had kept cherished mementoes in that box. Reminders of past joy. Birthday party invitations, tickets to Astley's Amphitheatre, courtesy of a generous impulse on the part of Richard when she was ten, letters, even a few from her mother after she had been banished to Aunt Maria, despite Aberfield's orders to the contrary. David's letters. And some things that had given her pain…like the brief, factual note her father had written informing her of her mother's illness and death, after the funeral had taken place.

That had been almost the last thing she had put in apart from David's letters. For the past year or so she had not even dared to look inside, just shoving each letter in and locking the box again.

But now…now she had things to put in it again. Invitations. Notes from Diana—telling her that friendship could endure. There was a little pile of papers down in the drawer of the *escritoire* in the drawing room. She would take the box down there and sort it out. When she had glanced into it before leaving Yorkshire it had been a terrible mess. It was time to sort it all out. She rang for a maid to help her with her stays.

She found the drawing room occupied.

His back to the door, Richard was sitting near the window in one of Almeria's prized Egyptian chairs, complete with gilt crocodile arms. Not odd in itself, but the chair was placed squarely in the middle of a raft of newspaper sheets. A faint scraping sound gave her the clue, and she understood; Richard was carving. He had the tea table beside him, and on it she could see several knives, a cloth and several small wooden objects on more spread newspaper.

Silent laughter welled up. He hadn't changed at all. Except that he obviously thought of the newspaper for himself now, rather than after Lady Arnsworth scolded him for making a mess.

She cleared her throat and he glanced round, frowning.

'Ah.' The frown disappeared. 'Ring the bell.'

She did so, and then asked, 'Why?'

'Myles will bring some tea now you are awake. Did you sleep well?'

She nodded. 'Am I disturbing you?'

'Idiot. What have you got there?'

A blush heated her cheeks. 'My collection, for want of a better word.' Heavens! He'd think all this rubbish…well, rubbish!

'Collection?' He looked curious. 'I had no idea you collected something. What is it? Sea shells? Roman coins? Max and I used to find them around Blakeney when we were boys.'

'Nothing so exciting,' she told him, and explained.

To her complete surprise he wasn't in the least dismissive. 'When you're an old, old woman, your grandchildren will find that fascinating. It will tell them something about how you lived.'

She set the box down on the *escritoire,* and said dubiously, 'I suppose so.' Perhaps David's grandchildren.

He laughed. 'Would you believe the British Museum has an extensive collection of ephemera, courtesy of old Miss Banks?'

'Miss Banks?' She lifted the lid of the box.

'Sir Joseph Banks, the naturalist's, sister. After she died a few years ago her entire collection came to the museum.' He paused. 'All nineteen thousand items of it.'

Thea dropped the lid with a bang. 'Ninetee—! Good God!'

'Quite,' said Richard with a chuckle. 'Visiting cards, invitations, admission tickets, you name it—she kept it.'

Thea looked at her own collection. 'I think I need a new box.' She opened the lid again and lifted out some of the contents.

His husky laugh warmed her. 'I'll make one for you.'

'Would you?' The warmth spread, and she reached into the box again. Her fingers felt something small and hard, irregularly shaped, at the bottom. Curious she delved and drew it out— 'Ohh…'

In her hand lay a small wooden bird, rather crudely carved, its beak open, wings half-spread. Richard had made it for her, and all these years it had lain forgotten in the box, the unheard song stilled. She had thought it left behind when she went to Yorkshire.

'What have you got there?'

Blinking hard, she turned and held out the little bird on the palm of her hand.

For a moment he seemed not to understand. Then, 'You've kept it all these years?' There was an odd note in his voice.

Scarlet, she said, 'I had forgotten all about it.' Desperate to change the subject, she asked, 'What…what are you making now?'

'Something to hang over the cradle for my godson or god-daughter,' he answered. 'Max and Verity's child. Tell me what you think.'

She went over to the table and a gasp of delight escaped her. Five gaily painted little wooden horses, in various attitudes, pranced there. A sixth, as yet unpainted was in his hand. 'Not very exciting,' he said. 'I did think of dragons, but these pieces of wood insisted on being ponies. I'm just doing the finishing touches to this one before painting it.'

'They are lovely,' she said softly. 'And I think your godchild will treasure them.' She reached out and stroked the nose of one pony with her forefinger. 'They're like my box of clutter—one day your great-nephews and nieces will look at these and think of you.' Perhaps even his great-great nephews and nieces. And so on until the children no longer knew anything about the man who had carved these dancing ponies so long ago. But they would know the toy had been made with love.

Just as she had remembered the wooden bird.

Very softly, she said, 'I shall like to think of you making something like this for your own children one day, Richard.'

He went very still as her words fell into a deep silence within him.

Until a year ago he had assumed that one day he would marry. There was no reason not to, but marriage had never been compelling. He had been busy, satisfied with his life, and his role as Max's steward. Indeed, that role was still his. But ever since Max's marriage he had been increasingly aware that something was missing in his life, and that it was time to fill the void.

'Thea—' Unsure what he was going to say, only knowing that words were there, he reached for her hand.

The door opened without warning.

He slewed around in his chair.

'Damn it, Myles! What the devil do you want now?'

Myles looked severely shaken. 'Mr Richard—there…there is a magistrate in the front hall—'

There came a sharp gasp from Thea. Richard reached out and took her hand, enveloping it in his, shocked to feel her trembling.

'A *what?*' Surely Myles hadn't said—

'A magistrate, sir. Sir Giles Mason. From Bow Street. Requesting an interview with Miss Winslow.' Myles swallowed. 'I know her ladyship will not like it, but, sir, perhaps you—since her ladyship isn't here?'

Her ladyship would probably have apoplexy when she found out, reflected Richard, but he couldn't see any alternative. Thea's hand, still lost in his, was trembling, although when he looked up at her, she appeared perfectly calm.

'I'd better see him, I think,' she said. Her voice was perfectly calm too. Turning to the butler, she continued, 'Tell Sir Giles that I will see him in the dining—'

'Show Sir Giles up, Myles,' said Richard, cutting straight across Thea. He eyed her in flat-out challenge. 'If you think for one moment that I am going to permit you to see a magistrate alone, you have some more thinking to do.'

'But—'

'But nothing,' he interrupted. 'Call me a coward, but I have no intention of admitting to Almeria that I let you face this alone!'

The door shut behind Myles.

'Thea…' he caught her other hand, holding them both in a gentle clasp '…do you have any idea what this might be about?'

She shook her head, and her eyes met his unflinchingly, but a deep, slow blush mantled her cheeks … He swore mentally and let out a breath he hadn't realised he'd been holding.

'I hope,' he said grimly, 'that you can lie a great deal more convincingly for Sir Giles's benefit.'

Sir Giles was a tall, grizzled man with a slight stoop. In his late fifties, Richard judged. Shrewd green eyes looked over the top of half-moon spectacles and flickered down to a sheaf of papers he had produced from a small case.

Polite greetings over, he got straight down to business.

'Miss Winslow, I am sure this must be a shock for you, and I am very glad that you have a responsible friend to support you in this. Painful though it must be for you, I must ask you some questions about your late, er, betrothed, Mr Nigel Lallerton.'

Shock jolted through Richard. He stole a sideways glance at Thea. There was not the least hint of surprise, manufactured or otherwise.

'Yes, sir.'

Sir Giles looked at her closely. 'That doesn't surprise you?'

'Your being here at all is a surprise, Sir Giles.'

The magistrate cleared his throat. 'No doubt. Now—did anyone dislike Mr Lallerton? Have a quarrel with him?'

She hesitated, then said, 'I am sure there were many, sir.'

'*Many?*'

'No one is universally popular,' she said, her hands shifting restlessly in her lap, pleating her skirts.

Richard reached out and took possession of one hand; instantly the other lay utterly still.

'Hmm. I meant,' said Sir Giles, 'was there anyone in particular who might have had a grudge against Mr Laller—?'

'Would you mind informing Miss Winslow of the reason for these questions, Sir Giles?' said Richard.

The older man's mouth tightened. 'We have received information, sir, that, far from dying in a shooting accident when his gun misfired, Mr Lallerton was murdered.'

'Information? From whom?' asked Richard.

'As to that,' said Sir Giles, 'the information was anonymous.' Richard froze, but said nothing. Sir Giles continued. 'We have made some enquiries into the matter, and it would appear that further investigation is in order.'

'You take notice of anonymous information?'

Sir Giles shrugged. 'Information is information, sir. Naturally we would not hang a man on the basis of an anonymous submission, but as a starting point for investigation, it is perfectly normal. Now, Miss Winslow—on the subject of your betrothed's popularity—did you know of anyone who might have wished him ill?'

'I know of no one who wished him dead,' said Thea in a low voice. She met his eyes squarely, her face pale.

'I see. And your own feelings…' Sir Giles shifted in his seat '…were you on good terms with Mr Lallerton? Happy about your coming marriage?'

Faint colour rose in Thea's cheeks as she said, 'I was counting the days, Sir Giles.' Her hand in Richard's shook.

'And tell me, Miss Winslow—where were you when Mr Lallerton died?'

'I was at my father's principal seat in Hampshire. My mother was giving a house party.'

'At which Mr Lallerton had been a guest. I understand he left rather precipitately and returned to London?'

'That is correct, sir.'

'And he had an accident in which his gun discharged and hit him in the leg, so that he bled to death?'

The pink deepened to crimson. 'So I was told, sir.'

The green eyes were steady on her. 'You can tell me nothing more, Miss Winslow?'

'No, sir.'

The magistrate nodded. 'Very well. If you should think of anything, please send a message to Bow Street. And I must warn

you that I may question you again as the investigation proceeds.'
He rose. 'I'll bid you good day, Miss Winslow.'

His mind reeling, Richard saw Sir Giles out, accepting his
repeated apologies for the intrusion.

Closing the front door, he faced the inescapable fact that Thea
had not been in the least bit surprised by the direction of Sir Giles's
questioning. Which of itself suggested that there was something
to find out, despite her neatness at sidestepping questions. He did
not for one moment doubt that Sir Giles would return.

His mouth set grimly as he went back up to the drawing
room. Hell's teeth! If Nigel Lallerton had been murdered, how
had it been covered up? Good God! Surely his family would have
noticed if there had been anything suspicious about his death?
And how the devil was he meant to protect Thea from this if she
wouldn't confide in him?

His jaw set in a state of considerable rigidity, he stalked into
the drawing room, only to find that the bird had flown. Thea had
taken her box and gone. Probably to her bedchamber. Well, if
she thought that was going to stop him—from below came the
sound of the front door opening...then,

'Who called?'

Almeria's outraged shriek came up to him in perfect clarity.
He swore. Invading Thea's bedchamber and forcing some
answers from her was no longer an option. Hearing the sound
of hurrying feet on the stairs, Richard braced himself, pushing
to the back of his mind the realisation that of all the questions
to which he wanted answers, the most pressing was not directly
connected to Lallerton's death.

He dearly wanted to know exactly what Thea had meant when
she told Sir Giles that she was counting the days until her wedding.

'Richard!' Almeria hurried into the drawing room. 'What is
this that Myles tells me? What were you thinking of to permit
such a thing?'

'That admitting Mason was preferable to having him summon
Thea to Bow Street,' he told her.

'But, surely…' Almeria's voice trailed away. 'Good God! A pretty thing that would be!'

'That's what I thought,' said Richard.

Almeria sat down, frowning. 'It might be worse. Myles assures me that none of the other servants is aware of Sir Giles's identity, and of course *he* won't gossip. As long as that is the end of it.' She eyed Richard in blatant speculation. 'I understood from Myles that you remained with Dorothea—thank you, Richard. I am most grateful.'

'Not at all, Almeria.' Damn. Now she was extrapolating all sorts of things from his intervention.

'I will be attending Lady Heathcote's assembly with Dorothea this evening,' she informed him. 'After a dinner at the Rutherfords. Will you—?'

'I will join you there, if you wish it,' he assured her. He could see absolutely no need to acquaint Almeria with the fact that he had already been planning to attend whatever entertainment Thea might be gracing that evening. That would only serve to encourage her.

Breathing with careful concentration, Thea forced her hands to steady enough to remove the stopper from her ink bottle and dip the quill. Then she stared blindly at the blank paper. What should she write? If she were quick, she had enough time before she needed to bathe and dress for the dinner and assembly she was attending with Lady Arnsworth that evening.

Dearest David—a magistrate from Bow Street questioned me this afternoon and I lied faster than a fox can trot?

Or perhaps:

Dearest David—Bow Street is asking questions about Nigel Lallerton's death…

A dry little sob escaped her. There was nothing she could write that might not be construed as a warning, suspicious in itself, unless… Her quill hovered above the paper and common sense finally broke through the fog of panic. What a ninnyhammer she was being!

She wrote quickly:

Dearest David—Sir Giles Mason, a magistrate, called this afternoon. He asked some very odd questions about Nigel Lallerton's death. You will understand that I found it most distressing. I would like very much to discuss it with you at the earliest opportunity. I will not be home this evening; we are to attend Lady Heathcote's assembly.

Your loving sister,

Thea

Quite unexceptionable, really. After all, there was nothing unusual in a sister asking her brother's advice on such a matter. Ringing the bell, she summoned a footman and asked him to deliver the note to Jermyn Street immediately.

She could do nothing further.

To her relief, David approached her within ten minutes of her arrival at Lady Heathcote's assembly. He came up and greeted them politely, chatting on general topics for a few moments. Then, 'Lady Arnsworth, I wonder if I might steal my sister away from your side for a little?'

Lady Arnsworth looked a little dubious, but said, 'Of course, Mr Winslow.'

He smiled and bowed, then led Thea away, saying in a low voice, 'I received your note. We had better talk.'

'Is there somewhere we may be private?' she asked, just as softly.

'Come with me.'

He took her to a small parlour on the next floor. Closing the door, he turned to her. 'Very well—tell me.'

She did so, leaving out nothing.

He listened in shocked silence, his eyes hard. 'Hell and damnation!' he muttered. 'Where the devil did that come from?'

'David—what if you are arrested? You might hang!' That fear had been tearing at her with black claws all afternoon until she could think of nothing else.

He looked up, obviously surprised. 'Hang? Me?' He took one look at the distress in her face and gave her a swift hug. 'Don't be a peagoose! It was a duel, not murder, and the only reason it was hushed up was to prevent your name coming into it. If it had become known that I had fought a duel with my sister's betrothed, the next question would have been—what caused it? Someone would have worked it out.' His mouth twisted cynically. 'Even old Chasewater didn't want that—some of the mud would have stuck to them as well.'

'But—'

'Thea, even if it comes out, I'm in no real danger. There are enough witnesses to prove that it was a fair duel. Yes, I might have to face a trial, but they would be unlikely to convict me. I'm safe enough, even if there is a bit of gossip.' His mouth flattened. 'What *is* of concern is the danger to you. You're the one who will be ruined if this—'

'I don't care about that!' said Thea.

'Well, I do!' he informed her. 'You said Richard Blakehurst was there—what did you tell him?'

The world rocked. 'Nothing,' said Thea.

He sighed. 'You'll have to tell him in the end, you know.'

'No,' said Thea. 'I won't.'

David's mouth tightened. 'I think Richard Blakehurst is a better man than you give him credit for.'

Thea turned away and closed her eyes. He was. And that was precisely the problem.

Richard found Almeria almost as soon as he arrived. She was seated on a *chaise longue,* chatting to Lady Jersey, making frequent use of her fan in the stuffy, overheated salon. Full battle regalia, he noted. The famous Arnsworth diamonds blazed and dripped from every conceivable vantage point. Thea was nowhere to be seen.

His stomach clenched. Walking up to Almeria in front of Sally Jersey and demanding to know where Thea might be had as much appeal as strolling naked along Piccadilly. Sally Jersey might never stop talking, but that didn't mean she wasn't as shrewd as she could hold together…

He looked round again, and saw Thea slip into the salon with Winslow. David Winslow looked calm enough, but Richard could see him scanning the room, as though looking for someone in particular. He leaned down and murmured something to Thea, who frowned and looked straight across at him.

What the devil was she frowning at *him* for?

'Evening, Ricky.'

He looked around. Braybrook stood at his elbow.

'Julian.'

'Something bothering you?'

Not for the first time, Richard cursed the blessing of a friend who knew you too damn well.

'You might say that.'

'I did,' said Braybrook drily. 'Ah, here comes Winslow with his sister.'

Sure enough, Winslow was escorting Thea straight towards them. Tall and slender, in the poppy-red muslin with gold trim.

He waited for them with Braybrook.

'Blakehurst.' Winslow greeted Richard with a quick handshake. 'Can I trouble you to escort Thea back to Lady Arnsworth? I need a word with Braybrook.'

'Of course. It's no trouble at all.' He smiled at Thea and offered his arm. Hesitantly, she took it. The light touch of her gloved hand, despite two layers of cloth, jolted through him like a lightning bolt. Some soft summery perfume laced with the sweet temptation of woman wreathed him.

And she only had her hand on his arm. He shuddered to think what the effect would be if he waltzed with her. He found himself wondering if this became less incapacitating with custom, if, after they were married, his reaction to her sheer proximity might be more manageable. Given that Max could function in a reasonably normal fashion now with Verity around, he had to assume that— shock hit him. Apparently he'd made his decision about offering for Thea without his mind being involved anywhere in the process.

'I've told David what happened,' she said.

That focused his mind very effectively. 'What did he say?'

'That I ought not to worry about it too much.'

Good God! Was Winslow insane? A ripple like this could overturn a woman's reputation in a flash. And Thea, damn it, looked as though at least part of the load was off her mind.

He flung a glance after Winslow and Julian. The pair of them were standing by themselves, conversing with their heads close. Winslow looked taut, almost feral as he gesticulated. Whatever he might have said to reassure Thea, plainly it hadn't convinced *him*. As he watched, the two of them were joined by Fox-Heaton, who looked as though he'd swallowed something unpleasant. The three of them made for the door.

He looked back at Thea. Her gaze followed Winslow and the other two as they left the room. The combination did not seem to surprise her one whit. Which was more than could be said for himself. While Winslow taking Julian into his confidence might come as no surprise, what the devil did Fox-Heaton have to do with it?

Memory supplied an unwelcome suggestion—Sir Francis had been a very close friend of Nigel Lallerton's…if Lallerton's death had *not* been an accident… Icy foreboding crawled up and down Richard's spine. Fox-Heaton was exactly the sort of fellow who would ask some very awkward questions if any rumours began to circulate. This had all the makings of a scandal *extraordinaire*.

A surge of protective fury roared through him. No matter what it took, he was going to keep Thea safe from whatever folly her brother had committed…

'Richard?' Thea's fingers tightened on his arm. 'It's Lady Chasewater.'

'Confound it!' muttered Richard, as he saw the Dowager Countess of Chasewater heading straight for them. 'Don't tell her about it. Not here.' She turned dazed eyes on him, and he laid his hand on hers, squeezing it in reassurance. 'Keep your chin up, and we'll get through.'

Arranging a polite smile on his face, he said, 'Good evening, Lady Chasewater.'

She gave him a distracted look. 'Mr Blakehurst.' She turned at once to Thea.

'Dear Dorothea! Such a dreadful thing! I must tell you before someone else does!'

Hell and the devil! Surely not?

'A magistrate, Sir Giles Mason, called on me to ask about poor Nigel,' said Lady Chasewater in tones calculated to turn heads.

Several heads did turn, but she continued regardless. 'It seems they are not after all quite happy about the way he died. There has been some suggestion that it might have been murder!'

Richard swore under his breath. No one nearby was making even a pretence of not listening, as her ladyship went on, 'Can you imagine it? Who could possibly have wanted to kill my poor boy? Why! 'Tis unthinkable!'

Not any more it wasn't. The blasted female had just made sure the entire *ton* would be thinking about it by breakfast time.

Thea's chin lifted. 'Yes, a very dreadful thing.'

'And so distressing for you, my dear!' went on Lady Chasewater, apparently oblivious to the fact that by now at least fifty people had drawn closer the better to hear what she was saying.

Richard gritted his teeth. The cat had its head out of the bag now—how the hell could he shut her up before the whole beast escaped? 'Ma'am, perhaps you would like to speak to Miss Winslow a little more privately? You might—'

'And I understand he plans to call on *you,* my dearest Dorothea.' She caught at Thea's wrist. 'Why, whatever would you be able to tell him?'

Shocked murmurs rippled outwards.

In a steady voice, Thea said, 'Very little, ma'am, I am afraid. Sir Giles called this afternoon.'

'Oh, my dear! You must let me know if I can be of the least help,' she told Thea, clutching her wrist convulsively.

Keeping your tongue still would have been a start! It was far too late now. The cat was right out of the bag and scurrying around the room, leaving murmurs and exclamations of astonishment in its wake.

Fury sang in every fibre. Damn the blasted woman! Dimly he could feel pity for her; she had lost her son, and this must be upsetting for her, but didn't she know better than to reveal the whole affair like this? Had she no discretion? All he could think was that the shock must have addled her wits.

By the time Richard left the assembly, scarcely anything else was being spoken of save the shocking news that Nigel Lallerton had apparently been brutally murdered.

'Slaughtered, they say, my dear!'

He ignored several offers for snug games of cards and a bottle of brandy and walked home.

Hell's own broth was brewing around him, and he had no idea how to get out of it. And getting out didn't matter a damn beside the far more pressing need to protect Thea.

He wasn't her brother, curse it! Winslow was the one with the right to defend her, but it seemed that Winslow was leaving it to him. Aside from her brother, there was Aberfield... Richard dismissed that idea. Any father who could view Dunhaven as a suitable husband for his daughter was worse than useless. And as for Dunhaven, who had been hovering all evening—Richard's teeth ground savagely as he trod up the steps of Arnsworth House.

The only way to circumvent Dunhaven's plans was for Thea to be married, or at the very least, betrothed. To someone else.

Someone like himself...

His latch key missed the keyhole.

He tried again, this time managing to unlock the door. Why hadn't he seen it earlier? A simple solution was often the best, and the simplest way to protect Thea from the attentions of Dunhaven, and her father's machinations, was to offer for her himself. Immediately. Otherwise, his power was limited. At least if they were betrothed he could deflect much of the inevitable gossip. And there was another thing—once they were betrothed, Thea might confide whatever she knew about Lallerton's death to him, which would mean he could help her.

Closing the door, he acknowledged that there were other things motivating him. He liked Thea—more than liked. He *cared* about her. About the woman who had kept that badly carved little bird all these years. About the woman whose eyes spoke sometimes of a pain he could only guess at. And who could wipe him off a chessboard. He smiled as he picked up a candle from the hall table and lit it from a taper. It was the only candle there so Almeria and Thea must be in already. He blew out the taper.

Yes, the more he thought about the idea of marrying Thea, the more right it seemed. Once he could get past the idea of facing Almeria's smug gloat. *No point cutting off your nose to spite your face.* There would probably be a certain air of well-fed-cat-picking-its-teeth-with-yellow-feathers about Braybrook too. Not even that had the power to bother him.

Not beside the anticipated delight of Thea as his wife, his bride, his lover… Desire kicked sharply as he trod up the stairs. If they were married, instead of passing her room with every muscle, nerve and sinew straining at the leash, he would be opening the door and stripping quietly, before sliding into bed with her…to hold her, love her gently… His blood burned and he realised to his horror that he had actually stopped at the door.

He took a shuddering breath. Tomorrow morning he was going to propose to Thea Winslow. It might be the only way to retain his sanity.

Chapter Seven

Thea stared blindly at her teacup. A piece of toast, reduced to crumbs on her bread-and-butter plate, bore mute testament to her lack of appetite. A sleepless night had left her with a crashing headache, and a churning stomach. The Heathcote assembly had turned into a nightmare with everyone speculating on the possible truth behind Nigel Lallerton's death.

Perhaps she had been mad to admit that Sir Giles had called, but once Lady Chasewater had made the suggestion, there had seemed little point hiding anything. Aching pity stirred inside her. How hard this must be for the woman…she had adored Nigel…

'Miss?'

The footman, James, stood just inside the door of the breakfast parlour, holding a silver salver. 'Yes, James?'

'A note for you, miss. It's just been delivered.'

She set her teacup down carefully, with only the slightest of rattles. 'A…a note?' No. It couldn't be. Foolish to think it might be another note like the one the other day…what purpose could such notes possibly serve now? All the damage had been well and truly done.

'Thank you, James.'

He brought her the note and she took it, seeing instantly that it was addressed to her in the same scrawl as the last one. A chill slid through her. 'That will be all, James.' Her own voice, calm, oddly distant.

'Yes, miss.'

She put the note by her plate, refusing to look at it until the door closed. Shivering now, she picked up her cup of tea and sipped, savouring it. There was more tea in the pot, and she poured herself another cup, adding milk with careful precision.

The note sat there. Unavoidable. She didn't have to read it. There was a fire in the grate. She could drop it in there unread. That would be the sensible thing to do. Swiftly she rose, picked up the note and hurried over to the fireplace.

She stared at the dancing flames. *Drop it in. That's all you have to do.* Only she couldn't. After yesterday, and last night…what if the note contained a threat? A demand. Something that ought to be dealt with. She shivered—what if—?

With shaking fingers she broke the seal—first she would read it, just in case. Then she would burn it… Fumbling with cold, she unfolded the letter.

Did they tell you that the child was dead? Were you relieved, Slut?

The room spun around her in sickening swoops as she crushed the note. Dear God…bile rising in her throat, she bent down and placed the crumpled note on the fire. It hung there for a moment and then the edges blackened, slowly at first, and then in a consuming rush as the flames fed hungrily. It was gone in less than a minute, paper and ink reduced to ashes.

Only, it wasn't gone. Not really. Because she had been fool enough to read it. She could not consign knowledge to the flames and the words remained, branded on her soul—but what could they possibly mean? The phrasing—*Did they tell you…?* What else should they have told her? Unless…unless they had lied.

She dragged in a breath, shutting her eyes as she fought for control.

The door opened.

'Thea?'

She straightened at once and her breath caught. Richard had come in, dressed for riding, dark eyes fixed on her. Dear God…if he had read this note! Her glance flickered to the fire, half-expecting to see the accusation writhing in the flames.

'Good…good morning, Richard.'

He frowned at her as he came into the parlour. 'Did you sleep at all? You should still be abed. Are you all right?'

She forced a smile into place. 'I was…just a little cold,' she lied. Change the subject, quickly. 'Have you been riding?'

He sat down at the table. 'Yes. Thea—about last night—'

'You must be hungry then.' She rushed on. 'Shall I ring for coffee? Were you up very early?' Heavens! She was babbling like an idiot in her attempt to sound vaguely normal.

'Thank you, but Myles knows I'm in. He'll bring me some coffee, and I breakfasted before riding.' He looked across at her. 'Thea, don't pretend with me. About last night—we need to talk. Privately.'

'Oh.' Her heart gave a funny little leap. She squashed it back into place and ordered her thoughts. Very carefully she said, 'Is that wise, Richard?'

His gaze narrowed, and she flushed, remembering a comment of Diana's about how peculiar it was to see Richard in town at all, let alone attending so many parties. Diana seemed perfectly certain that there would be an announcement at any moment—and that wagers had been laid that, finally, Lady Arnsworth would succeed in her dearest ambition.

'After all, you can't wish to…raise expectations, and…and then—'

His brows lifted. 'Expectations?'

She could not quite identify the undercurrent in his voice.

'Am I raising your expectations, Thea?'

He didn't sound concerned, but then he was always in control of his thoughts and feelings.

'Not mine!' she clarified. 'Society's expectations.'

What Richard said about society had a certain eloquence to it.

'You're my friend, Thea,' he told her. 'And I don't give a damn about anyone else's expectations,' he added, still with that odd, intent look. 'Yours would be a different matter.'

A friend. Her heart, foolish organ, glowed. Should she tell him about this note? Not because she wanted him to do something about it, but simply to tell someone. So that she did not feel quite so alone.

No. She couldn't. She could hear the conversation now.

Another note? What did this one say?

Oh, nothing much. Just…it was just nasty.

Nasty, how?

No, she couldn't tell him what it had said. The other one had looked like general spitefulness. This one was more directly aimed. He would want an explanation. Yet another explanation she couldn't give.

'Thea? Thea! Are you all right?'

To her horror she realised that he had been speaking to her, trying to gain her attention.

She flushed. 'I'm sorry, Richard. I…I was wool-gathering.'

'With a vengeance,' he agreed.

She pinned a bright smile in place. 'What did you wish to say?'

He didn't look at all convinced, but said, 'I planned to drive out towards Richmond this morning in the curricle, if you would care to join me. We do need to talk.'

'Driving…but…' Her voice died in her throat and the walls of the present dissolved, memory flooding through the breach. Another offer to drive out on a sunny day…another curricle… shame, embarrassment, and terror stretched out their tentacles, pulling her back in time …

Come, Thea, you cannot possibly believe that I mean you the least harm. Your mama is perfectly happy for me to drive you out. She wishes you to entertain me… At least you might tell me the reason for your change of mind…

'Thea? Thea? Is something wrong?'

His words made no sense. He had never asked before if anything was wrong. She tasted fear, sour in her mouth, and felt her knees buckle.

'*Thea!*'

Strong hands gripped her, lifting her, and then she felt herself being lowered, helpless—

'It's all right, Thea. Here—just lie still.'

Just lie still, you stupid girl!

No! Not this time. She *wouldn't* submit. Even as she felt the sofa beneath her, she squirmed, struggling wildly, clawing, striking out in panic.

The blackness cleared, dissolving to reveal an elegantly appointed breakfast parlour, and, instead of *him,* Richard Blakehurst bending over her, his cravat askew and a livid red mark on his left cheek.

Horror stabbed her.

'I...I—' The words dried up in her throat. There was nothing she could say in answer to the question in his shocked dark eyes. Cold flooded her from the flash of memory, and the disbelief on his face. What had she done?

Very slowly he straightened up.

'You will perhaps be more comfortable if I take my coffee in the back parlour, Thea.'

Thea sank back on the sofa, shivering. But not from the resurgence of nightmare and fear. Horror seeped through her at what she had seen in his face.

What had she done? She had insulted one of the most honourable men in London in the worst possible manner.

Richard Blakehurst was the last man on earth who would take advantage of a woman. Anywhere. Let alone in his godmother's breakfast parlour. She owed him an apology at the very least. And what could she say if he demanded an explanation?

I didn't see you. *I saw* him. *Felt his hands on me. Heard his voice, telling me to lie still...his weight crushing the breath out of me. His strength...*

She choked off the flow of memory, before it could become a nightmare. Not for years had she had a reversion of memory like that—the nightmare leaping to hellish life in her waking mind. Once the slightest unexpected touch had been enough to cast her back into hell...she had thought she was past that. Plainly she was not. But for now it could not be allowed to matter. She had to find Richard and apologise.

And when she had done that, she must decide what she was to do about this last note.

Having retreated to the back parlour, Richard pulled a letter he was writing to his sister-in-law out of the small desk he used. Unfortunately, all he could see was Thea's blanched terror, her dazed eyes.

How had he got himself into such a confounded mess? He'd thought she must be ill, that she was about to faint...dammit! She *had* fainted. If he hadn't caught her, she would have landed on the floor.

He gritted his teeth. Plainly he should have let her hit the floor and simply walked out. Apparently his chivalrous behaviour in catching her and laying her on the sofa had been interpreted as attempted ravishment!

He took another sip of coffee and reached for his pen. Putting words on paper had never been so difficult.

The soft knock on the door startled him so that the pen sputtered all over his half-written letter.

'Come in,' he called.

The door opened and Thea slipped in.

'Richard?'

He waited. He had no idea what to say anyway. Dammit! *She* had come looking for *him,* after as good as accusing him of attempting to rape her!

She looked stricken and his conscience accused him of wanting several pounds of flesh. At which point his body started speculating on which particular pounds he might start with. Banishing his fantasies forcibly, he consigned his conscience and good manners to hell, and waited, his mouth set grimly.

'I'm...I'm sorry, Richard. I would like very much to drive out with you. That is, if you still wish it.'

All the offended fury melted in the face of her distress. And something else, deep inside him that he couldn't even have put a name to, responded with a surge of tenderness.

'I think that it is for me to apologise,' he said quietly. 'I frightened you. I'm sorry, Thea.'

She shook her head. 'No, Richard. You are not to apologise. I think I'd feel better if you raged at me. It was not your fault. I know that you would never...never—' She took a shuddering breath, and said in something approaching her normal voice, 'It was just that I felt dizzy for a moment and became confused.'

He didn't believe it for one moment, but smiled and said, 'Then if you truly wish to drive out, I will order the curricle.'

'Yes, please. It would be lovely. As long as Lady Arnsworth does not object.'

He couldn't help laughing. 'Almeria? I should think you'll find her ready to hand you up into the curricle!'

She blushed.

'In half an hour, then?' he said.

'Yes. Thank you. I'll tell Lady Arnsworth now.'

Richard leaned back in his chair as Thea left the room. God help him; if Almeria knew what was in his mind, she'd be sending instructions around to Doctors' Commons within ten minutes.

Which would definitely be jumping the gun. They weren't anywhere near the point where a special licence was required. He'd intended proposing to her this morning. Suggesting that they marry quickly. Perhaps he needed to step back a little; discuss the idea with her. Point out the rational reasons for a match between them. If he could focus on them through the haze of fury that enveloped him when he thought of Dunhaven. Or the desire that tightened his loins every time he laid eyes on Thea.

Had she seen his thoughts in his eyes as she regained consciousness? If he were to be brutally honest with himself, he couldn't swear even now that he wouldn't have kissed her. He *thought* he wouldn't. He *hoped* he wouldn't! Surely he wasn't such a cad as to take advantage of an unconscious woman? But he wasn't quite sure. She'd exploded in panic before he'd been put to the test.

The worst of it was that little though he might like to admit it, the thought had been there. Oh, not to actually ravish her! But feeling her soft weight in his arms, breathing the fragrance of her hair, seeing those soft pink lips parted and vulnerable—his whole body had tightened with the urge to taste, his fingers had itched to caress her cheek and find out if it really was softer than silk. Not to mention the graceful curve of her throat.

He swore. If he kept on like this he'd be a basket case before ever they reached Richmond.

Thea was awaiting him in the hall, fashionably attired in a carriage dress of deep blue twill when he brought the curricle around to the front door. Almeria came out with her.

'Thank you, Richard,' she said, as he got down. 'A drive is just what will do Dorothea good after last night. A dreadful business. I cannot believe that Laetitia Chasewater, of all people, was so lost to all sense of decorum! And I am determined that tonight we shall attend only Lady Fairchild's *musicale.*'

'A very sensible decision, Almeria.'

He understood perfectly. It was vital that Thea continued to be seen, but at a *musicale* chatter was perforce limited. Of course there would be supper afterwards, but, knowing Lady Fairchild, it would be a small, select affair. All the better if it were.

He handed Thea up into the curricle and hid a smile to see that Almeria, even if she hadn't precisely pushed Thea into the vehicle, was reaching up to pat her on the hands.

'Enjoy your drive, dear. And a little stroll along the river. I am sure you will find it refreshing.'

She stepped back and Richard gave his horses the office, putting them into a slow trot the moment his groom, Minchin, had swung up behind.

Impossible to have any private conversation with Minchin there, so he kept the talk to indifferent topics as he threaded the curricle through the streets and out on to Piccadilly. There the traffic rendered any conversation impossible, until he was past Apsley House and the Knightsbridge Turnpike.

They trotted on, out through the village of Chelsea and on down through Walham Green to cross the river at the Putney Bridge before turning west again to go around to Petersham. It was a glorious day, sunny with a gentle breeze and with London far behind them. Thea relaxed. It seemed that every bird in England was singing for joy in the hedgerows at the fragrance of wildflowers and damp grass, driving out all fear, all memory. She pushed it away, determined, if only for this one perfect day, to live entirely in the moment and not worry about what might be around the corner, or what lay shadowed in the past. Right here, right now, she was happy.

'A penny for your thoughts.'

Richard's voice broke in on her trance-like state. She sighed. 'I was thinking that it would be lovely to live out in the country, somewhere like this, not too far from London so that one might come up easily to visit friends or go to the theatre.'

'But still live peacefully away from the crash and clatter?'

She looked at him gratefully. 'Yes, that's it exactly. I think when all this is over, after my birthday, that is what I shall do.'

'Your birthday?'

'Once I turn twenty-five, under the terms of my uncle's will, I receive two hundred pounds a year whether I marry or not, and whether Aberfield likes it or not. I can do as I please.'

'I see.'

'Do you disapprove?'

He laughed. 'Would it make any difference to you?'

She hesitated, and Richard waited, oddly aware that her answer was somehow important. At last she said, 'No. Not if I thought I was right. I should be sorry to disappoint you, but even if I make a mistake, it would be *my* mistake.'

He could hardly quarrel with that. It was his own creed— make your own mistakes and learn from them. His heart leapt in recognition. This could work. More than work.

Encouraged, he began to talk about his plans for his property, what improvements he had made in the house, how sheltered it was from the worst of the Channel storms. 'A little further from London than this,' he said, as he drew his horses up outside the inn in Petersham. 'But still close enough to come up easily for a visit.' Minchin sprang down and went to the horses' heads. 'And don't tell Almeria,' he added, 'but I've just bought a small town house.'

'Don't tell her? She'd be delighted,' said Thea.

He let himself down carefully to the road, aware that his leg had stiffened slightly. 'Not when she finds out where it is, she won't be.'

Thea looked her question.

'Bloomsbury,' he confessed.

Laughter rippled. 'Near the museum?'

'Mmm. She'll probably have palpitations.' Then, casually, 'Should you mind?'

'No, of course not.'

She looked at him oddly and he held up his hands to help her down. Time to change the subject. 'Are you hungry?' he asked. 'We could have something to eat here and then stroll along the river.'

The river slid past, deep and tranquil. They hadn't walked very far. Richard had produced a bag of old bread from the curricle. In her childhood a drive out to Richmond or Petersham with a picnic and a walk along the river to feed the ducks had been a high treat. Standing there on the bank, throwing bread to the quacking, squabbling ducks, she could almost forget her worries and how many years it had been since last she did this.

Richard's deep quiet voice drew her back. 'Has it occurred to you how similar our plans are?'

She threw a piece of bread to a duck. 'Standing beside the Thames feeding greedy ducks?'

He laughed. 'No. Although that's part of it. Neither of us wants any sort of public life—we both plan to live in the country, at not too great a remove from town.'

A swan moved in, its grace belied by its quickness in lunging for a scrap of bread.

'A quiet life,' he continued.

She threw bread to the swan. 'I'm not planning to run an estate and breed sheep,' she said.

'You could learn to help, though,' he said. 'And I'd enjoy teaching you.'

Shock hummed through her as she began to see where this was leading.

'Richard—you…you can't possibly be suggesting that—you said I could have twice the fortune, and—'

'Dammit, woman! I'm proposing to *you!* Not your blasted fortune! I'm asking you to marry me. Share my life.'

Share my life.

Those simple heartfelt words tore at her like a twisting knife. Share his life…and what did she have to share in return? A sordid secret in her past? And the way things were developing, a sordid and far-from-secret scandal here in the present.

'No,' she said.

Richard's heart landed with a thump in his boots. Owing to the extravagant poke of Thea's bonnet, gauging her expression was impossible, but a glance at her gloved hands showed them clenched together. No doubt the knuckles were stark white.

That was it? No?

He supposed it had the merit of being succinct. None of that nonsense about being honoured by his proposal, and—

So much for being rational. There was a moment's silence, in which he had an eternity to curse himself for the clumsiness of his address.

'This is not because of those silly notes? You do not feel that you must offer for me because of that?'

'Of course not! Lord, every mama in the *ton* would be sending anonymous letters in that case!' He dragged in a breath. 'Thea— I'm offering because I wish to marry you.'

The quacking of the ducks fell into the well of silence that had opened up between them.

'I am very sorry, Richard, but I cannot possibly marry you.'

He held back all the things he wanted to say. All the far-from-rational things that were burning a hole deep inside him. Somehow, he realised, it had not really occurred to him that she might refuse.

'Will you tell me why you cannot?' He flicked a glance at her, but she was staring straight ahead, her face hidden again by the poke of her bonnet. 'After all, we have always been good friends, you must know that I don't give a damn about your fortune, and—'

'Of course I know that!' She turned to him in obvious surprise, and he saw the pain in her eyes. 'It's nothing to do with that. It's just...just that I cannot...it never occurred to me that you could want to marry me!'

He waited, but she fell silent and looked ahead again.

'I frightened you this morning, did I not, Thea?' he asked quietly.

'No!' She faced him again, her face absolutely white. 'The truth is, Richard—' She stopped. He saw the convulsive movement of her throat before she turned away again. Her voice came again, utterly devoid of expression, 'Yes. I was frightened. But it was *not* because of you! Only because I did not realise that it was you.' Her mouth twisted. 'I know that sounds foolish and I...I cannot explain, but I do thank you for your offer. No one who knows you could possibly imagine you would offer because of my fortune.'

'Don't delude yourself, love.' The endearment hung between them, alive and shimmering. *Love.* He had called women that before, of course. One did in bed. It had been a meaningless endearment. But when had he ever really heard himself say it? When had it ever rung like a bell?

She looked up at him, soft lips curved in a trembling smile. 'They do not know you then, do they?' she said quietly. 'I said anyone who knows you, Richard. Would your brother, or Lord Braybrook, make that mistake?'

No. Not even if he lied. They would know. And apparently Thea knew...

'Are you sure, Thea?' he asked gently. 'Ungentlemanly of me to press, I know, but—'

'Quite sure,' she whispered, looking straight ahead again. 'It...it is not possible...if it were...that is...' Her breath came raggedly, as though she breathed glass. Her voice when it came was utterly steady and expressionless. 'I have no intention of marrying. Ever.'

Had she loved the fellow so deeply? She had only been sixteen when they were betrothed; seventeen when Lallerton died, and he had always assumed the match had been arranged by Aberfield and Chasewater, but...perhaps it was time to resurrect his rational proposal.

'Thea,' he said carefully, 'I quite understand how you must feel, but surely after seven years—' He felt her stiffen beside him and altered tack slightly. 'Have you considered that one may marry for friendship, as well as love? We have always been good friends. And this would solve your problem—I may not be a brilliant catch like Dunhaven in your father's estimation, but I'm perfectly eligible.' Only half-joking, he added, 'You wouldn't have to bother with toads like that any more, at least!'

Thea swallowed hard. She knew he would protect her. And it was tempting, so tempting... No! She didn't dare. To marry Richard, she would have to tell him the truth. 'I cannot, Richard,' she whispered. 'Please, will you take me back now?'

'Of course.'

They walked back along the path in silence. In the silence of her mind she railed at fate that had brought her here to this moment and mocked her with his proposal.

As they arrived back at the inn, he said quietly, 'Thea, just because you have refused my offer of marriage does not mean that we cannot continue friends, does it?'

She flinched, and, to her horror, tears sprang to her eyes. Forcing them back, she stared fixedly ahead, not trusting her voice. It would shake like her gloved hands, locked in front of her.

'Thea?'

'Friends—of course, Richard.' Her voice did wobble. Despicably. Friends told each other the truth. Trusted each other. She hated that she was deceiving him so deeply.

You could tell him the truth.

No. She could not. Not to save her life could she tell him that. It would be worse than death to see the pitying contempt in his eyes. And what if he didn't believe her? No one else ever had, save David. And perhaps David had believed her partly because he had disliked Nigel so much.

She shut her eyes. It would be better if David had not believed her either. If he had not, he would not be in such danger now. It would also be better if she did not have to see Richard again. Especially now. Now when she wasn't even sure that *she* knew the whole truth. *Did they tell you that the child was dead?*

With Minchin up behind them during the drive back, any further private conversation was impossible. Thea did not know whether to be glad or sorry. Richard was very quiet, speaking only to point out landmarks, or comment on the state of the roads.

Only when they reached Grosvenor Square and he escorted her up the front steps of Arnsworth House did he refer again to what lay between them.

'Lallerton was a very lucky man for you to have loved him so deeply.'

Not the slightest hint of bitterness. No anger. Just the kindest understanding of the lie that she and her family had cultivated to screen the truth. So easy simply to nod. To accept what he had said and agree. It stuck in her throat. Even if she dared not tell Richard the truth, she would not lie to him. Not in any way.

She turned to face him fully. 'I did not love Nigel Lallerton. Ever. Not then. Not now.'

And she opened the front door and fled into the house.

Richard stared after her, stunned. She *hadn't* loved Lallerton? Then why in Hades had she remained in seclusion for seven years? Why had she set herself so flatly against marriage?

There was something odd here. She had *said* simply that she hadn't loved Lallerton. But her tone of voice had said a great deal more...

Her perfect day was over. Thea sat with a smile of polite interest plastered to her face as she listened to the violinist Lady Fairchild had engaged for the evening. She should be enjoying this, but as the violin sang and soared, her thoughts spun wildly between doubt and searing conviction. Richard had not attended and Lord Dunhaven's presence beside her served only to increase her distraction.

Could they have lied about her child's death? Yes. Easily. And why, oh, why had she been fool enough to tell Richard that she hadn't loved Lallerton?

Had Lord Dunhaven moved his chair slightly? He was too close, especially in the overheated room. Her temples began to throb.

His lordship leaned closer, murmuring something about how much he enjoyed Mozart.

'Haydn,' she told him, and had the dubious pleasure of seeing him turn a dull brick-red. Dunhaven hated being contradicted—especially when he was wrong.

Would they have lied?

Over something like that? With the honour of the family involved? With David at risk? Oh, yes. They would have lied. In a moment.

The accusation of that morning's note hung before her in letters of fire: *Did they tell you that the child was dead? Were you relieved …?*

The sonata ended and the audience applauded with well-bred enthusiasm.

Yes. She had been relieved. For a moment. A day. And then the grief had come. The grief she had not been allowed to show. And the guilt.

But what if her child had survived? How could she find out?

Chapter Eight

She came down to breakfast the following morning to discover Richard already there. He had plainly finished his bacon and eggs and progressed to the toast-and-coffee stage.

Richard smiled at her over his paper. 'Good morning.'

Was it her imagination, or did he look somehow careworn? 'Good morning,' she replied.

'Shall I bring some more toast, Miss Thea?' asked Myles.

'Yes. Yes, please,' she said. She doubted that she could face eggs.

Myles disappeared.

Richard said, 'Thea—about yesterday—'

Myles burst back into the parlour.

'Mr Richard!'

Richard dropped the paper into his toast.

'Yes?'

Myles was holding out a letter. 'A messenger brought this. From Blakeney, sir. His lordship's writing—'

Richard had shoved his chair back, leapt to his feet and was breaking the seal with fumbling fingers before Myles had finished speaking. Thea stared, dumbfounded. He looked…he looked frightened, his eyes dark in a white face, his mouth a hard, set line as he scanned the letter. Then—

'YES!'

Thea's tea sloshed into the saucer as Richard's howl of triumphant delight rent the air. Then, the letter floating to the table, Richard seized Myles and practically waltzed around the room, his face alive and brimming with joy.

'Mr Richard! What is it?'

With which breathless question Thea heartily concurred.

'A boy, Myles! It's a boy! I'm an uncle. And her ladyship is perfectly well! She's come through safely, *thank God!*'

Her heart contracted. His sister-in-law, Lady Blakehurst, had come safely through the birth of her child. A small hidden corner of her soul echoed his words: Thank God.

She shook her head, refusing to acknowledge the memories pouring through her. They came anyway, relentless, raking her painfully. She forced them away, concentrating on the unknown countess, Richard's sister-in-law, Verity. What was it like to hold your child at the end, to see it after the months of waiting, of feeling it kick and wriggle inside? To rejoice in the *birth* of your child, rather than...

Strong, lean hands plucked her from her nightmare and out of her seat.

'Thea! Did you hear? I'm an uncle!' He whirled her around, laughing, alight with joy. His strength startled her; he seemed to hold her effortlessly, spinning her around so that her feet left the floor. She clutched at his shoulders, feeling hard muscles surge under the superfine of his coat, wildly aware of his hands on her waist, spanning her ribcage.

Her heart pounded, her mouth dried and his eyes laughed into hers as he set her down. 'I'm an uncle. And—' he cleared his throat '—about to be a godfather.'

He still had his hands on her waist, not gripping now, just resting there, as though...as though they belonged there. Intimate. Possessive.

'That's...that's wonderful, Richard,' she faltered, gazing up at him. He was close, so close. Sensation splintered through her, leaving her dizzy and breathless.

The laughter faded from his eyes as he stared back at her, stared as though he saw her for the first time, his mouth suddenly hard. His hands tightened slightly at her waist, fingers shifting in a way that sent heat flying through her. It reached her cheeks in a fiery blush as she realised the intimacy of his hold, that her breasts were nearly brushing against him. That they ached. And then, to her utter shock, that she wanted to lean forward, to press the ache against him. That did frighten her.

Richard knew instantly; saw the moment her eyes widened, heard the sudden startled breath as she realised how close they were.

He forced his fingers to relax, his hands to drop to his sides. But his body remained taut with the tension that had exploded when he felt the softness of her body in his hands, saw the delicate flush on her cheeks as he swung her around. Hell! He wasn't supposed to feel like this!

Like what?

As though he wanted to take her back into his arms and kiss her until they were both breathless, until her mouth and body melted under his, and…

Stop right there! This was insane. Surely he couldn't possibly be standing here—in his godmother's breakfast parlour, no less!—struggling against the urge to kiss Thea Winslow senseless? After she had categorically refused his offer of marriage the previous day? Apparently he was. And no matter what honour, not to mention common sense, thought of the idea, his body was making its opinion strongly felt. Visible too. *He* certainly didn't need to look and he hoped to heaven that Thea *wouldn't*.

She was still standing there, her hands resting on his chest. Why the hell wasn't she using them to push him away? And why was she looking up at him like that, with that wide-eyed look of disbelief, when she should have dealt him a ringing slap and kicked him in the shins?

He could, of course, step back himself. He did so, feeling as though part of him had been ripped away to leave weeping raw flesh. As if his retreat had broken a spell, Thea backed up too, her face scarlet.

And just in time.

Almeria walked in, a letter in her hand.

'Richard! Have you heard? Did Max write to you—oh!' She saw the letter on the table. 'You know already.'

Richard smiled. 'Yes. Wonderful news, is it not?'

Almeria cleared her throat. 'Naturally one must be glad that Max's wife has come through the ordeal, and write a letter of congratulations,' she said stiffly. 'Very obliging of Max to inform me.' She sniffed. 'If it can be called a letter! I could scarcely read it!'

Richard laughed. 'Yes, mine is a trifle incoherent as well. I'm not sure if it mentions the baby's name. If it doesn't no doubt he'll tell me when I see him.'

'See him? Will you be going to Blakeney?' asked Almeria.

He hesitated. He didn't want to leave town right now, but—

'You should go, Richard,' said Thea gently.

Almeria frowned. 'Of course you will have to go down, Richard. Whatever his failings…' she sniffed '…Blakehurst is your brother. I am sure that Dorothea and I can manage for a day or two.' She turned to Thea. 'I thought to visit Bond Street this morning, my dear, and would like you to accompany me.'

'Of course, ma'am, if you wish it,' said Thea.

Refolding her letter, Lady Arnsworth tucked it away in a pocket.

'Almeria, Max mentions in his letter that he has asked you to stand as godmother to the baby,' said Richard.

Lady Arnsworth flushed. 'Yes, his letter to me mentions something of the sort, but of course I cannot accept. Impossible to leave town at the moment with Dorothea to chaperon. It would be most remiss of me. No, I am afraid it is not to be thought of. I shall write to Blakehurst presently and inform him. Although I doubt that he can really want me to attend!'

Turning to Thea, she said, 'I shall be ready to go out in half an hour, dear.' And sailed from the room, leaving a thunderous silence behind her. It held for a moment and then detonated as Richard said several things that Thea had never heard before.

Given the shaking fury in his voice, she rather thought she ought to be blushing.

'Damn it!' he went on, slightly more moderately. 'She knows quite well what the gossip will be like if she *doesn't* attend the christening!'

'But why should there be gossip?'

Richard sighed. 'Because, to put it mildly, there was quite a bit of scandal attached to Max's marriage one way or another. The most popular version was that Verity trapped him. Almeria has even openly wondered if the child is *his*.' His jaw seemed to turn into solid stone.

'But—'

'Don't worry,' he said shortly. 'It is. Verity…well, you'll understand when you meet her.' His face softened. 'She is the best thing that could possibly have happened to Max. And she suffered enough with her own family. Max will never overlook a slight to her from Almeria.'

'I'm sorry—'

He stared. 'Why should you apologise? Oh. That nonsense about being your chaperon? No. That was an excuse so that I could not rip up at her. Nothing to do with you.'

But he was frowning as he took his leave, and Thea could not but see that she was a confounded nuisance one way or another.

Richard retreated to the back parlour upstairs, shaken by the near cracking of his control. Having Thea in his arms like that…he wanted her. Had wanted to tip her face up and kiss her until she had forgotten whatever reasons she had for not marrying.

He forced his mind back to Max's letter. Almeria had actually taken the fell tidings much better than he had anticipated. He suspected that she was feeling rather small and foolish after her behaviour towards Max's bride, that she did not wish to climb down for a generous serving of humble pie. He thanked God that Max had actually written to her directly, rather than relying on him to make the announcement. Perhaps in a day or so she would be a little more resigned over the birth of… He frowned, attempting to decipher a little more of his brother's scrawled letter…ah, William Richard. He grinned. As long as Almeria could be persuaded to attend the christening, all would be well.

A discreet cough interrupted his thoughts.

'Mr Blakehurst, sir?'

He turned and looked at the young footman standing in the doorway. 'Yes, Edmund?'

The young man shifted from one foot to the other, as though unsure of himself.

'I've a note here for Miss Winslow.'

'She is still in the breakfast parlour, I believe.'

'Yes, sir. It's just, well, after that one t'other day—you asked me about who brought it, and I think this might be another from the same person.' He proffered the note to Richard. 'An' from what James says, there was another one for Miss Thea.'

Damn. He should have told Edmund to alert James, but what excuse could he possibly have given for checking Thea's correspondence?

'Thank you, Edmund. I'll take it.'

The same excuse he was going to give now—none.

But what the hell was he to do with it once he'd opened it? Hand it over to Thea? Richard stared at the sealed note, his gaze narrowed. It looked like the same scrawl as on the first notes. The seal a plain blob of wax. And Thea had received another…which she hadn't mentioned to him. Why not?

'When did the other note come for Miss Winslow?' he asked slowly.

'Yesterday, James said,' answered Edmund. 'He reckons he gave it to Miss Thea at breakfast.'

Yesterday at breakfast? His stomach lurched. And Thea had fainted. Damn it! She'd been upset by one of these blasted notes. No wonder she'd been upset and confused.

But why hadn't she told him about the note? He already knew about the first one, so—? He'd wanted to find out who it was, and stop it. Thea hadn't wanted that. Why? Good God! Did she imagine he'd believe the sort of person who would pen filth like that? And was he really going to hand more of this filth to Thea? The hell he was!

His decision made, he broke the seal and opened the note. The ugly words slashed across the paper: *SLUT! How many times did he have you, you filthy little trollop?*

Searing rage gripped him. Bad enough that his own note had accused him of bedding Thea, but to fling the muck at her—something akin to a snarl escaped him.

'Sir?'

'Pushed under the door again, was it?' It was all he could do to keep his voice calm. He wanted to smash things.

'Yes, sir.' Edmund hesitated, then said, 'Only this time I saw him, sir. I was coming back from taking a note for her ladyship an' saw him at the door.'

'You did? Do you know him?'

'No, sir. Not to say *know*,' said Edmund. 'No livery. But I've seen him about. Often holds a horse for a penny. Anyway, I hope I've not done the wrong thing, sir, but I've taken him round to the mews.'

'You've done *what?*'

Edmund looked uncertain. 'You did want to speak to him, didn't you, sir?'

'Oh, yes. I definitely want to speak to him,' answered Richard, crushing the note and shoving it in his pocket.

He was going to deal with this before leaving for Blakeney. Thea might have refused his offer of marriage, but she was going to have his protection and help whether she liked it or not.

The boy, who laid claim to the name of Jacob, stared at up at Richard from his seat on an upturned bucket in mute confusion.

'Dunno, sir.'

Richard tried again. 'Well, a man or a woman?'

The lad's brow cleared. 'Oh. A lidy, sir. A *real* lidy,' he added. His gaze wandered around the stable yard, and became openly admiring as Richard's chestnuts were led out of their stalls.

Richard waited with scant patience as the boy cast a worshipful eye over the horses. 'And can you describe her?' he prompted at last.

The boy jerked his attention away from the horses with obvious reluctance.

'Wore black,' he said. 'Black dress, black hat, and one of them veils. Real heavy one it were. Couldn't see her face hardly at all. Gloves too.'

Richard frowned. 'So you couldn't tell me if she was old or young?'

'Oldish, I think, sir,' said the boy hesitantly. 'It's her voice. Dunno why, sir, but she sounds older now I think on't.'

Richard suppressed a curse, mindful of the boy's wide-eyed gaze.

That did narrow the field somewhat, but not enough. Which of the ton's tabbies would have something to gain from destroying Thea's reputation? And the letters were not aimed at Thea's reputation, but directly at Thea herself. Did it have something to do with this bizarre tale that had sprung up about Lallerton being murdered?

'I can show you where she lives, if you like, sir.'

'You can—' Richard stared at the boy. Children were like that, he reminded himself. They answered the question asked. He hadn't thought to ask about where she lived…

Twenty minutes later Richard gazed disbelievingly up at a small house in Half Moon Street.

'*Who* did you say lives there?'

The hurrying footman he had stopped obligingly repeated himself and then went on his way.

The house seemed to gaze back benignly—the epitome of discreet elegance. Impossible. There was no reason—surely! Yet…the connection was there…

He looked down at the boy who had brought him here. 'Are you certain, Jacob?'

The boy bristled at his dubious tone. 'Aye. *Told* you; I followed her.'

Perhaps there was a strange logic to it after all, albeit twisted and bitter. Which shouldn't surprise him, given the content of the letters. He grimaced. Indeed, a very ugly pattern was beginning to emerge.

'Very well.' It couldn't be coincidence that Jacob had led him here. He handed him a half-crown. 'There you are. Take care of it. And remember what I said; don't hang about here for a while and if you see her again, keep clear.'

The boy rushed off with a wave of thanks, and Richard trod up the steps to the front door to tug on the doorbell. He waited, bracing himself for what promised to be a most unpleasant interview.

A footman answered the door.

Richard handed him his card. 'Inform Lady Chasewater that Mr Richard Blakehurst has called.'

He was shown into the hall. 'Please to wait here, sir, while I see if her ladyship is at home.'

'Thank you.'

He supposed he could understand Lady Chasewater feeling bitter about her son's death, but why take it out on Thea? Could the woman resent that her son's chosen bride was alive and well? Was she perhaps a little mad?

A moment later the footman was back. 'You are to come up, sir. Her ladyship will see you.'

He was ushered into a dimly lit drawing room. Lady Chasewater was seated on a sofa beside the fire. Clad in black, spine ramrod straight, her mittened hand rested on the top of a jewelled cane. She inclined her head. 'Mr Blakehurst. Do, please, be seated. To what do I owe this pleasure?'

He met her gaze levelly. 'I doubt that *pleasure* is quite the word to use, and I think I shall remain standing. This is not a friendly visit.'

He brought the three notes out of his pocket. 'Do you have some explanation for this filth, ma'am? Beyond sheer vindictive cruelty, that is. What did you think to achieve?'

A cold smile twisted her mouth. 'Ah. Miss Winslow worked it out at last, did she? And ran to you, begging you to stop me. I expected the brother, you know.'

His fist clenched. 'Miss Winslow worked it out when she saw your first note, ma'am. And all she said was that the person who had sent it was unhappy.'

A muscle twitched in the sunken cheek.

Richard continued. 'She did not, however, identify you, and to the best of my knowledge, her brother knows nothing of the notes. I should also tell you that she has not, and will not, see this one. I repeat, Lady Chasewater—what did you think to achieve?'

She ignored the question. 'If Miss Winslow didn't tell you, what made you think of me?'

He'd thought of this. Lying seemed contemptible, but the last thing he wanted was this vindictive old woman going after the boy. 'I set someone on to watch the boy you used. You were seen handing the note to him this morning.' All true enough, but slightly expurgated.

'I wore a veil.'

'And came back here.'

A harsh laugh escaped her. 'As easy as that. Well, no matter. I suppose you are here to tell me not to send any more letters? Very well. You may rest easy on that head.'

Suspicion flickered. That had been too easy.

'And may one assume—'

'You may assume whatever you please, Mr Blakehurst, but there will be no more letters. I've tastier fish to fry.' She reached out and rang the bell. 'I think we have nothing more to say to each other, Mr Blakehurst, save perhaps that I think you are a fool. Good day, sir.'

Anger seared every vein, all the hotter for being impotent.

'You hide behind your sex, madam,' he said coldly. 'I assure you that only that, not your age, saves you from a direct challenge. But understand this—if you distress Miss Winslow by any other means, I will find a way to strike at you.'

A cold smile played about her mouth. 'Then, Mr Blakehurst, we shall see what manner of fool you are. A chivalrous one, or an ignorant one.'

* * *

'Of course, I won't be attending this…this christening party!' announced Lady Arnsworth as she stepped into the barouche for the planned visit to Bond Street. 'Really, I cannot think why Blakehurst has asked me to stand as godmother. He must have known what my response would be. And it is not as though he wishes me to do so. He has asked only because he feels obliged!'

Catching a glimpse of the footman's unconvincingly stolid face as he put up the steps and closed the door on this announcement, Thea winced. Lady Arnsworth never seemed to make the connection between gossip and talking unguardedly in front of her servants. Then again, perhaps she did. She looked a little self-conscious. 'You will not repeat that to Richard, will you? He has some ridiculous idea that Max's marriage is a good thing. Even though he is disinherited!'

She wouldn't need to. From the footman to Richard's groom, to Richard? He'd have heard about it before he left London.

'But, surely Richard never expected to inherit the earldom?' queried Thea. Perhaps another, disinterested voice might make itself heard?

'Certainly not,' said Lady Arnsworth. 'And neither did Max, but after Frederick's death—why, it was *clearly* understood that Max would remain unwed for Richard's sake.'

Judging by Richard's support of his twin's marriage and delight at the birth of the child who had supplanted him, Thea took leave to doubt that Richard had been counting on this at all. She cast a nervous glance at the coachman's very rigid back. A wonder that his ears weren't visibly flapping.

'And anyway, I wouldn't dream of leaving town at the moment with this dreadful story flying about,' said Lady Arnsworth. 'No, no. It is not to be thought of. Having undertaken to chaperon you, I must not be thinking of my own pleasure!' She leaned over and patted Thea on the knee. Drat! Richard was right. Lady Arnsworth was going to hide behind her chaperonage of Thea as an excuse. But people would know… Thea felt a jolt of sympathy for the unknown countess. Richard liked her. Richard was determined that his aunt should attend the christening, not simply because of potential damage to the family name and status, but because he was fond of his sister-in-law and didn't want her hurt.

But what could she do to help? It would take a very strong motive to shift Lady Arnsworth from London to Kent... Thea gulped. The reason that occurred was devious if not downright shabby. It might, however, take the trick.

What had Richard said of his sister-in-law? *Verity suffered enough with her own family.*

No matter the shabbiness of the stratagem, Lady Arnsworth must not refuse to attend. The gossip if she did so would be horrific.

'I have always heard that Blakeney is very lovely,' said Thea thoughtfully. 'I wonder if Rich—er, Mr Blakehurst, will return before the christening? I understand he has been asked to stand as godfather. He seems very happy about it.' She heaved an audible sigh. 'I dare say *you* will very much miss having him about the house.'

She found that she was holding her breath. Would the bait be snapped up? Or had she overdone it?

Lady Arnsworth was looking at her in a very startled fashion. 'Ah, yes. Yes. Of course.' A slight pause. 'You know, dear— Blakeney *is* very lovely at this time of the year. A shame to miss it.'

'I should so much like to see Blakeney one day,' said Thea, injecting a tone of wistfulness into her voice.

'Oh. Well, I suppose...of course...' Her ladyship's expression gave new layers of meaning to the word *smug*. 'Richard grew up there, you know.'

'Yes,' murmured Thea.

'And his own estate is not so far off.'

'Richard—I mean, Mr Blakehurst mentioned that he had purchased an estate,' said Thea.

Lady Arnsworth waved dismissively. 'Only a small one.' She sniffed. 'And after all my hopes! He bought it last year, after Max married. He said he had meant to buy his own place for quite some time, but really, there was no need until—' She pursed her lips and gave Thea a considering glance. 'You know, my dear, I do think you must stop calling me Lady Arnsworth and call me Almeria. As Richard does. After all—' She broke off and then started again. 'Ah, yes. Where was I? You know, I dare say that if I were to write and explain the *circumstances,* Blakehurst would be more than happy for you to come to Blakeney. So sad for Richard to be cut out, but one must make the best of it! And I shall depend upon you to choose a suitable christening gift for me. So difficult to know what to buy a boy. For a girl, of course, a gift of jewellery is most appropriate.' She beamed at Thea, and changed the subject. 'I think, dear, that a pretty travelling dress would be in order. So important to make a good first impression. And you ought to take a nap this afternoon. We must have you looking your best, must we not? Yes—a little nap will freshen the colour in your cheeks. You have been looking positively wan the past few days. I am sure Richard has noticed, my dear!'

Clenching her teeth at the grating archness, Thea accepted what she had done—namely, encouraged Lady Arnsworth's...damn! *Almeria*'s...expectations that she and Richard would make a match of it. She shuddered to imagine precisely what circumstances Almeria would explain to Lord Blakehurst.

She sighed. Apparently she was going to attend a house party. Complete with a christening. Which meant that she too had better purchase a christening gift. A thought occurred to her— she would have to tell Richard what she had done to assure Almeria's attendance. She could only hope he would deem the game worthy of the candle. The bitter irony of the fact that she might indeed have been attending the christening as Richard's betrothed seared her like a brand.

A christening. A celebration for the birth of a longed-for child. Lucky child. Pain welled up within her. Somehow, before she left town, she had to find out the truth about her own baby. There had to be a way.

Chapter Nine

Lady Chasewater's ambiguous capitulation exercised Richard's mind all the way down to Blakeney the following day. What other fish did Lady Chasewater have to fry? Had she stirred up the trouble with Bow Street? He pushed the horses hard, changing at each stage, using the horses Max kept stabled between London and Blakeney, and arrived in the early evening.

He walked up from the stables through the gardens to the terrace outside the library. Mellow lamplight poured out of the French doors to spill gold on the stone flags. The doors were closed against the cool evening and he looked in to see Max at his desk, writing. He grinned and rapped on the glass. Max's head jerked up and there was a flurry of barking from the pair of spaniels who had been dozing at his feet.

Max leapt up and strode to the door in the spaniels' wake. He opened it and the dogs shot out, leaping up at Richard, barking in delight.

'Get off, you idiots,' he said, bending to pat them. 'Calm down.'

'Speaking of idiots,' said his twin, 'what in Hades are you doing here?' The huge grin on his face belied the words.

Richard laughed. 'Don't gammon me, Max. You knew damned well I'd be down. Congratulations. When am I allowed to see my godson?'

Max gripped his hand. 'As soon as you like. We were expecting you. In fact you've lost me a wager with Verity. She would have it that you'd be down by tonight—*I* credited you with more sense and bet on tomorrow.'

Ten minutes later Richard was staring down into a carved wooden cradle at a ridiculously small swathed bundle with a shock of black hair. A watchful nurse sat knitting by the fire surrounded by racks of drying cloths.

'He's tiny,' he said, awed.

'Eight and a half pounds is not tiny,' Max informed him drily.

Richard shook his head in wonderment at the sleeping baby. 'And Verity? She is well, your letter said.'

'Yes. Exhausted, but well. She's sleeping now. That's why I was down in the library.' The relief in Max's voice hinted at the knife edge of recent fear. Max reached into the cradle and lifted his son out very carefully. 'Would you care to hold him? He was fed not long ago, so he's unlikely to wake.'

Richard took the child with shattering care. So little, so light. Ridiculously long, dark lashes lay on red cheeks. A tiny hand, with nails like pale pink shells, peeped out of the top of the wrappings. Inside him some strange new emotion swelled and burst in benediction. His nephew, hopefully only the first of a string of nephews and nieces who would add to Max and Verity's joy. For the first time in his life, he felt envy for what his twin had. No. Not envy—a bitter, poisonous draught, that. There had never been envy between them. No, this was a longing, a yearning to experience the same deep joy and peace he could see in Max's face.

He looked up to find Max watching him, wry amusement glinting in the amber eyes. 'It's a bit like that, isn't it?' said Max. 'I may become accustomed to it some time in the next ten years or so.'

Richard looked from his brother to his nephew and back. 'Or not?' he suggested.

Max laughed. 'Or not,' he agreed.

* * *

Thea tossed restlessly in her bed, haunted by the memory of Richard's joy at the birth of his nephew. Folly! she berated herself, to lose sleep over a dream, a might-have-been. She had a far more pressing problem—how to discover the truth about her baby and not alert Aberfield to her suspicions. This was reality and only she could face it and resolve it. Imperceptibly pallid grey light banished the darkness, bringing cold counsel with the dawn. The only person who would know the whole truth now was her father. And Aberfield would never tell her. He would lie without hesitation if it suited him. Somehow she needed to find out for herself.

Lord Aberfield's butler opened the door to her and stared in surprise.

'Miss Thea!' Carnely said. 'Are you come to visit his lordship? I am afraid he has just left.'

Since Thea, watching from the drawing-room window of Arnsworth House across the square, had seen her father not ten minutes ago leaving in his curricle, this did not come as a surprise.

'Oh, dear,' she said mendaciously. 'Will he be long?'

Carnely looked genuinely sorry. 'He's gone out to Richmond for two nights, Miss Thea. I can send one of the grooms if it's urgent.'

Thea shook her head. 'No need for that, Carnely. I shall leave him a note to find when he returns. I'm sure there must be pen and ink in the library.'

'Of course,' said Carnely. 'I shall send some tea and cakes to the library.'

Curse the fellow! Why did he have to be so beastly well trained? How on earth did anyone ever manage to burgle a fashionable residence with servants dripping from the chandeliers, offering cake and cups of tea at every turn?

'No, thank you, Carnely. I'll just write the note. That will be all.'

'Very good, Miss Thea.'

Once inside the library she closed the door, turned the key and stared around the well-remembered room. How she *hated* it! She could almost feel Aberfield's presence in the ordered rows of books, the painfully tidy desk, not a paper out of place. Controlled. Disapproving. As though it knew what she was doing. She steadied her nerves. It was only a room. It could neither know, nor betray her purpose.

Her conscience informed her in no uncertain terms that what she intended went well beyond shabby this time and into the realm of the utterly dishonourable. She gave her conscience short shrift, consigning it to oblivion. Not terribly successfully, but an occasional twinge wasn't going to stop her now.

Where should she look first? What was she looking for?

She looked at the *bureau plat* with loathing. Everything perfectly ordered, the standish set just so. Aberfield was the sort of man who never spilt the inkpot and whose pen never sputtered. Methodical, organised… Her eye fell on a ledger placed neatly in the centre of his desk. She opened it…it was his accounts book, detailing expenditure… Her mind raced. If Aberfield were supporting an illegitimate child there would be expenses at regular intervals…the quarter days. She checked the date on the book. Yes. This was the book for this year, 1823. So…swallowing hard, she turned the pages, forcing herself to read the entries and dates…here it was, March 25th, Lady Day. Her entire body felt cold, frozen to the marrow, despite the fact that a fire still crackled in the grate and the room was warm… Her finger ran down the list of quarterly expenses: bills, servants wages…her own allowance, David's allowance, and—a payment to Miss Dale's Seminary for the Daughters of Gentlemen. The cold inside her spread further, leaching out from the dark. A quarter's fees for SG. So; she knew something already—the child was a daughter, with initials SG.

There were other explanations. The child need not be hers. It could be David's. Or even Aberfield's. She clutched at the frail hope. Yes, that would be the answer. David's child. No. David would look after his own child. More likely Aberfield himself. She needed more information. This ledger only had the current year's expenses.

She found the ledgers for previous years easily enough in a neat row in a bookcase near the desk. Pulling out the last one, she discovered that sure enough, it was for the previous year. A quick glance at the quarter days revealed payments to Miss Dale's Seminary for SG at Christmas and Michaelmas.

At the midsummer quarter day there was a change in the pattern. A final payment, together with an extra amount noted as a bonus was paid to a Mistress Kate Parsons for… 'the succour and housing of SG'. And something else '…monies paid for the removal of SG from…' her eyes widened '…Kelfield to Bath.'

Ice condensed in her stomach, a hard painful lump. Kelfield was only a few miles from Wistow, where she had lived with Aunt Maria. No. It was not possible. They had *told* her…

Shaking, mired in disbelief, Thea took down more ledgers. She had to trace those payments to their beginning. If they went back too far…or not far enough…either way she would have her answer. Year by year she traced the payments back through the ledgers until she could find no more. Fear, nausea, shuddered through her as she confirmed the dates in the last ledger. It couldn't be. Perhaps he had missed a couple of quarters… Frantically she checked the ledger for 1815. Nothing. The payments began at the end of March 1816…seven years ago.

Seven years ago. Within days, *days* of… She choked off the memory. *NO!* She wouldn't believe it! She couldn't, mustn't think about it. Fear rose up, choking her. And with it, the memory of pain. Terrible, racking, rhythmic agony, laced with shame… and Aunt Maria's cold voice reminding her of the wages of sin… And later, when she recovered consciousness, the rector, reading her that passage from Exodus about the iniquities of the fathers being visited upon the children…and the child of David and Bathsheba—struck down for his parents' sin…

Shaking, she checked another date in the 1816 ledger…back and forth in the adjacent pages, until she found something…

monies paid to Aunt Maria for engaging the services of a midwife…she shivered, remembering…a doctor…and the rector? Why would the rector of the parish need to be paid if the baby had died without baptism? She looked again at the detailed amounts: twenty pounds to the midwife, fifty pounds to the doctor and another fifty pounds to the rector. The amounts were staggering for the services rendered. Unless they were bribes… Aberfield would have paid well to hide the family's shame.

With clumsy, shaking hands she replaced the ledgers, making sure they went back in the correct order. Where to look next? Her numbed brain moved slowly. Where did he keep letters, correspondence?

A row of deed boxes on top of the bookshelves caught her gaze. Squinting up, she moved along the bottom of the bookshelves. They were all clearly labelled. Swiftly she scanned them…SG. Shifting the ladder was the work of a moment and she had the box in her hands.

She sat down at the desk and stared at the box.

A quiet, eminently reasonable voice whispered to her: *Do you really want to know? You could put it back. No one need know.*

But if she put it back…she might never have another chance to slip in here. And she already knew the truth…there was no possible explanation beyond the one pounding in her brain.

Why does it matter anyway? What can you possibly do?

She recognised the calm, reasonable little voice: cowardice, pure and simple.

The box was locked.

For a wild moment Thea contemplated breaking the lock. Madness. Someone might hear it. And even if she got away with it now, the box wasn't dusty. Plainly the maids dusted up there regularly; even if they didn't, Aberfield would discover it the moment he needed that box.

Footsteps in the hall panicked her. Her heart slammed against her ribs. If she were caught with the ledgers and Aberfield found out…if he realised that she knew… Shaking, she scrambled back up the ladder, replacing the box exactly as it had been. She had still to write some sort of note to explain her having been in here.

She frowned, pulling paper and the standish towards her. Dipping the pen in the ink, she pondered...something plausible...some concern about the unpleasant rumour that Nigel Lallerton's death had not after all been an accident. She scratched away busily for a moment. Did he know anything of the matter? What else? Ah, yes...the information that she was to be invited to a house party—that would round it out nicely. Swiftly she sprinkled sand on the note and glanced around. Was everything in place? Nothing to suggest she had done anything but write a note to him? Nervously she adjusted the position of the current ledger to the exact centre of the desk. Folly! If he did note anything a trifle out of place he'd think it had been bumped when the maid dusted.

She sealed the note and left it propped against the standish, addressed simply: Aberfield.

Richard spent two full days at Blakeney, leaving after an early breakfast on the third morning.

'Why not stay down longer, Ricky?' urged Max over a final cup of coffee. 'You know you are welcome here, and your house is nearly ready, I understand. No need to go back.'

Richard shook his head. 'I've a few things left undone.' An understatement if ever there was one—something about his brief encounter with Lady Chasewater had left him very suspicious of what her next move might be. Quite apart from that, he wouldn't care to wager that Almeria would accept her christening invitation if he wasn't there to bring her up to scratch—which begged the question of where Thea was to go.

He took a deep breath. 'When I return with Almeria for the christening, would you mind very much if her other house-guest came too?'

The suspicion of a smile played about Max's mouth. 'Miss Winslow—Almeria's latest candidate for the position of Mrs Richard Blakehurst? Not at all, since the suggestion comes from you. At least she's found a candidate who can give you a good game of chess this time.'

Richard finished his coffee and stood up, conscious of heat on his cheekbones. There was absolutely nothing in the fact that someone, probably Braybrook, had kept Max informed. Nor that Max had remembered Thea's liking for chess…but that faint, amused smile was unnerving…he resisted the urge to tell Max there was nothing in it, or at least not much. And definitely not as much as he wanted there to be in it.

Richard arrived back in Grosvenor Square that evening to discover that Almeria and Thea had already left for a ball at Monteith House.

'And that was just delivered, Mr Richard,' said Myles, indicating a note on the hall table. 'For Miss Thea and marked urgent, it is. Her brother's man brought it around. Very distressed, he was.'

'Distressed? What about?'

'He wouldn't say. Just that I was to see Miss Thea received the note.' Myles looked uncertain. 'I did wonder if I ought to send the note around to Monteith House, but if it's bad news—' He left the sentence unfinished.

Richard frowned. 'I'll take it. I'll go up and change. Have some hot water sent up.'

He arrived at Monteith House to find the ball in full flight. Judging by the cacophony, everyone who was anyone was in attendance. Weaving his way through the crowded rooms and halls, he exchanged brief greetings with several acquaintances.

'Excellent news, old man!' said one friend, clapping him on the back.

'Er, yes. I'm delighted,' said Richard, wondering how Barnstable had heard about the baby. Almeria must have talked, he supposed.

Another voice broke in. 'Richard! Richard Blakehurst! How delightful! Congratulations, dear boy. And, of course, dear Almeria is in *alt!*'

Every nerve and instinct suggested that now would be a good time to bolt as he politely acknowledged the Dowager Lady Whinlatter. 'Good evening, ma'am. I am afraid, though, that I have not the least idea why I am to be congratulated.'

She laughed. An arch, tinkling sound that made Richard wonder if Whinlatter had cocked up his toes merely to escape it.

'Now, Richard! You must not think to pull wool over my old eyes! Such an old friend of Almeria's as I am! And I am *sure* Lady Chasewater must be mistaken, and that Miss Winslow is everything delightful…'

He only just managed to choke his natural response into submission. Instead, 'I *beg* your pardon?'

Her conspiratorial smile broadened. 'Well, of course I know nothing is *settled,* Richard,' she said, tapping his arm with her fan. 'And naturally, Almeria did not precisely *say* anything, even to me, but of course one *understood!*'

He dragged in a breath—prepared to deny everything categorically—and let it go again. What was he supposed to deny, without adding fuel to the gossip that was doubtless burning unchecked? What the *devil* was Almeria about? Not to mention Lady Chasewater. Extricating himself from Lady Whinlatter's fulsome delight without actually committing himself took several minutes of tact and diplomacy, but he was finally free and headed for the ballroom, smiling at people as he slipped past, but not stopping for so much as a 'good evening'.

He was a trifle late. From the top of the stairs leading down to the ballroom, he could see that the dancing was already underway. He needed to find Thea. His eyes found her almost immediately. Waltzing. With Dunhaven. He went cold all over and could only thank God it wasn't a waltz.

'Ah, Richard. Congratulations, old chap.'

Richard turned, reminding himself that punching Tom Fielding on the nose would not only create a scandal, but would be highly unfair.

'For what?' he asked irritably, looking back at Thea. Even at this distance her pallor struck to the heart. Nothing else betrayed her—just that balanced, expressionless mask.

Aberfield stood waiting nearby, watching them. The chill of warning intensified. Something was afoot here…he had to get to her.

'Er, your betrothal?' His attention snapped back to Fielding. 'What!'

Fielding gave the impression of backing up without actually moving an inch. 'Charming girl and all that.'

'And who told you I was betrothed?'

Fielding visibly relaxed. 'Oh, secret, was it? Well, everyone's talking about it. And although Lady Chasewater's sayin' no man of honour would have Miss Winslow for double the money—no one's takin' her seriously, mind you.'

'I see,' he said, his brain working furiously. This, then, must be what Lady Chasewater had meant by having tastier fish to fry. Hell and damnation. If she was now openly destroying Thea's character between sips of ratafia, to deny a betrothal would be tantamount to pouring oil on the blaze. He had to say enough to avoid committing himself, yet not so much that he gave the least credence to Lady Chasewater's attack on Thea.

'Yes, well, this is all rather premature, Tom,' he said calmly.

'What? Oh, yes—no announcement yet? I take you.' Fielding grinned comfortably. 'M'mother knows, of course. Well, I had to have some reason for not pursuing the woman! A trifle put out that I've let another eligible bride slip past, but never mind. Always another one.' He looked at Richard carefully. 'Something the matter with your teeth, old chap?'

To his horror, Richard realised that the loud crunching noise just happened to be his own teeth grinding. 'One infers, then, that your interest in Miss Winslow was purely pecuniary, Fielding?'

'What? Oh, lord, yes! Nothing personal, take my word for it. Charming girl, but not quite my style. And seeing you smitten—'

'Seeing me *what?*'

'Er, is that—yes, it is! Excuse me, old fellow. Have to dash.' He gave Richard a clap on the shoulder. 'Chappie over there I simply must see! Do hope Miss Winslow enjoys her stay at Blakeney, and m'mother says to congratulate you!'

And with that, Fielding hurled himself into the crowd.

Leaving Richard in a state of total confusion. How the hell did Fielding know about Thea's prospective visit to Blakeney? And what the devil had been going on to give so many the impression that a betrothal was imminent?

By the time the dance ended, several more people had offered oblique congratulations to him and it was only the glimpse of Lady Chasewater, seated on a chaise at the side of the room, that had prevented Richard from denying the betrothal. Loudly. The old woman's eyes were blazing with triumph.

'Thank God, you're back!' came a relieved voice and he turned to find Julian Braybrook at his elbow. 'There's been a most unfortunate development.'

'Oh, really?' That was one way of putting it.

'Winslow was arrested earlier for the murder of Lallerton.'

Richard went cold all over. The note burning in his pocket was explained if Winslow had been arrested, and every instinct urged him to find Thea. Fast. He knew now what fish Lady Chasewater had been frying.

The end of the dance came at last, and Thea, every nerve raw, stepped back out of Lord Dunhaven's arms.

He reacted swiftly, imprisoning her hand and clamping it on his arm. 'You will honour me with your company at supper, of course,' he said. 'I believe your father plans to join us.'

Nausea churned. Somehow she had maintained her self-control during the dance, but she had reached her limit. Forcing calmness and a smile, she said, 'How lovely. But if your lordship might excuse me for a few moments? I…I need to retire. I will join you as soon as I can.'

He looked at her consideringly. 'Of course, my dear,' he said at last, and released her.

Quickly, she slipped away through the crowd, making for the supper room.

Monteith House was huge, but Thea had visited there often as a child and knew it well enough to find her way out into the garden from the library. With a sigh of relief, she leaned against the wall of the house and breathed the soft fragrance of the garden. The roar of the gathering inside was strangely muted.

Just a few moments and she would go back.

'What a charming spot you have found, my dear.'

Thea's blood congealed at the soft purr, as she realised too late what a fool she had been to come out here.

He was between her and the door back inside.

'Lord Dunhaven,' she infused her tone with ice, 'this is most improper. You should not have followed me out here.'

He shrugged. 'What does it matter? We are to be married, are we not? Your father has given me his blessing. All that remains, my dear, is to decide the wedding date.'

His arrogance stiffened her, banishing fear and replacing it with coruscating fury. Controlling it, she said lightly, 'I think there is something you have omitted, my lord. Is it not traditional to ask the woman if she wishes to marry you?'

'If you wish, but we both know you have little choice. Very few men would be prepared to overlook your…state, shall we say?' His voice mocked. 'So, my dear; will you make me the happiest of men and consent to be my wife?'

'No, my lord. I will not. Now if you will excuse me—'

'I think not, Miss Winslow,' he said. 'Perhaps you have failed to understand your situation. You have obviously not heard the news? Such a tragedy it will be for your family if someone with the right connections does not step in.' His smile was all teeth and triumph.

Thea fiddled with her reticule. 'What news is this?'

'Why, your brother, my dear,' he said. 'Such a hurried note I received from Aberfield this evening—of course, if we act quickly it will all come to naught, but naturally I could not possibly have cause to intervene at Bow Street without a *family* connection.'

'Bow Street?' She summoned indifference to cover the frantic pounding of her heart, the chill fear that clogged her brain. 'And what has that to do with me?'

'Oh, not you, my dear,' he told her. 'Your brother—arrested early this evening for the murder of Nigel Lallerton, and it would be so unfortunate if *your* little indiscretion with Lallerton were to leak out. Such a powerful motive for murder, is it not?'

'What are you suggesting?' Her lips felt cold and stiff.

He shrugged. 'It's simple enough; your father and I have agreed on the match, and that is precisely what is going to happen. You have no choice. Naturally, as your betrothed I will use my influence at Bow Street on your brother's behalf.' He smirked. 'For which service your father is disposed to be *most* generous in the marriage settlements.'

Thea sucked in a breath. It was just possible that he was lying, but not likely. Could she get away with agreeing to a betrothal, and then jilting him once David was safe? She shuddered. Too risky. He would sue for breach of promise and take half her fortune. She couldn't risk that. Not now. There was the child to provide for.

'You will understand, sir,' she said carefully, backing away and trying to ease around towards the house, 'that I would prefer to discuss this with you at a more appropriate time.'

'No doubt,' he said, closing the distance. 'Your father warned me about that though, so my preference is for here and now.' He lunged for her just as she dodged. Her foot slipped and she found her wrist caught in a brutal grip.

'We'll settle this now,' he told her, hauling her close.

She fought him, kicking and scratching as he tried to force her away from the house, further into the garden. His odour nearly overwhelmed her; rank and sour, it was worse than during the dance, and the light from the library gleamed on a trickle of sweat at his temple.

She bit his hand savagely as he tried to clamp it over her mouth, and, twisting to face him, brought her knee up hard. She missed, striking his thigh, but he jerked back.

'*Bitch!*'

His grip loosened and she tore free, whirling to run.

He caught her again, but, even as she dragged in her breath to scream, a voice sheathed in ice lashed through the night.

'Take your hands off her, Dunhaven.'

Framed in the glow from the library two tall figures stood. One came forward, his steps slightly uneven.

'What the hell's it to you, Blakehurst?' snarled Dunhaven, but his hand dropped from Thea's wrist.

She cradled it, and saw the flare of rage in Richard's face. Saw the lines of his face harden to steel.

He came forward and without hesitation she went to him. 'Are you all right?' His voice was harsh, raw, strangely at odds with the gentle, shaking touch of his fingers on her cheek.

She nodded. 'Yes, but he says David has been arrested. He—'

'Tried to use it as a lever?'

She nodded again and Richard realised that his control hung by a single, burning thread, stretched to breaking point. He reminded himself that calling Dunhaven out would inflame the rumours already circulating. That the news of Winslow's arrest would just about blow the lid off an already bubbling pot.

'Obviously the word "gentleman" has not the least resonance for you, Dunhaven,' said Richard. 'I suggest you get out of here before I lose my temper.'

'Does the fact that I have her father's permission—?'

'Not unless you have hers, Dunhaven,' said Richard coldly. 'And in my understanding, when a woman uses that last trick, her permission is unlikely to be granted.'

'A whore's trick!' spat Dunhaven. 'Used by a soiled little dove, who's already been—'

The rest of Dunhaven's vitriol was lost as Richard's fist slammed into his jaw, sending him staggering backwards against the balustrade.

Swearing sulphurously, Dunhaven struggled up, his fists clenched, an ugly look on his face.

Braybrook stepped in. 'That will be enough for now. Dunhaven—you will accompany me back into the house.'

'The hell he will,' said Richard softly. 'Take Miss Winslow back inside, please, Braybrook.'

Thea's eyes widened at his voice. Deathly quiet, it rang with suppressed violence.

Terror shot through her as she realised where this was going. No! Not Richard too. She couldn't let him!

She dragged in a breath, but Lord Braybrook spoke first.

'No, Ricky. Leave it! It will cause even more gossip if she's seen coming back in with me!' He turned to Dunhaven. 'After you, Dunhaven.' He spoke quietly, but his voice held the ring of cold, tempered steel.

Breathing heavily, Dunhaven obeyed, cradling his fast-swelling jaw.

Relief sighed out of Thea. They were going to let it drop, thank God!

Richard's voice lashed out. 'Don't think you've heard the last of this, Dunhaven.'

His meaning ripped into Thea; he still intended to call Dunhaven out.

His lordship looked around. 'If you think it worthwhile, Blakehurst,' he spat out. 'I assure you, I wouldn't.'

He turned and strode back inside.

Braybrook glanced back. 'Don't stay out too long, Ricky,' he said, and followed Dunhaven.

Shaking, Thea turned to face Richard, her breath catching as though on powdered glass at the thought of the whole tragedy unfolding again. Whatever the cost, she had to stop this now.

She was safe. Richard felt some of the riptide ebb. Then he looked at Thea properly and it surged again. Even in the poor light he could see that she was blanched, her eyes huge and strained in her pale face. Her gown, although not torn, was dishevelled. Carefully, refusing to let himself dwell on what he was doing, he began to put it to rights with deft, gentle touches. She stood quite still, her eyes on his face. He could feel her gaze even as he concentrated on his task. Feel the fear and panic leaving her, as he fought the instinct to gather her into his arms and just hold her.

At last, he said, 'That's better. And now—' He dragged in a ragged breath. 'What the devil were you thinking?' he growled. 'To come out here with a loose screw like Dunhaven!'

'I didn't come out with him,' she said. 'I came out alone. I...I didn't feel well, so I slipped away. I don't know how he found me.'

'The same way we found him, no doubt,' said Richard savagely. 'Asked a servant. Are you sure you're all right?'

She nodded. 'Yes. Just...cold.' Her voice shook.

Stifling the urge to take her in his arms and warm her, he said curtly, 'Then we had best go back inside.' He couldn't answer for his own control if he touched her again.

'Richard?'

'Yes?'

'Please don't call him out. Please. It's not worth it. Promise me.'

'Forget about it, Thea,' he said gently. 'No challenge has been issued.'

She came to him then, laying her gloved hand on his arm. He stiffened, the light touch, muffled by kid gloves and his coat and shirt, searing bone-deep. Even as his blood leapt, her other hand lifted hesitantly to his chest.

'Thea,' he whispered. Just that—her name breathed over soft fragrant curls as he covered the trembling hand with his, holding it captive over his pounding heart. He abandoned the struggle and his other arm went around her, instinctively drawing her into his warmth, cradling her against his aching body.

'Richard, please don't call him out.'

He didn't answer the plea. Holding her was so sweet. He gathered her closer, resting his cheek on her hair.

'Richard—promise me!' Her voice broke on a sob.

He took a very careful breath, cursing himself for being such a fool as to make his intentions plain in front of her. Now she was frightened for him.

'Give me one good reason why I shouldn't,' he said grimly.

He felt her go utterly still, every fibre of her being frozen in his arms. Then came a shuddering breath.

'One good reason?' she asked, her voice a mere thread. 'Just one? And if I give it to you, will you swear to let this drop? That you'll not challenge him?'

'That would depend on the reason,' he answered. There was no answer that he could think of that would change his mind.

She pulled away and reluctantly he let her go. The soft curve of her mouth trembled, making him long to drag her back and cover her lips with his own, kissing her senseless until she agreed to be his.

She took another ragged breath, that pierced him to the core.

'It is the same as the reason why I cannot possibly marry you,' she said steadily. 'Or any other man like you.'

He went very still. 'Like me?'

Her gaze never wavered as she said, 'A man of honour.' Her voice sounded dead, bereft of all expression. 'Lord Dunhaven spoke only the truth when he called me a…a soiled little dove, Richard.'

Chapter Ten

She stepped back, drawing away from him, and, totally confused, he let her go.

Now her gaze did falter. She looked away and said simply, 'I am not a virgin, Richard. That is why I have never married and why I refused your offer.'

Shock slammed into him. Of all the reasons she might have given for not marrying him, that one had never even crossed his mind. What the hell was he supposed to say? By every tenet of society, unless he took a widow to wife, he had every right to expect that his wife would come to him untouched.

His brain whirled. So much now made sense. Her unwillingness to marry. Lady Chasewater's bitterness...Winslow's arrest. God! What a coil! Of course at the time it would not have seemed such a terrible thing. The betrothal had been announced—the marriage imminent. It probably happened more often than one would think. Only this time it had gone horribly wrong, because David Winslow had found out and quarrelled with Lallerton over it.

According to society's rules, his reaction was laid out for him...

A little voice murmured in a corner of his mind: *Thou shalt not be found out.* Society's unspoken, immutable law.

He glanced across at Thea. She looked white, her underlip

gripped firmly between her teeth. His heart clenched. He forced himself to look at the situation logically.

He wasn't a virgin himself. And no one jumped up and down about his lack of chastity. Except Almeria, of course, and even she had only ever glared daggers at whichever of society's widows he happened to be bedding at any time. More, he suspected, because she had feared he might one day offer marriage to one of them.

What the hell should he say? She had been honest with him. Brutally honest. She could have accepted his offer and said nothing. Instead, she had refused it because her honour demanded it. And she had only told him now to stop him issuing a challenge to a man who had insulted her.

He looked at her again and his heart ached as he saw the glistening silver track on her cheek. Just one, where a single tear had escaped. She expected him to condemn her for a single misstep in her youth? When he had made the same step over and over?

What should he say? There was only one thing he could say in all fairness. He went to her and reached out to wipe away another tear.

'Neither am I, Thea.'

She flinched slightly at his touch, but then turned to face him and he saw the pain in her eyes. And confusion.

'I…I beg your pardon? Neither are you what?'

'A virgin,' he said. He managed a smile. 'Thea, it was Lallerton?'

She nodded wordlessly.

'And this is why you have never married?'

Again she nodded.

'We had better return to the house,' he said quietly. What was the point of averting one scandal, only to cause another, if they were caught out here? His brain had numbed anyway, refusing to think at all, let alone rationally.

Carefully he asked, 'Were you aware, by the way, that the news of our betrothal is the latest item of gossip?'

'*What?* But we aren't!'

'So far three people have congratulated me on it,' he told her. 'Apart from this coil, what the devil have you been up to?'

'Almeria,' she whispered. 'But it's all *my* fault.'

Sick understanding washed through her. She had allowed their godmother to believe that there was an understanding between them. Almeria had doubtless told just one or two of her dearest friends—in strictest confidence, of course. And, equally of course, no doubt with many an arch smile and discreetly fluttering fan, the story had been wafted on its way, to be further enlivened by Lady Chasewater's innuendoes.

'Just what did you do?' The tone of bland enquiry did little to disguise the steel behind the question.

She met Richard's eyes. 'I…I gave Almeria to understand that I…that I would miss you when you left for Blakeney—that I had heard how lovely Blakeney is, how much I would like to see it one day, and…and…I think…she believed that—' In the face of his patent disbelief, she burst out, 'Damn you, Richard! I was trying to find a way of persuading her to attend your nephew's christening, and that was all I could think of! Some way to give her an excuse to go so that she wouldn't lose face over it!'

'I beg your pardon?' Tone and expression were unreadable.

'I'm sorry, Richard. I never imagined this would happen. She must have told people, and—'

'You have persuaded Almeria to go to Blakeney?'

She nodded.

'Why?'

Fellow feeling for your sister-in-law. She thrust that response back into the shadows.

'You were worried about the Countess and the potential gossip if Almeria refused to attend. How it would hurt *her*—not how it would affect your brother's standing, or the family—'

'Just how it would hurt Verity,' said Richard softly. 'But why should *you* care? You've never even met her, Thea.'

Thea shook her head. 'No, but you like her. Don't you?'

He smiled. 'Yes. I'm very fond of Verity.'

She went on, 'And you once said she had borne enough from

her own family…so, I…I just wanted to help. I'm sorry, Richard.'

He shook his head. 'No. Don't be sorry, Thea. Getting Almeria to Blakeney is a major victory. Worth any amount of embarrassment.' He frowned. 'To me, anyway. But you, Thea—this rumour—we can deny it, but it's bound to be damaging. To you more than to me.'

She shrugged. 'If I don't care, why should you?'

His glare was a revelation. 'Because you, or I, would be labelled a jilt. Probably you, since Lady Chasewater is doing her best to ruin you! Can't you just hear them? *Running true to form…* And I do care about that!'

Her hands were taken in a strong grip, and she found herself moving towards him again. Close enough that the sharpness of his cologne breathed about her with the scents drifting up from the garden, close enough that she felt surrounded, enveloped by his presence, by his sheer caring. It was a potent spell, woven of moonlight, fragrance and the gentle pressure of his fingers, and bound together by the ache in her heart that longed to sink into it.

Her mind fought free of the spell. He shouldn't care! Not like that. Not as though he cared about *her,* rather than the likely damage to his own reputation. Safer if he didn't care, if he read her a lecture on the dangers of…of deceit and…and loss of reputation, rather than looking and sounding as though he cared about Thea Winslow, who was not at all the sort of female he should care about.

And he certainly shouldn't be holding her hands like this and leaning forward…and nor should she be simply standing here, waiting, waiting for his lips to brush hers. Not just waiting, but yearning…

'*My goodness me!* Oh! Oh, good heavens! Oh, it's you, Richard.'

Hell's teeth! Instinctively Richard stepped across Thea, sheltering her from view with his body. And realised that he had effectually taken her into his arms—in front of Lady Jersey, who looked as if she had been granted a high treat.

'Really, I couldn't quite make out what Lord Dunhaven was

saying,' said Lady Jersey, her bright gaze flickering between them. 'Which might have had something to do with his jaw—it did look a trifle swollen.' Briefly her glance touched Richard's grazed knuckles. 'He seemed to feel there was some impropriety, but since you and Miss Winslow—' She waved airily, 'Well, it's no bread and butter of mine!'

Resisting the temptation to swear loud and long, Richard placed Thea's hand on his arm and said to Lady Jersey, 'I fear Miss Winslow has just received some very disquieting news, ma'am. You will understand she did not feel capable of discussing it in the ballroom.'

Lady Jersey looked intrigued. 'Oh? I am so sorry, Miss Winslow. Shall we all stroll back together? And, of course, I must wish you happy!'

Thea's fingers tightened on his arm, and he brought his other hand across to cover them. Whether the gesture was one of affection or protectiveness, he had no idea. All he knew was that it felt right. That the shocking idea that he was betrothed to Thea, like it or not, felt anything but shocking. And why should it? He had asked her to marry him days ago. Only, he had not quite intended a public announcement of this nature.

Lady Jersey kept up a flow of chatter as they made their way back through the house towards the ballroom. Richard suppressed with difficulty the instinct to throttle her. Better if they did look to have been chaperoned, and from the sound of her chatter the countess was disposed to be lenient with this breach of propriety. But he had that damned note in his pocket—somehow he had to give it to Thea.

They stepped into the ballroom and there, just inside, stood Lord Aberfield. Bitter resignation stood in the faded eyes, and scorn curled the thin lips.

'My congratulations, Mr Blakehurst.' His voice cut through the murmuring to an expectant silence. 'Of course, in my day it was considered polite to ask a father's consent. Which Lord Dunhaven had obtained.'

Banked fury leapt to blazing life. Richard fought it down and said in tones of cool courtesy, 'So I understand, my lord. He forgot the most important thing, however—the lady's consent. An offer of marriage is just that: an offer. It suggests that a refusal is possible.'

Almeria hurried up. 'Dorothea! I have just heard the news about poor David! Dreadful! But I understand Lord Braybrook and Sir Francis have the matter in hand—oh! Good evening, Lord Aberfield. Such a shocking thing—but I am quite persuaded it is a simple misunderstanding—naturally my *other* nephew, Earl Blakehurst, will look into it also should it become necessary.'

Aberfield's teeth grated. 'I assure you, I'm counting on it, ma'am.' He did not look as though the promised interest of that particular earl afforded him the least satisfaction.

In the quiet of her bedchamber, Thea looked back on the utterly disastrous evening. David had been arrested and society believed her to be betrothed to Richard Blakehurst. A rumour her father had deliberately confirmed. She understood why—Earl Blakehurst's influence was far-reaching. He was unlikely to sit back and twiddle his thumbs while a potential scandal threatened to wash over his family.

Only she wasn't family. Nor had she the least claim on Richard beyond this insane false betrothal.

False from her perspective, that is.

She knew his sense of honour well enough to realise that, as far as he was concerned, the betrothal would stand. He had made that quite plain in the few moments he had taken with her in the hall after Almeria bid them goodnight—in the sort of absent-minded tone that suggested she was already planning the nuptials.

'Thea—it is not so bad as all that. You must know that for me to draw back would seriously damage you. We can sort it out, away from prying eyes, at Blakeney.'

He had held her hand for a moment and said, 'Promise me that you will not repudiate the betrothal yet, Thea. Let us discuss it rationally down at Blakeney. You already know that I wish to marry you. That I am not standing by this betrothal out of duty.' And when she hesitated, 'Come—would I really be that terrible a husband?'

Mutely, she shook her head.

'Then, I have your promise?'

He was still asking, assuming, forcing nothing. Except what he perceived to be for her own safety.

'V…very well.' It was all she could get out.

His smile was the sort that ought to have been outlawed. Relief, tenderness, and comfort tore at her heart.

'You honour me with your trust, sweetheart,' he said quietly.

Before she could answer, he had feathered a gentle kiss over her cheek and left her.

Even now her fingers stole over the place his lips had brushed. *Sweetheart.* How could such a simple endearment shred all her defences and leave her longing for nothing more than to hear him say it again?

He had given her that note from David, too, apologising for not giving it to her sooner. Her fingers closed on it convulsively.

Aberfield. He considered the matter closed. He thought that her money would be enough for any gentleman to overlook the fact that he was receiving *soiled goods*. Maybe to some men the money would be sufficient—but she didn't want a man like that. Blinking back tears, she acknowledged what she did want— someone who would believe her, someone willing to accept her as she was. Someone who loved her.

The tears leaked from beneath her tightly closed eyelids. She wanted Richard, who was probably resigned to the marriage because he was fond of her and needed a wife. But what if in the end, despite his kindness and tolerance, he came to resent her? There was no point even wondering. What she planned to do in the morning would see to that. The final words in David's brief note were seared into her…

On no account, Thea, are you to do anything foolish. I am perfectly safe and this will all blow over soon enough. You are to remain out of it…

But what if it didn't blow over? She could not take that risk.

She slipped into bed, blowing out the candle. Past three, and sleep seemed impossible. Her mind lurched back to the struggle with Dunhaven. Sweat broke out on her body and nausea roiled her stomach, as though she could still smell his breath, feel his hand fumbling at her breast, taste his foul breath as he forced her mouth open. Forcing her memories open…

If Richard had not come…but he had come. She was safe. Safe as long as she remained awake.

Her eyelids felt heavy…she drifted on the verge of sleep… and jerked herself back. She mustn't sleep. Not now. Not tonight. She didn't dare. Despite her body aching with exhaustion, she forced herself to keep thinking, putting off the moment when she must sleep…

Nightmare raked her with black claws, draining her of strength. She fought it, struggling for her voice, choking on her terror…

'*Thea…Thea!*'

Loud knocking punctuated the harsh voice. She sat up, flinging off the clinging shreds of fear, aware that she was sweating, her heart beating frantically.

The knocking came again.

'Y…yes?'

The door opened and Richard, in his nightrail and dressing robe, came in bearing a candle. Swiftly he closed the door behind him. She stared. He was out of breath, as though he had been running, and came across the room with a quick, uneven stride. Perhaps Almeria was unwell?

She clutched the bedclothes to her. 'Is something wrong, Richard?'

He blinked at her as he set the candle down on her bedside table. 'Wrong? Thea, you were screaming. What happened?'

She had been screaming? Shame, embarrassment, flooded her. 'I…I must have had a bad dream.'

He frowned. 'You don't remember?'

She never did. Not really. The details always faded when she woke, leaving only strangling terror. But then, she didn't need to remember the dream. She *knew*. What her dream memory lost, waking memory could supply in endless detail.

Richard's mouth tightened. 'It's all right, sweetheart. Here.' He swept up her dressing gown from a chair and came towards her. Before she could protest, he was wrapping it around her, and pulling up the counterpane to snuggle it securely around her shoulders.

She still felt cold, clammy from the nightmare. She had not dreamed like this for several years, waking terrified, sometimes crying, but with no real memory of the dream beyond paralysing fear.

Richard was sitting beside her on the bed, one arm cradling her. 'Shh. You're safe.' Shocked, she realised that she was still shivering, her breath shuddering through her. Ashamed, she fought for control, trying to still the shaking. 'It's all right, Thea. Just breathe deeply. Come, relax. There's no need to fight it. Nothing can harm you.'

She barely heard the words, just felt the deep, soothing voice, easing her, banishing fear. The strength of the arm holding her against his shoulder. And his hand, stroking her hair, pushing back the tangled, sweaty locks in a gentle hypnotic rhythm. Somewhere at the back of her mind a warning sounded: impropriety. She dismissed it. No one would ever know. And it felt so good, so right, to be held and cared for. Richard's limp and his spare frame, she vaguely realised, were utterly deceptive. One did not expect his strength. On the heels of this realisation came another; that it was not only his physical strength that one tended to overlook—his quietness masked the fierce strength of his will. Men like Dunhaven overlooked him.

Slowly the shaking stopped. Yet he still held her. His own warmth infused her, body and soul. With a shock, she knew that she had not felt this safe for years. That she had become so used to the inner tension of the guard she set on herself that she had forgotten it was there. Until now when, twice in one evening, Richard's arms had banished it to the shadows along with fear.

'Better now?' His voice sounded husky, very close to her ear. His cheek, she realised, was resting on her hair.

'Yes.' It wasn't precisely a lie. She did feel much better. And it was hardly Richard's fault if in her foolishness she wished they could remain like this for longer.

'Good.' He released her and settled her back against the pillows. 'Stay there. I'll be back very soon.'

Her eyes widened. 'Back?'

He smiled. 'Yes. With something to help you sleep.' Gentle fingers brushed her cheek. 'I'll be as quick as I can.'

The door opened and closed behind him.

How had he known? How *could* he know that sometimes after a bad dream sleep would evade her? Her mind churned with questions as she wriggled down further into the feathers. No doubt he had gone to fetch a glass of brandy, or possibly laudanum. She shivered. She ought to have told him that she hated the stuff. The last time anyone had given her laudanum... She pushed the thought away. No doubt Aunt Maria had thought she was helping.

He returned about twenty minutes later with a glass in his hand.

She sat up. 'I don't want laudanum,' she said immediately, as he closed the door.

He raised his brows. 'That's good. I wasn't going to give you any.'

'Oh.' She subsided. Now she thought of it, he wouldn't take this long to pour a couple of drops into a glass of water. Or to pour a glass of brandy. So what ...?

He came to her and sat down on the bed again.

'Hot milk,' he said blandly, holding it out to her. 'I invaded the kitchen.'

'*Hot milk?*' Instinctively she accepted the glass, feeling its warmth seep into her fingers.

'Hot milk,' he confirmed. 'Much better for you than laudanum.'

'I suppose you dose yourself on hot milk when you can't sleep?' she suggested, between sips.

A husky chuckle greeted this. 'A gentleman, Thea, is supposed to dose himself with brandy.'

She flickered a glance at him. 'You ought not to be here, Richard. If anyone came in…'

He sighed. 'No. I ought not. But never fear; that innocent little glass of milk is our chaperon.'

'*Chaperon?*'

'There's an echo in here somewhere,' he teased. 'Yes, chaperon. Name me just one self-respecting seducer who offers his victim a glass of hot milk! I have it on the best authority that hot milk is considered most unseductive. Now, had I been foolish enough to give you brandy, or laudanum—! As it is, no one will ever believe that I came in with the intent of ravishing you.'

Laughter welled up in Thea, warming her even more effectively than the milk. Except for that tiny jolt of disappointment—that he had *not* wished to ravish her… She swallowed. Where had *that* thought come from? She couldn't possibly *want* him to ravish her. That warmth, unfurling within, wreathed around her certainty, dispelling it.

'That's much better,' said Richard. He stood up carefully. 'Don't forget to brush your teeth again,' he said, further dispelling any idea that there might have been anything more than brotherly concern in his care of her.

'I'm not a child!'

At her outrage his smile deepened. 'I'd noticed. A friendly word of advice, that's all,' he said. 'If you don't, your mouth will feel like the bottom of a birdcage in the morning.'

She had to laugh.

'Is that the voice of experience?'

He grinned. 'Bitter experience, I'm afraid. Only not gained with anything quite so innocent as a glass of hot milk. Goodnight.'

'Goodnight,' she whispered. She would be quite all right now. So why was she holding out her hand to him? Why did she want to cry out, begging him to stay? To hold her again. She was perfectly all right now. She didn't need comfort. Yet it had felt so good in his arms. Warm, cherishing.

A large hand enveloped hers with gentle strength. 'Thea?' As though her unspoken longing had found an answer within him.

She forced her voice to function. 'Thank you, for…for everything.' *For being here. For being you.* But he had to leave. If he were found here, it would trap him.

He bent down. Surprise sang through her. Surprise, but not fear, as long fingers slid into her hair, tilting her face up to his. Breathless, eyes closed, she waited for his kiss. And it came: warm, firm lips brushing lightly over her temple and brow, and finally, finally, a gentle feathering over her lips. Heat shot through her and she gasped, her lips softening, parting… His hand holding hers shook, she felt the backs of his fingers caress her cheek, her throat. Then he straightened and stood back. Her eyes opened and she saw him watching her, a queer taut expression on his face.

'No more, Thea. This is not…wise.' His voice sounded odd, too. Strained.

But he was right. This was not wise. It was madness.

'Goodnight, Richard.'

He turned to go. Then swung back. 'Thea—I should not have kissed you. I hope that you will not—'

She cut him off. 'I quite understand, Richard, that your offer of marriage is no longer open. You need not fear that I will misconstrue anything.'

His jaw seemed like to crack for a moment. Then, very carefully, 'What I wished to say was that I hoped you would not think I kissed you because what you told me had altered my view of you! Or that I intended to take advantage of it!' He glared at her. 'You have a remarkably unflattering notion of my character!'

He swung around, stalked to the door and left, closing the door behind him with commendable control for a man in what looked to be a considerable temper.

Damn, damn and double damn! A rare bumblebroth he'd made of that.

Richard removed himself and his aching erection from Thea's chamber, after a surreptitious glance into the corridor. He resisted the urge to bang the door. The last thing he needed was to be caught coming out of there dressed in his nightrail and dressing gown. In that sort of situation Almeria wouldn't accept the company of saints as sufficient chaperonage, let alone a glass of hot milk. She'd have them fronting the altar before the ink had dried on the special licence. And God help him if she'd caught him kissing Thea! What in Hades had possessed him?

He reached his own room, dropped his dressing gown on a chair and got back into bed.

He swore and thumped the pillow. He knew what had possessed him: desire, burning like a brand in his gut. He could only thank a merciful God that Thea had been far too upset by her dream to notice the state he was in.

It had been all he could do not to *really* kiss her. And he'd wanted to. Like hell burning. And he'd wanted other things—soft sighs, a silken body shifting beneath him… The violent pain of his arousal pointed out that his desire was not even slightly in the past tense. He still wanted her.

And she, apparently, had not had the least idea of the effect she was having on him. With another curse he leaned out of bed to blow out the candle on the bedside table. Just as well she hadn't realised. After Dunhaven—had that been why she'd dreamed? He grimaced. Having a lecher like Dunhaven sniffing around would be enough to give anyone bad dreams.

Hell's teeth! Just how far had the oily brute been willing to go to force the marriage?

At best, he'd simply been trying to compromise Thea technically. Ruining her reputation in order to give her no choice.

At worst…the thought sickened him, but there were other ways to force an unwilling woman into marriage and Thea would not be the first woman coerced like that. The surge of fury, of sheer primitive rage, that roared through him came as a complete shock. He lay there, shaken, waiting for it to subside. It did. To a steady rolling boil. Ready to erupt again at the least provocation. Thinking about Dunhaven coercing Thea into marriage was more than provocation—it was incendiary.

He forced himself to think of other things…Winslow's arrest…the magistrate's visit the other day. No wonder Thea had been upset. Had she suspected this might happen? Did that mean Winslow *had* killed Lallerton? Or simply that Thea believed he had done so? But why? Why kill his sister's betrothed?

He rolled on to his back and stared up into the darkness. Sleep was going to be a long time coming, he realised. Not that he was any stranger to sleepless nights; over the years his leg had given him quite a few. His leg ached a little right now, but that wasn't the reason sleep eluded him—seared on his memory was Thea's white face as she told him why he need not challenge Dunhaven. She had told him for one reason only—to save him. And she expected him to despise her for what she had done.

Thea felt battered as she faced Lady Arnsworth and Diana Fox-Heaton in the drawing room the next morning. The events of the previous evening, coupled with far too little sleep, had left her drained, but deep within a vein of determination beat a steady, sustaining rhythm. It flowed through her. The worst was over; she had told Richard the truth. Beyond securing David's safety, nothing else mattered now.

Richard stood by the mantelpiece in silence, his face grim, set in hard lines, with the dark eyes shuttered. Pain stabbed her. He'd had time to think, to realise what a lucky escape he'd had…and as she had always known it would, his rejection left the world grey and bereft, as though the sun had abandoned it.

Diana Fox-Heaton was speaking. 'Sir Francis believes that this meeting with the magistrate is vital,' she said. 'He thinks that Sir Giles wishes to ascertain whether or not a trial would have any chance of success, that it is possible the case might be dropped if Sir Giles is of the opinion Mr Winslow would be acquitted.'

Thea's breath jerked in, but Richard might have turned to stone. Not by so much as a flicker did he react to Diana Fox-Heaton's message.

Lady Arnsworth was not so restrained.

'Really! This is most improper, Diana!' she fussed. 'Dorothea cannot possibly appear at Bow Street!' She glared at Diana Fox-Heaton in a way that suggested that Diana was running the gauntlet of all the risks associated with being the bearer of bad tidings. 'Surely this is all a mistake and Mr Winslow will be released anyway.' When no one answered she demanded, 'Why *does* Sir Francis think her presence necessary?'

Diana shook her head. 'He didn't say, ma'am. You know what men are. Explanations are not a strength, unless one insists, and he *was* in a hurry. All he said was that if Thea knew anything that might assist her brother's case, she should attend.'

Thea waited, her hands linked carefully in her lap. In an odd way she felt completely detached from the situation. This discussion could not make the least difference to her course. She already knew what she had to do. She had known since finding out about David's arrest the previous night, but she had neither energy nor inclination to argue with Lady Arnsworth. Nor did she look again at Richard, still standing silently by the mantelpiece. There was a measure of peace in having her decision so clearly laid out for her this time—a calm certainty that she was doing the right thing.

'Richard!' said Lady Arnsworth. 'Surely you must see the impropriety of this!'

At that, Thea turned to look at him. The dark gaze was focused on her, still shuttered.

'Thea?' was all he said.

Shock burned through her. He was not going to attempt to influence her one way or the other. This decision, for good or ill, was hers and he knew it.

'I have to go,' she said.

'Dorothea!'

'Enough, Almeria!' Richard moved then, coming to stand beside and slightly behind Thea's chair. 'This is her decision to make. Winslow's life is slightly more important than matters of propriety.'

Lady Arnsworth favoured him with a polar glare. 'And you *approve?*'

From the corner of her eye, Thea saw tension take him.

'It is not my place to approve or disapprove,' he said gently. 'But whether Thea likes it or not, I will go with her to Bow Street.' She turned to stare up at him and his hand, warm and strong, gripped her shoulder. 'As a friend,' he added.

Heat stung and burned her eyelids. He had come to her last night, comforted her. It seemed that he refused to judge her, despite what she had told him. And now he would stand her friend. If there had been any judging, it had been done by herself.

She had completely *mis*judged the depth of his loyalty. And now he would discover the rest of the truth. She did not think she stood a chance of persuading him to remain outside Sir Giles's chamber.

The cab rattled over the cobbles towards Bloomsbury. Richard had thought it better not to advertise their visit to the entire world by using a crested carriage. Thea sat spear-straight beside him, her face hidden by the poke of her bonnet and a veil. Almeria had insisted on the veil. Thea had agreed, but not, Richard thought, because she thought it a good idea. He didn't think she cared one way or another. Her whole being was focused on what was to come.

As they swung around into Bow Street, he asked himself yet again if, in supporting her decision, he was doing the right thing. Telling the magistrate the truth handed him an iron-clad reason to send David Winslow for trial. Duelling—he assumed it would have been a duel—was frowned upon; the magistrates wanted to crack down on it. If it were decided to make an example of Winslow…he bit his lip. Thea would never forgive herself.

They drew up outside Number Three, Bow Street, and Thea turned to him and spoke for the first time since she had thanked him for handing her into the cab.

'Will you forgive me, Richard?' She reached out and her hand hovered over his.

He captured it swiftly. 'Forgive you? For what?'

She bit her lip. 'For not telling you quite everything. Please believe that it was not because I did not trust you. Just that...I have to tell Sir Giles...' She swallowed and her fingers trembled. 'But this is not something I can talk about easily.'

'Of course not,' he said quietly. 'There is nothing to forgive.'

He opened the door and stepped down to pay off the jarvey before handing Thea down.

She took a deep breath and squared her shoulders. Exactly, thought Richard, as one might imagine a person would face a firing squad.

They were ushered into Sir Giles's private chamber and found Winslow, Sir Francis Fox-Heaton and Lord Braybrook already there.

Winslow's mouth went white as he saw Thea.

'Damn you, Blakehurst!' he said. 'This is no fit place for her! Why didn't you stop her?'

'With what authority?' asked Richard.

'It was my choice, David,' said Thea. 'Good day, Sir Giles. I hope we have not kept you waiting.'

The magistrate rose. 'Not at all, Miss Winslow. Thank you for your message.'

'Message?' She looked puzzled.

Richard intervened. 'I sent a groom.'

The glare Winslow shot him was lethal. 'Thought of everything, didn't you?'

Ignoring this, Sir Giles said, 'Miss Winslow, this is a very serious matter. As you know, we received information that Mr Nigel Lallerton, to whom you were betrothed, was murdered. That initial information suggested that you might be able to shed light on the matter. Since then, more information has been provided, directly accusing your brother of cold-bloodedly murdering Mr Lallerton.' He paused. 'I must ask you, Miss Winslow,' he continued, a steely bite in his voice, 'if you know of any reason your brother might have had to murder your betrothed?'

'Leave her out of this!' snapped Winslow. 'Yes, I killed him, but it wasn't murder! It was a duel, properly conducted according the Code of Honour. Will that satisfy you?'

'I will remind you, Mr Winslow,' said Sir Giles, 'that duelling is now illegal, no matter how properly conducted, and that my question was directed to your sister. I want the whole truth. Miss Winslow?'

She glanced at Winslow. 'It's better this way, David.'

'Thea—!'

Something in her gaze quelled his protest and he fell silent. Richard swallowed as Thea turned to Sir Giles. If it had taken courage to tell him the truth, how much more must it take to confess here?

'It was my fault, sir. I ask you to remember that I was not quite seventeen at the time—'

'Dammit, Thea!' snarled Winslow, shaking off Braybrook's restraining hand as he surged to his feet. 'It was not your fault that the bastard raped you!' He turned on Sir Giles, naked fury in his face. 'That's what happened—now are you satisfied ?'

Chapter Eleven

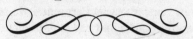

Shocked silence hung there thickly. For a moment no one moved. Sir Giles's shrewd eyes rested on Thea, who met the searching gaze unflinchingly.

Richard felt as though an avalanche had swept over him, as odd little things tumbled into place...

'Is that true, Miss Winslow?'

Something about Sir Giles's voice had changed. There was a gentleness in it that had not been there earlier. But the underlying steel remained. The sword might have been sheathed, but it remained a sword.

'Yes, sir. That is the truth.'

Her soft reply lacerated Richard as though he had swallowed powdered glass. Why hadn't he seen it? She had *told* him that she had never loved Lallerton...her dazed terror the other day when she had fainted and come to on the sofa and found him leaning over her...even her reluctance to marry might stem from a fear far more elemental than worry over a bridegroom's reaction to her lost virginity... Hell's teeth! If Lallerton weren't already dead... His fists clenched involuntarily. A pistol would be too quick.

Movement drew him back.

Sir Giles had risen to his feet and gone over to a small side table that held a decanter and glasses. He poured something into a glass and came back, placing the glass gently in Thea's hand.

'Brandy. Miss Winslow, I understand that this must be distressing for you. If you can bring yourself to speak of this…I can make no promises, but it may help your brother.'

She looked up and nodded. 'Yes, sir. I…I know.'

'You *were* betrothed to Mr Lallerton, were you not?'

She hesitated. Then, 'Yes, Nigel Lallerton and I were betrothed—that is, our fathers had arranged the match. I…I was not entirely happy about it and had expressed my doubts to my father. I asked for more time to…to become better acquainted with Mr Lallerton.' Richard saw her swallow. 'Instead, my father announced the betrothal and an early date for the wedding.'

Sir Giles's hand shifted on the desk. 'Go on.'

'I panicked and told Mr Lallerton that I did not wish to marry him. He…he appeared to accept my refusal, but asked me to drive out with him. There was a storm, and we were forced to shelter at an inn for the night…'

Not caring what anyone thought, Richard reached out and took one clenched hand from her lap, cradling it protectively.

'Damn it, Mason!' he snarled. 'Hasn't this gone far enough?'

Shrewd green eyes met his furious gaze. 'I think so,' said the magistrate quietly. 'Miss Winslow, if it were necessary, would you be prepared to tell me the rest? Even in open court?'

Richard felt the hand in his tremble, and protested, 'For God's sake! You cannot mean to make her go through such a confession in court!'

Sir Giles shook his head. 'I am not asking that of you at the moment, Miss Winslow—but if it were necessary, would you give that evidence?'

She dragged in an audible breath. 'Yes.' Firm and clear, although her face was blanched and she was visibly shaking.

He nodded, turning to Winslow. 'Very well. It seems you had sufficient motive to challenge Lallerton, Mr Winslow.'

'The hell I did!' snapped Winslow. 'Lallerton had exactly

what he wanted—my sister in a position where she had no choice but to marry him. How the hell could I challenge him?'

'I beg your pardon?' Fury seared through Richard. His jaw felt as though it might crack.

Winslow turned on him. 'What the devil was I supposed to do, Blakehurst? Think about it! And believe me, I had every intention of being the brother-in-law from hell!'

'Are you saying that you did not issue the actual challenge, then, Winslow?' asked Sir Giles.

Winslow's teeth grated. 'I did not. Lallerton had been staying with my family in the country up to that point. Everyone was in an uproar over them being out all night, and he returned to town.' He glanced at Thea. 'At first my sister said nothing. Literally. Until our father said that he had told Lallerton to return with a special licence, that she had no choice now. She ran from the room. I followed to try to make her see sense.' He broke off and swallowed.

'That was when she told you about the rape?' asked Sir Giles.

Winslow nodded. 'More or less. I noticed bruising on her wrists, one on her cheek.'

A savage growl escaped Richard.

Winslow glanced at him. 'Precisely.'

'And what then did you do?' pressed Sir Giles.

A mirthless smile curved Winslow's lips. 'I followed him up to town with the intention of beating him to a pulp! When I reached town, Lallerton was not at his lodgings—his man told me that he was dining with Fox-Heaton, so I went round there.'

The magistrate turned to Sir Francis. 'Can you confirm or deny this?'

Sir Francis nodded. 'Certainly. Winslow arrived at my rooms in a rage and forced his way in past my servant. There was a fight in which Lallerton sustained a black eye and lost several teeth.'

Richard failed to suppress an approving mutter, and the magistrate gave him a quelling glare.

'Did Mr Winslow give any indication of what the quarrel was about?'

'He did not,' said Sir Francis. 'And nor did Lallerton. He told Winslow in very offensive terms that he would meet him and that was that. Winslow told him not to be a damned fool, and—'

'I beg your pardon?' interrupted Sir Giles. 'What did you say?'

'Winslow told him not to be a damned fool?'

'Yes—that. Very well. Go on.'

Sir Francis shrugged. 'There's very little more to say. Lallerton accused him of not having the stomach for a duel and Winslow then agreed to the challenge in even more offensive terms and told me that his second would call on me.' He nodded at Lord Braybrook. 'Braybrook called the following morning. Neither principal was prepared to back down, the duel went ahead and Lallerton was killed. Both Lord Aberfield and Lord Chasewater decided to hush the matter up.' He hesitated, then said, 'In fact, although I had my suspicions, I was never sure, until just now, what had occasioned the quarrel between Winslow and Lallerton.'

'And you, Lord Braybrook? What can you add to the story?' Sir Giles's voice was non-committal, but Richard could see a muscle flickering at the corner of his mouth.

Braybrook shrugged. 'What can I add? Very little, sir. Winslow called on me early the following morning to request that I act for him in the affair. He told me that he would not under any circumstances apologise and to make sure we arranged a surgeon.' He glanced at Thea, and said, 'Like Fox-Heaton, I had my suspicions about the cause of the quarrel—especially when Miss Winslow vanished so completely from society. I did not communicate these suspicions to anyone.' He shot an apologetic look at Richard.

Richard nodded in acknowledgment. He could hardly fault Julian for that.

Braybrook continued. 'As Fox-Heaton told you, we arranged the meeting. Both combatants fired at almost the same instant— Winslow was hit in the left arm and Lallerton high in the leg, severing an artery. The surgeon was unable to stop the bleeding.'

There was a moment's silence. 'Mr Lallerton did not delope? He shot to kill?' asked Sir Giles. He sounded shocked.

Braybrook exchanged a glance with Sir Francis. 'That would be my opinion. Left side, on a level with the heart—yes. He only missed by a few inches. Fox-Heaton?'

'Agreed,' said Sir Francis shortly. 'He had an ungovernable temper at times and this was one of them. I will say that I did my best to dissuade him from the duel, fearing that he meant to kill Winslow. He would not listen, so I dealt with Braybrook accordingly.'

'And you, Winslow—had Lallerton retracted his challenge and...apologised...?'

Sir Giles watched Winslow closely.

Winslow bit his lip. 'What choice would I have had? Had he withdrawn, I must have accepted it—faced with his challenge, I had no choice but to shoot. To wound.' Bitterly he added, 'Whether or not it helped my sister is another matter.'

Silence fell, broken only by the drumming of Sir Giles's fingers on the desk, as a deepening frown creased his brow. 'If this had come before a court,' he said at last, 'the most likely result, Winslow, is that you would have been acquitted. Duelling may be illegal, but there is very little chance that you would have been convicted, especially given the particular provocation—' he glanced at Thea '—and considering the fact that the challenge was not actually yours. Therefore one must conclude that the main reason it was covered up was to protect Miss Winslow's reputation. Am I correct?'

Winslow nodded. 'Yes, sir. My father feared that even if it were possible to keep my sister's name out of it, the attendant speculation would ruin her and the family. Chasewater agreed.' His lip curled. 'He too feared the scandal if any of it came out. It did not paint his son in a flattering light.'

Sir Giles continued, 'Under the circumstances, while I am far from approving of such an affair, I can see little benefit in proceeding any further. To bring you to trial when you would almost certainly be acquitted would serve only to ruin your sister.'

He looked at Thea kindly. 'Miss Winslow, I can only honour you for having the courage to come here today and tell me this.

Given that neither Sir Francis nor Lord Braybrook have breathed a word of their suspicions in the past eight years, I think you may be assured of their continuing discretion. For myself, I can promise that no word of what has been said in this hearing will ever pass my lips.'

'Then...David is free to go?' she asked dazedly.

Sir Giles nodded. 'Quite free.'

Except for Lord Braybrook, who had ridden, they all squeezed into Sir Francis's carriage to return to Mayfair. Conversation was sporadic. Thea felt incapable of speaking.

Sir Francis handed her down and bowed over her hand. 'I understand you are going down to Blakeney soon, Miss Winslow.'

'Yes, sir.' No doubt he would be relieved that she was unlikely to see much more of Diana.

He smiled. 'Enjoy your stay. Perhaps you might dine with Diana and myself when you return?'

Her jaw dropped. 'Sir?'

'Let Diana know when you return to town. Good day.'

Descending from the carriage with her as well as Richard, David held out his hand to Sir Francis. 'Thank you, Fox-Heaton.'

Fox-Heaton shook his hand. 'Not at all, Winslow. That affair has bothered me for years. I'm glad to have it settled at last.'

The carriage rolled away, and Richard, David and Thea looked at each other. David let out a breath. 'I had best go and relieve Father's concern that his heir is about either to dance a hempen jig or take up permanent residence on the continent.' He enveloped Thea in a hug. 'You never should have put yourself through that for me.'

She shook her head. 'How could I not?'

He looked awkward. 'Yes, well.' He turned to Richard. 'I'll leave her with you. Thank you, Blakehurst. For everything. And I suggest you hone your authority!'

He strode off around the square towards Aberfield House, and Richard escorted her inside.

'That's it then,' he said. 'Your brother is safe thanks to your courage. You can rest easy now.'

She did not contradict him. Yes, David was safe. But there was still something left that she must face.

Half an hour later, Thea gave a hastily written letter to Almeria's footman. 'You will deliver this to the lawyers, Sydenham and Beckett, in Lincoln's Inn Fields. You will make sure that it is delivered directly to Mr Sydenham and you will await a reply.'

'Yes, miss.'

She gave him money for a cab and a little extra. 'The reply is to be given directly to me, James. It is understood?'

'Yes, miss.'

She nodded. 'Thank you. You may go.'

She sat back with a sigh as he left the drawing room. It was all she could think of. Somehow she had to discover the truth about her child. Was she safe? Happy? She only hoped that she could set it all in motion before she had to travel into Kent. Which reminded her; she had yet to buy a christening gift... Her heart faltered. A gift for a baby. Had anyone bought her baby a christening gift?

She didn't even know the child's name. An innocent life, blighted because she had been too frightened...

Shivering, she remembered her father's reaction: *Damned missish behaviour. Of course the marriage must go ahead! As fast as possible from the sounds of it! What the devil did you* think *happened? Nothing happened that wouldn't have happened in the marriage bed! You'll marry Lallerton and there's an end of it!*

The end of it had been that she had threatened to refuse her vows at the altar and state her reasons. Publicly. Even now, the memory of her father's fury and her mother's disbelief...*but, dearest! He's so suitable...*remained a gaping wound.

Only David had truly understood and believed her. The only one prepared to defend her... He had been in exile on the continent by the time her pregnancy was realised—by the time she realised how reckless she had been in refusing the marriage. The definition of a Pyrrhic victory.

If David had never known the truth, would she have married Lallerton? Probably. Her soul shuddered in horror at the idea, at the memory…yet an innocent child had been condemned as a result of her decision…she didn't know. She just didn't know… Hindsight, she thought bitterly, was a two-edged sword.

No one had ever suggested to the terrified sixteen-year-old girl that she might be pregnant. Would she have listened? Would she listen now? Condemn herself to the hell of marriage with a man who would force an innocent girl? Would she give that advice to another? She still didn't know.

Had they lied about the child to spare her shame? Or because Aunt Maria had found her that day, not long before the birth, her hand on her distended belly, feeling the baby's squirming, watching it through the fabric stretched over the mound of her pregnancy. Through her fear and humiliation there had been wonder that a life was blossoming within her. She could feel no hatred for that life, only wonder…curiosity to meet it. Had Aunt Maria seen that? She had certainly read her errant niece a savage lecture on the fruits of sin…and Aunt Maria had tipped that dose of laudanum down her throat after the delivery. Yes. It was more than possible. But did she have the courage to find out? What would she do with the knowledge? Would it be better not to know any more? Even now it was possible to back away. When Sydenham's letter came, she could write that she had changed her mind, no longer needed…

A very quiet voice spoke behind her. 'Thea? I thought you would be resting.'

Richard.

'Are you quite all right?' There was a world of gentleness and concern in his voice.

Determinedly, she turned, daring the tears to fall. She saw his mouth twist, saw his hand stretch out to her and stepped back, lifting her chin. If he held her, it would all come spilling out, all the pain, the guilt, the terrified confusion…

She summoned a smile. 'I...I was just wondering, thinking about a christening gift for your godson. Do you...do you think something for a baby would be acceptable or ought I to choose something for the future?'

His hand dropped to his side and she rushed on, covering the stab of pain. 'Of course, a girl would be far simpler; jewellery, you know. Although I dare say it would be sadly dated, by the time—'

'Are you feeling quite the thing?' he asked, cutting into her babble. 'Thea—if you are thinking that because I wish our betrothal to stand—you must know I would never force anything upon you, no matter how much the idea of marrying you might tempt me—'

He stopped, an odd, taut expression in his eyes.

'Of course I know that,' she assured him. 'It...it is as I said— the christening gift. Indeed, once I have made my decision I planned to summon a maid to accompany me out to buy the present.'

'Consider me summoned,' he said with a wrenching smile.

'You! But you're not—'

'Not a maid. No.' He heaved a lugubrious and wholly spurious sigh. 'I suppose it is rather obvious, but I did hope you wouldn't hold it against me.'

'But—'

That smile—the one that a merciful providence should outlaw—demolished all her defences, all the cogent reasons why she should not accept his escort. Like the fact that it would give further credence to the belief that they were on the verge of announcing their betrothal. Although after last night accepting his escort was a mere bagatelle. Richard had publicly nailed his colours to her mast last night and this morning. And she would have to tear them down. Just as publicly.

'What do you think I should buy?' She gulped. Why on earth had she asked that? Thinking about babies and all the might-have-beens in connection with Richard was guaranteed to shred the remaining rags of her peace.

He smiled. 'Well, I made those little horses to hang above the cradle. What about something to hang with them?'

She remembered the little bird she had found in The Box. If things had been different, would she have given it to her child? The child she had condemned…perhaps wilfully. Would God have been more merciful if not for her foolish pride and fear? Could she simply alleviate the lot of *SG* without ever seeing her…a child was a child after all…perhaps helping her lost baby anonymously would ease that pain so long denied…?

She forced the pain back, back into its dark corner, and faced Richard. 'I could buy some bells to hang above the cradle with them.'

His smile reached deep. 'A wonderful idea. Shall we go now?'

Thea blinked. 'But where?' For the life of her she couldn't think where one might go in London to buy such a thing.

Richard raised his brows. 'Weren't you ever taken to see the beasts at the Exeter 'Change when you were little? And then permitted to spend your pin money at the stalls downstairs afterwards? It's exactly the sort of place to find bells.' He grinned. 'Unless you had something more ambitious in mind and planned to steal them from St Paul's belfry?'

'The Exeter 'Change will do very well,' she told him primly. 'Shall we walk or do you prefer to take a hackney? I know you won't wish to keep your horses standing.'

'Walk, if you would like,' said Richard. 'We can always take a hackney home.'

A funny little spurt of pleasure buoyed her: walking meant more time spent with him. Quietly. With no one to disturb their friendship. She bit her lip, banishing a flicker of hope that their friendship might be something more. For both of them.

She could not in honour encourage his suit. But still that little voice whispered: *Why should he ever know?*

Chapter Twelve

They found the bells easily enough as it turned out, at a fascinating stall in the Exeter 'Change on the Strand. Richard watched Thea surreptitiously as they strolled around the stalls afterwards. She appeared perfectly in command of herself, but he could not banish the memory of her eyes when she turned to him in the drawing room. For an instant, before she began babbling about christening gifts, he had felt that he was gazing into a well of utter despair. For a moment her guard had been down and he had seen a pain she hid from everyone. Even from him.

The instinct to go to her, to hold her, had been nearly overwhelming, but the memory of her terrified reaction the other day had held him back. That day she had scarcely seemed to know where she was, let alone who he was. As if she had been flung into a waking nightmare…and the horror in her eyes when she realised that it was him… He swallowed—that haunted him.

He had held her since then, of course, but today had been like that day—as though she had looked into a living hell. All that babble about a christening gift! Had she thought to throw dust in his eyes? Or simply to hold herself together after what she had been through already that day? Lord, her courage shamed him.

'Shall we leave now, Richard?'

He looked down at her and smiled. A little sadly. He had

enjoyed just being with her like this. Quietly. But she looked tired, her eyes shadowy.

'Did you sleep again last night, Thea?'

'Of course,' she said.

There was no 'of course' about it. Except possibly that, of course, she was lying.

He gave her a considering sort of look and her eyes fell before it.

'Hmm. You do know that you are a terrible liar, don't you? We'll take a hackney.'

Her gloved hand tightened on his arm. 'Please, couldn't we walk a little of the way back?'

'You are tired, Thea—' he began.

'Yes,' she said honestly. 'But I have so enjoyed this. And if you are…are not returning to town from Blakeney, we will not be able to do this again, so…' her voice trailed off.

The idea that she was enjoying her time with him had a warm glow spreading right through him.

'Then we can walk,' he said.

They could walk together at Blakeney too. It would do her good to have some gentle walks and rides on the Downs in the fresh air. Come to think of it, he wouldn't take it amiss either.

'Thea, about last night, my offer of marriage—even before I knew…before you told Sir Giles what had happened—'

She looked up swiftly as they left the building. 'No. Please. I know what you would say. But there is not the least need for you to make me another offer. It is not such a disaster. I do not wish to be married.' She bit her bottom lip. 'Least of all because you feel obliged to rescue me. So, we will go to Blakeney and no doubt when I return to town there will be some other scandal to amuse people. They will forget soon enough.'

He should, of course, have been heartily relieved. No man wanted to find himself compelled by scandal to take a bride. So why did he feel so completely bereft that she would not consider marriage as a solution? His body made a very definite suggestion, which he promptly quelled. Leaving his body's disgraceful urgings out of the question—difficult with the object of his urgings strolling beside him—his feelings were in a complete tangle, pulling him in several different directions at once. But right now, only one predominated: somehow he had to find a way to protect Thea from the scandal. Whatever it took, he would do it—short of forcing her into marriage.

He couldn't bear the idea of Thea being forced into anything…she deserved better than that after what that bastard Lallerton had done to her.

And he definitely didn't like the idea of Thea returning to town after the visit to Blakeney. But she would have to when Almeria returned… Unless Verity were to invite her to stay on… Verity would do it if he asked. In her own way, Verity was as eager to see him married as Almeria, but her interest never bothered him. Probably because she wouldn't have dreamt of throwing an heiress at him, even if she knew one.

Yes, that was it. Ask Verity to invite Thea to stay on. He would only be a few miles away… He blinked a little at the suddenly violent need surging through him to remain close to her, not to let her slip away.

He set his jaw, firmly ignoring what his body was telling him. He was fond of Thea—and she was in trouble. As for this extremely inconvenient urge he had to sweep her into his arms and kiss her senseless—that was completely irrelevant. Or ought to be.

If he wanted Thea like that, he'd have to persuade her to marry him. Preferably before he disgraced himself and seduced her. Because…?

Because he loved her…

His mind came to a complete halt, as he discovered that, almost without realising it, he had come to an understanding, or acceptance, of what he felt for Thea.

He loved her. Thea Winslow—an heiress? Good God!

The small, irritatingly logical part of his brain left functioning pointed out that Thea was a woman, before she was an heiress. That his body was not responding to Thea's fortune. That he was worried about *Thea;* Thea sleeping badly, Thea in distress because of the visit to Bow Street. It wasn't her damned fortune cutting up his peace—except, of course, the worry about other men courting her for it. He felt as though he'd been hit with a brick. Could love creep up on one like this? With a woman one had known for years? Without one even realising it?

He thought about his twin. Love had hit Max like a thunderbolt. There'd been no creeping about it. It had been obvious to everyone. *Everyone except Max, of course.*

Oh, rot! Maybe Max hadn't noticed, but he was far more rational than Max! Surely he'd have noticed if he was falling in love!

A sudden scuffle on the pavement ahead drew him back to reality. Two mongrel dogs, sniffing in the gutters, had disagreed over territory and were circling, stiff-legged. A black horse, hitched to a waiting gig, shifted restlessly, flinging his head up and down, plainly unsettled by the snarling dogs.

Watching them all closely, Richard hurried Thea past, placing himself between her and the dogs.

She cast a surprised look up at him. He returned it with raised brows.

'Thank you,' she said simply.

He managed a smile. This couldn't be happening. He couldn't have fallen *in* love. Could he? All the way in love?

Behind them the volley of snarls exploded into outright battle.

Richard would have walked on, a dogfight was a dogfight, and well behind them now. But Thea stopped and glanced back, as the scream of a frightened horse combined with a sudden clatter of hooves and wheels to mask her sudden gasp.

He swung around, every nerve taut.

Frightened, as the snarling dogs rolled into the roadway under its hooves, the restless black hitched to the gig reared up snorting, jerking the reins from the boy holding them. Taken by surprise, he lost his grip on the bridle and stumbled in the gutter, startling the horse even more. With a rattle of hooves and wheels the horse leapt forward, swerving to avoid a carriage going the opposite way; the near-side wheel mounted the pavement, scattering goods and yelling pedestrians.

No time. He had no time. The horse was bearing down on them and there was no doorway to dodge into. Seizing Thea, he crushed her against the nearest wall, holding her there with his full weight, his arms wrapped over her head.

He shut his eyes…the clatter of hooves bearing down…if it struck them… He pressed her into the wall, using his entire weight to keep her there. A glancing blow ripped him away, sending him spinning…a brief vision of the wheel flashed past as he hit the pavement and rolled, the impact slamming all the air out of his body.

'Richard!' The scream burst from Thea's throat as she felt the blow from the gig shudder through his body, protecting hers, and felt him torn away, saw him spin like a rag doll and hit the ground.

For a heart-stopping eternity she saw him lying motionless on the dusty pavement, his eyes closed, his hat sitting nearby.

No. Not Richard. Not him. God, why did you let him…?

Terror, agony, fury all swept through her as she flung herself away from the wall and dropped to his side.

His eyes still closed, a totally blasphemous and, she suspected, quite graphic phrase escaped his lips. They were the sweetest words she had ever heard, uttered in a voice that reeked of annoyance and discomfort rather than anything worse.

The brown eyes opened and he tried to sit up. She helped him, unable to control the shaking of her hands as they carefully dusted him down. The gathering crowd barely existed, the excited cries and mutterings a meaningless blur.

'Are you…are you hurt?' she managed. 'Your leg…'

'My leg is perfectly well,' he lied. It pained him like the very devil. 'And I'm not hurt in the least,' he said reassuringly. 'Or not in places I'm meant to talk about,' he added with a wince. 'Let's just say that I'm going to be stiff and I might not sit down too comfortably for a few days.'

Relief breathed through her, loosening terror's icy claws. There was a smudge of dirt on his cheekbone. With shaking fingers she pulled off her gloves to brush at it uselessly. And realised that the dirt was an excuse, she needed to touch him; needed to touch the warm, living flesh, to reassure herself that he was alive, that he hadn't been taken from her.

Barely conscious of what she did, she felt the slight scratchiness of his cheek under her wondering fingertips, the hard line of his jaw…and then the touch of firm, warm lips. Her breathing shattered; he had turned his head to kiss her fingers… The sensation rippled through her…such a simple innocent caress, to release a flood of heat and pent-up longing.

She drew her hand back, gently, her gaze never leaving his.

Experimentally, Richard began to get up. A dozen hands, apart from Thea's, appeared to assist him. He ignored them all. Without explanation, or apology, in the full view of the crowd he put his arms around Thea and held her.

'And you? You're not hurt?' His voice was husky. Shaken, as she had never heard it.

'No. Thanks to you.' He had saved her. At the risk of his own life. Protecting her with his own body. And now he still sheltered her with his body, comforting the fading fear, the trembling that she could not control. Not fear for herself, but the fear she had felt in that dreadful moment she had thought him dead. His death at her door.

She felt safe, completely and utterly safe, here in his arms. Better than safe. The closeness of his hard body was a delight, a bone-melting joy she had never imagined. And the memory of that body crushing her against the wall, his full weight on her…heat pooled, deep and mysterious inside her.

The glorious sensation of holding, and being held by, another human being flooded her. She did not think she would ever be able to let go again.

But she must. Of course she must.

Richard felt the beginnings of tension in the soft body pressed against him. What the hell was he doing, embracing Thea Winslow in the middle of a public street? Rebellion screaming in every fibre, he released her. Well, sort of released her. He kept one arm about her, assuring himself that it was mere chivalry.

Not the wild conviction that to release her was to lose her for ever.

Losing Thea…his stomach churned.

A burly jarvey came forward from the gathered crowd and held out his hand. Automatically Richard accepted it.

'Ye're a ruddy hero, lad,' said the jarvey. 'You 'op up into my cab and me an' the old nag'll get ye both safe 'ome. An' I won't take a penny, s'welp me. Can't let the lass walk 'ome after that.'

His sentiments exactly.

Thea put up no protest at all about being bundled into the cab. A phenomenon Richard unhesitatingly ascribed to her concern about him. He was well enough, although bruised and rapidly stiffening, but the dazed look in Thea's eyes…shock. A cup of tea and a biscuit were what she needed.

Someone handed him his very dusty and battered hat, and he stepped into the cab and closed the door. After checking that they were comfortable, the jarvey mounted the box and they set off.

Safe. She was safe. The thought that he might have lost her pounded through him, along with the memory of her body pressed between his and the wall…to lose her and never know the sweet joy of holding her again, of making slow, aching love to her, of feeling her response…and knowing that she was his for ever… The truth of his feelings swirled through him now with all the violence he could possibly have wished or expected: he truly did love Thea Winslow. He'd probably always loved her, since he couldn't think when his feelings had changed. Just like Max, he hadn't noticed himself falling in love.

He was definitely noticing now.

He *wanted* to marry Thea. Just that. He wanted her. And he also wanted to spend the rest of his life with her. Two desires which added up to marriage.

Shaken, he faced the truth: he loved her. Deeply, irrevocably.

Beyond helping himself, he found his hand seeking Thea's, needing to touch her. For a moment her hand lay still, and then, in a gesture whose sweetness stole his breath, her hand turned into his, slim fingers sliding between his, clinging, as though she too needed the comfort of touch.

He leaned back against the seat, closing his eyes to banish the vision of soft, pink lips, slightly parted; gritting his teeth against the urge to haul her into his arms and possess those lips, taking her mouth as he longed to take her, body and soul. Too soon. It was too soon to propose again. And he dared not give rein to his need until she had agreed to marry him.

She trusted him, cared for him. Now he must teach her to desire him.

Thea retired to her bedchamber when they reached Grosvenor Square. Her mind refused to function, lost somewhere between the terror she had felt and the shattering memory of Richard's body holding her trapped and safe, the feel of her own body rioting in shock, his lips on her fingers, his hand reaching out in comfort on the way home. Madness. He would have protected any woman. It was not that she was special in any way.

That didn't help at all. Knowing that he was the sort of chivalrous idiot who would risk his life without question for another was not exactly a discouraging thought.

He was an honourable man. He probably would have flattened Lady Jersey or a scullery maid against that wall if the situation had arisen.

Would he have kissed her fingers?

Stupid question. Neither Lady Jersey nor the scullery maid would have been fondling his cheek, and nor should she have done so. Richard was kind. They had both been shaken. There was nothing more to his tenderness than that. There was nothing to fear…

No. Thea stripped off her pelisse. She did not fear Richard. What she feared was not having the strength to refuse if he really offered for her again.

He wouldn't. He'd made it clear that her fortune held no interest for him. And men didn't fall in love with childhood friends with reputations for jilting suitors.

Just as well. For she could never marry him.

A tap on the door was followed by the entry of a maid. 'Oh, miss! Mr Blakehurst was after telling us what happened. A tea-tray will be up in a moment. And her ladyship sent her smelling salts!'

Thea eyed the proffered vinaigrette with considerable suspicion. She hated the things. Still…she took it gingerly. 'Do thank her ladyship and assure her I shall be perfectly recovered after a cup of tea.'

'Yes, miss. There's this too. Just come while you were out.' She produced a letter from the pocket of her apron and held it out.

Her fingers suddenly unsteady again, Thea took the letter. The familiar, precise writing leapt out at her: Mr Sydenham.

'Thank you, Becky. That will be all.'

'Yes, Miss.' Becky bobbed a curtsy and went out.

Thea ripped open the letter and quickly scanned the contents. The little lawyer's disapproval dripped from every clipped sentence, but he had done as she asked. The meeting was arranged for two days hence. Just in time. She would be off to Blakeney two days after that.

With a shock, Thea realised that all her indecision was gone. Not her misgivings, just the indecision. She must know the truth. This afternoon she had nearly been killed. If not for Richard, she would likely now be dead and cold in the street.

Mortality brushed past, ruffling her skirts, leaving her chilled to the soul.

If she had a child, then she must provide for it. She must make a will, and to do that she must know the child's name. Her mind refused to go any further, refused to dwell on the forming thought that to know the child's name might be dangerous, might bring her perilously close to wanting more…

Chapter Thirteen

'Miss Winslow.' Mr Sydenham appeared from his office to greet her. 'You received my note, I see. Ma'am, all the arrangements are made. The individual you requested is here, but really! This is all most irregular! If you would give me your instructions, I could pass them on without you having to demean yourself, and—'

She cut him short. 'Sir—I asked you to find the most reliable, discreet man available. You have done so?'

'Well, yes, but it is not fitting that a *lady* should involve herself with such—'

'My business is private, sir. I need not reiterate that if I find word of this has reached Lord Aberfield, I will be searching for a new man of affairs when I attain control of my fortune.'

'No, ma'am. But surely his lordship would be the most fitting person—'

'No. You will conduct me to this gentleman and leave us.'

Mr Sydenham looked thoroughly disapproving, but obeyed, ushering her into an office occupied by a burly man with small, shrewd eyes.

He arose as she entered the room.

Sydenham floundered, his respectable soul evidently harrowed by the situation. 'Er, Rufton, this is, ah…'

Thea took pity on Mr Sydenham's mortification and stepped

forward. 'I am Miss Winslow, Mr Rufton. I understand you may be able to help me.' To the little lawyer, she said simply, 'Thank you, Mr Sydenham. You may leave us.'

As the door closed behind him, she said, 'Do sit down, Mr Rufton.'

He did so and said, 'Thank you, ma'am. But as to helping you, I couldn't rightly say. Mr Sydenham refused to tell me what it is you want. All I've been told is that someone wanted to hire me. Privately.'

'That,' said Thea, 'would be because Mr Sydenham has no idea what it is that I require of you. And I wish it to remain that way. All I told him was that I wished to hire a Bow Street runner, and that the man must be utterly honest, reliable and discreet.'

Mr Rufton looked gratified. 'A private matter, would it be, ma'am?'

'Very private,' she assured him.

He nodded. 'Well, then, there's one or two things you need to know first. One: I won't step outside the law. Two: if I find something that does step outside the law, I'm duty bound to report it. Three: any foreseeable expenses, travel and suchlike, need to be paid upfront. Begging your pardon, ma'am, but I've got my family to think of.'

She nodded. 'Very well. I accept your conditions. My conditions are simply that you are to say nothing of this to anyone. You will report your findings to me in writing.'

He looked at her keenly. 'One thing, ma'am—be very sure you want to know whatever it is.'

'I've thought of that, Mr Rufton.' She took a very deep breath. 'I wish you to trace a child for me. A...a girl.'

He flung up a hand. 'Ma'am—no matter if it's inside or outside the law—I'm a married man with childer of my own. I won't be party to anything that brings hurt to a child!'

At that moment the last of Thea's doubts about what she was doing melted. This was a man she could trust.

'Good,' she said. 'I shall explain what I require and you shall be the judge. She is currently a pupil at Miss Dale's Seminary for the Daughters of Gentlemen in Bath. I believe her to be about seven years old with a birthday in…late March.' Her heart contracted. She knew the date. None better, but it was possible it had been changed to avoid questions.

'A name?' asked Rufton quietly.

'Her initials are SG,' said Thea. 'I wish you to discover as much as you can. I believe she was brought up at Kelfield in Yorkshire by a Mistress Kate Parsons, but I wish you to check. Find out, if you can, where she was born and if…' the words backed up in her throat '…if she is happy.' *If she is my daughter…* She couldn't say that. Surely Rufton would be able to discover enough for her to know. One way or the other.

'It is *Miss* Winslow?' said Rufton slowly.

She nodded. 'What has that to say to anything?'

He looked at her gravely. 'Wouldn't be the first time a monied lady wanted to find out about something on the quiet like this. Like I said, I won't be party to anything that might bring hurt to a child. Ain't the child's fault her father had no proper respect. No more it mightn't have been the mother's fault neither.'

Thea shuddered. 'Mr Rufton—I wish to be assured of the child's welfare above all. I give you my word. I…I wish to know if…if there is anything…anything I can do to help her.'

After the near accident the previous day she could not take the risk. Mortality had breathed an icy warning. Only Richard's courage and swift response had stood between her and death. If her child were alive, then she must know it and make a will…one worded beyond all fear of challenge.

For a long moment he stared at her, as if summing her up, weighing her in the balance of his mind. She felt the colour surging in her cheeks, as if he read all her secrets with those shrewd eyes. Proudly, she held his gaze.

Finally he nodded. 'I'll take it on then.'

Her sigh of relief shocked even her. She had not realised that she was holding her breath. 'Very well. You will please to take this money for your expenses. It is a generous sum, but if I have not allowed enough, you must tell me. Here also are three names—a midwife, a doctor and the rector at Wistow, near Kelfield.' She handed him a sealed note. 'They may perhaps have information. Naturally your travelling expenses there would be defrayed if you needed to go there.'

Rufton took the purse she held out and the list of names. 'I'll be needing an address, ma'am.'

'Send the report here,' she said. 'Mr Sydenham will have it sent on. I shall also instruct him to pay whatever you are owed. One thing—'

'Ma'am?'

'The money in that purse—that is separate to your fee. You will render that in full and separately. If any of the expenses money is left, you may keep it with my goodwill.'

'Now, ma'am—'

'Keep it, sir. You will buy something for your wife and children. I shall like to think of that.'

His eyes bored into her. 'Ma'am, you are sure?'

He did not, Thea knew, refer to the money.

She lifted her chin a notch. 'Quite sure, Mr Rufton.'

She stepped out of the dimness of the chambers to find it drizzling and looked around for the hackney before descending the few steps to the pavement. It stood a few yards away on the opposite side of the road. The horse had a nosebag on and was munching rhythmically while the jarvey consumed his own lunch. She breathed a sigh of relief that he was still there as she adjusted her veil. Not that she was likely to meet anyone, but… Scarcely had she framed the thought when she saw a tall, very familiar figure strolling along the pavement towards her.

In the shadow of the veil her eyes widened, as she froze halfway down the steps. What on earth was Richard doing here? He'd said something at breakfast about being at the museum this morning. She did a mental calculation—the museum wasn't all that far. Obviously he'd had some business. Thank God she had decided to put the veil down inside. He'd never recognise her like this—probably wouldn't even look her way. Why should he?

At that moment Richard, seeing the hackney waiting for her,

stepped across to it. The jarvey shook his head and to her utter horror she heard him say, 'Sorry, guv'nor. The lady there asked me to wait. Bound to be someone along in a mo' for yeh.'

Richard turned to look at her. She stopped dead. At this distance he couldn't possibly recognise her... Yes, he was turning away, nodding to the jarvey in acceptance of the situation. Without hurrying, she started across the pavement—and Richard's gaze snapped back to her. His jaw dropped.

Then he was striding across to her, staring intently.

How on earth? He couldn't have recognised her. He couldn't!

He stopped in front of her, still staring.

The best defence...

'Good morning, Richard. Whatever brings you here?' she asked.

He blinked. 'It is you! What brings me—? Some papers to sign for my house. And what about you? You know quite well that you shouldn't be here unescorted.'

She lifted her chin. 'I was visiting my own solicitors and my business was private.'

'You should still have brought an escort,' he told her.

To her shock she realised that he was handing her into the cab.

'The lady and I are acquainted,' he told the driver. 'Grosvenor Square, if you please.' And stepped in after her.

'Richard—'

He shut the door. '*I* didn't ask *you* anything about your business,' he pointed out gently. 'Only why you were here unescorted.'

She bit her lip. 'I'm sorry...'

A large hand enveloped hers as the cab pulled away from the curb. 'No. There's no need. I've not the least right to question your actions. Have I?'

Regret echoed in his voice and her fingers clung to his instinctively as she forced herself to give the answer she must. 'No,' she whispered. But, oh, how she wished he had! That it was not so impossible...

He sighed and released her hand. She felt utterly bereft and was grateful for the screen of her veil for what she had to say next.

'Richard—I'm not going straight home. Please ask the driver to take me to Half Moon Street before taking you on to Grosvenor Square.'

Shock sliced into Richard, but he put his head out and called the change of destination up to the driver.

'Right y'are, guv.'

'Half Moon Street, Thea?'

Beside him, she nodded. 'Yes. I must.'

'Thea—'

'No, Richard!' she burst out. 'Don't tell me I can't, or ask me to let you deal with it. This…this is something I have to do. For myself as well as David. Alone. I have to try and ensure she never does this again.'

She turned to him and raised her hands to the veil. As he watched, she lifted it and put it back over her bonnet. Resolution was steady in the blue eyes, in the lift of her chin and set of her mouth.

'Alone?' Couldn't she understand how he felt? That he wanted to stand between her and the whole world? Between her and anything that might harm her, be it a runaway horse or Lady Chasewater. By now the woman must know that her attempt to ruin Winslow and Thea had failed. He told himself that Lady Chasewater could hardly hurt Thea, whether he was there or not. It was just…just that he could not bear the thought of her facing the old dragon by herself, facing more of Lady Chasewater's bitterness and rancour. He looked at her again, and remembered…there were things, some things that one had to face—

'Alone,' she repeated, finishing his thought. And shyly she reached out to touch his hand. Swiftly he caught it in a gentle grip.

'I owe her that much at least,' she said in a low voice.

Anger stirred. 'You owe her nothing!' he said savagely, his grip tightening. 'It is she who owes you—an apology amongst other things!'

She shook her head. 'No, Richard. None of this has been her fault, although it is not completely mine. Or David's. But none of it is hers.'

Her hand returned his clasp, and he fought the urge to haul her into his arms and kiss her resistance, her scruples into oblivion.

'You're asking me to let you walk into the lion's den alone?'

It was important to her. He understood that. That fierce drive to stand unbeholden and independent—only, that didn't have to mean alone.

She nodded. 'Not because I do not trust you. It is just one of those things, that—'

'—one has to do for one's self,' he finished for her. 'Thea, I have not the least right to ask this, but would you mind if I came in with you…' He saw the denial forming. 'No,' he said quickly, 'not to see her. Just let me wait downstairs for you. Whatever you have to say to her will remain between the two of you, I'm not asking for an accounting afterwards—' he smiled at her wryly '—you neither owe me one, nor do I require it. Whatever you are doing will be the right thing—just let me wait. As a friend. No more.'

He could not know how that simple request affected her.

'As a friend?' she whispered. He was asking nothing. Except that she allow him again to stand her friend. In some odd way— her second. It was her battle, all the way.

Richard held her back slightly as she made to descend from the cab in Half Moon Street.

'Your veil, Thea.'

She gave him back a straight look. 'I don't need it now.'

Because of you. She left that unspoken. She didn't understand it herself. She had intended entering Lady Chasewater's house veiled. Quite why she could not now remember. There was no reason to hide this visit. There never had been beyond her own cowardice.

She knew as she trod up the front steps at his side and rang the bell that she did not need the veil now. Not because Richard was coming in with her. But because his unswerving trust had shown her that there was no need to sneak into Lady Chasewater's house in secrecy. She would discharge this obligation openly; if Lady Chasewater refused to receive her, then she could do so—openly.

As the door opened, she took a deep breath and said very clearly to the butler, 'Miss Winslow. To see Lady Chasewater.'

She was ushered into the drawing room.

'Miss Winslow, my lady.'

The door was shut behind her.

Lady Chasewater was seated upon a sofa with a small black pug, which leapt yapping from its place and rushed growling at the visitor. Thea stood still and waited until the little dog reached her and sniffed around her skirts. Then she bent down and offered a lightly closed fist. The pug sniffed, bared its teeth and then scampered back to its mistress.

'He doesn't like you,' observed Lady Chasewater coldly.

'He doesn't have to, Lady Chasewater,' said Thea. 'And neither do you.'

The old eyes narrowed in their nests of wrinkles. 'No. I don't. Like you, that is. Whether I have to or not.' Bitterness curved the thin lips. 'And there are plenty to tell me that there are fifty thousand very good reasons why I should like you. Or at least tolerate you. What have you done with young Blakehurst? I take it that it is he who came with you? Is he not coming up to threaten me again?'

'Again?'

'Didn't tell you that, did he? Oh, he came. Warning me off as though you were a perfect nosegay of all the virtues. But you and I know better, don't we, Miss Winslow? He'll soon know the truth.'

'This is nothing to do with him,' said Thea, drawing off her gloves. 'For what it's worth, Richard Blakehurst already knows the truth, but this is for you and me to settle.'

Lady Chasewater stared at her. 'For God's sake, sit down, girl!' she snapped. 'I've no need for a stiff neck staring up at you! No. Wait.' She lowered her voice. 'Give the door a good hard thump. With your fist. Just about the keyhole.'

A little puzzled, Thea complied. The muffled grunt on the

other side and retreating footsteps spoke volumes for Lady Chasewater's acumen. Thea stared at her unwilling hostess, reluctant amusement bubbling within.

'I've no idea what Almeria Arnsworth's servants are like, but mine are a pack of busybodies!' said Lady Chasewater disgustedly.

The amusement deepened, entwined with regret. Under other circumstances she would have liked this outspoken old woman.

'You may sit over there.' Lady Chasewater indicated an open-armed chair at least three yards from her own sofa. 'And then you may tell me the reason that you have demanded to see me. And why this is none of Richard Blakehurst's business.'

Thea seated herself and gave the old lady back stare for stare. 'I made no demand, Lady Chasewater. I have merely called upon you because there is something I wish to explain to you. And Mr Blakehurst accompanied me as a friend.'

The old woman gave a harsh bark of laughter. 'A friend! And you make no demand, eh? There is merely something you wish to explain.' Her lip curled. 'How you can imagine anything you might say would influence my opinion of you is beyond me!'

'You mistake, ma'am. I could not care less whatever your opinion of me may be. You are welcome to think of me as you will.'

'Then what the devil do you want of me?' flashed the old woman.

'I want you to listen to the truth.'

Cold eyes bored into Thea. 'And you think this will alter my opinion of you?'

Thea shook her head. 'No. You think as my father does. His opinion has not altered in eight years. Like you, he has fifty thousand reasons to acknowledge me. The truth is not one of them.'

'I don't imagine it is!' mocked Lady Chasewater. 'Very well then, girl: what is this "truth" that you would tell me?'

'Eight years ago when...' She swallowed and tried again. 'Eight years ago, your son, with the approval of my father and his, offered me marriage. I was not quite seventeen.'

Lady Chasewater snorted. 'If you think youth excuses—'

'I did not initially refuse him.' Reminding herself that the old lady had been Lallerton's mother, she said quietly, 'But I was uncertain about marrying him. He was very much older, and I asked for time to think. To come to know him. Just that.'

'At sixteen you should have accepted that your father knew what was best for you and thanked God for a respectable match!' snapped Lady Chasewater.

Thea gritted her teeth. That was the view many people would take. She had expected nothing more. 'As you know, my father and Lord Chasewater were determined that the match should go ahead; my father told me that the match was settled.'

'As it should have been! Does it make you proud to know that *your* intransigence caused the death of my son?'

Thea continued. 'He also told your son that the match was a settled thing. That I would be brought to see reason. A day or so later, your son invited me out driving. Since I had requested the opportunity to come to know him better, I went. Your son drove some miles, it was late afternoon, a storm was coming on, and although I kept telling him we were too far from home and should turn back, he ignored me and we ended up seeking shelter at an inn. There was no choice but to remain there for the night.'

'So you were compromised.' Lady Chasewater's voice spat contempt.

'So he told me.' Thea hung on to her composure, her coldness, the icy armour that was her only defence against the searing humiliation and choking terror. It had happened to someone else, a girl who no longer existed, a stranger. She was telling someone else's tale.

'Perhaps foolishly, I told him that I would not marry him, that if he had engineered the situation to force my consent, it would not work. I retired to my bedchamber for the night with one of the maidservants. In that way, I thought, the worst of the scandal could be averted.'

'Thought of everything, didn't you?'

'Everything except your son bribing the girl to leave the chamber in the middle of the night—'

'What rubbish!'

'He admitted it, ma'am. Proudly. As though he had done something clever. Straight after he raped me.'

She had said it aloud. For the first time ever, she had said it aloud to someone. Always before she had shied from the actual word. Even in the silence of her own mind, she had flinched from the ugliness of that particular word. No longer.

'You were betrothed,' said Lady Chasewater with a shrug. 'No doubt he should have waited, but with your father sanctioning the match, what right had you to—?'

'I refused him.' Thea forced her voice to remain cold. Steady. Unflinching. 'I had refused his suit and when I realised...when I woke up to find him in my bed, I refused...I refused—'

She broke off. Shutting out the memories that rose black and monstrous to engulf her. The heavy body, crushing her struggles, the hand stifling her screams, his triumphant grunt as her thighs were forced apart...and the pain and terrified humiliation as he violated her body, swiftly and completely. She forced the memories away. Back behind the icy wall that must contain them.

'Oh, good God, girl! What do you imagine happened that would not have happened on your wedding night?' The words, the impatience, echoed Aberfield. 'Do you think this changes my opinion of you for the better? Little fool! Having lost your virtue to Nigel, you had much better have married him!' Her lip curled. 'No one else would have had you, knowing the truth, and if you think to sway my opinion of you with this tale, you have missed your mark.'

'Ma'am, as I said at the outset, your opinion of me is irrelevant.'

'Then state your purpose in coming and have done.'

'Ask yourself this question, ma'am: how would you expect any man of honour to respond on hearing that his sister had been raped?'

Lady Chasewater's mouth opened. And shut again. Her lips thinned.

'I see. You expect me, then, to accept your interpretation of Nigel's behaviour, and—'

'No,' Thea cut in. 'I do not expect that. Nor do I wish it. You may think as you please of me. You may believe that it was not rape. But do you have the imagination to accept that David believed me? That my brother believed that I had been raped, and acted accordingly? I ask you again: how should a man of honour respond? You have a daughter—how would your son have behaved if the positions had been reversed?'

Bitter silence cried out between them as the ravaged old face hardened.

'What do you want of me?'

'Very little. Sir Giles Mason has dismissed the case against my brother. You, however, can still ruin him by innuendo and gossip. If you were to let it be known that it was all a mistake, a misunderstanding—'

'You must be mad!'

Thea took a deep breath. 'Then I will have no choice but to tell people the reason for the quarrel—whether or not I am fully believed, the scandal will ruin you.'

'And you too,' said Lady Chasewater. Yet she sounded uncertain, shaken.

'But I don't care,' said Thea. 'And your son's name will be smeared. You have a daughter to establish.'

There was a long silence.

Then, 'Your brother behaved as a man of honour, and I will do what I can to stem the gossip. Does that satisfy you?'

'Yes.'

'Then let me tell you this: you disgraced your name, your family, your birth. In refusing to let my son make an honest woman of you, you disgraced your sex. You were not worthy of my son's regard! Nor of your brother's!'

Thea rose. 'There is one further thing. In one of your letters you mentioned a child. A...a daughter—'

Thea broke off as Lady Chasewater's eyes blazed.

'You admit it, do you?'

Pain banded around her heart. 'I was told the child died, but now I have made it my business to find out the truth. I believe that she is alive, and once that is confirmed and I have all the particulars, I will make a will in her favour.'

'Pah!' spat Lady Chasewater. 'What good will that do? Your marriage to Blakehurst will invalidate a will; betrothed to him, you can make no legally binding disposition of your property!'

She had considered that. It had been the final death blow to her unborn hopes. If the child in Bath was hers…

'There is no betrothal. Nor will there be. That was a misunderstanding. There is nothing to prevent me making such a disposition.'

Lady Chasewater stared. 'No betrothal? He is awaiting you downstairs.' Her mouth curled in a sneer.

'No,' said Thea quietly. 'There will be no marriage.'

Lady Chasewater stared at her, and Thea swallowed. There was pain, aching, grieving pain in the old eyes.

'I see.' Lady Chasewater's throat worked and her hands tightened in her lap. 'I dare say that I have no right to ask it, but perhaps you might send me news of the child…from time to time. If you visit her, that is.'

'I…I could do that,' said Thea, dazed. Then, not quite knowing why, she asked, 'Do you wish to see her?' Seeing shock in the older woman's face, she added hurriedly, 'Not to acknowledge her, but just to see her—if it could be arranged discreetly?'

There was a long silence, stretching, breaching the gulf between them. At last Lady Chasewater said, 'I'll think about it. Good day.'

Accepting her dismissal, Thea turned to go.

As she reached for the door, Lady Chasewater spoke again. 'Does Aberfield know yet of your intention?'

Thea looked back. 'Not yet. I'll tell him when I have all the information. I wish to give him no chance to hide the child again.'

A harsh laugh broke from the old woman. 'Very wise. I only knew of her existence after my husband's death. I found a letter from Aberfield, but he refused to give me any information. You will tell me if he causes any difficulty. Now go!'

* * *

The door shut behind her. She began to shake uncontrollably as the enormity of what she had done hit her. It was over. David would be safe now. Lady Chasewater had accepted that David had acted in all honour. She forced herself to breathe deeply, willing the shivering to stop. And, slowly, it did. Because she had said it must.

And not only was David safe, but there seemed now to be a queer, tacit understanding between herself and Lady Chasewater. She looked back to the bitter, frightened woman who had arrived in London a few weeks ago. Could that woman have walked into Lady Chasewater's drawing room, spoken the truth and forged this resolution?

She didn't think so. That woman had found it difficult enough just to hold herself together behind her façade. Somehow, somewhere, she had discovered her strength. And the courage to use it. Twinkling dark eyes and a crooked smile formed in her thoughts. Richard. He would never know how much he had helped—simply by being her friend.

He was waiting in the front hall, seated exactly where she had left him. As she came down the stairs he looked up and stood swiftly. His eyes seemed to search her, inside and out, for the least trace of harm. Then he smiled.

'Dragon slain?'

She shook her head. 'Not exactly.' Unless it had been within herself, nothing had needed slaying. Accepting his offered arm, she said, 'Understanding seemed better.'

The dark brows lifted. 'It often is. Come. I'll walk you home.'

The walk was just what she needed to order her thoughts. Richard didn't speak, but she was aware of his quiet strength beside her, somehow surrounding her while not being in the least overwhelming. A friend. And more, something much more that could not be acknowledged.

'You are leaving for Blakeney tomorrow?' she asked as they turned into Grosvenor Square.

'Yes.' Wry amusement touched his voice as he said, 'According to Max, my godson will be making all sorts of amazing progress that I simply must see.'

A strangled laugh escaped her. 'Of course.' Inside she bled, thinking of the child in Bath whom no one had wanted. The only thought at her birth had been to hide her. Even from her own mother.

'And you and Almeria will come down the day after. I'll look forward to that,' he told her. Gently, he said, 'Stop worrying, Thea. We can sort it out it. Talk it through.'

It would be so easy to accept what he offered—surely he would understand her desire to provide for the child first?

If you visit her… Lady Chasewater's words haunted her. She had thought only to ensure the child's safety. Children needed more than that. Her own father had kept *her* safe—according to his code of conduct he had done his duty by her—and more. Many fathers would have simply flung her out. He had at least provided for her.

Safety and security—but no love.

Didn't her own child need more than that? If she accepted Richard's offer, would he permit more than that?

Chapter Fourteen

Richard relaxed back in his chair by the French doors in the library at Blakeney, Max's spaniels at his feet. It was a glorious evening and the doors onto the terrace were open. All the sounds of the dusk drifted in, the cry of an owl, a faint whinnying and stamping from the stables. Scent wafted up from the garden, lavender, rosemary. It had been a warm day and the fragrances lingered on the air with a promise of the coming summer. He always felt at ease here, at home. This house, this room particularly, had been home all his life. Not any more. Oh, he still felt perfectly at ease, with the familiarity of long acquaintance. The room had still its welcome for him, as did the house.

But it was no longer home, much as he loved the place and always would. He had known that for some time. His brain had known it from the day Max announced his imminent marriage to Verity. His heart had known it from the moment he had realised the reality of his brother's marriage.

This house might hold his past. Another must hold his future. Everything was in readiness over at Tarring House.

Not that Verity or Max had shown the least eagerness for him to leave. On the contrary—they were delighted for him to remain. Verity especially had been upset, worried that he might have thought *she* wanted him gone.

He smiled, remembering her worry.

Verity, you goose! I need my own place. This is what I should have done years before the gudgeon met you.

That had been the truth. Max had seemed to see it. Only Max-like, he had decided it was all his fault.

I suppose I have been selfish keeping you here so long.

He hadn't called Max a goose. It had been a good bit more direct than that.

Max came back into the room. He had been upstairs with Verity, seeing little William Richard safely into his crib.

'All tucked up?' asked Richard gravely. Lord! Who would ever have thought to see Max such a doting father! As for the sudden ache in his stomach, and pricking behind his eyes, when Verity had placed his godson in his arms this evening—well, he just wasn't going to think about that. Thank God Max hadn't seen.

'Oh, shut up, Ricky,' said Max without the least rancour. 'Don't think I didn't notice how dewy-eyed *you* were over your godson when Verity gave him to you!'

'Dewy-eyed?' Richard protested. 'Damn it! You make me sound like some feather-brained débutante!' Good God, had it been that obvious?

His twin chuckled and said, 'Speaking of which, are you betrothed or are you not?'

'Thea Winslow,' said Richard, with a tolerable assumption of diffidence, 'is not a feather-brained débutante.'

Strolling over to a side table, Max said, 'Drink?' And proceeded to pour two very large brandies without waiting for a response.

He gave one to Richard and continued, 'I'd be surprised if she was. I seem to recall that by the age of ten she could give you a damn good game of chess.'

Richard smiled. 'That hasn't changed.' He sipped the brandy. 'This is good. The "Gentlemen", one assumes?'

Max gave a wry grimace at this reference to the local smuggling gang, as he lowered his large frame into a chair across from

Richard. 'Who else? They keep on leaving the curst stuff right behind the stables, despite any number of messages I've sent that it really isn't necessary. They must know by now that no self-respecting Blakehurst would inform on them. The other day they left scent and a length of lace too!'

Richard grinned and raised his tumbler. 'To tradition!'

Max snorted. 'I understand that there's a barrel or two awaiting your arrival at Tarring House, by the way.'

Richard burst out laughing. 'Is there, indeed?'

'Apparently so. And no doubt if you play your cards properly the lace and scent will follow in due course. Now stop changing the subject, and tell me about this betrothal of yours.'

Richard sighed. 'It's not exactly a betrothal. If you must know, it's hell's own mess.'

Max's black brows rose and the amber eyes glinted with amusement. 'So I gathered from the somewhat incoherent letter I received from Almeria telling me that she would be delighted to come to Will's christening, that she had a houseguest—to wit, Dorothea Winslow—and it would be most unfortunate if we all missed such a splendid opportunity to secure your lasting happiness, and, er—dare I say it?'

'Fortune?' suggested Richard.

'In a word. I was all for telling Almeria to go to the devil at that point, but since I'd already told you Miss Winslow would be welcome…' He shot Richard an amused look. 'I received the impression from Almeria's letter that Miss Winslow was positively yearning to see the beauties of Blakeney.' He shook his head. 'However it came about, I'm relieved that Almeria is putting aside her disapproval to come.'

'That, twin, is one of the reasons Thea is coming to visit,' said Richard and explained what Thea had done.

When Max had stopped laughing, or at least had subsided to an unholy grin, and occasional chuckles, Richard went on, 'Not being perfectly *au fait* with the extent of Almeria's obsession with seeing me married to the largest available fortune—' he waited patiently while Max regained some semblance of self-control '—she didn't realise that our mutual godmother would consider the whole thing as settled,' he finished ruefully.

'Either of you could have denied it,' Max pointed out, swirling the brandy around his glass and inhaling beatifically.

'No,' said Richard shortly. 'At least, I couldn't. Not at that point. And I persuaded Thea not to.'

'No, I suppose not,' said Max. He ventured nothing further. Julian Braybrook's last letter had given him the gist of the massive scandal that hovered over Thea and David Winslow. He was sure there was more to it than Winslow's arrest and subsequent release, but hesitated to probe as to the reason *why* Winslow had ended up in a duel with Lallerton. Richard would tell him in his own good time if he could.

And there was that earlier letter from Julian...

Of course, without you in town to distract her, Lady Arnsworth is interfering in Ricky's non-existent matrimonial plans— flinging heiresses at him hither and yon. But oddly enough, this time she seems to have got it exactly right. For all the wrong reasons, one might add. Fifty thousand of them, in fact. In the face of which, one can only pray that the almost terminal stubbornness of the Blakehursts will not blind the gudgeon to what is as plain as day to the rest of us...

Leaving aside that quite unwarranted jibe about the infamous Blakehurst stubbornness, apparently Braybrook thought Miss Winslow had something to offer Ricky beyond her fortune. And observing Ricky's abstraction since his arrival that afternoon, Max had a sneaking suspicion that Julian could be right.

Never before had he seen Ricky so silent, or so preoccupied. At least, he had, of course, but only over his books. Never about a woman. And on the occasions when Richard had struck up a liaison with a woman, never had his emotions been engaged.

If indeed they were now. Verity said Richard was in love. Max did not pretend to know *how* she divined that from the simple fact that while letters from half their acquaintance had mentioned Ricky's interest in Miss Winslow, Ricky himself had not so much as mentioned her once in any of his letters. But Verity was sure. And Max was inclined to agree.

One thing in particular convinced him: never in all their lives had Richard been loath to offer a confidence to his twin. He stretched out his legs, sipped his brandy and silently wished the half-remembered Miss Winslow luck. He looked forward to renewing his acquaintance with her on the morrow. They would all arrive then. Almeria was coming post with Miss Winslow, and Julian was driving himself down. The christening was set for the following week.

He wondered if it would be tactful to thank Miss Winslow for her efforts. Without the lure of marrying Ricky off, he suspected that either Almeria wouldn't have come at all, or her visit would have been of the most fleeting. As it was, she planned to remain for at least a week. He laughed suddenly.

Ricky's gaze narrowed over his brandy. 'Yes?'

'Nothing. I was just thinking—it's not surprising that Miss Winslow can still give you a good game of chess, if she manoeuvred Almeria that neatly.'

Not entirely to Max's surprise, his twin let that one pass.

Thea stepped out of the chaise the following afternoon, smiled her thanks at the footman who had let down the step, and heaved a sigh of relief. Not just for the physical relief of being able to stretch her legs, which were tired and cramped from the journey, but for the mental relief of no longer having to sit in the same space as Almeria.

Listening to her godmother casually enumerate all the best silk mercers and warehouses for brideclothes had imposed enough of a strain on her self-control. The musings on whether or not Princess Charlotte's example, some seven years earlier, of silver brocade must be considered a trifle outmoded, had tried her even higher.

She had acidly pointed out that Her Royal Highness's death in childbed the following year was not a good omen.

Very true, my dear. Not a lucky bride at all.

But the monologue between Canterbury and Blakeney on the

advantages of being married in the cathedral, as opposed to St George's Hanover Square, interspersed with reflections upon the advisability of employing a wet-nurse, had nearly broken her restraint. Never mind counting chickens before the eggs were hatched, Almeria Arnsworth hadn't even managed to get the rooster into the hen-run.

Almeria stepped out behind her, leaning heavily upon the hapless footman.

'Really! One would think that Max would at least—oh.'

She broke off at the sight of her nephew coming out of the front door.

Thea blinked. She had forgotten how alike the Blakehurst twins were. Not identical by any means, but the resemblance was still a shock.

Earl Blakehurst came down the steps with a lithe grace, a delighted smile on his face.

'Here you are, then. I've just given orders for tea to be served in the library.' He took Almeria's hands and bent to kiss her cheek. 'We're delighted you could come, Almeria. Verity will be down in a moment, I am sure. She was having a rest, but insisted I send a maid to awaken her as soon as you arrived.'

Under Thea's fascinated eye, Almeria thawed visibly. 'Well, I'm sure I would not wish to be disturbing her rest.'

Blakehurst chuckled. 'If you don't, I can assure you that our son will do it anyway! Come along in.' He turned to Thea. 'Miss Winslow. I'm delighted to renew our acquaintance. Welcome to Blakeney.'

'Thank you, my lord. It looks beautiful.'

It did. The house, a rambling Tudor mansion standing in extensive flower gardens, seemed to have sprung out of the landscape.

His smile reminded her of Richard's. 'Thank you, Miss Winslow. Please come in. Ricky is about somewhere and Braybrook arrived a couple of hours ago. I trust you have been enjoying your Season.'

Almeria said primly, 'It is very good of you to invite us, Blakehurst. While I continue to deplore the notoriety that accompanied your marriage last year, one can only be grateful to Verity that marriage has curbed some of your more obnoxious habits.'

Thea didn't know where to look. She knew exactly what Almeria meant by obnoxious habits, but it was not at all the sort of knowledge she was meant to betray. On the whole she thought an expression of blank uninterest might be best.

Blakehurst ruined that.

'Oh? Which habits would they be, Almeria?'

Thea stifled a choke of laughter and Almeria favoured Lord Blakehurst with a quelling glare. 'You know perfectly well to which habits I refer, Max!'

'Ah! *Those* habits,' said his lordship urbanely. Gesturing for Almeria to precede him, he offered Thea his arm. 'Come and meet Lady Blakehurst, Miss Winslow. She has been looking forward to your visit very much.'

Thea's assumption that the countess's eagerness to meet her was a polite fabrication on the part of Lord Blakehurst died in the face of Lady Blakehurst's very genuine delight and pleasure when she came into the library to find Almeria and Thea already fortifying themselves with cups of tea.

The countess was utterly lovely, thought Thea, with her dark hair and deep grey eyes. Small and slender, she still looked rather pale and Lord Blakehurst leapt to his feet, hurrying over to hand her to a chair.

'You slept well?' he asked, before she could say a word.

An ache spread through Thea at the concerned tenderness in his voice, the fleeting caress of his fingers on his wife's hand as he led her to a chair. This was how it should be.

'Yes, thank you, Max,' said the countess. 'Good afternoon, Aunt Almeria. How nice to see you here again.' Her voice was lovely too. Husky and musical. Finding Lord Blakehurst putting her into a chair, she ventured a protest. 'But I should be greeting our guests properly, not languishing in a chair!' She made to get up, but was firmly held back by her husband.

'You may greet them from there,' he said. 'You know perfectly well I think you ought still to be in bed! Verity, this is Almeria's goddaughter, Miss Winslow. Miss Winslow, this is my wife, Lady Blakehurst.'

'He's a tyrant, you know,' said Lady Blakehurst with a perfectly straight face. 'I was never so glad of anything when Richard went up to town because he was almost as bad! I have never been so fussed over or cosseted in my life! How do you do, Miss Winslow? I am so happy to meet you.'

Thea curtsied. 'Thank you, Lady Blakehurst. I am honoured.'

'Blakehurst,' opined Almeria, 'shows a very proper concern and regard for your health, Verity. I congratulate you on the birth of The Heir.'

Lord Blakehurst smiled. 'A secondary concern from my point of view, I assure you, Almeria. Speaking for myself, I was delighted with the birth of my child.'

'A sentiment which does you great credit, Max,' allowed Almeria. 'But naturally you must have been relieved that it was a son.'

Another voice broke in from the open doors onto the terrace. 'Actually, I don't think he was, Almeria.'

Richard strolled in with Lord Braybrook. 'Judging by the letter he sent me, anyway. All the first three paragraphs said was that a baby had been born and that Verity was perfectly all right. The baby's sex was almost an afterthought!'

To Thea's delight, Blakehurst reddened. 'Oh, go to the devil, Ricky! Wait until your turn and see how *you* like it.'

Lord Braybrook chuckled. 'Ignore them, Miss Winslow. Sometimes they are worse than this. Servant, Lady Arnsworth. Miss Winslow. I trust you had a comfortable journey down?'

'Most comfortable, thank you, Lord Braybrook,' said Almeria. 'And when, Verity, may we see—William, is it not?'

Lady Blakehurst smiled. 'Very soon, Aunt. He woke up about half an hour ago. I fed him and Nurse said she would change him and bring him down.'

Almeria's jaw dropped. 'You feed him yourself? My dear Verity, this is most unnecessary—a wet-nurse is far more—'

'I prefer it, Aunt,' said Verity quietly. 'It was my decision.'

Lord Blakehurst, still standing beside his wife's chair, laid his hand on her shoulder, saying, 'And one which I fully endorse.'

Much to Thea's surprise, given the very decided views on the subject aired in the chaise, Almeria subsided at once. 'Naturally, Max, if you approve, then there is no more to be said.' Then, rather diffidently, she added, 'As long as it does not tire Verity unduly.'

Thea rather thought that Lord Braybrook looked distinctly relieved that the subject was to be shelved. Even Richard looked to have relaxed somewhat. Although that might be more due to his worry about this meeting. His glance flickered back and forth between his brother, Almeria and the countess.

Then, without warning, his gaze rested on her and his heart-stopping smile dawned, lighting the dark eyes from within. His lips moved silently as he lifted his teacup in unspoken salute. *Thank you.*

All Thea's defences shook to their foundations, to the very core of her being. And if he ever suspected what she felt for him… Somehow she managed to smile back. Brightly. *Happy to have helped.* As though it meant nothing.

The door opening to admit the nurse with a small, shawl-wrapped bundle, was akin to a relieving troop of cavalry approaching a citadel under siege.

Lord Blakehurst strode across the room and the nurse, with a suspiciously primmed mouth, delivered the bundle into his arms.

'Thank you, Nurse. We'll let you know when he is back in the nursery.'

'Yes, m'lord.' She curtsied and went out.

The reason for the nurse's suppressed amusement was not far to seek. When Lord Blakehurst turned back to his guests, the expression of undisguised, tender pride on his face stabbed into Thea with undiluted pain, tearing at wounds she had thought healed and forgotten.

No one had ever looked at her child like that.

The countess spoke. 'Perhaps…perhaps Aunt Almeria might like to hold him, Max?'

Slowly, his lordship turned to his aunt. 'Almeria?'

'I…I should like that very much, Max.' Her voice, utterly expressionless, fell into a breathless hush.

Lord Blakehurst bent down, carefully depositing the babe in her arms. 'His…his head needs support, you know—'

'Max—I have held a baby before,' said Almeria with asperity. 'You, for one.' She shot a glance at Braybrook. 'Even you. In fact—' she settled the baby in her arms and drew back the shawls a little '—the only one of you here that I did *not* hold as a babe would be Verity.'

Silence fell as Almeria examined the baby. A very careful, elegant finger stroked gently, and a corner of the severe mouth flickered.

The knife twisting inside Thea dug a little deeper. No one had rejoiced at the birth of her daughter. Not even reluctantly. She had been hidden away, her very existence denied. She clenched her hands in her lap, willing the hurt to subside, forcing her face to remain calm, politely interested as they waited for Almeria to say something.

Then, 'Thank you, Max. I do not know how it may be, but the title Great Aunt seems far more ageing than that of Grandmother.'

Lord Blakehurst grinned. 'It must be the "Great", Almeria. Shall I take him again?'

'You may.'

He bent down and scooped up the little bundle effortlessly.

'That,' pronounced Almeria, 'is a very healthy and well-developed child, Max.' She turned to the countess. 'You have done very well, Verity. Very well, indeed.'

'Thank you, Aunt,' said the countess.

Almeria frowned. 'Verity, it is time and more that you ceased to call me "Aunt", if you please.' The frown deepened. 'I dare say that I have been very foolish in the past year. I hope that—'

'Almeria,' said Lord Blakehurst quietly, 'your presence here is a great pleasure to us. No more needs to be said.'

Almeria looked even more pokered up. 'You are generous, Max. Thank you.'

For an instant time stood still and Thea knew that, although doubtless there would be disagreements and Almeria might never fully approve of Lady Blakehurst, there was healing and acceptance, that the family was no longer split.

Involuntarily she met Richard's gaze. Quiet pride, gratitude and, oh, God—that something else that she dared not acknowledge.

Lord Blakehurst broke the spell. 'Miss Winslow, would you care to hold him?'

Hold the baby? Panic assaulted her. She couldn't—not a baby. Bad enough looking at every small child and wondering, endlessly wondering what her child might have been like...tall, fair? Mischievous, obedient? But to actually hold a baby... Only, that was *her* voice, saying politely how much she would like to hold the child, and Lord Blakehurst was already bending down and there was the weight in her arms, the weight she had never felt before, only imagined.

Such a tiny weight.

She was holding Richard's nephew and godson-to-be and all she could feel was rage. And pain. Rage that this had been stolen from her, that—no.

She would not feel bitterness. Not with a child in her arms. Not with the sweet, milky scent wreathing through her. There could be pain, yes. But not the bitterness of envy. This little one had done nothing to deserve that. She forced herself to focus on the tiny face. A small fist was stuffed into his mouth and she found herself smiling into the sleepy unfocused eyes blinking up at her.

Joy swept her, lighting the darkest corners, burning away all else in its path. Instinctively she found herself rocking gently, patting in the same rhythm, and before her wondering eyes, the child fell asleep, still with his fist stuffed in his mouth.

Richard saw the wonder take her, the amazement, the awe. In that instant he saw everything he wanted for himself. And for her. The knowledge shook him to the very foundations of his being and he knew what he had to do. He had to convince Thea that he wanted her. He had to convince her that his offer of marriage, when he made it again, had nothing to do with honour and chivalry, and everything to do with love.

A swift movement drew his attention. He glanced sideways, to catch Almeria dabbing moisture from her eyes. She caught his gaze and glared, stuffing—the only word for it—her lacy hand-kerchief into her reticule.

'There must be something drifting in from the garden,' she said defiantly, 'or perhaps those flowers on Max's desk!'

'Of course, Almeria,' he agreed gravely, not daring to look at Max.

He looked back at Thea, her head still bent over the baby, her arms and hands cradling the bundle in absolute safety. And the tenderness in her expression—as though she held her own child.

The thought of her holding her child, *their* child, hit him in a rush of possessive desire. Every muscle in his body turned to steel as he hardened. It was all he could do to remain in his chair. He wanted her. In his arms, his bed. His life.

She looked up, as if he had spoken her name. Her expression was dazed, shocked. He thought he knew exactly how she felt; as though her world had turned upside down, and quite possibly inside out.

An odd sound from Max recalled him to his surroundings. Tearing his gaze from Thea, he met his twin's eyes. Amused understanding glinted in the amber.

'Always such a shock,' murmured Max.

Lord William Blakehurst having been duly christened and welcomed into the church, and having yelled his lungs out the whole time, his relatives and well-wishers removed themselves from the church in a laughing, joyous crowd.

Lord Braybrook, holding his squalling godson, appeared more than marginally harassed. 'Lady Blakehurst, I swear, it's nothing *I'm* doing!'

The countess smiled. 'Here. I'll—'

'Give him to me,' said Max and took his son, who immediately yelled louder.

'It's the baptism,' said Richard, trying not to laugh as they strolled across the churchyard. 'I'm sure I have heard somewhere that if they yell, it means the devil is leaving them.'

'Which begs the question why Max yelled and you didn't on the occasion of your joint baptism,' said Almeria very drily.

Richard choked and turned instinctively to share the joke with Thea, whose soft blue eyes were indeed full of laughter. For an instant the corner of her mouth lifted in the beginnings of a smile, a smile that caught at his heart, that brought every suppressed longing raging to the surface. She immediately looked away.

As she had done for the past week.

Ever since that moment in the library when their eyes had locked over the baby in her arms, she had avoided him. Oh, not completely, but she had made quite sure that they were never alone together, never paired except in the most general way.

She had been the most charming and delightful of guests, leading several of Max's neighbours to comment that the rumours that had reached them from London must have been greatly exaggerated.

Even now she was chatting sensibly to old Lady Aldicott, a stickler if ever there was one. The old lady caught his gaze on them and smiled knowingly. 'And you're staying on at Blakeney, then, after Almeria returns to town?'

Thea denied it quietly, although colour rushed to her cheeks.

Not for the first time Richard cursed Almeria's not-entirely-accidental indiscretion in London. How to tell if Thea truly did not wish to marry him, or simply wished not to see him obliged to marry her out of duty?

His jaw hardened. All week he had held back, and she had slipped further and further away. It was, he understood, difficult for a woman to wear her heart on her sleeve if she were not quite certain of a man's affections. And for Thea, perhaps, impossible.

Screwing his courage to the sticking place, he strolled over to Thea and Lady Aldicott.

The old lady smirked. 'Well! And about time too that a new generation of Blakehursts came along to plague us!' She poked Richard with her walking stick. 'I'll look forward to seeing you do your bit.' Heat flared on his cheeks as the old she-devil nodded to Thea. 'I'm pleased to have met you, my dear. I'll look forward to continuing our chat some time. I'm off home now. My old bones need a rest. Good day to you both.'

She stumped off, and Richard turned to Thea. 'We need to talk,' he said. 'Quietly, privately and honestly. You know I won't lie, and that I won't force either of us into an unwanted marriage—'

'Richard—'

'We need to talk,' he repeated. 'Before you return to London. That is all I ask.'

'Very well,' she said. 'Now?'

Now? In the middle of a christening party? 'After dinner,' he said.

Chapter Fifteen

When the gentlemen joined the ladies in the library after dinner, Thea was not there. Richard frowned as he glanced round. She had looked very pale during the meal. Perhaps she had retired already.

Verity glanced up, smiling, from her conversation with Almeria and the rector's wife. 'Are you looking for Miss Winslow, Richard? She is on the terrace. I think she has the headache a little.'

Almeria shot him a severe glance. 'I dare say a little fresh air will not go amiss, Richard. I know that I can trust you to take Dorothea for a gentle walk in the gardens.'

An excellent idea—if only he could extend to himself the same trust!

Sure enough, he found her just outside, gazing out over the velvety darkness of the gardens from the balustrade. Mingled scents of flowers and newly cut grass came up to them, twining with the rippling song of a fountain. Such a fragile peace.

She looked up at him as he came up beside her. 'It is lovely here, is it not?'

'Beautiful,' he agreed. 'Should you care to come for a walk with me?' What they needed was a little privacy. Somewhere they did not have to worry about being interrupted and he could tell her…tell her—his heart felt as though steel bands were tightening around it—he needed to tell her that he loved her.

She did not answer immediately and a shaft of foreboding stabbed into him. Surely, surely he had not been wrong about this—

'Sir…that is, Richard—I do not think that would be advisable, you see—'

He laid his hand over hers on the balustrade, felt the fine tremor and the tension. 'Thea, we need to talk.'

'There is not the least need, Richard. And indeed it is not wise. Almeria will find it hard enough to believe when our supposed betrothal comes to naught.'

His heart clenched. 'Must it come to naught, my dear?'

It was all he could do to keep his voice light, and his hands still when every instinct urged him to drag her into his arms and kiss her until she knew the truth he knew—that she was *his*. He forced himself to remain still. After what had happened to her, Thea was the last woman in the world to be won over in that way.

She bit her lip. 'Yes. This…this is not what I want…to be manipulated and forced into marriage to satisfy society.'

Put like that… If Thea felt that she was being constrained—his throat tightened around the aching loss. More fool him. He had thought that beyond the impossible situation in which they found themselves, beyond the affection he knew she felt for him, that there had been something else, the possibility of something more.

Could she believe that he was offering a marriage without love?

'Thea…in marrying you, I would not be bowing to the dictates of society—'

She flinched, tugged her hand from under his. 'Please, Richard. No more. I…I cannot marry you. It is not possible.'

He could not mistake her determination. Nor that his suit distressed her. Her eyes were bright with unshed tears, yet she was facing him squarely, proudly.

She smiled, a wobbly travesty of a smile, but still a smile. 'Your wife, Richard, will the luckiest of women. But it cannot be me. We are dear friends—let it remain that way.'

Resolutely he faced the truth: that *his* truth might not be hers. That if he truly loved her, he would not bind her to him.

From somewhere he dredged up a semblance of a smile. 'Then we must wish each other well?'

Thea nodded, her eyes full of pain.

Somewhere deep inside him there was pain also. Pain he thought he might carry for the rest of his life. Unable to help himself, he reached out his hand, lifting it to her face. This must be the last time. He would not touch her again. Gently he traced her jaw, memorising the silky softness, the delicate whorls of her ear and the line of her brow. Desire, longing, flooded him. It would be so easy to take her in his arms and kiss her. He must not. Slowly, carefully, he brushed over the curve of her mouth with his fingertips…never again…never…and it should not be happening now.

He forced his hand to drop, seemingly relaxed.

'So be it,' he said quietly. And left her.

With his departure, Thea released the death grip she had kept on herself. She had never imagined that it could be this painful. Or that the hurt she saw in his eyes would threaten her resolution far more than the knife twisting in her own heart.

The following day brought Thea a letter from Aberfield. She stared at it for several minutes before slipping out into the garden and finding a quiet corner in which to open it. Her fingers trembled as she smoothed out the folds and read.

It wasn't all bad. The news that Lady Chasewater had spoken to David in public with every appearance of civility sent a jolt of relief through her. Thea could only imagine what that had cost her. But then she came to the part that concerned her directly.

I cannot but feel that, in leaving town before sending the notice of your betrothal to the Gazette, *Mr Blakehurst has been unwise. I say nothing of his failure to obtain my consent. You have been at pains to make it clear this means little to you. I dare say he has taken that as his cue.*

In any case, such a marriage will be convenient in many

*ways. As a younger son, without the family honour to uphold,
one may assume that he will be somewhat more lenient in certain
areas and your earlier indiscretion need not be considered. He
is a sensible man, and will no doubt accept this as the price of
an alliance otherwise beyond his expectations. I have no doubt
that you will deal well together.*

There was more, but she could not bear to read it all. The brutal
assumptions chilled her to the bone. Her marriage to Richard
would have been a convenience to Aberfield, settling the problem
of how to manage her fortune, scotch any remaining scandal. It
suited Aberfield; oh, and in marriage to a younger son, her—how
did he put it? She glanced again at the letter—*your earlier indiscretion need not be considered…you will deal well together.*

She walked on, through the gentle fragrance and humming
bees of the knot garden, the letter crumpled to a ball in her hand.

Marriage to Richard. Aberfield's reasoning sickened her, but
in a way he was right: Richard was the one man to whom she
could have given herself.

And now she knew what she would have wanted in marriage
to Richard. Love. The sort of love that blazed between Max and
Verity. That was what her heart had been trying to tell her about
Richard. A shiver went through her. Her heart and her body had
both tried to warn her.

Carefully she smoothed out the letter and folded it back into
the original creases, tucking it into her reticule. She had chosen
her course. No good could possibly come from mourning over
a might-have-been. Even if Richard had come to care for her in
that way, it was impossible. She knew now, had known from the
moment she held Richard's nephew in her arms, what she had
to do. And doing it would cut her off from Richard for ever.

It was not something she had any choice about. It simply was.
Her decision was made, and there could be no going back from
it. Not if she wished to live at peace with herself. She went into
the house by a side door and made her way towards the library.
Verity was usually to be found there often with little William.

At first the library seemed empty, but then voices drifted in through the open doors from the terrace. Smiling, Thea went towards them. And then, in the doorway, she froze to utter stillness. A comfortable-looking *chaise* had been placed in a shady corner of the terrace. Verity was there and Lord Blakehurst, who held his son cradled in one arm. The other encircled Verity as he kissed her, so tenderly it brought tears to Thea's eyes. Blinking, she stepped back behind the curtains. Back from the incarnation of all she could never have. All she would have most desired.

Impossible now to remember the way she had felt when she returned to London, wanting nothing more than her freedom and peace. That had been a safer ambition. One she could achieve. Now…she could never have what she now desired.

She was about to slip away when male voices floated up from the garden. Richard. And from the sounds of it, Lord Braybrook. Returned from their ride.

Booted feet sounded on the terrace steps, one set uneven. She sighed. There was no reason now to walk away.

'Hullo, Max.' Lord Braybrook's light baritone. 'Servant, Lady Blakehurst. Sorry to be so long. Ricky dragged me off to see his house.'

'Oh, did you like it?' Verity's soft tones.

Thea stepped out of the shadow into the open French door.

'Just the thing for Ricky, I should think,' said Braybrook. 'Sort of place that even had *me* thinking of marriage and families.'

'Julian?' That was Richard.

'Yes?'

'Stubble it.'

'Well, it's true,' averred Braybrook. 'It did. Gave me quite a turn, I assure you! I shall have to offer for Miss Winslow and—'

Thea froze in place, her wits whirling.

'Ah, Julian—' Earl Blakehurst's bright amber gaze was on her, his mouth twitching. Thea pulled herself together.

'Be refused?' she suggested, taking her cue and stepping out onto the terrace.

Lord Blakehurst gave a muffled crack of laughter. 'Very

sensible, Miss Winslow. Do come and join us.' He rose to his feet, still cradling his son, and came forward to greet her.

His smile gave not the least hint that he and his wife had been interrupted, that he might be wishing his guests at the devil.

'I wanted to see you. I understand that Almeria intends returning to town the day after tomorrow. There is not the least need for you to leave at the same time. I, that is, *we* would be most happy if you chose to extend your stay.'

A queer sound escaped from Richard. She glanced at him and found him staring at his twin with a totally disbelieving expression on his face. Outraged, even.

Despite knowing that she could not stay, pain slashed through her to know that the thought of her staying did not endear itself to Richard at all. Probably he'd heard quite enough speculation on the subject of their non-existent betrothal by now. Not that Lord Blakehurst would have made that mistake. He must know his brother better than that.

'Thank you, my lord. I will give that some thought.' Best to be non-committal.

'Do come and sit down, Thea,' said Verity. 'There is plenty of room here on the *chaise*.'

'Actually, I thought I might go for a walk,' she said. 'Up on to the Downs. It is such a beautiful day. Is there a path I could follow?'

Lord Blakehurst frowned. 'There is, but you were not thinking of going alone, were you?'

Thea flushed. 'I...I don't want to inconvenience anyone. Surely—'

Lord Blakehurst grinned. 'I can assure you that I will be more than inconvenienced when Almeria hears that we let her precious charge wander unescorted over the Downs!'

'Dear Miss Winslow,' said Braybrook. 'Behold your escort. No—don't demur. It will give me a chance to propose in private and you a chance to—'

'But you promised that you would play piquet with me!' protested Verity in some indignation. 'Richard may take Thea.' She turned to her brother-in-law with a ravishing smile. 'Won't you,

Richard? You could take her up through the beech woods. It will be lovely up there today.'

Richard, Thea swiftly realised, was in as impossible a situation as she was herself. He could scarcely refuse without the appearance of rudeness, and, having said she wished to go for a walk, *she* could not now draw back. Not without publicly rejecting Richard's escort.

Meeting his gaze, she saw wry amusement there, and resignation. He rose to his feet. 'If we are to go up on to the Downs, Thea, you will need to change your shoes. And find a bonnet that ties on securely. It will be windy up there.'

Thea bowed to the inevitable.

By tacit consent they talked very little on the walk up through the woods. Indeed, Thea scarcely had breath by the time they reached the top of the valley and left the trees behind. Up and up they climbed, until Thea's legs ached and her lungs burned. Just ahead she could see the crest of the hill…only a little further… She took a deep breath before the wind could whip it away, and pushed on to the top.

Once there the view snatched away the remnant of her breath. Around them spread the Downs. Above them swung the blue arc of the sky. In the distance the Channel shifted and glimmered in the late afternoon light.

'We should turn back,' said Richard, coming up with her, not sounding in the least winded, although his limp was slightly more apparent. Her own lungs were burning at the climb and she felt utterly exhausted. Her face must be scarlet and her legs felt as though they might actually drop off.

But the view was worth it. Blue and green and limitless. Up here it was almost possible to believe that if one only spread one's arms and leaned on the wind one could fly. Up here all the problems and trivialities of the world fell away. Oh, they still existed, but they could not *touch* you up here.

She sighed. 'Yes. But I needed this. Needed to get out. Feel space around me. London—' She broke off, not quite sure how to express herself.

'Cabined, cribbed, confined?' he suggested.

She nodded. 'Yes. This—' she gestured wildly '—this is beautiful. You can be alone without being lonely.' She knew he would understand. He always did.

A faint smile curved his mouth. 'It's called solitude. At least that's what I call it. My mother didn't like it at all. She hated Blakeney. Said it was too isolated. She spent as much time as she could away from it.'

Thea remembered the late Lady Blakehurst. And thought of the present Lady Blakehurst.

'I don't think Lady Blakehurst minds.'

'Verity?' Richard smiled. 'I doubt she'd mind where she was, as long as Max was somewhere nearby. But, yes. She loves Blakeney.'

Slowly they descended, following the faint path down until they reached the beech woods. The cool green shade welcomed them, the light breeze sighing, rippling above. Caressing. Gentle. The way Lord Blakehurst had kissed Verity.

She pushed the thought away. And then faced it. Yes. That was how a kiss could, *should,* be. The new-found knowledge ached inside her. This was something she would only ever be able to guess at. Something she could never know for herself. But at least she now knew that with the right man, there was nothing to fear. Richard had taught her that.

She tripped on the thought. She really ought to thank him. But how? What to say? To Richard of all men.

And there was the rub. Richard. The man she loved. The man she would always love, so deeply that he seemed a part of herself. Even if he never knew it. She shut her eyes against the prickling tears. He must never know it.

But somehow she must thank him for what he had taught her. For what he had forced her to see. Here, still high above the world, she could see what she had known deep down for weeks. The day he had swung her out of the path of the gig, holding her afterwards as if he would never release her; the night he had come to her during her nightmare and comforted her; his protective fury when he rescued her from Dunhaven; the day he had swung her around in joy at the news of Verity's safe delivery. Above all, he had accepted her as she was; he had stood by her. He had not judged. Oh, yes; she had been in love with him for weeks, yet, held prisoner in the darkness of her own fears, she had been too cowardly to acknowledge it.

But now in the sunlight, she knew: with Richard there would have been nothing to fear. The world misted and she blinked furiously. It was impossible. She had made her choice—and yet…

The woods were thinning. Soon the house would be in sight and this was the sort of thing that she would much prefer to say very privately indeed.

'Richard?'

'Mmm?'

'The other day—when you asked me to marry you…' She hesitated, struggling to give words to her thoughts. 'Even though I can't possibly marry you—I wanted to thank you, for…for believing me, and even before that…for not judging me.'

His smile tore her heart from her breast, deepened, reaching places within her that she had thought lost. Dazed, she realised that he had taken her hands, that he was bending towards her, that he was going to…

His lips brushed across hers in the gentlest of featherlight caresses. Her whole being leapt and surged unbidden as he straightened and drew back. She felt as though a flame leapt and burned within her, dancing in joy.

He had kissed her. Just.

And her whole being yearned for him to kiss her again. Properly.

He said in an odd, tight sort of voice, 'We had better keep moving.'

Automatically she followed him, shockingly aware that her lips felt bereft, incomplete, that she was like a moth dancing around a lamp. Certain to be singed, but dancing all the same and yearning for the touch of flame on its wings just once more.

Would he mind? Just to show her? It would be utterly shameless, of course, but what did she have to lose? Her virtue?

'Richard?'

'Yes?' Very curt.

Perhaps he *would* mind. Nevertheless Thea took a deep breath and asked huskily, 'Would you kiss me again?'

He stopped dead in his tracks.

'I beg your pardon?'

Stubbornly she met his disbelieving gaze. 'Please…if you wouldn't mind…would you kiss me again. P…p…properly this time.'

He was having difficulty just breathing, but he managed to say, 'I think I might just about be able to cope.' Dear God in heaven—what the hell did she mean by *properly?* Unfortunately, the way—*all* the ways—he wanted to kiss Thea Winslow came under the heading *im*proper. Extremely improper. Now was probably not the right moment to point out that he'd been wanting to kiss her properly for some time. And it certainly wasn't the right moment to lose all control. She had refused even to listen to his last offer of marriage. So why in Hades did she want him to kiss her?

'Here?' he suggested, keeping his voice very neutral. At least his voice was under control. It was about the only part of him that was. Apparently the shreds of his control had been used up keeping that last kiss within the bounds of propriety.

She looked about. 'Y…yes. Here would be nice.'

Nice? Richard took a shuddering breath. *Here* would be perfect. He suspected that *here,* in the sun-dappled green of the beech woods, was about to become the most wonderful place on earth. Slowly, he raised a hand and brushed his fingers along the elegant line of her throat and jaw. So soft. So silky. He couldn't remember any woman's skin ever being that soft. He couldn't remember any other woman at all for that matter. She, and only she, filled his memories, his heart, his soul. And she had asked him to kiss her. Just kiss her. If anyone had ever offered him anything sweeter, he didn't remember that, either. Carefully he cradled her jaw, smoothing his thumb over her lips. They parted on a soft gasp and heat shot through him.

Just a kiss, he reminded himself.

Thea waited, shivering in wonder at his touch, her mind reeling with shock, that she had actually done something so outrageous as to ask a gentleman to kiss her. Properly. Only…having asked him to kiss her, she now had absolutely no idea what the next move should be. She didn't even know what *properly* involved. Fortunately it was obvious that Richard *did* know.

His fingers, light and caressing, drew tingling magic from deep within her, melting her shyness in the warmth of his tenderness. Gentle, featherlight kisses caressed her temples, her closed eyes. Controlled strength drew her closer, nestling her against his body as that teasing mouth brushed fire along the line of her jaw, until, in sudden frustration, she turned, clumsily capturing his lips with her own.

A moment's stillness as their mouths met, then his lips moved in a heart-shaking entreaty, the silky heat of his tongue tasting, teasing her own lips open. So different, a melding this, and she responded to the heat spreading within her, parting her lips, opening her mouth in acceptance.

His tongue slid deep, stroking, and heat burst inside her as she felt the aching pulse deep within, echoing the possessive surge and retreat of his tongue.

He took, but he also gave. And she could sense his restraint. In the taut strength of his arms, cradling her so tenderly. In the low groan deep in his throat as she tentatively returned his kiss, tasting, probing with her own tongue.

Her bones melted. Every fibre softened in delight and she clung, pressing against him, closer than sunlight, feeling joy and love pour through her, illuminating every dark corner, flinging back the shadows.

Finally, far too soon, he drew back, releasing her mouth and settling her cheek against his chest. She could hear his heart hammering. Beating to the same wild, burning rhythm as her own. His hand stroked her hair, soothing, gentle.

His voice came, utterly calm. 'Was that what you meant by properly?'

Her heart steadied slightly.

'I…yes…I think so. Yes.'

Her own voice wobbled despicably. Properly? Yes, oh, yes! If properly mean shot with fire and life and a promise that could never be fulfilled.

She took a careful breath, forcing it past the aching lump in her throat. 'Thank you, Richard.' At least the wobble was gone from her voice. She wished she could say the same for her knees. Regardless she pushed gently against his chest, asking wordlessly to be released. She could stand alone.

She would have to.

He released her the moment he felt her desire to be freed, and wondered if some part of him had ripped free of its moorings, for ever to swing rudderless. He had known that he desired her. Hell! He had even known that he loved her.

But he had not put the two together. He had not realised what it would be like to kiss her in the full knowledge of how deeply he loved her. To hold her in his arms and feel the wild sweetness of her response to him. To feel the tenderness restraining his own wild ardour.

And then to release her, knowing that it might be for ever.

She had asked him to kiss her. She had wanted to know.

Knowledge. Not possession.

His soul flared in rebellion: not yet, he promised himself. But it was a start. That kiss had allayed his greatest fear: that Thea's refusal to marry him might spring from fear. Fear and distaste for what would happen in the marriage bed. Believing that, he had resolved not to press her, but surely now she could not deny what lay between them, and her own response to it, any more than he could. And he could as soon deny his own breath.

He wanted her. Wanted to see her in his home. *Their* home. He wanted to see their children growing around them. If he could tell her that…or better, show her. He thought he understood what was holding her back. Doubt and fear. Doubt that he could possibly want her. A fear that his offer sprang from chivalry and pity, that he might one day come to resent her.

The idea slipped into place very simply. He needed to show her. Show her that she lay at the heart of what he wanted. And then, perhaps, he might be able to find the words to say what was in his heart.

Tucking her hand into his arm, he began walking again. He didn't have long. Almeria had finally decided to return to town.

'Thea, would you ride with me tomorrow afternoon?' he asked.

'Ride?'

'Yes, echo! Ride with me.' He took a deep breath. 'If Almeria intends to return to town the day after tomorrow… A last outing? Just the two of us?'

Chapter Sixteen

'Where are we going, Richard?' asked Thea, pushing her mare into a trot to keep up.

He grinned across at her. 'You'll see. How do you like Fidget's paces?'

'Very nice,' she said. 'What else would I expect from an earl's favourite mare? Don't change the subject! Where are you taking me?'

'Over the hills and far away?' he suggested. 'I'll tell you when we get there.'

Thea sighed. She ought not to have agreed to this ride. Being alone with Richard again like this was not wise. Not wise at all. Her treacherous heart sang and danced in joy that he wanted to be with her, had leapt wildly at the thought of riding out with him this afternoon. Even his teasing refusal to tell her their destination only added to her delight.

It was so long since anyone had arranged a surprise for her.

They cantered on in companionable silence over the Downs, past the great flocks of sheep, hearing the calls of larks riding the wind high above and further away the crash and roar of the sea boiling around the cliffs.

They came over the brow of a hill and Richard flung up his hand.

'Here we are,' he called, as they reined in.

He pointed down. Thea looked. There below in the valley, nestled in a beech wood, stood a house. An old rambling manor house; over the years it had been added to until it appeared to have simply grown there along with the trees and gardens. Smoke curled up from a chimney.

'Who lives here?' she asked. It felt familiar, yet she was sure she had never been there before.

He flashed her a smile. 'You'll see. Come along. And mind the track down. It's a little steep here. This is the back way in. Much faster than coming round by the roads.'

She followed him, letting the mare have her head, but prepared to gather her up in event of a stumble. At the bottom she found that they were in an orchard. Gnarled old apple trees were laden with blossom. She gazed around in delight as the mare followed Richard's gelding. They clattered into a cobbled stable yard and an old man came out, blinking.

'There yeh be, Mester Richard,' he said, without the least evidence of surprise, taking the bridle of Richard's horse as he dismounted.

'Good afternoon, Sam. This is Miss Thea. Thea, may I present Sam Decks?'

Thea smiled, masking her puzzlement.

'How do you do, Mr Decks?'

He touched his cap. 'Nicely, ma'am. Nicely.' Jerking his thumb over his shoulder, he said, 'Ye'll find the missus inside, sir. Been like a pea on a griddle, expectin' yeh this last hour.'

Richard's eyes twinkled. 'I'd better not keep her waiting any longer then.' He came over and Thea's heart and stomach pirouetted in a mad waltz as he set his hands to her waist and prepared to lift her down.

'Richard! I...your leg!'

He grinned. 'These are my arms, Thea. Nothing wrong with them.'

Memory stirred...his arms...remembered delight rippled through her—no, there was nothing wrong with them at all.

A wheezy laugh from the old groom drew her back, and she was being lifted to the ground in a gentle, inescapable grip. For a fleeting instant she met his eyes. Heat, wild and unbidden, leapt within her at their expression. Dark, intent. Breathless, she dropped her gaze. To his mouth. To the firm lips that had swept away the world and replaced it with a new one.

One in which she could not dwell.

Mercilessly she fought back the urge to lean against him, refused to believe that the strong, tender hands had lingered on her waist, that the withdrawing fingers seemed to trace and caress the curves.

No. It was impossible.

'What…who are we visiting?' she asked, wishing she didn't sound so breathless.

Richard didn't appear to have heard. He was leading her across the cobbles and out of the stable yard.

'We'd better go around to the front. Mrs Decks will skin me if I bring you through the kitchens this time.'

'Richard! Who is Mrs Decks?'

And what was so special about this time?

His smile was half-guilty. 'Well, she was my nanny. Mine and Max's, that is. Now she's my housekeeper.'

The world seemed to contract around her to utter stillness, even though she was still moving, following him along a flagged path around the house and its flowerbeds. Bees hummed, a blackbird flashed past them. At the front of the house a rather weedy carriage drive swept up to the front door. No wonder it felt familiar—it was exactly as he had described it. But why in the world had he brought her here?

'It's a trifle neglected,' said Richard ruefully. 'But it's gradually coming into order. I'll be moving in this week. All the staff will be here tomorrow, but today it's still just Sam Decks and his wife.'

The front door stood open and with a smile and bow, he ushered her over the threshold into a dim, flagged hallway, then called out, 'Nell?'

Firm steps were heard and an elderly woman came bustling into the hall.

'Well and surely! 'Tis about time, Master Richard.'

Bright eyes looked Thea over and Richard said, 'Nell, this is Miss Thea. She came down from London with Lady Arnsworth for the christening. I thought she would like to see the house.'

He turned to Thea. 'Thea, may I present Mrs Decks. She ruled Max and myself with a rod of iron. Terrorised us, I give you my word!'

Mrs Decks went scarlet. 'Oh, you and your nonsense! Pleased to meet you, I'm sure, miss. Enough to turn your hair grey, this one and his lordship. Looks like you just missed the rain and all. Setting in it is, Sam reckoned.'

Richard frowned. 'Hmm. Not precisely what I wanted. We might have to make a very quick tour and head back earlier than I planned. If it really blows in…'

Thea supplied the rest mentally—they would be in for a very wet ride back to Blakeney.

Turning to her, Richard said, 'Come and see the house, Thea. Then we can have a cup of tea and, if I know Nell, she will have baked a cake.'

Mrs Decks smiled fondly. 'I'll bring it all to the parlour in half an hour then, Mr Richard.'

Richard's house.

Thea followed him around, listening.

'I bought it a few months ago, but it needed work, so I stayed at Blakeney while it was done. There's quite a bit of land attached. Enough to keep me occupied. In fact, some of those sheep we saw on the way were mine.'

'Oh.' It felt so right for Richard. She could see him here, managing his land, reading his books…but—this was a house for a family. Gazing out the window of one of the bedchambers, she could almost see and hear children racing through the garden…wicked, dark-haired little boys who spent more time in mischief than out…one could have a swing under that big oak, and Richard's dogs would love it…he'd always had dogs. And the stables, now empty but for their mounts, would be full of horses. The whole place would be alive, brimming with joy, echoing with noise.

She bit her lip.

'Thea?'

'It's…it's lovely, Richard. I'm sure you will be very happy here.'

He smiled and came to her. 'Will I, Thea?'

She backed away. 'Yes. I am sure you will. Goodness! Just look at that sky! Positively threatening! Perhaps we should keep moving?'

Richard glanced out of the window, saw the clouds piling up in dark masses, and frowned. 'Damn. It does look murky. We'll have to gulp our tea and go.'

Mrs Decks had laid out a meal in the parlour, cakes, biscuits, bread and butter. A fire crackled in the grate, casting its golden dance about the room so that shadows shifted and played.

Richard watched as Thea poured tea. The light caught in her soft, coiled, tawny tresses, so that he longed to reach out and scatter her hairpins and release her hair and the light to tumble around her shoulders. He forced the thought down. Seducing Thea was not an option. She looked so…so *right* here. Somehow he had to convince *her* of that. Convince her that she belonged. Not *to* him. But here—*with* him. There was a slight rattle of the teacup in its saucer as she handed it to him and their fingers brushed.

Her eyes were wide, questioning. Lord! If the eyes were truly the window to the soul and she could see what was pouring through him, surging at the constraints of honour, she'd flee. At least with the tea table between them, she wouldn't see any more tangible evidence of the direction of his thoughts.

Thanking God for whoever had invented tea tables, he eased in his chair just as the rain began to patter fitfully against the window. Standing up again, he went to look out.

One glance at the sky settled his decision. Black clouds were piling in from the Channel. Even as he watched there was a distant flash, followed by a rumble of thunder. It wasn't going to be a gentle spring shower. This one meant business. Already gusts of wind were flinging the rain harder against the window panes.

'Richard?'

He turned to her. 'I'm sorry, Thea, but I rather think we're caught.'

'Caught?'

He nodded. 'There's no riding home in that, and I've no carriage here yet. It's going to blow, and blow hard. It's too exposed to take the short way over the Downs and if we go around by the roads it will take hours. I doubt the rain will let up much before morning.'

Another roll of thunder, closer this time, drove home his point.

Her face was white. '*Morning?* But…Richard, if we don't go home… I…we…' Her voice trailed off.

He didn't need the problem spelt out. Her reputation. Hell and damnation! This was the last thing he had wanted, for Thea, when he offered for her again, to have the least reason to think he offered out of the promptings of honour. Or worse, that she had been tricked because he wanted her fortune.

Very carefully he said, 'You know, it's not as bad as it looks at first sight, my dear. Nell is here. She can sleep with you. That should preserve the proprieties. And the only people likely to hear about the whole thing are those at Blakeney and I really can't see Braybrook, let alone Max and Verity, making an issue of it!'

'And Almeria?'

Yes, well. There was the rub. Almeria would be practically dancing a jig at the thought of a marriage between the pair of them.

'I can handle Almeria,' he lied. As long as he could make her see that delivering a long-winded discourse on duty and propriety would be just the thing to have Thea digging her heels in.

Judging by her raised brows, Thea didn't believe him.

He temporised. 'Very well, of course Almeria would do everything possible to force a marriage between us. And yes, she will see our non-return tonight as a blessing from heaven.' He smiled wryly. 'She'll be in alt! Thinking that I will be obliged to offer for you and that you will be forced to accept. And all the while she will be having a marvellous time deploring the moral turpitude of our generation in general and Max and myself in particular.'

'What a charming evening for your brother and sister,' said Thea, trying not to laugh.

Richard grinned. 'That's better! They won't mind. Make a pleasant change, I shouldn't wonder, to hear Almeria condemning *my* morals instead of Max's.'

Good. She was distracted.

'Then you won't be making another formal offer for my hand in the morning?'

That brought him up short. Obviously she wasn't distracted enough, confound it. He had every intention of making an offer for her hand the next morning. Not necessarily particularly formal, though. Kissing properly was one thing, but he wasn't sure how to kiss formally. This required some out-and-out duplicity. He summoned up his best glare. 'Thea Winslow, do you, or do you not, trust me?'

She glared back. 'Well, of *course* I trust you!'

Thank God for that!

'Then you may trust me when I say that I will make another offer of marriage to you, when I have fallen tail over top in love with you, and not before!'

'And…and you're not going to do that?'

Was there just the faintest hint of disappointment there?

'No,' he said firmly. 'I am not going to do that.'

But only because he'd already done it. Although he wouldn't like to swear that he mightn't fall even deeper into love with her. On his current record the whole thing seemed to become more overwhelming by the minute.

She met his gaze. 'I…very well, then. Should we—should *you* inform Mrs Decks?'

Yes. He most definitely should inform Nell. And warn her not to open her budget to Thea. Warn her that he hadn't offered yet, so that she didn't accidentally put her foot in it. One thing, he knew he could rely on Nell to keep her own mouth shut, along with keeping Sam's shut for him.

Nell, of course, thought it all highly romantic when he found her in the kitchen and explained matters.

Her face beamed. 'Well, of course I can dress a dinner for you. There's a chicken can be killed and don't you worry about a thing. What's that? Sleep with Miss Winslow?' Her eyes twinkled. 'No, we won't have any nasty gossip. Never you fear. I'll get on now and make up the rooms. And when will the pair of you be moving in for good?'

'Nell!'

'Oh, go on with you!' she said crossly. 'Think I can't see you're nutty on her? I won't say a word to your young lady, but don't you think to pull wool over my old eyes!'

Never before had Thea realised how dangerous a room could be. The parlour they retired to after dinner was full of temptation of the worst sort. The curtains had been drawn against the storming darkness, muffling the blattering of the rain. Mellow candlelight lit the room and a fire danced in the grate. Even the shadows were friendly in this cosy, intimate chamber.

That was the danger. The intimacy. Oh, not that she believed for one moment that Richard had designs on her non-existent virtue! But she felt so comfortable here. So at home. She had a dreadful feeling that through all the years ahead, the memory of this room would stand for all she had lost and could never regain.

Angrily she shook herself mentally as she sat down. That sounded remarkably like self-pity. Better to think of this room with joy. Not the bitterness of regret. It would be good to be able to picture Richard here. To know that he was happy.

'A game of chess? Or piquet?' offered Richard.

'Yes, please.' Anything to take her mind off what she really wanted—for him to kiss her again. She knew Richard's sense of honour. If he believed that his behaviour had in any way compromised her, the promise he had made earlier would be swept aside in what he would view as the greater obligation to her.

Ironic. The one man she could have given herself to joyfully was the one man from whom she must, at all costs, avoid an offer.

So, chess.

Except that she found herself distracted; watching him surreptitiously as he considered his moves, loving the concentration on his face, the half-frown as he watched her moves; nearly breathless as the long fingers took hold of a piece and she remembered the way he had touched her face, the tingling magic flickering in their wake.

Even the memory had warmth unfurling inside her, an ache of unbearable longing. Her fingers trembled as she reached for her queen and knocked several hapless pawns and Richard's bishop flying.

Flushing with embarrassment, she began to pick up the pieces, fumbling as she did so. A gentle hand closed over hers, stilling it, and every nerve quivered to life.

His large warm hand enveloped hers, his thumb caressing. Unconsciously her fingers clung as she lifted her gaze to his face. Dark need burned in his eyes, in the hard line of his mouth, in the fierce tension she sensed in his body. It should have terrified her, not awakened an answering need in her own body. Yet his hand held hers so gently.

Knowledge came to her then; she could stand up, leave the room and he would not make a single move to stop her. Indeed, he would open the door, summon Mrs Decks and bid her a goodnight.

If only…her heart cried out within her.

'I must have been mad,' he whispered, as he stood up, releasing her hand.

'Why?' she asked softly.

He came around the table to her and drew her to her feet.

'This.' He took her in his arms, brushing his cheek lightly over her brow. 'It's no good,' he said huskily. 'I've tried, but—if you will look at me like that…'

He broke off, drawing her against his hard body, soft curves fitting as though they belonged. She should stop him; this way lay madness. She knew that. But her heart and body were at odds with her common sense. There would be time later for sanity. A whole lifetime.

She could spare a few moments for madness.

Madness was a gentle mouth, caressing and possessing hers; steely arms supporting and cradling her body, tightening instantly as she melted against him. Madness was the joy of his hands, trembling as he released her curls in a pattering of hairpins and tangled his fingers in the thick coils that tumbled around her shoulders. Madness was her own response; her arms reaching up to pull him closer to her own, hot twisting need, her fingers sliding into his hair, her mouth and tongue answering the temptation of his.

Her name was a groan in his throat as he deepened the kiss, sending streamers of heat rippling through her core. She should stop him. She knew that. But she could no longer recall the reason.

He should stop. He knew that. But soft fingers brushed over his jaw in wondering tenderness, banishing the knowledge to oblivion. Such a simple touch to set the fire inside him blazing higher. He wasn't quite sure how they had ended up on the sofa together. A remaining particle of sanity and honour raised a feeble protest in some corner of his brain. He ignored it, heart and body intent on the same thing—the loving, intoxicating response of the woman in his arms. All fire and burning sweetness, she returned his kisses with a trust that consumed him.

He definitely ought not to be unbuttoning the bodice of her riding habit. But his fingers had other ideas and continued regardless. Shaking, he pushed the halves of her bodice apart, reaching in to cup a soft, full breast through the fine muslin of her shirt. The nipple sprang to life in his palm and every muscle in his body tightened in response.

He'd never known it could be like this. Desire, yes. He knew about that. But this was not merely desire. This was need, burning him alive as he clumsily unbuttoned her shirt, and sought the drawstring of her chemise. One tug dealt with that, and his fingers met silky, yielding flesh.

Her response was a sigh of pleasure that his mouth absorbed, and a shift of her body that pushed her breast more firmly into his hand. With an aching groan he released her mouth. Soft husky cries spilled from her lips as he slowly kissed his way down her throat and over the creamy curve of her breast. He should stop. He knew that. He even knew there was a reason. He just couldn't recall what it might be. Shuddering with need, he closed his mouth over the taut nipple and sucked gently.

Her whole body stiffened in shock. Not resistance. Simply shock.

It was enough. Honour won.

And not just honour. Love. And the need to protect her. Especially from himself.

She had not struggled. Nor had she protested. His conscience informed him pithily that she should not need to. With a wrenching effort, he forced himself to stop. For a moment he fought for control, for breath. This was Thea. His Thea. His love. He had sworn not to compromise her. And he was willing to swear that, despite all, she knew very little of the passion between a man and a woman.

Swearing mentally, he lifted from her.

'Richard?' Her voice was ragged, husky. Breathless.

'No more, sweetheart,' he said hoarsely. 'We mustn't. Not like this.'

She deserved a bed. Or at the very least his wedding ring on her finger. He wouldn't answer for making it as far as the bedchamber with her.

Her dazed eyes gradually focused. He saw the moment when control, and understanding, returned.

'I…I'm sorry,' she whispered. 'This…I never meant to make you do something you would regret…'

Regret?

'You didn't.' Every muscle locked with restraint, he leaned over and kissed her gently. 'But if I hadn't stopped—' his body roared a protest just thinking about it '—if I hadn't stopped, then we would have been anticipating our wedding vows.'

The moment the words were out, he realised his mistake, even before the look of shock hit her face and she began to struggle with the buttons of her bodice as she sat up.

'But—you promised! You said we wouldn't be compromised!'

'Dammit, Thea! That was before I kissed you!'

Slight understatement there, but there was no need to go into details. She knew perfectly well what he'd done.

'But, no one has to know you…kissed me!'

The blush on her face as she said it, her hesitation, nearly undid him.

'I'd know,' he said simply. 'But that's not the point.'

'And the point is?' She managed to do up two more buttons.

She was going to make him spell it out? Did she think he normally went about kissing innocents like that?

'The point is that I want to do it again!' he said shamelessly. Her blush deepened. He eyed it appreciatively, adding, 'And next time I don't want to have to stop!'

Her eyes widened and he took advantage of her shock to say, 'No more now, Thea.' He reached for the bell pull by the chimneypiece. 'I'll ring for Nell and you can go up with her. But let us have one thing straight: my offering marriage has nothing to do with our situation tonight, and everything to do with what just took place on that sofa! And why it took place.' He ran his hands through his hair. 'Think about it. Why do you imagine I brought you here to show you my home?'

He took one step towards her and stopped at the look of horror in her eyes. It cut him to his core.

'Sweetheart?'

Sweetheart. She swallowed convulsively, still fighting with her buttons. No. Not this. Not with him. The knife twisted relentlessly in her soul, slicing it open, as she saw the truth in his eyes.

Denial leapt, useless, to her lips.

'No, Richard. No. You can't!'

He smiled. A smile to tear a woman's heart from her breast. 'Oh, yes, I can. I do. I love you, Thea. That's why I brought you here. To see my home. To convince you that I love you. That you belong here. I was planning to ask you again to marry me tomorrow. Spending the night here was *not* part of my plan! I never wanted you to feel coerced.'

No. She knew that. Richard neither wanted nor needed her fortune. And even if he had needed it, he would never have coerced her into marriage. It was worse than that.

Richard had been all too convincing. He wanted *her*. Thea Winslow. Because he loved her.

In silence she finished setting her clothes to rights, then she drew a ragged, slicing breath.

'Richard—'

A gentle tap on the door announced the arrival of Mrs Decks, who bustled in cheerily.

In the morning. She would tell him everything on the way home, including the decision she had made. After which she supposed she would never see him again.

Never before had Richard felt like banging a door in Nell's face. All he could do was bid Thea goodnight and wonder what in Hades he had set loose. She couldn't, *couldn't* believe he'd trapped her for her fortune! And she certainly couldn't believe that if he had been frightened of compromising her further, that he would have been fool enough to touch her, let alone…kiss her. All right, let alone nearly bed her on the sofa!

So, why? *Why* was she still so dead set against marriage to him? That had been another refusal quivering on her lips. If Nell had not walked in just then—

He cursed. Given Thea's response, he refused to believe she didn't care. She was not the sort of woman to give herself lightly. Could it be that she still doubted *his* love? That she believed he would in the end resent her lost virginity? Would cast it up at her?

He could think of nothing else. Taking a deep breath, he looked around for a brandy decanter. And realised there wasn't one. It was definitely going to be a very long night.

Chapter Seventeen

The storm had largely blown itself out by the following morning. Heavy clouds still scudded overhead, but there was little rain, and Sam Decks, when consulted, gave it as his expert opinion that there would be little in the time it would take Mester Richard and his young lady to ride back to Blakeney.

'Better set out sharpish,' he opined. 'His lordship'll have a search party out by now, like as not. If so be as he don't come hisself. Be in a right tizzy with you not comin' back lars' night.'

Richard stared. And realised the truth of this statement. In fact, he wouldn't put it past Max to be saddling a horse right now, if he wasn't already halfway across the Downs.

He swore, eliciting a shocked look from old Sam, and strode back to the house. They had to start early. He had a very great deal to say to Miss Dorothea Winslow for which he most definitely did not desire an audience.

Thea went down to breakfast conscious of a headache, scratchy eyes and the sort of roiling stomach to be expected after a largely sleepless night.

Little beyond the commonplace was said over breakfast. With Mrs Decks coming in and out to see that they had everything they needed, it was impossible. For which she could only thank God.

No doubt he would open the subject of their marriage the moment they were out of the stable yard and she would have to tell him why she couldn't marry him. She thought he would understand even if he couldn't accept it. In the end, it didn't matter. On this she had to follow her conscience—that still, quiet voice that had lead her to this decision.

It was a lovely morning. Everything looked fresh and damp. Thea breathed it in deeply as she followed Richard around to the stable yard. Raindrops glistened and sparkled on flowers, turned cobwebs into nets of enchantment.

An illusion only. The enchantment was not for her.

Richard said nothing as they trotted out of the stable yard and back through the orchard and the tension gripping Thea tightened. She concentrated on the skittish mare, keeping her well up to her bit and curbing her early morning freshness.

Despite her edginess and longing to have the whole thing over with, she was grateful for Richard's silence as they rode up the now slippery track out of the valley to the Downs. But once on top she could put it off no longer.

'Richard, you must understand that I cannot possibly marry you,' she began quietly. If only he would accept that.

He nodded. 'Mmm. So you said last night. Or words to that effect. What you haven't explained is why.'

Her throat tightened.

He went on. 'You know perfectly well that I never intended to trap you into a compromising situation, do you not?'

She swallowed and nodded. It was unthinkable that she should take that way out.

'And after last night…' his voice softened to a caress '…you would be wasting your breath trying to convince me that you don't love me.'

'You can't know that,' she whispered.

His smile deepened. 'I can know that, Thea. Last night…if you didn't care for me, you would have stopped me.'

'It's partly because I care for you that I cannot marry you,' she said. Her cheeks burned. 'Richard—you cannot possibly want me. One day you would come to resent me. It would always lie between us. Perhaps even now you are wondering if…if my response to you last night was that of a…a wanton.'

She looked away. Surely that was enough. She stared straight ahead between the mare's ears and kept riding through the silence that stretched between them. Outside the silence a falcon screamed high overhead. Away on the Downs a flock of sheep grazed, the bleating of lambs drifting to them on the wind. And always the distant hushing of the sea around the cliffs.

Eventually he would say something. She bit her lip, conscious of the heat pressing behind her eyes, the choking sensation in her throat. Now, more than ever, she regretted last night's descent into madness. She felt cold all over, as though the sun had been put out.

'Thea Winslow,' he said fiercely, 'if you *ever* refer to yourself in that way again, I swear I'll put you over my knee and spank you! Who the hell put all that filth into your head? Your father? Your aunt?' He dragged in a breath. 'All last night tells me is that you love me.' He released the breath. 'You can't possibly think that I would condemn your behaviour when mine was exactly the same.' He grimaced. 'Worse! I was the one doing the actual seducing!'

'You can't know that I love you!' she flashed, quelling the agonising flare of hope. 'I…I might behave like that with every man who kisses me!'

'Then you wouldn't be telling me so now. And you wouldn't have told me the truth to stop me challenging Dunhaven.'

'This…this is impossible,' she whispered.

'No, it's not,' he said. 'Thea, I love you. Come, sweetheart. Can you not trust me a little bit further?'

In all her nightmares Thea had never imagined this—that Richard would accept her lost innocence so completely. That he would still be prepared to marry her. She *couldn't* accept. Not yet. Not now. There was the child…she had to make sure that her child was safe, provided for. Once she accepted Richard's offer, she could no longer make any disposition of her own property…and if he did not agree, there would be nothing she could do, except break the betrothal.

A yell brought her head up. Galloping towards them were two horsemen.

'Damn!' muttered Richard. 'Max and Julian. We can't talk about this now, Thea. When we are back at Blakeney. But understand this—I am not holding to my offer of marriage out of some idiotic notion of chivalry or pity or whatever other excuse you can dream up. I'm offering because I love you!'

'How can you?'

His answer nearly destroyed her.

'How? God knows. Why does anyone fall in love? Why does Max love Verity? He'd tell you all the wonderful things about her. Her courage, her loyalty, her honesty.' He grinned. 'Her temper. All things which I can see and love in her. But I am not *in* love with her. So, no, Thea. I cannot tell you why I have fallen in love with you. Only that I have. But you gave me the truth. You could have simply refused me. Or if you wished to marry, you could have said nothing.' He flushed. 'Sometimes…sometimes these things are not obvious, you know. I certainly would never have suspected.'

He met her eyes. 'But that never occurred to you, did it? Instead you told me the truth because you foolishly thought that would stop me challenging Dunhaven. It didn't. What stopped me was the knowledge that doing so would worsen any scandal for you. Thea—what happened eight years ago is done. Past. It wasn't your fault. Leave it there, sweetheart, and we can have the future.'

Lord Blakehurst and Lord Braybrook had reined into a trot and brought their mounts around in a wide circle to join them.

'Blast you, Ricky,' called Lord Blakehurst as he came up. 'Do you have any idea of how worried Verity was last night when you didn't come home?'

'Verity?' scoffed Lord Braybrook. 'It wasn't *Verity* talking about saddling a horse and coming out to look for them. At midnight, no less!'

'Oh, shut up, Julian!'

Richard grinned. 'We were safe enough. We were still at Tarring when the storm hit. Nell Decks looked after us.'

'Well, I thought that would be the case,' said Blakehurst, looking slightly embarrassed, 'But still…oh, very well! I was concerned! But only about Miss Winslow and my mare!'

Despite her pain, Thea laughed. Lord Blakehurst didn't fool her for one instant. Of course he had been worried about his brother. The link between them was almost palpable. Pain slashed at her; he would be even more worried if he knew what sort of woman his brother wanted to marry.

Lord Braybrook grinned. 'Nell Decks? Your old nanny?' His expression became mournful. 'Poor Lady Arnsworth. At least half the pleasure of her evening has been cut up!' He continued, 'Naturally she started out by condemning your carelessness, Ricky, not to mention your morals! I must say I was astonished at the details of your life that she seemed to know. You really ought to be more discreet. Anyway, by the time the tea-tray was brought in—and I do suspect Lady Blakehurst of ordering it early!—she was planning the wedding.' He cocked a brow at Richard. 'Obviously with Nanny Decks to play gooseberry, there's not the least need?'

'None,' said Richard flatly. 'At least not on that head.'

'Oh?' Lord Braybrook looked intrigued.

Richard's mouth tightened.

'Julian?'

'Hmm?'

'Shut up.'

Lord Blakehurst broke in. 'Before you call each other out and have to decide which of you has me as a second—there's something I have to tell Miss Winslow.'

She turned to him with relief.

He smiled. 'Ignore them. Especially Richard. What I have to tell you is that a letter arrived for you shortly after you left yesterday. An express.'

Thea's stomach clenched and chills washed through her. Only one person would have sent her an express. Rufton. He must have completed his investigation and sent in his report. And Almeria's butler had sent it on.

'Might I suggest we pick up the pace a trifle?' said Lord

Blakehurst. 'If Miss Winslow is agreeable, of course. It is just that Verity was a trifle concerned about you both.' His mouth twitched. 'And Almeria, of course.'

'Certainly, sir,' said Thea, forcing herself to appear calm. The sooner she knew the contents of that report, the better.

The child was called Sophie Grey. *Sophie*—her own middle name.

Numb, Thea stared at Rufton's report. And found the words blurring before her eyes. It didn't matter. Their accusation was seared into her heart. The child's age—they had not, after all, altered the birth date... The village where she had been raised—not five miles from Aunt Maria—by the daughter of the midwife who had attended the birth. And then an unknown benefactor had sent her to Miss Dale's Seminary in Bath last year. It all fitted.

All these years... They had lied to her, all of them. Even the doctor and rector. For her own good, no doubt. And she had believed the lies without ever bothering to question.

Sophie.

The rector's cold comfort echoed... *God has been merciful. 'Twas better that the child died rather than being born into such sin. Indeed, 'tis possible that the child's death is punishment for the sin of its parents. The Good Book tells us that it must be so: the sins of the fathers shall be visited upon the children unto the last generation...*

A child's life and death seen as an instrument of punishment. And used as a lie. Her mouth tasted sour with bile and her unspoken hopes crumbled to ashes. The nausea intensified.

Sophie. Her child's name was Sophie...

She was as guilty as the rector, guilty in that she had hoped, *prayed,* that her suspicions were unfounded, that the child was indeed her father's bastard. In doing so, she too had wished the death of her own child.

She could not sleep. She had dozed in the afternoon and dined on a tray in her bedchamber. Now, long after midnight, she knelt at her window sill, staring out into the dark of a moonless night. Only it was not truly dark. Above, the heavens sang with cold light. Not enough light to see by, but a reminder that the light was there. Beyond her reach.

It had always been beyond her reach, that particular light.

Or was it? She did have a choice. The letter did not mean that she had to act. It had given her the truth. At the start that was all she had wanted. Only she had not reckoned on the fact that truth was not inanimate. It had its own life and demands. It could not compel her. But it could destroy her. She understood now what Rufton had meant when he warned her to be quite sure she wanted the truth.

She had sought out the truth and now she must live with it. If she did not, she would have to live with her own conscience instead.

She closed her eyes, exhausted, leaning on the sill. Sounds came to her; the bark of a fox, the wind sighing in the beech woods, just as it must be over at Tarring House. It was all so lovely. And it would remain so, despite her own pain. Yet she could not find it in her to regret what had passed.

He truly loved her. Her heart ached in joy as she permitted her mind to drift. For the first time in years memory was not a nightmare beast dragging her into horror; it took her only as far as the previous night, when Richard had shown her what might have been. If only, she dreamed, if only he had not stopped. She wished, oh, how she wished… Her head slipped and she jerked awake as her brow bumped the sill. She had nearly fallen asleep, she realised. Stiffly she rose to her feet. Lady Arnsworth was returning to London in the morning. She would return with her.

There was, after all, only one choice that she could make. And it was not a choice that any honourable man would be able to countenance.

'Are you sure, Thea?' asked Verity, worry clouding her grey eyes. 'You need not go simply because Almeria must return. If there was a reason…I mean, if you wished to stay, we would

all—' she broke off, catching herself up '—that is, Lord Blakehurst and I would be delighted for you to remain.'

Thea bit her lip. This was dreadful. She had raised expectations and they were all expecting her to stay on. And she could
not.

'I am sure, Verity. I must go. There…there is something I must
do.'

Verity brightened. 'Is that all? Well then, you may come back
afterwards. It is only a few hours' travel. I'll send the carriage
up for you.'

Disappointing Verity was nearly as hard as hurting Richard.
She shook her head. 'I'm sorry, Verity. For everything. There will
be no going back.'

Verity blinked. 'Thea, what are you talking—?' She broke off
and heaved a sigh of relief. 'Here he is! Richard—do come and
talk some sense into Thea. She is insisting that she must return
to London.'

Thea faced Richard. His face was weary, as though he had
slept as little as she these past two nights.

'Perhaps you would walk with me in the garden first, Thea,'
he suggested. 'Almeria is unlikely to depart for another hour at
least.' He turned to his sister-in-law. 'If you will excuse us, Verity?'

She smiled. 'Of course. I must go upstairs to the nursery and
see to Will. You will not let Thea go without saying goodbye?'

He shook his head. 'No. Off with you. I'll take care of Thea.'

He meant that in every sense of the phrase. He wanted to take
care of her. Always. But he could see in the lift of her chin, in
the set of her mouth, that her decision was made. But why? She
knew he loved her, and he no longer held the least doubt that she
loved him. So it must be fear that he could not truly accept her,
that he would resent her past…

The fragrance of the gardens breathed around them in the soft
sunshine. He took her to the knot garden, dreamy and pungent
with herbs, its low lavender hedges weaving about the rainbow-
filled fountain at its heart.

Sitting on a wooden bench, she told him without preamble, truth like a slashing knife cutting across the song of the water. His brain froze with shock and for a moment he was utterly speechless as he grappled with it.

Finally, 'A *child?*'

She nodded.

Numbed, he took a very deep breath and waited for the knowledge to sink in, to feel something. Anything. He did not know *how* he felt. Anger, perhaps. Confusion, certainly.

'Why did you not mention this earlier?'

'I…I did not know.'

'A little hard to miss, I would have thought.' For the life of him he could not prevent the sarcasm slicing through. He saw her flinch, knew that it had cut deep, but still he could feel nothing. Until she lifted her eyes and he saw her pain.

And even then, he did not know what the emotion was that he felt. Only that it was likely to tear him apart.

'When I…when the baby was born…I…they gave me laudanum…straight after the delivery. Before I even held the…her. I *didn't* hold her. When I woke up finally, it was the next day…and they told me—'

Her voice cracked and before he could think, he was kneeling beside her, enveloping her cold hands in his, knowing only that she was hurting, that she had never told anyone this.

She dragged in a breath and continued in a hard little voice. 'They told me the baby had died. Had died and was buried. They would not even tell me the child's sex. They said…they said it was better not to know. When I asked about the grave…they said *it* died without baptism, that the grave was unmarked.'

'And you did not know this yesterday?'

'Not…not definitely,' she whispered.

Understanding flared then. 'The letter?'

She nodded. 'Yes. One of Lady Chasewater's notes had made me wonder. Apparently she discovered after Lord Chasewater's death that the child lived.' She shuddered. 'I did not wish to believe her, but I knew my father could have covered it up, so—'

'You asked him?'

A savage laugh ripped from her. 'Asked him? No. He would have lied. I searched his study for information. When I had it, I hired a runner to find her for me. I knew the school she was, *is,* placed at. And her initials. At first I merely wished to ensure that she was safe, and happy. But now—'

Struggling to cope with the enormity of what she had told him, Richard held her hands gently, feeling her tension. There was more. He knew that.

'What now?' he asked quietly.

'You must see, Richard...I cannot leave it like that. Apparently my father has provided for her all this time, but—'

'Of course,' he said. Typical of Thea. She wished to support the child herself. He could understand that. 'We can arrange to have all her expenses met. Set aside some of your fortune as a dowry so that she can make a respectable marriage. You can make enquiries about the school. If you are not happy, she can be moved. This need make no difference—'

'It makes every difference,' said Thea. 'She needs a family...a mother, at least, so—'

'*No!*' Denial burst from him. 'Dammit, Thea! It's too much! No man would stand for it! If you really wish it, then you may visit your child occasionally. Anonymously. You cannot ask me to accept the child of the man who raped you!'

'I have not asked that of you, Richard,' she said steadily. 'And I will not.'

He took a ragged breath. 'I...I beg your pardon, if I misunderstood.'

She shook her head. 'No, you have not. Only that I am not asking you to accept Sophie.'

'Sophie?'

'That is my daughter's name.'

'Then—'

'Richard, I cannot marry you—'

'You are refusing my suit because I will not—*cannot!*— accept your...your child?'

'No. I am refusing your suit because *I* will not ask you, or any man, to accept my base-born daughter. She is mine. And her illegitimacy is at least partially my fault.'

He could hear the pain. Feel it. Hers as well as his. And, steady despite the pain, he could hear her determination.

'*Your* fault?'

She nodded. 'Yes. Had I not let David know the truth, I think I would have been too frightened not to marry—she would have been legitimate.'

Conflicting emotions stormed inside him. He couldn't name even one of them. All he could think was that he had lost her, that her decision was made and that there would be no turning her back from it.

'Thea, I need to think,' he said very softly. 'I am sorry if—'

Thea's breaking heart stilled. He was going to apologise.

'No!' she said vehemently. 'You will *not* apologise!' Tears stood in her eyes. She held them back, refusing to let them fall. 'You are such a *good* man! You offered so much more than I had any right to expect, but…it is just, there are some things…'

Some things that one's conscience cannot bear. Some things that one cannot negotiate on. She left the words unspoken. She had said enough. Had she still doubted that Richard loved her, his shattered eyes and white face would have convinced her.

He turned away. His voice harsh, he said again, 'I need to think.'

She could not speak for the choking grief in her throat, could barely see him for the tears crowding, spilling over in silent loss. He walked away towards the house and the rainbows shimmering in fleeting loveliness in the fountain dissolved in mist as she whispered, 'God bless you, Richard.' She would not see him again and force him to say the words.

An hour later she was in the chaise travelling back to London with Lady Arnsworth. Verity and Lord Blakehurst had farewelled them. Richard was nowhere to be seen.

After an appalling journey, during which Lady Arnsworth progressed from reasonably subtle hints about the supposed forthcoming nuptials between Thea and Richard, to outright demands to know why in heaven's name Thea had not leapt at the chance to re-establish herself fully, Thea found herself back in Grosvenor Square late in the afternoon, facing Lord Aberfield. His shock was palpable as he read the report she had given him.

'You…you hired a Bow Street *runner?*' He seemed unable to believe it, his eyes wide with disbelief.

She shrugged, determined to seem unmoved. 'It seemed the obvious way to discover the truth.' She had not given him a chance to deny it all, simply flinging the report at him and demanding to know why he had lied to her.

Suddenly he seemed an old man as he sank down into a chair. 'Dorothea—you didn't think to ask me?'

Disbelief lashed her. 'Ask *you?* You *lied* to me. All these years I believed that she had died! Who arranged that?'

At that he seemed to recover slightly. 'We were trying to protect you!' he said angrily. 'Good God! It would have been better if the child *had* died! As it is, I have paid for her education and seen to her future. You need not concern yourself. She will remain at the school and be trained as a governess—'

'Have you ever seen her?'

'*Seen* her?' Had she suddenly grown three heads he could not have looked more shocked.

'Visited her,' said Thea evenly. 'Does she know that she has a family?'

Lord Aberfield frowned. 'This is excessive sensibility, Dorothea. Most ill judged. It is unnecessary to see the child. Indeed it would be most improper! One does not visit a child of *that* sort. Better that she remains in ignorance of her background. To regard her as a member of the family—impossible! To visit would only breed a…a spirit of resentment.' He shook his head. 'That is not how these things are done. If you wish, you may see Miss Dale's reports—'

'Does she think that Sophie Grey is *your* daughter?'

Aberfield's lips thinned. 'Very likely. I merely entered the child as my ward. I did not consider her parentage to be any of Miss Dale's concern.'

'Very well. Then you will write a letter to Miss Dale, asking her to release Sophie Grey into my custody, *as her mother*.'

'*What?*'

Thea faced him squarely. 'She is my daughter and I am well able to provide for her.'

'She is already provided for! For God's sake, girl! Think! Do you believe that Blakehurst will countenance this? He will never marry you—'

'There is no betrothal, nor has there ever been. We are agreed that we shall not suit.'

'*What?* Almeria Arnsworth assured me before you left London that—'

'She was mistaken, my lord,' she said quietly. 'There is no more to be said. The child is mine. You will write that letter. After which you need never see me again.'

'Dorothea—there is no need for this. I take it you told Blakehurst the truth, that you are not…that you…' He wiped his brow. 'Naturally he would not accept your, er…*explanation,* but I could still see him. After all, the match is still very much to his advantage, so I could—'

'Explain that you had given Lallerton permission to address me and he interpreted that as permission to rape me?'

'For God's sake, girl! All this talk of rape! You were betrothed! Naturally I would have preferred that he waited until you were married before bedding you, but it was not *rape!*'

Her stomach churned. 'Of course, you would know, my lord,' she said with savage irony. 'You were the one being held down, begging him to stop.'

He flinched. 'Dorothea—think!' he said. 'Years it's taken me to win back the position I lost when you refused Lallerton in a fit of missishness. And now it will be known that my daughter has a bastard!'

'No,' she said quietly. 'I am willing to use another name. No one need know. Unless you refuse to write that letter to the school. And you will also write a declaration that the child is mine. To be witnessed and held by my lawyer.'

'Damned if I will!'

She shrugged. 'No. Damned if you don't, my lord. And damned if you don't release enough of my money for me to live on comfortably. Because I will make the whole thing public.' Remembering something, she added, 'With Lady Chasewater's help.'

She watched with calm interest as his eyes bulged. It might take a few moments for him to realise, but he had no room to manoeuvre. The risk of scandal was too great. Without a word she strolled over to the chair by the window and sat down.

'What do you think you're doing?' he barked.

'Waiting for you to come to your senses and write the letter to Miss Dale,' she replied. 'You really have no choice.'

'And what about this other document?' he snapped.

She frowned thoughtfully. 'I shall speak to my lawyer and have it properly drawn up and brought to you for signing. There must be no doubt that you acknowledge the child to be mine and in my sole custody. For now the letter to the school will suffice.'

'And you promise to stay away from us and use another name?'

'You have my word. I do not wish to cause trouble. All I want is my daughter.'

Thin lipped, he stalked to his desk and began to write, the scratching of the pen the only sound. Finally he stopped writing and looked up.

'Do you wish to read it before I seal it?'

She shook her head. 'It should not be necessary. You cannot possibly desire a scandal over this. And there will be one if you have attempted to trick me.'

Silently he reached for the pounce box, sprinkled sand on the letter, then sealed it and held it out.

She stood up and drew on her gloves and went to receive the letter, tucking it into her reticule. 'Thank you, sir. My lawyers will draw up the other document as soon as possible. If you should wish to contact me at any stage, you may direct your request to them. I dare say we will not meet again.'

'Damn it, girl! You can't disown your family for a bastard child you didn't even know existed!'

She smiled then. 'Yes, sir, I can. As easily as you disowned your daughter for a sin she did not commit. Goodbye, my lord.'

Her interview with David the following morning was worse. She could no longer feel anything with Aberfield. But David…

'For God's sake, Thea!' he implored. 'Where will you live? Under what name? You realise you will have to pretend to be a widow? And what of Richard Blakehurst? I had hoped—' He broke. 'Thea?'

Pain streaked through her, all the hurt and misery that she had refused to feel.

'It is at an end.'

Not that she blamed Richard. It was not his fault. She had never expected him to accept her child. No man would be prepared to do such a thing. She had known that when she had made her decision.

David came to her and took her hands gently 'Are you sure this is necessary? I understand the child has been well provided for. She will be safe enough. For once in his life, perhaps the old man is right. Would it not be wiser—?'

'To leave her without a family?' asked Thea quietly.

'Damn it, Thea! That was not your fault!'

She shook her head. 'Yes, it was, David. Had I not been such a naïve little fool and realised that I might be with child, I would have agreed to the marriage. There would have been no other choice. And she would not now be a bastard. That bit in the Bible…about the "sins of the fathers"? I've always hated it. I can't condemn my own child for her father's crime.'

'Thea, must you—?'

'She needs a family, David. Even if it is only me.'

'You will permit me to visit you?'

Her heart leapt. 'You would do that?'

'I would do that. I shall like having a niece.' Bitterly he said, 'Blakehurst is a fool!'

Sudden fear consumed her. 'No. He is not. You will give me your promise, David, that you will not quarrel with him over this.'

'Dash it, Thea! I—'

'Your promise, David!' If he were to challenge Richard… Her heart lurched in terror at the thought.

He swore under his breath. 'Very well,' he went on. 'You have it.' He looked at her narrowly. 'You love him, do you not?'

'Yes. I returned his love.'

David stared. 'You returned—? And yet he will—'

She flung up her hand. 'Ask yourself: what would you do in his position?'

His eyes fell.

She smiled sadly. 'Precisely.'

Chapter Eighteen

The chaise rocked on its way and Thea sat huddled in the corner, staring out at the passing countryside, scarcely seeing it. All she could see was Richard's set face, the dark eyes resigned, full of pain. Pain that she had caused.

Maybe this was for the best. He deserved better than to be caught in a trap of his own decency. As perhaps he had been. She did not think she could have borne it if they had married and he had come to regret it or to resent her. His pain would pass. She had to believe that, and accept that one day he would find another woman to love.

Just as she had to accept that in comparison to her daughter's need, her own pain and despair could not be allowed to matter. There would be no one else for her.

She forced herself to think of Sophie Grey. The child she had borne; who had been taken away, brought up without knowing anything about her parents, believing herself unwanted.

Shame seared her. The memory of her initial relief when they told her the child had died—memory took her further back, remorseless. The day she had first felt the baby moving, an intangible fluttering within her and had realised it as a physical presence for the first time. Had realised that an innocent was condemned to bastardy.

Almost against her will, she had begun to wonder if it might be possible to keep the baby—and then the terror would take her, the fear choking her in nightmares that came each night, dreams when she relived what had been done to her. Feeling the child kick inside her then had terrified her.

She had been relieved when Aunt Maria told her that the babe had died. It had never occurred to her to doubt the lie. Why should she? Her parents and Aunt Maria had already settled it between them that the baby was to be fostered—she had been so dazed and panic-stricken at events that she had not so much as murmured a protest. All the protest had been shocked out of her. Yet in the end they had lied and told her the child was dead. Perhaps they had even meant it kindly, thinking to spare her.

And, yes, she had been relieved at first. And then had come more shame, more guilt, that she could have felt relief at the death of one who had been totally and utterly innocent of everything. Relief at the death of a baby who had been given no chance for life at all.

And now? Now she had the chance to put it at least partially right. She could give her daughter at least some part of the life that should have been hers.

If it was not too late.

Seven years. Seven years for Sophie to know herself unwanted by her family, an object of disgrace. Seven years knowing little but resentment. What if the child hated her?

A shudder racked her—what if her daughter resembled Lallerton? What if *she* could not look on her daughter without being reminded…no! She would not allow that to weigh with her!

She had made the right choice, the only choice, but the memory of Richard's hurt, and the knowledge of what she had lost, left an aching void within her.

Richard sat staring into the fire. He had not bothered to light the lamps. It was still light outside, but he had drawn the curtains early against the chill of the evening. A book lay abandoned on the wine table beside him. He didn't feel like reading—for once in his life the solace of the printed word had failed utterly.

Around him, Tarring felt empty, echoing. Which was patently ridiculous. He had moved in today and knew for a fact that it was full of people, his staff, all of them hell-bent on making him far more comfortable than he had any right to be. But in two days since Thea's return to London the whole world had felt like a sunless wasteland. He'd left Blakeney without a word to either Max or Verity, leaving a brief message. He'd needed to think, not talk. But now...

What in Hades was he to do, all by himself, in a house like this that had been intended for a family? The question had not occurred to him when he had bought the estate. He had vaguely thought that one day, he would marry, bring his bride here and set up his nursery. It had been a pleasant thought, something to look forward to in a comfortable sort of way.

That was before he had met Thea again. Before he had fallen in love. And before he had lost her. Now the house echoed drearily, where before its quietness had seemed to wait in anticipation. Now all the improvements he had planned seemed futile, a way to fill time that stretched out relentlessly.

She would never forgive him.

God in heaven, what a damned fool he'd been. What a blind, stupid, insensitive fool.

He took a sip of his brandy, and swallowed, watching the flicker of firelight in the amber liquid.

The door opened.

He didn't bother to look up. He knew who it would be.

'His lordship, sir.'

'Thank you, Minchin. I won't need you again tonight.'

'No, sir. Good night, sir.'

The door shut and Max said, 'For God's sake, Ricky. It's like a tomb in here. I received your message.' The bright eyes narrowed. 'What's amiss?' Then, urgently, 'Ricky, are you all right? Your betrothal—'

Trust Max to see straight to the heart of the disaster.

'Is off,' said Richard. Not that it was going to be off for long if he had anything to say about it, but at this moment that was the literal truth. It might remain the truth; it was entirely possible that Thea would tell him to go to the devil when he caught up with her.

'What the devil d'you mean?' rapped out Max.

Richard sighed wearily. 'Have a brandy…' he waved at the decanters on a side table '…and let me tell you a story.'

Max poured himself a glass of brandy, and sat down in the wingchair on the opposite side of the fireplace. 'Something tells me I'll be needing this.'

Richard avoided his eyes. The worried frown shamed him. Once Max knew…

Quietly, he told the story, as it had been revealed to him, leaving nothing out. Max sat listening, occasionally sipping his brandy. At the end he tossed off the rest and went to pour himself another. Richard waited.

'She refused to marry you for the sake of a child she had thought dead? A child most sensible women would be only too glad to ignore.' Max's voice was quiet, non-committal.

Richard nodded. A mother who would not abandon her child, regardless of the cost to herself. Exactly what he had wanted.

'She chose her child's happiness and safety over her own?'

Still Richard could only nod, his heart aching. Max had seen it immediately, as Richard had known he would. Why the hell had it taken *him* so long to see it? Was he so caught up in his own self-importance that he had not seen her courage? Her integrity?

'It won't be easy, Ricky,' said Max quietly. 'People will realise the truth. There will be some who'll never accept her. Are you willing to live with that?'

Yes. It made no difference to him.

He looked straight at Max. 'Will you support me?'

Max stared at him, jaw sagging, as if in utter disbelief. 'Confound it, Ricky! Did you have to ask? And would it make any difference?'

Richard's lips twitched at the outrage evident on his twin's face. 'Not the least. But I had to tell you. My mind is made up and there will be no hiding the truth. I don't give a damn what anyone says. Not even you. I'm going to marry Thea Winslow and her daughter will be accepted as my own.'

If Thea will have me now. If I haven't ruined everything with my stupid pride.

Max smiled at him. 'Good. I shall enjoy having a niece to spoil until Verity does her duty and provides me with a daughter or two.'

'A niece?' Did Max mean what he thought he meant? He had known that Max would accept his decision, would publicly support him, but...

Reading his mind, Max answered the unvoiced question. 'Your daughter will bear the name Blakehurst, will she not, Ricky?' He smiled. 'As such she will be my niece. Tell Miss Winslow that. Tell her that I will be proud to stand up for you. And to act as godfather to your *next* child.'

Calmly he tossed off his brandy and rose. 'I'm going home to Verity. No doubt you'll be making an early start tomorrow? I suggest that you bring them back to Blakeney before the wedding. It will take a couple of days to get the licence—shall we say, Friday week? That gives you ten days. I'll tell the rector.'

That was a bit much. Richard gave him a frosty look. 'D'you know, I think I can just about manage to get married without your advice, brother.'

Max raised a brow and grinned. 'Oh? The same way I managed to sort out my marriage?'

Richard laughed. '*Touché.* Lunacy must run in the family.'

Max snorted. 'Ah, well. At least we're doing our damnedest to breed it out. Congratulations, Ricky.'

Richard stood up. 'You haven't said it yet, Max.'

'Said what?' asked Max. 'Oh—that you're a damned idiot? It would be a case of the pot speaking to the kettle. Besides, you know it already.' He frowned and said slowly, 'There is one thing that occurs to me, though.'

'What?'

Max frowned. 'Stubble it...I'm thinking.'

Richard waited. Max's frown had deepened as he stared out of the darkening window.

'You know,' he said at last, 'society is really very hypocritical about these things.'

'Fancy that,' said Richard drily.

'Yes, they are,' continued Max. 'No one would turn a hair if you had an illegitimate child—except to mutter that they'd always known you couldn't possibly be as sober living as everyone thought.'

'Pardon?'

'And gloating over what a complete scoundrel you were to make up to Miss Winslow, convince her to marry you, and *then* foist your bastard daughter on her.'

All Richard could do was stare in disbelief at his twin, who grinned and said, 'I believe you pointed out to me last year that love had completely addled my wits? Welcome aboard, Ricky!'

Making an early start the following morning, Richard drove through the Knightsbridge Turnpike as dusk was falling. Carefully he guided his horses through the streets to Grosvenor Square, drawing up outside Arnsworth House.

He got down, passing the ribbons to his groom. 'Take them around to the stables here. Her ladyship won't mind. Have a fresh pair in the shafts first thing in the morning, I'll be making an early start.'

'Yessir.'

Richard stared across the Square. He'd sent a messenger ahead. Aberfield should be expecting him. Hoping that his self-discipline was up to the interview ahead, he walked around to Aberfield House.

Aberfield received him in the library, rising from his desk as Richard limped past the butler, still wearing his greatcoat, hat and driving gloves.

'Your coat and hat, sir?' asked the butler.

Richard shook his head. 'I won't be here long enough for you to trouble.' He jerked his head at the door. 'Out.'

'How dare you dismiss my servant, sir!' blustered Aberfield, coming around the desk towards him.

Richard raised his brows. 'I do beg your pardon, Aberfield.' He turned to the butler. 'You had better stay and listen, then.'

'That will be all, Carnely!'

Aberfield glared at Richard.

He waited only until the door closed behind the butler. 'You should be horsewhipped, Aberfield,' he said softly. 'What the hell did you think you were doing?'

The older man paled and took a step back reaching for the bell pull.

'I wouldn't,' said Richard, in conversational tones. 'You really don't want your staff speculating on the reason for my visit, do you?'

'For God's sake, man! There was no intent to deceive. Had you applied properly for Dorothea's hand, you would have been apprised—'

'Apprised? Apprised of what, Aberfield?' asked Richard, his voice a silken whip. 'What do you imagine to be the cause of my quarrel with you?'

'You feel deceived, naturally, now that Dorothea has confessed her lack of virtue.'

Richard's hands balled into fists. 'Her lack of virtue,' he repeated. 'I see.'

'You would have been told!' snapped Aberfield. 'Ask Dunhaven, if you doubt me! *H*e was told!'

With difficulty Richard restrained the urge to step forward and plant his right fist in the man's face.

'Really? You told Dunhaven that you had attempted to constrain your sixteen-year-old daughter into an unwelcome marriage and condoned Lallerton's actions when he raped her to force her consent.'

'Rape? Missish nonsense!'

Banked rage surged in every vein. 'And you told Dunhaven. You handed him a weapon so that he could coerce her! Do you call yourself a father? God help you, do you call yourself a man?'

'What the hell do you want, Blakehurst?' demanded Aberfield. 'You have declined to marry Doro—'

He broke off at the sound of the door opening.

'The hell I have!' snapped Richard, ignoring the door. 'What I want from you is the address of her daughter's school in Bath.'

'Why would you want to know that, Blakehurst?' came a cool voice from behind him.

Swinging around, Richard discovered David Winslow standing just inside the door, the grey eyes glittering.

'It's obvious, isn't it?' Richard said.

'Not entirely,' said Winslow, strolling over to the fireplace and leaning indolently against it. 'Spell it out.'

'I intend to marry her,' said Richard. 'What the devil did you think? That I would take her as my mistress?'

Winslow shook his head. 'You might have more success.' An expression of regret crossed his face. 'She seems quite determined not to marry you.'

Aberfield broke in. 'She's taken a foolish notion to raise the brat herself.'

Richard inclined his head. 'So I understand. Naturally I will acknowledge the child as mine.'

Shocked silence fell in the room.

Winslow straightened. 'You care that much?' His voice was oddly expressionless.

Richard didn't bother to reply. He was watching Aberfield, who had turned grey.

'You can't!' he whispered.

With a harsh laugh, Richard said, 'I've no desire to find out how thin your blood is, Aberfield, but I'm a Blakehurst. I can.'

'Damn your eyes, Blakehurst!' lashed Aberfield. 'You really must want that fifty thousand to counten—'

He broke off, backing away as Richard took a single step towards him.

With the speed of a panther Winslow got between them.

'Better not, Blakehurst,' he said, his voice tinged with regret. 'Much as he might deserve it, we can't afford the scandal if the servants get wind of anything.'

'Hah! There'll be scandal aplenty if he's fool enough to take the brat!' snarled Aberfield. 'From the reports I've had, the whelp's the spit of all the Winslows! Blue eyes, fair hair—you think people won't remember and put two and two together?'

Winslow swore softly, his hard gaze coming back to Richard.

Keeping his expression impassive, Richard said, 'You'd better hope they don't.' His voice hardened. 'Otherwise I'd have little choice but to let the entire story be known. And you wouldn't make a pretty showing, would you?'

It could only be a last resort. Unthinkable for the child to have the truth forced on her.

Something must have showed on his face, because Aberfield said with renewed confidence, 'Gives you to think, doesn't Blakehurst?' His expression became cunning. 'You persuade the girl to give up this ill-judged start and I'll arrange to release her money. No need to have it too carefully tied up.'

Richard opened his mouth to make an explicit and blasphemous recommendation about where Aberfield could go and what he could do with his offer when he got there.

Winslow's cool voice forestalled him. 'Not an insurmountable problem, sir.' He shot a steely glance at Aberfield, and turned to Richard. 'If I might make a suggestion?'

Richard nodded curtly.

A cynical glint in his eyes, Winslow said, 'What I propose, Blakehurst…'

Thea stepped out of the chaise and stared up at the narrow house. A shiver passed through her at the forbidding aspect.

The entrance hall was grey. Grey and respectable. A pall of silence hung over the house. She waited impatiently while the maid who had admitted her took her card to the headmistress. Eventually the study door opened and the maid returned, dropping another curtsy.

'Miss Dale will see you now, ma'am.'

Steeling herself, Thea entered. This woman's opinion did not matter to her, could not harm her. She did not care what the woman thought.

Miss Dale rose. 'Miss Winslow? I understand from your letter that you are come to remove Sophie Grey.'

Thea nodded. 'That is correct.'

'You understand that she is under the guardianship of…' The woman hesitated, plainly unwilling to divulge the child's guardian. She primmed her mouth. 'I cannot simply hand her over.'

Thea took a deep breath. She would not shirk any of this. Easy to hand over Aberfield's letter, which merely told Miss Dale that Sophie Grey was to be given into the charge of the bearer, Miss Winslow, but she *would* not. Sophie should be acknowledged as her daughter.

'She has been under the guardianship of Lord Aberfield. Here is his letter resigning the charge to me. I am Sophie's mother.'

A frown creased Miss Dale's brow as she took the proffered letter. It deepened as she read it. When finally she looked up, her eyes were cold. 'I see. Very well, there is nothing more to say. I will have the child sent for and a maid shall pack her belongings.'

She rose. 'You will excuse me, I am sure, *Miss* Winslow.'

'Certainly,' said Thea. 'There is one thing—Sophie will not be told who awaits her, just that she is to be taken away to a home of her own. You will leave it to me to explain who I am.'

A chilly nod was the only reply and Thea could have sworn the woman drew her skirts aside as she passed.

She waited, fear creeping through her tiredness. What if the child disliked her? What if she looked like her father? What was she to do if she could not love the child? Sophie; her name was Sophie. She was not 'the child' any more. She was a little girl with a name, and soon there would be a face with the name, a personality…it was not possible to hate a child of seven, no matter what her father had done.

The door opened and the maid came in. 'Miss Sophie.' Then, over her shoulder, 'Come along now, do. She's not about to bite you. In you go.'

A small child came through the door with obvious reluctance, her eyes huge in a pale face.

The maid gave her a kindly push over the threshold. 'There

you are then, lass. Don't be shy. The lady's come to take you to a real home.'

For a moment Thea simply stared as the maid closed the door. The soft fair curls were familiar, blue eyes gazed back as a small hand crept to the mouth.

'Sophie?'

A nod. Nothing more.

'Did they tell you anything? Who I am?'

The head shook faintly.

'No, ma'am. Just that…just that you are taking me away…to your home.'

At the wobble in the child's voice, Thea's heart shook. Would she hate being taken away from here, from her friends?

'Shall you mind that? Living with me?'

A vigorous shake this time. 'No, ma'am. Is it true? Will I have a real home like Lucy said? Not just here?'

'Yes, Sophie. Your own home.'

'With you?'

'Yes.' Her throat had developed a choking lump. There were things that must be said; but how to say them when her throat ached and her eyes stung viciously?

'Why?'

And there it was. The question that could not be fudged, and certainly could not be put off.

And in the end, the words came easily enough past the choking lump, breaking, but clear. 'Because…I am your mama.'

The child, Sophie, took two hesitant steps forward. And one back. The eyes were shuttered, suspicious. 'I don't have a mama. At least, not one who wants me. That's what they said.'

'No, Sophie,' said Thea, blinking back tears. 'That is not true. I do want you. But I didn't know about you until a few days ago. They told me you had died.'

'But I didn't,' said Sophie, plainly puzzled.

'No. And I do want you.'

'Are you really my mama?'

Thea shut her eyes, trying to hold back the tears.

'Yes. I really am.'

Sophie nodded solemnly. 'Am I allowed to call you Mama?'

No name had ever sounded sweeter, ever pierced so deeply. 'Of course, Sophie.'

Two more steps forward. And two more. And a small, sticky, inky hand reached for hers, clutched tightly. Gently Thea drew her daughter into her arms for the first time; held her safely for the first time since the child had left the sanctuary of her body. This was right. Completely and utterly right. Feeling, looking at the soft curls tucked beneath her chin, the small, warm body pressed against her, she knew, deep in her heart, that there could have been no other way.

For a moment there was a gentle silence, an aching regret for all the lost years, the lost achievements, the first smile, the first steps, the first words. And then came a fierce joy in this first meeting, in all the achievements to come. There would be other firsts to balance those which were gone beyond recall.

'Will I have a papa, too?' asked Sophie, lifting her head from Thea's shoulder.

Thea breathed deeply. She had known this question must come. For now at least, a half-truth must suffice—that her father had died…

She began carefully. 'Your father—'

'Is disgracefully late,' chimed in a familiar deep voice from the open door. 'For which I beg your pardon most humbly.'

Dazed, the world and certainties she had built up so diligently on the journey shattering about her, Thea stared at Richard limping towards them.

Sophie took a step backward, pressing into the shelter of Thea's body.

'Is this…Mama, is this my papa?'

There were no words. Not for the questions, nor to express her confusion, and no words to lead her through the morass of uncertainty. She could only stare at Richard, his eyes suspiciously bright as he knelt down beside them. Sophie's small hand clutched hers, hard.

He made no move except to hold out his hand to Sophie.

The child repeated her question, this time to Richard. 'Are you my papa?'

He smiled, his dear crooked smile that melted glaciers and made her heart turn over. 'Yes, sweetheart. If you will have me. And if your mama will have me. We have a home in Kent just waiting for the three of us and I suspect by now that there is a pony in the stable waiting for you.'

And finally Thea understood. Understood the depth of his love. The depth of her love. And the depth of understanding that had brought him to her. To them. There were no more questions. Only his arms reaching out to encircle them. And hers, also encircling her daughter—no, *their* daughter at the centre.

An hour later in the chaise, Sophie lay sound asleep in Thea's arms, lulled by the rocking and worn out by excitement.

'Is she heavy?' asked Richard. He sat back in the opposite corner, long legs stretched out.

Thea nodded. 'Yes, but I don't mind.'

He smiled. 'No, but when your arm starts to mind, let me know.'

She finally gave voice to the question that had been plaguing her. 'Richard?'

'Yes, love?'

'Where are we going?'

He looked a bit surprised. 'Well, home, of course. But first we are going to Blakeney.'

Several more certainties came crashing down. '*Blakeney?* But, your brother—surely—'

'Is, and I quote, looking forward to having a niece to spoil, and acting as godfather to my *next* child.' He leaned forward and possessed himself of one hand. 'In the meantime, he has professed himself content to be my groomsman and Verity is more than happy to be your matron of honour.'

'But—'

'But we're Blakehursts,' he said with a faint grin. 'If you ask me, Max is so disgusted that anyone could have a worse scandal than a Blakehurst scandal, he thought it my duty to marry it into the family.' His smile deepened and he reached out to caress her cheek.

'Richard, no one else will ever accept Sophie, you will be ostracised!'

'For what? Acknowledging my daughter?' he asked, smiling.

'*Your* daughter?' A glimmer of understanding came to her then, telling her just how far he was prepared to go.

'My daughter,' he confirmed. 'As Max pointed out, society is very usefully hypocritical over this sort of thing. While condemning *me* for a heartless libertine, they'll be turning *you* into an angel for accepting my daughter so graciously.'

For a split second joy sang through her. And then she saw the hitch. 'It won't work, Richard. Look at her! She is the image of—'

'The Winslow family,' agreed Richard. 'So at the same time as I acknowledge Sophie there will be an even more scurrilous rumour making the rounds: that Sophie is actually neither your, nor mine, but your brother's child and that by taking her in we have both behaved like saints. A bit embarrassing for your brother, but it *was* his idea. Apparently he has supported the child and her mother, but with the mother recently dead, he was at a loss.'

Her silence terrified him. 'Thea, I understand that you want her to be yours, but this way she is safe—even with the rumor about your brother, officially acknowledged as my daughter she will be more readily accepted.'

'You would do that for me?' she whispered.

He went to her then, taking her into his arms, settling her where she belonged. It felt as though the jagged edges of a wound had come together and were knitting. There was still pain, but it was the pain of healing.

'That and more,' he told her. A man had betrayed her in the worst possible way and yet…he touched the soft cheek of the sleeping child with careful fingers. Soft, silken, utterly innocent…

'There you sit,' he said huskily, 'with his child in your arms. You would have sacrificed everything for her.'

'She had nothing,' said Thea. 'Nothing except shame and the knowledge that her family didn't want her. I could not knowingly abandon her to that.'

'No,' he said, his arms tightening, 'you could not. And when I understood that, I knew what a fool I had been to hesitate.' Her sigh trembled through him.

'I cannot think of her as his,' said Thea softly. 'She is mine, and ...' She hesitated, a tension he could feel creeping into her.

'Mine,' he affirmed. 'Yes, love. I meant it. Not just legally, but in every way. That little girl in your arms is Sophie Blakehurst. *Our* daughter.'

He cradled them both in his arms, his heart full as he lowered his head to brush his mouth across hers. Hesitant, trembling, her lips parted, accepting his caress, offering her own. Joy singing, burning within, he took and gave in equal measure.

'Who giveth this woman to be married to this man?'

Thea smiled shakily up at David as he gave her into the keeping of the rector. He smiled back tenderly as Richard took her hand. Then he stepped back with a little nod of approval.

'I, Richard Alexander, take thee, Dorothea Sophie, to my wedded wife, to have and to hold, from this day forward, for better or for worse...'

Behind her, Thea was aware of Verity holding Sophie's hand, and beyond Richard, Max, standing proudly at his brother's side. And Richard himself, his voice deep and firm, pledging himself to her '...to love and to cherish, until death do us part...'

She could not help the tears sliding down her cheeks. They blurred her vision and choked her when it came to her turn to repeat her vows. In her heart the vows had already been made. Yet here in this old church, the words rang out, alive, burning between them, perhaps given more strength by being spoken and received.

Richard slid the ring onto her finger and held it there as he spoke the final vow. 'With this ring, I thee wed, with my body, I thee worship, and with all my worldly goods, I thee endow...'

* * *

The wedding breakfast was over, the farewells said. David had put the new Mrs Richard Blakehurst into her husband's carriage with a hug and a kiss. Together with Sophie they had come to Tarring House for their wedding night. Verity had offered to keep Sophie for the night, but Richard and Thea had both thought the child better with them. It was all so new to her and confusing, that she clung to Thea as if afraid that her new life would vanish if she let go.

Their wedding night… Richard stood at the window of their bedchamber, waiting. Thea had gone to settle Sophie for the night and tell her a story. When she came back… His body tightened. He wanted her. Wanted her until it was a fire in his blood.

He had wanted women before. But not like this. Love changed everything. And beyond that was the knowledge of how deeply she loved him, how deeply she trusted him to give herself. He stared out at the darkening sky, at the stars leaping to life one by one.

There had been so little chance to speak to her in these days before their wedding. She had remained at Blakeney, of course, and he had been here. Was she afraid of what was to come?

The door opened and he swung around. Thea stood there in the doorway, plainly hesitant. His heart contracted. Shyness? Or fear? She had been a long time with Sophie…

She came further into the room, which was lit only by the flickering dance of the fire and a branch of candles on the chimneypiece. Warm, laced with intimate shadows.

'I…I am sorry to be so long. She wanted me to stay for a little. It was all so strange for her. I waited until she slept.'

His own fears, for they had been fears, vanished. He held out his hand and she came to him at once.

He drew her into his arms. 'Our wedding night,' he said softly, one hand teasing the hollow of her spine as the other removed hairpins, freeing the silken curls to tangle around his fingers.

'Yes.'

'You are sure then? You do not wish to wait?'

'Quite sure,' she whispered. 'What would I wait for? To love you more? To…to *want* you more?'

His breath caught. 'You want me?'

Her smile tore at his heart. 'Richard—that night when we were here and you nearly seduced me in the parlour, you knew then that I wanted you. Nothing has changed. I still want you.'

His heart nearly shattered with love. For a moment it was all he could do to breathe, then she whispered, 'Richard—if *you* do not want this…'

There was only one answer.

He took her hand very gently and raised it to his lips, tenderly brushing kisses over her suddenly trembling fingers. Then slowly, his touch light, he guided her hand down his hard, aching body. Even through the heavy silk of his dressing gown the touch of her hand set fires under his skin. Finally her hand rested on his thigh, inches from the taut flesh that screamed his need.

The next move must be wholly hers.

His voice harsh with restraint, he said, 'Men can lie about nearly everything, Thea. But not this. Touch me. See, *feel,* how much I want you.'

An instant's hesitation. He felt the flaring shock in the sudden tension in her body and prepared to draw back. Then a gossamer touch through the silk. A single, curious finger trailed over the aching length of his need. He shuddered at the fierce leap of desire, trying desperately to curb the response of his flesh under that delicate touch.

He didn't succeed and heard a soft gasp from Thea.

Fighting the urge to tip her face up to his and kiss her sense-less, he reached for her hand, covering it, drawing it away. 'It's all right, sweetheart,' he managed. 'You don't have to—'

The touch of her lips silenced him, trailing along his jaw until he turned his head and captured them. She gave her lips willingly, sweetly and took his in return. He opened his mouth, tracing her lips with his tongue, licking delicately until they parted on a sigh. With a shuddering groan he deepened the kiss, sinking into the heat and taste of her.

She pulled her hand from his and touched him again, still lightly, still hesitant. Pleasure that was nearly pain sang through him, beating in his blood to an ancient rhythm. He had to touch her.

His fingers shaking, he tugged at the ribbon holding the bodice of her nightgown together. It gave, exposing the soft, creamy breasts.

Thea barely noticed, so entranced was she by the feel of him. Through the silk, the hot surge of flesh and blood under her exploring fingers held her enthralled. His mouth, possessing hers so deeply, told her of the other way he needed to possess her and heat swirled through her own body in response.

Gentle fingers on her breasts, tantalising, caressing, releasing fire that spread from his touch. More. She wanted more—a firmer touch—and instinctively arched her back, pushing her breast more fully into his hand. She felt his smile through their kiss as he cupped the tender offering and rubbed his thumb over the aching crest. Delight pierced her and she cried out, the sound captured by their kiss. He released her mouth and murmured, 'You like that?'

'Yes, oh, yes,' she whispered, scarcely able to speak for the hot pleasure flooding her. And not just her breasts, but aching and pooling lower, in her belly, between her thighs. She arched again, pleading for more.

He feathered kisses over her face, her jaw, tracing the curves of her ear, breathing gently so that she melted, her knees shaking until she would have fallen if not for the steely arms cradling her. She clung to him, all her fears gone, her world remade in the joy of their embrace.

'One more promise, Thea,' he whispered, drawing back a little.

'I promise,' she gasped, not wishing him to stop, not caring what promise he wanted.

'Look at me,' he insisted.

Somehow she opened her eyes to meet his gaze.

He stepped back, holding her at arm's length and said, very softly, 'There is never a moment, Thea, when you cannot ask me to stop. I will have your promise that if I do something, anything at all, to frighten you, anything you do not wish, you will stop me.'

She stared, dazed. She could feel his need, the urgency of his desire. And she could see something else too. In his eyes. Love, tenderness, all that. And with it, fear. The fear that in possessing her, he might lose her. If she had needed any further proof that he loved her, this was it.

'Only if I have the reciprocal promise,' she whispered, smiling up at him as she reached for the sash of his dressing gown.

He caught her hand. 'And that would be?'

She tugged at one end of the sash. 'That you don't stop again otherwise.'

His dressing gown fell open and she gazed speechless at the lean, hard strength of him, etched in shadow and firelight.

His heart hammering, heat pounding in every vein, he said, 'I think I can safely make that promise.' And led her to the bed.

She had not known that it could be like this. Sweet and wild, his strength and weight exciting. She had not known all the hot textures and tastes of a man. Never imagined that desire could sing, a deep, aching beat in her body. Fierce, open-mouthed kisses blazing over her throat and lower, until with lips and tongue he circled her nipple, teasing and biting gently. Her body melted and she sobbed, writhing against him, her fingers sliding through the dark locks, pressing him closer, wanting more and not knowing what *more* might be, until with a groan of pleasure he drew her nipple deep into his mouth and suckled.

A cry of shocked pleasure burst from her and her fingers clutched at his head, holding him to her.

His hand slid lower, over her belly, the long fingers caressing and exploring, telling her with each touch how lovely she was. Further, until he reached the soft curls nestled in the apex of her thighs.

He took her mouth again and she opened for him as he deepened the kiss, his tongue moving slowly, rhythmically…his hand on her thigh stroking to the same rhythm. The same rhythm as the throbbing emptiness within her. So that it seemed the most natural thing in the world to open her thighs to his tender urging.

His fingers shifted, seeking the aching heat and emptiness, teasing, parting soft folds. Liquid pleasure welled up and she cried out in shock as it spilt over, his fingers now sliding easily…

'Richard?'

'Beautiful,' he whispered hoarsely. And his touch told her again. Endlessly seeking and loving. Her body was no longer hers to control. It had melted, softening into delight as he discovered a place where every nerve in her body seemed centred, ready to explode in fire and light. A choked cry escaped her as he pressed lightly and stars shattered about her.

'More?' His voice was a husky breath against her lips. She couldn't speak, only lift against him in frantic entreaty as he teased, circling her softness. Then…a gentle pressure and one long finger slid within, a tender invasion of her body's secrets. Slowly, so slowly he stroked as thought fled, leaving only sensation and shattering emotion as the heat of desire and need swept her body.

Shuddering need raked its claws through Richard as he felt her surrender. Felt it in the molten liquid welcome of her body, sensed it in the utter trust of her surrender, knew it in the delight of her giving.

He could take her now. She was ready. Soft, wet, her body trembling on the point of release. And his body was screaming for it, aching to be sheathed in her clinging heat and feel her shatter around him. Shaking with need, he withdrew from her sweetness and nudged her thighs further apart.

Desire hammered in his blood with every heartbeat, redoubling at every breath. But—a queer realisation came to him—this was, in some strange way, her first time. Lallerton had taken her by force, stripping her of her virginity. She had never had a lover. Only violence and betrayal.

And she lay now in his arms willingly, giving herself

without reservation, trusting him utterly—her lover. Her only lover. Her husband.

Pushing himself up on one elbow, he looked down at her, continuing to stroke gently. At her body, flushed and ready for his possession, lifting to his touch. At her face, eyes closed, her trembling mouth, swollen with his kisses. As he watched, her eyes fluttered open.

'Now?' she whispered, and he felt it, the slightest tension in her body.

'So impatient?' he murmured, bending to kiss her breasts again, trailing lower over the damp heated skin of her belly, nuzzling into the soft curls. He slid between her thighs, holding them apart with his shoulders.

Shock held her speechless as she felt the hot caress of his breath and realised what he intended. No. She had to be wrong. He couldn't...

He did; and she nearly died at the fiery delight that speared her, the intimacy of his mouth and tongue. Tender, teasing and demanding. A fierce giving and a wild taking she could never have imagined. Gentle hands holding her in a tender vice for his loving. His worship. And she burned, helplessly, in wanton abandon, pleasure and need pulsing through her.

She was frantic, her body afire before he surged over her and she felt the hot seeking of his body, pushing into her hungry flesh. Not enough. Not nearly enough. She needed to feel him within, deep inside where she ached to hold him.

'Thea?'

'Yes. Please. Now.'

The naked plea nearly broke what was left of Richard's control. He hung on, his jaw cracking with strain as he fought the urge to ravish her, to sink deep.

He came a little further, stretching her, giving himself with a slow penetration. She gasped, lifting against him in a silken surge, taking more of him. He groaned. She was so tight that he feared hurting her. He withdrew a little and she cried out, wrapping her legs around his hips.

His control snapped and his loins surged, sheathing himself to the hilt in her soft depths.

Deep. He was so deep. Her softness shivered around him in the sweetest caress, yet she lay so still, her eyes closed.

'Are you all right?' His voice was harsh, shaking. He pushed a lock of hair from her eyes with trembling fingers, spreading it out on the pillow, framing her face with his hands. If he had hurt her... He ignored the hammering of his blood, the pounding urge to have her utterly, and held still.

Her eyes opened slowly and her fingers slid into his hair.

'Yes,' she breathed. 'You promised not to stop.'

Her hips shifted against him, seeking, pleading.

'I love you,' he whispered, brushing his mouth over hers.

He moved then, deep within her, taking her mouth as he took her body, gently, completely. Soft moans punctuated each stroke, mingling with his own huskier voice. Loving her with every fibre of his being until her breath fractured into desperate need and her body tightened around him in urgency. Loving her slowly, thoroughly, holding deep and still as her release shattered around him and his own consummation welled up in an explosion of love and joy.

Thea awakened in the dawn. Pale streamers of light gilded the room and the bed where she lay entangled with her husband. She was cradled in his arms, her cheek pillowed against him, one thigh nestled between his. Contentment held her. Every fibre hummed with relaxed pleasure. She snuggled closer, pressing a kiss on his shoulder, and felt his arms tighten.

'Awake?'

It was a soft murmur. Not enough to disturb her if she had been asleep.

'And if I'm not?'

He chuckled. 'I'll have to wait a little longer.' A brief pause. 'Or wake you up.'

He'd awakened her in the night, invading her dreams with tender passion... She smiled against his chest. 'I'm asleep then.'

She felt the laughter deep inside him as he eased himself around and began to wake her. To life, to joy and to the bright world that lay before them.

Epilogue

The clatter of hooves on the carriage drive roused Thea from her doze in the shade of the oak tree. Blinking sleepily she looked up and saw Sophie trotting towards her, Richard a length or so behind.

'Mama! Papa taught me how to jump a log! And Uncle Max said it was an excellent jump.'

The child drew the pony to a halt beside the chair. The pony promptly dropped her head in Thea's lap and blew noisily, demanding largesse.

Laughing, Thea rubbed the velvety nose. 'And what did Papa say?'

Richard dismounted. 'Papa says that his daughter is an unconscionable baggage who has her uncle Max twisted around her little finger.'

His daughter. Her heart swelled in joy at the love in his voice. The complete acceptance. Not even the birth of little Davy six months ago had changed that, except perhaps to deepen the ties binding all of them.

He bent to kiss her gently. 'And how is Davy?'

Thea glanced fondly into the baby carriage beside her chair. 'Asleep. I just fed him. Did you ride as far as Blakeney? How is Verity?'

'We didn't go to Blakeney,' said Sophie as she dismounted. 'Uncle Max was out by himself. He says Aunt Verity isn't allowed to ride at the moment and she doesn't want to go in the carriage because it makes her sick.'

Thea stared up at Richard, who grinned at her unspoken question.

'Yes,' he said, a wicked twinkle in his eye. 'Max informed me that I'm going to be an uncle again. I think he's determined to catch up. Actually accused me of cheating!'

Thea smothered a chuckle. 'Oh, how lovely,' she said. 'What a marvellous idea. Perhaps we should do a little bit more cheating?'

He kissed her again. 'Another baggage. I'm surrounded by them.'

Sophie looked up from an inspection of her baby brother. 'He sleeps a lot, doesn't he?'

'He's growing,' said Thea, smiling at her daughter. 'Just like you. Why don't you run inside and ask Nell for some milk and cake?'

Sophie bent a stern look on her. 'I have to take Astra to the stables first,' she said firmly. 'Papa says always to see to my pony first.'

'Good girl,' said Richard. 'Off you go and have your milk and cake afterwards.'

Sophie led her pony away as Thea and Richard watched fondly.

'She is so happy, Richard,' said Thea softly. 'Thank you.'

He smiled down at her. 'For what? Having the good sense to marry the woman I love and gain a daughter?'

'For being you,' she said simply. 'And for having sense, if you must put it like that!'

'I'll find another way to put it later on,' he promised her, dark eyes full of wicked, smiling promise. He reached down and pulled her out of the chair, sitting down in it himself and settling her in his lap. With a deep sigh of contentment, he untied her cap and dropped the lace-edged confection on the grass, to bury his face in soft tawny tresses.

'Sometimes,' he said, kissing her ear, 'I can't believe you actually forgave me for being stupid enough to hesitate.' It still horrified him that he had come so close to failing her.

She twisted in his arms to nestle closer. 'That,' she told him, 'was *my* good sense.'

His arms tightened. He'd thought to find contentment in marriage, and he had. But this deep, aching joy that spread through everything, even backwards so that everything that had led to this moment, and this woman in his arms, was somehow a preparatory blessing. Heaven, he supposed, just might be retroactive.

*Lord Braybrook's
Penniless Bride*

Chapter One

Julian Trentham, Viscount Braybrook, bit his tongue, figuratively speaking, and reminded himself that his stepmother, Serena, considered tact the best way to deal with his wayward half-sister. Telling Lissy she sounded like a second-rate actress in a bad tragedy was not tactful.

'But it *isn't* fair, Mama!' said the Honourable Alicia furiously. 'Julian only met Harry for five minutes yesterday and—'

'Half an hour,' said Julian, sitting down on a sofa. 'Long enough to ascertain that, apart from his post as Sir John's secretary, he has no prospects.' He eyed the tabby cat seated on Serena's lap out of the corner of his eye. The blasted thing was convinced he adored cats. It couldn't have been more mistaken.

'*Five minutes!*' repeated Lissy, 'and poor Harry is declared *unsuitable*. Whatever that means!'

'Amongst other things, it means you'd run the fellow aground inside of a month,' said Julian, unmoved. 'Have sense, Lissy.'

The cat stretched, brilliant green eyes fixed on Julian.

Lissy glared. 'I would not!'

Serena chimed in. 'Lissy dear, I feel quite sure that charming and pleasant as Mr Daventry may—' She made a grab for the cat, but it was already flowing off her lap. 'Oh, dear. Now, where was I? Yes, Mr Daventry, I am sure he is not at all well off, so—'

'What does money matter? And anyway, he *has* an income!' protested Lissy.

'Two hundred a year?' Julian suppressed a snort. 'And, no, money doesn't matter. Just as long as *you* learn to manage without it. Otherwise you will find it matters a great deal when the bailiffs take your furniture and the landlord kicks you into the street.'

'Harry has his *own* house,' said Lissy. 'In Bristol. He told me.'

'A man of property, then,' said Julian. He watched, resigned, as the cat strolled with offensive confidence towards him. His setter bitch, Juno, sprawled at his feet, lifted her head and then lowered it with a doleful sigh.

'Well, I wouldn't marry Lissy,' piped up six-year-old Davy from the corner, where he was endeavouring to put together a puzzle map of Europe. 'I'm going to marry Mama.'

Somehow Julian preserved a straight face. 'Excellent notion, old chap,' he said. 'Only not unless you want to land in Newgate!'

Lissy looked as though she might have giggled, had she not been trying so hard to look affronted.

The cat sprang into his lap and made itself comfortable. Very comfortable; its claws flexed straight through his buckskin breeches.

'Never mind, dear,' said Lady Braybrook to her youngest son. 'You won't want to marry me when you are old enough anyway.'

'No, indeed,' said Julian. 'After all, Lissy no longer wishes to marry me. Do you, Liss?'

'I never did!' exploded Lissy.

'You proposed to me when you were about five,' said Julian, reminiscently. 'It was most affecting.' He turned to Davy. 'Why don't you trot off to the kitchens and see if Ellie has something for you to eat?'

Davy leapt to his feet, scattering Europe to the corners of the drawing room, and decamped before his mother could veto this excellent idea on the grounds of education or indigestion.

As soon as the door shut behind him, Lissy burst out again. 'It isn't fair, Julian! Why should you have any say in it?'

'Probably because I am your guardian,' he said. 'For my sins,' he added. 'Calm down, Lissy. You're too young to be thinking of marriage.'

'I shall be *eighteen* soon!' she cried, making it sound like a death sentence.

'You turned seventeen less than three months ago,' Julian pointed out. 'You're not precisely on the shelf.'

'What if it were one of your rich, titled friends?' she countered. 'Like Lord Blakehurst?'

Julian blinked. 'Since he's married, I'd shoot him! Believe it or not, I would refuse my consent to any binding betrothal until at least next year.' The cat in his lap rolled, displaying its belly in furry offering. Resigned, Julian kneaded the shameless creature.

Lissy stared. 'But, *why?*'

'Because you're too young,' he said. 'And don't tell me again that you're nearly eighteen!'

Deflated, Lissy said, 'But we *love* each other. It isn't fair. Just because he isn't wealthy—'

'Lissy—Daventry can't afford to marry you!' He strove for patience and nobly squashed his instinctive, and more cynical, reaction. 'Not with bills like the ones sent to me from Bath last month,' he said.

Lissy blushed. He hoped some of his pithy comments on the advisability of keeping a check on expenditure had sunk in. 'It *is* unfair, though. If we cannot see each other, then—'

'I didn't forbid him the house!' said Julian irritably. 'For God's sake, Lissy! Stop acting as though you were in a bad tragedy!'

Serena coughed, and Julian gritted his teeth, remembering the tact. He added, 'He seems pleasant enough, and I believe I can trust *him* not to go beyond the line.'

'You mean, we may meet?'

He fixed her with his best steely glare. 'If he is invited to the same entertainments, then of course you will meet. He may call here. Occasionally. But you may not meet him unchaperoned, nor exchange correspondence. And I would make the same conditions for any man courting you, even if he were a veritable Midas!'

'I suppose you think you're being generous!'

He nodded. 'Yes. Now that you mention it, I do. And if at any time you are tempted to view me as a callous tyrant,' he added, 'you might care to ponder the fact that our father would have shown Daventry the door with a horsewhip, set the dogs on him, complained to his employer, and confined you to your room for a month. At least. And think—once you are twenty-one, I will be powerless to prevent your marriage.'

Faced with this very accurate summation, Lissy set her mouth in a mutinous line. In trembling tones she said, 'If you had the least idea about *love*, Julian, you would understand the *agony* of being obliged to wait!'

She swung around and stormed out.

Serena, Lady Braybrook, said, 'I thought we agreed to be tactful?'

Julian snorted. 'Tactful? Lissy needs a dose of salts!' He removed the cat from his lap. 'What has she been reading, Serena?'

Ignoring that as wholly unimportant, Serena regarded her stepson. 'Tell me, dear—when you were seventeen—'

'Yes, all right, very well,' said Julian hurriedly, recalling some of *his* youthful peccadilloes. He looked away from the cat, which was staring up at him indignantly. 'At least I never wanted to marry any of them!'

At Serena's choke of laughter heat flared on his cheekbones, and the cat took advantage of his distraction to reinstate itself with fluid ease.

'So I recall,' Serena said, still laughing. 'Is Tybalt annoying you? Just put him out.'

He grimaced. 'I think I can survive one cat.' Even if it was stretching its claws on his breeches again. Serena was fond of the thing. 'Was I that much of a nuisance?'

'Worse,' she assured him. 'Whenever news of your misdemeanours at Oxford and then, after you were sent down, London, reached us, your father nearly had apoplexy.' She smiled reminiscently. 'The worst was the rumour that Worcester was about to call you out for your attentions to Harriette Wilson.'

Julian blinked at this unabashed reference to one of his youthful follies. 'Dash it, Serena! Where did you hear that?'

'Oh, was it true, then? I told your father it was more than likely a silly invention and not to give it a moment's thought. Was I wrong?'

'He *told* you?' He hadn't even realised that his father *knew*!

Serena stared. 'Well, of course! How else could he ask my advice?'

'He asked your advice?' Julian tried, and failed, to imagine his father discussing his son's involvement with a notorious courtesan with Serena.

Grey eyes twinkling, she said, 'Frequently. Which is not to say he took it very often.' Her mouth twitched. 'Not intentionally, anyway.'

Julian decided he didn't want to know. 'Hmm. Well, I'm here now for the rest of the summer, and Lissy and Emma are off to Aunt Massingdale in the winter. Surely we can keep Lissy out of mischief until then.'

'You're staying until Parliament resumes?'

He shrugged. 'Mostly. I do need to see Modbury about some business. I'll go to Bristol for a few nights next week. Since I'm meeting with him I'll write first and ask him to find out something more about Daventry. This house, for one thing.'

'Yes, that surprised me,' said Serena.

'Modbury should be able to discover something if Daventry does own property,' said Julian. 'Apparently, Alcaston is his godfather and settled the income on him.'

Serena frowned. 'Alcaston? The duke?'

'Yes. He recommended Daventry for the post with Sir John,'

said Julian. 'Will you be all right while I'm away? Are you sure you don't want Aunt Lydia to visit? Or—'

He broke off under the fire of Serena's glare.

'I may be stuck in this wretched chair, Julian, but as I've said before, that does not mean I require someone hovering over me the entire time,' she told him. 'And since that is exactly what Lydia would do, no—I do not want her to visit!'

'Very well,' he said. 'No Aunt Lydia.'

He'd have to think of someone else, because with her daughters off to Bath for the winter Serena needed a companion. He looked at her with affection. Her confinement to the *wretched chair*, as she put it, limited her physical independence. While he could see her point in categorically refusing her widowed sister-in-law as a companion—Lydia would fuss mercilessly and bemoan ceaselessly the unfairness of fate—who else was there?

'Julian—I don't want *any* well-meaning relatives fussing over me.'

'No. I understand that.' Sometimes he wondered if she could actually read his mind…he'd have to think of something else. Meanwhile he'd best write to Modbury and ask him to find out what he could about Daventry.

Chapter Two

I think I've found the house you wanted, my lord. Only Daventry I could find. It's on Christmas Steps.

Yes?

Only thing, my lord—there's a young woman living there from what I could find out...a Mrs Daventry ...

Good Lord! Julian stood at the top of Christmas Steps and wondered if he was insane even thinking of descending the alley. Modbury had thought so, and Julian could see his point. The alley was positively medieval, and so steep someone had actually built steps. According to Modbury it led down to the old quay, and at least once had housed the sort of establishments sailors on shore leave frequented—brothels and taverns.

You can't visit, my lord!

The hell he couldn't. Gripping his umbrella, Julian started down the slippery steps. There were two possibilities. Either Daventry kept a whore down here—it was not unknown for a woman to use her protector's name—or he was already married. On the whole, Julian thought a conveniently distant wife more likely; a mistress was only convenient if she were close enough to bed regularly. Either, however, would settle Lissy's idealistic infatuation, if a description of the alley wasn't enough.

It was dark in the alley and a dank chill closed in, with a reek of cabbage, fish and sour humanity on the breeze rattling the shop signs. The old, timbered houses with their cantilevered upper storeys loomed over the street, holding light and fresh air at bay. A couple of seedy-looking taverns were the only hard evidence of the street's former reputation. There were few people about, but suspicious eyes followed him from doorways and windows. He consulted the address Modbury had given him—there, on the opposite side, just before the next set of steps between a fishmonger and an apothecary, was the house he sought.

A one-eyed, moth-eaten cat sheltering in the lee of the building flattened its ears and hissed, slinking away as he approached the open door.

A voice was raised.

'Now be sensible, missy. I got Mr Daventry's letter and it says, right here, "the house and all its contents"! See? *All* its contents. Not "all its contents if no one else happens to want them". So—'

'Well, I assume you're not planning to put *me* on the auction block along with my clothes and hairbrush as part of the contents!' came another voice. A prim, schoolmistressy voice a man would think twice about annoying.

The voice went on. 'And if you can make that distinction, then you should be capable of exempting the rest of my personal property.' Irony gave way to anger. 'And since Mr Daventry is my brother and not my husband, he owns neither them nor me!'

Blast! Probably not wife, then. Mistress remained a possibility…

The angry woman continued, 'When you return next week, you may *have* the house and all its contents because I shall have removed myself and *my* possessions to lodgings!'

Through the open door Julian could now see a large, beefy-looking man, in the old-fashioned knee breeches and frieze coat of a respectable tradesman. He had his back half-turned, but there was no mistaking the rising annoyance in the set of his jaw.

'Now see here, missy!' he growled, all attempt at reason abandoned. ''Twas unfortunate I misunderstood how things were, but there's no call to take that tone! I'll be calling in the sheriff and bailiffs if you remove more than your clothes and hairbrush. Everything, the letter says, and I've made a list, I have!' He brandished a piece of paper, presumably in his unseen opponent's face. 'If aught's missing, I'll have the law on you!'

It was none of his business, Julian told himself. Common sense dictated that he remain out of any legal brangle between Daventry and his *sister*. Only this wasn't Daventry…and exactly what situation had the man misunderstood?

The woman spoke again. 'You may leave, Goodall. I suggest you clarify your instructions with my brother. In the meantime my solicitor will call upon you.'

Goodall, far from being abashed, took a step forward, presumably towards the woman.

'Are you threatening me, missy?' His voice had turned thoroughly unpleasant.

'Leave!' Sister or not, the undercurrent of fear in her tone flung Julian into action. Three swift strides took him over the threshold.

'Goodall!' he rapped out.

The man swung around. 'Who the hell are you?'

'The lady told you to leave,' said Julian coldly. 'As an acquaintance of Daventry, I suggest you do so before I speak with the magistrates on his behalf about entering this lady's home and harassing her. Out.'

He strode past Goodall with scarcely a glance at the woman. All he could see was that she was of medium height, bespectacled and clad in dull brown. His attention was on the aggrieved Mr Goodall, and he deliberately interposed himself between them.

Goodall flushed. 'Now, see here—'

'Out.' He delved in his pocket and pulled out his cardcase. 'As for who I am…' He took out a card and handed it to Goodall '…I'm Braybrook.'

He gestured to the door and Goodall, his face now as pale as it had been red, swallowed.

'I'm sure…that is…I didn't mean—'

'Out!'

Goodall went.

Julian closed the door and turned to receive the heartfelt gratitude of his damsel in distress—

'I have no idea who you may be, but you will oblige me by also leaving.'

Frost glittered at him from behind unbecoming spectacles. And there was something odd about her direct gaze, something faintly disconcerting—as though she had the ability to see straight through. Right now he wouldn't have wagered a penny on her liking what she saw.

As for what *he* saw—the woman was a quiz. Her hair colour remained a mystery under an all-enveloping and extremely ugly cap. As did whatever figure she might possess beneath a gown remarkable only for its sheer shapelessness and being the drabbest brown he'd ever seen.

Any lingering hope of her being Daventry's doxy faded. No self-respecting doxy would wear the gown, let alone the spectacles.

And she faced him with her chin up, her jaw set, and her mouth a flat, determined line.

'No gratitude, ma'am?' he drawled.

Those queerly penetrating eyes narrowed. 'I'm reserving it until I know who you are, and why you entered my home without my leave,' was the icy rejoinder.

'Well, you won't discover either of those things if you kick me out into the street,' he pointed out with what he freely acknowledged to be unforgivable logic.

It seemed she concurred. One small fist clenched and the pale cheeks flushed. Otherwise her control held.

'Very well. Who are you?'

He supposed she could not be blamed for being suspicious.

He took out his card case and extracted another card, holding it towards her.

There was a moment's hesitation before she moved, and then it was warily, watchful eyes on his face as she took the card. At once she stepped beyond his reach behind a settle before examining the card.

He watched, fascinated. There was something about her, about her face—what was it? Apart from that she looked cold.

She was glaring at him again.

'So, Lord Braybrook—assuming you are Lord Braybrook and not some scoundrel—'

'I'm obliged to point out that the two are not mutually exclusive,' he said.

She positively bristled. 'That I can well believe!' Then, 'Oh, for heaven's sake! One of my eyes is blue and the other brown! And now perhaps you will stop staring at me!'

One was blue, the other... So they were. He could see it now; behind the spectacles one eye was a soft, misty blue and the other hazel brown.

'And, no, I am not a witch,' she informed him.

He smiled. 'I assumed you weren't, since Goodall left in human form rather than as a toad.'

For a split second there was a flare in her eyes that might have been laughter. A lift at the corner of the mouth, which was, he suddenly saw, surprisingly lush. Soft pink lips that for a moment looked as though they might know how to smile.

The impression vanished like a snowflake on water.

'Frivolity,' she said, as one who identifies a beetle, all the softness of her mouth flattened in disapproval.

'Ah, you recognised it,' he said with a bow.

This time her eyes widened, but she controlled herself instantly.

Intrigue deepened. What would it take to crack her self-control?

'Do all your rescuers receive this charming response?' he

asked. 'It's true, you know; I am acquainted with Harry. As for my motives; I was coming to call on you and overheard Goodall. I interfered out of disinterested chivalry, Mrs Daventry.'

'Miss Daventry,' she corrected him.

He watched her closely. 'Oh? I understood a Mrs Daventry lived here?'

Her expression blanked. 'Not now. My mother died some months ago.'

'I beg your pardon,' he said quietly. 'My condolences.'

'Thank you, my lord. Will you not be seated?'

She gestured to a battered wingchair by the empty fireplace. The leather upholstery bore evidence of several cats having loved it rather too well. The only other seat was the uncomfortable-looking wooden settle opposite with a damp cloak hung over it. He took the settle and, at a faint startled sound from her, glanced over his shoulder to catch the surprise on her face.

'What?' he asked. 'You can't have thought I'd take the chair!'

Her mouth primmed. 'I've noticed gentlemen prefer a comfortable chair, yes.'

His opinion of Harry Daventry slid several notches. 'Then they weren't gentlemen, were they?'

Her mouth thinned further. 'And you are?'

He laughed. 'Usually. I'll warn you if I feel the urge to behave too badly.'

'Very obliging of you. May I offer you tea?'

Prim. Proper. As calm as though she entertained the vicar.

Tea, though. He didn't like tea at the best of times. And imagining the quality of tea he was likely to receive here sent shivers down his spine. His spine's concerns aside, however, good manners dictated acceptance. And Miss Daventry looked as though a hot drink would do her good.

'Thank you, ma'am. That would be very pleasant.'

She nodded. 'Then please excuse me. My servant is out.' With a graceful curtsy, she left through a door at the back of the parlour.

Julian took a deep breath and looked around the cramped room. This was what he had come for, after all: to judge Daventry's condition for himself. And if Lissy could see this, the circumstances to which she would be reduced if she married Daventry, it might give her pause for thought.

It was spotless, though, he noticed. Absolutely spotless. As though dust dared not settle in a room tended by Miss Daventry. Everything gleamed with care. Wood waxed and polished. Not a cobweb in sight. Against one wall was a bureau bookcase, crammed with books. Julian frowned. It was old now, but it spoke of one-time wealth.

Interesting. Other things caught his eye. An old-fashioned drop-sided dining table against the wall held a lamp. Brass candlesticks that once had been silver gilt. A battered wine table, piled with more books beside the wingchair. Every sign that the Daventries had once been well to do, commanding the elegancies of life and, in sinking to this address, had clung to a few treasured reminders. Perhaps the crash of the '90s had brought them down. He could even sympathise with their plight. His own father had steered clear of those shoals, but had not been so canny in recent years... Lord, it was cold in here!

His mouth hardened. Harry Daventry would not restore his family's fortunes at the cost of Lissy's happiness. No doubt Daventry's sister would be quartered in his household... His eye fell on the books tottering on the wine table—sermons, probably, and other improving works. He picked up the top volumes and his brows rose. Sir Walter Scott—*Ivanhoe*. He looked at the next couple of books, poetry. So Miss Prim had a taste for the romantical, did she? He picked up the final volumes—Miss Austen's *Northanger Abbey*. Serena had enjoyed that...

He set the books down, frowning. Contradictions lay hidden

beneath the layers of brown sobriety and the cap. Strolling back to the settle and sitting down, he wondered what colour her hair might be. Not so much as a strand peeked from that monstrous cap. Mousy? It would suit the spectacles and that prim mouth with its iron clad composure. Although it wasn't quite iron-clad, was it? What would it take to breach it utterly?

She would return soon. Miss Respectability, laden with a teatray needing to be put somewhere… Below the window was a small tea table.

With a sigh, he rose, shifted the table, placing it between the wingchair and the settle. Good manners, he told himself. A gentleman did these things. It had nothing to do with Miss Daventry herself or wishing to show her that not *all* men were inconsiderate oafs who took the only comfortable chair, leaving their sister the wooden settle. Definitely nothing to do with *her.* It was simply the right thing to do.

He looked at the empty grate. It *was* cold, after all.

It was the work of a moment to lay a fire, find the tinderbox and have a small blaze going.

He had barely sat down again when the door opened and Miss Daventry came in bearing a small tray.

Shock sprang into those disquieting eyes as she saw the fire. 'Oh, but—'

Julian rose and took the tray from her, setting it down on the table before turning back to her.

She hadn't moved. She was staring at the little table as though wondering how it had arrived there. Then she looked at the fire. All the tension in her face, all the taut lines, dissolved, leaving her, he saw with a queer jolt, looking tired, yet as though something far more burdensome than the tray had been lifted from her.

Almost immediately she recovered, saying in her primmest tones, 'How kind of you, my lord. Please do be seated.'

She bent over the tray and poured a cup. 'Milk? Sugar?'

'A little milk, please.'

She handed him his cup, poured her own, and sat down, her back ramrod straight.

Julian took a wary sip, and acknowledged surprise. The tea, if one liked the stuff, was perfectly acceptable. And the teacups, although old and chipped in places, had once been the height of elegance and cost a small fortune. Yet apart from mentioning Alcaston as his godfather, Harry Daventry made no play with grand connections or past glory.

'Perhaps, my lord, you might explain how you know my brother.'

Miss Daventry's cool voice drew him out of his thoughts. Did she know about Lissy? If so, then it probably had her blessing. She was no fool. The advantages of such a match to her were obvious. She might make a decent match herself from the connection.

'Your brother has become acquainted with my sister.'

Miss Daventry's teacup froze halfway to her lips. Her face blanched. 'Your sister—?' The teacup reversed its direction and was replaced in its saucer with a faint rattle. 'Would your sister be Miss Trentham?'

'Yes. My half-sister.'

Spear straight she sat, her mouth firm and a look of mulish obstinacy about her chin. The air of dignity intensified, despite the pallor of her cheeks.

Hell! No doubt she would defend her brother's marital ambitions to the hilt. Why wouldn't she? Such a connection would be a lifeline for her.

His mouth set hard.

He had to protect Lissy. Nothing else mattered. Even if he had to batter Miss Daventry's pride into the dust.

'How very unfortunate,' she said, her voice calm. 'I trust you are doing all in your power to discourage this?'

Unfortunate? From *her* perspective? *He* had every reason to disapprove of Mr Daventry, but what possible objection could *she* have to Lissy?

With freezing hauteur, he said, 'I am at a loss to know how my sister merits your censure, Miss Daventry.'

'Never having met her, I do not disapprove of Miss Trentham,' said Miss Daventry. 'Merely of—' She broke off, staring. Faint colour stained the pale cheeks. 'I think I understand the purpose of your visit, my lord. A warning to Harry? "Stay away from my sister, and I'll stay away from yours." Is that it?'

Outrage jolted through him. 'I *beg* your pardon?' Thank God she hadn't divined his original suspicions!

She faced him undaunted. 'If that is not the case, I beg your pardon. I can think of no other reason for your visit.'

Could something of his reputation have reached Miss Daventry via her brother's letters?

'No doubt, Miss Daventry. However, I *am* a gentleman. Whatever you may have heard to the contrary.'

'Your reputation is of no interest to me, my lord,' she informed him, picking up her cup and sipping her tea.

'And what leads you to believe that I have a reputation, Miss Daventry?' His reputation, after all, was not the sort one discussed with respectable females.

She gave him a considering look over her tea cup before answering.

'Everyone has a reputation, my lord. All that remains in doubt…' she sipped, '…is the nature of that reputation. Naturally, since you are a gentleman, yours is not the sort of reputation in which I interest myself.'

'Yet you referred to it, ma'am.'

The brows lifted. 'I, my lord? Hardly. You alluded to the possibility that someone might have mentioned you in unflattering terms. Thus suggesting that, deserved or not, you have a reputation.'

Julian nearly choked on his tea. Did she dot every 'i' with a needle? Serena, he realised, would have been cheering the chit on.

She changed the subject. 'We were speaking of your sister,

my lord,' she said. 'As I said, I do not disapprove of Miss Trentham. How should I? I have not the honour of her acquaintance. But I do disapprove of my brother's interest in her.'

'A fine distinction, Miss Daventry,' he said. 'Would you care to voice your objections?'

If possible, she sat up even straighter. Her chin lifted.

'There is a looking glass over the chimneypiece, my lord. Examine yourself in it. Bring to mind your home. Your estates. Recall your rank. Then look about you. Tell me what you see.'

He didn't answer. Her cold, blunt assessment rivalled his own. The obvious, brutal response was that everything about her and this room spoke of impoverished gentility. But faced with her quiet dignity, he simply couldn't say it. Which was foolish beyond permission since the words had been on his lips.

After a moment she spoke again. 'Your silence is answer enough. Harry and Miss Trentham are from different spheres. You cannot wish your sister to make such a step. I assume that is what you are come to tell me, and also that you have refused to permit Harry to see your sister again.'

'Not quite, Miss Daventry,' he said.

He'd intended exactly that, but Serena had talked him out of it.

She stared and he felt the corner of his mouth twitch. That had rattled her.

'You *can't* approve such a match!' The disbelief in her eyes echoed in her voice.

'Naturally not,' said Julian. 'But my sister has a stubborn streak and in four years when she gains her majority, I will not be able to prevent the match. Your objections tally with my own. Your connection to the Duke of Alcaston notwithstanding—'

'My *what*?'

'Your brother's godfather, Alcaston,' said Julian, eyeing her spectacularly white face. 'Are you quite well, Miss Daventry?'

'Yes…yes, perfectly.' Some colour returned to her cheeks. 'He told you that, did he? It makes no difference, surely?'

'None,' said Julian. 'Your brother is still ineligible as a match for my sister, even with the income his Grace has settled on him.'

She nodded. 'So. You have forbidden Harry the house, and—'

'No. I have not.' Serena had pointed out that the fastest way to encourage clandestine meetings was to ban legitimate ones. He could see the logic, but…

'*No?* What sort of brother *are* you, then?'

That caught Julian on the raw. 'A good one, I hope!' he snapped. 'Yes, of course I could forbid them to meet! And where would I be when Lissy hoaxed herself into the role of Juliet and the young fools eloped?' Serena again.

'Lissy?'

'Alicia,' he said.

'I beg your pardon,' she said. 'I did not mean to tell you how to order your sister's life—'

'Ouch,' he said drily. 'I hope that I do not *order* my sister's life, as you put it.'

She flushed. 'I'm sorry, that was—'

'If you don't stop apologising, I shall start to think you are buttering me up.'

'Nothing, *my lord*, could be further from my intentions!'

'No. I thought as much,' he murmured.

That silenced her. If one discounted the draconian glare, which fairly scorched the air between them.

He grinned. He couldn't help it. He wished—oh, how he *wished*!—Serena could hear this exchange. He tripped on the thought—Serena would like this prim, outspoken woman. A woman who was about to be kicked out of her home…and Lissy needed a sharp dose of reality to convince her that life with Harry Daventry would not be love's young dream at all, but a nightmare. Yes. This might work. Two birds with one shot. He almost patted himself on the back. And then remembered that not only had Miss Daventry not accepted, but that he hadn't made the offer.

'Miss Daventry,' he began, 'I gather you intend to seek lodgings when this house is sold.'

'Until I can secure either a position as a companion or a teaching post.'

Better and better. 'In that case, I wonder if the offer of a position might be acceptable—'

'No! It most certainly would *not*!' she flared.

He stared at her scarlet face. 'I may live on Christmas Steps,' she continued furiously, 'but that does not mean—!' She broke off, biting her lip.

And he realised that—whether or not his reputation had preceded him—an unspecified offer from a gentleman might well be viewed with suspicion by a respectable female living on Christmas Steps.

'My stepmother requires a companion,' he said. And waited.

He was disappointed. Apart from her blush deepening, Miss Daventry maintained her composure, or, rather, regained it.

'Oh. I see,' she said. 'I cannot think, my lord, that you really want me as a companion for your stepmother.'

No explanation. No apology. She moved straight on from the potential quagmire of embarrassment. He had to applaud.

'Why not?' he asked.

'Only consider the consequences!' she said. 'If I were living in your house, Harry would use that to—'

'Precisely,' he said softly. 'You would be an unexceptionable reason for your brother to call. Most illuminating for Alicia.'

Her eyes flew to his. 'You mean—'

'Meeting you, knowing you must earn your living—'

'Would give your sister food for thought,' she finished.

'Yes.' She had caught the point in a flash. He added feelingly, 'It would also relieve me of the stigma of being thought a mercenary, callous brute by my sister, because offering you the position would signify my approval of you and, by extension, your brother.' But it would force Alicia to view Daventry in a different light—a young man who could not provide for his sister.

Another silence. She was thinking about it. He had seen enough of her to know that otherwise she would have rejected the suggestion out of hand. Miss Daventry had a mind of her own and reserved the right to use it.

'I doubt that I would be a suitable companion for Lady Braybrook,' she said.

If the lady in question were anyone but Serena, he would have agreed wholeheartedly. As it was…

'You would amuse her,' he said. 'Meekness bores her, and I think we can leave *that* out of your list of virtues.' An understatement if ever there was one.

Amused at her blush, he went on. 'An accident some years ago left her unable to walk. I want someone intelligent to keep her company. I was considering older females, but I think she would like you. You mentioned teaching—do you have any teaching experience?'

'Yes.'

'I have another sister still in the school room and a six-year-old brother. At present they have no governess, so you could help there.'

Miss Daventry looked sceptical. 'That will hardly answer once the summer is over and they require more lessons. I cannot be in two places at once.'

He shrugged, dismissing the objection. 'Once another governess is hired, you can be available on her days off, or if she is indisposed,' he said. 'Naturally, were you prepared to take on this dual—or should I say triple?—role, I would pay you accordingly. Shall we say, one hundred pounds per annum?'

While he did not precisely expect Miss Daventry to leap at his generous offer like a cock at a blackberry, she would no doubt be somewhat flustered. Most governesses or companions were lucky to receive a quarter of that.

The soft, rosy lips parted slightly and he felt a jolt of what he sincerely hoped was mere gratification....

'You cannot possibly pay such a ridiculous sum to a companion who relieves the governess,' she informed him.

The devil he couldn't! He bit that back, opting for icy civility. 'I *beg* your pardon, ma'am?'

'It is ridiculous,' she repeated, her mouth re-primmed.

It was, was it? Just how much more did the harpy want?

'Moreover,' she went on, 'it would be grossly unfair to the other governess, who might well be older and far more experienced, were I to be paid such an astronomical sum!'

His jaw dropped. 'You're complaining that I'm offering too *much*?'

She frowned. 'What did you think I meant?'

He shook his head in disbelief. 'Miss Daventry, permit me to inform you that most people would not concern themselves in the least if I offered too much. My offer stands.'

Her eyes narrowed. 'Fifty,' she said.

His mouth twitched. Good God! He was actually arguing—haggling like a merchant outside the Corn Exchange—with a potential governess, trying to persuade her to accept a higher figure!

'Miss Daventry, your scruples are admirable, but your value to me lies far beyond the companionship you will offer my stepmother, or whatever knowledge you may impart to my younger siblings.'

'But I might fail,' she pointed out.

'One hundred per annum,' he insisted, battling the urge to laugh at this dowdy, honest woman with her disturbingly pink, prim mouth and earnest mismatched eyes. 'If it helps, no one besides ourselves will know how much you are paid. Certainly not the other governess.'

'No. It doesn't,' she said at once. 'It is still unfair, whether the other governess knows, or not. *I* would know.'

He gritted his teeth. Damn the wench. Could she not strangle her scruples and accept his generosity? 'Miss Daventry, upon occasion I play cards. I bet. Shall we say twenty-five pounds per annum as a companion? A further twenty-five as a governess. I'll gamble the other fifty against you being able to dissuade my sister from marrying your brother.'

Her eyes narrowed again behind those frumpish spectacles. 'Very well, on one condition…'

He might have known it. 'Which is?'

'If I am still in Lady Braybrook's employ when your sister marries, the extra fifty pounds ceases. And should she marry my brother, I repay you—'

'Not bloody likely!' he said. And couldn't believe he'd said it. What was he about? He *never* swore before females, but something about this one tipped him on to his beam ends. As for Miss Daventry—the ladylike façade was in ruins, her mouth parted in shock.

'I *beg* your pardon?'

Sheet ice encased her voice. As for her eyes…that was it—the eyes were tipping him off balance. And she was angry, furiously angry. Beneath that calm exterior was someone quite different.

'Er, certainly not,' he corrected himself. 'Otherwise, Miss Daventry, it would not be gambling. Would it?'

Under his fascinated gaze the fiery creature was visibly subdued and closed away. Prim Miss Daventry stood in her place. 'I disapprove of gambling,' she informed him. 'You can hardly expect—'

'Damn it all!' he exploded. 'What I expect seems to be going by the board! I *expect* you to accept my generous offer. I *expect* you to be ready to accompany me when I return to Herefordshire in three days. I *expect*—'

'Three days?' Fire licked through the cracked façade. 'I cannot possibly pack up this house in three days! Nor—'

'My man of business will handle it,' said Julian, pouncing on her implicit acceptance of his offer.

'Nor could I possibly accompany you to Hereford!'

'Why the d—why not?' he corrected himself. 'How will you take up your position if you do not?'

'Oh, don't be so literal!' she said. 'I meant I cannot travel alone with you. We should have to spend a night on the road.'

It was his turn to feel outraged. 'Dammit, girl! Believe me, I've no designs on *your* virtue!'

'It wouldn't matter a scrap if you did or not,' she said frankly. 'My reputation would be ruined either way! I am twenty-four, Lord Braybrook. I cannot travel with you alone.'

'You expect me to engage a *chaperon* for you?'

He couldn't quite believe it. Five minutes ago he had offered this impossible woman respectable employment and they had been arguing ever since. Somewhere he had lost control of the transaction.

'Of course not,' she said impatiently. 'I shall travel on the stage, and—'

'The deuce you will!'

'Lord Braybrook, I have frequently travelled on the stage—'

'Well you shouldn't have!' he growled, adding, 'And you won't this time.' Which was so illogical as to defy comprehension. Companions and governesses always travelled on the stage.

'Yes, I will,' she said.

Julian gritted his teeth in barely concealed frustration. 'Miss Daventry,' he ground out, 'I begin to see why you consider yourself unsuited to the position of companion!' The inescapable fact that she was perfectly right about the situation didn't help in the least. Nor the defiant chin that said she knew she was right, and that she knew that he knew… He halted that train of thought at once.

'Ma'am, I cannot agree to a lady under my prot—' one look at her outraged countenance and he corrected himself before the façade exploded in flames '—for whom I am responsible, travelling on the common stage. Or the Mail,' he added, before she could suggest it. 'You will travel with me!'

'Not unchaperoned!' she shot back.

'Very well!' he snapped. 'Will it be acceptable if a maid shares your room at the inn we put up at, or must I inveigle a Dowager Duchess into service? I've no designs on your virtue, but even if I had, seducing the governess in my travelling coach is *not* one of my favoured pastimes!'

Miss Daventry flushed. 'There is no need to be horrid about it. I am not at all concerned about *you*. Merely how gossip might construe it. I have no wish to find myself the object of vulgar curiosity and censure! A servant at night will be perfectly adequate. Naturally I will pay for my own accommodation and—'

'You will do no such thing,' he stated with deadly calm. 'As of this moment, Miss Daventry, I consider you to be in my employ. Any expenses incurred on your journey will be borne by *me*. Are we clear?'

For a moment the prim mouth took on a mulish set, but she dropped a slight curtsy. 'Yes, my lord.'

Discretion, ever the better part of valour, suggested it was time to beat a hasty retreat. Before he strangled her, or worse, swore at her again. Having solved several problems in one stroke, he was in no way minded to have his plans upset by Miss Prim and Proper deciding she could not enter the employ of a gentleman so dissolute as to swear in front of a lady, let alone allude to the possibility of seducing her in a travelling coach.

'I will bid you a good day then, ma'am.' He set down his cup and rose. 'I have business tomorrow and Wednesday. We will depart on Thursday. My carriage will take you up at seven a.m.' He bowed. 'If you do not object to starting early.'

She had risen too.

'I will be at the top of the steps outside the Chapel of the Three Kings. Will a trunk and valise be too much?'

He raised his brows. 'You will pack whatever you require. If it does not fit, a carrier will bring it.'

He held out his hand. A polite gesture to seal their bargain.

Nothing more. For a moment she hesitated and then placed her own hand in his. Awareness shot through him. Her hand fitted his as though they completed each other. Startled, he met her gaze. Behind the spectacles her mismatched eyes widened, as though the same awareness had taken her. For a shocking instant their gazes linked as tangibly as their hands. Then her lashes swept down, veiling her eyes, closing him out.

He released her hand and stepped back. 'Good day, ma'am. My man of business will call.'

'Good day, my lord,' she responded quietly.

Having seen Lord Braybrook out, Christiana Daventry closed the door behind him with trembling fingers and leaned against it.

Had she run mad? What was she about to accept his offer of employment? What if he wasn't Lord Braybrook at all? And what was it about him that had broken her usual self-control? Not since she was sixteen had Christy lost command of herself like that. It hadn't done any good then, either. Not that she cared. She could manage without being beholden to anyone.

She fished Lord Braybrook's card out of her pocket, frowning. Anyone could have an elegant card embossed. Except, how could anyone but Lord Braybrook know of Harry's interest in Miss Trentham?

Miss Trentham, who, according to the perfunctory description in Harry's last letter, had blue eyes and black hair—Christy muttered a distinctly unladylike word—just like Lord Braybrook's. Indeed, if they were anything like her brother's blue eyes and raven hair, then Miss Trentham would be nothing short of a beauty. She had never realised eyes could actually *be* that blue, outside the covers of a romance from the Minerva Press. Or that penetrating, as though they looked right into you and saw all the secrets you kept hidden… Oh, yes. He was Lord Braybrook right enough. And she had accepted a post as companion to his stepmother and a sort of fill-in governess. It must be a most peculiar household, she reflected. Most ladies of rank would hire their own companions and the governess.

She snorted. It was all of a piece with his arrogant lordship. Marching into her home as though he owned it. Taking up far too much of her parlour with his shoulders…why on earth was she thinking about his shoulders? It hadn't been his shoulders that had forced Goodall to back down, it had been that stupid card with his name and rank on it. *Lord* Braybrook. A title and Goodall had been bowing and scraping his way out backwards. Where was she? Oh, yes. His arrogant lordship, telling her what to do, taking the beastly uncomfortable settle instead of the wingchair, taking the tray and moving the tea table for her— lighting a fire she could not afford, although if she was leaving on Thursday there was enough fuel to last.

At least she was warm now. It had been a kindness on his part. Of course some men were considerate, but she must not linger over it as though he had done it for *her*.

Drat him! Cutting up her peace, arranging her life to suit his own convenience, dismissing her concerns about propriety in the most *cavalier* way, and—

Well, he did come around in the end…

Only because he had to, or you wouldn't have accepted the position!

Which begged the question: why—despite his desire to have her give Miss Trentham's thoughts a more proper direction— did he still persist in thinking her a proper companion for his stepmother and younger siblings?

She had flown at him like a hellcat, been as rude as she knew how and argued with him when he showed a wholly honourable concern for her comfort and welfare on the journey to Hereford.

Why hadn't he simply retracted his offer of employment and walked out?

And why was she even bothered about it? Why not do as he suggested and accept his money without argument? In a ladylike way, of course.

The seething, rebellious part of her mind informed her that she was going to have trouble accepting any of his lordship's dictatorial pronouncements without a great deal of argument. Ladylike or otherwise.

In the meantime, due to his lordship's rearrangement of her life, she had not enough time for everything. Certainly there was no time for pondering the odd feeling that she had just made the most momentous decision of her life. Or had it made for her. As for the ridiculous notion that Lord Braybrook was somehow dangerous—nonsense! Oh, she had no doubt that to some women he might be dangerous, but she had heard the scorn in his voice.

Believe me, I've no designs on your virtue.

That stung a little, but when all was said and done, she *was* a dowd. Perhaps a little more so than was necessary, but that was all to the good if it deflected the attention of men such as Lord Braybrook.

There had been that look, though, the feeling that he truly saw *her*, Christy, not merely Miss Daventry… She shut off the thought. Only a fool needed a lesson twice. The last thing she wanted was for him to notice her at all. Men seemed to have difficulty in comprehending when *no* was short for *no, I don't want to go to bed with you* rather than *no, you aren't offering enough.*

Crossly she pushed away from the door. She would not be sorry to leave this house. Once it had been happy enough, when Mama had been alive. But now it was filled with memories of nursing her dying mother. One must go on. And apparently, come Thursday, that was precisely what she would be doing.

As for Harry—was he mad? How could he imagine himself a suitable match for the Honourable Miss Trentham? A viscount's sister, no less! The least investigation… She knew the answer of course: his Grace, the Duke of Alcaston. The Duke's patronage had given Harry ideas dizzyingly far above his station.

Why could Lord Braybrook not behave like any normal man, forbid the match and see that the importunate suitor was denied the house? She had that answer as well; he thought it might drive his sister into revolt, and if his sister was as used to getting her own way as he was, then he had a point.

Unless... There was one way in which she might ensure Lord Braybrook could take that action without his sister uttering a word of protest. A single letter to his lordship would suffice. She looked at the bureau bookcase, hesitating.

Writing that letter would work, but at the cost of an appalling betrayal. Telling tales under a self-righteous cloak. And it was important for Harry to acknowledge the reality of his situation. Somehow she had to persuade him that his course of action was wrong. She needed to see him. Harry would ignore her letters to him. She must see him, try to persuade him of the wrongness of his intention to ensnare Miss Trentham or any other woman without telling her family the truth.

It might even ruin Harry if the truth were generally known. She wasn't sure, but she could not take that risk. As a last resort she might have to tell the truth, but it would drive a wedge between them and she had no other family. None that she cared to acknowledge.

And there was another consideration—the money Lord Braybrook offered. She did have some money. Enough to manage if she were very careful, and prices didn't rise. But there was little left over to hoard against illness or chilly old age. With this position, she could add to her meagre nest egg. Even if it were for a year or less, she would earn far more than she could in any other position, and she would save her keep as well.

She could pack up her books and take them with her. Braybrook had said his man of business would help; very well, she would ask him to sell the furniture bequeathed to her by Mama. It might not fetch very much, but every penny helped, and she was *damned* if she'd leave it for Goodall to sell on Harry's behalf!

Accepting Lord Braybrook's offer was the sensible thing to do. As long as she remembered her place. Separate. Apart. If only she could succeed in teaching Harry that lesson.

There was no real choice. She must go into Herefordshire and make Harry see the truth—that a greater gulf than mere money lay between the Daventrys and the Trenthams. If she failed, then, in the last resort, she must tell Lord Braybrook the truth herself.

Despite the fire warming the room, she shivered, imagining his disdain, the brilliant eyes turned icy. She stiffened her spine. It didn't matter. There was no question of her being upset by his contempt.

That sort of thing only hurt if one committed the folly of allowing someone too close. A warning voice suggested that in breaching her reserve and triggering her temper, Lord Braybrook had already stepped too close. She must ensure he never did so again.

Chapter Three

Three days later an elegant equipage pulled up St Michael's Hill to the Chapel of the Three Kings. Julian sat back against the squabs, still not quite able to believe what he had set in motion. On the seat opposite sat his valet, Parkes, stiff with disapproval, apparently determined to remain so for the entire journey. The news that he was required to sit inside, rather than on the box hobnobbing with his crony the coachman, had been ill received.

Not a chaperon precisely, thought Julian. For a young lady of quality, Parkes would be thoroughly inadequate. For the governess, however, his presence would dampen gossip. Besides which, Julian still felt uneasy about Miss Daventry. Something had sparked between them. Something dangerous, unpredictable. He found himself thinking about her at odd moments, smiling slightly at her stubborn independence.

He should have put her in her place, reminded her of the abyss between them. But that had been impossible with her cool façade shattered. They had spoken as equals. That must never happen again. No matter how much it piqued his interest.

She was just a woman with a temper that she had learned to control. Nothing more. There was no mystery behind the prim glasses that would not upon closer acquaintance fade to mundanity. In the meantime, it was safer to have Parkes, rigid and disapproving, on the opposite seat beside Miss Daventry. If nothing else, it would serve to remind her of the gulf between master and servant.

The carriage drew up outside the Chapel. Glancing out, he discovered Miss Daventry had foiled his plan to assist with her baggage. She was seated on one of a pair of trunks and accompanied by a female of indeterminate age and generous proportions. Julian wondered how the devil the pair of them had got the trunks up the street.

Miss Daventry had stood up. 'Goodbye, Sukey. Thank you for your help. I wish you would let me—'

'Oh, go on with you!' said the woman. She shot a suspicious glance towards the carriage and lowered her voice to the sort of whisper that could cut through an artillery engagement. 'Now you're quite sure all's safe? Can't trust these lords. Why, only t'other day—'

She broke off as Julian stepped out of the coach. Miss Daventry, he was pleased to note, flushed.

'I'm sure it will be all right, Sukey,' she said, darting a glance at Julian. 'Good morning, my lord.'

'Good morning, ma'am. My valet is within the coach,' said Julian, with all the air of a man setting a hungry cat loose in a flock of very plump pigeons. 'I do hope that allays any fears your friend has.'

The woman's eyes narrowed as she stepped forwards. 'Aye, I dare say it might. *If* so be as he ain't in your lordship's pocket, in a manner of speaking. If you *are* a lordship an' not some havey-cavey rascal!' She set her hands on her hips. 'I ain't looked after Miss Christy this long for her to be cozened by some flash-talkin' rogue! Why, only t'other day a chap persuaded a young lady into his carriage and had his wicked way with her. Right there in the carriage! An' her thinkin' it was all right an' tight, just acos he had another lady with him. Lady, hah! Madam, more like!'

'Ma'am, I assure you that I have no designs upon Miss Daventry's person,' he said with commendable gravity. 'Her brother is known to me and my only object is to convey her to her new position as my stepmother's companion.'

Sukey snorted. 'Easy said!'

'Sukey,' said Miss Daventry, 'I am sure it's all right. Truly.'

Clearly unconvinced, Sukey stalked to the coach and peered in, subjecting the scandalised Parkes to a close inspection. She stepped back, clearing her throat. 'I dare say it's all right.' She looked sternly at Miss Daventry. 'But you write soon's you arrive. Vicar'll read it to me, like he said. And keep writing so's we know.'

'Sukey—!' Miss Daventry appeared completely discomposed.

The older woman scowled. 'Can't be too careful, Miss Christy. You do like we said an' write!'

'Yes, Sukey,' said Miss Daventry meekly.

Julian blinked. There was someone in this world to whom Miss Daventry exhibited meekness?

'This is everything, Miss Daventry?' he asked, signalling to the groom to jump down.

She looked rather self-conscious. 'Yes. But one of the trunks is only books, so if there is not room—'

'There is enough room,' he told her.

The groom hefted one trunk into the boot along with the valise. The other trunk was strapped on the back.

Sukey came forwards and enveloped Miss Daventry in a hug. To Julian's amazement the hug was returned, fiercely.

Finally Sukey stepped back, wiping her eyes. 'Well, I'm sure I hope it'll all be as you say. You be a good girl. Your mam 'ud be real proud of you. You take care, Miss Christy.'

'I will. You have the keys safe?'

'Aye. I'll give 'em to that agent fellow. Off you go, then.'

Ignoring Julian's outstretched hand, Miss Daventry stepped into the coach and settled herself beside the valet.

Julian found himself facing judge and jury. He held out his hand. 'Goodbye, Sukey. You may rest assured that Miss Daventry is safe.'

Sukey accepted the proffered hand, after first wiping her own upon her skirt. 'I dare say. Miss Christy—Miss Daventry—she's a lady. Just you remember that, my lord. I'm sure I hope there's no offence.'

'None at all,' Julian assured her.

He stepped into the coach and sat opposite Miss Daventry. They moved off and Miss Daventry leaned out of the window, waving until they turned the corner and she sat back in her seat. Her mouth was firmly set, her expression unmoved. Yet something glimmered, trapped between her cheek and the glass of her spectacles. Julian watched, wondering if her emotions might get the better of her, but Miss Daventry's formidable self-control prevailed.

Relieved she was not about to burst into tears, he performed the introductions. 'My valet, Parkes, Miss Daventry. Parkes, this is Miss Daventry, who is to be companion to her ladyship and also assist as governess at times.'

Miss Daventry smiled. 'How do you do, Parkes?'

'Very well, thank you, miss.' And Parkes relapsed into the proper silence he considered appropriate when circumstances dictated that he should intrude upon his betters.

Seated in his corner of the carriage, Julian picked up his book and began to read. There was no point in dwelling on the fierce loyalty Miss Daventry had inspired in her servant. Nor her obvious emotion at Sukey's protectiveness. Of course Miss Daventry had feelings. Nothing surprising nor interesting in that. Her feelings were her own business. He had not the least reason to feel shaken by that solitary tear.

On the other side of the carriage Christy watched as his lordship disappeared into the book. She had not bothered to have a book to hand. If she dared to read in a carriage, the results would be embarrassing. Especially facing backwards.

She steeled herself to the prospect of a boring journey. There was no possibility of conversation with the elderly, dapper little valet. He had all the hallmarks of a long-standing family retainer. He would not dream of chattering on in the presence of his master, even if Christy herself did not fall into that limbo reserved for governesses and companions. She knew from experience that her life would be lived in isolation, neither truly a member of the family, nor part of the servants' hall. Neither above stairs, nor below. An odd thought came to her of generation after generation of ghostly governesses and companions, doomed to a grey existence on the half-landings. Just as well, too. It made her preferred reserve far easier to maintain.

Her stomach churned slightly, but she breathed deeply and otherwise ignored it. It was partly due to tiredness. With all the work of packing up the house, she had scarcely had more than five hours sleep a night, and last night she had barely slept at all. She never could sleep properly the night before a journey, for dreaming that the coach had gone without her and she was running after it, crying out for it to wait, not to abandon her…

She wondered if she dared lower the window and lean out. No. It would be presumptuous, and she would become sadly rumpled and dusty. Not at all ladylike. She set herself to endure, leaning back and closing her eyes.

Leaving Gloucester midway through the second day, Julian knew Miss Daventry was not a good traveller. He had without comment lowered all the windows. Not that she complained, or asked for any halts. But he could imagine no other explanation for the white, set look about her mouth, or that when they stopped, she would accept nothing beyond weak, black tea. She hadn't eaten a great deal of dinner or breakfast either.

He knew the signs from personal experience, only he had outgrown the tendency. There was little he could do about it, he thought, watching her. She was pale, and her eyes were closed, a faint frown between her brows. Oh, hell! 'Miss Daventry?'

'My lord?' The eyes opened. He blinked, still not used to their effect. The shadows beneath them were darker today than yesterday. It shouldn't bother him. *Noblesse oblige*, he assured himself. Nothing personal.

'Miss Daventry, perhaps you might change seats with me?'

Somehow she sat a little straighter. 'I am very well here, my lord. Thank you.'

He was not supposed to feel admiration—she was the governess-companion, for heavens' sake! His voice devoid of expression, he said, 'I think "well" is the last word that applies to you at this moment. Certainly not "very well". Come, exchange places with me.' Determined to expunge any misleading suggestion of personal feeling, he added, 'I cannot sit here any longer feeling guilty.'

Blushing, she complied, scrambling across past him.

'Thank you, my lord,' she said, still slightly pink.

He inclined his head. 'You are welcome, Miss Daventry.' Detached. Bored, even. 'Of course, should it be necessary, you will request a halt, will you not?'

She squared her shoulders. 'That will not be necessary, my lord. I should not wish to delay us.'

He raised his brows. 'I assure you, Miss Daventry, a brief halt will be a great deal more preferable than the alternative—won't it, Parkes?'

The valet, thus appealed to, permitted himself a brief smile. 'Indeed, sir. I've not forgotten how often you used to ask to be let down.'

Julian laughed at Miss Daventry's look of patent disbelief. 'Perfectly true, Miss Daventry. But I became accustomed eventually.'

A small smile flickered, and a dimple sprang to life. 'I fear I did not travel enough as a child then. I remained staidly in Bath.'

'Bath? I understood from your brother that your home had always been in Bristol.' Where the devil had that dimple come from?

Miss Daventry's pale cheeks pinkened again and the dimple vanished. 'Oh. Harry was very small when Mama moved to Bristol. And I went to school in Bath when I was ten. When I was older I became a junior assistant mistress.'

She subsided into silence, turning her head to watch the passing scenery.

Julian returned to his book, glancing up from time to time to check on Miss Daventry. He told himself that he was not, most definitely *not*, looking for that dimple. He had seen dimples before. But, really, for a moment there, the staid Miss Daventry had looked almost pretty. Spectacles and all. And her mouth was not in the least prim when she smiled. It was soft, inviting…

There was something about her. Something that made him want to look again… The eyes. That was all. Once he became accustomed to them, she would have no interest for him whatsoever. In the meantime she was suffering from carriage sickness and it behoved him to care for her. No more. No less.

Reminding himself of that, Julian reburied himself in his book, only glancing over the top every ten pages or so.

Aware of his occasional scrutiny, Christy tried to ignore it, repressing an urge to peep under her lashes. Her heart thudded uncomfortably; the result, she assured herself, of having so nearly revealed too much. Her pounding heart had nothing to do with those brilliant eyes that seemed to perceive more than they ought. It wasn't as if he cared about her, Christy Daventry. She was in his charge, therefore he owed it to himself to make sure she was comfortable. If she were not, it was a reflection on himself. He was being kind to her in the same way he would care for any other servant. Or his dog or horse. Admirable, but nothing to make her heart beat faster. *Noblesse oblige.* That or he was ensuring she wasn't sick in his beautifully appointed carriage.

But the bright glance of his blue eyes was hard to ignore. She was infuriated to find herself drifting into a daydream where his lordship's remarkable eyes were focused on her.

And not because he was concerned she might be sick all over his highly polished boots.

Ridiculous! She knew nothing of him. Except that he was thoughtful enough to find a companion for his stepmother, kind enough to change seats with the carriage-sick companion, and sensible enough not to drive his sister into revolt. Heavens! She was rapidly making him out to be a paragon.

Lord Braybrook was no paragon. The lazy twinkle in his eyes, combined with unconscious arrogance, suggested he was the sort of man a sensible woman steered well clear of. Assuming he had not already informed the sensible woman that he had no designs on *her* virtue, as though the idea were unthinkable. And a very good thing too. Christy had a sneaking suspicion that when his lordship did focus his attention on a female, good sense might come under heavy fire.

Oh, nonsense. He was probably horrid on closer acquaintance, the sort of man who kicked puppies. Yes. That was better. No one could like a man who kicked puppies. Or kittens. A pity she was having so much difficulty seeing him in the role. Much easier to see those lean fingers cradling a small creature… rocking it.

She smothered a yawn. Such a warm day…rocking…like a cradle. No, that was the coach. It was beautifully sprung and she felt much better now, facing forwards. Far less disconcerting to have the breeze from the open window in her face and see the world spinning towards her and away, rather than just spinning away in front of her…rocking, rocking, rocking…

Later, some time later, she was vaguely aware of being eased down to the seat, gentle hands removing her bonnet and spectacles, tucking a rug around her, a light touch feathering over her cheek…a dream, a memory, nothing more. Christy slept, cradled in dreams.

She awoke in near darkness to a touch on her shoulder and a deep voice saying, 'We are nearly there, Miss Daventry.'

Dazed, she sat up. Strong hands caught her as the coach swung around a turn. Coach? Where…? Blinking sleep away, she clutched at the strap hanging down, and the hands released her. Some of her confusion ebbed. This was not Bristol. She was in a coach, with Lord Braybrook and his valet. Why had she been lying down with a rug tucked over her? And where were her glasses? Everything was blurred.

Worried, she felt along the seat. They must have fallen off while she slept. And how dreadful that she had dozed off in front of Lord Braybrook and been shameless enough to lie down! And her spectacles were probably broken if they had fallen to the floor.

'Miss Daventry—is something amiss?'

She flushed. 'My spectacles must have fallen off. I can't see without them.'

'Of course.'

He reached into his pocket and drew out a small object, offering it to her. Confused, she reached for it and he placed it in her hand. Immediately her fingers recognised her spectacles, wrapped in a handkerchief.

'I thought they were safer in my pocket,' said his lordship.

Her fingers trembled slightly as she unfolded the handkerchief, shaken by a memory of gentle hands making her comfortable. Had her dream not been a dream? Had he laid her down on the seat and removed her spectacles and bonnet? And tucked the rug over her? She swallowed. He must have. But the caressing touch on her cheek had certainly been a dream. Hadn't it?

'Thank you, my lord,' she said, putting the spectacles on. The darkening world came back into focus. 'You are most kind.' She schooled her voice to polite indifference. His *noblesse oblige* again. If she remembered that, good sense would prevail. Not the foolish dream of tenderness. She handed him the handkerchief.

He pocketed it. 'Not at all, Miss Daventry. We shall be at the house in a few moments. Your bonnet is on the seat.'

His cool tones revived her wilting common sense. She retrieved the bonnet, and attempted to tidy herself, securing stray tendrils of hair with hairpins before replacing the bonnet. She thought that she must be sadly rumpled after the day's journey and sleeping in the carriage, but there was little she could do about it.

Julian dragged his gaze away from her to look out of the window. He could see the house now, lights glimmering in the dusk, its bulk dark against the deepening sky. Home. Concentrate on that. Not the impossible softness of her cheek under his fingers as he removed the bonnet and spectacles, not the jolt to his gut as he finally saw the colour of her hair, a rich tawny brown, rigidly scraped back and confined with a battalion of pins. Nor the queer protective sensation he had felt watching her sleep, her mouth relaxed and soft. Definitely not the odd pang he had felt when she awoke and sat up, clothes and hair askew, and that vulnerable sleepy look in her eyes.

She was in his employ, a servant to all intents and purposes. He had no business feeling anything for her beyond a sense of general responsibility. Indeed, to judge by her cool response to him, that was precisely what she expected and preferred.

She would neither expect nor wish him to be thinking about a little girl left at school in Bath. It was none of his concern. It should not come near him, let alone touch him. Ridiculous to feel sympathy for that long-ago little girl. He had gone to school himself at eight…memories poured back. His confusion at his first return for the holidays to find his mother gone. The servants' evasions of his questions. His father's bitterness and refusal to explain and the slow realisation that there was to be something scandalous, and expensive, called a 'divorce'. That he probably wouldn't see his mother again. And he hadn't. After the divorce she had married her lover and lived on the Continent, dying when he was fifteen. By then he had understood. His father's attitude had been quite clear when he married Serena as a matter of convenience to breed a couple of back-up heirs. Better to marry for reasons less likely to sour on one than love—property, connections and duty. One needed to like and respect one's spouse. Anything more was damned dangerous, and passion and desire were best served by taking a discreet mistress.

Still, he remembered the child's sense of abandonment and loss. Worse for a girl, of course. Boys were better able to cope with such things. Look at Davy, longing for the day he went to school. Not until he was ten, though. Serena had insisted and, since he knew his father had agreed, that was that. Besides which, he liked having Davy about the place. All of them, in fact.

Christy sat up straighter as they bowled up the avenue, the horses finding a second wind so close to their stable. They rattled over what appeared to be a stone bridge, under an arch into a narrow passageway and out into what must once have been a castle forecourt. Obviously someone had been watching for them, because as they drew up at the front door several people and a dog raced down the steps.

To Christy's startled eyes Lord Braybrook appeared to be surrounded by a mob as he stepped out of the coach into the light of the carriage lamps. She had the oddest sensation that thick glass reared up, allowing her to see, but slicing her apart from the bright circle.

'Did you bring us anything?'

'Why didn't you come back sooner? You *said* you would be back yesterday!'

Lord Braybrook fended off the barking black-and-tan setter, swung a small boy up into his arms and said, 'For heaven's sake, be still, you three! Get down, Juno. Anyone would think I'd been away for a month! How are you, Davy? Have you behaved yourself?'

'Yes.' The small boy nodded vigorously.

'Liar!' said an older boy of fifteen or so. 'He's been a little pest, Julian. He glued himself to the front steps last night so he wouldn't have to go to bed until you came home! The bottom of his nankeens is still there!'

'Yes,' chimed in the girl. 'And Mama made *us* pull him out of them when they wouldn't unstick! She said it was our fault he got the glue because we were supposed to be minding him!'

In the dusk, Christy had the distinct impression that his lordship was trying to preserve a straight face. Laughter bubbled up inside her.

'Davy?' His lordship's voice was mild enough, but something about it hinted at tempered steel.

'Well, you *said* you'd be back!' muttered the little boy.

'Hmm. I was delayed. Next time go to bed when you're told.' A stern voice, one to be obeyed, but affectionate. Caring.

'Oh, very well. That's what Mr Havergal said. *Did* you bring us something?'

'Who is Mr Havergal?' asked his lordship.

Davy shrugged. 'Just a friend of Mama's. Don't you know him? He calls quite often.' He tugged on his brother's lapel. 'Did you bring us anything?'

'No. I brought your mama something instead.'

'Mama?' came the chorus from three throats.

Lord Braybrook put the little boy down, patted the dog, an elegant bitch, and turned back to the coach. 'Permit me to assist you down, Miss Daventry.'

Christy stood up, and discovered herself to be appallingly cramped from the long journey, her legs barely able to hold her. Carefully she moved to the open door.

A strong hand gripped her elbow. Heat shot through her. Shocked, she looked up.

The firm lips curved a little, not unsympathetically.

'I dare say you are a trifle stiff, Miss Daventry. I am myself.'

Christy took leave to doubt that. The wretched man had leapt down as lightly as a stag, without any hint of stiffness.

'I…thank you, my lord.' Tingling heat still spread through

her. Folly! She was tired. Imagining things. She was chilled and his hand was warm.

He assisted her down from the carriage, steadying her as she stumbled a little.

'This is Miss Daventry,' he said. 'Miss Daventry, these are my youngest sister, Emma, and my brothers, Matthew and Davy.'

Christy summoned a smile, despite her tiredness. 'Good evening, Emma, Matthew, Davy.' The dog came and sniffed at her and she bent to fondle the silky ears.

'And Juno,' said his lordship. The dog returned to him, tail waving.

'Good evening, Miss Daventry,' said Emma politely.

'Good evening, ma'am,' said Matthew, bowing slightly.

Davy scowled. 'Did you make Julian late?'

Now she thought about it, she probably had. 'I am afraid so, Davy,' she admitted. 'His lordship kindly gave me an extra day to ready myself before leaving Bristol.'

Davy looked unimpressed. 'Mama was cross with me because of my nankeens,' he informed her. 'I had bread and butter for my supper, and no cake.'

Lord Braybrook stifled an odd sound and leant down to give his small brother a not unkindly swat on the behind. 'Don't blame Miss Daventry for your misdoings, scamp. Now, off with you. It's long past your bedtime.'

Lord Braybrook kept his hand close to Christy's elbow as they went up the steps into the mellow lighted hall, closely attended by Juno, who seemed to feel she must remain as close as possible to her restored master.

A butler bowed. 'Welcome home, my lord.'

'Good evening, Hallam,' said Lord Braybrook. The butler glanced at Christy but his well-trained visage betrayed not the least surprise or curiosity.

She stared about her. The hall was enormous. She had the impression of great age, a high-vaulted ceiling and pinky-brown weathered stone. A branching stone staircase at the back led up to a gallery

'Welcome to Amberley, Miss Daventry,' said Lord Braybrook.

Her response was lost in a startled exclamation from the back of the hall.

'Good heavens! Who is this, Julian?'

Two people were there. One a tall, slender young lady who must, Christy surmised, be Miss Trentham. Black curls, loosely arranged and confined with a pink bandeau, framed a vivid face with the family eyes. The other was an older woman, seated, her legs covered with a shawl, and a large tabby cat in her lap. An instant later, she realised that the chair had wheels—a Bath chair.

The woman was staring at her in amazement. And, she thought, disapproval. Her new employer. Lady Braybrook herself.

'Julian, what have you done?' This in tones of deep suspicion.

His lordship went to her, bent down and kissed her on the cheek. 'I suppose you will think I have been far too precipitate and should have discussed it with you, but—'

'No doubt!' said Lady Braybrook.

Lord Braybrook smiled. 'This is Miss Daventry, Serena—your new companion.'

If Lady Braybrook had looked puzzled before, she looked positively stunned now. Her jaw dropped and she said, 'But I told you! I don't want a companion! Even if I did, I would very much prefer to choose my own!'

Christy blinked. She had known he was autocratic—arrogant, even. Her lips set. Yes, she had definitely known he was arrogant! But this! He had completely bypassed his stepmother's views on the subject!

Anger, and hot embarrassment, overcame the little voice warning her that she'd better bite her tongue.

She lifted her chin and said in the sweetest tones she could muster, 'Thank you, my lord, for a most interesting, if wasted, journey. Perhaps next time you might have the goodness to take account of the views of *all* the persons involved before embroiling anyone else in your schemes. I do trust that I may be offered a bedchamber for the night rather than trudging back immediately!'

Chapter Four

Lady Braybrook's eyebrows nearly disappeared into her elegant cap, but Christy didn't care. To hell with what anyone thought of her. She was tired after two days' travel, and now she had the journey back. She probably wouldn't even have time to see Harry before being bundled off and she would have to dig into her slender savings to stay at an inn while she found lodgings.

Then, 'Oh, well done, dear! Julian, for heaven's sake, stop standing there gaping and see that Miss…Daventry, did you say?'—a swift glance at Miss Trentham— 'Yes, have Miss Daventry's baggage taken up. She may have the guest chamber along from me. That will do very well.'

She held out her hand, saying, 'You must be famished, Miss Daventry, so do not worry about changing.' Bemused, Christy came forwards to accept the proffered hand.

'Lissy dear, show Miss Daventry where she may wash her face and hands. Then bring her to the small dining parlour.'

Christy permitted herself to be led away by Miss Trentham and heard Lady Braybrook say in tones of steely determination, 'In the meantime, Julian, shall we discuss this privately? Matt—take Davy upstairs and see that he goes to bed.'

* * *

Miss Trentham smiled at Christy in a very friendly way as she led her out of the hall and asked, 'Are you really Miss Daventry? What a coincidence! I...*we* know a Mr Daventry. He...he is a most particular friend.' She blushed prettily.

'No coincidence at all,' said Christy. 'Harry is my brother. Lord Braybrook sought me out intentionally. Since he was under the erroneous impression that your mother required a companion, he thought of me.'

Miss Trentham's blue, blue eyes opened wide. 'But, surely *you* need not work?'

There was no scorn in her voice, only shock.

First trick to his lordship, thought Christy, following Miss Trentham down a passage. Probably the last one though, given Lady Braybrook's reaction to his high-handed efforts. She elaborated, feeling she might as well partially earn the quarter's wages that Lord Braybrook would undoubtedly insist she accept. 'But of course, Miss Trentham. Harry must make his own way in the world and I cannot be a burden on him.' Miss Trentham looked a little self-conscious, and Christy went on, 'At this stage of his career he has quite enough to do to support himself. Our—' She caught herself and went on, 'His godfather is generous, but it does not extend to supporting a sister.'

'Oh. I...I see.' The dazed tone suggested that Miss Trentham was gaining a whole new view of matters beyond Harry's good looks and charm. 'Here we are,' she said, opening a door. 'This is the garden room. Mama insists the boys come inside through this room and there are always soap and water here.'

Removing her bonnet to lave her face and hands, Christy thought Lady Braybrook sounded extremely practical. Kind, too, and probably a far more pleasant employer than her last. Christy sighed as she dried her face. She wouldn't be getting much of a reference out of this one either.

To Whom It May Concern:

Miss Daventry arrived to be my companion on Friday evening. After raking down my stepson, she returned to Bristol on Saturday morning.

Yours etc., etc.

As a reference, it had limitations, she acknowledged, re-pinning her hair. And as a position, this must be a record: dismissed before she had begun. Her hair as neat as she could make it, she turned back to Miss Trentham.

'Are you ready?' asked the young woman. 'It will be famous having you here, you know. Leave your bonnet. One of the maids will take it up to your bedchamber.'

Christy left the bonnet and followed Miss Trentham from the room. 'Ah, Miss Trentham, I believe Lady Braybrook said that she did not want a companion. I dare say I shall be dispatched back to Bristol tomorrow.'

Leading the way along the corridor, Miss Trentham shook her head so the black curls bounced. 'Oh, pooh! Of course you won't. That is what is so particularly annoying about Julian—he persuades people to do precisely as he says! Even Mama. And he is always so…so insufferably certain that he knows what is best. Mama says he means well, but if you were to ask me, he's a tyrant!'

'Explain, if you please, Julian.' There was a distinct bite in Serena's voice.

Julian had wheeled her into a small parlour off the hall. 'A ploy,' he said, closing the door and turning to face her. 'The companion part is a blind. She's actually here to keep Lissy in order.' Bringing up a chair for himself, he explained his reasoning.

Serena's eyebrows rose. She was silent for a moment, thinking it over, and he waited.

'I see,' she said eventually. And he had the sneaking suspicion that she did see. Every single machination anyway. He hoped to hell she couldn't see the inexplicable attraction Miss

Daventry held for him. Not that it mattered, because he wasn't going to do anything about it.

'I suppose she's dowdy enough for a companion-governess,' said Serena thoughtfully.

Dowdy? 'Nothing of the sort,' he said stiffly. 'She is still in mourning for her mother, Serena!'

Amusement crept around Serena's eyes and mouth. 'Oh,' she said. 'I see. Well, I dare say some of my own mourning garb can be altered to fit her. It will certainly give Lissy pause for thought.'

'She stays, then?' What the hell was that jolt of relief in his midriff?

Serena blinked. 'Oh, I think so, dear. I'm sure she will suit admirably. She's not at all mealy-mouthed, is she?'

'No.' Along with meek, that was the last adjective he'd use to describe Miss Christiana Daventry.

Christy tried not to let her shock show. Lit with more candles than she would have used in a year, the small dining parlour was somewhat larger than the entire ground floor of the Christmas Steps house. And, since these were wax candles, without the reek of tallow.

'Ah, here they are.' Lady Braybrook was already seated at a circular table with his lordship and Matthew, who both rose politely.

'Come and sit beside me, Miss Daventry,' said Lady Braybrook. 'I apologise for my lack of tact earlier. You must have thought yourself in a perfect madhouse! Unfortunately Braybrook did not see fit to apprise me of his intentions.' She glared at her stepson, who had strolled around the table to pull out a chair for Christy.

Christy managed to look demure and murmured her thanks as she seated herself. There was no faulting his lordship's manners, even if his high-handed assurance left a great deal to be desired.

'I beg your pardon, Serena,' said Lord Braybrook, sitting down again.

Christy doubted the sincerity of his lordship's contrition. And she observed that, far from kicking puppies, his lordship was obviously very fond of dogs. The setter, Juno, lay as close as possible to her master's chair, chin resting on a stretcher.

'Mama,' said Miss Trentham, 'Miss Daventry is Mr Daventry's sister!' Her eyes sparkled. 'Should I send him a note to say she is here?'

Christy caught Lord Braybrook's eye, and said, 'How kind, Miss Trentham. On accepting his lordship's offer, I took the liberty of writing to Harry myself.' Spurred on by malice aforethought, she added, 'I would be most grateful if you were to inform him that I have returned to Bristol and will write again soon.'

An odd choking sound came from Lady Braybrook. Christy turned quickly and her ladyship patted her lips with her napkin. Laughing grey eyes met hers.

'No, no, Miss Daventry. That will not be necessary. Now Braybrook has explained *all* the particulars, I am delighted to have you here.' She glanced at her daughter. 'Yes, Lissy, Julian explained the connection. A kind thought to assist Miss Daventry in this way. And so pleasant for me.'

Miss Trentham brightened. 'Oh, famous! You see, Miss Daventry—I told you Julian would talk Mama around. I'm sure Mr Daventry will come to see you as soon as may be.'

Christy had not the least doubt of that. His lordship was one of those annoying persons who always contrived to achieve their ends.

Lord Braybrook met her gaze blandly. 'Naturally, ma'am, when he does so, you must take a morning or afternoon off to spend with him. I dare say you have not met for some time.'

'No,' said Christy. 'We have not.' *Not since Mama's funeral.*

It had rained unrelentingly. And they had stood there, soaked to the skin, wondering if *he* would come. If he would have the decency…well, *she* had wondered. Harry had thought it unlikely. Indeed, unnecessary.

Don't be a peagoose, Christy. I dare say he has much to occupy him.

She would never forgive Alcaston for that. Never. Not to come to the funeral. Nor send so much as a wreath. Discretion, of course. That had been his reason for not attending little Sarah's funeral all those years ago…but she had foolishly thought that he would attend Mama's funeral. She shivered. If anything further had been needed to drive home the necessity of standing alone, that had been it.

'Miss Daventry?'

Horrified, she realised that his lordship was speaking to her and that she had been staring into space.

The bright eyes were focused on her, faintly frowning.

'I beg your pardon, my lord. I was woolgathering.'

Heat pricked behind her eyes, but she kept her voice steady. He was still watching her, with eyes that peeled away too many defences.

'I fancy Miss Daventry is very tired, Julian,' said Lady Braybrook. 'I'm sorry, my dear. Your room will be prepared by the time you have finished your supper and you may go to bed. We need not arrange anything tonight. Do have some chicken soup. And, Lissy, please pass the rolls to Miss Daventry.'

As she helped herself to the soup and accepted a roll, Christy wondered what sort of establishment she had landed in. A greater contrast with her previous live-in situation could not be imagined. A sense of dislocation niggled at her. Rather than treating the governess-companion as a lesser being, Lady Braybrook treated her as if she were a favoured guest. If she were not on her guard, she would forget her place. Never before had that been a problem. Never before had she imagined herself belonging. Not caught forever on the half-landing. She *must* remember that, all kindness aside, Lady Braybrook was her mistress.

And Lord Braybrook her master?

She gritted her teeth. She was a dependant. Not their equal. If she could not remember that, how could she convince Harry?

Christy spent the next morning unpacking, or rather she spent twenty minutes unpacking, and the rest considering how best to fit into the household. Lady Braybrook, she discovered, did not usually leave her bedchamber until late morning, when a footman carried her down to the drawing room. This was explained by Grigson, an unsmiling female whose fashionable clothes proclaimed her Lady Braybrook's dresser, when she came to tell Christy that her ladyship awaited her in the drawing room.

Lady Braybrook was seated by a sunny window, the tabby cat enthroned on her lap. 'Thank you, Grigson. That will be all. Good morning, Miss Daventry. You slept well? You look much better this morning. Braybrook mentioned that you were uncomfortable in the carriage.'

Christy curtsied. 'Thank you, ma'am. I slept very well. His lordship should not have concerned himself.'

'Hmm. Well, I am glad you are feeling better. Do come and sit down and we can discuss your duties. You really only have Davy and Emma. Matthew is home from school, so you need not worry about him. Lissy has her French and Italian conversation and her music to practise. And she should do some sketching. You are able to help her with those?'

'Of course, ma'am.'

'Excellent.' Lady Braybrook beamed. 'With Matt on holiday, Emma and Davy need not have many lessons. Emma must practise her music and Davy must continue his reading, French and a little arithmetic, but until Matthew goes back, there is little point in more. Davy would play you up dreadfully, I dare say!'

'I assure you, he would not get away with it,' said Christy.

And mentally kicked herself. Adoring mamas did not commonly like to know their high-spirited darlings needed discipline.

'Excellent,' said Lady Braybrook. 'From the way you gave Braybrook his own last night, I didn't imagine you would have any difficulty with Davy.'

Christy blinked.

The cat rose, stretching, all elegant muscle and sinew. Lady Braybrook made no effort to hold it, and it leapt down, stalking towards Christy.

She eyed it sideways, wondering if her pet's desertion would offend Lady Braybrook. Unblinking emerald eyes stared back.

'Ma'am, if you do not dislike it, I have given some thought to my role here—' She broke off as the cat sprang into her lap. Oh, drat! She could hardly tip the creature off and it had been so long since she had been able to have a cat.

Lady Braybrook smiled over her embroidery, as the needle continued to flash. 'My dear Miss Daventry, why should I dislike it?' A faint twinkle appeared in her eyes. 'After all, you have had more time to become used to the idea than I!'

Christy blushed, and petted the cat, who had settled down purring.

Lady Braybrook laughed. 'Oh, don't feel embarrassed. Believe me, I know how autocratic Braybrook can be when he is arranging everything for one's good. Maddening, is he not? Now, tell me: what were you thinking?'

'Well,' said Christy, 'I noticed this morning that you did not come down until quite late and—'

She broke off at Lady Braybrook's wry smile.

'These silly legs,' she explained. 'I take my bath in the morning, and of course it does take a little time. Such a nuisance...'

'Ma'am, I did not mean—'

Lady Braybrook chuckled. 'Of course not. Tell me what you have in mind.'

'I wondered if I taught the younger children in the morning, before you came down, if that would work?'

'An excellent idea,' said Lady Braybrook. 'Then I shall steal you for the rest of the day. Although after lunch you might accompany Lissy and Emma for their walk.'

'Naturally I would be happy to do so,' said Christy, 'but if I am to be your companion—' The amused look on Lady Braybrook's face stopped her.

'You have other duties, Miss Daventry,' pointed out Lady Braybrook.

Christy flushed. 'Lord Braybrook explained, then?'

'Braybrook,' said her ladyship, not mincing words, 'is the most devious and annoying man imaginable. I haven't decided if he is disguising your true purpose from Lissy, by pretending that you are my companion, or disguising your true purpose from *me*, by pretending you are here to help open Lissy's eyes!'

Christy found herself smiling. 'He used both arguments with me. Perhaps I am merely a convenient stone to be hurled at two birds.'

Lady Braybrook's lips twitched. 'He's not completely blind, Miss Daventry. I doubt he believes you to be made of stone.'

To this cryptic remark, Christy said nothing. There was something unsettling about the amusement in Lady Braybrook's voice. The cat rolled in her lap, offering his belly, eyes closed to blissful slits as she obliged and kneaded.

'Another thing, my dear. That striped creature is Tybalt— Tyb. He has an absolute genius for making up to people like Braybrook who loathe cats. If you dislike him, or he makes you sneeze, for heaven's sake, tip him off.'

Again the sense of dislocation swept her. She felt not at all like a dependant. Lady Braybrook was doing everything in her power to make an outsider feel at home. She had even given her one of the best bedchambers.

'Thank you, ma'am, but I love cats.'

Lady Braybrook smiled. 'Excellent. Braybrook, like most

men, prefers dogs. I must say I have never worked out why so many women love cats, and men profess to loathe them, but love dogs.'

'That,' said Christy, caught off guard, 'might be because cats are independent, not slavish like dogs. Perhaps we women admire an independence and power few of us will ever know. Your Tybalt may sit in my lap, but he is the one conferring a favour. Cats are rather like aristocrats. They have staff.' Oh, dear. Should she have said that?

A ripple of delighted laughter broke from Lady Braybrook and she laid aside her embroidery. 'Oh, goodness. I'd never thought of that, but you are perfectly right. Although many women love dogs too.'

'And that,' said Christy, wildly aware that the conversation had somehow become far too personal, 'is because we are far more flexible than gentlemen and are capable of loving creatures for quite opposite reasons. Cats for their dignity and independence, and a dog for its loyalty.'

'Good morning, Serena. May I interrupt?'

Christy froze. As a lesson in the perils of unguarded conversation, this would be hard to beat.

Julian had enough sense to pretend he hadn't heard the comment about aristocrats and cats, but he was pleased to see he had been correct in his estimation that Serena and Miss Daventry would suit.

'Of course, dear,' said Serena. 'Miss Daventry was just observing how much you and Tyb have in common.'

Julian took one look at Tyb's current position, sprawled with considerable indelicacy in Miss Daventry's lap. He wasn't sure any reply was safe. His mouth dried at the sight of Miss Daventry's slender fingers kneading that furry abandoned belly. He'd never realised all the advantages of being a cat before.

Miss Daventry, of course, was taking no notice of him whatsoever. Although he thought there was a faint flush of colour in her cheeks.

Piqued, he said, 'Good morning, Miss Daventry, I trust you slept well?'

'Very well, thank you, my lord.'

Prim. Proper. Precisely what she ought to be. Not speaking until spoken to, evincing a becoming respect for her betters. But under the dowdy façade lurked quite a different creature. One who was not Miss Daventry at all. One who argued, and refused to be put in her place. Who sat kneading a cat's belly in a slow hypnotic rhythm that sent heat curling through him. Christy. That was the woman he wanted to know. And he wouldn't mind switching places with Serena's cat either. His body tightened. Hell! If Miss Daventry could read his thoughts, her cheeks would ignite in fury.

'Do you require something, Julian?' asked Serena.

He turned to her, realising that he had been staring at Miss Daventry. Somehow he had to relegate the woman to her proper place.

'No. I merely came in to see that you were well. I will be in the library if you require me. Just send Miss Daventry.'

Serena sent him a very straight look. 'Thank you, Julian. I believe I need not use Miss Daventry like a page boy. We will see you later, then. Good morning.'

Julian removed himself, before he could put his other boot in his mouth. It was the cat's fault. If the blasted creature hadn't been lolling in Miss Daventry's lap so brazenly, he would never have been such a fool.

His agent's reports would banish his wayward thoughts. Anything to rid himself of this fancy to find out what, beyond a sting like a wasp, hid behind Miss Daventry's prim façade.

At luncheon Julian congratulated himself on an excellent choice of companion. Serena seemed brighter, happier than he had seen her in a long while. Not that she was ever self-pitying, but he had thought for some time that she had lost something of her sparkle.

Miss Daventry was worth her hire for that alone.

'I think, this afternoon, Miss Daventry might accompany Lissy and Emma for their walk,' said Serena, sipping coffee. 'She must learn her way about.'

'We intended to ride this afternoon, Mama,' said Lissy. 'Of course, Miss Daventry may still come with us. May she not, Julian?'

He glanced up, trying not to appear at all interested. 'Miss Daventry ride? Yes, if she wishes.' As an invitation it left a great deal to be desired, but his unbecoming interest in Miss Daventry must not be indulged.

Miss Daventry cleared her throat.

Bracing himself for the inevitable, Julian said, 'I collect you have an objection, ma'am. Please state it.'

Miss Daventry's eyes narrowed. 'Not precisely an objection, my lord. An observation.'

Did she *have* to be so damned pedantic?

'Yes?' He didn't like the snappish tone of his voice, but Miss Daventry seemed not to notice.

'I don't ride,' she said.

'Don't ride? But *everybody* rides!' Lissy's disbelief was palpable.

'Not everyone, Miss Trentham,' said Miss Daventry gently. 'I have always lived in a town and we couldn't afford a horse.'

'But Harry, I mean, Mr Daventry rides. He told me he had ridden since he was a child—'

'Enough, Lissy.' Julian was at a loss to explain the revulsion sweeping him. This was precisely why he had hired Miss Daventry—to demonstrate to Lissy the gulf between them. To force her to realise all she would be giving up. Now, hearing Miss Daventry explain the reality of genteel poverty with quiet dignity, he suddenly didn't like it. The opposite side of the equation was laid brutally bare—Miss Daventry's humiliation.

He had never intended to rub *her* nose in the gulf between herself and Lissy. If he were honest, it had not occurred to him. And yet, he could see Lissy thinking, looking at Miss Daventry's dowdy appearance with new eyes, applying it to herself. And Miss Daventry seemed unperturbed.

Why wouldn't she be? She's had years to accustom herself to her station and you are paying her fifty pounds extra for the privilege of having her nose rubbed in it.

Part of him rebelled against this cold logic. Surely, even if only as part of her remuneration, she was entitled to some enjoyment in her life. It might ram the message home to Lissy all the faster, he told himself. Yes, that was it.

He looked across at Serena. She raised her brows, dearly.

'We still have Merlin in the stables,' he said, wondering what the devil was so entertaining.

She smiled. 'Dear Merlin. I dare say he will be glad of a little outing. By all means, dear. I'm sure it will be very beneficial.'

Beneficial for whom? wondered Julian. Something about Serena's smile had alarm bells clanging. He turned to Miss Daventry. 'Ma'am, if you would care for it, you may ride Lady Braybrook's old mount. He is very quiet, used to carrying a lady.'

Miss Daventry demurred. Of course.

'Thank you, sir, but I will be more than happy to remain with Lady Braybrook. I—'

'No, dear. Go with them,' said Serena. 'I would be much happier if you learned to ride. Lissy is for ever giving the grooms the slip when she rides out, but I fancy she will not be so rag-mannered with you! Especially if she knows you to be inexperienced.' She shot a glance at her daughter. Who blushed.

In one final attempt to avoid her fate, Miss Daventry said, 'But I have no riding habit!'

Serena—Julian silently blessed her—dismissed that with a wave of her hand. 'Oh, pish! You may have my old one. It will be a little large, but the colour will suit you. It's quite a dark blue, so you need not scruple to wear it despite your mourning. And there are any number of mourning gowns in my dressing room. Heaven knows I wouldn't fit into most of them any more.' She smiled ruefully at Miss Daventry, and added, 'I have a tendency to put on weight sitting in this horrid chair. It would be better, of course, if I were not so fond of cakes and made more use of my exercise chair.'

Julian looked at Lissy. His sister was watching Miss Daventry, an odd expression on her face, as the companion accepted politely.

Chapter Five

Christy frowned at her reflection. The riding habit was slightly too large, but the wretched thing was almost flattering. She had an observable figure. Most of her gowns deliberately disguised that. Wearing gowns in any way related to one's shape was, in the crudely expressed opinion of her former employer, 'asking for it'. Too-large gowns—which were easier to button up un-assisted—the caps, and the spectacles all helped. Not that the spectacles were mere disguise—she would trip over her own feet without them.

No one looked beyond a dull, shapeless gown, the cap and spectacles. They saw only the dowdy paid companion or gover-ness. It was safer that way.

Only she had the uncomfortable sensation that, like his lordship, Lady Braybrook saw Christy, not Miss Daventry. She had been right about the habit suiting Christy. The deep blue gave a little colour to her cheeks, although that might be the country air. She fingered the braid up the front of the habit. It was beautiful, so elegant. She had never worn such clothes in her life. Perhaps it didn't matter. She was still the companion-governess. Borrowed plumage did not make fine birds, she told herself as she went downstairs.

'There you are!'

Lissy and Matthew were waiting in the hall, which Christy had learnt was the Great Hall. Apparently Amberley was very old indeed and the Trenthams had been here for ever.

'You do look nice,' said Lissy, and Christy bit her lip not to smile at the new hint of patronage. 'The horses have been brought around. We have Mama's old hack for you. He's terribly quiet.'

'Not a slug, though,' put in Matthew. 'You could have ridden another horse, but Julian said it was better to be safe than sorry. He said he didn't want to bury you.' Not a hint of patronage there.

'An unwelcome expense, no doubt,' said Christy.

Matthew grinned. 'He didn't put it quite like that.' The grin turned impish. 'It was more the inconvenience.'

Christy peered over the top of her spectacles at him, in a manner she had found to be very effective with youngsters. They never seemed to realise it was a bluff; that without looking through the lenses she could see very little.

Even so, she could see Matthew's grin; and those blue eyes, very like his brother's, continued to twinkle.

'Julian's outside, with the horses and Emma and Davy,' said Lissy, cheerfully. Not at all as though this were the brother she had described as a tyrant the previous evening.

No doubt he meant to see them off, thought Christy, wishing she had not agreed to this ride. No doubt she would make a complete fool of herself. Wasn't one meant to learn to ride as a child? Probably little Davy was more accomplished than she would ever be.

Sure enough, when Lissy and Matthew took her out on to the front steps, Davy was already mounted on a chestnut pony with a pretty head and lively eye. Emma was mounted on a bay. His lordship stood close by, holding the reins of a tall black horse, and a lead rein attached to the bridle of a sleepy-looking dappled grey. Not a horse, really. More a large pony.

Grooms held two other horses. Mentally counting, and looking at the quality of the black horse, Christy came to a dead halt at the top of the steps as an appalling realisation struck her. She had assumed a groom would accompany the riding party and attend to her instruction. Apparently not. His lordship was dressed for riding. Which meant...she gulped...he was planning to teach her to ride.

Schooling herself to reveal nothing, she met his lordship's limpid gaze. And saw the glimmer of unholy amusement.

Drat him!

He knew, to a nicety, just how embarrassing she would find this and he was enjoying it!

His greeting confirmed it. 'Miss Daventry—I'm sure you understand that I prefer to ensure your safety myself.'

She smiled. Sweetly. 'I am very grateful for your lordship's condescension.'

His brows snapped together, and his mouth hardened. Then his gaze flickered to Lissy, listening avidly, and he said, 'Not at all, ma'am. Come and meet Merlin.'

Meet Merlin. As though the creature were of some account to him, like his dog. Christy watched, fascinated, as Lord Braybrook petted the old horse...something told her Merlin was no longer in the first flush of youth. His lordship's hands were gentle, rubbing the ears, stroking the arched neck. Then something was produced from a pocket and whiffled up out of his hand with an appreciative crunch and snort.

'Come.' His lordship spoke abruptly. 'Hold out your hand. Quite flat and still.' She obeyed and he placed a sugar lump on her palm. Horrified, she stared at it. Old though he might be, judging by the noise he'd made munching the last lump, Merlin had teeth. Large ones. In perfect working order. But before she could protest, or drop the sugar, soft whiskery lips took the treat with amazing delicacy. The teeth, again, dealt with the offering in a fashion anything but delicate.

A delighted thrill went through Christy. Without thinking she stroked the long nose and found it velvety. Liquid dark eyes blinked at her wisely, and then...that same velvet nose was shoved against her chest and rubbed up and down with great enthusiasm.

Caught unawares, Christy staggered back hard against an immovable wall. A wall with arms that steadied her effortlessly. A shocking warmth stole through her and for one heart-stopping instant she relished the male strength surrounding her. A delight promptly banished by hot embarrassment, but before she could react, strong hands grasped her shoulders and eased her away.

'I beg your pardon, Miss Daventry,' said his lordship in obvious amusement. 'Merlin *is* a gentleman, but he is very fond of sugar. Are you all right?'

'Perfectly,' she said, ignoring her racing pulse.

Davy, from his perch on the little chestnut, said in pleased tones, 'Look, Julian! Merlin has slobbered all over her chest.'

Christy looked down. Sure enough the braided front was a mess. She gulped and met laughing blue eyes that were pointedly *not* looking at her...chest.

'Don't worry, Miss Daventry. I'm sure it will come off.'

'But, Lady Braybrook won't like—'

'Nonsense,' said Lord Braybrook. 'She always grumbled about that trick of Merlin's. He has slobbered on it before. Besides, she gave you the habit. It's yours now.'

Christy flushed. Besides the habit, Lady Braybrook had given her a number of gowns, saying she never wore them and that they were unsuitable for Lissy. They were even more unsuitable for the governess. Of course, a lady's maid was given her mistress's cast-offs, so perhaps it wasn't *too* improper.

'Can we go? *Please?*' begged Davy.

Matthew had mounted, and one of the grooms was about to put Lissy up. Christy gulped as the groom linked his hands for Lissy's booted foot and threw the girl into her saddle. Dear God. If he did that to her, she would go straight over the saddle and land on the ground.

'Miss Daventry?'

Lord Braybrook's voice sounded oddly distant.

'Is there…is there not a mounting block? I don't think the way Miss Trentham was—'

'I'll put you up, Miss Daventry.'

Unresisting, she was led around to the saddle. Balanced against Merlin's side, clutching the stirrup, she lifted a foot. His hands grasped her waist and lifted her. She gasped, and found herself perched on the saddle. For a moment his hands stayed at her waist, then dropped to her hip, steadying her. That was all. Wasn't it? Her body hummed, as if…as if he had caressed her. Nonsense! He was making sure she was safely in place. She sat up as straight as possible, and the disturbing hands released her. She sighed in relief, thinking her ordeal over.

Wrong. His lordship was busy arranging her right leg safely over the pommel, long fingers gripping her knee as he pushed it into position. She froze, desperately trying to ignore the intimacy of his touch. Ridiculous. He was merely showing her how to sit. There was nothing intimate about it. Then his hands were on her left ankle as he adjusted her foot in the stirrup. She had to remind herself that she was wearing a boot. That he was not really touching her ankle. More accidental touches as he shortened the stirrup leather. Then he caught her foot again.

'Keep your heel pushed down, Miss Daventry,' he instructed, doing it for her. 'That helps to keep your, er, *seat*, firmly in the saddle.'

That was a relief to know. She felt like a bug perched up there. Merlin seemed a great deal taller than he had from the ground.

'Now—your reins.'

Christy looked down at the reins. She had picked them up. She knew that much. But what should she do with them?

His lordship showed her. 'Just hold them lightly,' he said, long fingers guiding hers to the right position, and showing her how to shorten the reins. 'They are not to help you balance. Only to guide him. You must only feel his mouth. A light contact. And keep your thumbs on top.'

Her hands were gloved, but his touch felt just as shockingly intimate as it had on her legs. He stepped back and looked her over. She blushed.

'Very well. At least you don't have to be told to keep your back straight,' he commented. He walked around to his own horse and mounted with fluid grace.

Ridiculous to glow at such off-hand praise. Determinedly she sat even straighter in the saddle.

Merlin snorted and took a couple of steps. Stifling a gasp, as her balance shifted, Christy clutched at the saddle, but Merlin came up against the end of the leading rein and stopped. She straightened at once and glanced across at his lordship, but he seemed not to have noticed.

Any more than he had noticed how scared she was. Stupid. It was years since she had fallen off that horse of Harry's, and Merlin was much quieter, but still…she forced herself to breathe deeply.

All women had waists, Julian reminded himself. Discovering Miss Daventry's waist under the slightly-too-large habit might have been a surprise, but not one that should have had his hands lingering, marvelling at the suppleness of the curve, and then drifting to her hip.

With a swift glance at Miss Daventry to assure himself that she was secure in the saddle, he tugged gently at the leading rein and put his own mount into a walk. Miss Daventry's face blanked as Merlin moved, but she gave no other sign, beyond sitting very straight and still.

He had been trying to believe that Miss Daventry must be as shapeless as her gowns. But she wasn't. She disguised her body as effectively as she hid her true nature. Under the dowdy clothes she was slender and lissom as a willow. She would be sweet, warm…*sweet*? Hell's teeth! If she knew what he was thinking now, and as he settled her in the saddle, she'd be a virago!

Miss Daventry might have an elegant figure and a neatly turned ankle, but she was a bundle of prickles. For which, he admitted, she could not be blamed. A wise woman in her position avoided drawing mens' attention, unless she wished for a career in the *demi-monde*. Governesses and companions always held themselves slightly apart.

A lonely existence…

'Where shall we go,' asked Lissy, bringing her mare up beside them. 'Miss Daventry, you choose.'

Julian noted that Miss Daventry looked somewhat startled at being consulted. She demurred.

'Oh. That's very kind, Miss Trentham, but I do not know this part of the country at all, so—'

'I like the river,' said Davy, hopefully.

Lissy sighed theatrically. 'Not the river again, Davy!'

'No, Davy!' said Emma. 'Not everyone likes waiting while you watch for trout that never appear.'

Davy scowled.

About to vote for the river and bring down a deluge of fury on his head, Julian was forestalled by Miss Daventry.

'A river? With trout? Real trout?'

Davy's scowl vanished as hope rekindled. 'And salmon. Really big ones,' he said, dropping his reins to demonstrate. He shot a glare at his sisters as he caught up the reins again. 'And they do appear. Julian owns them.' This last with great pride.

Miss Daventry's mouth barely twitched. 'Then of all things, that is what I should most like to see,' she said firmly. 'I had no idea his lordship was important enough to own fish and make them appear.'

Emma giggled, and Matthew shouted with laughter.

'There you are, Julian. When do you try holding back the tide?'

'As I recall,' said Julian, trying not to laugh, 'that wasn't King Canute's idea! The river then. Come along all of you.'

They rode towards the river, all thought of quarrelling forgotten.

He had to hand it to Miss Daventry. She had averted a quarrel very neatly. Lissy was far too well brought-up to argue with her. He was amused to see that Lissy's attitude to Miss Daventry was just what he had hoped it would be. Sympathetic affection laced with pity. Which should be enough to have Lissy entertaining second thoughts about her infatuation for the dashing Mr Daventry. In his experience pity was a death knell to passion.

As for Miss Daventry, he listened with deepening respect as she took shameless advantage of Davy's momentary gratitude.

'Davy, what is the French word—' beyond a faint smile she ignored a groan '—for "fish"?'

His littlest brother stared, and wrinkled his brow. *'Pou... poussin?'*

'Nearly,' said Miss Daventry. 'That is a chicken, but it does sound similar. *Poisson.'*

They rode on towards the river and Julian listened in utter disbelief as Miss Daventry proceeded effortlessly to enlarge not only Davy's French vocabulary, but Matthew, Emma and Lissy's as well.

Talking about fish.

By the time they reached the woods, Christy felt a great deal safer on horseback. Lord Braybrook had insisted on keeping to a walk, but now permitted the younger members of the party to ride ahead.

'Very neat, Miss Daventry,' he said, as the youngsters raced off whooping. 'I had no idea Davy knew that much French.'

She smiled. 'You are paying me handsomely, my lord. I should use my time to the best advantage.'

'There is that,' he said. 'Sit up straight, Miss Daventry. We'll essay a trot.'

Before she could utter a word of protest, he had urged his mount to a trot. Trotting, she discovered, was a great deal harder than walking. Merlin bounced, and so did she. His lordship, she observed, riding astride, was able to rise and fall to the rhythm. In a side saddle she had no such option.

She gritted her teeth, sat up even straighter and tightened her right leg around the pommel. As far as she could see, she was going to earn every last penny of her one hundred pounds per annum.

They had not gone far before the younger members of the party were well out of sight around a bend in the woodland ride. The sound of pounding hooves and faint laughter floated back. Breathless from the bouncing, Christy managed to say, 'Should we not catch them up, my lord?'

He flicked her a glance. 'You'd break your neck at that hell-for-leather pace.' He frowned. 'If you wish to stop bouncing, sit straighter and keep your heel down. It will keep your…seat in the saddle.'

Her…seat was already so sore that the last thing Christy wanted was to have it in closer contact with the saddle, but she obeyed, and, sure enough, she bounced less. Whether or not she was any more comfortable was a moot point.

'I cannot but think that Miss Trentham will find riding with me in attendance somewhat boring, my lord,' she said a few moments later.

'Probably,' he said.

She flushed, suddenly aware that he too must be finding the restricted pace a bore. 'I am sure if you wish to catch up with the children, that I will be perfectly safe. Merlin seems very quiet.'

His brow rose. 'Certainly not, Miss Daventry. Whatever my shortcomings, I have a little more consideration than that.'

Christy subsided. Surreptitiously she patted Merlin's neck, finding it warm and silken. Despite still feeling like a bug perched on top of him, she found that she rather liked Merlin. She liked the friendly way he occasionally swung his head and blew at Lord Braybrook's mount. And once or twice lipped at Lord Braybrook's breeches. At least, she assumed he was only using his lips.

It would be nice to ride him again.

She flinched away from the thought. Becoming fond of Merlin would be as foolish as becoming fond of Lady Braybrook's cat. Or feeling herself to be part of the family. This was not her place. The landing—that was her place; no matter how kind and considerate the family might be, she was not one of them. She would do far better to take her cue from his lordship's hauteur and remember that she was not riding for her own pleasure. That was incidental. His lordship had insisted because it made her more useful to him.

'Dare you attempt a canter, Miss Daventry?'

This appalling suggestion broke in on her thoughts just as they came out of the woods on to a sunny watermeadow.

'A canter?' He'd said *dare*, curse him! 'Of course, my lord.'

Something that might have been a smile flickered across that impassive countenance. 'Very well, then,' he said. 'Shorten your reins a little, but don't put any more pressure on his mouth. It is just to give you a little more control *if* you need it.'

Carefully she followed his instructions.

'Good. Now—sit up, and give him a kick.'

She did. Merlin remained in a trot.

'His ribs are quite strong. You won't break him,' came the comment.

She tried again. And found herself swinging along a great deal faster, his lordship's horse keeping pace beside them. It was...exhilarating. She could feel the wind rushing past, feel the power of the horse surging beneath her, part of her. It was like...like flying.

It was also a great deal more comfortable. Nowhere near as much bouncing.

'I'm doing it!' she said in breathless delight. 'And I'm not bouncing any more!'

'Merlin's paces are particularly smooth,' was the dampening rejoinder.

Killjoy.

'I *beg* your pardon?'

Blushing, Christy realised she had spoken aloud.

Buoyed by her delight, and determined not to be cowed, she repeated obligingly, 'Killjoy.' And flicked a glance at him.

He was grinning. Laughing with her. Something leapt inside her, bubbling, part of the mad delight of the swinging motion beneath her and the glorious summer's day.

Killjoy? Julian fought not to laugh out loud as he rode beside her. He should have known. He'd taught both Emma and Davy to ride. How could he have forgotten that moment of joy on their faces when they first broke out of a trot? How could he have forgotten his own first canter? The sudden realisation of power coiled beneath him. The sensation that one had somehow harnessed the wind…

He set his jaw. He had not forgotten. But Miss Daventry was the governess. The companion. He had no business to feel her triumph so keenly. No business to note the flush on her cheeks, the sparkle behind the spectacles. Definitely no business remembering the firm suppleness of her waist, the dainty ankle in Serena's old boot. He took a deep breath and willed his blood to steady. He certainly had no business thinking of another way to bring a flush to her cheeks.

He rode on in silence, ignoring her, except for necessary instructions. For her part, Miss Daventry appeared to have taken the hint. She volunteered nothing further, but obeyed him in silence. Exactly the way it should be. Except she was still flushed, smiling. After half a mile he said, 'Sit up straight and feel his mouth by closing your fingers, then pull him in gently.' He watched carefully as she obeyed, matching his pace to hers. Somewhat to his surprise, she managed quite well, Merlin responding to her hands. They came to a halt. 'Well done,' he said. 'In fact, I think we can dispense with this.' And he leaned down and removed the leading rein. Looking up, he met Miss Daventry's shocked gaze.

'But—'

'If he really decided to go, I probably wouldn't be able to

hold him,' he told her. 'That was just until you felt in control. He's very quiet. You know how hard you had to kick to make him canter.' Seeing that she still looked slightly nervous, he said, 'Miss Daventry, whatever you may think of my duty of care to you, trust me when I say that I do not take risks with my horses!'

Behind the spectacles her eyes narrowed. Not a flicker of her mouth as she said, 'A point indeed, my lord.' But that blasted dimple was there—hidden laughter. Hidden pleasure beckoning unbearably.

With a curt nod to her to follow, he rode on.

The river slid and sparkled beside them, the wooded hills rising on either side. Further up, the river went into a gorge and they would meet the others coming back. Unless they took a track up into the forest, but he hoped they would wait before doing that. Being alone with Miss Daventry was dangerous. Not because he thought she had the least idea of entangling him, nor yet because he intended to entangle her, but because the curiosity to know what would happen if he did so, shocked him.

So where in Hades were his siblings?

Laughter and hoofbeats came from the trees and sure enough, a moment later, they appeared. The little group had been enlarged. Two young men now rode with them.

Julian recognised them. Harry Daventry and Ned Postleton—the squire's son—riding either side of Lissy. Neither man was bothering to look ahead towards where he sat awaiting them with Miss Daventry. Both were competing for Lissy's attention.

But as he watched, Lissy leaned towards Daventry and spoke, nodding and pointing with her whip. Daventry looked towards them and even at fifty yards Julian saw puzzlement on his face. Lissy said something else, and the puzzlement vanished. Every line hardened as he stared towards his sister. With a brief word and nod to Lissy, he spurred forwards, then pulled up beside them, his face grim. 'Good afternoon, my lord,' he said. The young horse he rode fidgeted, tossing its head and mouthing the bit.

'Good afternoon, Daventry,' returned Julian. 'I don't need to introduce you to our companion, do I?'

'No, my lord. You do not.' It was said between gritted teeth. Daventry turned to his sister. 'What are you about? What are you doing here? Why are you not in Bristol?' His voice indicated the complete opposite of delight. A surge of anger rippled through Julian. No matter how shocked the cub was, at least he could greet his sister civilly! He waited for Miss Daventry to annihilate the boy.

'Did you not receive my letter?' she asked in diffident tones. 'I sent it last week, as soon as I knew I was coming. It should have reached you.'

Daventry flushed. 'I...a letter came yesterday.' His scarlet deepened. 'I have been very busy. Sir John has had a great deal of work for me.'

There was just the slightest pause, before Miss Daventry said, 'Of course.' There was no hint of reproach or hurt in her tone, but Julian shot her a glance. Her mouth was more than ordinarily firm, controlled. As though she held something in check.

'Then this is a pleasant surprise for you, Daventry,' said Julian. He fought to keep anger from his voice. If Daventry chose not to open his sister's letter, it was no business of *his*.

'As you say, my lord,' said Daventry, his lips stiff. 'I should like to speak to my sister privately, if you—' He broke off as his horse danced and flung its head up at the approach of the rest of the party.

'Is this not a lovely surprise, Mr Daventry?' called Lissy. 'I told the others not to breathe a word when we saw you! Miss Daventry is to be Mama's companion and my governess. Oh, Miss Daventry, this is Mr Postleton.'

Davy scowled. 'She's my governess too! She's teaching me French.'

Lissy ignored that. 'And Mama says that when she is unable

to chaperon me, Miss Daventry may do it, so I dare say you will see a great deal of her, sir.' She smiled at Harry.

Neither Mr Postleton nor Mr Daventry looked in the least gratified by the intelligence that in future Miss Trentham's chaperon would have the use of her legs.

'Didn't know you had a sister, Daventry.' Postleton's eyes slid over Christy. Julian bristled as Postleton raised his hat, his eyes weighing up and assessing charms. 'Afternoon, ma'am.'

'Good afternoon, sir.' Miss Daventry acknowledged the greeting with cool good manners.

Julian edged his mount closer, for some unspecified reason wishing to shield Miss Daventry from Postleton's attention. The younger man's gaze swung his way and became a knowing smirk.

He turned back to Miss Daventry. 'Braybrook's mounted you well, I see.' His voice was all innocence, but Julian froze. Better not to react. It was possible that Postleton had made the remark innocently.

'As you see,' said Miss Daventry in an expressionless voice. 'This is Lady Braybrook's old hack. I have not ridden before.'

'Ah. Dare say you're not up to a gallop, then.'

Harry frowned slightly, staring at Postleton, but nothing in Miss Daventry's expression suggested that she saw anything suggestive in Postleton's remarks.

Postleton turned to Lissy. 'Miss Trentham, would you care for a gallop? Slow going when Braybrook's got your governess to consider.'

'Oh, well…' She glanced at Miss Daventry and then at Julian for permission. He nodded. 'Yes, you and Emma and Matt if he wishes it.' Postleton might indulge in crude innuendo over the governess, but he was not fool enough to pass the line with Miss Trentham of Amberley.

Postleton looked less than enthused at this addition to the party, saying merely, 'After you, Miss Trentham, Miss Emma.'

'Can I go?' pleaded Davy.

'No,' said Julian, and before his little brother could object, said, 'You are going to have a jumping lesson over that log while Miss Daventry speaks to her brother. Off you go. I'll follow, but no jumping until I say so. Not even by accident. If you can't stop Star, I'll put you on this leading rein and mount you on a complete slug for a month.'

Davy brightened and trotted towards the log.

Julian glanced at Miss Daventry, who said, 'I think you covered everything, my lord.' The dimple flickered.

He snorted. 'You have to with that one. Be warned, ma'am!'

Chapter Six

Christy watched for a moment as he followed his brother and then turned to her brother, who was staring at her, his mouth hard.

'He seems mighty familiar with you. Dammit, Christy! How am I supposed to support the character of a gentleman, if my sister is seen to be—'

'Seen to be what, Harry?' she snapped. 'Supporting herself and saving for her old age? What was I supposed to do when you sold the house? Starve politely?' She dragged in a breath, reaching for self-control at the same time. 'No. Don't let us quarrel. Shall we try again?' She managed a smile. 'It's lovely to see you. Are you well? Is that your horse?'

He shrugged, still looking annoyed. 'I'm well enough. And this is one of Sir John's youngsters. His Grace mentioned in his letter of recommendation that I was good with young horses. What the devil are you doing here, Christy? Why, of all positions, did you apply for this one?'

'I didn't,' she said. 'His lordship visited me. I explained it all in my letter.'

'*What?*' His jaw hardened. 'Why the hell would he do that? Dammit, Christy! His reputation—' He broke off. 'How did he find you? I suppose he's been nosing around—spying!'

She shrugged. 'I have not the least notion. But he called while your friend Goodall was there. We talked, and he offered me the position. After he had sent Goodall on his way.'

'He *what*?'

She held his gaze. 'Some of the contents of the house were *mine*, Harry. Goodall seemed not to understand that.'

'Dash it, Christy!' he said furiously. 'What need did you have for them if the house is to be sold?'

'None,' she told him. 'But I do need the money. I have arranged for their separate sale.' She saw no need to inform him that she had kept some of the smaller items their mother had left her, as well as most of the books. Better that he thought them sold and gone.

His eyes shifted a little. 'Well, of course I would have given you your share of the money. And that does not explain why you accepted this position!'

'Why should I not?'

'Because he's using you to get at me! Surely you can see that? *Leave my sister alone, sir, and yours is safe*—it's obvious!'

Christy thanked a benevolent deity that Harry had not realised the full deviousness of Lord Braybrook's plan.

'And I suppose he wants you to spy on myself and Al—Miss Trentham!' snarled Harry.

Christy bit her lip. She'd known he wouldn't be overjoyed to see her, but this bitterness…

'No more than any other governess or chaperon,' she told him, denying the small dagger of hurt. 'And what is there to spy on? You are always at pains to assure me that you are a gentleman. Therefore I can expect you to behave as one, can I not?'

'Dammit, Christy! That is not what I meant!' He changed the subject. 'How do you know Braybrook means honestly by you?'

'He has given me no reason to distrust him,' she said quietly. 'My bedchamber is two down from Lady Braybrook's own. I am to spend my days with either Lady Braybrook or with the younger children or Miss Trentham. Beyond my function within the household, he has no interest in me whatsoever. He is hardly the sort to threaten *me* because he disapproves of *you*!'

Harry snorted. 'And just how many governesses do you imagine Braybrook has favoured with a riding lesson?' he snapped. 'Not to mention a new riding habit! I know *you* would not have purchased such a thing.'

Christy flushed. 'Since her maid would have little use for it, Lady Braybrook gave it to me so that I could ride with her daughters. His lordship was kind enough to give me a lesson for the same reason. Apparently Miss Trentham is in the habit of giving the grooms the slip and riding alone.' She watched him, wondering…

Harry said nothing, but his shifting gaze and sulky mouth were answer enough. Easy enough for Alicia to know Harry's day off and ride out, or walk out if necessary. Especially with her mother chairbound. More anger at Harry bubbled up. She held it down. No need to say anything. It would be harder for Alicia to play that trick now.

'Now don't jag his mouth this time! That's it! Well done!'

Glancing over, Christy saw Davy bring his pony around, and canter back to face the jump again, blazing triumph on his face. She knew exactly how he felt. A glance at Lord Braybrook discovered an equal triumph and pride on his face, as he watched his younger brother. A rush of warm delight stole over her. Such a simple foolish thing—

'Christy! Are you listening?'

She dragged her attention back from his lordship. 'I'm sorry. What did you say?'

'That it would be better if you resigned. Returned to Bristol.'

She stared. 'On what pretext?'

He scowled. 'Anything. Say you've received a better offer. Or that you don't like the country. Lord knows you never have!'

'I've never had the opportunity!' she said. 'And I find that

I like the country very well.' She did too. She had not realised how hemmed in, confined she had felt by town.

'Well, a better offer then.'

With the wage he was paying her, his lordship would know that for a lie instantly. 'As governess *and* companion I am being paid better than I could hope to achieve elsewhere. His lordship is not an idiot. Besides, where should I go?'

Harry was still trying to come up with reasons for Christy's swift departure ten minutes later when Alicia and the others came trotting back.

Alicia smiled at them benevolently. 'You must ride over on Wednesday, Mr Daventry,' she said. 'I am sure Mama will be able to spare Miss Daventry for an hour or so.'

'Wednesday?' queried Christy.

Harry scowled. 'My day off,' he said, not sounding pleased with Alicia's suggestion. At her startled glance, he forced a smile and added, 'Perhaps you could ask for Wednesdays off, Christy. Then we could meet for part of it. Sometimes.'

Summoning all her powers of diplomacy, Christy said, 'I shall mention it to Lady Braybrook.' Along with the information that it was Harry's day off. She could just imagine how many times he would fail to arrive at an arranged meeting with his sister and later plead an unavoidable engagement!

Lord Braybrook trotted up with Davy. 'We should be going home now, you four. You may ride ahead if you like.'

The four younger members of the party rode off, waving farewells.

Braybrook turned to Harry and Postleton. 'Good day, gentlemen. Daventry, I'm sure Lady Braybrook will be amenable to you visiting your sister.'

Christy forced a smile. 'Thank you, my lord. I'll see you soon then, Harry.'

'Yes. Yes, of course,' he muttered.

She nodded to Mr Postleton. 'Goodbye, sir.'

'Say rather, *au revoir*, ma'am,' said Postleton, in an appalling accent, as he bowed extravagantly. 'French, y'know. I'm sure we'll meet again,' he said, as though he thought it a high treat for her.

Christy's temper jerked on its leash. 'I am a governess, Mr Postleton,' she informed him in tones of sweetest condescension. 'I *do* recognise the French language when I hear it spoken.'

Julian choked. Definitely time to go.

'Good afternoon, Postleton,' he said, in as urbane a tone as he could manage for the laughter welling up. 'Come, Miss Daventry. We had best follow those four.'

They set off back along the meadow at a trot. Once out of earshot, he said, 'I would advise you to be wary of Postleton, Miss Daventry. He does not always keep the line with... women.' With women he considered his inferiors would be closer to the mark, but he could not say that.

Miss Daventry snorted. No doubt she understood exactly what he had left unsaid.

He felt his mouth twitch. 'Could this be another reason why you consider yourself a failure as a companion.'

She pulled Merlin up. He turned, startled, to find her glaring at him, her cheeks absolutely scarlet.

'Do you think that, my lord?' Her contempt stung. 'Then I dare say that you will not be in the least surprised when I inform you that Mr Postleton, no matter how distinguished his lineage, or ample his fortune, is no gentleman to indulge in such innuendo with women present! Have you no regard for your sisters?'

That caught him on the raw. So she had understood Postleton after all.

'But they did not understand, Miss Daventry. You did. What does that say about you?'

Her eyes narrowed. 'Exactly what it says of you—that I am not ignorant. And that I cannot afford the luxury of being as sheltered as your sisters!'

She nudged Merlin with her heel and rode on. At a trot. Precisely as he had taught her. For some reason that irritated him.

'What the devil do you think you are doing?' he snapped, bringing his horse alongside.

'Going home!' She bit her lip. 'That is—back to Amberley.' She said nothing further, but her colour remained high.

What was it about her that got under his skin? Ready to strangle Postleton himself, he'd ripped up at her for saying very much what he was thinking. She was right; innocence would leave her easy prey for men like Postleton. Or himself. What would it be like never to trust anyone fully? Never to let anyone close, because you did not really belong anywhere or with anyone. Damn it! He was becoming maudlin. He forced his mind back to practical matters.

She sat as straight as ever in the saddle, but something about the set of her lips reminded him that they had been out quite a while. She was going to be sore.

'Feel his mouth, Miss Daventry. We'll slow to a walk.'

They did so without mishap.

'Is he tired?' asked Miss Daventry, patting Merlin's neck. 'He's old, isn't he? I'm not too heavy for him?'

Unwilling approval stabbed through him. And wry amusement. Miss Daventry hardly weighed enough for Merlin to notice. He had noticed, though. Noticed how sweet she felt as he lifted her to the saddle. Noticed the faint fresh scent of lavender that hung about her. Lavender and something else that he didn't want to think about. Something that was Miss Daventry herself.

'No, Miss Daventry,' he said tightly. 'My concern is for you. You are going to ache quite enough.'

She nodded and they rode on in uncomfortable silence.

To Julian's relief, Davy awaited them on the other side of the woods.

'Star is tired,' he informed them. 'The others *would* go too fast.'

'Very wise,' said Miss Daventry, smiling. 'Do you call her Star for that pretty mark on her forehead?'

Davy looked affronted. 'Star is a *gelding*, Miss Daventry. Don't you know the difference?'

Now, how would prim and proper Miss Daventry get out of that? wondered Julian.

'I'm afraid not, Davy,' she said calmly. 'I am dreadfully ignorant about horses. You tell me.'

Davy's explanation of the differences between mares, geldings *and* stallions, not to mention their significance, was startlingly comprehensive. Julian concluded that Davy was picking up a good deal of information of a decidedly agricultural nature on his visits to the stables.

And all the blasted female did was nod and murmur encouragement from time to time. Quite as if none of this surprised her. Which he admitted, it probably didn't. If she'd understood Postleton's less than delicate insinuations, this should hardly stretch her understanding. And at least she wasn't enlarging Davy's French vocabulary on the subject.

By the time they reached the stableyard, Christy knew that she had been out far too long. She looked at the cobbles. Down, it always looked further, but how to dismount? Slide? Even as she wondered, his lordship dismounted, tossed his reins to a groom and moved towards Merlin.

Her body tensed, remembering his hands on her waist, her ankle. No. She kicked her left foot from the stirrup, unhooked her right leg from the pommel, and slid.

It was much further than she had realised and the cobbles a great deal harder. Her legs gave way, collapsing under her.

He caught her, hauling her against his chest before she actually hit the cobbles. Shocked, she clung to him, conscious of the mingled odours of horse, leather and warm, slightly sweaty male.

'What the devil did you do that for?' came the clipped, furious voice. 'I warned you that you would be sore!'

Annoyed, she pushed to be free, but her legs wobbled despicably and his lordship ignored her feeble attempt and kept an arm around her.

'You didn't warn me my legs wouldn't work!' she said crossly.

He snorted. 'Given that they must feel like chewed string, I didn't think it necessary!'

'Is Miss Daventry all right, Julian?' came a younger voice.

Matthew stood there, his jacket slung over one shoulder. 'Shall I help her up to the house?'

'Yes,' said his lordship. 'If you have seen to your horse.'

'Oh, yes. We walked the last bit to cool them down,' said Matthew. 'Take my arm, Miss Daventry.'

He held it out and Christy took it gratefully, trying an experimental step. Chewed string, indeed! She was furiously aware of Lord Braybrook hovering. Not exactly protectively, more like a hawk waiting to swoop. Her legs held and she tried another step.

'That's it, Miss Daventry, said Matthew encouragingly. 'You shouldn't have jumped down like that, though. Lucky Julian was there. I thought you would land on the cobbles.'

'Damned lucky,' came a mutter from behind her.

Determinedly Christy looked back and met the blue eyes.

His lordship's face was set hard. She repressed a shiver, trying to ignore the memory of his body, hard and powerful, pressed against her own. As though…as though he owned it.

'Thank you, sir. For the lesson, and your patience.'

The line of his mouth flattened even further.

'You're welcome, ma'am. Good day.'

He caught up Merlin's bridle and led him away.

Christy turned back to Matthew. She could recognise a dismissal when it slapped her.

Julian watched her go from the refuge of Merlin's stall. God help him, he could still feel the imprint of that slender body. Small breasts crushed against him, the faint, rising scent of lavender. And a wisp of escaping hair, curling around her brow. Tawny brown glinting gold. Startled, mismatched eyes behind the misleading spectacles, and soft, slightly parted lips.

He'd wondered what she would taste like. Not only wondered, but considered finding out. It would be better to see as little of her as possible. Not that there was any danger of seducing her, but he could do without the inevitable frustration of not being able to do so, if he didn't squash this inexplicable attraction.

Miss Daventry was dangerous. The more so because she had not the least idea of it. She didn't even realise the danger *she* was in. Not that she was in any danger. He was not, definitely *not*, going to seduce his stepmother's companion.

'Miss Daventry!'

Christy turned carefully at the autocratic summons, conscious of stiff, aching muscles. She had spent the rest of the afternoon sewing and talking with Lady Braybrook until it was time to change for dinner. Now she wondered if she might have to eat her dinner off the mantelpiece. She could almost hear the creaking protest of overused muscles with every movement. As for the stairs, they were a penance.

'My lord.'

He was frowning at her. 'That is one of Lady Braybrook's gowns.'

She felt heat steal over her cheeks. No doubt he thought she was dressing above her station in this soft grey silk. Her skin flickered at his intent stare. She twitched the heavy embroidered shawl Lady Braybrook had given her, drawing it a little closer across her bodice.

'Her ladyship wished me to wear it.' Her ladyship had more than wished. She had ordered. On pain of being sent back upstairs to change, should Christy dare to rebel and appear in one of her old gowns? How could she refuse? She couldn't remember when she had last talked, really talked, with another woman apart from her mother and Sukey. It was frighteningly easy to believe, to pretend, that she belonged here.

Her last employer had considered her as more of an errand girl, only addressing her when she required something. Lady Braybrook's notion of a companion was far more…well…*companionable* than Mrs March's had been. It touched a chord inside her, an unacknowledged yearning that had been better left sleeping.

'And you obliged her.'

There was something odd about his voice, but she forced herself to respond calmly. 'As you see, my lord.'

Her tone was even, quite indifferent. Which, given that her lungs had apparently lost their capacity, was remarkable. There was nothing, she told herself, *nothing* about Lord Braybrook to make her breathing hitch.

She had seen handsome men before. Men with blue eyes. Well-dressed men. There was no reason in the world for her waist, hands and—her stomach fluttered—legs to remember how carefully he had settled her in the saddle. There had been nothing intimate about it.

'And the cap, Miss Daventry—'

'Is my own,' she informed him stiffly.

He didn't doubt it. Not for one moment. Serena wouldn't have been seen dead in the monstrosity. And not a scrap of hair was to be seen. For which he ought to thank every god in the pantheon. Three ruined cravats on the floor of his bedchamber were testament to his distraction over whether or not Miss Daventry's hair could possibly be as silken as it looked.

Clearing his throat, he gestured for her to precede him into the drawing room. And averted his gaze from the lure of her slight figure. *Voluptuous*, he reminded himself. He preferred voluptuous. Ripe, seductive, *womanly* curves. It would help enormously if he remembered that, rather than the supple curve of Miss Daventry's waist.

To his relief Serena, Lissy and Matthew were already down.

Finding himself alone with Miss Daventry… His cravat tightened in the most unaccountable way, and he wondered what excuse he might have used for abandoning her.

'Ah. There you both are.' Serena smiled. Then frowned. Direfully.

Julian blinked. And glanced down to check that he hadn't forgotten some vital item of attire. Like his trousers.

'No, dear. *Not* a cap. Not with that gown.'

He choked back a laugh, and risked a sideways glance to see how Miss Daventry was taking this admonition.

Meekly. Not a flicker of rebellion. For some reason that irked him. She'd bristled like an angry cat when *he* mentioned it.

'Julian, for heaven's sake, remove it!'

Remove it—? Remove Miss Daventry's cap? His fingers itched.

Playing for time, he said, 'Remove what, Serena?'

'Miss Daventry's cap!' said Serena in pained tones. 'Now, Julian!'

Rebellion sparked then all right and tight. Miss Daventry clutched at the cap…just a split second after Julian's instinctive response to an order that would have made a troop sergeant jump.

The cap dangled in his hand, and Miss Daventry stared up at him in disbelief, minus the remnants of her dowdy disguise.

'Much better!' declared Serena.

Part of Julian's brain agreed. The witless part that took one look at the gleaming tawny coils of Miss Daventry's hair and wanted to slide his fingers into it. The other part of his brain, the part that recognised Miss Daventry as Disaster-Made-Flesh, told him to return the cap without delay, and tell Serena to mind her own misbegotten business.

'Give it to me, Julian,' said Serena. Stunned, he obeyed. And groaned mentally as she shifted in her chair and sat on the cap. Not even the redoubtable Miss Daventry was going to retrieve it from there.

'And let that be the last of these caps that I see,' Serena said cheerfully. 'You may wear them at my age.'

Lissy giggled. 'But, Mama—Mr Havergal said they were repellant at your age too!'

Havergal again? Who the devil *was* this Havergal fellow?

He couched it a little more tactfully. 'Who is Havergal and what does he have to say to your mother's choice of headgear, Liss?'

'Nothing at all,' said Serena.

'Oh, he's an old friend of Mama's,' said Lissy. 'He plans to settle not far from here and rides out from Hereford to visit Mama every few days. Haven't you met him?'

'Not yet,' said Julian. An oversight he planned to correct very soon. He glanced at Serena. 'I'll look forward to making his acquaintance.'

'I'm sure you will soon,' said Serena, her cheeks faintly pink. 'Now where was I? Oh, yes. Miss Daventry—at twenty-four, a cap is an abomination. And when you have such pretty hair, 'tis a crime to hide it. Isn't it, Lissy?' She favoured her daughter with a stern look.

Lissy blinked. 'Pardon, Mama? Oh, yes. Miss Daventry, you look much nicer without the horrid thing!'

She did. Years younger and damnably pretty. Even with the spectacles. None of which deflected him from the fact that Serena had purposely changed the subject. Whoever Havergal was, she didn't want to talk about him.

'If we are finished correcting Miss Daventry's lamentable taste in caps,' he said, 'perhaps we might have our dinner.'

Over the next few days Christy settled into the rhythm of the house. In the mornings before Lady Braybrook came down, she taught Davy and Emma. After lunch she walked with Lissy and Emma, practising French or Italian conversation, or sketching.

She saw little of Lord Braybrook. She suspected he had

taken a dislike to her. He never spoke to her unless he absolutely had to. And she had not been asked to accompany him out riding with his sisters again.

On the afternoons he escorted his sisters riding, she remained with Lady Braybrook. When he could not ride with them, she accompanied them with an elderly groom called Twigg, who instructed her patiently and seemed to like her.

This was how it should be, Christy told herself, as she escorted Alicia and Emma out to the garden for some sketching practice about a week after her arrival. It didn't matter if his lordship liked her or not. For all his faults, he was too fair-minded to dismiss her if she did her job well. Since Lady Braybrook was happy with her, she was safe. After all, his plan was working perfectly. There were innumerable opportunities for Alicia to be faced with the reality of what marriage to Harry would mean...such as this sketching party.

'You know, we *have* sketched Amberley before,' grumbled Emma, as they walked across the park.

Christy was not about to be deflected. 'Excellent. Then we can compare what you have sketched. It's interesting how different people can all draw the same familiar scene and produce completely different pictures. And if you hunt out the old sketches, we can see how you have improved and how your style may have changed.'

Emma scowled. 'I'd rather go to the stables and draw one of the horses.'

This notwithstanding, she settled down and silence reigned while the three of them sketched. At length Christy called a halt and looked at her pupils' efforts.

She was hard put to it not to chuckle. Both sketches said as much about the artists as Amberley. Emma's was very exact, down to the precise number of windows visible and including every tree and shrub as well as a stray gardener. Alicia, however, had shown Amberley as a rearing mass of stone with a turbulent background of non-existent clouds.

'But it's sunny today, Liss!' protested Emma when she saw this.

Alicia glared. 'Who cares? Amberley looks so romantic when there's a storm coming. Like something in *The Mysteries of Udolpho*.'

Emma rolled her eyes. '*That* silly book?'

'It's not silly! You haven't even read it!'

'Only because Mama won't let me!' said Emma. 'Anyway, Matt said it was silly.' She turned to Christy. 'May we see yours, Miss Daventry?'

'Of course.' Christy passed her the book.

'But this is not Amberley,' said Emma frowning. 'You said "our home".'

'Amberley is your home,' said Christy. 'This is *my* home. Or it was. It is to be sold now.'

'Oh,' said Emma. 'Liss, it's awfully good. Do look.' She tilted the book to give Alicia a better view. Christy held her breath. She had drawn the house meticulously, showing its size, its position between the apothecary and the fishmonger, the very unaristocratic nature of the street. It was, above all, completely unromantic.

Alicia looked rather daunted. 'You lived *there*?' she asked, as though such a thing were unimaginable. 'But I thought…a town house, Mr Daventry said.'

'Well, it's in a town,' said Christy cheerfully. 'Right in the middle of Bristol near the quay. Rather noisy. Wealthy people live in Clifton for the most part. I lived in that house after I left school, although I became a junior mistress for a year first. Then I was at home with Mama before I took a live-in position as a companion out at Clifton. I came home to nurse her.' No need to mention the more unpleasant aspects of earning your own living. Such as being considered fair game by your employer's son. At least she did not have to contend with that here.

Emma was still examining the picture. 'Is that an apothecary beside your house, Miss Daventry?' she asked.

'An apothecary?' Alicia sounded stunned.

Christy nodded. 'Yes. Very useful when Mama was ill. And a fishmonger on the other side. Smelly, sometimes, but it was a very convenient house. Not so large as to require more than one servant to help with the housework, and close to all the shops. Shall we pack up?'

Alicia was notably silent as she packed up her sketching gear, nibbling at her lower lip, and frowning as though deep in thought.

'Is something bothering you, Alicia?' asked Christy gently.

Alicia flushed. 'Oh, no. That is one of Mama's old dresses, is it not, Miss Daventry?'

'Yes,' said Christy. 'Thanks to Lady Braybrook's kindness I shall not have to make myself new dresses for years. Quite a saving.'

Alicia's eyes widened. 'For—?' She broke off, staring past Christy. 'I…I think…is that not Mr Daventry coming towards us?'

Christy turned. Sure enough, Harry was striding towards them from the direction of the house.

Alicia went pink, casting a nervous glance at Christy. 'How…how lovely. I mean, for you, Miss Daventry.'

Harry bowed as he drew near. 'Good afternoon, ladies. Lady Braybrook said I would find you here. Sketching, is it?' He bestowed an extra smile on Alicia.

Alicia smiled back, but Christy thought there was just a touch of reserve in her expression.

'We sketched Amberley,' said Emma, 'because Miss Daventry said that we should draw our home, only of course she drew *your* old home in Bristol. It's awfully clear. You can even see the apothecary next door!'

It did not appear that this information afforded Harry the least pleasure. 'Can you?' He looked at Christy. 'Lady Braybrook has given you permission to walk with me in the grounds. She says Miss Trentham and Miss Emma should return to the house.'

'Of course,' said Christy. She smiled at Emma. 'Perhaps you might take my book and pencils back to my room, Emma?'

She watched as the girls departed and then faced her brother. 'Why the hell did you do that?' he demanded.

She raised her brows. 'You don't think Miss Trentham deserves some inkling of what is in store for her if she marries you? Of course, had you not led her to believe that you owned a *fashionable* town house—'

He scowled. 'It's no business of yours! You'd be better off having a care for your reputation! People are talking about Braybrook squiring you around! Of course, I assured Sir John that there was nothing in it, but—'

'You *what*?' Christy's temper spilled over. 'How dare you discuss my affairs!'

Stubbornness crept into his expression. 'He's a rake. Everyone knows that around here! Why, he's even got—' He broke off, and cleared his throat. 'Well, mum for that, but even though Sir John says Braybrook isn't the sort to seduce the chambermaids, let alone the governess, people are talking.' He gave her a scathing glance. 'Although you're not the sort to attract him, so there can be nothing to worry about—unless he was bored.'

'His lordship,' said Christy with a decided snap, 'appears not to have sunk to such ghastly depths of *ennui* as that!' She denied the ignoble urge to ask what it was his lordship had got. It was none of her business. Besides, she could hazard a very fair guess that his lordship had a mistress tucked away close by. Hereford, perhaps. That was how these things were done.

'Well, you might give a thought to *my* position,' growled Harry. 'It won't help my standing if people are whispering that my sister must earn her own living!' He went on. 'And there is no need for you to do so! His Grace would help you. If you would only—'

'No.' She cut him off. 'I want nothing from him! Harry— be sensible!'

He snorted. 'Sensible? I am being sensible! The quickest way to establish myself is by an advantageous marriage, and—'

'You cannot marry anyone without telling the truth! Let alone Miss Trentham, who is accustomed to all this!'

All this, she gestured to include, meant the pinkish-brown bulk of Amberley, the grounds and the woods stretching down to the glimmering stretch of river. And not just Amberley itself, but all it represented—Lissy's place in the world. A world from which she and Harry were barred.

In this world, being the illegitimate son and daughter of a duke made every difference.

She had always known that. No one had cushioned the truth for her. She had known it at eight when people pointed and whispered in the street. And at ten when she had gone to school in Bath with strict instructions that her 'father' had died and where they were from. That the Duke of Alcaston was Harry's very generous 'godfather'. And she had known it at eighteen when she had fallen in love for the first and last time. For some, love did indeed alter when it alteration found.

Although perhaps for Harry it was slightly different. He at least could make his way in the world and be known according to his own actions. She, on the other hand, would always be judged on her mother's status as a duke's mistress. Tainted. A potential whore. The sins of the mother were very definitely visited on the daughter.

Harry seemed to read her thoughts. 'And what came of it when *you* told the truth? If you hadn't been so high minded—'

'I told the truth!' she snapped. 'I prefer to manage honestly and upon my own terms. How will you support Miss Trentham?'

He shrugged. 'I daresay his Grace would increase my allowance if I married. Especially if I married well. And she has a dowry.'

Her teeth clenched.

'She has a dowry if her brother chooses to release it!' she said, not bothering to disguise her contempt for his attitude. 'And you have no claim on Alcaston at all. You cannot rely on him.'

'Since I was never fool enough to antagonise him as you did,

I'm not worried he'll cast me off.' His mouth hardened. 'I see no reason why my birth should make a difference. As for Braybrook—' he shrugged '—he's fond enough of Alicia not to let her starve. He'll know damn well that it's better to help me than cast her off.'

Christy's fists clenched, but she said in a calm voice, 'I hadn't thought of that. How convenient for you that Braybrook is devoted to his family.'

Harry went scarlet. 'I didn't mean it like that! Just that— look, Christy, don't make such a piece of work of it. A good marriage for me would help us both. If I can persuade our father into settling some money on you, then you could live with us. You can help Alicia with the household.'

'How very generous,' she said carefully. 'This certainly puts things in a different light. I'll think about it.'

Harry looked relieved. 'You do that. You'll see it's for the best. It's not as if I'm going to seduce Alicia or elope. Her connections won't help my career if she's disgraced.' He pulled an elegant timepiece from his pocket. 'I must be off. An engagement in Hereford. Just thought I'd call on my way past.' He put the watch away. 'Change your day off next week. We could go into Hereford together. Sir John has a gig that I am permitted to use.'

She smiled. 'I am afraid not, Harry. Wednesdays seem not at all convenient for Lady Braybrook.'

Chapter Seven

Christy said goodbye to Harry at the stables and then walked up to the house. He was determined, then, to snare Alicia. The situation was worse than she had thought. She had believed that she could influence Harry, make him see the wrongness of deceiving Alicia and her family. She was a fool.

Perhaps she ought to be grateful Harry was clear-headed enough to see that an elopement or seduction would damage Alicia and by extension himself. Instead she felt sick. Cold calculation held him back, the realisation that a disgraced bride would be a burden. And inside her churned the knowledge that if he'd claimed more altruistic reasons for not seducing Alicia or eloping with her, she might not have believed him.

Her course was clear although she had time before she might have to act. Any hint that Alicia was likely to do something foolish, and she must tell Lord Braybrook the truth. Armed with that information, he would be able to forbid Harry the house and even the headstrong Alicia would agree he was correct to do so.

It would ruin Harry if Braybrook made the truth public. He would probably lose his position. And the story would travel. Even with Alcaston's support, it would be difficult, if not impossible, for Harry to find another position. It was even possible that Alcaston, to whom discretion was all, might cast him off as he had her...

She wouldn't come out of it well either. Her position here would be finished and possibly all other positions, unless she changed her name, which would mean she had no references at all... No. That couldn't be allowed to matter. Perhaps, since the truth would save Alicia, Lady Braybrook might agree to write her a reference under an assumed name? But what about Harry?

She opened the side door that led into the garden room and walked slowly back through the hallways that led to the Great Hall. Could she bring herself to ruin Harry so entirely?

The answer came easily—if it saved Alicia from a crashing mistake, then yes, she could. She could not bear to see the family torn apart by Harry's ambition and Alicia's folly.

There would be no point threatening exposure; Harry might simply pretend to agree and become more secretive. The knowledge that he was capable of using a girl's affections so coldly sliced deep. That was worse than the rest—if Harry had truly loved Alicia, then she would sympathise. But he didn't. Alicia was a means to an end and he had weighed her brother's affection for her in his plans.

She came out under the musicians' gallery and turned towards the main stairs. She must return to Lady Braybrook and the girls. Continue opening Alicia's eyes to the truth. Not just the life she would lead, but the far more bitter truth that Harry felt no affection for her.

'Miss Daventry?'

Startled, she spun around. Lord Braybrook rose from a seat at the huge oak refectory table to one side.

'My lord. I did not see you. Were you looking for me?'

He came towards her, frowning. 'Is something bothering you?' There was no suspicion in his voice. Only concern.

Something inside her tilted as he walked towards her. Quaked in fright that he read her thoughts and feelings so easily.

'Of course not!' she said too quickly, summoning a bright smile. 'Whatever should be bothering me? You will excuse me, my lord. I must return to my duties.'

'A family quarrel, perhaps? I saw your brother.'

Her smile froze and she spoke as coldly as possible. 'I do not believe that is anything to do with you, my lord.' The lie tasted sour. Her quarrel with Harry was very much his business. Should she simply tell him? Get it over with?

He reached out, carefully smoothing between her brows with one finger. Shock jolted through her. Then, lightly, he touched the finger to her lower lip, traced the curve.

For a moment she stood, unable to move for the torrent of sensation. Then she stepped back, her eyes lowered. She forced herself to concentrate on a patch of sunlight glowing on the Persian rug beneath her feet. 'Is that all, my lord?'

His hand dropped back to his side. 'I'll bid you good day,' he said. And turned, walking swiftly away.

She shivered as he disappeared through a door under the gallery at the back of the hall. Why had he done that? Worse, why did she feel as though a thousand chrysalises were hatching into butterflies in her stomach? Not just her stomach either—her entire body hummed, fluttered at the memory of his touch.

His reputation. He's a rake!

His touch had driven everything else out of her mind. No, not just his touch—he had been concerned about her. He had noticed her distraction. That was temptation itself.

It was not so much that she mistrusted him, but herself. Mistrusted the little voice murmuring that he had truly *seen* her. Enough to see her distress. As though it mattered to him. She could not afford to think that. The half-landings might be a trifle dull, but it was safer to remain on them.

He was going to stay away from Miss Daventry. Under no circumstances would he wait for her in empty passages. Nor would he risk finding her alone by coming down early for dinner. Or any other meal. Nor would he permit himself to wonder about what brought a frown to her brow or a worried look to her eyes. It was not his concern.

None of which resolutions explained why, the following morning, Miss Daventry's empty place at the breakfast table felt like a void.

Julian carved more ham for himself, refilled his coffee cup and glared at the empty place. Was she ill? And why was he wondering about it? He'd been insane to touch her yesterday—how could touching a woman's brow and lower lip with a single finger feel more intimate than—?

'Is the ham disagreeing with you, Julian?'

Serena's amused voice broke his reverie. And that was another puzzle—why the devil was Serena downstairs at this hour?

He shrugged. 'I merely wondered why Miss Daventry is not down.'

Serena's lifted brows had him adding hurriedly, 'After all, she's not much of a companion to you lying abed.' And immediately had to banish images of Miss Daventry lying abed, tawny tresses spread in silken abandon on a pillow—*his* pillow. He strangled the forming vision, cleared his throat and pulled his chair closer to the table.

'Since Lissy and Emma have gone to spend the day with Lucy Pargeter, we decided that Miss Daventry should have her day off,' said Serena. 'I dare say she is preparing to go out.'

'Out? Where?' And how? As far as he was aware, Miss Daventry could not drive so much as a gig.

At that moment the door to the breakfast parlour opened to admit Miss Daventry. Julian stared. She was wearing one of her old gowns, an unadorned grey cambric with a deep blue spencer. A plain straw bonnet hung from her arm by its strings. There was not a cap in sight, however, and the coiled tawny tresses seemed to capture every stray gleam of sunlight. A single wisp had escaped, drifting against her cheek

He swallowed, his fingers itching to tuck the wisp back, brush his fingers over the soft cheek, feel the warmth of leaping blood under her skin.

Not a good idea at all.

'Ah, Miss Daventry.' Serena's smile was unabashed. 'His lordship was wondering where you were. Have you thought where you might go for your day off?'

Casting a suspicious glance at Julian, Miss Daventry said, 'I thought to go for a walk, ma'am.'

Julian frowned. A walk sounded harmless, but what if she became lost? The forest stretched for miles.

Matthew looked up. 'There's a nice path up through the woods just beyond the village,' he said helpfully. 'Then you follow it back along the ridge and down to the river, and it brings you home the way we rode the other day. I'll draw you a map.'

Which put paid to Miss Daventry losing her way; Matthew's maps were generally very good, but still— 'That is easily a walk of four miles, Matt,' he said irritably. 'A great deal of it uphill. She will be exhausted!'

'Oh,' said Matthew, plainly crestfallen. 'Well, I suppose it's a bit steep, but—'

'*She,*' said the cat's mother, sweetly deferential, 'enjoys walking. And *she* is quite capable of deciding for herself how far she can walk. Thank you, Matthew. That sounds lovely. I shall take my sketch book and pencils.'

A very odd choking noise escaped Serena, but all she said was, 'You had better take food with you. And some water. I know that walk and a great deal of it *is* uphill.' She smiled. 'And you might like to take a basket with you for blackberries.'

'Blackberries?'

'Oh, yes!' said Davy, muffled by a mouthful of toast. He swallowed hastily. 'There's a jolly big clump just where you get back down to the river.' He added, 'Only you get a tummy ache if you eat more than you put in the basket.'

Miss Daventry's dimple made the briefest appearance. 'Do you?'

'You do,' said Serena, absolutely straight faced. 'A medically proven fact. And the juice is very hard to get out of clothing. Not exactly medically proven, but you might like to bear it in mind.'

There was that dimple teasing him again. Curse it, she wasn't even looking at him, so why should he feel so enchanted by it?

'Thank you, ma'am.'

And not just the damned dimple—laughter in her eyes and voice, and the corners of her mouth lifting into the loveliest smile, one that he could imagine stained purple with blackberry juice, lips as sweet and luscious as the most forbidden of forbidden fruit, softening, parting… What the hell was he *doing*? Indulging in erotic fantasies about Christy Daventry and blackberries was bad enough, but at the breakfast table with her and his family it was lunacy!

'Just don't become lost,' he said coldly. 'Searching for you would be inconvenient.'

'Your lordship is all consideration.'

He breathed a sigh of relief as the dimple vanished and prim Miss Daventry returned in glacial propriety. As long as he didn't think about melting the ice… He blocked that from his mind as Matthew explained the route, tearing a page from a small notebook in his pocket. Melting this particular glacier was out of the question. It didn't want to be melted. He had seen that yesterday. He had seen the flash of awareness in her eyes before she stepped back behind her walls.

Perhaps he could tempt her out again, but if she didn't want to play, then that was that. He was past the age where an uninterested woman was a challenge. Wasn't he?

He pushed back his chair and Juno, sprawled behind it, leapt to her feet, tail waving. 'Coming, Davy?' he asked. 'I'm looking over some crops this morning. You can come if you wish and your mother doesn't mind.' Davy's constant chatter would drive all thought of Miss Daventry out of his head.

Davy's face lit and he turned pleading eyes on Serena. "Mama? May I? Please?'

A smile twitched at the corner of Serena's mouth. 'Oh, I think I can manage, Davy. You may go.'

Julian eyed Serena. 'You won't be lonely?'

'Not at all,' she assured him, pouring another cup of tea.

He left it there. Every instinct shrieked that she was up to something. But what?

Davy finished his toast in record time, wiped his mouth and jumped up, giving no further time for speculation.

Julian grinned and held out his hand as his little brother came around the table. The small fingers that slid into his hand were sticky. Definitely sticky. He was going to end up with jam all over his breeches, no doubt. 'We'll stop by the kitchens for some food on the way to the stables.'

Unable to help himself, he glanced towards Miss Daventry. She was watching Davy with an odd smile. She looked up. For an instant their gazes held and then, still with that queer, twisted smile, she turned away.

For a moment she had looked…well, *longing*. But what would a woman like Miss Daventry long for? Riches? Status? Probably. Who could blame her? Her future was insecure in the extreme. He pushed the thought away, giving his attention to Davy's questions as they left the room together. But he could not quite banish the niggling question—*what would happen to her after she left Amberley*? For she would. One day she would be gone. Where would she go? What would she do? And why did the image of her alone in lodgings, eking out every penny, leave him cold and shaken?

Sticky with perspiration, damp tendrils of hair clinging to her brow, Christy forced her aching legs up the last of the incline. Lungs burning, she leaned against an oak at the top to catch her breath. Below her the track wound away down through the oak woods. She had come out on a broader track, a ride, stretching in either direction along the top of what she supposed was a ridge. Matthew had explained it all as he drew the map for her.

Just turn right when you reach the top. It will bring you to a lookout over the river after a couple of miles. You could eat your lunch there. Another two hundred yards on, you'll find a track leading you back down to the river where we rode that first day and you follow the river home. It's very easy.

Easy.

Except for the pull up that hill. Matthew's *a bit steep* didn't even begin to describe it. Taking out her water bottle, she uncorked it and had a couple of mouthfuls, letting it trickle down slowly. Goodness, she was hot! Her bonnet dangled from her arm by its strings. She had taken it off less than a third of the way up the hill. There was no point worrying about sunburn in the green cool of the woods, and the lining would be ruined with perspiration if she did not.

She was hot, sticky and, she suspected, rather grimy. Her hair was dishevelled, and her gloves were stuffed in her pocket. Ladylike Miss Daventry had remained at the bottom of the hill. Or perhaps back at Amberley. Up here there was no need for her. Up here there were only squirrels and birds to see Christy. A rabbit hopped across the path. She smiled—very well, rabbits too. She looked about. It was just a wood. Trees. But the sunlight slid through the leaves in dappled green light and there was such a feeling of freshness, of damp earth, of things growing and simply being. And it was all hers. Every sun-dappled scrap of it. In this moment the trees, the damp growing earth, the birdsong and the occasional scurryings of small creatures were all hers. She stood quite still, drawing it in, wishing she could remain right there, in that place and time. For a moment her whole being sang with joy and delight at merely being alive.

Still with that delight brimming over, she set off along the ridge for the promised lookout. She found it easily enough, a rocky outcrop where she perched high above the valley and could see the river far below, a shining ribbon slipping along towards its rendezvous with the mightier Severn at Chepstow, and at last the sea. All connected, all of a piece. Boats, like a child's bath toys, came and went as she munched her bread, cheese and apples. Apples that had grown in this same earth, warmed by the same sun pouring down on her head and shoulders. Folly to imagine that somehow she was part of it, but the idea lingered of being held, cradled, for once belonging. She should, she knew, put her bonnet back on—she was going to be sadly freckled, even a little bit sunburnt. She didn't care. Even her spencer had been discarded and folded away in the satchel. She couldn't think when she had enjoyed a day more. And all she had done was go for a walk. In Bristol when she had walked there had always been streets, noise and smells. Here she had the forest track and instead of noise, the song of birds and the occasional sounds floating up from the village below nestled in the trees on either side of the river. She watched a small ferry being poled across. Lady Braybrook had said something about organising a boating picnic for the children in a few days. She had no doubt that her ladyship would announce that she had absolutely no need for a companion that day and insist that she went with Lissy and Emma.

She sighed. That was the greatest danger of all. This affection she felt for all of them. Not just Lady Braybrook, but the children. Matt with his quiet scholarly ways, yet still with the streak of boyish mischief, Emma and Lissy, so merry and confident, and little Davy with his hero-worship of his eldest brother. Christy pushed away the memory of them going off together that morning, Davy chattering like a magpie and his lordship, dark head bent to catch all those whirling words, his little brother's no doubt sticky hand safe within his, and the dog at their heels.

Foolish sentiment, she told herself. It was not for her. They were kind, friendly, but they were not her family. Eventually she would leave and have to depend solely upon herself. That was constant. She had known it at eighteen when she had fallen in love—

No!

She grabbed the satchel and pushed herself to her feet. That bitter memory would not spoil this golden day. It would be over soon enough and she would have to wait for her next day off, which might be pouring with rain. Picking up the basket she had brought for blackberries, she set off.

Today there was only today, with no regret for yesterdays and definitely no worry about tomorrows. She was going to pick blackberries. She was going to enjoy the day's gifts and hoard the pleasure like a squirrel with a nut, every scrap of sunshine, every touch of the breeze on her hot face, every birdcall and every blackberry that didn't get as far as her basket.

Two hours later, picking blackberries, Christy acknowledged that one of the day's memories would be blackberry brambles. She wouldn't have believed how viciously the wretched sprays could cling. As for connected, the problem was to *avoid* being connected. They clung to everything, her hair, her skirts; her bare arms were well and truly scratched. Her basket was two-thirds full and that had taken an hour, although she admitted it might have been quicker had she not eaten so many. She loved blackberries and these, bursting with sunshine, were temptation itself.

She was slightly damp, having cooled her face in the river, but it was so hot she would be dry again by the time she reached Amberley. Although she would still slip in by the side door. She was a mess, but she was having so much fun. Never had she been able to roam like this for a whole day. Always she had been kept within doors, living in town. Either with her mother or at school or in her jobs. When she had gone out, it had been to do an errand. There had never been a chance simply to *be*. And blackberries had always been bought.

Moving around the patch, she saw a particularly luscious bunch over her head. Standing on tiptoe, she reached up, carefully lifting a prickly shoot out of the way…and felt it catch across the tops of her breasts through the cambric and linen of her gown and chemise.

'Bother!' she muttered and twisted around to release the clinging barbs. More snagged on her hair. With a curse she reached up to remove them. And froze as something on the ground caught her gaze. There, coiled lazily in the sun, was a greeny-coloured snake. She pulled back with a startled gasp, lost her balance and fell against the brambles. The snake didn't move.

One eye on the snake, Christy tried to pull free, but discovered that she was held fast. As soon as she loosened one set of barbs, another gripped with even greater tenacity. The snake appeared oblivious, until it suddenly uncoiled, raising its head. Briefly the forked tongue flickered and then with a rustle of grass and fallen leaves it slithered away towards the river.

Christy breathed a sigh of relief, and continued to battle the brambles, only to hear the sound of approaching hoofbeats. She muttered a curse as she twisted to look over her shoulder. Riding towards her on his tall black gelding was his lordship, sitting easily in the saddle as if he had grown there.

Spending the rest of the afternoon entangled in a bramble bush because she was too proud to call out would be stupid. Drawing a deep breath, she yelled. He raised a hand and his horse altered course towards her.

'Miss Daventry, is something—?' He broke off and the blue eyes widened. 'Ah.' He barely suppressed the grin, but swung down and came towards her swiftly. 'Are you all right?' His gaze fell on her scratched arms and his mouth set hard. 'What the devil were you doing to get that scratched?' Even as he spoke he fished an odd-looking tool out of his coat pocket, unfolded it to reveal a blade and began cutting her free.

'I was reaching for *those*…' she indicated the dangling blackberries '…and overbalanced.'

He gave a disgusted look as he caught a spray snagged on her hair, cut it and cast it away. 'Miss Daventry, the first rule of blackberrying is that no fruit is worth falling into the brambles for.'

'There was a snake,' she said, feeling foolish. 'I dare say it was harmless, but it startled me.'

'A snake?' He began to unhook a shoot that had caught across her breasts, the small barbs digging mercilessly. She froze at the shocking feel of his fingers, brushing with apparent uninterest over her breasts. Her breath locked in her throat; she looked down. The long, lean fingers worked carefully, detaching the clinging prickles. She swallowed. She felt surrounded by him, by the mingled odours of leather, horse and something warm, spicy and very male. This close she could see the faint dark shadow along his jaw, even though he would have shaved that morning. It looked scratchy, tempting, as though it invited curious fingertips. She clenched her fists, denying the thought, denying the sensation of his fingers brushing her breasts. Several layers of cloth should have muted his touch. They didn't.

His hands stilled. 'I'm sorry. Did I hurt you?'

'Wha—pardon?' She gulped. His right hand rested very lightly on her right breast. Heat rose, aching in both breasts.

'Your hands clenched. Did I hurt you?'

'Oh. Er, no. Of course not.' She forced her hands to relax. She wasn't used to being so close to a man. That was all.

He frowned as though not quite convinced, but continued. 'What colour was it?'

'Colour?' Frantically she pulled her senses back from the accidental caress of those long brown fingers. 'Oh, the snake—greenish. It was quite long, too. A yard?' No doubt he would think she was exaggerating and tell her that snakes didn't grow to that size.

'A grass snake, then,' he said. 'Harmless.' There was a ripping sound as one stubborn barb tore her gown, a small, three-cornered tear. His breath hissed in.

'Blast. Did that scratch you?'

'N…no.'

'Good. Hold still, we're nearly there.'

A moment later she stepped free, stumbling slightly. He steadied her. 'You should wash those scratches. Mrs Higgs will have some comfrey salve in the stillroom.'

She nodded. 'Thank you, my lord.' Her breath came uncertainly. He still held her. Not to steady her now. There was something intangibly different about the grip of his hands just above her bare elbows…something extremely unsteadying. She should step away. Should have already stepped away. Even as the thought flickered, his grip loosened, slid up her arms, his gaze questioning. And every speeding heartbeat she remained in his hold gave him the wrong answer.

'Someone in the bible found a lamb in a thicket, did they not?' His voice caressed. Hungry.

Oh, the temptation of that dark hunger! Not just his voice, but in his eyes. Her reason floundered for some sort of footing. 'Abraham,' she said. 'And…and it was a ram, not a lamb. He sacrificed it instead of his son.'

Heat flared in his eyes. 'As long as I am not expected to sacrifice you…'

Chapter Eight

His blood hammered. Surely she knew where this was heading?

Awareness flared in her eyes. He took a deep breath. She knew, then. Knew and had not stepped back... Slowly he raised his hand to her face, brushing the backs of his fingers over the silk of her jaw, her throat...soft, warm...tawny tresses tumbled over his wrist. Any moment she would pull back, the golden, sun-warmed enchantment broken by reality.

Reality which said she was not for him. That she was respectable, unmarried, probably virgin—his sisters' governess, his stepmother's companion. In a word, forbidden. Dangerous.

Some dangers were worth risking. Behind the spectacles, her mismatched eyes were dazed. He drew her closer, one arm sliding about her waist, bringing her to him so that the small, rounded breasts just brushed against him. A taste. Just one taste of those sweet, berry-stained lips...

His intent was clear, and every instinct shrieked a warning to Christy. Folly! Exactly what she had guarded against. She should stop him. Say no... But she was discovering that virtue was a simple matter when there was no temptation to sin. And Julian Trentham was temptation incarnate. It glinted in the brilliant blue of his eyes, now blazing with desire, caressed her with fire in the touch of his fingers on her throat, and trembled within her at the hard promise of his body, so dangerously close as his lips sought hers.

One word—*no*—was all it would take.

His lips touched hers and her wits whirled.

A kiss. Just a kiss. She'd been mauled about before by an employer's son. *A bit of sport*, he'd called it. It had meant nothing to him, less than nothing to her. Only this man did not maul, and a kiss was definitely not just a kiss. Warm, firm lips feathered and caressed, promising ravishment, yet teasing with light touches before settling properly. The tip of his tongue traced the quivering seam of her lips, exploring, probing at the corner of her mouth. Gentle strength enveloped her, cradled her, all heat and restrained fierceness…and against all received wisdom, her head sank back against his arm as her mouth opened under his.

His control shook as he felt the flowering of her lips, the softening as they opened. Quelling the urge to ravish her mouth, he took it gently, absorbing the gasp of shock as his tongue penetrated the sweetness, sliding deep. Honey, sweet wild honey, intoxicating—her very hesitance, even clumsiness, made it all the sweeter. All the more dangerous… With his final, fading shred of sanity Julian broke the kiss. He stared down into her flushed face, and nearly lost control again as she blinked up at him from behind her spectacles.

'This,' he informed her, 'is not a good idea.' With difficulty he forced his arms to release her and stepped back, clutching a few returning shreds of common sense, not to mention honour.

'N…no.' She seemed to be having as much difficulty breathing as he was.

No man of honour seduced innocents. He hauled in a breath. This was neither the time nor place to say what he needed to say to Miss Daventry. Especially since he couldn't straighten his wits enough to think what that might be.

The blackberries she had been trying to reach caught his eye. Sweet, luscious and ripe. He stretched up, plucked them carefully, one by one, and deposited them in the basket.

'Your berries, Miss Daventry. I'll bid you good afternoon.'

Before he continued where he had left off and disgraced himself any further. She said nothing and, with a nod, he went to his horse and mounted.

Pushing Conqueror into a trot, he rode away, suppressing the urge to look back. Desire had been riding him with spurs for days, but kissing Christy Daventry was tantamount to insanity. Her birth and character rendered her untouchable. Or they should. Marriage was out of the question. Seducing her unthinkable.

But there were other open, honest offers that could be made to a woman. Offers that did not rely on the sweet lies and falseness of a cold-hearted seduction. He could have her as long as she understood exactly what was offered and was not permitted to delude herself with romantic dreams. As long as he didn't cheat her with lies.

Christy watched him ride away, shivering despite the warmth of the sun. She touched her lips. How could a kiss— just a kiss!—make her feel like this?

Like what?

As though she were about to melt. As though his hand still cupped her breast, and his mouth still plundered hers. As though her world had tilted on its axis and started spinning in the wrong direction.

Her world would be tipped upside down if she let him seduce her. She knew that. Why, then, was everything in her whispering that it might be worth the risk? It was worth nothing. The only guarantee was a parting.

So? that insidious little voice murmured. *He's rich. You could get a settlement from him that would mean you never had to work again...you would have what you want: security.*

She might also have a child, and not willingly would she start the cycle again. Oh, there were precautions that could be taken. She knew that. None better. She also knew that they were uncertain at best. Harry was proof of that. And there was further proof, a headstone in a Bristol churchyard…a little sister. She blinked back tears at the memory. She had been sixteen when eight-year-old Sarah died of measles. Sarah would be sixteen now, earning her own living. Worrying about scraping enough together to survive on. Perhaps it was as well…

She couldn't do it. She would not risk bearing a child with no rights. *Filius nullius.* A child who did not exist in the world's calculations. A child who would have to lie every time someone asked about her father. Whose father would not bother to attend that child's funeral… The old anger rose, but she forced it back. There was no point. There never had been. Even when she had said all that was to be said on the subject. Said it to the Duke of Alcaston's face.

And she could not bear to sell, for cold hard cash, what she had once refused to give for love. Desire was not love. This aching, restless need would not last. It would fade, as love had once faded. Until it did, her hard-earned and usually un-shakeable self-control would have to do double duty.

Somehow all the delight had gone from the day, although around her the sun still poured golden, birds still sang, and blackberries gleamed darkly in the hedgerow. Bending down, she picked up the basket. She had enough in there. Some fruit was out of her reach; the rest was not worth the pain, and if she knew which ones Lord Braybrook had plucked, she would leave them behind for the birds.

After a long walk she should have been hungry. Instead, every spoonful of soup was an effort. The problem was sitting to her left, and he didn't appear to be off his food at all. Certainly he did not look as though he were aware that the woman he had kissed witless near a blackberry patch a few hours earlier was seated beside him. Not right beside him, of course, but a quarter of the way around the table.

There were only four of them that evening: herself, Lady Braybrook, Matthew and his lordship. Alicia and Emma were spending the night with Miss Pargeter. It should not have made any difference. Unlike her previous position where she had always dined alone if her employer had family or a visitor, she was expected to take her meals with the family.

She felt comfortable with them usually, except for the queer off-balance feeling that his lordship caused, but she ignored that, pretending it didn't exist. These family meals at the round table held little of formality, and it never seemed to matter who sat where. No one ever minded if the conversation bounced back and forth across the table and became somewhat noisy. The affection between them all glowed as golden and mellow as the candles on the table and in the wall sconces. Just being there and seeing it gave her a sense of peace, even though she was not really part of it. Not inside. It was not that they ignored her. Far from it. They made her welcome. But she still did not *belong*, although the light touched her.

Now, listening to Lady Braybrook explaining what needed to be done before the Summer Ball in three weeks, she knew what a fool she had been—that even while denying it, she had let herself believe that she *was* somehow included. The Incident—a cold, indifferent word chosen deliberately—by the bramble patch had jolted her out of her folly.

She nodded. 'Of course, ma'am. I will see that the bedchambers are prepared as well, if you wish to give me the list of guests staying overnight.'

Lady Braybrook smiled. 'Thank you, dear. It will be so much easier with you to help. I positively look forward to Braybrook marrying and his wife taking this sort of thing off my hands!'

Lord Braybrook looked up from his conversation about winter crops with Matthew. 'Serena, if the ball is too much—'

She waved him to silence. 'Nonsense. Not now I have Miss Daventry. Ah. Thank you, Walter.'

The servants cleared away the first course and brought in the second. Matthew's eyes lit up.

'I say! Blackberry pie! Excellent!' He grinned at Christy. 'Did you pick those?'

Her cheeks reddened. 'Yes.' She had delivered the berries to the kitchen, expecting them to be transformed into nicely anonymous jam or jelly. Not placed on the table before her, a tangible reminder of idiocy. Anger spiked. No doubt to his lordship they were merely blackberries. A tasty treat. Just as she would be if she weren't careful.

'A family tradition,' said Lady Braybrook cheerfully. 'One's first full basket of blackberries is always served for dinner. I gave the instructions this morning that if you came in with enough we were to have a pie.'

Christy felt the barbs dig into her again, mocking even as they drew her on.

'Looks jolly good,' said Matthew. 'Thank you, Miss Daventry.'

'They are…they are just blackberries,' she said. 'I thought they would be made into jam.' It was just their way. She would not fall into the trap of self-delusion again.

'Certainly not,' said Lady Braybrook. 'One's first blackberries should be memorable, Miss Daventry. Don't you agree, Julian?'

'Definitely,' he said. 'They look delicious, Miss Daventry.'

Cheeks hot, she met his gaze.

Beyond a polite greeting, it was the first remark he had addressed to her all evening. She wished he had refrained now. There was something disturbing in his gaze. Something that said he was thinking about the taste of more than blackberries.

She swallowed, cold and shaken as the blush ebbed. More than ever she felt apart, separate.

Matthew frowned. 'That walk was not after all too much for you, was it?' he asked. 'You're awfully quiet this evening. Pale, too.'

Aware of his lordship's intensified gaze, she managed a smile for Matthew. 'Nonsense. I am a little tired, but it is a nice sort of tired.' Or it would have been. 'And I saw a great many birds,' she added, desperate to change the subject. 'Just as you said. Only I didn't know what the half of them were.'

'Oh, we can't have that,' he said cheerfully. 'You'd better borrow Braybrook's bird books.' He turned to his brother. 'That will be all right, won't it, Julian?'

'Of course,' said his lordship. He turned to Christy. 'Indeed, there is something I wish to discuss with you, so if you come to the library after dinner I will give them to you.'

Oh, *God*! Why hadn't she bitten her tongue? She could just imagine what he wished to *discuss*. His etchings probably.

'Perhaps another time, my lord,' she said. 'I believe Lady Braybrook wishes to arrange the details for the Summer Ball, so—'

'Nonsense, dear,' said Lady Braybrook, cutting off her retreat. 'That can wait, but you do put me in mind of something.' She turned to her stepson. 'Julian—your marriage.'

Julian's wineglass paused halfway to his lips as he stared as Serena.

'My *what*?' he asked, in disbelief. Where the devil had that come from? They had been talking about blackberries. Sort of.

'Marriage, Julian.' Serena sipped her own wine. 'I am sure I can speak freely. Matt will not repeat anything and of course Miss Daventry would not.'

A quick glance told him that Miss Daventry looked as stunned as *he* felt. 'Nevertheless, it's hardly—' he began.

'It really is time you considered marriage seriously,' said Serena, ignoring his attempt to change the subject as she served some pie for herself and Miss Daventry. 'At thirty-two, it's high time you were settled. Before it's too late.'

He set his wineglass down with a distinct click. 'Are you telling me that I'm on the shelf?'

Matthew spluttered.

'Shut up, Matt.'

'Sorry.' Matthew didn't sound in the least bit sorry.

'Not precisely on the shelf,' said Serena. 'But if you leave it much longer they'll all be far too young for you. Think about it! All the eligible…that is, well, well-bred, well-dowered, *pretty* girls are snapped up at once.'

He stared at her.

'That is what you want in a woman, after all. Isn't it?' she said.

Those were precisely the qualifications that he had always taken it for granted that his *bride* would possess. Only right now he wasn't thinking about a bride. In fact, given his current intentions, discussing a possible marriage seemed highly inapposite.

'Have some pie, dear,' she said, passing it to him. His brain reeled. Those were still the qualifications he required. Blackberry pie had nothing to do with marriage…

'So,' continued Serena, as Julian helped himself to pie and then passed it along to Matt, 'it appears to me that as you have not met anyone suitable in London, then you might as well consider local candidates—the Summer Ball is a perfect opportunity for you to look them all over and make a selection.'

Good God! He took a spoonful of pie, its sweetness bursting in his mouth. She made it sound like buying a filly at Tattersalls! And he couldn't fault her for that, because, on the rare occasions he had considered the matter, that had been his own approach.

'Intelligent,' he got out and took another spoonful of pie. It was delicious, delicately spiced with nutmeg, and, violently aware of Christy's silent presence, he was enjoying it about as much as a bowl of dust and ashes.

Serena raised her brows. 'I thought that went without saying?'

And the rest *didn't*?

'Anyway, dear—give it some consideration. The obvious choice is Miss Postleton, but—'

'*Anne?*' asked Matthew, the serving spoon clattering against the pie dish. 'Shouldn't have thought she was quite Julian's sort, you know. She's not…I don't know…*kind*, really. Snubbed poor old Flint horribly in the village the other day when he asked her if he might dance with her at the Summer Ball. Liss spoke up to save his feelings and said *she'd* dance with him.'

'Oh, well,' said Serena. 'I do not say that I am set on Anne—that will be for Braybrook to decide…'

'Really?' he said with just the faintest hint of irony.

Serena sipped her hock. 'Don't be sarcastic, dear. I am merely pointing out that, unless you actually think about it, nothing will happen.'

'Better him than me,' muttered Matthew, casting Julian a pitying glance and pouring a generous dollop of cream over his blackberry pie.

Christy's faint hope that talk of marriage might have given his lordship's thoughts a more proper direction died as they rose from the dining table.

'Serena, if you will excuse me, I have some work to do this evening. If I may borrow Miss Daventry for a few moments, I will find those books for her.'

'Of course, Julian,' said Lady Braybrook, clearly oblivious to the possibility that her companion might have to defend her virtue. 'And, Miss Daventry, the ball can wait. This is still your day off, you know, and you look quite tired. I think you should go up early. Goodnight, dear.' She signalled to the footman who waited to carry her up to the drawing room. Matthew rose to wheel her out, saying, 'Goodnight, Miss Daventry.'

Once the door was safely shut behind them, Christy swung to face Lord Braybrook. 'You will excuse me, my lord. I have nothing to discuss with you. If you are happy to lend me the books, you may send them to my room. Goodnight.'

Devils danced in his eyes. Gritting her teeth, she turned to go.

'I'll bring them up myself, Miss Daventry. Just as soon as I find them. I suggest you don't prepare yourself for bed quite yet.'

'Wha—?' Recovering, she veiled fright and anger under frosty disdain. 'I *beg* your pardon?'

'Miss Daventry—I wish to speak with you. Now. You may choose the venue. My library. Or your bedchamber.' The corner of his mouth twitched. 'Or mine if you prefer.'

She went cold all over. Sometimes a man's kisses meant worse than nothing…

'On the whole I recommend the library,' he went on. 'You may sit beside the bell pull and I will sit far enough away to give you ample opportunity to use it should you deem it necessary.'

She stared at him. He might be lying, but she thought not. She simply couldn't imagine him telling a lie. Which might mean that her imagination was sadly lacking. 'The library, then,' she agreed. If he was lying, he would discover that she was not entirely without defences.

True to his word, Lord Braybrook made no effort to join Christy by the fireplace, but sat behind his desk.

'You know why we are here, Miss Daventry,' he said. 'But first let me assure you that I have no intention of seducing you here in the library, or indeed under this roof.'

'You don't?' Then what had that kiss been about? If ever a kiss had promised sinful indulgence…

'I wish to make you an offer.'

Shock robbed her of speech. He couldn't, it simply wasn't possible! And even if he did—

'I am offering you the position of my mistress.'

That on the other hand was eminently possible.

After a moment she said carefully, 'No doubt you will explain the difference between this and seduction, my lord, but—'

'The difference is honesty, Miss Daventry,' he told her. 'I am not offering lies about kisses and moonlight, nor about undying devotion. I am not tricking you into anything. I am not even trying to trick your body into anything. I desire you and wish you to be my mistress. After that kiss this afternoon, there is no point in denying our mutual attraction. Is there?'

She shook her head. One moment of idiocy. And God help her, the memory of it, the tender promise of his arms and kiss could still tempt her even in the face of his cool, businesslike proposition.

He was speaking again. Cold. Rational. 'Obviously you are not the sort of female to whom I can offer marriage—but you would be well provided for.'

She swallowed that without flinching. It was no more than the truth. Indeed, it was truer than he knew. She waited.

'I have several comfortable houses in nearby towns. A lease would be settled on you, along with an annuity, and I would visit you. Discreetly, of course.'

'Of course,' she echoed. *Discretion*, the duke's watchword. The reason he had not attended her mother's funeral, or Sarah's. Yet all her neighbours would know exactly what she was and she would live isolated except for his brief visits. Visits that would grow further apart until they ceased entirely and then one day she would receive a note from him to inform her of what her heart already knew: that it was finished. She would be her mother all over again. Mistresses were for bedsport only and when their charms faded, their lovers faded away too. Her mother had been lucky the duke had continued to support her.

'You would not find me an ungenerous lover, Miss Daventry. In any way. There would be a proper contract drawn up between us, including provision for any child. Nor would you be dismissed when I marry.'

'I see. A charming prospect for your wife.'

He actually flushed. 'You misunderstand. The requirements for wife and mistress are very different. In my world fidelity is not demanded, nor am I hypocrite enough to expect something of my wife that I am not prepared to give in return. Once the succession is assured, she may please herself discreetly.'

She had never heard it spelt out so brutally, and she had

never heard of a contract, but she understood all about the difference between wife and mistress in his world. A wife brought breeding and fortune. A mistress was for bedsport. *And love...?* She choked that off. Love had no part in either arrangement, despite lip service in the marriage vows.

'Miss Daventry?'

She rose to her feet, conscious of aching regret, mingled with gratitude that he had made his offer openly, that he had not seduced her with sweet lies and kisses. Tenderness would have been the ultimate temptation. Now more than ever, she understood her mother's mistakes, understood her believing that it was different. Because the memory of this afternoon's kiss promised delight and tenderness. Even in the face of his cold, calculated offer, that kiss whispered of so much more. That with *him* it would be different.

'No, thank you, my lord. Goodnight. I will give Lady Braybrook my notice in the morning.'

'I beg your pardon?' He looked as winded as if she had landed a blow to his stomach.

'I am refusing your generous offer, my lord—'

'Yes, I understood that,' he said impatiently. 'But why are you leaving?'

She struggled for words. For coherent thoughts.

'My lord, you have offered me the position of your mistress. Surely you neither expect nor wish me to remain here?'

He frowned. 'I thought I made it clear that I was not going to seduce you? If you are refusing me, then that is an end of the matter. I'm not about to creep into your bedchamber to have my wicked way with you against your will. You have refused. So be it. Do not imagine, Miss Daventry, that I am fancying myself in love, nor that I am incapable of controlling my desires. You are perfectly safe under my roof.'

Safe? Perhaps in the way a mouse was safe from a well-fed, sleeping cat...but something about the very quietness of his assurance rang true.

He could be lying. But she still couldn't imagine it, and she liked being here. It was the most dangerous illusion of all, but here she felt comfortable. Which was stupid. His lordship's dishonourable proposal had showed her exactly how far from his world she was.

'Very well. I will remain.'

For now.

'Good.' He stood up and strolled across to the bookshelves, pulling out three octavo volumes. 'And you are quite sure that you will not reconsider your refusal?' As though he had offered to buy something material. Which perhaps he had.

'Quite sure, my lord,' she said evenly. 'It is not a life that appeals to me.'

He turned, the books in his hands, and frowned at her. 'I thought you were insulted, but you are not, are you?'

She considered that. Was she? Beneath the numbness she felt something, but she doubted it was anger. What right had she to be insulted? Even if he didn't know it, she was illegitimate, a duke's by-blow. She used the ugly term deliberately, reminding herself of reality. He had been honest with her. That in itself implied some sort of respect. He had not simply attempted to take what he wanted, either by stealth, or force. The choice was hers. She must make it wisely.

'No, my lord. You were honest with me. I appreciate that. But if it's any consolation, I have no experience or talents that would render me at all suitable as a mistress.'

He seemed to freeze, but an instant later laid the books on his desk, placing them with careful exactitude in the very middle. 'Ah. I believe these to be the volumes you wanted, Miss Daventry.'

'Volumes?'

Long, lean fingers brushed lightly over the calfskin, reminding her of the magic they could summon from a woman's body…

'George Graves, *British Ornithology*. In three volumes. Lady

Braybrook will wish to know if you are enjoying them.' His voice was cool, remote. Aristocrat to humble dependant. Probably she would have been expected to call him *my lord* in bed… 'Matthew is our resident expert if you have any questions.'

She dragged in a breath, banishing fancy and regret. 'Of course, my lord. Thank you.'

The other subject was closed, then. Dismissed. No doubt from his mind as well as from discussion. Which was exactly what she wanted. Wasn't it?

Aware of his gaze on her, she came forwards and picked up the books. A slight movement behind the desk startled her. She looked up at him sharply.

'If you are not insulted, Miss Daventry, and you admit your attraction—will you tell me why you refused?'

His voice betrayed only mild curiosity, but something about the set of his jaw, the line of his mouth, had her backing away, heart pounding. And not in fear. Her mind was blank. Why *was* she refusing?

Words came without conscious thought. 'You warned me yourself, my lord.'

The black brows snapped together. 'Oh? When?'

'This afternoon. When you told me that no fruit is worth the pain of falling into the bramble patch.'

His mouth twisted. 'I see. Well, should you change your mind,' he said politely, 'you have only to say so and I will arrange it all.'

She inclined her head. 'You are all kindness, sir.' Then, clutching the books, she beat a dignified retreat.

Chapter Nine

Julian shut his eyes and clenched his fists as the door closed. That was that. The refusal he had half expected. Without even bothering to find out what he was prepared to offer. What *was* it about Christy Daventry? She wasn't a beauty—but he had never wanted a woman more. She was honest enough to raise blisters when she abandoned her reserve. And the thought of her abandoning her reserve in bed raised something even more painful.

But she wasn't his usual sort of woman. She was neither one of his discreet aristocratic lovers, nor a woman he would set up publicly in London, an acknowledged ladybird—a voluptuous prize to flaunt before the world, at the opera, in the Park. He couldn't see her in that milieu at all. He wanted her all to himself. *His.* Here.

Well, not *here* precisely. That was impossible. But somewhere close to Amberley so that he could ride over and spend a few days with her at times…which was foolish beyond belief. He had never done anything like that in his life. When he visited a mistress it was to have sex. Not because he wanted to spend time with her. Damn it! Why had he wanted to sit down with those books and help her find the birds she had seen today? And suggest other birds to watch for. Why did he want to find out how to make her laugh, banish the sadness he some-times saw in her eyes? Why did he even notice the sadness?

She had refused him. And it was not the sort of refusal that gave him the least hope she would change her mind. Her decision had been made, and voiced, with cool deliberation. No tears. No reproaches. She hadn't even been decently shocked.

No fruit is worth the pain of falling into the bramble patch.

That spurred something inside him startlingly close to shame. He knew damn well it was true. In these *affaires* all penalty was on the woman's side. Any social costs and hurt would be borne by her. Miss Daventry had decided that he wasn't worth the risk. And having assured her that she was safe from him, he must honour that promise. Her assurance that she had no experience didn't help in the least. Quite the opposite—he was doubtless about to spend a sleepless night imagining all sorts of ways in which he could redress her inexperience.

Enough! He had promised not to seduce her. Blackberries were off the menu.

For the next few days Julian buried himself in estate business either in the library, or about the estate, listing jobs to be done before winter. Cottages to be repaired, wood to be cut, a farmer's widow to re-house. He took Davy with him and spent as little time in Miss Daventry's company as possible. He saw her at breakfast and in the evenings, always in company with Serena or one of his siblings. She said *good morning, good evening*. Beyond that she scarcely even looked at him.

Which was a good thing, he assured himself as he tightened his horse's girth one morning ten days after the ill-advised ren-dezvous by the blackberries. Miss Daventry was doing the job for which she had been hired. She ran errands for Serena, helped with teaching Davy, supervised Lissy and Emma at their music, engaged in French and Italian conversation with them, and, according to Serena, was a great help with the ar-rangements for the swiftly approaching ball. This morning she had been sent off to the village shop to buy some embroidery silks. Serena had given her the errand at breakfast. He had been tempted to order his curricle instead of riding to his meeting with Sir John Postleton so that he might offer to take her up. He was an idiot.

Out of sight, out of mind. That's how it was meant to work. That was how it always had worked in the past.

This time dismissing a failed conquest from his mind was nigh on impossible, he thought, riding out of the stable yard. He snorted. Conquest? A more inappropriate word could not be imagined. Miss Daventry was not the sort of female one conquered. He still wanted her. Only that wasn't why he had thought of offering to drive her into the village. He had simply wanted to be with her. Talk to her. Perhaps tease her into one of her sharp comments. He must be mad. Barking, in fact. Especially since he was quite sure she would not have stepped into the curricle.

A bell clanged as Christy pushed open the door of the village shop. She blinked as her eyes adjusted to the dimness after the blaze of sunshine outside. The shop was crowded, shelves towering to the ceiling, laden with goods ranging from shoes to cheeses. More expensive wares, such as tea and spices, were stored behind the counter to be dispensed by Mr Wilkins on request. Flitches of bacon hung from the rafters and the whole shop breathed the yeasty warmth of new-baked bread.

Everything was spotless, from the windows to the floor, including the small, neat man behind the counter, subjecting her to a searching scrutiny. Recognising her, he relaxed and permitted himself a slight bow.

'Good day, Miss Daventry. May I help you?'

'Good day, Mr Wilkins,' she said. 'Some embroidery silks for her ladyship, if you please, and some cambric for myself.' She needed to hem new handkerchiefs.

Mr Wilkins bustled from behind the counter and in a very

short time the embroidery silks were laid out for her inspection. Pulling Lady Braybrook's samples from her pocket, Christy began the painstaking task of selecting matches. Some blues were needed…that pale sky blue? Yes. But not that royal blue. This one? Perhaps… About to ask if she might take the silks to the window, she heard the bell ring again as the door opened. Mr Wilkins, setting out some cambric for her inspection, looked up and his mouth pursed as though he had bitten into something unpleasant.

'What is it, child?'

The cold, dismissive tone drew echoes from the past, and Christy turned to see who had entered.

Shock slammed into her.

In the drawing room at Amberley there was a set of miniatures of Lady Braybrook's children. All painted as five year olds, all staggeringly alike with the Trentham dark hair and blue eyes, luminous on ivory.

It was as though the portrait of five-year-old Alicia had sprung to warm, glowing life and walked into the shop. The same glossy black curls and bright eyes—only this child's complexion was tinged golden with the sun.

'Well?' snapped Mr Wilkins. 'What do you want?'

There could only be one explanation for the child's resemblance to the Trenthams and Mr Wilkins's attitude. With condensing pain, Christy saw the little girl's nervousness.

'Please, sir—a paper of pins for Mam, and…and a pink riband.' The piping voice sounded breathless, and the child cast a quick glance at Christy. 'I've enough money.' She opened her tightly clenched fingers to show a shilling clutched there.

Mr Wilkins looked affronted. 'You'll have to wait. This lady is before you.'

Her voice indifferent, Christy said, 'There's no need for that, Mr Wilkins. I am not done with my selections. Serve the child.'

'Well—' Mr Wilkins found a paper of pins and wrapped

them up. 'There. You can't have the riband. I'll not have you pawing through my goods, dirtying them.'

Within Christy long-buried rage uncurled, stretching its wings.

The little girl said nothing, just swallowed and handed him the shilling.

'Mr Wilkins,' said Christy in creditably neutral tones, 'I believe my hands are clean. Perhaps if I were to look through your ribands and the child were to point out the right colour?'

Purple, Christy reflected, was particularly unflattering on a man's face. 'There's no need, Miss Daventry,' began Wilkins, 'I assure you—'

The door jangled, but Christy did not bother to look around.

'Mr Postleton! Miss Anne!' Mr Wilkins started towards them, bowing low, his face wreathed in obsequiousness.

Miss Anne… Christy glanced over her shoulder—she had met Miss Postleton at church—briefly. Anne Postleton had acknowledged the introduction with a supercilious *oh?* and continued on her way. It was a wonder the shop ceiling didn't cave in with the shock of having the young lady under it along with the woman Braybrook desired as his mistress. Not to mention the child.

'Oh, Mr Wilkins!' said Miss Anne. 'I am in such a bother! The Summer Ball at Amberley, you know! And I am to have a new gown, so I should like to look at your silks, if you please!'

'But of course, Miss Anne!' he said at once, starting towards them, wreathed in unctuous delight. 'If you would just tell me which colours, I will fetch them down this instant!'

The final thread restraining Christy's temper snapped.

'The ribands, if you please, sir!'

Shocked faces turned towards her, and she shamelessly added, 'I should not care to keep Lady Braybrook waiting for her silks either, Mr Wilkins.'

Mr Postleton stared. 'What the deuce! Braybrook's governess, ain't it?'

'Miss *Trentham*'s governess,' Christy corrected him, willing herself to ignore the smirk.

A faint sneer curled Miss Postleton's lip. 'Oh, yes. The *governess*.' Oozing disdain, she turned back to Mr Wilkins. 'I won't keep you long, Mr Wilk—'

Mr Wilkins, however, had found the ribands and placed the box on the counter with a bang. 'Thank you,' said Christy, and turned to the little girl with a smile. 'A pink riband, was it not? And I don't think I know your name?'

The child looked up her hesitantly and nodded. 'Nan,' she whispered.

A stifled titter came from behind them. 'Oh, really! Ned! Do you see who it is?'

A muffled crack of laughter came from Mr Postleton. 'By Jove!'

The child, Nan, flinched. At the sight a slow fire ignited in Christy's gut. She remembered, oh, *how* she remembered the murmurs in Bath when she had been a child—the people who turned away, the shopkeepers who seemed not to see one. Whose arithmetic in working out the change had so often disagreed with hers. Then she had not understood. Now, she understood only too well. And this child…she was how old? Five? Six? And already condemned.

She summoned a smile. 'How do you do, Nan?' she responded. 'I am Miss Daventry. I work at Amberley.'

Selecting several different pinks from the box, she set them out. Beyond them at the far end of the counter, Mr Wilkins tenderly laid out lengths of silk for Miss Postleton. Christy ignored them, but Ned Postleton's occasional glances were an unpleasant itch between her shoulder blades.

The child, Nan, subjected the ribands to a close inspection, then, careful not to touch, she pointed and said, 'That one.'

It was a deep, rich colour, almost raspberry.

'Perfect,' said Christy. She could imagine it glowing in the raven curls. 'Is it for you? It will look very pretty.'

Nan nodded. 'Because I've been good.'

Such a simple delight, thought Christy. She put the other

ribands back and looked toward Mr Wilkins, who was hovering over Miss Postleton, complimenting her on her taste as she scowled over the merits of jonquil yellow and palest pink. His back was firmly turned to Christy.

She dragged in a breath and prepared to do battle.

'Mr Wilkins—'

'Might as well serve the lady, Wilkins,' drawled Mr Postleton, lounging against the counter and running his eyes over Christy. 'M'sister could be hours.' He gave Christy a wink.

Miss Postleton glanced up, cast a condescending glance at Christy and shrugged. 'Oh, as you please. I am sure it makes no difference to *me*!'

Mr Wilkins came over and grudgingly measured out a length of pink delight while Nan watched, breathless.

She paid for the riband and pins and then, stowing her treasure safely in a pocket, smiled shyly at Christy. 'Thank you, miss.'

With a jingle of the doorbell, she was gone, trotting off up the street. Christy watched her for a moment—torn between an aching sense of fellowship and a searing desire to hit the man whose careless pleasure had condemned his daughter to a half-life. Nan could have been herself all those years ago…or Sarah. Or her own child had she been fool enough to accept Braybrook's offer. An innocent, condemned by the world as tainted, impure.

Her chin up, she turned to Mr Wilkins. 'What a pretty child,' she said. 'Such blue eyes—I've never seen anything lovelier.'

Another titter escaped from Miss Postleton.

Let them make of *that* what they would! She knew exactly where those blue eyes came from and she would wager her year's salary that neither Mr Wilkins nor Miss Postleton had ever snubbed the father!

'Very pretty,' muttered Mr Wilkins, as though the words were dragged from him.

'And so well mannered,' continued Christy with malice

aforethought, handing him Lady Braybrook's embroidery silks and her own cambric. 'One can tell so much from the way a girl conducts herself with others.'

Miss Postleton looked up from the dress lengths, her face stiff with outrage.

Casting discretion to hell, Christy continued pensively, 'Heritage does tell, does it not? Her parents must be very good sort of people.'

Mr Wilkins's mouth flopped open and closed like a fish on a very nasty hook, as he did up Christy's purchases in a neat parcel. Ignoring a stifled snort of laughter from Mr Postleton, Christy handed the money to Mr Wilkins.

Mr Wilkins gulped, and wiped his brow. 'Ah, yes. Jane Roberts…she's, er, widowed. As it were.'

'As it were, Mr Wilkins?' She tucked the parcel safely into her satchel. Never before had she quite understood the pleasure there could be in taking a pound or three of flesh.

The little man swallowed. 'Er, yes. He died—old Tom Roberts, her husband. Child was born a few months later.'

'How very sad,' said Christy. 'Such a misfortune. Well, thank you for your help, Mr Wilkins. Good day to you.' She nodded politely to Mr Postleton and his sister as she walked to the door.

A spiteful voice followed her. 'I dare say poor, dear Lady Braybrook will be *most* interested in the company her servants keep.'

Christy looked back. 'Oh, do you think so? I *had* thought her mind to be above village tittle-tattle, but if you think it will amuse her to know that I met you here, Miss Postleton, I will mention it. Good day to you.'

Without waiting for a response, she left the shop in a furious jangle of bells. She was shocked to find herself shaking. Not for years had anything slid beneath her guard; she had learnt to ignore that sort of jibe. For herself at least…only not since Sarah's death had she seen another child on the receiving end.

She pushed the memory away. Sarah was at peace in that little churchyard outside Bristol, a white rose dreaming over her. It *was* better that way. Or so she always told herself.

Out of the corner of her eye she saw his lordship riding into the village from the direction of Amberley. Rage bubbled up, scalding…all the things she wanted to say searing on the tip of her tongue. Just as they had boiled up at the Duke after Sarah's death. She had said it all then. She must not this time. She was not sixteen, and it was none of her business. Slamming the lid down on the roiling cauldron, she turned resolutely and forced herself to walk in the opposite direction. Fast. She ought to return to Amberley, but if she passed him, if he stopped and spoke—God only knew what she might say. All the years of self-discipline had incinerated in moments. She wasn't sure enough of her control to risk an encounter with him now.

And why on earth should she be surprised at this? It happened all the time. Why this sense of disappointment? Would she have expected him to rear his illegitimate daughter with his younger siblings? Hardly!

A mocking catcall pulled her out of her abstraction. Fifty yards ahead a small group of village boys milled around a low stone wall. Pressing close, they shoved and jostled, apparently engrossed in something beside the wall. A puppy with a brick tied to its tail? A kitten? Something small and helpless they could torment? Christy's already swift stride lengthened.

'Givin' yerself airs, eh?' came a jeering voice. 'Yer just a little bastard, my dad ses, an' yer mam's nowt but a rich man's fancy piece!'

'Leavin's, yeh mean, Bob,' came another voice. 'Everyone knows he don't come next or nigh her no more. 'Ere! Gimme that!'

'No! They're me mam's!'

Christy broke into a dead run.

Unhesitatingly her hand fell on the shoulder of the largest boy, a tall, well-grown lad of perhaps thirteen, twisting him towards her. Caught off-balance, he staggered and bumped against another boy.

'Stop it!' she ordered. Her rage scorched. Nan cowered against the wall, her curls dishevelled, dress dusty and a trickle of blood showing on one leg. The little parcel of pins lay in the dirt.

The boys turned and eyed Christy in patent wariness. The big boy she had grabbed, shuffled and wrenched his shoulder loose, saying defiantly, 'We're not doin' no harm.' Ignoring that, she pushed him aside as she went to Nan, picked up the package and handed it to her. Then she turned to face the boys again, her hand on Nan's shoulder.

The big boy looked around at his mates, as if for reassurance and swaggered slightly. 'Just a bit of a game,' he went on, 'ain't it, Nan?' The others snickered in agreement.

The little girl, her cheeks tear-streaked, hesitated.

'Ain't it, Nan?' he repeated through gritted teeth.

'Yes,' whispered the child, pressing against Christy's skirts and reaching for her hand.

Disgust sour in her mouth, Christy stared hard at the boy, brows raised until his gaze dropped and his mates began edging away.

'Just a bit o' fun!' he insisted.

'Odd sort of fun,' came a deep voice, 'that leaves a little girl bleeding and in tears, wouldn't you say, boys?'

Christy spun around with the boys at the familiar voice.

Braybrook stood there, his horse's reins looped over his arm, his face hard, the mouth set in an implacable line.

He glanced at Christy. 'Thank you, Miss Daventry, for your intervention. I regret its necessity, and so will these lads once I have spoken with their parents.' His voice did not lift above its usual level, but the boys exchanged nervous glances.

'Just so,' he said quietly. 'You will, each and every one of you, apologise to both Miss Daventry and Nan.'

Under that cold blaze the boys shuffled past, muttering apologies.

When the last of them had gone, Braybrook seemed to relax

slightly. Very slightly. When he turned to face them, tension remained in the hard lines about his mouth.

Yet his voice was gentle as he bent down to Nan. 'May I see that scrape?'

Despite her rage, Christy found his diffidence oddly touching. As though *he* were unsure of his rights. Still clutching Christy's hand, Nan nodded wordlessly, and with gentle hands Braybrook lifted her skirts to expose a skinned, bruised knee.

'Fell over running,' whispered Nan. 'Banged my knee.'

Braybrook said nothing, but Christy saw a muscle flicker beside his jaw. Without a word, he produced a handkerchief, and dabbed carefully at the graze.

'I've some water,' said Christy, finding her voice. She let go of Nan's hand and opened her satchel, bringing out the water bottle.

'Thank you.' Braybrook took the bottle and uncorked it, pouring a little water onto the handkerchief and using it to wash away the streaked blood and dirt.

'There,' he said at last. 'That's better. All clean now.' He straightened up, his expression unreadable.

Some of Christy's anger, momentarily deflected by his gentleness with the child, returned.

'All injury avenged,' she said coolly. 'I'll walk Nan home, my lord.' He might have come to the child's assistance, but she doubted that he would care to be seen walking through the village with her.

He looked down at her, frowning. Then, 'Yes. You do that. I have a couple of other things I must attend to.'

All of Christy's fury re-ignited.

It took every ounce of her self-control to say only, 'Of course you do, my lord. Good day to you.'

She held out her hand to Nan. 'Come along, sweetheart. I'll see you safely home. Do you think your mama will make me a cup of tea?'

* * *

Julian left the forge half an hour later, reasonably certain that not one of the boys would be able to sit down to his dinner. Whatever their parents might think of Jane Roberts, or suspect about her daughter's paternity, they had no doubts at all about the unwisdom of offending the lord of Amberley, who happened to own well over half the village.

Simple enough as far as it went. Which was not nearly far enough. His visit to Jane would not be simple at all.

Jane Roberts opened the door and flushed when she saw him. 'Good day, my lord.'

He tensed at the barely veiled hostility, but said politely, 'Good morning, Jane. How do you go on?'

Dark eyes wary, she said, 'Well enough. Is there something you want, my lord?'

He shook his head. 'No. Merely to say that I have spoken with all the boys and their parents and I doubt that there will be any more of this morning's trouble. I take it Miss Daventry explained when she brought Nan home?'

Jane's defensive air eased slightly. 'Yes. Thank you.'

'Tell me, Jane—has anything like this happened before?' he asked.

She shrugged. 'Only to be expected, wasn't it?'

'The hell it is!' he retorted. 'When you told me to stop visiting, I warned you about this sort of thing! Don't you think I'd have dealt with it, if I'd known?'

'Very obliging of you, I'm sure.'

'Obliging be damned!' he snapped. 'For God's sake, Jane! Would it not be better if you moved? Started somewhere else, where people won't take one look at Nan, and—'

'Call her a whore's daughter?' finished Jane. 'Why should I be driven from my home?'

'I'm not trying to drive you out,' he said wearily. Every time they spoke this came up. 'I want only what's best for both of you.'

Her face hard, she said, 'Twould make little difference. A

"widow" with a child and a mysterious source of money, moving where no one knows her? Have me pegged in no time, they would. Might as well put out a sign sayin' "whore".'

'I'm sorry, Jane,' he said quietly. 'I wish for your sake it were otherwise, but—'

'Ten years!' she burst out. 'Ten years of marriage an' no child!' She bit her lip. 'D'you wonder I thought myself barren?' Savagely she said, 'An' even then it might not have mattered, if…if—'

'If she weren't the living image of her father,' finished Julian. 'May I see her?'

Jane hesitated, then shrugged. 'If you like. Nan! Nan!'

Flying steps sounded in the passage behind her and the small face appeared, peering around Jane's skirts.

He smiled down at her, feeling as always, absurdly guilty. 'Good morning again, Nan,' he said gently. 'Are you feeling better now?'

The child nodded solemnly, but remained silent. Julian had heard the whispers, that she was slow, a dullard—the bright clear gaze belied it.

He persevered. 'I've spoken to Bob Pratchett and his friends. If it happens again, your mama will send a message to me. Yes?'

Again the nod.

'That's a very pretty ribbon,' he said. The deep pink set off the glossy dark curls. 'Is it a new one?' He had no idea whether it was or not, but it looked pretty, and she'd not been wearing it earlier.

'Yes.' The merest whisper. He had to bend to catch what she was saying. 'Miss Daventry helped me choose it. Mr Wilkins thought I'd dirty his things.'

'Did he?' Julian kept the anger from his voice with an effort. That was another call he'd have to make. Damn it all to hell and beyond! The person least to blame in this hellish muddle was Nan.

He straightened. 'I'll speak to Wilkins,' he said, more to Jane than to Nan.

She shrugged. 'You might also mention that I don't appreciate being charged extra in his shop.'

Anger tightened sharply. 'I'll do that.' He looked at her hard. 'In future, Jane, keep me informed. I don't shirk my responsibilities, but if you don't tell me, I can't help much.'

She flushed. 'You've supported us when you had no obligation. What more could I expect?'

Anger and guilt warring, he said shortly, 'Let me know next time there's trouble and you might find out.'

Her mouth twisted. 'Forget I said that. You've been good enough to us.' She frowned. 'One thing…that Miss Daventry—you'd best warn her not to call here. Don't rightly know that she understood how it was. Bringin' Nan back's one thing, but she did insist on coming in. Had a cup of tea an' all. Not that I grudge the tea. Kind, she is. But you warn her not to do it again. I don't want trouble for her after what she did.'

He snorted. 'Tell Miss Daventry what she may or may not do? If I survived the encounter, you'd have to scrape me off the walls!'

Chapter Ten

Julian rode through the village, conscious that he was late for his meeting with Sir John Postleton, and that the latest gossip would have circled the village at least twice.

The servant who opened the door bowed, saying, 'Good morning, my lord. Sir John is expecting you, but my lady requests the favour of a private word first.'

'Very well, but please inform your master that I am here.'

'Very good, my lord.'

Lady Postleton received him in the drawing room, her smile a polite fiction. 'Good morning, Lord Braybrook.'

'Good morning, Lady Postleton,' he said warily. Quite apart from Serena's comments on the subject of his marriage, he knew he figured largely in Lady Postleton's matrimonial plans for Anne. No doubt this interview was another skirmish in her ongoing campaign to secure the prize. Usually the young lady concerned was draped in a becoming pose around the chronically out-of-tune harp in the corner.

Seeing his eyes flicker to the harp, Lady Postleton said with a satisfied little smile, 'You are disappointed not to see Anne. I must tell you that she is laid down upon her bed with the headache, so overset was she about this morning's little contretemps.'

'Is she?' Julian waited. She couldn't have got wind of Nan's business and what affair was it of Anne's anyway?

'Yes.' Lady Postleton's smile glittered. 'And while I hesitate to upset poor Serena, it would be as well if you were to drop a hint in her ear. This Miss Daventry she has taken up is not at all the thing!'

Julian stiffened.

'I am given to understand that she was quite impertinent to my poor Anne this morning, putting herself forward in a most odious way and actually had the effrontery to insist on being served first in Mr Wilkins's shop!' Her mouth primmed. 'Quite the grand lady! I wish you will tell Serena that she is sadly mistaken in the young person's character and would be well advised to turn her off immediately.'

It took fifteen minutes of polite evasions to extricate himself from Lady Postleton's clutches. That he had done so without signing an agreement in his own blood to dismiss Miss Daventry the moment he laid eyes on her, was in the nature of a miracle. Of course, remarking on how much he personally would enjoy welcoming Lady Postleton to Amberley helped enormously.

Julian took his leave, conscious of a burning desire to know exactly what Miss Daventry had said to cause offence. Of course, it was also possible that Miss Daventry had a burning desire to box his ears, he realised, knocking on the door of Sir John's book room.

'Come in! Come in!'

The baronet looked up from his ledgers as Julian entered.

'Hah! Late!'

'I beg your pardon, sir,' said Julian. 'An urgent matter I needed to attend to.'

Sir John snorted. 'Don't bother sparing my blushes! Heard all about it already. Best to move the Roberts woman on. Don't know why you haven't. Not as if she's anything to you now.

Just causes trouble. Pity it's so obvious, but if you moved her on, there'd be an end of it.'

Julian controlled himself with an effort. 'That is not my decision to make, sir.'

Sir John looked pained. 'Ought to be your decision, boy! That's the point. Your cottage, ain't it?'

Julian said merely, 'It is.'

'Yes, well. There you are. And of course my wife wasn't best pleased with Miss Daventry's actions in Wilkins's shop. Dare say that's what she wanted to speak to you about. Not Miss Daventry's fault—how was she to know who the child was?'

Julian froze. *Miss Daventry helped me choose it. Mr Wilkins thought I'd dirty his things.*

'Nan Roberts was in the shop?'

Sir John went slightly red. 'Er, yes. Dare say the lady wife didn't like to say. As I said, not Miss Daventry's fault. *She* wasn't to know.'

Miss Daventry not know? Did Sir John think she was stupid? Blind? Of course she knew. Or thought she knew...

Sir John pulled a pile of papers to the front of his desk. 'Fact remains, lad, if you moved them on, these situations wouldn't arise. Just as easy for you to provide for her elsewhere! And let's face it...' he cleared his throat, looking self-conscious '...awkward for your bride when you marry. Having it in her face, so to speak. Not,' he added hurriedly, 'that it's any business of mine!'

'Quite,' said Julian. 'Now, sir, I have the figures on the expected cider-apple yields. If you have yours to hand, we can see about this brewery.'

Clearing his throat, Sir John said, 'Oh, aye. I can take a hint. None of my affair, although—' He broke off. 'Very well, then—to business. Not a bad idea, you know, a brewery. A few more jobs. Stop some of 'em going off to the cities and getting into trouble. Bring up a chair, boy!'

* * *

An hour later, his head full of plans and figures for new plantings, Julian made ready to leave.

'Met that fellow Havergal yet?' asked Sir John.

In the process of ordering his papers, Julian stiffened. 'Not yet, sir.'

Sir John looked thoughtful. 'Seems to call out this way quite often. Visits Serena, Lady P. says. Odd sort of chap.'

'Odd, sir? In what way?'

'Hmm? Oh, well, as to that he's pleasant enough. Taken lodgings in Hereford. Came before me on the bench t'other day.'

'*Havergal* came before you?'

'Yes—some young rascal picked his pocket, if you please. Bold as brass! Wouldn't have the boy charged, though. Just hauled him along for a warning. A warning, I ask you! He wanted the boy to attend some charity school. Waste of time, if you ask me! God knows where it will all end.'

'With one less child transported, or ending on the gallows?' suggested Julian.

Sir John gave a dubious grunt. 'He came to see me a day or so later. Told me the boy was at school and off the streets. Interesting chap. Been in India the last twenty-odd years. Just thought I'd ask if you'd met him. Since he calls on Serena.'

Deep in thought, Julian took his leave. Who was this Havergal? A fortune hunter? Surely he wasn't labouring under the misapprehension that Serena was wealthy in her own right? Like most widows, she lost her jointure if she remarried. He'd have to meet Mr Havergal, and make a few things very clear.

Christy left Jane Roberts' cottage, cursing her own folly. Once more Christy had stepped out from behind Miss Daventry, this time to deal a set-down to Miss Postleton. And her temper had still had the whip hand when Lord Braybrook appeared.

She walked back through the village, wondering if she had

lost her mind. She had not bothered to hide her contempt. Oh, she might not have said anything, but her face, her tone of voice! She was an idiot. With a position that bordered on miraculous, she had jeopardised it by allowing her feelings to show. One thing to defend Nan. It was quite another to betray her scorn and contempt for Miss Postleton and her brother. Let alone her anger with Braybrook.

And she was, she realised, leaving the village behind and turning into the road for Amberley, still angry. Deep within fury and disappointment melded in a cold, bitter lump.

Disappointment? Anger, yes. But disappointment? That implied surprise, that she had expected something else. Yet what was surprising about a wealthy, handsome aristocrat taking his pleasure with a respectable woman, with no care for the consequences she would face if she bore his child? What was surprising about said aristocrat showing little interest in his child and leaving the mother to manage alone in a community that largely shunned both her and her daughter? Why should she have expected anything else of him? Had he not offered to take *her* as his mistress? And with just the same cold indifference to all but his own pleasure?

She was nowhere near finding answers when she reached the stile that gave on to the path leading through the woods to Amberley. About to climb over, she heard hoofbeats from the opposite direction and turned to see who was coming.

Around the bend came Harry on a tall bay. She was about to wave, but he saw her immediately and reined his mount in hard. For a startled moment his expression looked one of shock and fury.

Then he waved and rode up to her, saying with a friendly smile as he halted, 'It's not your day off, is it? Are you on your way to the village with an errand?'

Had she imagined the anger? 'Yes and no. I'm on my way back. Can your horse jump the stile? If you aren't in a hurry, you could walk me to the end of the path. It would be nice to talk.'

'Oh, er, no. Better not. Sir John will be expecting me, you

know.' Harry flushed and for a moment Christy thought again that there was a faint hint of annoyance in his face. Then another smile. 'I'll call on my day off. And of course there is this party at Amberley next week—I am invited, did you know?'

'Yes.' She had helped write the invitations.

'Not having any trouble with him?'

'Definitely not.' Even if she *had* been tempted to succumb to the lure of his lordship's disgraceful offer, this morning's revelation had served as a timely warning.

'Well, that's good,' said Harry. He raised his whip in salute. 'Bye, Christy.' With that he pushed his horse into a trot and was gone.

Christy stepped down from the stile and set off towards Amberley. Her stride lengthened as her temper mounted again. This time directed at herself, for being foolish enough to think that Lord Braybrook was somehow different. That he was not the man to evade his responsibilities.

A more moderate voice made itself heard. *He did intervene with those boys. And looked after Nan's scraped knee.*

She didn't want to think about the gentleness with which he had tended the child. Or the odd, blank expression on his face as he knelt in the road. Better to remind herself that he had left her, a stranger, to take the little girl home and explain matters to the mother. That he had preferred to limit his time with his daughter.

He is very protective of Lady Braybrook. And his sisters.

She dismissed that. Many men were protective of their sisters and mothers. Or stepmothers. Unfortunately they failed to make the leap to being protective of someone else's sister. Or wife.

Especially when the woman in question was lower in the social scale. Apparently it didn't count in those circumstances. And why that should be a surprise, let alone a disappointment to her, she couldn't begin to imagine.

Right now, even if she still had a position, keeping it might depend on her ability to cloak her emotions again. Miss Daventry, prim, proper, only-speaking-when-spoken-to Miss Daventry, had to mask Christy's fury.

Somehow she had to rebuild the façade. This was not a subject that ever needed to be raised with Braybrook. It was none of her business, and nothing she said would make a ha'porth of difference. Her business was to amuse Lady Braybrook, teach the younger children and keep an eye on— She stopped dead as she came around a bend in the path. The path ended at another stile which led into the park. Beyond it deer grazed, the pinky-brown bulk of Amberley rearing up in the distance against the summer sky.

Seated on the bottom step of the stile was Alicia—staring at her in consternation. Christy's brain whirled. No wonder Harry had been annoyed! Somehow they had planned this. Yesterday Alicia had walked to the village with Matthew and Emma. Lady Braybrook considered that safe enough. She opened her mouth, and closed it. She had no proof. It could be coincidence. And saying something might put Alicia on her guard.

'Good morning, Miss Daventry.' Alicia appeared to have recovered her composure. 'Have you been to the village for Mama?'

Christy hesitated. 'Yes. Embroidery silks. Shall we walk back to the house together?'

Alicia's gaze flickered to the path leading back through the woods. 'Oh. Er, yes. I…I was just going back.' She stood up and forced a smile. 'Did you see anyone interesting? In…in the village, I mean.' Again she cast a nervous glance back down the path.

'Your friend, Miss Postleton, was in the shop with her brother. And I ran into Harry.'

'Oh. How…how nice for you.' A telling blush crept over Alicia's face.

Christy decided to say no more. She would have to tell his lordship. And the last thing she desired just now was a private interview with *him*.

* * *

Julian arrived back at Amberley, still smarting from the unspoken contempt in Miss Daventry's gaze. Not unvoiced though. Her icy tones had been eloquent. He dismounted in the stableyard and loosened the girth.

Of course you could tell her the truth.

The truth? Why in Hades should he? It was none of her business!

It might make her think a little better of you.

Since when did he care for the governess's opinion? Even if she had agreed to be his mistress, her opinion was irrelevant—as long as it remained unexpressed. He removed the saddle and handed it to a waiting lad. 'Thank you, Billy.'

An interested nicker caught his attention. He glanced around and saw an unfamiliar face with a white blaze looking out over a half-door.

'Billy!' he called to the lad taking his saddle to the tack room for cleaning, 'Whose horse is that?'

Billy looked back over his shoulder. 'Beg pardon? Oh. That's Mr Havergal's Rajah. Called about an hour ago.'

'Ah.' Julian strolled over to look at the horse.

The nondescript bay gelding looked back. Average points, nicely put together—there was nothing wrong with the animal precisely—but there was no hint of quality either. An adequate hack, probably with comfortable paces. Several cuts above a job horse, but not an expensive beast. Rajah. An Indian prince. He patted the horse absent-mindedly. *Well, well, well.*

It shoved its nose at him hopefully.

At long last he was going to meet the mysterious Mr Havergal.

The drawing-room door was open, voices and laughter drifting through. Curious, he stood in the doorway. Serena, Davy and a man he assumed to be Havergal were sitting round a tea table, the backgammon set in front of them. Davy was frowning at the board.

Havergal was speaking. 'Look, Davy—this point has only one of my checkers. Land there and you force me on to the bar. Which means I can't do anything until I get off.' Average height, his hair grey and his face deeply lined and tanned—a man who had perhaps spent many years in a hot climate?

Davy grinned, and moved his checker. He looked up, smugly. It jolted Julian to see the likeness to Matt at the same age. And just as delighted to outscore an elder.

'That's it,' said Havergal. 'Now, I have to throw the dice so that I land on an unoccupied point in your homeboard—and since you have them nicely filled, I can't move. Your roll again.'

A shaft of irritation went through Julian. He'd taught Matt to play. Somehow he'd not yet got around to it with Davy and here was this…this *outsider*, this Havergal, doing it. Taking his place.

He watched unnoticed as the game continued. Their father had taught him. Would he have taught Davy too had he lived? He tried to be a father to Davy, not just a much older brother. Davy had no memory of their father… The grey head and the small dark one bent over the board in fierce concentration. An odd thought surfaced—what did Serena think of this? He glanced over and her face ripped him wide open.

She watched both of them, and in her eyes was regret such as he had never imagined. As though she were looking at something irrevocably lost to her. As though all the might-have-beens in the world mocked her. For a split second her fingers whitened on the arms of her Bath chair and she sagged back, her eyes closed…

Havergal's voice, instructing Davy, faltered slightly and he looked up. At once Serena's usual cheerful expression fell into place and she smiled at the fellow.

Julian's heart ached. Serena, infinitely cheerful, infinitely patient with her lot in life… He had known she must find her disability frustrating, but she refused to speak of it, was always so uncomplaining. She made it easy to believe her acceptance complete.

He must have moved slightly, because she looked around.

'Julian—there you are! Come and meet Mr Havergal, a very old friend of mine. We grew up together.'

An old friend…?

Havergal had risen and was holding out his hand.

'How do you do, sir?' said Julian, shaking Havergal's hand. What, precisely, was meant by an old friend?

'Very well, my lord. I am pleased to meet you at last. Whenever I call you seem to be from home,' said Havergal.

The merest glimmer of Serena's smile, and Julian realised with a stab of shock that she had somehow engineered it that way. Hell's teeth! He thought back; on Miss Daventry's last day off, Serena had managed to get rid of the entire household!

'I don't think I recognise your name, sir,' he said mildly. Serena had been her father's sole heiress; he now owned the small estate and visited it on occasion—surely if they had grown up together the name Havergal should be familiar to him?

'My father was the Rector,' said Havergal.

'You are not in the church, yourself?' asked Julian.

Havergal shook his head. 'No. I was a great disappointment to my father there, but my uncle found me a place in his business.'

'Mr Havergal lived in India, Julian,' said Davy, his eyes shining. 'And he has a tiger! A real one!'

Havergal chuckled. 'You will be giving your brother a very strange notion of me, lad! A real tigerskin *rug*, is what I said. And I did *not* shoot the poor beast myself. It was a gift.'

'I should like to see it,' said Davy hopefully.

Havergal smiled. 'Another time, Davy. It would be a little awkward to carry while I'm riding. My poor horse would have a fit! Some time I shall hire the gig and bring the rug out for you.'

'Very kind of you,' remarked Julian. Obviously not a well-inlaid nabob if he had to hire the landlord's gig. It fitted with the quality of his horse.

'Can we finish the game, please, sir?' asked Davy.

'Of course.' Havergal sat down again. He glanced up at Julian. 'You will excuse me, my lord?'

'Certainly.'

Havergal, noted Julian, was obviously a very skilled player. While he won, it was by a narrow enough margin for Davy to be very, very pleased with himself.

'I'm improving, aren't I, sir? Can we play again next time?' he asked as they packed away the set.

'If your mother permits,' said Havergal, with a faint smile at Serena. 'I should be going now. Perhaps you will walk with me to the stables?'

Davy jumped up. 'Yes, sir. May I, Mama?'

'Yes, dear.' Serena smiled at him. 'And don't nag about that tiger!'

'I'll come with you as well, if I may, Havergal,' said Julian, rising.

Davy glared at him. 'I was only going to *ask*,' he said. 'It's all right to *ask*.'

Havergal chuckled. 'Quite right, lad. No harm in asking. But let's put your mother's mind at rest and consider me asked. I promise you shall see that tiger. Come along. You may ride Rajah down the carriage drive, if you like.'

He took his leave of Serena, and Julian's hackles rose at the way the fellow bowed over her hand. He didn't kiss it, but the way he held it, the intimacy of their parting smile, set alarm bells clanging.

Havergal bowed slightly to him. 'No need to see me out, my lord. Davy will do admirably.'

And as they left the room, Julian felt a sharp twinge of jealousy to see his small brother according a stranger the hero-worship usually reserved for his elder brothers.

'And what are your plans for the rest of the day, Julian?' asked Serena cheerfully.

He raised his brows. 'Manures. I have a new book on the

subject to study. Shall I bring it up here in Miss Daventry's absence?'

'Not on my account, dear,' said Serena. 'I am sure she will be back shortly.'

'Serena—this Havergal—'

'Is a very old and dear friend,' she told him, her face closing up, and much of the remaining glow dimming. 'You need not concern yourself. I am neither planning anything foolish, nor indiscreet.'

'Of course not,' agreed Julian. In the face of such a clear *mind-your-own-business* sort of response, he dropped the subject. 'I shall remove myself to the manure heap, then.'

'You do that,' said Serena. 'And, Julian—remember, I am forty-two, not seventeen. And a widow to boot. As you are well aware, widows are not subject to the same restrictions as young girls.'

The book on manures failed to engage him. Bad enough having to worry about Jane Roberts and Nan. Like it or not, they were his responsibility. He had to find a better solution for them that Jane could accept.

And now Serena! *Widows are not subject to the same considerations as young girls…*hell's teeth, he knew that. None better. But…*Serena*? He just couldn't picture it—Serena taking a lover. And she was crippled! The doctors had spelt out the risks of another pregnancy after her accident. That was why…of course there were other possibilities, ways of giving and receiving pleasure, but… His cheeks scorched. Damn it! This was *Serena*! His stepmother!

Pushing these thoughts aside, he forced his attention back to his book and began taking notes. He had not made much progress before there was a knock on the door.

'Come in,' he said.

The door opened to admit Miss Daventry. Another, even more disturbing distraction. Whatever she wanted, he doubted it was to tell him that she had thought the better of her refusal to become his mistress. Meeting Nan Roberts would have settled that.

He laid down his pen, ignoring the immediate distraction in his breeches. 'Yes, ma'am?'

'If you have a moment, my lord, I wish to discuss Alicia with you.'

He repressed the urge to swear. 'Very well. Leave the door open.'

She flushed. 'If you wish. I do not doubt your word, my lord.'

He shrugged. 'Better safe than sorry.' He gestured to a chair. 'Please be seated and tell me what is troubling you.'

He listened in growing anger. 'You believe a meeting was planned?'

'Yes. They could have arranged it yesterday when she walked to the village with Matthew and Emma. A brief meeting in public—neither Matthew nor Emma would have thought anything of it.'

'Damn your brother!' said Julian furiously. 'He must have told her that he would be passing and cozened her into the meeting! Of all the dishonourable—'

'She agreed!' Miss Daventry replied. 'And Harry's intentions are perfectly honourable!' she went on. 'Which is more than I can say—' She broke off, her face crimson.

Julian snorted. 'I'd be better pleased if his intentions *weren't* honourable. Lissy wouldn't be such a little fool as to fall for that!'

'Thank you.' Shards of ice splintered in her voice.

He realised belatedly that he had expressed himself badly. Very badly.

'The cases are different, Miss Daventry.' Hell! That sounded even worse, and, judging by her narrowed eyes and flat mouth, Miss Daventry concurred.

'Quite, my lord. I have no aristocratic family to disgrace, do I?'

'No! That is…damn it! That is not what I meant at all!' he said, aware that he was digging an abyss. 'Lissy is my sister; I'm supposed to protect her!'

'But your protective instincts don't extend to other men's sisters.' She looked at him directly. 'Or wives. It doesn't matter to you that the consequences for a woman who becomes your mistress might be as disastrous for her as for Alicia if she marries unwisely.'

'Did you just call me a hypocrite?'

Silence hung quivering. Would she attempt to wriggle off the hook? Back down and apologise?

Her chin went up. 'Yes. I suppose I did.'

He breathed carefully, and tried to analyse the emotions pouring through him. Fury. Because her words stung. Her contempt burned. Admiration because she had the courage to hold her position. And through it all the lick of desire. The urge to find out if he could still kindle the same response in her. To reassure her that she was wrong. That she didn't understand…that he would look after her…the word *always* hovered. He shoved it away.

He *never* offered reassurances to women. Just a straightforward offer of intent. Take it or leave it. Definitely not pure, but very simple with no room for misunderstanding. And *always* had nothing to do with it. Ever. Yet with Christy Daventry he was in constant danger of overstepping these boundaries.

He changed the subject. 'Very well. What do you suggest we do about this situation, Miss Daventry?'

Her hands clenched. 'That I consider you a hypocrite?'

'No. Lissy's foolishness.'

'Why would you wish for my opinion?'

Why, indeed? Because she was so brutally honest that he valued her judgement? He shied away from that. 'So far you've had little hesitation in stating your opinion,' he said. 'Why stop now?'

'Leave it and remain alert,' she said. 'There is no direct

proof. If I am wrong and you act, it will increase Alicia's resentment. If I am right and a meeting was planned, then the fact that it didn't work and they were so nearly caught might make her too wary to attempt it again. Especially if she is left uncertain about our suspicions and I keep her busy.'

'Say nothing?' he asked. 'Convenient for your brother.'

She stood up swiftly, jaw set and her eyes blazing. 'You asked my opinion. I have given it. And if I were concerned with protecting Harry, why tell you in the first place?'

He hung on to his temper. There was something else he had to say to Miss Daventry. 'Very well, ma'am—one more thing—'

She remained standing. 'My dismissal?'

His teeth ground audibly. 'No. My thanks for your kindness to Nan Roberts.'

She stiffened. 'Unnecessary, my lord. Visiting the sins of fathers on the heads of children is not a failing of mine. And I had a little sister—' She broke off, her face blank.

His gut clenched. 'Had?'

'Sarah died of measles when she was eight. I was sixteen.'

Her voice was expressionless. He could only guess at the agony it hid. He remembered the consuming fear when Davy had caught measles. 'I'm sorry,' he said. The fear had been bad enough…and Christy had not been spared the grief.

Her glare blazed straight through him. 'Sorry is an easy word. And in Sarah's case you have nothing for which to be sorry. *She* was not your responsibility.' She walked out with her head held high.

Julian stared out the window, his heart aching for the death of a child he had not even known.

Chapter Eleven

The next few days saw Amberley in uproar as the Summer Ball approached. Although it seemed to Julian that far fewer problems required his intervention this year, he saw far too much of Miss Daventry. She appeared to have a list permanently in her hand as she directed the staff scurrying about with furniture and linen for the guests who would remain overnight.

Alicia, too, seemed very much taken up with the arrangements. He found her in the library one morning going through menus with the housekeeper.

She looked up as he came in. 'Oh! I'm sorry, Julian. Are we in your way?'

'Not at all,' he said, bemused.

'Good,' said Alicia and turned back to Mrs Pritchard. 'The duckling, then, and green peas. And I think the apricot tart to round the course off.'

'Very good, Miss Alicia,' said the housekeeper, tucking her notes away and rising. 'I'll tell Cook.'

'Thank you, Pritch,' said Alicia. 'Tell her I'll come down later to see that all is well.'

'Very well, Miss Alicia.' The housekeeper dropped a curtsy and left.

'You're doing a good job, Liss,' said Julian.

Lissy flushed. 'It's not me. Mama handed it all to Miss Daventry and Miss Daventry asked me to help with the menus. I'm just doing as I'm told.'

She hadn't realised that she was being kept out of mischief, thought Julian. Miss Daventry had been right. A warning to Lissy would have resulted in sulking and fuming. Probably trying to come up with ways to sneak out and meet Daventry. Instead she was happily doing something useful.

'It's fun, really,' said Lissy, gathering up several pieces of paper. 'I thought it would be frightfully boring working out who should sit where at dinner, and what we should eat, but it's not.'

'You'll make some lucky man a very fine wife and hostess one day,' said Julian, pulling at a glossy curl as he passed behind her chair. Lissy giggled.

'More likely Miss Daventry would,' she said. 'I had the easy job with Pritch. Christy's out breaking the news to Hickson that he will have to provide flowers for the floral arrangements! I did warn her that he'd probably take a garden fork to her, but she said she could manage one crotchety old gardener!'

'Christy?'

Alicia shrugged. 'It's her name. Short for Christiana. I asked if I might use it, and she said yes.' She frowned. 'It's friendlier, and she's such a nice person.'

'I see. Well, if you finished your menus, I am going for a ride. Should you care to come?'

Her face fell. 'Oh, I'd love to, but I mustn't. I promised Christy that I would help with the sewing while she gives Davy his French lesson. Thank you, though.'

Nice? He thought about that after Lissy left the room. It seemed such a bland, boring word to describe Christy—*Miss Daventry*, he corrected himself. Stubborn, blindingly honest, kind. She took people as she found them, whatever society's opinion. Witness her response to Nan Roberts. Damn it, he supposed she was nice.

He doubted very much that she would return the compliment. Not that he was bothered by that of course, he assured himself. As a hired dependant she could count herself lucky to still have her position. He ignored an irritating little voice demanding to know how the hell he could have dismissed her for speaking the truth as she saw it. She was a companion, for God's sake! She wasn't paid to *have* a mind, let alone speak it. And it didn't bother him at all if she didn't think *he* was nice.

Nice. It *was* a boring word, and very likely closer acquaintance would prove it suited Miss Daventry admirably. Right now he was going for a ride. And he was not going to spare her another thought.

Hallam greeted him in the hall when he returned. 'You will find her ladyship in the drawing room, my lord. Mrs Pritchard is recovering from her turn, but she is of the opinion that The Creature will give Master Davy nightmares.'

'What creature, Hallam? What the devil are you talking about?' asked Julian, stripping off his riding gloves and dropping them with his whip on the refectory table.

'The Creature Mr Havergal brought,' explained Hallam. 'He met Mrs Pritchard on the stairs with it and she Had A Turn. Most unfortunate for the tea tray her ladyship had ordered.'

'I see,' said Julian, not seeing at all. 'I'll go up to the drawing room then, shall I, and see this, er, Creature for myself.' He started for the stairs.

'A very good idea, my lord,' said Hallam, gathering up the gloves and whip.

Julian found a scene of considerable confusion in the drawing room. Sprawled before the fireplace, snarling ferociously, was…a tiger, upon which Davy sat in glory, Matt and Emma scowling at him. Miss Daventry, seated beside Serena on a sofa, looked as though she were trying hard not to laugh. That cursed dimple flickered in and out of sight, causing his heart to beat painfully fast.

Seeing him, Davy leapt up, flushed, eyes sparkling. 'Look, Julian! Just look! And it's *mine*. Not Matt's or Emma's.' This last with a triumphant glare at his siblings.

'As if *I* want the horrid thing,' said Emma with an unconvincing sniff.

Matt didn't bother to deny anything. His lustful gaze at his small brother's treasure said it all. Julian was conscious of a twinge of envy himself. Of all the things guaranteed to thrill a small boy, a tigerskin rug, complete with snarl and positively lambent glass eyes, had to take the prize. He noted with some satisfaction that Tybalt had retreated to the back of the sofa behind Serena and was fluffed up to twice his normal size. Some very peculiar noises emanated from the affronted cat.

'Where the devil did that come from?' he asked Serena, who, to his surprise, blushed.

Davy answered. 'Mr Havergal brought it. Remember? He told me all about it last time, and I asked if I might see it? And now it's mine! He said it had belonged to another boy, but he didn't need it any more so he thought that I should have it.'

'I see,' said Julian, casting a very thoughtful look at Serena.

She returned his gaze, her blush deepening. 'It was very kind of Mr Havergal, Julian.'

'I'm going to have it in the nursery,' announced Davy. 'Mama, may I go into Hereford to thank Mr Havergal? Twigg would take me if I asked.'

Julian stared. 'I should hope you had thanked Mr Havergal when he gave it to you!' His mind was working furiously. Could Havergal, who was patently *not* well off, be misinformed as to the terms of Serena's jointure?

'I wasn't *here*,' said Davy. He cast Miss Daventry a very dirty look. 'I was in the schoolroom doing French verbs.' His aggrieved tone expressed to a nicety what a waste of time he thought *that*.

'*Mea culpa*,' said Miss Daventry. 'Unfortunately, Davy, no matter what you think of my ability to see out of the back of my head, crystal gazing does not come within the purlieu of a respectable governess!'

Julian choked back a laugh.

'So he left it with Mama,' said Davy. 'He couldn't stay because he'd hired the landlord's gig to bring the rug out, and had to take it back. Really, Julian, don't you think that I *ought* to go and thank him?'

'Oh, I think so,' said Julian. Taking Davy to Hereford to thank Havergal would provide the perfect excuse to call upon the gentleman and apprise him of certain facts. Which, if he were not much mistaken, would see an immediate cooling of his attentions to Serena.

'In fact, Davy,' he continued, 'if Miss Daventry has drilled enough French verbs into your head for one morning, we shall go at once.'

Miss Daventry raised her brows. 'Can you doubt it, my lord?'

Serena laughed. 'Miss Daventry, may I trouble you to help Davy take the rug up to the nursery first? And Matt, Emma, you may take yourselves off. I require a word in private with Julian.'

His stomach clenched. A private word. About Havergal?

As soon as they were alone she went straight to the point. 'Before you visit Nigel breathing fire and brimstone, you should know that he has asked me to marry him and that I have accepted.'

Marriage?

He tried to assemble his thoughts. 'Serena, you know I only wish you to be happy. Are you—?'

'Perfectly sure,' she said. 'We were in love when we were young, but he had no money and my father would have disinherited me for making such a match. I chose not to be a burden on him and he went out to India. Eventually I married your father. Not a love match, but he was kind and very honest about his reasons for remarrying. Convenience and spares in case something happened to you.'

He frowned. 'Serena—' he began, but she flung up a hand.

'No, Julian. You need to understand. We still love each other and there is nothing to keep us apart. He came home because he heard I was widowed—'

'How convenient.' He could hardly keep the cynicism from his voice.

Her eyes narrowed. 'We intend to be married very soon. He assures me that my lack of fortune will not be a problem, that he can support me comfortably.'

'And the children?' he asked. 'They are in my wardship. Where will you live? Here? That will make supporting you very easy! Can't you see? The fellow's using you!'

Sparks spat from the grey eyes levelled at him. 'If I could reach, Julian, I would box your ears for that! Listen to yourself! Don't think me ignorant of all the reasons it is unlikely anyone should wish to marry me. He knows that I bring nothing to the marriage—'

He snorted. 'So of course he'd assume I'd let you starve! He'd have me over a barrel, and he knows it even if you don't!'

Julian left his curricle and pair in the tender care of Jack Fichett, the head ostler at the New Inn and, hand in hand with Davy, strolled around to the cathedral. Mr Havergal, he understood, had lodgings nearby. Jack had been very informative. Mr Havergal had his own horse stabled at the New Inn, and indeed he had returned the landlord's cob and gig not an hour since. 'Pays his shot reg'lar, an' tips fairly. Horse ain't nuthin' special. Comfortable enough ride, I dessay, but not quality like your lordship's.' He stroked the silken nose of one of Julian's horses affectionately. 'Pair o' beauties, these lads.'

It all spoke of a man in modest circumstances. A man looking to better his situation. Bedamned if Havergal was going to attempt that to Serena's hurt. Better to choke this off now, before things went any further.

They found the house easily with Jack's directions. A solid timber-framed building, its cantilevered upper floors bulged over the street. A respectable-looking woman opened the door, took one look at Julian, and dropped a curtsy. Upon being informed that Lord Braybrook had called to see Mr Havergal, she became even more flustered, and conducted them up two pairs of stairs to the top floor and knocked on a door.

Havergal opened it and smiled. 'Ah. Good afternoon, Braybrook,' he said politely. Then he caught sight of Davy. 'Well, this is pleasant. How do you do, Davy? I understand Miss Daventry was doing her worst when I called.' He turned to the landlady. 'Mrs Philpott, if it would not be too much trouble, could you bring up coffee for his lordship and myself, and milk for Master Trentham. And some cake?'

'Why, of course, sir,' said Mrs Philpott. 'It's no bother at all.'

'Thank you, ma'am,' he said courteously. 'Do come in, my lord. Come along, Davy.'

'Sir, thank you very much for the tigerskin!' burst out Davy as the door closed. 'It's splendid! I'm to have it in my room, and Matthew is as sick as a cushion about it!'

Havergal chuckled. 'Perhaps you might lend it to him on occasion? Please sit down, my lord.' He gestured Julian towards a chair.

Davy looked unconvinced. 'Well, I *might*,' he said.

They conversed for several minutes, with Davy asking as many questions as he could about India. 'I should like to go there,' he said.

'Later, lad,' said Havergal. 'The climate is not good for boys your age.'

The coffee arrived, along with the cake and milk for Davy. Julian sipped his coffee and watched his small brother with Havergal. Davy plainly liked the fellow, now telling him between mouthfuls what he had been doing and asking when Mr Havergal was going to visit again—fury soared through him.

'Oh, I'll ride that way again in a few days,' said Havergal easily. 'I am invited to your mother's party, too, but no doubt you will be abed.' He caught Julian's suddenly focused gaze and added, 'Davy, why don't you bring your cake and milk through into the other room. I've something there for you to play with.'

Julian watched in rising annoyance as his little brother's eyes sparkled.

'Another present, sir?' Davy asked.

Havergal laughed. 'No, Davy. These are mine—but you are welcome to play with them while your brother and I talk of boring grown-up things.' He stood up and held out his hand. Davy took it immediately and followed him into the other room.

A moment later Havergal was back, closing the door behind him.

'Here to warn me off, my lord?'

Julian set his coffee cup down with great precision. 'Do I need to?'

The corners of Havergal's eyes crinkled. 'That would depend on your point of view.'

'My point of view,' said Julian, 'is that I consider Serena to be in my care.'

'One does wonder what Serena said to that?' mused Havergal.

'That is neither here nor there, sir,' said Julian coldly. 'I am here to put an end to your pursuit of Serena.'

'How very gallant,' said Havergal. 'Would it allay your fears to know that my intentions towards Serena are perfectly honourable?'

'No. She told me of your offer. Cultivating Davy was very clever, wasn't it?' Havergal's eyes blazed, but he said nothing and Julian continued. 'You might like to consider that Serena's jointure is conditional upon her not remarrying and that her children are in my ward.' His gaze swept the room, taking in the modest furnishings and simple style. Bronzes and ivories were scattered about and there was a very fine rug on the floor. Interesting, but no doubt in India they could be picked up for a song. Havergal himself was neatly turned out, but his clothes were clearly well worn.

Havergal had straightened in his chair. 'Yes, she was at some pains to ensure that I understood that. More coffee, my lord?'

'Thank you, no.'

'Ah.' Mr Havergal poured himself some more and sipped, watching Julian over the rim of the cup. 'I have to inform you, my lord, that in this instance I am concerned only with Serena's point of view.'

'And your own.'

Havergal inclined his head. 'That too, but not quite as much as Serena's.'

Julian did not bother to repress a disbelieving snort.

'You become offensive, my lord,' Havergal informed him calmly. 'Let me assure you that Serena was most prompt to inform me of her circumstances. Nor did I give Davy that ti-gerskin to curry favour. I gave it to him because I thought he would like it and he reminds me of another small boy.' A slight pause. 'The boy who owned it originally was my son.'

His voice did not change, but Havergal's very stillness warned Julian that he was treading on dangerous ground.

He took a deep breath—damned if he'd back down. He spoke softly, but with lethal intent. 'I'll be blunt, Havergal. Like it or not, Serena is in my care. And I'm damned if I'll let her be cozened by you or anyone else!'

Havergal's fists clenched. 'Admirable sentiments, my lord. Believe it or not, I am perfectly well to pass, and have abso-lutely no need to prey on wealthy widows to support myself!'

Julian raised his brows. 'Do you expect me to take your word for it?'

Havergal didn't answer. Instead he rose, went to an untidy desk and began writing. A moment later he sprinkled sand on the letter, stood up and handed it to Julian, along with a card.

'Authorisation to ask whatever questions you like of Hammerfield, my man of business. You may also wish to ask about me with the East India Company. I don't work for 'em any more, but they know all about me. I ask only one thing—that you don't tell Serena what you learn. I'd rather tell her myself.'

Julian stared at the brusque note ordering the unknown Hammerfield to inform Lord Braybrook of whatever he wished to know about Havergal's circumstances…and Havergal had been in India for over twenty years…was well known to the East India company…

If it wasn't a bluff, Havergal must be wealthier than he looked.

'Not all men choose to display their wealth, Braybrook,' said Havergal, apparently reading his mind. 'That brings its own inconveniences. Serena knows that I am well able to support myself, but I have not told her the extent of my fortune. She was having quite enough difficulty in seeing herself as a suitable wife for me.'

'A suitable wife,' repeated Julian. He shot a glance at the door to the other room, wondering if Davy was about to reappear. 'Havergal, a man with a fortune generally wants an heir. It may not—'

'Serena made that plain,' said Havergal quietly. 'I am not marrying for an heir.'

Julian frowned. If not for an heir, or money, then what the devil *was* he marrying for? It was not a question he could ask. As long as Serena was safe and happy—something else occurred to him.

'The children are in my wardship,' he said. 'Literally, my responsibility.'

Havergal smiled. 'We discussed it. I understand Serena chose not to move into the Dower House and of course she will no longer have a right to it, but perhaps you would lease it to me? Will that serve?'

Julian teeth clenched. '*Assuming* I am satisfied that Serena will be happy with you, then the Dower House lease is my wedding gift!'

* * *

He drove back to Amberley, returning automatic answers to Davy's chatter about the set of ivory elephants he had been playing with. 'Hundreds of them, Julian! Big ones and little ones. All in a big golden box. Only Mr Havergal said it was brass. And he says I may play with them again some day.'

Why did Havergal want to marry Serena? It defied all the logical, rational reasons for marriage.

He looked very hard at the question. From all angles. And discovered that he didn't much like the man who had asked it. Serena was a kind, attractive, loving woman. The sort of woman who would make any man a wonderful wife …

She is crippled. She will never walk again. She cannot give him an heir, nor does she bring any money to the marriage.

Havergal didn't care about these things.

Love. That was the only reason left.

To Julian marriage was a matter of wealth and convenience. Yet at least two of his friends had married for love, shrugging at the lost opportunity to increase their wealth and position.

He liked their wives, too, and when he thought of the way Thea Blakehurst smiled at Richard, or the way Verity's eyes lit up when Max entered a room…it wasn't for him. He wanted an impeccably bred wife of suitable fortune, and a mistress for bedsport. And Christy Daventry, who declined to fit either compartment.

He forced his mind back to Serena's likely marriage. Havergal was taking her for no more than the use of the Dower House. He was also offering to find positions for Matt and Davy if needful. Julian didn't deny that having such careers laid out for his brothers would be a blessing. His first reaction had been refusal, but Havergal's expression had stopped him…

I thought that I would never return to this country…there was a native girl. Padma. She was to be burned on her husband's funeral pyre as is the native custom. I rescued her and, well, she couldn't return to her own family, they would have killed her. So I offered to take her, and she stayed with me.

We had a child, a son. I would have remained with them, but they died of cholera some years ago...I told Serena when I brought the rug out this morning...

He glanced down at Davy, sitting beside him on the curricle seat, happily examining a little bronze tiger... Havergal's son had owned the bronze and the tigerskin rug. And had the boy or his mother lived, Havergal would never have returned. Even knowing that Serena was free, he would have remained in India, loyal to the native girl he had saved and their son...and Serena had loved him all these years, despite her marriage and unswerving loyalty to her husband and stepson. He faced a staggering realisation—and it went against all custom and received wisdom: if Havergal had not been wealthy enough to wed Serena regardless, he would still have ended up supporting the marriage, giving them the use of the Dower House and allowing Serena at least part of her jointure.

It was insanity. He could only be thankful that a merciful deity had probably spared him such foolishness. The Summer Ball was ten days away. If he sent urgent letters enquiring about Havergal tomorrow, he should have a response by the day of the ball. If Havergal's claims were borne out, then he supposed he would be making an unexpected announcement.

Amberley was ablaze as dusk fell on the night of the Summer Ball. With the weather set fair everyone who was anyone for miles around had come and laughter and chatter spilled with golden light from open doors and windows. The musicians hired from Hereford were installed in a corner of the forecourt to accompany the dancing and the Great Hall brimmed with merriment.

Julian looked around the Hall. Everyone seemed to be enjoying themselves. He glanced over to where Serena was seated by the refectory table, Havergal in close attendance. She caught his eye and raised a brow questioningly. He nodded. The waltz in the forecourt was nearly finished. After that it would be supper. He intended to make his announcement just as soon as the company was seated.

It would raise some eyebrows. News of Havergal's wealth had leaked out. Several matrons with daughters to establish had taken pains to make themselves known to Havergal that evening, parading their virtuous treasures under his nose. He'd muttered to Julian that he'd be relieved when the announcement was made and girls young enough to be his daughters stopped making sheep's eyes at him.

Lady Postleton had not swelled the hopeful throng, but probably only because she had Anne aimed at Julian's head. He had obliged by leading Anne out for one dance, and that was enough. He couldn't imagine why Serena thought the girl would suit him. Certainly she was well bred, well brought up, well dowered, dutiful and attractive...*everything you wanted in a wife, in fact.*

Except that, as Matt had said, she wasn't very kind. He tried to imagine her...*what*? Storming in to defend Nan Roberts from being bullied? Ridiculous. He had heard her not five minutes ago laughing openly at another young lady's unbecoming gown, encouraging others to laugh.

His gaze went to Miss Daventry. Gowned in soft grey cambric, she sat near Serena. Did she waltz? An irrelevant question. Even if she accepted, dancing—let alone waltzing!—with the governess would cause an uproar. And she would not accept. The only invitation she had accepted had been from her brother. Harry had lead her out for a country dance. She had declined all other invitations.

The Hall was filling up, most people were seated, only a few still looking for somewhere to sit down. He rang a small bell. 'If I might have your attention, ladies and gentlemen,' he said. The stragglers whisked themselves into whatever spots were left. 'First, thank you all for coming tonight. Lady Braybrook and I are delighted to welcome you to Amberley. And now, I have an announcement. Of a betrothal.'

There was a startled gasp and hum of speculation, swiftly suppressed.

'Yes, a betrothal,' he went on. 'For the past several years, Lady Braybrook has insisted that she wishes to retire to the Dower House and leave the running of Amberley to someone else.'

Another murmur. Speculative eyes rested on Miss Postleton, whose face was utterly frozen.

'Having now despaired of me ever making myself agreeable enough for a woman to accept, Lady Braybrook has found another solution. I am delighted to announced the betrothal of Serena, Lady Braybrook, to Mr Nigel Havergal. I would ask you all to raise your glasses and wish them well.'

The shock had died down to speculative murmurs by the end of supper. Christy, looking for Harry, supposed the surprise was inevitable—most people seemed incapable of understanding that Mr Havergal's reasons for marriage might have more to do with the heart than monetary advantage.

'Well, Miss Daventry—your employment here will soon be at an end, will it not?'

Startled, she turned. Anne Postleton stood there, her gaze patronising.

'I beg your pardon, Miss Postleton? My employment?'

Miss Postleton smiled. 'My dear Miss Daventry, a newly married woman has little need of a *hireling* for company. And since David should be off to school soon and Alicia and Emma to Bath this winter—well, there is nothing left for you. My mama commented on it just now. Such a shame for you.'

'I pray you won't lose any sleep over it, Miss Postleton,' said Christy drily. There was no point in assuring the girl that Davy's departure for school was not imminent.

Miss Postleton smirked, turned on her heel and strolled off.

Supressing the urge to throw her reticule at Miss Postleton's retreating curls, Christy looked about for Harry. Lady Braybrook had given her permission to retire for the night and she wanted to say goodnight. She frowned. Where on earth was he? Carefully she scanned the crowd. He wasn't in the Hall. Neither, when she went out on to the steps, could she see him in the forecourt…and nor, she realised on a surge of concern, had she seen Alicia Trentham anywhere.

'Looking for someone, Miss Daventry?' Matthew stood at her shoulder.

'Yes. My brother, and…my brother,' she finished.

'Oh. I saw him leave through the back of the Hall. Said he wanted a breath of air. Through the garden room, I think. Quieter out there.'

No doubt.

Christy stared at the door to the garden room. As a venue for an assignation it had a great deal to recommend it. Privacy. Well away from the party. No one was likely to want anything from it. And she hoped to God that she was a nasty-minded, spiteful old spinster and completely and utterly wrong.

Drawing a deep breath, she opened the door and walked in.

For a moment neither Harry nor Alicia realised she was there. They were completely involved in their kiss. They broke apart as she closed the door.

'I beg your pardon,' she said coldly. 'I think you had better return to the party, Alicia, before anyone else realises you are missing.'

'Damn you!' cursed Harry. 'You were spying on us! *Spying!*'

'And you were both breaching Lord Braybrook's trust!' she replied. 'Damn yourself, Harry. You claim to love Alicia, yet by arranging clandestine meetings you expose her to the risk of censure and ruin! If you cared for her in the least, you would see that!'

She turned on Alicia. 'As for you! Have you no common sense?'

Scarlet-faced, Alicia began, 'It is none of your—'

'Business?' suggested Christy, anger routing any tendency to mince words. 'Tell me—do you think being caught would force your brother's hand?'

Alicia's expression became mulish, and Christy swept on. 'Bear in mind that Harry cannot support you. What would you live on? *Where* would you live? His lodgings in the village?'

When neither of them returned any reply, she continued. 'Don't you realise Braybrook would be more likely to call Harry out for this, than permit you to marry him? And you tell me it's none of my business?'

Alicia paled. 'What are you going to do?' she whispered. 'Are you going to tell Julian?'

Christy considered. Now was not the right moment. 'Your mother's betrothal has just been announced. You should be with her. Go.'

White faced, Alicia obeyed.

'Full of orders, aren't you?' burst out Harry, as the door closed. 'Blast you, Christy! Just because you're such a damn cold fish—'

'Better than being a dead one,' she told him.

'Got orders for me, too?' he sneered.

'No. But this isn't the first time you've tried to meet Alicia, is it? The other day, when I met you at the stile.'

He shuffled. 'What of it? There was no harm in it!'

She held his gaze. 'No harm? It would have ruined Alicia had someone else caught the pair of you just now! Did you care about that at all?'

'Damn it, Christy! What am I supposed to do?'

She shook her head. 'Behave like the gentleman you claim to be, perhaps?'

His throat worked convulsively. *'Bitch!'* he spat at her, and slammed from the room. Christy leaned back against the wall with a shuddering sigh. There was no choice. Braybrook must be told the truth. Armed with that knowledge, he could ensure that Alicia no longer viewed Harry as a possible match. Heat pricked at her eyes. She hadn't wanted this. But what else could she do?

'Well, well, well,' came an amused voice from behind her. She whirled and found Ned Postleton standing in the open outside door. 'What a stirring scene, Miss D.' His eyes mocked. 'Dare say Braybrook won't be too happy, eh?'

Chapter Twelve

Fighting shock, Christy said nothing, but watched warily as Postleton strolled into the room, closing the door behind him.

'Very high in the instep about these things, Braybrook is,' he went on. 'Quite the fire eater. Nothing wrong with a fellow entertaining himself in the right quarters, of course.' He smirked. 'But Braybrook's sister ain't the right quarters. Eh?'

Christy found her voice—inextricably entwined with her temper. 'What are you suggesting, Mr Postleton?'

His gaze crawled over her and she felt unclean. 'Oh, I just thought you might like to devote a few moments to modifying my memory, eh? Amazing how a pretty woman can muddle a man's mind.'

'You think I won't tell Braybrook?'

He spluttered with laughter. 'Tell Braybrook? You won't tell him! He'd call Harry out! Think—Harry's tongue halfway down the chit's throat, his hand up her skirts fingering the goods.'

'That's a lie!' she exploded.

'Now, now, Miss D.' His eyes jeered. 'Think it over. It would make pretty telling.' He shrugged. 'Lose Harry his position, too. The Pater's quite the puritan over these things.'

He came a step closer and Christy snatched up a little gardening fork from the shelf beside her.

Postleton stopped, his startled gaze on the gleaming tines. 'Put that down!' he snapped, lazy mockery gone.

'When you leave,' said Christy. She stepped aside, indicating the inner door with her free hand and making sure there was room for him to pass easily. 'You'll want to be very sure of your story before you retail it to Braybrook.' It was a long shot. She had no idea which way Braybrook would incline, but if she could shake Postleton's confidence…

His expression twisted. 'You think he'll believe *you*?'

She assumed an attitude of amusement. 'A risk, isn't it? You see, he might wonder why *you* didn't intervene when you saw Harry taking such dreadful liberties. Why Harry isn't already sporting a black eye? And how you managed to see so much through a closed door?'

The stunned look on Postleton's face told Christy that this had not occurred to him. She held her breath. There were gaps in her bluff that you could have driven a coach and four through. But it might buy her time to reach Braybrook first.

'He's tupping you,' said Postleton suddenly. 'Braybrook's already dipped his wick! That's why you're so sure he'll believe you.'

She merely raised her brows, quelling the panic bubbling beneath the surface. The expressions he'd used were unfamiliar, but their meaning was clear.

'He'll tire of you fast enough' said Postleton. 'And then you'll be out on your ear, probably with his brat in your belly. Wouldn't be the first time.'

'Leave' she said. 'Now.'

His eyes narrowed. 'Oh, I'm going. I'm not fool enough to meddle with any wench Braybrook's bedding.'

He strolled towards the door and Christy tracked him with her eyes, moving to allow him passage, stepping back to remain behind him, the garden fork still levelled.

Then the door closed behind him and with a shudder she sagged against the shelves. Whatever riptide had seared her

veins, allowing her to face him down, it had subsided to leave
her cold and shaking. She stayed there, wrapping Lady Braybrook's old shawl close. The riot of birds, butterflies and
flowers still shimmered, but now their loveliness served only
to mock. She stared at the garden fork. Would she really have
stabbed him with it, had he attempted to force her?

Yes. In a heartbeat.

On the thought the inner door opened behind her. Fury,
spurred by fear, ripped through her and she levelled the fork
as she whirled.

Julian retreated from the virago confronting him.

'Christy!'

Even as he spoke she sagged back against the shelves, the
garden fork clattering to the floor. He took in her white face,
the trembling hands, heard her breath rush out.

'I…I'm sorry, my lord. I thought…I didn't realise it was you.'

The shaky words scorched him and he put it together in a
surge of searing fury. Whoever she had expected she would
have greeted him with a garden fork levelled at his guts…

'What did Postleton do to you?' He scarcely recognised his
own raw voice.

She flinched. 'Postleton? How—?'

'Damn it, Christy! Trust me!' Then he forced his voice to
gentle and said, 'He passed me in the hall. Look, if you were
wielding a garden fork you were hardly a willing participant!
What happened?'

Her eyes searched his face.

'Harry and Alicia were here too.'

'I beg your pardon? I thought Postleton—' Her words sank
in. 'Harry and Lissy? Explain.'

She did. In a detached, clear voice, her gaze steady.

'Bloody young fools,' he muttered to himself. Then, realising he'd spoken aloud, 'I beg your pardon. Go on. Where does
Postleton fit into this?'

'He threatened to tell you.'

'Not much of a threat since you've told me anyway,' he said.

'An exaggerated version.' Her cheeks flamed.

'Oh?' They were coming to the nub of it. For the first time her eyes wavered. Focusing on a point beyond his left shoulder, she said, 'He intended to tell you that Harry had his...his tongue halfway down her throat, and his hand...his hand—'

'Very well,' he said. Her distress was palpable and he had the gist of it.

She went on. 'He offered to keep silent on certain terms.'

'What terms?' grated Julian, although he thought he knew.

She met his gaze. 'There is only one thing a gentleman wants from a woman of my station, my lord. As you well know.'

Anger roared through him. Anger at the thought of Postleton, or any other man, so much as thinking of touching her, let alone threatening her. And sheer, blistering hurt that she saw his own offer in the same tainted light.

'I did *not* attempt to coerce you!' he ground out.

'No,' she acknowledged. 'But there was no difference in what you wanted. Just that you wanted it for longer and were prepared to pay generously for your entertainment.'

Entertainment? This hot twisting in his gut was *entertainment*?

He opened his mouth, prepared to scarify her, rage at her...

'I'm sorry,' he said very quietly.

She stared, clearly confused.

She wasn't the only one. What was he sorry for? Postleton's insults? His own offer? All he knew was that behind the calm exterior she was hurt, upset. That she had been exposed to insult and danger in his house and he wanted to hit someone for it. Unfortunately, beating Postleton to a pulp would only cause more trouble. Quite possibly for her.

After a moment she cleared her throat. 'It doesn't matter,

my lord. And this was certainly not your fault.' She swallowed, the movement of her throat convulsive. 'But there is something else I must tell you—'

'Whatever it is can wait until morning,' he said. The set of her jaw told him that whatever it was would cause her pain. 'You've had enough. Go up.'

She hesitated, biting her lip. After a moment she nodded. 'Very well. Goodnight, my lord.'

He meant to let her go. But as she drew level he saw the fine trembling of her mouth, that she clutched her shawl as if the warm night had turned chilly.

He muttered a curse and reached out a hand, laying it gently on her wrist. She stopped, but didn't look at him.

'My lord—please.'

He pulled her into his arms, felt the stiffness of her body, the shivering. He would just hold her for a moment. To comfort her. Nothing more. He slid his fingers into the warm silk of her hair and pressed her cheek gently against his chest. For an instant she resisted, her hands pushing back against his chest, but then with a little sigh, she relaxed, yielding to his embrace. 'Shh. It's all right,' he murmured, and rested his own cheek on her hair. It felt right. She fitted—against him, against his heart, in a way no other woman ever had.

He took a deep breath, trying to steady the rising beat of his blood, but breathing in was a mistake. Her soft, warm fragrance, mingled with the soap she used, slid into him and he was lost. He gathered her closer, turning her face up to his. Behind the spectacles her eyes were huge in a pale face.

'My lord?' she whispered again.

He should say something. Something reassuring. Comforting. But again all that came out was, 'I'm sorry.' And whether he was apologising for what he had already done, or for what he was about to do, he didn't know.

Slowly, giving her every chance to pull back or stab him with the fork, he lowered his mouth to hers.

Christy's mind whirled even as her lips softened, returning his kiss. She should say no, pull away. This was insanity. Steely strength surrounded her, yet it was not that which held her. His gentleness, his restraint, the aching tenderness of his kiss held her in thrall. She was cradled, not confined. He would release her if she wished it.

She did not wish it. Rather, as she felt the seeking caress of his tongue against her lips, she parted them on a sigh of longing and he took her mouth. His tongue slid deep, touching hers, possessing her, in a rhythm that sang in harmony with her beating blood.

A large hand drifted over her waist as though entranced with the curve, lifting to cover her breast. Even through her gown and chemise, the sturdier defence of her stays, she felt it. Her body leaping to life as her nipples peaked in a burning rush, pressing against the confining stays in a hidden plea so that she pushed against him. With a groan his kiss deepened, his arms tightening around her …

Lord, she was sweet. Her shy, untutored kisses set him ablaze as nothing else ever had.

A violent crash broke them apart and he broke the kiss to see the door bouncing off the wall.

'You bloody hypocrite, Braybrook! Get your hands off my sister!'

Harry Daventry's words and his contorted, mottled face as he glared at them from the doorway dashed over Julian like cold, dirty water. Beyond Harry, Ned Postleton's smirk mocked. Beside him, Christy tried to step away, a small sound of distress escaping from her. It pierced him and instinctively he caught her wrist.

'Dear me. Are we interrupting something?' drawled Postleton.

Julian's fists balled. 'Get the hell out of here, Postleton,' he said, stepping forwards. 'This is nothing to do with you!'

Postleton grinned. 'Oh, come, Braybrook! Hardly the first time you've slipped away to enjoy a lady's charms. Romance in the air tonight?'

'Romance?' spat Harry, advancing on Julian. 'I'm not good enough to raise my eyes to *his* sister, but mine is good enough for his amusement! Thanks for the tip-off, Postleton!'

'Harry! No!'

Christy stepped around him, facing her brother. Damn it! Was she protecting *him*? He caught her shoulders and pushed her behind him. 'Don't be an idiot!' he told her, and swung to face Daventry. At this point nothing mattered but protecting Christy from the consequences of his own stupidity.

'I'm willing to offer whatever satisfaction you like, Daventry, but this is neither the time nor place unless you *want* to see your sister's reputation ruined!'

'A fat lot *you* cared about—!'

'I say, sorry to interrupt, Mr Daventry, but have you seen my brother?' Matthew appeared in the doorway. 'Oh, there you are, Julian. Mama was wondering where you'd vanished…' His voice trailed off as his widening eyes took in the scene. 'Er—'

'I'll tell you where he'd vanished to!' roared Harry. 'Seducing my sister! That's where!'

A dull flush rose on Matthew's cheeks and he flung a hasty glance back over his shoulder. 'Um, George—why don't you go back? I've, er, found him now.'

And George Endicott's voice. 'Oh, ah, right you are, Matt. I'll see you later, then.'

Julian swore under his breath as Mr Endicott's footsteps retreated swiftly. Doubtless in a hurry to pass the story on to his sisters, who would tell all their friends. And so on. The story would be all around the ball within half an hour and all over the county inside of a sennight.

'Sorry,' said Matthew.

Behind him he heard Christy draw a shaky breath. He swung around, jaw set. 'We'll talk in the morning—' he began.

'Talk?' snarled Harry. 'What's to talk about! You'll marry my sister or answer to me!'

Christy's mind reeled. 'Harry—are you *mad*? I don't want to marry him!'

Braybrook shot a startled, measuring glance at her. Damn him! Did he imagine she'd marry a man who preferred her in the role of mistress?

Harry glared at her. 'You should have thought of that before he tupped you!'

'He didn't—'

'One more insult to your sister, Daventry,' snapped Braybrook, stepping forwards with clenched fists, 'and *you* will answer to *me*!'

Oh, this was ridiculous! They were like two dogs snarling over a bone! She had to stop it before one or the other of these *idiots* said something from which there was no backing down.

'Well, my lord?' growled Harry, 'Which is it? Pistols or marriage?'

'It will be neither!' said Christy. Dragging in a breath, she steeled herself to deliver the final blow. And saw Ned Postleton lounging in the doorway.

Her breath caught. There was still a chance that if she told Braybrook the truth privately, Harry could retain his position and she might scrape a reference. But if Postleton learnt the truth their ruin would be absolute.

'Get rid of him,' she told Harry, indicating Postleton.

Postleton's smirk intensified. 'No, no, Miss D. Independent witness, you know!'

'Exactly!' blustered Harry. 'Damned if I will. Postleton's stood my friend this evening, and—'

'He deliberately stirred up trouble!' snapped Christy. 'I'm warning you, Harry—it makes little difference to me, but it might make a difference to you.'

A split second of incomprehension, then Harry's face drained of colour. 'Christy, you…you wouldn't! You *can't*!'

'I can,' she said softly. 'Get him out. And make sure he doesn't listen at the door as he did to your tryst with Alicia!'

Harry stared.

'That's right,' she said, beyond caution. 'He tried to blackmail me over it!'

'A misunderstanding, Daventry,' Postleton assured him lazily. 'But we might as well leave the lovebirds to settle the date.'

With that parting shot, he strolled out. Harry cast a panicked look at Christy and followed.

'Daventry!' said Braybrook quietly.

He looked back from the doorway, his expression blank.

'You had better call tomorrow afternoon, or rather *this* afternoon, to discuss the matter.'

His face grey, Harry nodded and walked out, closing the door.

Letting out a breath he hadn't been aware he was holding, Julian turned to Christy.

Spear straight, she faced him. 'Wait a moment, then check that Postleton is really gone,' she told him.

He did so, but the passageway was empty, the only sound the distant drift of music and laughter. He closed the door again and turned back to her. His course was laid out for him, straight and uncompromising. Only he had never envisaged himself making an offer of marriage in the garden room on the heels of an argument and in the teeth of unprecedented scandal.

'Christy—Miss Daventry—' He broke off, searching for words, and settled on blunt formality. 'Miss Daventry, will you do me the—?'

'No.' She flung up a hand. 'There is not the least need for this, sir. You do not need to make me an offer of marriage.'

He sighed. 'Miss Daventry, we both know better than that,' he said. 'While marriage was not what I had in mind, I play by the rules. You are a gently bred lady in my stepmother's employ. By breakfast time, thanks to your brother, half the county will be speculating about our relationship.'

'You think he did that *on purpose*?'

The shock and anger in her voice was matched with clenched fists.

'That is irrelevant,' he told her. 'What is relevant is that either I marry you, or your reputation in this neighbourhood is destroyed.'

'If it doesn't matter to me—'

'It matters to me,' he told her. 'I am sure you do not expect me down upon my knees, so—will you make me the happiest of men, and do me the honour of becoming my wife?'

'No.'

He suppressed the urge to swear.

'Miss Daventry, we have no choice in this.'

'You may not. I do. No.'

Some of his certainty vanished. His offer to take her as his mistress was one thing. He could understand her refusing that. But he was offering marriage now. An offer far beyond anything she could ever have dreamed. 'Miss Daventry—'

'No!' She flung the word at him, took a deep breath and continued, 'Harry and I are illegitimate, my lord.'

'What?'

'Precisely, my lord. The Duke of Alcaston is our father, not Harry's godfather. That circumstance relieves you of any obligation. It should also dampen your sister's enthusiasm for marriage with my brother.'

He stared at her, dumbfounded. She faced him unflinching, her chin up, cheeks burning with embarrassment.

'That is what I was going to tell you earlier. Now, if you will excuse me, I must begin packing.'

She walked towards the door, the shawl clutched around her. Stunned, he let her go. She was illegitimate. Her brother was illegitimate... Even Lissy would acknowledge that that rendered Harry Daventry ineligible. And as for Christy Daventry, that simple statement was his salvation; no one in their right mind would consider that he owed her marriage now.

Serena's grey eyes resembled nothing more than twin gun barrels after the house was quiet and he confessed to what had happened and told her the truth of Christy's birth. Nigel Havergal, seated beside her, said nothing and his expression said less. But Julian had never seen Serena angrier.

'I have very little choice, Julian,' she told him quietly. 'And apparently Miss Daventry herself knows it if she has said that she is leaving.'

'*No.*'

Serena raised her brows. 'What else is to be done? With her reputation destroyed, I cannot employ her without damaging your sisters' reputations.'

'It wasn't her fault!'

Serena laughed mirthlessly. 'Julian, in these cases it is *always* the woman's fault. Especially when it isn't. You know that. All I can do is give her a reference. And even that won't help her once the story is out, whether you seduced her or not—'

'I didn't!' He dragged in a breath. 'She refused me.'

Serena raised her brows. 'A pity you didn't listen to her. There is nothing I can do, Julian. Unless you have another solution?'

He slept badly. Time and again he woke from dreams in which Christy was gone. Vanished into a swirling fog that consumed even her memory as if she had never been. Each time he reminded himself that he'd given instructions that no carriage was to be ordered for her unless *he* ordered one.

Unless she walked, without her possessions, she couldn't leave. He'd told himself that each time he woke sweating. Now it was time to face the day. And the consequences of his idiocy.

He saw Alicia first. Pale and subdued, she came to him in the library.

'Mama said you wished to see me.' Her voice was husky, as though she had been crying.

'Yes.'

She swallowed. 'I'm sorry. Mama told me what happened, and…and about Harry…that he's—' She took a shaky breath. 'I'm sorry, Julian…I didn't mean—'

'It's all right,' he said quietly. How could he allow Lissy to apologise when his behaviour had been much worse?

'Mama is writing to Aunt Massingdale in Bath, to see if I may visit earlier than planned.'

It was probably a sensible solution, but… 'What do you want to do, Liss?'

She stared and a tear trickled down her cheek. Dashing it away, she said, 'I agreed it would be best. So Mama said I should leave straight after the wedding. But Julian, is it—?'

'Wedding?'

Her cheeks reddened. 'Well, Mama's wedding. Julian—you…you aren't going to challenge Harry? Are you? Please, say you aren't—I couldn't bear it!'

What the hell could he say? There was every chance he would end up facing Harry over duelling pistols. 'I hope not.'

'Will you have to marry Christy?'

He gave her the best answer he had. 'I don't know, Liss.'

His fingers drummed on the desk as he waited for Christy. They had to settle this. Gossip must be flying already, by tomorrow the hunt would be up, with Christy the prey to be coursed and torn to pieces… *Yes, my dear—quite shocking…Of course, I knew how it would be. Always the same, girls of that order—cunning. Out for what they can get.* There would be plenty to join the cry. *Dreadful! Poor Serena! Carrying on the affair right under her very nose. Still, she should have known there was something more to it when Braybrook employed the girl. Dare say the slut will be gone by now…* The men would take a different perspective…sniggering, speculating… *Bit of sport, eh? Shouldn't have thought she was quite the type, but these quiet ones…eh?*

He stood up and went to the windows, staring out at a golden late summer's afternoon. He could step away from the situation. Christy's illegitimacy rendered his offer null and void. Drop the fact of her birth into the flood of gossip and the thing was done. She and her brother would be disgraced, and there would be no expectation that he should respond to a challenge from Daventry with anything but derision.

That was how the world would see it. There was even the possibility that with her character destroyed and nowhere to go, she would consent to becoming his mistress and no one would breathe a word of censure.

A light tap came on the door.

'Come in.'

Christy entered, and it was like a punch to the stomach. Even across the room he could see how strained she looked. How tired. As though she had not slept any better than he had.

'My baggage is in the hall, my lord,'

She was even making it easy for him…

Chapter Thirteen

A headache thumped behind Christy's tired, scratchy eyes. Sheer exhaustion had induced an hour or so of nightmare-ridden sleep. Dark, twisting streets in which she wandered alone, lost, searching, always searching for something that remained misty and formless.

Braybrook stood by the window. With the light pouring in behind him his face was shadowed and unreadable. She was unsure why he had sent for her. She supposed he might wish to dismiss her formally with her quarter's wages. Unless her altered status made her fair game for seduction now. Please God she still had the courage to refuse.

He came forward and she saw the gravity of his expression. 'Miss Daventry, my offer of marriage stands.'

Her world spun out of control, all her certainties reeling. Barely able to breathe, she stared at him. Against all precedent, all expectation, he was still offering marriage. She could neither speak nor think for the confusion storming through her.

Then, 'Why?' she whispered. 'Why would *you* be prepared to marry me knowing that, when even—?'

She broke off too late. Braybrook frowned, his gaze slicing through every barrier into her memories.

'Who was he?'

She struggled to rebuild the barriers. 'That is nothing to do with you, since I have no intention of marrying you.'

'Who was he?'

Anger stirred. 'Why? Are you worried in case I'm not a virgin?'

He frowned. 'Should I be?'

'Not unless I agree to marry you, and even then I doubt you have the right.'

His expression hardened. 'Since we *are* going to marry, I'd say I have every right!'

'Didn't you tell me once that you were not hypocrite enough to demand something of your bride that you were not prepared to give?'

He was silent for a moment. 'Very well. Shall we agree that I have no rights, merely a lamentable curiosity? Christy—who was he?'

Perhaps it was better to get it over with. Like cauterising a wound, or digging out a splinter. She shrugged. 'No one you would know. Jeremy was the son of a merchant. Not wealthy, but rising. I had been at school with his sister and...' she swallowed, barely able to say it '...we fell in love.'

'And?'

'He asked me to marry him, so I told him the truth.'

Braybrook nodded. 'Whereupon you never saw him again?'

Oh, how she wished that were the case!

'On the contrary, he came to me a week later.' She forced the words out. 'He still wanted me; only his terms had changed. I was to take lodgings for which he would pay.' She stopped, unwilling to go on. Of all men, he would know where this sordid tale was going.

'Did you?' There was no accusation in his voice.

'No.' She had wanted to crawl into a hole and die of shame. He had spoken to her differently. *Looked* at her differently. As though she were something to be bought. As though she had no right to want, let alone expect, something better.

'So why are you refusing to marry me?'

She stared. 'Why—? *You* wanted me to be your mistress too! Do you think I wish to marry a man who sees me that way?'

His fist clenched. 'Touché,' he said harshly. 'But you refused my offer. As well as refusing the man you apparently loved.'

She shivered. Had she loved Jeremy? How could she tell now? She had thought that she loved him. She had certainly liked him, had wanted to marry him. He would have been a safe husband. But love—?

'I refused because I was angry!' she snapped. 'Not because of any particular virtue!'

His mouth twitched. 'Yes, I'd imagine that you were angry.'

'Not because he declined to marry me,' she said. 'I understood that. I told him to give him that chance. It was because he wanted to have his cake and eat it.'

His lordship's eyes widened. 'He—? Of course.'

'And I did *not* refuse your offer because I was holding out for a better one!' She couldn't bear him to think that. 'All you need do is let the truth be known. No one will censure you.'

'Except me,' he said.

'You?'

'After refusing my original and dishonourable offer, you made sure we were never alone together again,' he said. 'In fact, you took pains to avoid me as much as possible.'

'What has that to say to anything?' She ached with weariness.

'It matters because you made it clear you did not want what I was offering despite the attraction between us.'

She didn't want to think about that. About the way her whole body, heart and soul had echoed in harmony when he kissed her. About the way he had made her believe, or wish to believe, that his kisses meant something. That *she* meant something beyond a passing fancy.

'Perhaps I was being coy,' she suggested.

'Coy?' he repeated. 'Christy, you are probably the least coy woman of my acquaintance!' He laughed wryly. 'Except possibly Serena.'

She was trying not to think about Lady Braybrook. 'The fact remains, my lord, that—'

'That you made it clear you would not have me, and I gave you my word you were safe. Instead, I ruined you.'

Her eyes blazed. 'You did not!' she shot back. 'It was a *kiss*, nothing more!'

'Your reputation, then,' he amended. 'Unfortunately, that is enough.'

'You *can't* wish to marry me,' she whispered. It was impossible that he should do such a thing.

His mouth twisted. 'Christy, this is not what either of us wanted,' he said quietly, 'but, there is little choice. I'm not going to announce your illegitimacy.'

She dragged in a breath, fighting to block all emotion and view the matter rationally. She could marry him, or leave in disgrace. If she refused and Braybrook would not use her illegitimacy to defend himself... She swallowed. Harry would challenge him. *One of them at least would die because you were too missish to accept a marriage that is entirely to your advantage...*

'You would have to meet my brother, would you not, my lord?'

Shock slammed into Julian.

'Christy—you can't think—! His quarrel with me is justified! I would—'

'Fire in the air?' She shrugged. 'Where's the difference? Harry is a very fine shot. Very well, I will marry you. You are not the only one with an inconvenient conscience, my lord.'

His breath caught. She understood he would not kill her brother. So if she had not agreed to marriage to protect Harry— his brain felt sluggish, clogged—it was *his* life she was concerned about. She had agreed to marriage to protect *him*. The realisation left him reeling.

You are not the only one with an inconvenient conscience, my lord.

'We are well matched after all, aren't we? Shall we say, in four weeks?'

She nodded, turned around and left the room without a word.

Julian stared at the closed door. He had wanted a bride without any romantical notions to complicate matters. It seemed he had got that with a vengeance. He had also gained a penniless bride with worse than no connections.

Now all he had to do was write a discreet letter to inform Alcaston that his unacknowledged, illegitimate daughter was about to become a viscountess.

'My lord?'

Julian looked up from his account books to find his butler fidgeting in the doorway. 'Yes, Hallam.' He frowned back at his recalcitrant column of figures.

'My lord, I thought you should know his Grace, the Duke of Alcaston, has called.'

'What?'

He straightened and set his pen in the holder. 'Alcaston? Of course I should know! Show him in!' He'd received a note from Alcaston's secretary acknowledging his letter and heard nothing more. By now he had assumed that Alcaston was going to ignore the matter.

Hallam swallowed visibly. 'I'm very sorry, my lord, but he said he'd see you afterwards—'

'Afterwards? After what?' demanded Julian, pushing his chair back.

'After he had seen Miss Daventry,' explained Hallam. 'He insisted.' Hallam hesitated. 'Not my place to say, my lord, but his Grace…well, he looked angry.'

Suppressing the urge to swear, Julian nodded. 'Very well. Thank you, Hallam. Where are they?'

'The drawing room, my lord.'

'Lady Braybrook is there?'

Hallam shook his head. 'No, my lord. Her ladyship went down to the Dower House with Mr Havergal to see the new furnishings.'

Christy stared, shocked at the duke, whose cold eyes surveyed her. 'I don't know what fairytale you spun Braybrook, girl, but if you thought I'd let it pass, then you're more of a fool than I imagined!'

She stiffened her spine. 'Fairytale?' She was going to remain calm and in control of herself. She wouldn't let him win.

Alcaston's eyes surveyed her coldly. 'How'd you do it? Trapped him? A mere compromising situation? Or did you play your only trump card?' He gave her a measuring look. 'I dare say that's it, isn't it? You let him swive you.'

She said nothing. She didn't care what he thought of her, and it would have made no difference anyway.

'I nearly let it go,' he told her. 'After all, if he's fool enough to marry a girl without connections or a penny to her name, let alone one who'll let him bed her, then he deserves what he gets.'

'So why are you here, sir?' She was mildly surprised to discover she felt very little for him.

A harsh laugh escaped him. 'Couldn't do it, could I? Couldn't let a man pollute his line when I could stop it!'

Once those words would have hurt. She would have felt rage. Shame. Now there was only emptiness. She could not think of him as her father. His seed had gone into her making, but she felt nothing. Not even regret for the void.

'And how will you stop it? Stand up in church and denounce me?' she suggested. 'It's hardly in keeping with your policy of discretion.'

His face mottled. 'I won't need to, girl. I'll give you one chance—tell him you've changed your mind. Break the betrothal quietly and I'll settle some money on you. Otherwise I'll tell him the truth myself and you'll get nothing!'

He thought she had deceived Braybrook. Lied by omission.

'You may go to hell, sir,' she told him.

For a speeding instant he looked stunned. He recovered swiftly. 'Words, girl! Do you think he'll marry you once he knows the truth?'

'What truth, your Grace?' came a cool voice.

Alcaston swung around. Christy's breath caught. Braybrook stood in the doorway. Tall, dark and somehow menacing. The planes of his face were hard and cold, the brilliant eyes fixed on the duke. He strolled forward. 'I do beg your pardon, your Grace.' The urbane voice belied the chill in his gaze. 'I am at a loss to understand why my butler should have shown you in here rather than bringing you to me. Most improper of him since Miss Daventry is not yet mistress of Amberley and Lady Braybrook is out.'

There was a pause. To Christy's amazement Alcaston looked chagrined. Even diminished.

'I believe I indicated to your man that I wished to see—that is, that I—' He broke off, jaw working. 'No matter,' he growled.

Braybrook's cold gaze never wavered and Christy was torn between admiration and horror. Alcaston was a *duke*, for pity's sake! Had Braybrook taken leave of his senses?

He spoke again. 'Obviously you read my letter at last. I dare say you were eager to wish Miss Daventry happy. I hope I see you well?'

Alcaston recovered the use of his tongue. 'Aye. I'm well enough,' he snapped. 'And I read your letter three weeks ago! You're damned lucky I decided to do something about it in the end!'

Braybrook raised his brows. 'Do something?' He reached Christy and took her hand, setting it on his arm, covering it with his other hand in a heart-shakingly protective gesture. 'I have already made a generous settlement on Miss Daventry, but of course if you wish to see the documents—'

'The devil I do!' growled Alcaston. 'I'd like to speak to the girl alone, if you please, Braybrook!'

'I don't please,' said Braybrook quietly. 'And you will mind your language in front of Miss Daventry,' he added.

Alcaston's jaw worked. 'Mind my—' He looked at Christy and his eyes hardened. 'Very well. I offered her a chance, but only to spare your feelings. I don't know what lies she's told, Braybrook, but she's no more fit to marry a man of rank than is a mongrel bitch. The truth is, she's a bastard. Her mother was my mistress. Sorry to be the one to break it to you, but—'

'Why would you assume I didn't know?'

'Because—' Alcaston broke off, jaw slack. 'You *knew*? Your letter didn't—'

'I was being discreet.' Braybrook's voice was icy. 'For your sake more than mine, I might add. I assumed your secretary would read the letter, so I referred to Miss Daventry as the sister of your godson. Naturally I am aware of Christy's birth.'

'How? How could you have known?' he rapped out. 'No one ever knew! Their mother passed as a widow.'

Fury at the memory of the lies her mother had been forced to live sang through Christy. 'Because I told him!'

The hand covering hers tightened. 'Leave this to me, sweetheart,' he murmured. Her heart shook at the endearment.

Braybrook's voice became colder. Harder. Yet his fingers still caressed hers reassuringly. 'You see, Miss Daventry was more honest with me than you were with her mother, Alcaston.'

Alcaston's eyes bulged and a vein stood out at his temple. His face was mottled. 'You'll marry her and soil your bloodline?'

Braybrook's voice lashed. 'I'll admit the thought of *your* bloodline doesn't fill me with delight. But since there is clearly very little of you in your daughter, I'll risk it. Was that all you came for?'

'Damn your insolence!' spat Alcaston. 'I take the time and trouble to warn you, and you meet me with insults? She's no daughter of mine, and you'll get not a penny from me!'

'You relieve me,' said Braybrook. 'Perhaps you might also relieve us of your presence?' Christy stared up at him, shocked.

He had snubbed a duke for her. One of his own class. Under the sleeve of his elegant coat, in the hand covering hers, she could feel every muscle hard and corded. His jaw resembled solid granite and her heart's defences shook.

'You *fool*!' ground out Alcaston. 'Go to the devil your own way!'

He stalked out, slamming the door.

Julian clung to the remaining shreds of his self-discipline. Frogmarching Alcaston through the house and flinging him down the front steps was out of the question. Instead he turned to Christy.

She looked calm, unmoved, as though her father had not just denounced and disowned her without so much as speaking her name. As though nothing had shifted in her world. Perhaps it hadn't. Yet he could feel her fingers digging into his arm. Fury? Hurt? As though reading his mind, she relaxed her hold.

'Thank you, my lord.'

'You're welcome. Come, sit down.' He urged her to a chair and then turned away to a small side table and poured a glass of brandy from a decanter there. 'Here—drink it. You'll feel better.'

She sniffed it suspiciously. 'I don't need it.'

'The hell you—' He broke off.

'Lost for words, my lord?'

He ran a hand through his hair, smiling ruefully. 'Having just called your fa—' Something in her eyes stopped him. He re-phrased what he had been about to say. 'Having called Alcaston to account for swearing in front of you, it would be the outside of enough to do it myself.'

Behind the spectacles something glimmered. He swallowed, turned away to pour himself a brandy.

'He's no father to me,' she said softly. 'My father would have attended Sarah's funeral.'

Sarah? Her sister? His heart twisted. 'I don't blame you,' he said. 'Christy, you've never told me about your mother. I didn't want to pry, but—'

'You have every right,' she said. He wasn't entirely sure that was true.

'After all,' she continued bitterly, 'she might have been a back-alley whore or a notorious courtesan.'

He shook his head. 'Unlikely. No back-alley whore could have raised you to be what you are—a lady. And if your mother *had* been a notorious courtesan, then it's unlikely Alcaston could have kept your existence quiet. Nor,' he added, 'would your mother have had to pretend to be a widow. Tell me.'

She was silent for a moment, but he did not think it was the silence of refusal. Her eyes were distant, remembering, thinking. At last she met his gaze and sighed. 'This is only in part what Mama told me. Some of it I pieced together from old letters and her diary.'

He nodded, and she continued. 'Mama was the daughter of lesser gentry living near Alcaston's principal seat. Her name was Catherine. Catherine Louisa Daventry.'

'It was her real name?'

She frowned. 'Yes. There were a couple of letters from my grandfather, and a diary she had kept before and just after her elopement.'

'Good.' Safer to ask. A false name could call the validity of their marriage into question later.

'From the diary she believed that Alcaston intended to marry her, but since the previous duke had contracted enormous debts, he contracted to marry the only daughter of an extremely wealthy merchant. Naturally he did not tell my mother this when they eloped. By the time her family found her, Alcaston was married to his heiress and I was on the way.' She shivered. 'There was a letter from her father disowning her.'

'They cast her off?'

She frowned. 'I think…when I was about six—it was after Harry was born—a man came to visit. We were in Bath by then. I think he was Mama's brother; she said at first to call him Uncle Harry, but that made him angry. After he left Mama said we'd be all right now. I suppose he gave her money. There was an annuity that died with her.'

He nodded. 'Did Alcaston support her?'

She bit her lip. 'After a fashion. He didn't visit often after Sarah was born. That was when he moved us to Bristol.' Her cheeks reddened. 'Easier to maintain the "widow" fiction if he moved us during each pregnancy.'

He didn't know what to say.

She continued. 'After Sarah died, he tired of Mama, but gave her the Bristol house.' Coldly, she added, 'Guilt, probably.'

Julian thought back over all he knew of Alcaston. Fear of exposure might have had something to do with it. It was common knowledge that Alcaston's father-in-law had been particularly strict on such matters. He'd have pulled the ducal purse strings uncomfortably tight had he suspected this. Probably Catherine's family had used that to force Alcaston to support her.

'Do you wish me to approach your mother's family?'

Some of her brandy spilt. '*No*. I wrote for her when she was ill, dying. A note came back from a Henry Daventry saying that he had no sister. I wrote again when she died and received no reply.'

He nodded. Families hid a daughter's disgrace at all costs. And sometimes the innocent paid.

'We'll ignore them,' he told her.

The ghost of a smile touched her lips. 'I doubt they'll notice.'

'Their loss,' he said lightly. And meant it.

Two days later Christy faced the altar of the village church as the Vicar expounded the reasons for matrimony, the words she had already heard that morning piercing her.

'Thirdly, it was ordained for the mutual society, help and comfort, that the one ought to have of the other, both in prosperity and adversity. Into which holy estate these two persons present come now to be joined…'

Early that morning Serena had married Nigel Havergal with

only the family present. Their faces had been alight with happiness, the rightness of their union unquestionable. The Vicar's words had been a blessing, a confirmation of joy.

But now those same words sounded a warning…

'Therefore if any man can show any just cause why they may not be lawfully joined together, let him now speak, or else hereafter forever hold his peace…'

She half-expected Alcaston to reappear. Folly. There was no legal impediment to the marriage. Merely social convention. She dragged in a breath to give her responses. Was she doing the right thing? Harry's belligerence suggested her chances of talking him out of challenging Braybrook had been non-existent. Braybrook himself appeared completely unmoved, and for some unstated reason Serena was delighted, welcoming the betrothal, dismissing her birth.

Unfortunate, but since you are exactly what he needs there is no point dwelling on it. It is nobody's business but your own.

Kind, generous words, but how could a bastard, a woman he had wanted as his mistress, be what he needed in a bride?

Harry was placing her hand in the Vicar's. A moment later the Vicar gave her hand into Braybrook's keeping. He took it in a firm, steady clasp. Just that formal touch demanded by the ritual, and her senses sang with awareness. His height, his strength, the hard line of his jaw, the hint of sandalwood and the spicy, masculine tang that was *him*. Every nerve thrummed with a terrifying anticipation…

The Vicar was speaking again.

'Wilt thou have this woman…?'

Had it been a foolish impulse on his part? Did he regret his decision already, or would that come later? A shiver ran through her.

Beside her, he frowned, the dark brows snapping together. She lifted her chin and met the piercing blue gaze.

'…and forsaking all other, keep thee only unto her, as long as ye both shall live?'

The frown deepened...then his fingers tightened.

'I will.'

Her heart shook as he made vows she doubted he intended to keep. Yet, unbidden, her fingers returned his clasp, and trembled as his thumb stroked gently over the back of her hand.

The wedding guests were gone except for those staying in the house and Christy stared out of her bedchamber window. The western sky flamed pink and gold on deep, deep blue, the trees beyond the park standing black against the glowing embers of day. The whole world, the very air was flushed golden pink. She leaned out, pushing the casement wide. It was still relatively early. Far too early to be in her nightgown. But her newly appointed maid had been waiting when she came up, had seemed to think that she ought to be arrayed in her nightgown. Ready.

Acquiescence was easier and a hot bath was unaccustomed luxury even without the various oils Beth the maid tipped into the steaming water.

Her ladyship—Mrs Havergal, that is, gave them to me specially, my lady. For tonight. A conspiratorial smile had accompanied the words.

There had been soap as well, its delicate fragrance a match for the bath oil. She would have loved it, even with Beth hovering, making sure everything was just so. But the rising, scented steam reminded her mercilessly that this was a ritual, that she was being readied. Adorned. Made fit for her husband.

She had rebelled, though, at the gauzy froth of silk and lace laid out for her on the downturned bed. Serena had given it to her, but the thought of appearing before Braybrook in the intimacy of her bedchamber half-naked sent panic skittering down her nerves. Her husband had been bedding London's beauties for years. She had no idea of inviting comparison. Instead she had folded it carefully away, selecting instead plain, modest, high-necked linen. It gave at least the illusion of safety.

A fragile illusion. Braybrook's chamber was next to this one with a connecting door and she had heard faint sounds of movement. Indistinct male voices. She had dismissed Beth at once, and the maid had departed with a curtsy, and barely concealed smile at the closed connecting door. That had been bad enough, but had Braybrook appeared with the maid still in the room…

A throat was cleared. 'Christy?'

Chapter Fourteen

Julian watched her from the door as she leaned out of the window, limned in light. The way she was seated sideways on the window ledge had his blood heating. One bare foot remained on the floor, steadying her; the demure nightgown—which should have concealed, but instead hugged breast, slender waist and curving hip—had slid up to expose a dainty ankle, part of her calf, graceful, shapely... She was half-turned away, her face hidden as she gazed out.

Desire bucked, but he hesitated; she had been nervous in the church. Yet during the hours since her composure had been absolute. A façade, he knew, something that could be broken. He had once wondered what it would take to break her quiet self-possession.

A wedding night was almost guaranteed to leave her self-possession in tatters.

And what about your *self-possession?*

He dismissed that. *His* self-possession had never been in doubt. Not with any woman. It was not now.

He cleared his throat. 'Christy?'

She did not move, yet where she had been still before, her stillness now held the quality of force. And when she turned to face him, the control in her movement cried tension. In the dimly lit room and with the flaring sky to frame her, he could not read her expression.

'My lord?'

That stung.

He came further into the room as she slipped from the window ledge and the nightgown fell around her in modest concealment. He gestured towards the door. 'Shall we?'

She looked blankly from him to the door. 'I beg your pardon?'

'Our wedding night. Or had you forgot?'

She flushed. 'Of course not! I…I just thought—' Her gaze flickered to the turned-down bed and he saw where her confusion lay.

'My bed,' he said quietly. Tonight at least it seemed fitting.

Her eyes widened, the faintest chink in her calm. Without a word she moved around the room, snuffing candles until the only light was from the window and the doorway behind him. She made to catch up the dressing gown lying across a chair.

'You won't need that,' he informed her. She wouldn't need the nightgown either, but he supposed it would be a bit much to tell her to leave that behind. As it was, she stilled and her head came up.

For an instant her hand hovered over the dressing gown, then dropped and she came towards him. He stepped back to allow her to pass through the doorway. Roses and honeysuckle, and soft, warm woman drifted by, the fragrance humming through him. He hardened his jaw against the instinct to haul her into his arms there and then.

What was the matter with him? She was a woman like any other. Why did she burn at his self-control? He forced his arms to remain at his sides. Better not to give her any hint of his urgency. She was probably nervous enough. Besides which, without a measure of control he would hurt her more than was inevitable in the loss of her innocence. And the thought of hurting her in any way lashed at him. How could he keep this marriage on a manageable footing when the thought of that un-avoidable, and probably slight, hurt knotted his gut?

He remained at the door, watching as she crossed the room. The chaste gown hid everything. In the dancing firelight there was not the slightest shadow cast through the heavy linen. No hint of the lissom body he knew was there. The long, slender legs, the rounded bottom and swell of her hips, made for a man's hand to slide over and possess. Why did he want *her* more than he had ever wanted another, so that desire itself burned anew?

He had always assumed that he would desire his eventual wife and enjoy taking her to bed. In a friendly, comfortable sort of way. Rather like his aristocratic lovers, but without the in-convenience of constant discretion. He'd also assumed his wife would be a woman of his world, bringing wealth and impor-tant connections to the marriage.

Christy was different—she brought nothing to the marriage. And all the power was his, to give or to withhold whatever he pleased. So why did he feel so at sea? As though he were in the grip of something larger than either of them? Something that swung him to and fro, bobbing like a cork in a tempest.

And why the hell did he feel that in some odd way, without even realising it, his powerless, inconvenient bride held the reins? Because he couldn't take his eyes off that demure night-gown? Because just watching her walk unhestitatingly straight to his bed had him hard and aching?

Christy stopped at the bed. Shock at being summoned to his room had propelled her across the vast expanse of his bedcham-ber. It was not sufficient to get her into that enormous bed.

Her legs rebelled and refused to go a step further.

Nothing in her experience gave any clue to what she should do next. She took a deep breath and another. But her insides still quaked. She knew what happened in the bed, but how was she to get into it? Climb in? Wait to be invited? She felt a complete fool that he'd had to summon her to her duty, but how was she to know where they were to…she didn't even know what to call it. *Making love* seemed inappropriate in the extreme. Consummate the marriage?

She turned and swallowed; he wore only a banyan. Beneath the heavy crimson silk was bare chest. She stared. His feet were bare too. Presumably he intended to remove his robe. Would he remove her nightgown? Or should she take it off?

Suddenly he looked larger, more powerful, his face harder, etched in shadows. A trick of the firelight, surely. He might resent the marriage, but he was not a man who would use his physical strength against a woman.

She supposed he would be careful in…in taking his pleasure, that he would not hurt her intentionally. There was nothing to fear—except even now, with him still on the other side of the room, she could feel her body's treacherous yearning, the melting heat. The memory of his fingers on her breasts sent heat curling through her. Would he expect her to touch him? Or would it disgust him?

She felt cold. Lost.

He had wanted her as his mistress. And had been forced to take her as his bride. She knew, none better, the yawning gulf between the woman a man would take as his mistress and the woman he would take willingly as his bride.

His gaze raked her from head to foot. And still he said nothing, made no move towards her. Perhaps she didn't look pretty enough. Perhaps she should have worn that confection of lace and gauzy silk—except she would have felt more exposed than if she had been naked. Bad enough standing here before him in this all-enveloping linen.

She still wore her spectacles. Slowly, hands shaking slightly, she removed them, and set them carefully folded on the bedside table. The room dissolved into a firelit blur, her husband—oh, God! her *husband*—an indistinct shadow near the door.

* * *

Julian took an uncertain breath as she laid her spectacles down. In a career dotted with beautiful women draped in various alluring poses and degrees of undress, he had never seen anything more erotically tempting. His bride, shrouded from neck to toes in plain, white linen, her soft tawny curls confined in a single braid hanging over her left shoulder almost to her breast. Christy, blinking at him uncertainly without her spectacles. His mouth dried.

She said nothing. Just waited. She was his, and his blood burned with wanting her. Every law and precept, all custom and tradition, said she was his. His by undeniable right. He started towards her, half-expecting her to step back. She didn't, but he could see the tension, the self-control she exerted not to do so. Instead her arms came up to cross defensively over her breasts.

He stopped, desire a heated ache, thickening in his groin. A hunger that he would soon assuage in the soft body of his bride.

She stood before him—a pale offering against the dark hangings of his bed.

'Our wedding night, Christy.' The words were out before he knew it, leaving him wondering why he had said them at all.

Silence stretched between them.

'Yes.' Her voice was quiet, expressionless. As if she merely agreed with his statement of fact. But something about her very stillness told him it was more than that. That in one word she had voiced her acceptance, her submission to what would take place in the shadows of the bed behind her.

Desire flexed its claws and he took the final steps to stand directly in front of her. She met his gaze unflinchingly, but her throat moved convulsively, the tip of her tongue moistening soft, trembling lips.

He fought the immediate, feudal urge to take and possess that mouth, ravishing it utterly. His self-discipline hung by a thread—if he touched her now, let alone tasted her, they would be on the bed. If he didn't just tumble her to the floor and take her there. He forced desire back into its cage. She was his bride—he had all night.

Slowly he raised one hand and set it to the ribbon securing the neckline of her nightgown. A gentle tug, and the bow surrendered. Need clawed at him. A row of buttons marched down the bodice of the gown to disappear under her tightly crossed arms. One by one he encircled her wrists in a careful grip, lifting them away from her breasts. Her eyes widened, dilating as he drew her hands down, holding them slightly away from her body. He kept his touch light, aware of the tension flickering through her, although she had not resisted.

'I wish to see you.'

Her breath came and went in a rush. She nodded and he released her wrists. Her hands remained at her sides. Without the protection of her arms he could see the veiled hint of sweetly rounded breasts. Soon he would taste them. Soon he would have her beneath him. His own breath shortened. Soon. Very soon.

Her chin lifted, exposing the slender column of her throat. So vulnerable, so tempting. He leaned forwards, touched his lips to the hollow at the base of her throat, flicking out his tongue to taste. Soft female fragrance exploded through him.

He straightened, and saw that her eyes were closed, lips slightly parted. His blood drumming, he set his fingers to the top button of her nightgown and undid it, forcing himself to be slow, deliberate. One by one the buttons fell victim until the gown hung open almost to her waist.

The sight had his blood roaring in his ears. Dainty, rounded breasts, half-hidden by the gown. He set his hands to her and pushed the garment off.

A startled gasp escaped her as she clutched at the gown, catching it at her hips. A simple matter to pull it away, leaving her fully exposed…instead he traced the curve of a creamy, uptilted breast with shaking fingers. Dear God, she was lovely—soft, silky flesh that begged his touch, shadows and firelight dancing over her.

Lightly, he touched one pink nipple; it tightened in reaction. He nearly forgot to breathe as he stroked again. A strangled sound brought his gaze back to her face. Her eyes were tightly shut, her lower lip caught between her teeth.

His conscience murmured. Slamming a door shut on the unwelcome voice, he slid his hand lower, over the gentle swell of her stomach, feeling taut muscles flicker. Pushing beneath the gown at her hips, his fingertips found the soft curls nestled at the juncture of her thighs.

She froze, every muscle locking.

He stopped, no longer able to ignore the truth. She was afraid.

She was his wife. She had not protested. Had not taken so much as one step away, let alone tried to stop him. His fingertips still rested on those soft curls.

Yet even as he watched, a tear slipped from beneath her tightly closed eyelids.

His conscience rebelled.

You can't! Not like this.

Why not? She is my wife. She has not refused me, and even if she had—she is still mine to take.

You can't do this. No matter that law and custom say you can. No decent man would take her like this.

He looked at her. She was shaking with the effort to hold herself still, her lower lip still gripped between her teeth.

There was no equivocating. No matter that he had every legal right to take her—he couldn't do it. It didn't matter that she had consented, that she was not fighting him, or even protesting.

She was not willing.

She has not refused me.

His conscience scoffed. *Why would she? She knows the law as well as you. She has no rights. She is yours and she knows it.*

He took a long look at the sweetly enticing body of his

bride. Never in his life had he taken a woman who was anything less than eager.

With a savage curse he withdrew his hand and turned his back.

'I can't do this,' he said tautly. 'Cover yourself and get back to your room. Quickly.'

Before he changed his mind and tumbled her to the bed. He tasted bitter self-loathing as he realised how close he was to doing that. The temptation hammered in his veins. Every muscle and nerve, every fibre growled in frustration as he listened to the flurry of movement behind him, heard the swift padding of bare feet, and the thud of the door.

Christy stood shaking in the darkness of her bedchamber. She leaned on the panelled door, clutching her spectacles, barely able to stand for the trembling of her limbs. He didn't want her, had ordered her out.

I can't do this.

Her breasts ached with need. He had scarcely touched her and she felt…she didn't understand what she felt. Or did she? Weak—liquid heat pooling low in her belly. An emptiness that cried within her. Body and soul, she felt as though something had been ripped from her core, leaving her cold and desolate.

Her eyes stinging with unshed tears, she faced the truth: he had scarcely touched her and she had wanted him. She had felt her whole body melting, like heated honey, at his light caresses. Her cheeks burned in the darkness. It had been all she could do to stand, unresponding, and not press against him.

His touch on her breasts, sliding over her belly, lower and lower, had been terror and delight. Knowing that he would soon touch her *there*, where she ached. *There* where she felt…with shaking fingers she touched herself, gasping at the bolt of sensation—*there* where she was wet and hot.

She was his wife, not his mistress.

Shame scorched her body. Had he reached just a little further he would have found that slick heat. He would have known. Known that she *wanted* him to touch her there. He expected his wife to behave as a lady. Which she was patently incapable of doing. Perhaps he had known, despite not touching her. Known and been disgusted.

She drew a shuddering breath. Foolish to remain here shivering all night. The room was pitch dark. She strained her eyes, staring into the emptiness, trying to remember where things were. The bed was directly opposite the door. She moved cautiously towards it. And stumbled over a chair.

There was a tinderbox near the fireplace, she recalled. Only the way her hands shook, she would probably end up burning down the house if she tried to use it.

She found the bed, fighting her way through the hangings, and dragged in a sobbing breath as she huddled under the bedclothes. In all her nervous imaginings of this night, it had never even crossed her mind that she might end it as she had begun— a virgin. He had expected her to do her duty, but apparently he had been far too disgusted to do his.

Julian stared up at the shadowy canopy of his empty bed. It was some sort of judgement on him, he supposed, that after years of seducing other men's wives, he now couldn't seduce his own. His closest friends would be hard pressed not to chuckle at his predicament.

He swore and punched his pillow as the clock on the chimney piece chimed endlessly. Midnight. Over two hours since he'd sent her back to her room. By now, if he'd behaved like any normal husband, his marriage should have been consummated, his bride irrevocably his.

Instead he was lying here, wondering if he should have continued gently and got the deed over and done with. He would have to do precisely that eventually. His stomach clenched at the memory of her white face. Never before had a woman feared him. Never. It was not a pleasant feeling.

It looked like being a very long night. And then there would be tomorrow. He was taking her down to Abbey House, a small manor he owned in Monmouthshire. It was a quiet, secluded place near the river. Ideal for a newly-wed couple head over heels in love. Precisely the impression needed to stem the murmur that a scheming little adventuress had trapped him. She didn't deserve that.

But what the devil did he say to her? How could he reassure her that he would not press his rights immediately? And what was he to do about this marriage all together? A marriage of convenience was what he had always intended and there was no reason he could not have it. Desiring his wife was perfectly convenient. As long as he didn't allow it to rule him.

As long as he remembered that a wife and a mistress inhabited two different spheres of a man's life and it was not wise to combine the roles in one woman.

Chapter Fifteen

Julian trod up the worn stone stairs of Abbey House the following evening, shielding his flickering candle from draughts. Had he been mad to choose this shabby old manor for the bride trip? It held memories of mad boyhood summers, when he and the Blakehurst twins had come here with Serena and run wild fishing, climbing trees, riding their ponies all over the place and not always coming home at night. Carefree holidays when all that mattered was who caught the biggest fish, jumped the highest fence, or climbed the tallest tree, and the next day might see the record fall to a new victor. Days his memory insisted had been endlessly sunny.

Why had he brought Christy here? Shouldn't he have taken her to Bath? Shown her off publicly as his chosen bride? Surely she would have preferred Bath where she could shop, meet people and be acknowledged as the new Lady Braybrook. Yet when he had suggested it she had demurred, saying she would prefer a quiet place. So he had thought of this house. But what would she do here?

And why hadn't he sent instructions for a second bedchamber? The housekeeper here, Mrs Braxton, was a farmer's daughter. In her world husband and wife shared a bed. A flash of memory came—when his father had joined them in the summer holidays he had always shared Serena's room. No, it would never occur to Mrs Braxton to prepare two rooms. Not for two newly-weds.

He reached the upper corridor. Who would he find in that bedchamber? The self-possessed woman who had bid him goodnight an hour ago? Or the terrified bride of the previous night? If the latter, he wasn't sure he could bear it.

He found his bride ready for, but not yet in, bed. Closing the door behind him, he surveyed his property. Never before had he questioned the legal decree that a man's wife was literally his property. Now he did. It seemed absurd. Even wrong.

Christy was...Christy. Herself.

She sat curled up in a wingchair beside the fire, wrapped in a pink silk robe. A wine table beside her held an oil lamp and a tumble of bright embroidery silks. The mellow light shifted and gleamed on the thick tawny braid hanging over one shoulder as she looked up from her sewing. Something flickered across her pale face, instantly stilled.

'Am I disturbing you?' he asked.

Her surprise was palpable. 'Of course not. This is your room too.'

He frowned. Was her calm real, or feigned?

'I did not like to say anything tonight,' he said, 'but tomorrow I shall speak to Mrs Braxton about a separate room for myself.'

Again that indefinable something flickered.

'You must do as you please, my lord.'

'Dammit, Christy! We're married! This is our bedchamber—you may call me Julian!'

He dragged in a breath. Yelling at a nervous bride wouldn't help.

'Does our marriage give me that licence?'

He stared. 'Of course it does!' He thought about it. 'In private, at least. Publicly you would call me "Braybrook" or "my lord" and refer to me with anyone but family or a very intimate acquaintance by my title.' He added, 'I think.'

'You *think*?'

Laughter welled up as he went towards a screen set up across a corner of the room. Of all the things to be discussing! 'That's just it,' he said. 'I don't think about it. It's automatic.'

'Bred into you, in fact.'

He shrugged. 'Yes.' And saw the barely perceptible withdrawal—if a woman as reserved as Christy could withdraw any further. Belatedly he saw where the conversation had gone as he stepped behind the screen. 'It's not very important, Christy,' he said from behind it.

'Not to you,' she agreed.

But to her most definitely. He eased his coat off and untied his cravat. The story of their suspiciously swift marriage was buzzing about with a sting in its tail. Any slip she made would be magnified and bandied about in every drawing room from Hereford to Ludlow and beyond. Discussed with smiling malice between ladylike sips of tea. A raised brow here. A knowing look there. The inevitable way of the world, he acknowledged as he unbuttoned his shirt and hauled it off over his head.

Sitting down, he pulled his boots off. The only reason a man of his rank would willingly marry a woman like Christy was if he had fallen head over heels in love. Ergo, in the eyes of the world, he had not been willing and Miss Daventry had trapped him most cleverly. Never mind that the whole damn thing had been his fault, he thought, stripping out of his breeches and drawers. A ewer of water and basin stood on a night table. He poured water and washed before donning the nightshirt left ready and walking out from behind the screen.

He didn't have to spell it out to the woman sewing in the pool of light. She knew. For the first time he wondered if she would be happy. He'd taken it for granted. Rank, wealth, security. What more could she want?

Climbing into bed, he looked at his bride. She was still sewing. Quiet, industrious—she appeared to be embroidering a handkerchief. Firelight flashed off her spectacles. Memory tossed up an odd scrap of knowledge gleaned from Serena—the light…didn't seamstresses often go blind sewing in poor light?

'Shouldn't you stop sewing soon?' he asked.

She finished setting a stitch and looked up, her face still. 'If…if you wish it, I will come to bed now.'

His stomach clenched. Did she think he was ordering her to his bed?

'That was not a command, Christy,' he said quietly. 'I was concerned that sewing in this light would hurt your eyes.'

'Oh. I thought—'

'I know what you thought,' he said shortly. 'And you need not worry. I've never taken a woman who was less than willing, and I'm damned if I'll start with my wife.'

Christy, sliding her needle into the handkerchief, looked up sharply. 'Last night,' she began, 'I thought you…that it was because I…that you did not want—' her face flamed, but she held his shocked gaze '—that I had somehow—'

'No!' He found his tongue and stumbled into speech, searching for words to reassure her. 'No. That was not a problem,' he said in careful understatement. 'I wanted you.'

She looked disbelieving.

'You were frightened,' he said simply.

She was silent for a moment, then nodded and said, 'But not unwilling. Just nervous.'

Nervous? She'd looked terrified.

'Nor am I unwilling now.'

Nor was she… His heart skipped a beat over the sudden, slow, heavy rhythm of his blood. Light caught in the thick braid over her shoulder, silken tawny fire. He could almost feel his fingers sliding through the mass, tumbling it over the pillow…her mouth, lush and sweet; his to ravish and plunder… No. That way lay madness with her. Her kisses, for all her inexperience, were incendiary and kisses were not necessary when making lo—having sex—he didn't want that intimacy, especially not now when it threatened to tear him apart.

'My lord?'

He drew a ragged breath. She was a virgin. He must not lose control and hurt her. 'Julian,' he corrected her softly.

She nodded. 'Julian, then. We must do this, must we not?'

'Yes.' His control would not increase with waiting—rather, the opposite.

An indrawn breath, as though she braced herself. 'Then I would prefer to get it over with sooner rather than later.'

Not the most flattering invitation he'd ever received from a woman, but tension cried out from every taut line of her body. And she was being as honest as she knew how. Painfully so.

'Come, then.' He flipped back the covers on the other side of the bed, his eyes never leaving her. She nodded and began to put away her embroidery. He watched, not missing a movement of the careful, clumsy hands that fumbled over the simple task, the heightened colour of her cheeks, or the way the silk robe flowed around her.

Dear God, he was hard to the point of pain, just watching her. Finished, she stood up and doused the lamp, leaving only his candle and the firelight. Slowly she slid her robe off, laying it neatly across the chair. Either the same demure gown as last night, or its twin, enveloped her.

His breath shortened. Familiarity wasn't helping. He remembered those buttons, the softness and fragrance of creamy, rose-peaked breasts. His groin ached.

'Come,' he repeated. If she could not come to him of her own free will, then he had no business taking her.

Panic shuddered through Christy. His expression was unreadable. He was very still, but there was no hint of relaxation in the corded tendons of his neck, and his eyes possessed her darkly.

If she could not walk to that bed and climb into it, she would have another day of strain to face. Folly! If she knew anything about him, she knew he was not a brute. That she remained virgin bore testament to that.

The room was not large. A shaky breath and a few steps took

her to the bed. She circled the foot, startled when he leaned over to blow out his candle. Just the firelight now. She reached the other side of the bed. Steps led up into it. A mountain to be climbed.

Trembling, she climbed up and slid under the covers beside her husband who lay propped on one elbow now, watching with dark intent...*and the two shall become one flesh*...he was so still, a statue, not flesh and blood at all...*one flesh*... Steadying her hands, she removed her spectacles and placed them on the bedside table.

There was a sudden movement beside her and she jumped.

He stilled again. 'Christy?'

'It's all right,' she whispered, but he made no move.

The previous night he had unbuttoned her nightgown... Clumsily she undid the top button.

'No.'

Embarrassment burned her. No?

'That's my privilege.'

He thought it a privilege?

Banners of heat unfurled as large, gentle hands took over, opening button after button until her bodice hung open and he carefully cupped one breast, stroking his thumb over the suddenly aching peak. She sat rigid, fighting her body's melting response to his caress and hot, hungry gaze. His free hand tugged at her nightgown, sliding it up over her legs.

'Lift up,' he said.

She suppressed an instinctive protest and wriggled so that the nightgown came free to be taken off over her head. Her breath caught and she slid lower into the bed. But he sat up, hauled off his nightshirt and came to her, pushing back the bedclothes. Skin to skin. Hot flesh to hot flesh...sparks flickered and leapt under her skin. She lay still, trying to control her trembling, reminding herself that he would not hurt her, that he would be gentle...but she was *naked*. And *he* was naked—lying against her, looking at her, touching her, undoing her braid, freeing the thick, unruly mass. She gasped as he pressed a knee between her legs, *opening* her. Her breath shortened as fires danced beneath his warm hands sliding, feathering over her so that she ached *there*, between her legs where she was becoming moist and warm as she had the night before. The same fear shook her—would she disgust him?

'Ssshhh,' he murmured. 'Relax.'

Relax?

She lay half under him as he leaned over her, one powerful thigh wedged between hers, holding her open for his hungry gaze and wicked, invading fingers on her inner thigh. She felt vulnerable, helpless. No—not helpless. One word would stop him, and she didn't want him to stop… Oh, but she had to force herself to lie still, wanting to touch *him*, fighting the surging need to lift her hips against his hand in restless wanting—and then his fingers were *there*, where she ached, sliding easily on slick flesh.

'Good,' he murmured, smiling down at her.

So he didn't mind the embarrassing wetness, it pleased him…it felt strange though…it should have felt immodest, but it felt good… Her whole body jerked and quivered as one finger pressed, and slid just inside the hot, slippery ache. She gasped, tensing against the cataract of sensation, of stretching.

He stilled.

'Does that hurt?'

'N…no.' She wanted…*more*.

He lowered his head to her breast, kissed the taut nipple, then drew it into the shocking heat of his mouth and sucked. She bit back a cry as bright pleasure speared from her breast to where he so gently penetrated her body. Involuntarily her hips lifted, her body winning free of her control to arch towards him, around him.

And she had *more*. Fierce strength took her, covering her, and she cried out in shock as his hard weight pressed her into the mattress, her thighs pushed wide, wider than she could have believed. Hot pressure at her core, stretching her, burning as he came into her and she gasped, biting down on sudden pain, closing her eyes against it.

A ragged curse, and he stilled.

Then, harshly, 'I'm sorry,' And he thrust the rest of the way.

Pain cut, tearing a choked cry from her throat, and he was still again. Blessedly still. She lay quietly, forcing herself to breathe, half-surprised that there was room for breath, she felt so...full. He was deep, so very deep inside her, pain easing to discomfort.

'Are you all right?' His harsh voice. At odds with the gentle, clumsy fingers sliding into her hair; *he* was shaking, she realised on a burst of shock. Actually shaking as he brushed moisture from her cheek...she was crying? She opened her eyes.

'Christy, are you all right?' His expression was urgent, taut. As though *he* were in pain.

'Y...yes,' she lied, shifting to ease that shocking fullness.

A groan tore from him. 'For God's sake—stay still.'

She tensed, staring up at his hard face, the blazing eyes. Sweat beaded his brow, a muscle flickered in his jaw.

He groaned again, shutting his eyes, and pulled back so that she sighed in relief, only to catch her breath on a gasp as he pushed in again. And again. Slowly. His eyes shut tight and sweat sheened his face. That first flash of pain over, she could bear it now. And he slid more easily, it was almost...almost pleasant, despite a lingering soreness. But he was distant. Closed away. Shut eyes in a taut mask. He was moving faster, his breath hoarse and ragged. Harder, faster so she felt the push and pull within her where his body invaded hers, until with a groan he pushed deep, his whole body shuddering and convulsing, before he collapsed on to her, burying his face in her hair.

Shudders rippled through him, and her arms curved around him, holding him safely to her, enjoying his weight, her hands shyly stroking his shoulders where muscles bunched and flickered beneath hot, damp skin. Briefly he turned his head and pressed his lips to her temple. Heat stung her eyes at the caress. Somehow she had thought kisses played a bigger part in the marriage bed.

She drew a breath. It was done. She had survived. She hoped he hadn't found her too gauche and ignorant. He was still inside her, his weight shifted slightly to one side, utterly limp in her arms. *In her arms.* Her arms still encircled him, held him to her. She was clinging to him. Carefully she released him, forced her arms to fall to her sides.

His head lifted at once. Heavy lidded eyes opened, piercingly blue. Please, God, he could not see her thoughts, know that she felt wanton. Bracing his weight on his elbows, he withdrew from her body and rolled away to lie staring up at the canopy.

She swallowed. There seemed nothing to say. A stolen sideways glance showed his mouth set hard. Anger? Disappointment? Perhaps she had done something wrong, but she had no idea what and no way of finding out. She was all for plain speaking in this marriage, but she baulked at asking her husband how she had erred, not five minutes after resigning her virginity to him.

She wondered if he would fall asleep soon. She wanted to wash. She felt sticky and tender there. *There* where he had been. And she supposed there would be blood…

He sat up, pushing back the bedclothes, and she watched out of the corner of her eye as he left the bed and shrugged into a robe, stepping behind the screen. She heard water pouring, and flushed. If she was sticky, then… Moments later he reappeared in his nightshirt and robe, a flannel in his hand.

Her breath jerked in as he came around the bed to her and reached for the bedclothes. She sat up, clutching them to her.

'My lord? Julian?' She pulled herself together. 'Thank you', and held out her hand for the flannel. Cheeks hot, she held his gaze.

His mouth twisted. 'As you wish,' he said, handing her the cloth and turning away.

Snatching up her discarded nightgown, Christy dragged it over her head and scrambled out of bed, trying not to wince at the ache between her legs.

Julian took a shuddering breath as she disappeared behind the screen. What the hell did he say? Apologise? Promise it would be better next time? Could he keep that promise? None of his lovers had ever had cause to complain, but they had all been experienced and had come to him willingly, not acquiescing because he owned them body and soul and they had no choice. Nor had he ever lost control like that.

He felt like a brute. A rutting brute. She had been a virgin and he hadn't even aroused her sufficiently not to hurt her, let alone bring her to pleasure as he ought to have done before taking her. Some pain had probably been unavoidable, but his conscience lashed him—she had cried. There was no need to look for blood where she had lain. The blood on his body had been accusation enough.

It had not been even remotely good sex. Certainly not for her. And yet he had never felt such fierce pleasure sliding into a woman's soft body, nor experienced such a shattering release.

Frustration. He'd wanted her too long. She had been a virgin too. He had never lain with a virgin. *Nothing like novelty to pique the appetite*, a sly, cynical voice murmured. Damn it! He'd never *wanted* to lie with a virgin before! And he hadn't wanted that now. He'd just wanted Christy, beyond all rhyme or reason. Because she was Christy? He pulled back from that thought. Of course, he had not had a woman for months. Not since leaving London. Logical answers, explaining everything. His loss of control. His response.

It didn't help. What sort of brute was he to have felt pleasure when Christy had felt only pain?

She reappeared from behind the screen, her colour high, her eyes shuttered.

He managed a smile. 'Come. You must be tired.'

Quietly she climbed into the bed and lay down.

'Goodnight.'

The catch in her voice tore at him. Unthinking, he leaned over and kissed her gently on the mouth, cradling her jaw, brushing his thumb over her cheek.

He felt shock leap through her and prepared to pull back, but her lips softened, parting, and he was lost. With a groan he accepted the invitation, his tongue surging deep. Fire exploded through him impossibly, searing every vein as his body hardened. So soft, so lovely. It would be better for her this time. Slower—

Damn it!

He released her mouth. He'd just taken her virginity, for God's sake! Bad enough to hurt her; rutting on her again would be unforgivable.

'Enough,' he said tightly, forcing himself back to his side of the bed. 'Goodnight.' Staring up at the canopy, he felt her roll away from him.

Reality crashed in on him. This was his wife. In his bed. Or was he in her bed? Christy had been a virgin, but this part was new to him. He'd never slept, actually slept, with a woman. When he spent the night with a mistress, it didn't involve sleep beyond brief dozes between bouts of sex. His aristocratic lovers had been literally drawing-room affairs—quick interludes snatched on a *chaise longue* fully clothed. This was different, lying sated and sleepy, listening to the whisper of a woman's breathing, feeling her weight depressing the mattress, aware of her warmth and the hot, musky scent of their lovemaking. Very different, and perhaps not wise…

He awoke in the middle of the night to realise that someone else was in the bed—the warm, sweet fragrance of woman mingled with roses was all about him. Sleepily he reached out and gathered her to him. Christy. His. With a sigh she snuggled into him and he felt the soft huff of her breath through the linen of his nightshirt. Complete, he sank back to sleep.

erness *felt* loving…his kisses…the gentle way he'd touched her, held her afterwards—close, as though he couldn't bear to release her. But her mother had warned her men were different. They could feel only physical pleasure where a woman felt as though her heart had left her breast.

That was my mistake, dearest. Don't repeat it.

Other women must have felt this way about him. Jane Roberts, perhaps. Coldness gripped her. Jane and her daughter, Nan—did he have other children? There was no point resenting his past involvements; she was the product of such a union herself. It was just that she was falling, or had fallen, in love. She was jealous. Possessive. She wanted him to be hers alone from now on, and he never would be. He had been very honest about that.

She had tried not to let this happen—even this afternoon she had tried to hold some small part of herself apart, inviolate, but afterwards he had coaxed her into the river, teaching her to swim, endlessly patient and encouraging. And, oh! The touch of his hands on her body through the wet, clinging chemise. She'd been too shy to swim naked, but in the end the chemise had been worse than nothing. A tremor coursed through her— it had not just been his hands, but the sensation of his wet, powerful body sliding against hers, and the hot, hungry touch of his gaze, and his laughter. His encouragement of her efforts and his delight when she could keep herself afloat and swim a few strokes.

She had to remember that to him it was nothing more than kindness.

They had walked back to the house, his horse trailing behind, hand in hand like lovers.

We are lovers, she thought. But only in the physical sense.

The opening door scattered her thoughts.

The sight of her husband seized her breathing. He stood just inside the open door, his expression serious, the dark hair tousled and slightly damp. Beneath his robe she could see only bare, muscled chest. Her lips parted on a soundless gasp—he hadn't bothered with a nightshirt. She steeled herself against possible disappointment; perhaps he had merely come to say good—

'May I come to you?'

Shock slammed through her. He had every right to take her whenever he chose. That even now he had not taken her consent for granted—the last little bit of her that she had tried to hold back was lost, utterly lost.

Joy flared, blocking her throat.

'Y…yes,' she stammered.

Then, seeing his hesitation, she repeated in a despicably wobbly voice, 'Yes, oh, yes—please.'

His eyes darkened. The door shut with a thump and he came to her.

Her mind shattered, dazed with pleasure, Christy opened her eyes to stare down at her husband, her lover—the man who lay beneath her, one strong hand on her hip more to share her rhythm than to guide, while his hot gaze and free hand caressed and loved her. He was so hard and deep inside her and she was burning, dying with need, yet she could not find her way over… *Please! Please!*

'Like this, sweetheart. Come to me, love. Now.' The hand at her hip tightened, bringing her down hard just as his questing fingers found that place, the special place hidden in her damp, soft curls, and pressed so the storm within her broke. She cried out, convulsing helplessly around him as her release swept through her and he was holding her, rolling her beneath him and the firestorm redoubled, roaring through her again as he drove to his own climax.

He had called her 'love'.

She lay exhausted in his arms, thoughts and emotions tumbling through inextricably tangled, but through the whole shimmering web one thread wove brightly…

I love you.

His arms tightened and she realised sleepily that she had spoken aloud. That the last barrier had fallen, and he had said nothing.

He should return to his own bed. But an hour later Julian lay sleepless, listening to Christy's quiet breathing.

I love you...

The sleepy words haunted him. Had she meant them? Or believed she meant them? Hell! Had she even been awake? Other women had spoken those words to him. Especially in the throes of passion. Often they thought love was the only ladylike reason for their own sexual desire. He understood that. But sometimes they actually believed it. He always tried to pull back gently from those *affaires*. It did not seem fair to tacitly accept a woman's love when he was not prepared to return it in any way. As he grew older he had learnt to recognise and avoid women likely to believe they had fallen in love, and he had been careful not to use the word *love* as an endearment. Nor to call what happened in bed *making love*. Sex was safer. Less open to misinterpretation.

He could not avoid Christy, though, and all his rules had flown out the window. He had called her *love*. The word had just come out, and he had called sex *making love*. Now he had to explain as gently as possible the terms of their marriage. After all, a marriage of convenience would be the safest thing. For her especially, he told himself. As long as he could assure her that her response to him was nothing to be ashamed of, that it delighted him, and she did not need to excuse it in any way.

I love you...

But the memory of the words, her sleepy, unfocused voice, pierced him. It was highly unlikely that she meant it. Making love—having *sex*—could be like too much to drink. One could find oneself saying and doing things one would not dream of normally. She might not recall saying it in the morning.

He should return to his own room. That was what one did

in a marriage of convenience…he yawned and her fragrance sank deep…one bedded one's wife and returned politely to one's own bed to sleep. His eyes drifted shut…he supposed he ought to leave…rolling towards her he hooked an arm around her waist, drawing her against him. She came with a sigh and a wriggle, all soft curves, and drifting curls tickling his nose. Brushing one aside gently, he breathed her sweetness and slept.

Sleeping with her had been a mistake. He'd meant to make an early start. And he had. Only it hadn't involved getting out of bed. He hadn't meant it to be like this.

Like what?

This…this warmth. The pleasure of looking forward to her company on the journey. The remembered intimacy of lying with her this morning, her silken body snuggled against him, limp with pleasure.

This was dangerous, Julian realised as he handed Christy up into the curricle. Bedding her, yes, but not sleeping with her. And he'd intended to ride today while Christy travelled in the coach. Somehow he had to create some distance between them. But she had barely touched her breakfast and he'd remembered her tendency to carriage sickness. Her unwillingness to make a fuss about it.

'Thank you,' she said, smiling down at him as she settled her skirts.

His wits fractured and he dragged in a breath.

Lust. Reduce everything to its component parts, and she was an attractive, innocently sensuous, responsive woman. He'd have to be dead not to desire her. But that didn't explain the aching tenderness, or splintering joyous agony of holding back to ensure her pleasure. Oh, he'd always been careful to please his partners. That was only fair. Part of the exchange. And their pleasure also increased his own.

He stepped up into the curricle and nodded to his groom to release the horses.

It was not like that with Christy.

He wanted *her* pleasure. For *her*.

Duty and his own gratified lust had little if anything to do with it.

He glanced at her as he set the horses in motion and guided them out into the lane. Her cheeks were softly flushed, and her mismatched eyes shone. His breathing shortened as he remembered those same eyes dazed and unfocused, the aftershocks of pleasure trembling through her this morning…and last night—those sleepy, haunting words…

I love you…

His blood surged and the horses snorted and tossed their heads as his fingers tightened on the ribbons. Quickly he eased the pressure on their mouths. He wasn't a green youth to be addled by a pretty smile or passion-induced declarations of love. He *had* to put this marriage on a proper footing. Bed was now satisfactory for both of them. Surely he could arrange everything else as neatly?

They liked—yes, *liked* and respected each other. The marriage would work, and it was time his bride—he stole another glance at her—understood how.

He drew a deep breath and began.

Christy listened to her husband's careful detailing of family finances, her gloved hands gripped painfully in her lap. He seemed quite unmoved as he explained his responsibility as head of the family to ensure everything was passed on intact to succeeding generations.

By marrying her he had made his task a great deal harder. Not that he had actually said that.

She glanced up at him. He was watching the road, as calm as though he had told her what he liked for breakfast. Not as though he had just explained why marrying her was the greatest mistake of his life.

She bit her lip.

He flicked a glance at her. 'You needn't look so downcast—I merely wished you to understand how things work.'

'We should not have married.' It was all she could say.

'I beg your pardon?' His voice was frosty.

'You can't afford me.'

The horses slowed.

'What the hell do you mean?' Anger incinerated the frost.

She struggled for the right words. 'When Harry insisted on that enormous settlement, and—'

'It was the right amount. What I would have provided for you without Harry's intervention,' he informed her. 'What do you mean—I can't afford you?'

'I brought nothing to the marriage,' she said. 'No dowry to provide for myself or my children. The money settled on me is money you should be using for your brothers and sisters. And for your property. Isn't it?'

His silence told her she was right, and she risked looking at him. He eased the curricle around a farm cart.

Safely past, he said, 'None of that matters. I didn't say I regret our marriage!'

No. He was far too polite. But it could not be far from the truth. From his explanation she had understood that what was left of Serena's dowry would provide for Lissy, Emma and the two boys. How were her own younger sons to be provided for? Where would *her* daughters' dowries come from? For Julian to hand on his lands and wealth intact he had needed a wealthy bride. Instead, he had her. Penniless, illegitimate Christy Daventry.

'How can you not?' she whispered. What a fool she was to have thought that what they had found together was something more than sex. And she had been fool enough to speak words he did not want to hear.

He pulled the horses into the hedge, transferred the reins to one hand and his free arm came around her. 'Damn it, Christy!

How can you believe that I regret it?' he demanded. 'After yesterday afternoon! And last night!'

She forced herself to meet the blue fire of his gaze, and swallowed, heating at the memory of his passion, her own passion leaping to meet it. The soul-wrenching delight as they made lo—

'You heard what I said last night, didn't you?' she asked painfully.

His mouth tightened. 'Yes. It's all right, Christy. You have never had a lover so you are unused to…physical pleasure. Naturally I understand why you said it, but it is not necessary.'

Nor wanted. Worse, it was actively unwanted.

'Then it is just…just—sex,' she said. 'Not—' She broke off, forced the choking lump from her throat and continued, 'You could find that with any woman.' Dragging in an aching breath, she added, 'You have always done so. I expect you will continue to do so. That was clear when you asked me to be your mistress and said that I should not be dismissed when you married.'

Blue fire froze to icy chips.

The arm withdrew and the horses were set abruptly in motion. She shifted away from him, not daring to look after saying something so shameless.

He drove on into the golden haze of sunshine and birdsong. The hedgerows towered above their heads, full of song and bustle. Beyond the hedges a cow lowed, a boy's voice called in the distance. It was all hollow—empty.

Eventually he broke the gaping silence. 'You are reconciled, then, to the possibility that I will be unfaithful to you?'

She fought the urge to deny it as heat mantled her cheeks. She did not have the right. She had known the truth before she agreed to marriage. 'Yes.'

'And will you be unfaithful to me?'

I am not hypocrite enough to demand something of my wife that I am not prepared to give in return. Once the succession is assured, she may please herself…

She was silent for a moment, trying to imagine herself in that situation. She couldn't imagine it. But what if Julian were to be unfaithful? Would she be able to imagine it then? Perhaps that was what marriage vows were for? To hold you firm when you *could* imagine such a thing. After all, her decisions about her behaviour were *hers*, were they not? Why should they be dependent on *his* behaviour? Those vows had been made not only to him, but to God.

'No. I do not intend it.'

He sent her a swift unreadable glance, but said nothing.

She gritted her teeth. He had not offered a similar reassurance. Nor would she ask. If he gave it, she would not believe him, and she would have pushed him into a lie to save her feelings. The one thing of value they had between them was honesty. She was not prepared to squander it.

Four mornings later Christy walked to the village for embroidery silks. She had spent the past two days receiving bride visits. News of their return had spread and it seemed everyone wished make the acquaintance of Amberley's new mistress.

She felt like a beetle pinned to a board for constant scrutiny. Oh, everyone was polite enough. Offering felicitations, saying how delighted they were to make her acquaintance—and all the while she could imagine the conversations once they were safely back in their carriages.

My dear! What did he see in her? No wealth! No connections! It's true, then? She trapped him?

Who had trapped whom? Did it matter? She was married. Safe. Secure. Her husband was kind to her. He was honest. Too honest to permit her to deceive herself with dreams of love.

He was being very careful to make his position clear. Despite coming to her bed each night to make—for *sex*, he did not remain afterwards. He bedded her passionately and skilfully, leaving her limp and exhausted with pleasure, and then he left. As though he wished to make sure his behaviour mirrored what he felt: nothing.

One day she might learn to be grateful for his honesty, rather than feeling as though a small piece of herself died every time he left her sleepless in an empty bed.

What mattered now was that they had an invitation to dinner the following night at Postleton Manor.

I should be delighted if you could attend, had gushed Lady Postleton. *It is not to be a grand occasion. Just a few people who would be honoured to make your acquaintance.*

The hypocrisy sickened her. *Not my acquaintance. It's the new Lady Braybrook they want...* Nothing would give her greater pleasure than to decline the invitation, but that was impossible. Julian had been pleased. *Good. You'll soon be established.* If they ever found out what she was, she would be unestablished in a heartbeat.

The bell jangled as she entered the shop and predictably Mr Wilkins greeted her with oily subservience, bowing low. To her annoyance he followed her around the shop, rubbing his hands together. By the time she left with her embroidery silks, having arranged the delivery of several dress lengths, she was urgently needing fresh air.

In the village street she saw Nan Roberts. On an impulse, she stepped across. 'Good morning, Nan. Are you well?'

Nan went pink, nodding shyly.

'And your mama? Is she well?'

Another shy nod. 'Yes.' Then in a rush of confidence; 'I've got a kitten. T'other Lady Braybrook gave her to me.' Nan bit her lip. 'You can come an' see her, if you like.'

Christy swallowed. Jane had been Braybrook's mistress. It might be awkward, but the child was looking up at her hopefully. It was not Nan's fault and Julian's previous *affaires* were none of her concern. She pushed away the thought that his future infidelities were also not to be her concern. 'I should love to see your kitten. If you are sure your mother won't mind?'

'Oh, no!' Nan assured her. 'Mam said you was nice.'

Which didn't necessarily mean Jane would welcome a visit. Christy thought Jane Roberts looked anything but pleased when she saw who had come to call, but she greeted her politely enough.

'Her ladyship wants to see my kitten,' said Nan.

Jane heaved a sigh. 'Does she now? Well, you find Puss quickly, then.

'You ought not to be callin' on me,' she informed Christy bluntly as Nan went off to find the kitten. 'Folks talk and his lordship won't like it.'

'If that's all that's bothering you, let me worry about it,' Christy told her. 'Has Nan had any more trouble?'

Jane shook her head. 'No. Thanks to you and his lordship. Didn't mean to sound unwelcoming, but I don't want trouble for you. Not after you were so good to Nan. But since you're here, you might as well come out in the garden. Should you care for tea or my blackberry cordial?'

'Oh, the cordial, please.'

Jane bustled about setting a small tray with glasses and a bottle of rich, dark cordial. Nan came back with a ball of wool and a tiny striped kitten, bearing a strong resemblance to Serena's Tyb. She showed the kitten to Christy with pride.

'She's all mine, an' she's going to keep all the mice an' rats away.'

'If she's ever allowed to walk anywhere, an' not carried and cuddled half to death!' said Jane wryly. 'Nan-love, you take her ladyship through to the garden, while I bring the tray.' Christy followed the child out into the small garden and sat down on a bench in the sun. Flowers and vegetables grew in garden beds and insects buzzed everywhere. At the end of the garden an old plum tree leaned against the wall, its leaves just beginning to turn. Nan took the kitten down there and played in the shade.

Jane poured a tumbler of cordial for each of them. 'I make this each year. No need to worry. It's not strong liquor.'

Christy sipped, tasting sunshine and blackberries as she watched Nan trailing wool for the kitten to pounce on.

'She loves that kitten,' said Jane. 'Good of her ladyship to bring it. She's always been kind, despite things.'

Christy said nothing. Of all women, she couldn't imagine Serena holding Jane to account because of Julian's affair with her. She just wished there was more she could do for Nan and Jane.

She turned, trying to think of something, something to say, to offer…and saw the wasp on the edge of Jane's tumbler. She reached out to knock it away, but it was already at the other woman's lips.

'Jane—!'

With a gasp of pain Jane dropped the tumbler and batted at her mouth, knocking the wasp away. Angrily it buzzed back and Jane cried out again. And again.

'Mam?'

'It's all right, Nan,' called Christy. 'Just a sting.'

She looked back at Jane. It wasn't all right. Jane's mouth looked queerly misshapen. Swollen. Swelling further as she watched.

'Jane! Does that hurt? Can I fetch something?'

The woman felt her mouth and looked dazed. 'Hurts,' she said in a queer constricted voice. 'My throat…can't swallow properly…'

Her throat… Christy felt the blood drain from her face. 'I'll send Nan for the doctor.'

Dr Wharton stared down at Jane Roberts, now fighting for breath, her face and throat impossibly swollen. 'Good God,' he muttered, bending over the bed. Christy had assisted Jane inside and applied a cool compress, but it hadn't helped. Jane was losing consciousness now as she wheezed, her face purple.

'A wasp, you say?' said the doctor.

'Yes!' said Christy. 'It was on her cordial glass.'

The doctor swore under his breath. 'There's nothing I can do,' he said. 'I'll stay with her until it's over. Keep the child out.'

Christy stared. 'What? Until…' Her stomach lurched. 'She's going to die?' she whispered.

The doctor nodded. 'Some people react badly to wasp or bee stings. Especially around the mouth and especially if it stung several times. I've seen it twice before.'

Jane's eyes opened, dazed, terrified. Her mouth worked, but only a desperate wheezing came out. Her tongue was impossibly swollen. She tried again, a frantic, choked sound, her eyes clinging to Christy's.

Christy knew what she was trying to say. What she herself would be frantic about if she were Jane. She went to the side of the bed and took Jane's hand. The woman clung with shocking, dying strength. Her own eyes blurring with tears, Christy choked, 'I know, Jane. It's…it's all right. I swear I'll keep Nan safe for you. Is that it?'

The dying woman nodded, tightening her grip.

'She will be safe,' repeated Christy. 'I'll look after her.'

Jane squeezed her hand again and then released it.

Christy looked up at the doctor.

'Go,' he said. 'You can do nothing more.'

Chapter Eighteen

A quarter of an hour later Dr Wharton came out of the bedroom, his face grim. Christy's unspoken hope faded. Nan, clinging to her, burst into tears at the doctor's expression and Christy held her, conscious of her own tears. There was nothing she could say.

'I'm sorry,' said the doctor. 'There was nothing to be done.' He looked at Christy and the sobbing child in her arms. 'Kind of you to ease her worries, but I'm aware of how embarrassing this could be for you. I'll make arrangements for the child, Lady Braybrook. No need to concern yourself. An orphanage will take her if her mother's family won't do it. My housekeeper will look after her tonight and I'll see to it all tomorrow.'

Sick understanding came to her, as Nan's grief-stricken sobs redoubled.

'You misunderstand, sir,' she said, rising to her feet with Nan still in her arms. 'Those were not empty words to comfort a dying woman; I meant it. By all means speak to Mrs Roberts's family, but unless Nan's maternal relations can provide her with a safe and happy home, she will remain with me. If…if you would speak to the Vicar to…to arrange the funeral? I will send a servant to collect Nan's belongings. She will come home with me now.'

The doctor's eyes widened. 'Ah, Lady Braybrook, it may…er, have you fully considered? His lordship—!'

The door crashed open, and Christy, her arms full of the still-weeping child, turned to find her husband in the doorway.

'What the devil is going on?' he asked. 'The village was full of some story that Jane is ill. Christy?'

Wharton stepped forward, his face stiff with embarrassment. 'My lord—a most tragic occurrence, but I fear her ladyship does not quite—'

'What tragic occurrence?' snapped Julian.

'Mam! Mam!' sobbed Nan.

A queer look crossed Julian's face and his hand stretched out to the child. 'Nan?'

Doctor Wharton spoke again. 'Jane Roberts is dead, my lord.'

The hand fell. Julian turned to the doctor, his face white.

'Dead? How?'

Christy intervened. Nan did not need to hear the details. 'My lord—is your curricle outside?'

'My—?' He looked at her. 'Yes. Yes, it is.'

'Good. Nan and I shall await you in it. Please bring her belongings and don't forget the kitten.'

His jaw dropped. 'Bring her—'

Doctor Wharton flushed. 'As I was saying, my lord, her ladyship does not comprehend the, er, *delicacy* of the situation. I can make all arrangements for the, er, *housing*—'

Christy moved towards the door and Nan, realising, screamed, *'Mam! I want Mam!,'* fresh tears pouring down her face. Christy's eyes burned as she held Nan securely, her own voice choking on useless words of reassurance. What comfort could there be? She stepped out into the small garden strip. It seemed impossible, wrong, that the sun still shone, that a blackbird was whistling in carefree abandon.

Julian's groom, Twigg, stared at them in surprise and Christy noticed a gaggle of curious villagers standing at a distance. She ignored them and went to the curricle.

'Stay at their heads,' she told Twigg, and lifted Nan to the seat, stepping in after her and lifting the child back into her lap. All she could think was that the child needed to be held. Her screams had died to a low sobbing, and she lay limp in Christy's arms, her face stained and her eyes reddened.

A short time later, Julian came out with the doctor. Between them they carried a small trunk. In addition, Julian held a small closed basket. The trunk they placed in the boot, but Julian handed the basket up to Christy. It yowled indignantly.

'The kitten,' he said in an expressionless voice.

Nan stirred at that and Christy spoke gently. 'Best to leave Puss in the basket so we don't lose her on the way home.'

In the act of stepping into the curricle, Julian looked at her sharply, but said nothing. Nan nodded, and lay, silent now, in Christy's arms.

'You'll make the funeral arrangements with the Vicar, then, Wharton,' said Julian. 'You may leave the rest in my hands.'

Wharton nodded. 'Yes, my lord.'

'Let 'em go, Twigg!'

'Where is Nan?'

Julian didn't turn around as he asked this question, but continued staring out of the window unseeingly. After arriving home he had told Christy to see to Nan and then to come to him in the library. That had been an hour ago.

'In the nursery. It seemed the best place for her.'

He turned, and his chest constricted at the pain in her white face and red-rimmed eyes. He braced himself to deliver the blow she must be expecting.

'Christy—this was unwise. She cannot remain here.'

Her eyes sparked defiance. 'Then Nan is unfortunate in her father!'

A blow straight to the heart of the matter.

Grimly, he reminded himself that his wife should have no say in this. He didn't even owe her an explanation—least of all an explanation she was almost certain to dismiss as a lie. And yet…

'You're quite correct,' he said quietly. 'Nan was unlucky in her father, but, contrary to what most people believe, she is not my daughter.'

Christy's eyes widened in shock. 'Not—?' she began. 'Oh, *please*—!'

He steeled himself against the bitter disbelief. Pain banded his heart. There was no reason for her to believe him. He did not doubt that in the end she would accept his word, but in the meantime—

'Your *father*?'

The icy bands around his heart snapped, and his fist clenched on the table.

'You believe me?' he asked.

'Yes,' she whispered. 'You've never lied to me. Not once. Why would you lie about this? To me of all people?'

He sighed. 'Yes. Nan is my half-sister,' he said. 'But most people believe her to be my daughter. You remember Jane was married to a farmer? His second marriage and he had three daughters by his first wife. Jane's marriage was barren. Naturally Tom blamed her.'

'How surprising,' said Christy with more than a touch of sarcasm.

Julian continued to explain. 'The fellow did have three daughters from the first marriage, remember.'

Christy didn't respond.

This was the tricky bit. 'Has Serena told you much about my father?'

She shook her head. 'No. I've, er, gathered he was somewhat autocratic.'

'He was indeed,' said Julian.

'A family trait, perhaps?'

Ignoring that, he went on. 'He was one of the old school. A good man, though, and after Serena's accident when the doctors said it would be extremely dangerous for her to have any more children, naturally he looked elsewhere for his—' He stopped, unable to think of a polite way of putting it.

'Amusements?' suggested Christy. 'Entertainment? I've noticed men do tend to think of women in those terms.'

Stung, Julian said bluntly, 'Shall we say sexual release, then?' Dammit! Did she believe he thought of *her* as entertainment?

She blushed crimson, but her chin lifted a notch. 'If you wish. It is at least honest. Do please continue.'

'My father had an affair with Jane and she became pregnant. She told him she was pregnant, and broke off the affair. Neither of them was particularly concerned. In fact, it was impossible to know for certain then who *had* fathered the babe. Jane was married, Tom still bedded her regularly and he was cock-a-hoop to think he'd finally got her with child.'

'And when Nan was born? What did he think then?'

'He was dead,' Julian told her. 'Nan was born in the winter, and he had died in a tree-felling accident the previous autumn. Under the circumstances, and Tom having been one of our tenants but with no son to take on the farm, my father provided for Jane with the cottage and a pension. When he died three years ago, I continued the arrangement. But by then it was obvious that Nan could not be Tom's daughter.' He hesitated. 'The resemblance—'

'Is remarkable.'

'Since Jane was my father's only indiscretion for many years, people assumed I was the father. My father asked me to let it stand.'

'Why?'

'He was fond of Serena. He didn't want her to be hurt, especially after her accident—and everyone assumed me to be responsible anyway.' he shrugged. 'My reputation helped.'

'And Lady Braybrook?'

'I assume she believes Nan to be mine.'

'I see.' She was silent for a moment. 'But this makes no difference. She is your half-sister instead of your daughter. As much your sister as Emma or Lissy.'

He had to make her see what it would cost if she kept the child. 'Christy, we are to dine at Postleton Manor tomorrow. Can you imagine the conversation? By then people will know of Jane's death, that you were with her and have taken her daughter. If you keep her, then people will whisper that I thought no better of my bride than to ask her to raise my by-blow! There has been enough talk about our marriage without that!'

She went white and an appalling silence echoed.

'And I suppose,' she said after a moment, in unconvincingly calm tones, 'someone might even discover that you had been obliged to marry someone else's by-blow?'

The ugly word festered between them.

'Damn it, Christy—I didn't mean it like that.' But how the hell *had* he meant it?

She appeared to share his scepticism. 'Oh? I wouldn't have thought there were so very many interpretations,' she said quietly. 'You will excuse me, my lord. I ought to return to Nan.'

Gritting his teeth, Julian managed a brief nod and watched as she left the room. Would Serena be able to talk sense into Christy? Make her realise the gossip she would face with her position already so precarious. Curse it! He was trying to protect her!

If he could arrange a decent home for the child…a decent home with Jane's brother and his wife. Carter was a good, upright fellow, if a trifle unbending. His wife was known for her good works, and they had older children. Nan would be safe with them. God knew he wanted her safe as much as Christy did. He could provide a weekly sum for her upkeep, even a capital sum in trust to serve as her dowry… He'd arrange it now and send for the Carters. If Christy met them, surely then she would see it was for the best.

And why the hell was he even hesitating? It was his decision and it *was* for the best. Particularly for Christy. He strode over to his desk and sat down, pulling paper and the standish towards him. He'd settle this here and now. A groom could deliver his letter and wait for a reply.

Christy found Nan still huddled in the chair she had left her in with the kitten sleeping in her lap, petting it, her face blank. Beth got up from her own chair as she came in.

'She's not said a word, m'lady,' whispered the maid. 'Just sits there stroking the kitten.' She shook her head. 'Poor little thing. What'll happen to her? Tisn't like anyone will want her, what with all the talk.'

Something inside Christy that had been close to breaking, stiffened, hardening into renewed resolve. *I want her.* 'Nan will be cared for.' She said it firmly, strongly. As much to convince herself as anyone else. She had given Jane her word.

'Shall I fetch some mending, m'lady?' offered Beth. 'I could sit with her a bit. She shouldn't be left alone, should she?'

'No, she shouldn't,' agreed Christy softly. 'I'll stay...' She hesitated. 'Fetch that mending, Beth. It would be nice to have someone to talk to, or I might have to leave.'

Beth dropped a curtsy and left.

How did you comfort a child whose mother had just died? She noticed the untouched bread and butter on the table. 'Do you want your bread and butter, Nan?'

A quick shake of the black head, but she said nothing. Only the small hands moved, stroking the kitten.

There were toys in the room, a plethora of them. A large, battered, dapple-grey rocking horse. In one corner stood a col-lection of wooden swords, ranging from quite well-carved efforts to a very simple one consisting of a short piece of wood nailed at right angles to a long one. A table with a dolls' house, elegantly furnished. An old Noah's Ark. A bookcase stuffed with books. Here were dreams and fantasies for a dozen children. But not this little girl whose small, safe world had fractured into nightmare.

Christy looked around desperately. *She* didn't know what to do. What did she know about small children? There had been Sarah...what had she done when Sarah had been sad? She had held her. Let her know she was safe and secure. And when Sarah had died, her small frame racked with fever, she and their mother had held her then too. So there should be someone to hold Nan. Someone to comfort her. What was God *thinking* to do this to the child? If He was going to take her mother, then He damn well should have provided someone else for her!

He had provided Christy.

So she walked to the chair, bent down, lifted Nan into her arms and sat down. There was a moment's frozen stillness and then Nan fought her, screaming, the unnatural calm broken into glittering shards. Shocked, the kitten leapt to life, scuttling for cover under a table.

Christy hung on, ignoring the feet battering her shins, holding the child's arms close to her body, speaking softly...nonsense... anything...aware her own tears had escaped, that she was crying as hard as Nan and that something inside that she had tried to hold inviolate had shattered irrevocably. And it hurt far more than she could have possibly believed.

Running footsteps sounded and Beth burst into the room, her eyes wide.

'Oh, m'lady! Here—I'll take her!'

Christy shook her head. 'No. I'll manage.'

At last Nan had fought and struggled herself into exhaustion and lay limp and sobbing in Christy's arms. Christy just held her silently, stroking the tangled black curls with a shaking hand. She had no more reassurances to whisper, and Nan seemed not to need it. The storm had passed for now and the child drifted towards sleep, the small body growing heavier in Christy's arms.

Beth who had sat quietly in a corner occupied with the mending, looked up.

'Asleep, is she?'

Christy nodded.

'Likely she needed that.'

'Yes.' She had screamed and raged after Sarah's death. At their father. Blaming him. For everything. For her life. For Sarah's life. Even for Sarah's death, which had certainly not been his fault. And hating him for not caring enough to attend the funeral. For being more concerned about appearances. He had ignored her after that.

Beth spoke again. 'I made up Miss Emma's old bed. It's all ready. No need to undress her. Just slip her shoes off. Even popped in an old dolly of Miss Emma's. Something to cuddle.' She shrugged. 'Better'n nowt.'

'Yes.' Bracing herself, Christy rose, Nan a limp weight in her arms. Together she and Beth tucked Nan safely into bed and stood looking down at her.

'You'll sit with her, m'lady?' Beth asked.

'Yes.'

'I'll fetch some tea for you. Anything else?'

She started to refuse, then a picture on the wall caught her eye. A portrait. Rather amateurish, but recognisably Serena. Without answering, she stepped closer. It was signed, *ET*— Emma Trentham.

'Yes. Yes, there is something, Beth. My sketching things.' Before memory faded for her or Nan.

It was dark before she had finished and the lamps were lit. Beth had brought her meal on a tray along with some soup for Nan, who had woken for long enough to be changed into a nightgown and tucked back into bed after having the soup.

She had fallen sleep clinging to Christy's hand, the kitten on the pillow beside her. Eventually the viselike grip had eased and the small hand relaxed on the covers. Now Christy sat staring at her sketchbook, knowing it was inadequate, but unable to do better.

'Will you remain here tonight?'

The deep quiet voice from the doorway startled her, so that she nearly dropped the book.

'Yes,' she said turning to face her husband's disapproval. He didn't look particularly disapproving just now, but he'd made his attitude clear that afternoon. 'She's only a little girl. Someone should stay with her.'

'One of the servants—'

'She trusts *me*.'

His mouth twisted. 'Sensible of her. Your maid told me what happened. Are you all right? She didn't hurt you?'

She thrust away the warm little feeling of delight that he'd asked. Duty. Cold, hollow duty. 'I am quite uninjured, thank you.' The sin of *her* birth could be hidden. Nan's couldn't. That was the only difference.

He came and squatted down beside her chair, reaching to cover her hand with his. His presence nearly overwhelmed her.

'You're sure? Your maid said the child was beside herself.'

The warmth of his hand stroking. He was only touching her hand, yet the gentle caress awoke other memories in her body. Fingers sliding on slick, wet flesh, seeking the hot, fierce joining of their bodies... It was only sex. It was not important and she was a fool to wish otherwise.

'Christy?' His lips spoke her name, but all she could think of was the dark, heated demand of his mouth on her breasts. Her own hunger answering his. And the longing and hunger that he did not answer.

'I'm perfectly all right,' she managed. She tried to focus on Nan, asleep in the bed.

'What's that?' Before she could stop him he had twitched the book from her lap and was examining her truly dreadful portrait of Jane Roberts. She had only met Jane twice and those last terrible memories had kept intruding, so that she had finally given up in despair. Just as she had with the sketch of Sarah... It was as like Jane as she could make it.

Julian was utterly silent as he looked at the sketch. Silent and unnaturally still. Would he understand why she had done it? To give Nan a way of remembering Jane clearly and knowing that someone else remembered her mother?

He handed the book back to her and stood up.

'Did you draw Sarah?'

Her throat ached. 'Yes. Before I could forget.'

Something passed across his face.

'I sent for Nan's aunt and uncle. They will come tomorrow. They are willing to take her.' His voice was distant and expressionless.

Pain sliced soul deep. She was going to fail in everything, then?

He went on. 'No doubt you will wish to meet them, assure yourself they will care for the child.'

Soothe my conscience? 'Thank you, my lord.'

He frowned, but did not correct her. Instead he reached out to stroke Nan's cheek with a careful finger. She didn't stir, but the sleepy kitten yawned pinkly and dabbed at his hand with a lazy paw. He touched it with that same finger and straightened.

'Goodnight, Christy.'

'Goodnight, sir.'

He left the room and she heard his swift strides on the bare boards of the nursery, the sound of the outer door closing behind him. He was gone, and she wasn't going to cry. She *wasn't*, curse it!

Julian forced himself to focus on his agent's report. He had an hour before the Carters could be expected and he ought to spend the time profitably. Workers' cottages. Needing repair. Before winter. Estimates of cost. Which had to be balanced against the money he had available for the repairs. It could be managed. With Serena remarried, the estate no longer provided for her.

But his thoughts refused to focus. He'd scarcely slept. Without Christy his bed was cold and empty. Which was ridiculous! It was no emptier, or colder than it had been before his marriage. It was exactly the same bed, with the same blankets and exquisite linen. Not to mention the same richly embroidered counterpane. Besides which, Christy had never been in his bed. He'd been going to her bed and returning to his own to sleep. Or not.

It wasn't only last night he'd slept badly. He kept waking and reaching for her in the night. When had he ever done that after leaving a woman's bed? When had he ever wanted to hold a woman—just hold her—while she slept? Why was everything suddenly so damned complicated? If only Christy would fit into the neat little box labelled 'wife'.

What was she doing this morning? He assumed she was still with Nan. He shut his eyes, trying to banish the image of his wife sitting by the sleeping child's bed. Of course Christy would sympathise with Nan's predicament. But it didn't alter reality.

He shoved his chair back from the desk and stood up. Why was he so on edge about a simple question of duty? He was doing the right thing in ensuring Nan's well-being. He was being generous in making a financial settlement on her. Providing a separate allowance to her aunt and uncle for her upkeep was more than generous, and adding a little extra as an incentive for them to treat her well was more than anyone would expect of him.

Except his wife.

He understood that. With her experience she did not see things in the same way.

Coldly?

Rationally. The solution she had proposed was unthinkable.

No. Not unthinkable. Royal bastards have always been well provided for.

I'm not royalty, and she isn't my daughter!

No. She's your sister. And it didn't matter a damn to Christy when she believed Nan was *your daughter.*

That in itself staggered him. Believing Jane to be his ex-mistress and Nan his daughter, Christy had still befriended them.

He walked over to the window, staring out at a blustery day. He was doing the sensible thing. The right and proper thing. Only he couldn't forget the blank, shuttered expression in Christy's eyes as she applied the term *by-blow* to herself.

By-blow—with all it implied. Tainted. *Filius nullius*—a child with no legal existence. Better unborn. Or dead. Like her sister.

He saw again Nan's pale face against the pillow, her eyes red-rimmed, and Christy sitting beside her. His Christy, sweet and affectionate. So blazingly honest and independent. Did he really want to contemplate his world without Christy in it? It might have been an easier world... No—it was too late for that. Christy was his.

I love you...

The opening door interrupted his churning thoughts.

'The Carters have arrived, my lord.'

His gut clenched. 'Show them in, please, Hallam. And send a message up to her ladyship asking her to bring Miss Nan down.'

'Certainly, my lord.'

A moment later the Carters were ushered in, dressed in what Julian assumed to be their Sunday best. Prosperous. Respectable.

Julian knew them by sight and reputation. Carter was Sir John's tenant, not his. He knew them to be well thought of. Upright. Decent.

He went forwards, holding out his hand. 'Carter. Mrs Carter. Thank you for coming. Please sit down. Lady Braybrook will be down shortly.' He hoped.

Carter frowned. 'Very kind of your lordship.' His wife murmured her agreement, and they sat down on a sofa, perching on the extreme edge and looking excessively uncomfortable.

'Please accept my condolences on the death of your sister, Mrs Carter,' said Julian politely.

The woman flushed and Carter spoke sharply; 'As to that,

it's all for the best, no doubt. We're decent, God-fearing folk, an' there's no denying that Jane—' He broke off, eyeing Julian in some trepidation. Julian said nothing, and Carter went on in a hard voice. 'Well, she's dead now, and a body shouldn't speak ill, but there's no cause for grief. The Good Lord moves in mysterious ways.'

Julian wondered if Carter felt God's wasp had left half the job undone. Hoping to reduce the tension, he began to talk about the harvest.

Carter was expounding his views on the advisability of planting more apple trees when the door opened and Christy came in, hand in hand with Nan.

While Julian had not expected Nan to rush forwards with shrieks of glee to greet her relations, it came as a kick in the gut to see her shrink closer to Christy's skirts at the sight of them. Shy, he told himself. She would adjust soon enough. But how did a child adjust to guardians who openly described her mother's death as divine retribution? He rose to present them to Christy.

The Carters greeted her civilly, but Julian caught the surreptitious and curious glances. Like the rest of the county, they were doubtless wondering exactly how she had prevailed upon him to offer marriage.

'And here is Nan,' said Christy, urging the little girl forwards gently. 'Come, Nan.'

Nan's murmured greeting tore at something in Julian. He smiled at her, but her eyes were downcast.

Carter grunted. His wife remained silent.

Christy's chin lifted. Julian stiffened, but her voice remained calm. 'She is a little shy at the moment. I am sure you understand her distress.'

Carter cleared his throat. 'As I was a-saying to his lordship, sometimes these things are all for the best. 'Tis hard on a respectable man to knowin' his sister-in-law isn't no better than—'

He caught Julian's eye and subsided. 'Well, mum for that. I'm sure your lordship has more important matters to see to. I understood from your lordship's note that you wish to put the girl under our care?'

Julian nodded, and said slowly, 'Yes. That did appear as the best solution.'

Carter's heavy shoulders squared. 'We'd best discuss ways and means, then. No denying it'll mean an extra mouth to feed.'

Christy spoke again. 'Mrs Carter—the care of Nan must come upon you. What do you think?'

Carter cleared his throat. 'Beggin' your pardon, m'lady, but I'm master in my own home,' he told her bluntly. ''Tis my decision, and no other's.'

'Carter!' Julian's voice slashed.

'My lord?'

'You will remember, Carter—Lady Braybrook's sole concern is Nan's well-being.'

Carter's face reddened. 'Beg pardon, my lord. I meant no disrespect.'

Julian nodded. 'Very well. Naturally I am prepared to contribute a weekly sum for Nan's board. In addition, a capital sum will be held in trust for when she weds, or comes of age.'

Carter scowled. 'Well, now. I don't say something for the girl's keep would come amiss,' he said. 'But there's no need for the rest. Setting her up over my own childer. Don't seem fitting somehow for a child like that.'

'Fitting?' Christy's voice had lost all semblance of gentleness, slicing into the sudden silence.

Mrs Carter spoke up. 'A child of sin,' she said. 'We don't need paying to do our Christian duty.'

Julian flinched. The word *duty* had never sounded colder. And Nan had shrunk back against Christy, as though someone had raised a fist to her.

'Of course not,' said Christy, her hand going to Nan's

shoulder. 'But St Paul believed that without charity, *love*, that is, even giving your body to be burnt would be an empty act.'

Mrs Carter's lips pursed. 'We've said we'll take the girl and do what's right,' she said in a low, hard voice. 'Bring her up strict among godly folks. 'Tis only right we do our best to make sure my sister's sin don't go no further. Look at that ribbon in her hair! Vanity!' She almost spat the last word.

'That ribbon,' said Christy, 'was her mother's last gift to her!'

Carter turned to Julian. 'Best we take the girl now, my lord. She'll forget quick enough.'

'No.' Christy's voice was sharp. Peremptory.

Julian took a deep breath. They couldn't have this conversation now. Not with Nan present.

Christy rushed on. 'A note came up from the Dower House, my lord. Your stepmother wishes me to take Nan to visit her. I sent a note back promising to do so.'

For a hastily concocted excuse, Julian thought, it was superb.

Carter frowned. 'Better not, my lady, beggin' your leave. Give the girl foolish ideas above her station. Best she comes with us now.'

'Aye,' said his wife. 'Start as we mean to go on.'

It made sense. Julian knew that. It was the sensible, rational way forwards, only—

'I am afraid my stepmother would have Lady Braybrook's head on a pike,' he said politely. 'And Nan's belongings will not be packed.' He couldn't believe he was saying this, and, judging by their expressions, neither could the Carters. 'I will send a message when all is arranged. Thank you again for coming. Let me show you out.'

Chapter Nineteen

When he returned to the library Christy was alone, sitting in a wing chair by the window.

'Where is Nan?' he asked.

'Don't you mean *the girl*, my lord?'

Never had he heard such bitterness in her soft voice.

'I sent for Beth to take Nan down to Serena, with a promise that I would follow.'

So it hadn't been an excuse.

'How *can* you?' she burst out.

'Christy—'

'How could you abandon any child, let alone your *sister*, to people like that?'

'The Carters are reputed to be honest, hardworking—'

'They didn't greet her, or speak to her. They didn't even use her name!' blazed Christy. 'Carter as good as said in front of her that Jane *deserved* her death! How do you imagine they will treat her? Even the ribbon in her hair was a crime!'

Anger flared. 'They will have me to answer to if she's not cared for!' he said. 'Once they understand their allowance is contingent—'

'Money!' she spat. 'Do you really think it can buy what Nan needs? Even if they don't mistreat her, how happy can she be if no one loves her? She's lost her *mother*! Don't you understand? You could settle a fortune on her, force people to be polite, fight a duel over it—and it would all be empty. Worthless!'

She stood up, her shoulders somehow slumped. She looked exhausted, defeated. 'You will excuse me, my lord.'

'Where are you going?' he asked sharply. The despair in her voice lodged deep inside him.

'To visit Serena,' she reminded him, walking towards the door.

Perhaps it was better to let her go and discuss the whole thing again when she was less upset. 'You recall we are to dine at Postleton Manor? We need to leave by half past four.'

'Of course, my lord.' She reached the door and looked back. 'If you believe me fit for such exalted company.'

'Hell's teeth, Christy!' he growled. 'That's ridiculous!'

'It is the truth,' she told him, opening the door.

'You're my wife!' he said.

She shivered. 'Yes. And perhaps it would have been much easier had that wasp landed on my glass, not Jane's.'

The door closed behind her with a terrible finality.

He'd read the blasted report and written instructions about the cottages. He'd been through his accounts and written a letter to Modbury about investing in shipping. He had responded to the Vicar's message setting Jane's funeral for the day after tomorrow. Bereft of excuses for avoiding the issue any longer, he shoved the standish away with unwonted force.

Did Christy really think he would have been relieved if she had been the one to die? Logic told him that she was hurt and had lashed out. But he had been the one to hurt her. And he was forced to admit a certain logic in her reasoning—her birth was, in truth, no better than Nan's.

But damn it all! He had defied her father, the Duke of Alcaston, condemned him for his behaviour to her...her father who had disowned her without ever speaking her name. Just as the Carters had not spoken Nan's name?

Was there nothing more binding them than duty and honour? And the passion they shared in bed? Was it just sex? She had said that the other day, and it had hurt, hurt unbearably. He had felt as though the world had emptied, become barren and void. What had Christy said to the Carters? It niggled at him—something about St Paul.

He pushed his chair back and strode over to the window, staring out over the parterres and park. From here he could see the Dower House, nestled in its trees. On the grass he could see small figures, faintly hear shrieks and yells as they batted the shuttlecock back and forth. Emma was there, with Matt and Davy. Not Nan. No doubt she was with Serena and Christy beneath that oak. He could see two people sitting there. The shade made it impossible to see properly, but he thought there was a smaller figure too.

Christy had said something about St Paul... He pushed the thought aside.

What the hell did he do now? Christy was right. He couldn't let Nan go to the Carters. His conscience wouldn't allow it. Would he have realised it if not for Christy? Without her he would have arranged everything at a distance. He might not have even seen the Carters in person. He had done that to reassure Christy.

And they were not bad people. Just unyielding. He did not think they would be intentionally cruel to Nan, but...he remembered his own confusion when his mother had left. No one had spoken of her. Her portrait had been removed and his father had ordered him to forget her. He hadn't. He'd just pretended to because it was easier. And then his father had remarried. He'd wanted to hate Serena, but that had proved impossible. Later, when the news came of his mother's death, it had been Serena who had comforted his forbidden, unspoken grief.

He'd been older. How could a little girl of five be forbidden to speak of her mother? Forbidden to remember her with love.

What had Christy said about St Paul? Irritated, he went over to the corner where the family bible was kept. He lifted it down, bracing himself against its weight and took it over to his desk. Lord, he was as bad as Ricky Blakehurst when a stray quote bothered him this much.

St Paul… He riffled through the New Testament. Something about love, or rather charity…he found it in Paul's letter to the Christians at Corinth…exhorting them to love…*if I have not charity…I am nothing…though I bestow all my goods to feed the poor…give my body to be burned, and have not charity…*

Charity. Love.

Hell and the devil! Not even the Vicar would interpret the passage in that way.

Christy had, though.

He went to stare out of the window again at the little group by the Dower House. There appeared to be some disagreement over the shuttlecock game. Davy was jumping up and down, a sure sign that he was cross about something.

From the chimney piece, a delicate chime rang out twice. He frowned. Two o'clock. Christy should be back soon if they were to leave on time. Perhaps he should walk down and bring them back.

How happy can she be if no one loves her?

The words flayed him.

Halfway across the park he realised that the adult under the tree with Serena was Havergal. Nan was there, sitting close beside Serena. She looked to be sewing and Serena was bending over her to guide and help, but Christy was nowhere to be seen.

She must have stepped into the house… He was within a hundred yards of the group when he noticed there was no chair set out for her. Davy had seen him and came tearing up, yelling and whooping.

'Have you come to play? Play on my side!'

Julian swung him up. 'Steady there. What are you up to?'

'Shuttlecock. Couldn't you *see*? Nan isn't playing. She's sitting with Mama and Uncle Nigel, because Mama says she's too sad.'

'Yes. I saw that. And where is your Aunt Christy?'

'She doesn't like being "aunt",' Davy informed him. 'She said to call her Christy.'

'And where is she?'

Davy wriggled and Julian set him down. 'I don't know. In the house? Are you going to play? Emma and I have been playing against Matt.'

'Perhaps.' In the house? Not very likely. If she were, Serena would be with her. Had she gone back to the main house already? But why leave Nan here?

'There's lemonade,' said Davy. 'Come and have some.'

Serena looked up, frowning as they approached. Havergal smiled, brandishing the lemonade jug. 'Your tipple, Braybrook?'

'Thank you, sir.' He smiled at Nan. She looked back gravely, saying nothing.

Serena said gently, 'You are doing very well, Nan. Keep the stitches nice and even, just like that.' She smiled at Julian. 'She is a far better pupil than Alicia and Emma were. Are you looking for Christy? She went for a walk. I am sure she will be back soon.' She reached for her parasol. 'In the meantime, you may take me for a walk.'

Havergal handed him a glass of lemonade, which Julian drained.

'Very well, Serena.' No doubt she was about to tell him why he could not permit Christy to raise Nan. She smiled, picked up her parasol and opened it.

Julian was used to pushing Serena's chair, but it was always disconcerting to converse with a pink, tasselled parasol.

They were barely out of earshot when she said calmly, 'I discussed the matter with Nigel, after Christy left, and if you really feel unable to take in your sister, she may come to us.'

Julian stared at the parasol's tassells fluttering in the light breeze. He supposed one day Serena might lose her power to shock him, but he couldn't imagine when. Hauling in a breath, he said, 'You *knew*?'

Hidden by the parasol, her expression could only be guessed at, but her snort was eloquent. 'My arithmetic is quite good, Julian. At the time Nan must have been conceived, you hadn't been anywhere near Amberley for months. In fact, I have letters from you in Paris for that period! Of course I knew. From the very first, as soon as I heard the talk. I asked your father and he admitted it. But he insisted that the story of your responsibility stood, because he didn't want me embarrassed.' She frowned. 'I didn't like it, but it wasn't hurting anyone, so I agreed.'

Good God!

All he said was, 'And you are prepared to raise her?'

The parasol snapped shut and Serena glared up at him over her shoulder. 'The person I was cross with was your father! Not Nan. Of course I'm prepared to raise her! Although I'd probably let the lie about her being your child stand. Then I'll appear a saint, not a fool. Naturally, if you and Christy are to keep her, we shall let the truth come out and I can be a martyr while you and Christy appear saintly.'

The idea that one day Serena might cease to shock him died a swift and painless death as he started to laugh helplessly.

'The trick, dearest, is not to give people the least reason for thinking *you* are at all perturbed by the situation,' she told him, putting up the parasol again. It twirled, tassells aflutter. 'Once you have decided, let me know. For now I suggest, since you and Christy are to be out for dinner, that you leave Nan with me. The poor child will be better for some company. Christy's maid may bring some things down for her.'

'Very well,' said Julian. 'I will think about it.'

The parasol twitched. 'Well, make sure you do think. Don't just take your prejudices out for exercise. That isn't going to help your marriage either. Now you may take me back to Nigel and Nan. And then you had best return to the house. I'm sure Christy will not be far behind. She had her watch in her pocket.'

But she did not return. By three-thirty Julian was concerned. Half an hour later he was panicking. They ought to be leaving soon. Where the hell was she?

He stared at Twigg. 'You're sure she isn't in the park?'

'Aye, me lord. Looked everywhere, we have. I've sent lads down along the river, but—'

Julian didn't hear the rest. The river. She didn't swim very well. If she'd fallen in… No. This might be her way of avoiding the dinner party. She'd been upset, suggesting he must believe her unfit to be in such company. She was angry with him. His fear eased a little.

'Bring Conqueror around,' he told Twigg. 'I'll look for her myself.

Four hours later, he hadn't found any trace of Christy. His voice was hoarse and fear crawled coldly in his veins as he stared around a clearing he had already been through twice— she might be home already. He needed to check. Wheeling Conqueror, he pushed him into a trot, heading for Amberley.

Reaching the edge of the woods, he rode out into the park and stared across the tree-studded expanse at the house. Dark against the deepening sky, it stood ablaze with lights.

If she hadn't returned, he'd go out again. But where? The forest was huge, stretching for miles. If she had left the path in there… His stomach churned. They might never find her.

He pushed the gelding to a canter. He was a hundred yards from the house when a yell went up. Hope unsheathed itself again, slicing at him, as he saw one of the undergrooms running towards him from the stables.

'My lord! She's here. Just gone up to the house!'

He had Conqueror in a flat gallop within six strides. He pulled up beside the lad and flung himself from the saddle.

'Is she hurt?'

The groom took the bridle and said cheerfully, 'Don't think so, my lord. Just went for a walk in the woods, she said. She's got a—'

He didn't hear any more. He was running for the house.

She'd been in the woods. And, having frightened him half to death, she'd reappeared too late to attend the dinner party.

He strode into the house by the side door and met Hallam. *'Where is she?'*

Hallam eyed him with some misgiving. 'In the Hall, my lord. But I think—'

What Hallam thought he didn't wait to find out. His whole mind was occupied by the blistering reprimand he was going to give his wife the moment he saw her.

Curse it! He'd been worried sick, and she'd been hiding in the woods because she didn't want to go to a dinner party. Did she think he wanted to go, damn it? Not likely. All he wanted was a chance to—he slammed the lid down on his preferred alternative. Reprimanding his bride while wreathed in lascivious visions of seducing her would be damn near impossible.

He stalked into the Great Hall and found his bride crouched over something on the hearth.

'Where the devil have you been?' he roared.

Belatedly he noticed the presence of his housekeeper and an assortment of maids and footmen.

'Out.' Couched in deadly soft tones, the command encompassed all of them. His boots echoed on the stone flags as he approached his kneeling bride. It was tempting to think her submissive posture betokened an attitude of becoming repentance, but, knowing Christy, he could imagine nothing less likely.

Sure enough, she glared up at him as he approached. At least, he assumed she was glaring at him. With candlelight glinting off her spectacles and her thick hair collapsing half over her face, he really couldn't be sure. And somewhere in his confused and befuddled mind, part of him was relieved to see

* * *

Christy awoke, warm, safe and comfortable. She dozed, aware of nothing but the sensation of being cradled, cherished... She snapped awake to realise that she was in her husband's arms, her cheek resting on the nightshirt covering his broad chest, and her nightgown around her waist leaving her shamelessly exposed, with a powerful thigh pushed between hers and a ridge of unyielding male flesh pressed into her hip. She felt that strange softening inside—the ache of...emptiness?

She looked up and met a hot blue gaze. Her breath shuddered out and her whole body turned to honey.

'M...my—Julian?'

A queer look, almost revulsion, crossed his face. He pulled back, disentangling them, and adjusting his nightshirt.

Her cheeks fiery, Christy straightened her own nightgown, pushing it down around her legs where it belonged.

'I am sorry. I...I am not used to—that is, I must have forgotten you were there, and rolled over.'

He stared. 'No. I—' He broke off. Then, 'No matter. What would you wish to do this morning? Ride?'

Christy hesitated, wondering what *he* would prefer.

He reddened slightly. 'No. I suppose not.' He reached out to brush the backs of his fingers over her cheek. His mouth twisted. 'I'm sorry.'

Her face heated. 'I'm not...I'm quite all right.' That other ache deepened, intensified at the gentle touch of his fingers.

He looked unconvinced and drew back, saying, 'Tintern Abbey is close. We could walk there, or drive if you are tired.'

His tone was polite. Friendly, even. But distant. As though she were an acquaintance—not the woman he had spent the night with. As though they had not awoken in a warm, drowsy tangle. Yet there was that hesitance, an underlying concern in his voice and eyes.

It's all right. I'm not sore.

The words froze on her tongue. Ridiculous, but she couldn't say it. It was too intimate, entwined with another ache whispering hotly deep within her.

'Tintern would be lovely,' she said, sitting up. 'And I should like to walk.' Surely that would reassure him their wedding night had not crippled her?

Polite, friendly. That would be the rule for their marriage and her idiotic, romantic longings for *more* were to be squashed flat.

Polite and friendly. Considerate. Attentive. By the close of the day Christy knew she had nothing to worry about. Her husband was courtesy itself. And she had never felt more alone. Which was ridiculous. He had spent the entire day with her. Being kind. Friendly. And distant.

She stared at the closed door of her bedchamber. Now most definitely *her* bedchamber. Julian had spoken to Mrs Braxton and arranged another chamber. Ten minutes ago he had wished her a polite goodnight at the door and continued down the hall to his own room.

She felt as though she had intercepted a bucket of icy water. Surely she hadn't been secretly hoping he would come to her again? Oh, yes, she had. All day. And lying to herself. Pretending she didn't want him, as if in doing so she could prevent him from ever realising that he had married a wanton.

Chapter Sixteen

Christy awoke alone on their last full day in Monmouthshire. Just as she had each morning after the first day. Although they had spent at least part of each day together, Julian had not come to her again at night. He had begun teaching her to drive a gig, they had ridden and walked. In the evenings he had read aloud while she sewed. Last night she had played the old harpsichord in the parlour while he listened. In some ways she knew him better now. She knew what he liked to read, what music he enjoyed, and that he loved apples. She knew he cared for his tenants and looked on his rank as more responsibility than privilege.

She knew *things* about him. She did not know *him*. And it seemed that was how he preferred it. His very courtesy was a barrier between them that she did not know how to breach. Or even if she should. She had thought consummating the marriage would make things easier.

They were not. Several times yesterday she had caught him watching her surreptitiously, his gaze so intent she had wondered if she were doing something wrong, or had a smudge on her nose. And still he had politely bidden her goodnight at the door of her bedchamber and gone to his own room, leaving her restless and far from sleep.

And now she was awake in a grey dawn. She pushed back the covers and went to the window. Outside mist rose from the river and birds rejoiced at the day's return. It could not be much past five, but sleep was far away.

Further down the river the dreaming arches of the abbey soared above the mist, as though nothing could ever disturb the ivy-clad walls and tumbled masonry. Later the ruins would echo with the voices and laughter of visitors, as it had the other day. It would be different now, lying at peace in the misty curve of the singing river. There would be the same stillness and belonging she had found on that day high above the river. Before Julian had kissed her for the first time, and the world had changed for ever.

It was only a mile to the abbey. She would be back in time for breakfast at eight easily. If she went now, it would just be herself, the birds, the murmuring river and the mist.

Julian blinked as the slender cloaked figure hurried out through the damp garden below towards the river path. In the pale light she looked insubstantial, a creature of the mist and dawn.

Yet he knew, none better, that she was a woman of flesh and blood. Last night he had nearly gone to her, tempted by the siren lure of warm, yielding softness. He had resisted. She had seemed edgy, restless. He thought he knew why; all day he had been watching her, wondering if it were too soon to take her again. It had probably made her nervous.

He flung off his nightshirt, washed and began to dress. All week he had taken her about, walking, driving, riding. Frustration aside, he had never enjoyed a week more. Just being with her had been a delight. He had taken her down to Chepstow one day to explore the castle. She had loved it, even crying when he told her about the final siege when Cromwell's forces took the place and shot the commander on the spot.

Can we come again?

There probably isn't time this visit.

Next time?

He hauled on his boots and stood up. He desperately wanted a next time, but without this frustration and guilt. All week he had avoided the subject of that night. Ashamed of himself, worried it would embarrass her. Hoping it would sort itself out was idiocy. His was the experience, however illicitly gained. If anyone was to put this right, it would have to be him.

He followed her easily, her tracks clear on the damp path leading from the house towards the river. He thought he knew where she was going. The abbey would be peaceful now, before visitors arrived.

She was seated on a fallen block of masonry, her expression calm, distant, as though fixed on something beyond the river in its misty cloak. He hesitated, wondering if he should go back, or just wait until she returned from wherever it was she had gone.

Before he could step back, she swung around and her eyes widened as she came to her feet. 'My lord? Julian?'

She still found it difficult to use his name, despite the fact that hers came to his lips so easily. He walked towards her.

'Is something amiss?' She flushed. 'I suppose I ought not to be here alone—is that it? I am doing the wrong thing?'

He stared. Did she expect a scold? He supposed it was true enough—she ought not to be here alone.

'No,' he said. 'I was awake and saw you leaving the garden, but I just wanted to talk to you.'

'Oh.' She relaxed a little.

'You like it here?' He sat down on the block she had vacated, leaving room for her.

'Yes.' She sat down again. Perhaps he had not left quite enough room. She was very close. The fragrance that had haunted him all week wove around him, insubstantial as the morning mist.

'Christy?'

She looked up.

The stilted little speech died in his throat. Very carefully he lifted one hand, brushing the backs of his fingers along the line of her jaw, tracing her lower lip with a knuckle. Her lips parted and he heard the uncertain breath as her eyes widened.

Somehow his arms were around her and he bent his head and took the kiss he had not known he was aching for. With other women kisses had been pleasant, but not necessary. With Christy, he realised on a wave of tenderness, kisses were vital. Perhaps for both of them. Her lips clung, the sweetest invitation. He fought the urge to deepen the kiss. For now this was enough—warm soft lips trembling under his, her body pressed to his, her arms holding him. This was right. But before there could be anything else he had to find the right words. Gently he broke the kiss and rested his cheek on the top of her head.

'I wanted to apologise for hurting you,' he said quietly. They were not the words he had planned, but they came easily. Like the kiss, they felt right.

'Hurting me?' She pulled back a little and stared up at him.

Denying the need to kiss her again, he brushed his lips over her temple and pulled her back against him. Somehow feeling her relaxed and trusting in his embrace made this easier.

'The other night.'

A tremor ran through her and he held her closer. 'Exactly. I wanted you to know that when I…when we come together again, it will not be like that. It won't hurt again. You don't need to fear me. I'll leave it to you to decide when you wish to come to me.' She stiffened, and he pressed a kiss on her hair. 'No, you don't have to say anything. Just come to me. And I'll do my best to make it good for you. That's all. I'll leave you in peace now.'

He released her and rose. 'I thought I might fish today, if you do not mind. I believe Mrs Braxton was going to show you some of her special recipes?'

Christy nodded. 'Yes. This morning.'

He smiled. 'I'll see you at breakfast then.'

He walked away. And prayed he had said enough.

* * *

Christy spent a glorious morning in the kitchen with Mrs Braxton and had a notebook full of jams and preserves as well as stillroom recipes. She had been busy and occupied, but her mind kept drifting back to that early morning tryst. Julian's gentleness. The sweetness of his kiss, and the reason he had not come to her bed again. She should have overcome her idiotic shyness that morning a week ago. Told him in plain words that she was perfectly all right.

She thought about it after lunch as she set out for a walk. He thought she feared him. Physically. That their coupling the other night had left her unwilling. So he had stayed away from her and spent a week worrying that he had really hurt her because she had been embarrassed. She followed a path she knew led to a quiet backwater partially shaded with willow trees, hidden from the main river. It would be peaceful there, and she could think.

She didn't doubt he had told her the truth. One thing she could count on with Julian—he always gave her the truth. She might not always like it, but that did not diminish the value of the gift.

He had left the ball in her court. She would have to go to him, and tell him when she wished him to come to her again because he did not trust himself. Something else he had said shifted beneath her worry about *how* to tell him.

Just come to me. I'll do my best to make it good for you.

Those words thrummed through her with all the glorious promise of his hands on her body the other night, his mouth hot and demanding, his body burning against hers. Did he mean *she* was to enjoy it?

She came out of the woods into the clearing and saw the familiar, black horse grazing. Conqueror. And then she saw her husband standing on the bank, facing the river.

She gulped. Julian had been swimming. It was the only possible explanation for him to be dripping wet and stark naked.

She could always retreat. He had no idea she was there. But

she stayed, her gaze riveted to his back. That one night, what with firelight, bedclothes and her own shyness, she had not seen him properly. Not like this. Broad shoulders gleamed wet, tapering to narrow hips and the taut curve of his buttocks, the long powerful legs. She had not realised that beauty could be masculine, encompass such power. She had not equated beauty with strength. She did now, and her heart pounded as heat rose inside her.

I'll leave it to you to decide when you wish to come to me.

He hadn't meant here on the river bank, for heaven's sake! But she could tell him…tell him what? She reminded herself to breathe. It would be all right to tell him that she wouldn't mind him coming to her bed again. Tonight, perhaps? Could she manage that without making a fool of herself? Without letting him know the mere sight of him had that hot ache twisting in her belly, and lower.

He should return to the manor, but the sun on his back was glorious after the chill of the river. As long as no one came along. But this backwater was very much on his land. Screened from the main river, few people knew it was here.

Conqueror whinnied, and Julian turned to see what had disturbed him. And found his wife, her eyes wide with what he assumed to be shock. They widened even more as her gaze moved down his body.

Naturally he did the only thing possible. He slid straight back into the river.

The chill was as shocking as ever, but he managed to find his voice. 'Were you looking for me?'

'Er, no. Not exactly. I mean, I didn't know you were here, but I'm quite glad to see you.'

She'd probably seen a damn sight more than she'd bargained for.

'Are you going to swim again?' She came towards him.

He gritted his teeth. 'No. I was about to get dry.'

'Oh.' She stopped. 'Do you…should I go away?'

Something about her voice suggested she was deferring to *his* sensibilities. Not that he had many. Except he didn't want to frighten her and right now, despite his assurance that the next time would not hurt, the sight of him probably *would* frighten her. Which confounded all precedent. Never before had he been violently aware of rampant, hard-edged lust while standing up to his chest in a distinctly chilly river. Only, he didn't want her to go.

And she didn't sound as though *she* wanted to go.

'Pass me the towel and shut your eyes,' he said.

She did as he requested and sat down, closing her eyes obediently. Right where he planned to get out.

He heaved himself out of the water and dried himself quickly. And carefully. He'd never realised quite how erotic a towel could feel. Swearing silently, he hauled on his drawers and breeches, and discovered a new problem. While he had on occasion been wearing breeches when this problem arose, he'd never had to button them up around it before. He struggled on, desperately ignoring the muslin-clad temptation beside him.

Finally succeeding with the breeches, he reached for his shirt.

Temptation spoke. 'May I open my eyes yet?'

He shut his own eyes. She sounded exactly like a little girl with a present. He wondered if he would survive the experience of being unwrapped by her.

Swallowing raw desire, he managed to say, 'If you wish.'

He couldn't help watching as she opened her eyes. Watching as her gaze travelled over him, the oddest smile trembling on her lips. A smile that made him long to kiss her, feel her lips flower and part for him. He breathed deeply, fighting to retain his sanity, clutching his shirt. If he kissed her now, it wouldn't end as chastely as it had this morning.

His shirt. He started to put it on.

'You don't need to put your shirt on, do you?'

The shirt dropped, forgotten, as disbelief radiated through him.

She reached out, curious fingers skimming his shoulder, the light tracery on bare skin shafting fire straight through him. He braced himself against the urge to take her in his arms and kiss her senseless. To ease her down into the grass and make love to her until she moaned with pleasure. Need slammed through him in slow, hot waves, mounting with every heartbeat.

Jumping back in the river wouldn't help. After all, he'd got into this state standing in the water. Instead of dousing desire, there would be steam rising off the water.

'Julian?'

'Yes?'

'When you kissed me this morning—well, I liked it.'

His heart began to pound. 'Did you?'

'Yes. I…I always like it when you kiss me.'

'You do?' A slow, hot, heavy beat.

'Yes. So, would you…would you kiss me again? Now? Please?'

Would he…? As he reached for her, she removed her spectacles carefully, folded them and set them on a convenient log.

Julian was drowning. Drowning in her taste, the sweet, wild response of her mouth, yielding to the passionate demands of his lips and tongue; drowning in the delight of her pliant body shifting beneath him, rounded arms drawing him closer.

Shaken to the core, he caressed the curve of her hip under the flimsy muslin and discovered that his fingers were bunching the material, pushing it out of the way.

He shouldn't do this. Not here. Not now. But his body refused to obey the dictates of mind and conscience. Tenderly he kissed her, drinking the soft cry as he caressed the silken skin of one thigh. Easy, so easy to part her thighs, but if he did… No. He mustn't. Not here. He hung on to the sliding reins of control.

She opened to him anyway. He forced his fingers to stillness, struggling for sanity. Her hips lifted. Very slightly. Just enough for him to feel the silent plea. This was the response he had wanted from her. Here. Now. His. All his for the taking.

With a groan, he surrendered. To her desire, not his, his seeking touch finding a softness that blossomed in liquid fire as he caressed her with growing intimacy. And she touched him, shy hands exploring and discovering, curious fingers finding his nipples, lingering to tease when he groaned in aching pleasure.

This was the sweetest kiss he had ever known. And then he remembered.

Would you...would you kiss me again?

She had asked him to kiss her. Not seduce her! And she was so damned innocent, she didn't have the least idea what she was doing to him! Where this would lead. Furious with himself, he tore his mouth free and sat up, shuddering with the need to tear his breeches off, push her thighs wide and sink into her wet, scented heat. Instead he grabbed his shirt, hauled it over his head and began to do it up with clumsy shaking fingers.

'No more,' he said, frustration roughening his voice. He tried not to look at her, but even so there were scorchmarks on the remnants of his self-control.

Forcing himself to his feet, he took several painful strides towards the bank.

'Cover yourself,' he said shortly. God help him if he turned and saw her lying there, dishevelled from his lovemaking. He shook at the thought.

She was his wife. She deserved better than to be tumbled on a river bank when all she had asked for was a kiss, just because he had all the self-control of a rutting stag.

'I'm...I'm sorry. I won't do it again.'

He didn't dare look at her. 'Won't do what?'

'That. Here. I mean, I won't—'

Her voice broke and he turned.

'*Christy.*'

The sight of her quiet self-possession dissolved into tears

lanced through him and three strides had him beside her, all control shattered by the need to comfort her.

'Christy, sweetheart, it's all right. I'm sorry. I never meant it to go so far. You don't have to be frightened of me.' His voice cracked as he rocked her. 'No matter how much I want you.'

She wriggled free and faced him. 'You *do* want me?'

He nodded, not trusting his voice, desperately trying to banish the memory of Christy yielding beneath him in the fragrant grass, her mouth soft with his kisses... Helpless, his fingers traced the line of her throat, feeling the warmth, the flickering pulse leaping to his touch.

'Then, why did you stop?'

Why? Directness was the only possibility. 'I stopped because you had no idea what you were doing,' he informed her. No idea she'd reduced his control to smoking ruins.

She reddened. 'I know, but how...how can I know what pleases you, or...or how you want me to behave, if—'

'*What?*'

The small part of his mind retaining a semblance of rational thought observed that her blush had deepened.

'Christy, I didn't stop because I wasn't enjoying what you— what *we*—' Dammit! Now *he* was blushing!

'I was enjoying it so much,' he told her, 'that I was within about two heartbeats of taking you.' It might have taken him a little longer to remove his breeches, but not much.

'Then, you...you didn't mind that I...that I was enjoying what you—' The break in her voice turned him inside out. There was light now at the end of a very dark and mystifying tunnel. He had no idea what was out there in the light, but if he went just a little further, committed himself to chance—

'Christy—I loved that you were enjoying it.' Her eyes widened and it was as though he had opened a gift early, breaking it in clumsy greed. But then someone had taken the broken gift and wrapped it again, renewing it, giving him a second chance.

A humming silence spread around them in which the golden late summer air fizzed and sparkled, rippling like the river, alive with promise.

Then she said, 'Well, you did say this morning…and I…I suppose there must be worse places, must there not?'

His mouth dried. He had told her this morning that he would leave it to her to decide when she wished to come to him. And what did she mean by *worse places*? Was she deliberately…?

He forced himself to ask. 'Worse places for what, Christy?'

She looked at him uncertainly. 'You didn't mind?'

'No, I didn't. Trust me. Worse places for what?' he repeated, unbuttoning his shirt again, just in case he was right.

She reached out and fumbled with a button. His heart contracted.

'Worse places to…to…' She floundered to a halt, obviously uncertain of what to say, what to call it.

'To make love?' he suggested, capturing her hand and taking it to his lips, drawing her to him.

To make love. He had never used those words. Not to any woman. Always, always it had been sex. No more. But the words sounded right with Christy in his arms, just as kissing her was right.

She hesitated and his heart nearly stopped beating. 'Only if…I mean, it's not the sort of thing you expected of your wife, is it?'

His heart tried to catch up and failed. He hauled the shirt over his head and dropped it.

'No,' he said, easing her down to the grass. 'I have to admit it never occurred to me I'd be lucky enough to marry a woman who would seduce me on a sunny river bank.'

'And you don't mind? Even though I am your wife—'

Pardon?

'—not your mistress.'

Wife, not mistress?

The painful words rocked him to the core, the wound he had

dealt her laid bare. He heard his own cynical voice outlining the roles of wife and mistress—he had convinced her that a woman's passion was something furtive and shameful, only acceptable in a mistress. That in his wife it was unwanted. That *she* was unwanted.

'The only thing I mind,' he said, sinking on to the grass beside her and taking her in his arms again, 'is that I was such a damned fool. This is what lay between us, isn't it? You thought I didn't want you to be like this?'

'Yes.' The merest whisper, as though she could barely draw breath.

He took her lips, teasing the sensitive curves with his tongue until she opened to him and he could ravish the sweetness within. By the time he lifted his head she was soft and yielding, half beneath him, and his senses were reeling again.

Dear God. All he'd had to do was kiss her?

'You thought wrong,' he murmured, and kissed her again.

Dazed by his kisses, Christy was still aware as wickedly skilled fingers unbuttoned her bodice, that he had lifted her in his arms and peeled the muslin away, leaving her in her stays and chemise. She blushed, but it was too late for modesty. He had turned her and was loosening her stays. Heat flooded her at his hot breath on her nape, his lips brushing warmly over the curve of neck and shoulder and her lungs seized as he nipped gently at her ear.

'Julian—'

One arm slid around her, drawing her against him, still nibbling as he fondled her breasts. 'Do you want me to stop?'

'No. Oh, no,' she breathed. She no longer cared about being a wanton hussy.

The arm tightened, his tongue traced the curve of her ear and her mind and body melted in delight. 'Thank God.'

Moments later her stays and his breeches were gone and she was in his arms, only her chemise between them. He cupped one aching breast through the fine linen, his thumb stroking lightly over the urgent nipple. Lightning shot through her and she cried out, arching. This time there was no need to hold back.

Slowly he lowered his mouth to her breast and kissed it, his tongue laving the sensitive peak until the fabric clung wetly.

He drew the taut crest deep into the heat of his mouth, suckling gently, then, as she cried out in pleasure, harder before turning his attention to its twin while one hand slid down her body, sliding up under the linen to tease gently over her belly.

Shaking hands stripped away that last barrier. Caressing. Learning. Loving.

His hand moved lower, reaching between her thighs and her breathing fractured as he cupped her and stroked gently into slick, aching need. Pleasure, bordering on agony in all it promised, rippled through every vein in torrents of fire. And at the centre of it all a shattering emptiness, crying out to hold him within her. Her hips lifted involuntarily against the wicked play of his fingers.

His control quaked at the pleading dance of her body, all soft, wet temptation, burning him alive. Lifting his mouth from her breast with a groan, he gripped her hip, stilling her. 'No. Just lie still.' Any more and he'd be buried in her, and he wanted to take his time, make it right for her…

She tensed, pulling away, and he knew what he'd said. With aching care he brought her back, gathering her close. 'No, Christy,' he whispered, feathering kisses over her face. 'Not that. Never that. It's just…I want you too much.' He kissed her, his tongue plundering gently until she sobbed in need and her hips lifted again, seeking, urgent against his teasing fingers.

He lifted his head, breaking the kiss. 'I want it to be right for *you*,' he said, tightly, continuing to ravish the slick heat that lured him. Groaning, he slid one knee between her thighs, opening her, feeling the sweet tremors shake her body as he settled in the intimate cradle. He braced himself on one elbow, reaching down between their bodies to guide himself to her.

'Julian?'

He kissed her. 'Yes, sweetheart. You're soft, wet—do you want me?'

'Julian…oh, God! Yes. Please!'

'Where, love? Here?' He pressed carefully against the hot entrance.

'Yes, oh, yes. There. Inside.' Her voice broke as he pressed into her, feeling the clasp of her body.

'Slowly,' he whispered as his control shook, whether in reassurance, or to remind himself, he couldn't have said. He withdrew a little, waiting. And it came—the urgent lift of her hips, following his retreat. He hung on, shaking, as her response, hot liquid silk, welled up, her breath trembling on her lips.

Her eyes opened. 'Please…now,' she whispered.

He lowered his mouth to hers, consuming her soft pleas as they fell from her lips. One thrust, deep and true, and he lay buried to the hilt in her sweet sheath. And held utterly still as her cry stabbed into him.

Her eyes were shut tight, her breasts rising and falling in trembling breaths. He hung on to control as she softened, hot and sweet around him. Slowly her eyes opened again, and he saw the dawning knowledge, the realisation of him buried deep within her body.

'Christy,' he whispered. 'Oh, Christy.' This then was what he had wanted. He had wanted her to let go. Steel bands contracted savagely in his chest. He had been forced to let go first. Tenderly, he pushed back a tumbled curl from her face, threading his fingers in the silken skeins, and feathered his lips over hers.

There were no words to express how she felt. She didn't know what she felt. Never in her life had she felt so helpless, so vulnerable as she did lying impaled beneath him, her body captive to his. It did not hurt this time. She had trusted him that it would not. But she had not thought, had not realised, that feeling him so deeply within her, filling her so tightly, a *part* of her, might be joy itself. She had not thought desire could leave her shaking, frantic with need, longing only for his utter possession.

She had not thought it could feel like this—his weight a heated intimacy, mingling with his musky masculine scent, lean fingers tangled in her hair, his thumb clumsily brushing tears from her cheeks…all her nervous embarrassment gone, replaced by aching need, to feel him move within her, to move herself. To give until nothing was left, except the need to give.

She had not thought at all.

Certainly she had not thought to see her own vulnerability reflected in his eyes, or hear it in his voice as he soothed her, nor expected his hands to tremble as he cradled her face.

'Julian—' Her voice broke as he shifted slightly within her, fire streaking through every vein. She wanted, needed, more.

He stilled, tension pouring from him—evident in the flickering muscles of his shoulders, the corded tendons of his neck.

'Am I hurting you? Do you want me to stop?' His voice, harsh with restraint, pierced her to the core. She could hear the need in his voice—taut, hungry; see it blazing in his eyes; feel it in the minute, helpless shifts of his body, ravishing hers, melting her senses in fiery delight. Those tiny movements, splintering in fierce pleasure, told her what she needed.

'No,' she whispered. 'Never. I want you.' And shifted against him.

He was lost. The silken caress of her body raked him with fire. So hot and soft and tight around him. The chains of control snapped and his mouth came down on hers, taking her sobs of pleasure as he began to move, claiming her, urgent and possessive. Yet still, at the very depths of his desire, one gossamer thread held true, stretching, never breaking, binding him as surely as iron chains; he took her with a fierce tenderness he did not understand, and had never imagined could exist.

She had not known, had never imagined it could be like this, her body winged, frantic for release, as he possessed her deeply, irrevocably in a rhythm that sang with time itself. Above her, on her, within her, he took her spinning into the heart of fire. The very edge of madness.

She tried to hold back, her fainting reason crying out, warning her that from this point, if she went any further, there would be no going back.

He would not let her hold back. He took her to the brink and held her there, breaking, then went with her as she shattered, her body dissolved in delight.

Chapter Seventeen

He lay, Christy asleep in his arms, staring up through the sun-dappled green, hearing the hum of insects and the call of birds. A faint splash from the river told him a trout had risen. The air fizzed gently. Alive. Glowing. He felt part of it as he never had before. As though heaven and earth had contracted to the space occupied by their bodies and infused them.

Something nameless within him had broken loose.

His arms tightened, and she wriggled against him with a sigh, sending shards of rekindling desire splintering soul deep. Whatever it was that had got loose shook again. The other night she had given him her innocence. Today, here on the river bank, she had given him herself.

Neither of which gifts he deserved. Could they start again? Could they have the marriage he had always intended for himself? True, she had not brought any money to the match, but she was intelligent, caring. She was interested in the estates and his people. Now their misunderstandings were largely behind them, surely they could create a solid, rational union.

A wry voice suggested the passion unleashed between them had nothing to do with rationality.

* * *

Christy stared at the book in her lap. The pages might as well have been blank. Even though she was alone in her bed, everything was different now, wasn't it? She had come up half an hour ago. Julian had been reading a report sent down by his bailiff.

It had been such a lovely evening. They had talked. Really talked. She had asked him about this house and he had told her about all the summers he had spent here as a boy. About his friends. About himself. She knew so much more about him now. It was as though what had happened on the riverbank had breached his barriers. It was not just the lovemaking…

It never occurred to me I'd would be lucky enough to marry a woman who would seduce me on a sunny riverbank…

She blushed. Had she really done that?

No, it was not just the lovemaking, although it had been… She searched for a word—beautiful? Shocking? Exhilarating? All of that. But now there was an intimacy between them. Julian—his name came so easily now—was so much more relaxed, as though he had been on his guard before. She supposed the same could be said for her. Indeed, she knew it; making love like that left all of herself, all she kept hidden, exposed to him.

It was terrifying.

Because that complete, unreserved, nothing-held-back physical intimacy had revealed her own unacknowledged longings. For tenderness.

For love.

She was falling in love with a man who had married her only because he had to. Worse—only because *he* thought he had to. His world would not have cared a scrap about her fate. His sense of honour, the unexpected streak of kindness, disarmed her. He hadn't cared about the world's opinion. Only his own.

He didn't love her. She must remember that. Only his tend-

she wasn't cowed. There was not the least hint of fear in her attitude.

Then he got a good look at the state she was in, and forgot all about whether or not she was glaring at him. His prim and proper, never-a-hair-out-of-place bride was a complete and utter mess.

Quite apart from her dishevelled hair, her cambric walking dress was torn and looked as if she had been lying face down in the mud. Her arms were scratched and filthy, and her hands—he blinked—she looked as though she had been digging with them. They were black, the nails, or what was left of them, encrusted with dirt. Fear lashed through him, all the worse for knowing it was too late for him to do a damn thing about whatever trouble she had landed herself in.

'What the *hell* have you—?'

The whimper stopped him cold, and he saw the dog. Well, he supposed it was a dog. A half-grown pup, actually—but its ancestry beggared the imagination. Thin, scruffy, its filthy white coat splotched with brown, one drooping and one flyaway ear—for a moment Julian was speechless.

Then, 'Where did *that* come from?' he demanded.

'*He,*' said Christy, with what Julian considered undue emphasis, 'is a dog. And *he*—'

'Are you sure of that?' asked Julian sarcastically. He should have known better.

Cheeks flaming under the grime, Christy said, 'Perfectly sure. Even I know bitches don't mark trees.'

Julian took that one on the chin. 'Thank you,' he said, suppressing the urge to throttle her. Or kiss her. 'And what evidence can you present that this…*thing*…is indeed a dog?' Seeing that she was silenced, he swept on, 'And where did you find this dog? For want of a better term.'

'In the woods,' said Christy in oddly muted tones. 'He…I…we were playing, with a stick, and chasing rabbits. At least, he was—'

'And you *conveniently* forgot the time. You decided playing with a stray mongrel was more important than fulfilling your social obligations, so you stayed out late—worrying me half to death in the process!' he finished savagely.

'Worrying *you*?'

She sounded as though the idea struck her as ludicrous.

'Of course I was worried! What did you imagine I'd think when you didn't come home? But much you care! You were out disporting yourself with a dog who should have been shot for trespass!'

'Stop yelling at me!' said Christy furiously. 'Can't you…can't you see he's hurt? And you're frightening him!'

Her voice shook, and to his horror a tear slid down her cheek, leaving a track in the dirt.

All his anger dissolved, leaving exposed the fear he had lived with for hours. His stomach clenched again, painfully. And tightened further as another tear fell.

'Just go away,' she said in a very wobbly voice.

He stared down at her, half-turned away from him. How indeed should she have known that he would worry about her? How could she know that his conscience was like a raw wound with salt burning it? How could she know he had spent the day going over his dealings with her and finding himself completely at fault?

'How is he hurt?' he asked quietly.

There was an aching silence. Then, 'His back leg,' she whispered.

Julian crouched down, eliciting a growl from the frightened pup.

'Gently, little fellow,' he murmured, holding out a lightly clenched fist for the pup to sniff. It snapped, and then whined piteously. He kept talking in a lazy sing-song voice, uttering nonsense, knowing only the tone mattered.

Christy herself was caught, enthralled by the change in him. Dazed, she listened to the soothing voice.

'You're lucky she found you. What stupid mess did you get into? Hmm?'

The pup sniffed cautiously at the outstretched hand.

'Yes, that's better. I don't really eat dogs—there. Yes, that's a good spot, isn't it, laddie? Softly, then.'

The lean, powerful hand scratched gently behind the pup's ears. Christy gulped, recallng the effect those caressing fingers had on her.

'Now, let's see…ah, so there's the problem. How did you do it, you silly creature?'

'What has he done?' asked Christy softly.

'Dislocated the hip,' replied Julian. 'Nasty. Never mind, little chap. How did it happen?'

It took Christy a moment to realise that he was asking her.

'Oh. I was on the way home—with him,' she added defiantly. 'And he chased a rabbit. There's a tree down in the woods. Just on the edge of a bank. He got in among the roots chasing it, and…' She hesitated. He was going to be furious.

'Go on.'

She took a deep breath. 'Well, it was odd, but there seemed to be tunnels in the bank, behind the tree, and—'

'What sort of tree?' he asked sharply. The pup cowered and he moderated his tone. 'Easy, little chap. What sort of tree, Christy?'

'Um, an oak. It was awfully smelly.'

'I know the place. It's an old badger sett that foxes use now,' he said grimly. 'Go on.'

'Well, he didn't come out when I called, but I could hear him barking…and then there was a sort of rushing noise and he was still barking, but it was muffled.' She shivered, remembering.

'You mean part of the sett collapsed?' asked Julian in a queer, tight voice.

She nodded.

'So how did he get out?' His eyes raked her ruined gown. Clearly this was not the behaviour a viscount expected of his bride.

'I…I climbed in over the roots and dug him out,' she said.

His face drained of all colour, and he said in a carefully expressionless voice, 'You're telling me you crawled into a badger's sett, in an unstable bank, that had already collapsed *twice*, to dig out this…this misbegotton excuse for a dog?'

Anger and hurt flared. 'I wasn't thinking about his ancestry at the time,' she said. 'No doubt you would have left him to his fate and strolled home without a care in the world!'

She didn't realise she was crying until shaking hands cradled her face and a gentle thumb wiped clumsily at a tear.

'Christy, he's just a dog.' His voice sounded strange. 'You could have been trapped! Killed! We had no idea where you were!'

She knew he was right, but— 'I couldn't just leave him!'

His breath came out in a groan. 'No. I don't suppose you could. Very well. We'd better patch up him.'

'How?' she asked. 'It looks dreadful.'

He grimaced. 'I can assure you, it doesn't feel very pleasant. I think we'll find Twigg knows how to put it back. He put my shoulder back in for me once when I was a boy. Ring the bell. We'll send for him.'

She reached up and tugged on the bell pull. Then she looked at her husband, sitting on the hearth, comforting a mongrel pup, his hands gentle.

'Julian?'

He looked up, his blue eyes somehow bruised.

'I'm sorry about the dinner. I don't suppose you will believe me, but I was coming back for it. Truly, I was.'

His jaw dropped.

Once he'd been sent for, Twigg appeared promptly. Julian rather thought Hallam hadn't been far away, given the swiftness of his response to the bell. Probably wondering if he would have to intercede on his mistress's behalf, thought Julian in self-disgust.

I don't suppose you will believe me…

Ice had condensed in his stomach at those words. She didn't expect him to believe her? What the hell could he say? He'd already said quite enough and there was the pup to look after now.

Twigg took one look at the shivering pup. 'Well, well. That's a nasty mess an' no mistake.' He grinned at his master. 'You'd know what that feels like.'

'Only too well,' said Julian drily. 'Can you put it back?'

'Oh, aye. Easy enough, if so be as you and the mistress can help. I could get a couple of the lads, but I dessay he'll feel better without too many strangers messing round with him.'

Christy swallowed. 'What do you want me to do, Twigg? I don't know anything about dogs.'

He smiled. 'You'll do just fine, m'lady. Now, first thing— since I can't tip a quart of brandy down his throat like I did with you, Master Julian, you'd best hold his head and shoulders.' He grinned at Christy and added confidentially, 'We'll give him that job, then it'll likely be him as gets bit.'

'Thank you,' said Julian wryly. 'Did you want a reference, or not?'

But Twigg's shrewd old eyes were on Christy's wrist. 'Looks like you already got a bit of a nip, ma'am.'

Julian focused sharply on the puncture marks. 'Damn it, Christy! How did that happen?'

'When I pulled him out,' she said. 'I must have hurt his leg. I could see it was all wrong, but the tunnel—' He drew a savage breath and she broke off, 'I was in a hurry.'

She was avoiding his gaze and his blood congealed. 'The bank collapsed again.' He felt cold, frozen to the marrow. If she hadn't got out…she wouldn't have stood a chance with the weight of the earth and possibly the fallen tree on her. She would be dead by now. Buried. They might never have found her. A world without Christy?

He gave vent to his feelings in a few blistering words that turned the air blue and earned him a dressing down from Twigg.

'Yeh talk nice in front of her ladyship,' he admonished. ''Taint no way to talk to any woman, leave alone your bride!'

He turned to Christy. 'Now, m'lady, once his lordship's got the pup firm, I want yeh to lace yer fingers together, and link them under his thigh—like so.' Gnarled old hands guided hers into position. 'That's it. With you bracin' him, I can twist the leg easier to get the joint back in. See?'

Christy gulped.

Twigg looked sympathetic. 'Just shut yer eyes. No need to look at what I'm doing. Happen he'll make a bit of noise, but it can't be helped.' He grinned. 'That'll just be dog talk for a few of the things Master Julian said a moment back.'

Christy managed a shaky smile. 'Very well.'

'Good girl,' said Julian softly.

Steadied by this praise, she felt better.

She did shut her eyes, but nothing could shut out the pup's terrified yelps. Tears ran down her face, but she hung on, and suddenly felt a click under her hands, and heard Twigg's triumphant, 'Ah! There 'tis! Well done, lass. We've done it!'

Sick to her stomach, Christy opened her eyes.

The leg was back in right relation to its owner.

'Now, he'll need to be kept warm and quiet for a few days,' said Twigg, with a glance at Julian. 'I can take him down the stables with me while that leg heals. What'll you do with him then?'

The question took Julian by surprise. He looked at the pup and repressed a shudder. 'Ask roundabout if anyone owns him; if not, I suppose someone might like him for a child. One of the farmers, perhaps.'

Beside him, Christy's breath jerked in and she froze to utter stillness.

In a very diffident voice—one she used, he was fast learning, to conceal hurt—she said, 'May I not keep him?'

Chapter Twenty

J ulian stared. Keep the pup? Rescue it—yes. Tend its injury—
by all means. But keep a misbegotten pup that looked as though
it had strayed off a dust heap?

'Christy, if you want a dog, of course you may have one,'
he said. 'A proper dog. Not—' He broke off.

'Is breeding so important, my lord?'

'Well, yes. At least—' He stopped—heard what he was saying.

Christy's odd eyes met his unflinchingly. 'Then he is quite dog
enough for me. He has a tail to wag when he sees me, ears to prick
when I call him, and eyes to tell me—' She stopped, blinked
several times and then went on, 'That is sufficient for me. I fear
I am not quite so nice in my requirements as you, my lord.'

He felt sick. 'Christy, I didn't mean…' But he had once
meant it, and her eyes told him that she knew it. The pup…
Nan…Christy herself.

'You really want him?' He could see his reputation going
straight down the sink.

She nodded.

He sighed. 'There can be no objection. He'll have to be
trained, though, if he is to be a house dog.'

Her smile broke through like sunshine after rain. Hesitant
and wonderful.

Twigg grinned. 'I'll deal with that. My missus'll like havin' the pup to fuss over and he can come back up here to the house when he's learned his manners nice.' He turned to Christy. 'You come down each day to visit him and take him for a walk when that leg's ready and he'll learn who's mistress quick enough.'

Delight flooded Christy. The pup was hers. She stood up, wanting to thank Twigg, but staggered as the Hall spun, a crazy blur of light and stone…

'Christy!'

Strong arms caught her.

She came to herself seated at the long refectory table, Julian beside her, holding her close. Twigg and the pup were gone.

'Christy—are you all right?'

'I'm…I'm quite all right, my lord. Just tired. I should go up now.'

'In a moment,' he said. Still with his arm around her, he looked into her face, frowning. She must look a complete fright. She blushed as his gaze travelled to her scratched and filthy hands. He touched one gently and she trembled.

She felt dizzy again. Julian seemed to realise, because his arm tightened. She shut her eyes, leaning against him. Perhaps in a moment he might let her go up to bed. She didn't like to think about how she was going to get that far.

A moment later she felt herself being swung up into his arms and carried upstairs. Whispers and movement penetrated the haze. And Julian's harsh voice ordering a bath to be drawn, cloths and warm water to be brought along with supper to her bedchamber. She sighed and rested her head on his shoulder.

She roused as she was lowered with infinite gentleness into a chair before the fire in her room.

'Here. Let me.' His voice was a soothing murmur, but her eyes snapped open as a warm, damp cloth touched her face. She was beyond protest as he bathed her face, then her arms and hands. Light, caring touches that insensibly eased her and cleansed more from her than dirt. It sponged away hurt and fear.

Behind them Beth bustled about, directing the footmen where to place the bath. It didn't interest her. The strong hands cleansing her held her utterly spellbound. She closed her eyes again, surrendering to his care, and a powerful arm cradled her close. It felt so good to be cared for in this way. Not since she had been a little girl and skinned her knee had anyone tended her like this.

It was not safe. His warmth and strength seduced her senses—she could withstand that. But his tenderness tore at her heart. It would be much easier if he were the cold, arrogant aristocrat. But behind the pride and chill was a man who could ravish the heart from a woman without even knowing, or wanting it.

He was being kind now because he felt guilty about hurting her. Desperately she reminded herself that he wanted a dutiful bride to give him an heir. He enjoyed her passion and her body, but the emotions battering at her held no value for him.

Folly to weave dreams around simple kindness, to imagine that his hands had trembled as he sponged away dirt from her face, that the long fingers had grazed her throat on purpose. She fought the urge to nestle closer, burrowing against him.

Beth's voice broke into her daze. 'Comfrey salve, my lord. Best for those scratches.'

'Thank you.'

Salve was rubbed in with a feather-light touch. Face, hands, arms.

By the time he had tended Christy's scrapes and the bite, Julian ached with arousal. He breathed carefully. Kissing her senseless in front of her maid was more than slightly inappropriate. Especially since he would end by carrying her to his bed and... He halted the train of thought right there. She was exhausted; she needed sleep.

Never before had he realised how deeply it was possible to

desire a woman. And it was not just that he wanted her *more* than any other woman. He wanted her differently. He wanted all of her. Everything he had pretended was unimportant. Her barbed tongue as well as her sweetness. Her blazing honesty that never backed down. Her pride.

He wanted *her*. Christy. His wife.

'Beg pardon, my lord. Bath's ready.'

He looked around. Christy's maid stood beside a steaming bathtub by the fire. Towels lay over a chair.

It required an effort of will to stand up.

'I'll be in my room,' he said. Everything in him roared a protest, that he should dismiss the maid and care for Christy himself, but he couldn't trust his control. He would come back when she was safely in bed to make sure she was all right.

Christy submitted to Beth's ministrations, clumsily washing herself with her left hand, but permitting the maid to wash and rinse her hair. Her bandaged right wrist ached, but overlaying the pain was the memory of Julian's gentleness as he had cleansed and tended it.

When Beth asked, she stood to be rinsed with a bucket of warm water. Once dry, she pulled on a robe and sat by the fire to rub her hair dry. Food was brought. A hot, rich soup, bread and cheese. She ate hungrily.

Beth took the tray when she was finished, saying gently, 'Bed, my lady?'

Bed. Obediently she got into bed and Beth drew the bed-hangings, leaving a small gap so Christy could reach the bedside table.

Slight sounds came to her. Hushed voices as two footmen removed the bath. Beth tidying up.

'Will there be anything more, my lady?'

'No. Just snuff the candles. Thank you. I will ring in the morning.' She felt as though she could sleep for days and still be tired. It wasn't just her body, tired though it was. Her very spirit felt weary, as though she had been confronted with something that she could neither walk away from nor ultimately win. She lay back against the pillows, listening as Beth moved about snuffing candles. Bit by bit the room darkened.

She had to be sensible. Not moping because she…because she what? Had a husband who worried about her and lost his temper when she had frightened him? Because she could depend on him to look after her? Because he would follow an honourable course no matter what?

The darkness swelled as Beth doused the lamp on the dressing table.

She had nothing to mope about. She had aimed at the moon and she had tripped. That was all. She hadn't hurt herself badly. Only broken a useless dream. Countless girls and women were sleeping in doorways tonight, and, but for Julian's sense of honour, she might well have ended up among them.

'Leave this one, my lady?' Beth was back, looking at the candle on the bedside table.

'Yes. Thank you. Go to bed.'

'Yes, my lady.'

Another door closed. The world seemed full of closing doors.

She had lost nothing. Only a dream she had never really believed in. Not for herself. It wasn't practical, or even safe to dream that particular dream. She would manage without it. Compared to her failure to keep Nan safe for Jane, it wasn't important.

She sat up, took off her spectacles, and leaned over to blow out the candle on her bedside table. Darkness poured over her. And with it, fear. Blind, unreasoning fear. Of the dark. Panic. Black, choking, as the tree shifted, earth and stones sliding around her, pattering over her, and she heard their hungry growl, knew she had only instants, seconds to get out before the consuming dark took her…

She forced herself to breathe. Clean, free air. She was safe. Safe in her own bed. Julian was in his room. If she called, he would come. But she would not call. Knowing that she could must be enough. Better if he didn't see any more of her weakness. A bright moon had been rising earlier. Moonlight was safer than falling asleep with a lamp or candle.

Flinging back the covers and hangings, she got up and went to the windows. The curtains rattled as she pulled them back. The clear, bright sky drove panic into retreat.

She turned away from the window and cried out in terror as a shadow moved by the door.

'Christy!'

He was across the room and had her in his arms before she could take another breath. His heat infused her, warming, comforting. Beneath her cheek his heart thudded. One hand held her close, the other traced her jaw, her lips, throat, and slid shaking into her hair, pressing her closer to the reassuring beat of his heart.

'Shh. It's me. I needed to see that you were all right. That you weren't frightened.'

She tried to summon a lie. Tell him she hadn't been frightened. But her trembling body betrayed her.

'You…you startled me. I wanted light…it was so dark. And it smelt awful—' She was babbling, unsure whether she meant her room or the sett. 'I'm sorry about the dinner—I was coming back for it. Truly.'

His arms hardened instantly. 'I thought I'd lost you.' His voice was rough. 'Then when you told me what had happened, and I knew how close you'd been to—' He broke off, and she felt a shudder rack him. Strangely, it steadied her. 'The things I said—I'm sorry. The dinner wasn't important.' His mouth brushed clumsily over her temple, her eyes. Then he released her and stepped back, his face etched hard in silver and shadow. 'Is there anything you need?'

She swallowed. Pride would help here. Pride would allow her to assure him that she was very well. That she had only needed fresh air…that she hadn't been frightened…

'Just you.'

Her voice was the merest breath, but she saw her words strike. Saw the shock in his expression.

His voice neutral, he said, 'You wish me to remain with you for the night? Just hold you?'

It would be easy to let him believe that was all. Safer. And untrue.

'No,' she said. 'I need to know that I am still alive. I need *you*.'

'Christy.'

It was all he said before his mouth claimed hers. Words were impossible, unnecessary, consumed in the fierce desperation of their kiss. Then she was swept up in his arms, being carried past her own bed and through the door to *his* room and *his* bed and tumbled on to it. There was scarcely time to gasp before he was with her, his weight, hot and hard, covering her, swift hands banishing her nightgown, his robe, until nothing remained between them. Nothing but fiery need, all restraint and distance incinerated.

Julian couldn't speak. There were words he needed to say, but his throat was hot and tight, choking him. Because she was kissing him, her cheeks wet with tears. And her hands, hesitant and a little clumsy, were a burning, soul-deep delight. Every shy touch echoing the words in his heart, the ones trapped in his throat.

He wanted everything. He wanted to give her everything. Everything given and received. Everything taken and offered. Because it had nearly been too late.

He kissed his way down her throat, licking and caressing, finding the frantic pulse beating at the base. Adoring the high, sweet curve of her breast, coming to the taut nipple and drawing it into the dark heat of his mouth to suckle fiercely so her body arched wildly and she cried out, a strangled sound of pleasure. Pleasure stabbing deep in his own body, driven by her response.

He shifted, burning, and reached between restless silken thighs. 'Open.' His voice harsh, demanding. But she obeyed and he pressed shaking fingers to hot, liquid silk as he took her mouth again, kissing her deeply in searing promise.

Everything.

He stroked and teased, finding the hidden nub, circling so that she moaned and pushed against him, pleading for more. He slid one finger inside, felt her body clench wildly, and pressed with his thumb. She convulsed, her cries spilling into his mouth as release took her, leaving her limp and trembling.

So easy, so tempting to take her now. But he'd wanted to give everything.

He slid down her hot, quivering body, kissing every slick inch. Breasts, sweetly curving waist, the gentle swell of her belly, flaring hips and finally the soft cream silk of her thighs, pushing them wide, wider, with his shoulders. She gasped, a high, shocked sound and tried to push him away. He captured her hands gently.

'No. Don't fight me. Trust me. Let me love you.'

The words stilled her startled resistance and Christy's mind fractured at the hot, open-mouthed kisses on her inner thighs, at the harsh sound of his breath...the warm caress of his breath...there—there where she was aching and burning again. It terrified her...the intimacy, the emotions pouring through her.

Let me love you...

Oh, please, please...

Strong hands held her hips captive, tilting her for an impossibly tender, shockingly silken caress.

Her hips bucked as dark pleasure speared her and her throat burst with a raw, choked scream at the hot pressure of his mouth. Her hands sought him, clutching, sliding through the silk of his hair. It shattered her, terrified her. It was unbearable, it was wonderful. She would die if he didn't stop. She would die if he did stop.

She broke, crashing into oblivion as ecstasy poured through her again, consuming her in a fiery cataract. She hardly heard his tender, loving words as her tears spilt. And she wanted more, she ached, felt empty.

'Please.' Her voice shook. 'Please. I want you…all of you.'

With a harsh sound he surged up her body and she opened fully to him, felt the hard press of him at her entrance.

Shaking, on the brink of madness, bathed in her taste and scent, part of him clung to sanity, to safety. He should be gentle with her, take her carefully.

She was having none of it. Even as he fought for restraint she lifted against him, hot, wet softness claiming the head of his shaft, long slender legs wrapping around his hips. Nails raked his shoulders and her voice broke on his name.

Control exploded into ruin as he thrust into her welcoming body and buried himself to the hilt. Lost, he took her again and again, feeling her pleasure as his own, feeling her catch and match his rhythm so that their bodies sang together. He knew when the end was upon her, when he could let himself go and be swept with her into the final crescendo. Consummation took him, all dark, fierce pleasure as he spilt deep within her convulsing body, blind and shaking.

With a groan he collapsed on her, and slid to one side, still holding her close, unwilling to let her go. Ever.

With his last remaining strength he pulled the bedclothes over them, sinking into a warm cocoon in a sweaty, sated tangle of limbs, Christy safe in his arms.

He woke to bright sunlight. Somewhere outside, high above, a lark was pouring its gift of winged song back to the world. He rolled over, reaching out, and made an unwelcome discovery—he was alone. She might be in her own room. He got up, pulled on his dressing gown and went to look.

There was no sign of Christy, but her maid's eyes first widened at the sight of him still tying his robe, and then dropped modestly to the floor, her face scarlet. He felt his own ears burn. Damn it! Why the hell hadn't he put on his nightshirt? The entire staff would be laughing over this.

He cleared his throat. 'Do you know where your mistress is?'

'Oh, yes, m'lord.' Was that a flicker of amusement? 'She went down to the Dower House to fetch Miss Nan. She's up in the nursery with her.'

'Thank you, er, Beth, isn't it?'

'Yes, m'lord.'

He beat a hasty retreat.

The nursery. He was going to have to face them both.

Back in his own room, Julian realised that at some undefined point either last night or this morning he had made a decision. Two decisions. About his marriage and Nan's future.

'I don't know, sweetheart.'

Christy's tired, defeated voice sliced into him. 'It...that may not be possible, but I...I promise you will be safe and well looked after.'

He tensed at the uncertainty in her voice as she made the promise. Was she wondering if she would be permitted to keep it?

An indistinct murmur followed—a child's voice. Nan. His sister.

'Yes. It must seem strange. I don't fit in very well here either.'

Not fit? His fist clenched on the door frame until his knuckles whitened.

Again, Nan's indistinct voice.

'Of course not, Nan! No one will mind if you ride it!'

He'd heard enough. He pushed open the door and walked in.

His old rocking horse had been pulled into the middle of the floor, and Nan was clearly attempting to dismount as Christy tried to stop her. Scarlet faced, Christy turned as Nan's eyes widened and her breath jerked in on a gasp at the sight of him. She slid off the horse and stood stiffly, her eyes downcast.

He felt sick, clumsy and completely useless.

What the hell could he say? To either of them?

Christy met his gaze. 'My lord. You should have sent for me.'

'Actually I wanted both of you.' He looked at his sister, who was still staring at the floor. 'Good morning, Nan.'

A quick glance up, a mumbled greeting.

'Am I interrupting your ride?' he asked very gently.

A silent shake of the black curls answered him.

He looked from the stiff, averted face to the rocking horse. He'd been a year younger than Nan when Twigg's father made it...Starlight. Named for the diamond blaze on the wooden face. Dapple-grey paint, chipped in places, worn and rubbed in others. The leather reins were soft and supple, the padded leather saddle showing where four gallant riders since himself had sat brandishing wooden swords, urging their noble steed to death and glory.

He reached out to touch the arched neck, remembered holding Lissy and Matt for their first rides. He supposed they had done the same for Emma and Davy. The once-flowing mane under his fingers looked a trifle ragged now, as did the tail. Probably due to five pairs of hands, firmly taught to care for their mount first and foremost.

At Nan's age he'd half-believed Starlight a real horse, enchanted to look like a toy by day, but resuming his true form once the house slept. So many dreams. He'd been Starlight's first owner—was he special to Starlight? The painted eyes had faded, but there was something about the expression... To a creature like this, all children would be special, a flying weight of dreams on his back, and small, loving hands grooming out yet more of his mane and tail every year. He accepted them all.

He gave the proud neck a last rub and stepped back. 'I called him Starlight,' he told Nan.

For a moment there was silence. Then, 'He's yours?'

He thought about it. 'No. Not really.' Any more than Amberley truly belonged to him. Perhaps it was actually the other way around. Or he was merely a guardian. Starlight had

passed happily to other children now. As one day he hoped
Amberley would pass to his son.

He looked around. His eye fell on Noah's Ark, set out on a
low table with the animals dutifully lined up in pairs, being
shepherded into the Ark by Noah, his wife and their sons. Only
the lion, at the head of the procession, was alone. The lioness
had fallen to lie forgotten beneath the table.

He crouched down before the table, and held out his hand.
'Come and look, Nan.'

She came hesitantly.

'This,' he told her, 'was made for our great-grandfather.'

He heard Christy's startled intake of breath, but his concentration now was on the child looking at him, uncomprehending.

'Your great-grandfather, sir?'

'Yes. And yours.' He drew a deep breath. 'I remember him.
Just. When he was a very old man he used to let me bring the
Ark down to the library after dinner. He said our father, yours
and mine, had liked it too.'

Her hand had remained at her side, but now Julian reached
out and took it. She looked at him, the blue eyes so like his own
full of bewilderment.

How the hell did one explain something like this to a child?

He tried. 'There was a time, you see, Nan, when your mother
and our father were both very sad and became friends. Your
mother was very kind to our father, and you were born. I've
always known that, but your mother obviously wanted you with
her. And that was right and proper. But now—'

He stopped. Nan's eyes had spilled over and his own
throat felt thick. Uncertain if it was the right thing to do, he
put an arm around Nan and hugged her gently. Fumbling in
his pocket, he found a handkerchief to wipe her eyes and
blow her nose.

'It…some people would say what they did was wrong, because
they were both married to other people—but that is in the past and
is not your fault,' he said carefully. 'And it means you are my

sister—my half-sister, like Lissy and Emma. And Davy and Matthew are my half-brothers. We all have the same father.'

He couldn't look at Christy. He didn't dare. A few days ago she had told him that she loved him—and he'd flung it back in her face. Reduced her gift to mere sex. Because her honesty had frightened the hell out of him. It had been easier to deny what she felt—deny *her*.

Just as it would be easier to let Jane's family raise Nan, and contribute to her upkeep, holding aloof from further entanglement. Easier. Safer. For he did not delude himself that his chosen path would be easy. It would not. There would always be people to censure him for this step and look down their noses at Nan. He couldn't help what they thought, but, by God, he would protect his sister.

'So, these toys, Nan,' he said. 'Some of them were made for me. Some for my father and aunts, and so on. They don't seem to mind which children play with them. They just belong here. Like the children. No doubt you'll have Davy coming over rather often, and in a year or so there might be another occupant—' He risked a glance at Christy, but she had turned away, was folding some clothes in a basket. With a deep breath he looked at Nan. 'You might have to share, but I don't suppose you'll mind that. They're yours to play with for as long as you want them, because this is your place now, and you belong here, just like they do.'

Nan said nothing, but she wriggled out of his hold, leaned forwards and picked up the fallen lioness. With careful concentration she set the creature upright beside her mate.

'That's it,' said Julian, his throat unaccountably tight. 'They'll be happier together.' He was aware that Christy had turned around, was watching them. 'Poor old Rex probably felt a trifle lost without her. He'll do better now he's got her to show him the way to go on.'

He looked up and met Christy's gaze.

Her breath caught in her throat at the smile in those blue,

blue eyes. She was being foolish, imagining too much into his words. He had decided to accept Nan—that was all. No—it was everything. The most wonderful thing that could have happened. Far more important than her foolish romantic dreams.

She said nothing and after a moment he murmured something to Nan and gave her shoulder a squeeze. He rose in a lithe surge and came to her. She forced herself to remain still as memories of the previous night washed over her. His fierce passion, his tenderness—it had just been sex. That was all. For him.

'Come,' he said, and led her from the room into the empty passage.

He spoke softly. 'Sometimes we have trouble seeing what's right in front of us.'

She took a careful breath. He was all around her, the musky scent that had wreathed her all night faintly overlaid with the sandalwood soap he used. He was right. Sometimes it was difficult to keep sight of things that were laid out clearly. Like the difference in their feelings. Last night had not been about love. Not for him.

Yet his touch, careful and light on her cheek, the gentlest tracery, said otherwise. *Let me love you.* Not more than physically. He was a consummate lover and once was quite enough to make a fool of herself in that particular way. And it shouldn't matter so much.

She stood rigid, trying not to let her heart show in her eyes under his magical touch. Yet still her heart yearned, not so much to hear him say it, but to be able to say it. To say it and not have it dismissed as a woman's excuse for enjoying sex. As gratitude.

Just dismissed. As something almost distasteful and rather vulgar. It was as though she had finally opened a door she had never wanted to approach, only to find herself trapped on the threshold, barred from the wonderful new country she had not even suspected.

'Christy?'

She managed a smile. He meant she had helped him to see the truth about Nan. He would never have done this simply to placate her. Rather he had listened, really listened. And he had changed his mind. She had his respect and that would be enough.

Only the bright world she could see through the door blazed and beckoned. She could still shut the door and turn away. It would be safer to do that. Far more comfortable to close it.

He reached for her hand, enveloping it as though it were infinitely precious. Her left hand, weighted with his ring, the symbol of their contract. Duty and honour. Cold, empty bedfellows, but they would have to be enough. She dare not ask.

'What was right in front of you?'

She scarcely recognised her own voice. It came from a great distance, as though she were not quite in control. As though some foolish, rebellious part of her had stepped out to take one last risk.

He lifted her hand to his mouth and kissed the heavy ring.

'That quote you flung at me yesterday—eventually I looked it up.'

Her mind tripped over the image of her rakish husband searching for a Bible passage.

'St Paul was somewhat unequivocal on the subject of love, wasn't he?' said Julian, a wry smile tearing at her heart. 'There was nothing there to let me off the hook. Even if I didn't have the courage to acknowledge my own feelings, I had no right to cheapen and dismiss yours.'

'Your feelings?' she whispered, hardly daring to believe what he was saying.

He drew her into his arms, into the warmth and safety. And it was he who sighed in pleasure first as she settled against him.

'Yes,' he said. 'I spent a great deal of time and effort trying to convince myself that there were many excellent reasons for wanting you and marrying you. Desire, duty, honour.' He kissed her gently. 'But in the end I had to admit I was being a fool.

Oh, I desired you right enough, but it became so much more.'
He broke off again, seeming to search for words. 'I care what
you think of me, I care about *you* and I don't give a damn about
your birth, unless it causes *you* hurt. Yesterday, when I realised
how close I came to losing you—' his arms tightened around
her '—it terrified me.'

He held her slightly away from him. 'Tell me it isn't too late,
sweetheart—tell me you still love me.'

'Yes, I love you,' she whispered. 'So much. I just wish...'
Her voice faltered.

'What do you wish, sweetheart?'

She struggled for the words. 'That I was not...my birth...'

Gentle fingers stopped her lips. 'No,' he said. 'Don't wish
that. Don't wish to be anything other than who you are and what
you are. That's the woman I love. The woman I will always love.'

Her eyes were blinded, the room dissolving into mist. But
he caught her chin and lifted it, then gently removed her spectacles, slipping them into his pocket. Through the blur she saw
his mouth twist.

'You gave me those words, and I didn't have the courage to
accept them, let alone return them. So I hurt you instead.' He
kissed her tenderly, on the eyes, the cheeks, capturing the
silvery tears. 'I'm not worth these,' he whispered.

She smiled through them. 'Not even tears of happiness?'

'Just as long as I don't cause you any more of the other sort,'
he said, holding her close.

More tears fell, but through the mist of joy she could see
the gleaming world stretching out, limitless. Full of mysteries
and unseen paths, probably not a few sorrows, dangers and
pitfalls, but it was theirs to tread and explore. Together.

REGENCY
Collection

*Let these sparklingly seductive delights whirl
you away to the ballrooms—and
bedrooms—of Polite Society!*

Volume 1 – 4th February 2011
Regency Pleasures by Louise Allen

Volume 2 – 4th March 2011
Regency Secrets by Julia Justiss

Volume 3 – 1st April 2011
Regency Rumours by Juliet Landon

Volume 4 – 6th May 2011
Regency Redemption by Christine Merrill

Volume 5 – 3rd June 2011
Regency Debutantes by Margaret McPhee

Volume 6 – 1st July 2011
Regency Improprieties by Diane Gaston

12 volumes in all to collect!

www.millsandboon.co.uk

REGENCY

Collection

*Let these sparklingly seductive delights whirl
you away to the ballrooms—and
bedrooms—of Polite Society!*

Volume 7 – 5th August 2011
Regency Mistresses by Mary Brendan

Volume 8 – 2nd September 2011
Regency Rebels by Deb Marlowe

Volume 9 – 7th October 2011
Regency Scandals by Sophia James

Volume 10 – 4th November 2011
Regency Marriages by Elizabeth Rolls

Volume 11 – 2nd December 2011
Regency Innocents by Annie Burrows

Volume 12 – 6th January 2012
Regency Sins by Bronwyn Scott

12 volumes in all to collect!

MILLS
BOON

www.millsandboon.co.uk